Magnolia Street

For
Jessie Brett Young
Because of Fraita

For
Francis Brett Young
Because of The Dark Tower

Magnolia Street

Louis Golding

www.fiveleaves.co.uk

Magnolia Street
by Louis Golding

This edition published in 2006 by
Five Leaves Publications,
PO Box 8786, Nottingham NG1 9AW
info@fiveleaves.co.uk
www.fiveleaves.co.uk

Magnolia Street was first published
by Victor Gollancz Ltd., in 1932
and is re-issued by permission of
The Orion Publishing Group,
the copyright holder of this title

Introduction copyright: Hugh Cecil

Five Leaves acknowledges financial support
from Arts Council England

Cover illustration courtesy of Manchester Jewish Museum
Cartoon of Louis Golding courtesy of Hugh Cecil
Five Leaves has been unable to trace the copyright
holder of the Louis Golding cartoon.
We would be pleased to correct this omission
in any subsequent edition.

Design and typesetting by Four Sheets Design and Print
Printed by the Russell Press in Nottingham

ISBN: 1905512007

Introduction

The celebrated novel of Jewish Manchester, *Magnolia Street,* was first published in 1932, by Victor Gollancz. From the start it was an outstanding hit, 18,000 copies selling within a few months, leaving the bookshop shelves at a rate of 800 a day. It came fourth on the bestseller list in that year and eventually one million copies were sold, translated into twenty-seven languages. In 1934 a play based on it was produced by Charles B. Cochran, with a star cast directed by Komisarjevsky. For all the glittering ensemble, it flopped, having too many characters and sub-plots to work satisfactorily on stage; but it was excellent publicity for the book, and a TV film, *Magnolia Street*, followed.

Louis Golding, the novel's author, was born in Manchester in 1895, the third son of Philip and Yetta Golding, Jewish immigrants from Cherkassy in the Ukraine, where his father had been a ritual orator. Visitors today to the Manchester Jewish Museum in Cheetham Hill Road can see, through contemporary photographs, the dire living conditions forced upon Eastern European families like the Goldings when first settling in their new country. They were one small element of the two million penniless Jews fleeing abroad from persecution in the Russian Pale of Settlement, between 1880 and the outbreak of war in 1914. In time, Louis' family was able to move to a modest but respectable home in Sycamore Street, Manchester, in the area known as Hightown — a neatly planned quarter of terraced houses, planted with trees. This was the model for the 'Magnolia Street' of his most successful novel, in which he described, in colourful detail, the relations between Jews and their non-Jewish neighbours, over 'the crowded years' from 1910 to 1930.

Between the two world wars, and into the 1950s, Louis was to enjoy widespread fame as a novelist, travel writer and commentator on Jewish life. He never broke from his origins and remained always a champion of English Jewish culture; but like his character, Max Emmanuel, in *Magnolia Street,* he led a sophisticated, religiously broadminded life in bohemian circles. He was the author of around forty books, of which well over half were novels or short stories; other publications including works on politics, boxing and haute cuisine.

1

From his infancy Louis delighted in writing, and only his death in 1958 put an end to his tireless flow. His precocious talent impressed teachers at elementary school, and in 1908 at the age of 12, he gained a scholarship to Manchester Grammar School. He proved a particularly promising pupil, and was devoted to the institution, throwing himself into the life of the school, both athletic and literary. He called the school camp in the Lake District in August 1913 'the greatest experience of my life', and told the High Master, J.L. Paton, that he intended to get an Oxford Scholarship 'if I have to use force'.

During this time he made close friends with a non-Jewish Manchester family, the Owens. Mrs Owen was a young widow with two children, May and Gareth. Louis now fully intended to become a professional writer and Mrs Owen ('Zzo', as he nicknamed her) had her own literary ambitions. Louis used to say that he came to tea and stayed with the family for the rest of his life. They 'adopted him' and he spent most of his time with them, though he never severed connections with his parents. In due course, when he went on to Oxford, he introduced the Owens to a contemporary of his, the future orientalist, Neville Whymant, whom Mrs Owen subsequently married. In later years Louis owed much to the Owens' help — but equally there is no doubt that the clever and charming schoolboy and undergraduate did a great deal for them. He injected, in his quiet way, a level of vitality and fun into their circle.

In 1914, he gained a classical scholarship to Queen's College, Oxford. There he cultivated new interests and contacts through sporting and intellectual societies, including the Fabian Society — addressed on one occasion by G.K. Chesterton. When not speaking at the Union or the Liberal Club, he was constantly engaged in arguments — mainly with fellow Jewish undergraduates — which meant more to him, it seems, than the lectures he was expected to attend. Even by the end of his first term he had provoked strong reactions in others, both favourable and unfavourable. To those who were critical he stood out as the archetypical aesthete, poking fun at 'priggish public schoolishness'. His room — which he had intended to be 'the most tasteful room in Oxford' — was repeatedly trashed by College 'bloods'. He was profoundly hurt, for he treasured the books, pictures and ornaments he had acquired at no little cost; and there was an anti-Semitic element in this vandalism. He talked of forming an 'Outsiders' club. All his life he had an underlying anxiety that people might suddenly turn on him. But he took such blows courageously and soon acquired a staunch circle of companions who responded to his resilience, wit, and gifts as a writer, as well as his intense appreciation of art, architecture and nature. At this stage of his life he saw himself, above all, as a poet.

He became a close friend of Richard Blaker, a fellow scholar from India, of probably partly Jewish extraction. Blaker's father was in the Indian Civil Service and the Blaker family had lived on the sub-continent since the early 19th Century. Blaker too had strong literary interests and the two men helped one another in their writing careers in later life, though Blaker, the author of the best-selling *Here Lies a Most Beautiful Woman* and a distinguished war novel, *Medal Without Bar*, never achieved Golding's sustained success.

At 18 Golding was a remarkable looking young man — beautiful-ugly — with huge deep-set dark eyes, heavy eyebrows, and intellectual forehead. As a youth he was small and slight — in contrast with his later barrel-like shape. In manner he was quiet and on first acquaintance exerted no particular magnetism. There was a certain reserve about him. He liked talking, but often preferred to listen, and his style was ironical and self-deprecating. Socially relaxed and friendly, the creative writer in him was also at work, observing, amused, appreciative. In his letters to friends, he adopted a bantering and effusive style, addressing them affectionately in such terms as 'you enchanting creature', 'my pet' or 'laddie'.

During the year following the outbreak of war in 1914, Louis' contemporaries at Oxford, including Richard Blaker, volunteered straight from the University. Jewish Manchester, too, responded to the war like the rest of the nation — with a great number of young men joining up immediately. There was a keen desire, where so many were of recently foreign extraction, to be accepted as true nationals by serving their country. For some, there were difficulties: one was Britain's alliance to Russia, whence so many families had fled; others were religious pacifists, taking seriously the commandment 'Thou Shalt not Kill.' In *Five Silver Daughters* (1934), one of his finest novels, Louis drew with great compassion the ordeal of Harry Stonier, the conscientious objector. In *Magnolia Street* and other works he also

3

described the xenophobia to which some Jews were subjected during the war because of their foreign-sounding names. This was especially so when the neutral American liner Lusitania was sunk by a German submarine, and at the time of the Russian Revolution of 1917; but the record of the Manchester Jewish community in supporting the war effort as workers or soldiers was to their advantage.

This path, towards reconciliation, is a principal theme of *Magnolia Street*, which celebrates enduring Jewish values and the eventual acceptance of Jewish immigrant neighbours by the 'Christian' residents. The author is far from blind to faults within his own community — narrowness, over-anxiety and at worst, disloyalty to their kind, and callous self-advancement; but central to the book too, is the message that the Jewish input into English life had a strengthening effect on the locality, and that the worst damage came through malice, dissipation, lust and intolerance within the 'native' English ranks. On both sides, however, loyalty and generosity of spirit triumphed over these evils.

Louis' family was no exception to the widespread Jewish response to the wartime call to arms. His brother Jack joined up as a soldier and was killed in April 1918 — drawing from Louis some of the more moving poems in his 1919 collection, *Sorrow of War*. Louis, though not passed fit for the army, settled, like Max Emmanuel in *Magnolia Street*, for work in the Young Men's Christian Association, which took him up to the front, spending much of his war in the Macedonia-Salonika sector, until sent home, severely ill.

The idea of a Jewish boy working for the Young Men's Christian Association may seem incongruous; but in fact the YMCA religion was classless and inclusive and, as a result, the favoured form of Christian worship with most British Protestant soldiers on the Western Front. It was the opposite of the hated Church Parade — enforced turnout for soldiers in any weather, in full equipment (including rifles until later in the war) and an oppressively conventional Anglican service complete with irrelevant sermon. By contrast the YMCA dispensed a cheery non-denominational religion, heartfelt prayers in homely language and familiar old hymns bellowed out in manly fashion. Otherwise what the Association meant for soldiers far from home were comforts — mugs of tea or beer, cigarettes, extra food, fruit-gums and concerts. In such breezy company, Louis, detached and amused, enjoyed himself and was well-liked.

For its staff, YMCA service in Salonika could not be described as the most dangerous kind of work but it was hard, disciplined and not free of risk, in so far as back areas did get bombed and shelled fairly frequently. Most painful was the loss of soldier friends killed in the small-scale but insidious and frightening border fighting which rumbled on along the Balkan lines.

A sensitive man, like Louis, would have found much on which to brood. As at Oxford, there were anti-Semitic incidents during his time with the YMCA. There were also spare moments for the writing of poetry and literary reviews. In a later commentary on world events, *The World I Knew* (1940), he described his great sense of release through this, his first taste of foreign travel. His encounter, in February 1916, with the Greek civilization he had long studied, thrilled him, as did the mountainous scenery on the Macedonian Front. For the rest of his life he was an adventurous voyager.

Immediately after the First World War, he returned to Oxford to finish his studies. He was already launched on his writing career. One of his friends later remembered 'on such a blue and silver evening in early summer, when the stars powdered the sky with brilliance and the moon revealed every tower, cornice and dome I saw Louis Golding sitting on the step of the Sheldonian Theatre, an open notebook lying beside him... Golding was not writing but sitting and dreaming; perhaps he, too, was caught by the magic of the night.'

The war had left its mark. With dreaming went introspection and eventually nervous breakdown. He was overworking; his second book of poetry, *Shepherd Singing Ragtime*, and his first novel appeared while he was still at Oxford, as well as his regular contributions to the *Manchester Guardian*. More importantly, his ambitions and affections had separated him from his parents despite loyalty to his roots. His attraction to a bohemian way of life, to living for the emotional and pleasurable moment, conflicted with his moral upbringing.

However he emerged from this crisis, strengthened in resolve. His 'other mother', Mrs Owen, and her children had moved to London, partly at his urging. Now she and her husband, Neville Whymant, helped to get him noticed in the right circles — by Arnold Bennett and Rebecca West in particular. From early on,

Louis' writing dealt largely with Jewish themes. His first novel, *Forward from Babylon* (1920), was the forerunner of many others, which appeared in the 1930s, concentrating on bringing the Sycamore Street and Jewish Hightown of his youth to a wider world. The further he travelled, he said, the more he was drawn back to the scenes of his childhood, set in a fictional Manchester, which he called 'Doomington'. The choice of name implied a mixture of repulsion and attachment — both a dread of the place and, at the same time, his 'doom' to be forever tied to it.

His uneasy relationship with Manchester lay at the heart of two memorable sides of his character. First, his restlessness: in his journeying he seemed forever trying to distance himself from the admirable, but constricting, world of his upbringing. Travel writing for such works as *In the Steps of Moses the Conqueror* took him to the Middle East and the Balkans and as far as Malaya. He was often in the USA before the Second World War, lecturing, negotiating book deals and visiting relations. He wrote his books in a great variety of places — New York; Suez and Paris; Ardgay in Scotland; Tunis; Mühlau-bei-Innsbruck and Capri; Bovingdon (Richard Blaker's village) in Hertfordshire. *Magnolia Street* itself was composed in Hamburg and London, then completely revised in Berlin.

Another side of his character, much remarked on, was his passion for getting something for nothing, which went back to the extreme poverty which had haunted his childhood. On visits to friends, he could often be heard making requests as he left: 'Any eggs? Any biscuits? Or could you make me a little sandwich for the train?' It was not greed — nor was it close-fistedness, for he could be very generous — but a compulsion arising from his feeling of triumph over a terrible obstacle. The impresario Victor Hochhauser once described him as 'the great *schnorrer*' (a cadger or scrounger), and there was indeed something grandiose about the way Louis successfully talked his way into one 'freebie' after another. He expected to be treated as a celebrity wherever he went, assuming that if he came to a country and had written or was going to write enthusiastically about it, he would be made very welcome. In this he was usually — if not always — correct.

One day in the 1950s, when he was being driven by a friend through Chatham, in Kent, they stopped for a drink and a stroll round the town. They passed a naval establishment with a parade ground and got into conversation with an officer. Louis spun a story about how he (a very important novelist) was writing a novel about the navy. This led to them visiting HMS *Dolphin*, which was the shore establishment for submarines, and being invited to go on board a submarine during manoeuvres. They were taken on an admiral's barge to a large ship, joined an official dinner and had a great many drinks after which they fell asleep. At 4am, somewhat hung-over, they were woken to have breakfast and conveyed, in a storm, to the submarine, HMS *Tiptoe*, and her sister ship HMS *Tulip*. Louis was not particularly interested in submarines but what really delighted him was that they were given an open invitation to visit the navy any time they were travelling around the Mediterranean, all for nothing save inventing a little story about a novel which he might never write.

He always worked with an intense imaginative concentration. To gain inspiration, he would wrap a green cloth over his eyes and wander round the garden blotting out everything except what was going on in his mind. On one occasion he had been writing for hours on end and broke off exhausted just before describing a Judas-figure hanging himself. He flung himself down on his bed only to awake with a sensation of being strangled. For years, though hugely industrious, his hours were irregular and he often laboured at several projects at a time. One, which had remained incomplete for months, he finished in a single colossal effort, not stopping to undress for three days and three nights.

He took great care in preparing his novels, making exhaustive notes on such topics as world economics, high finance, political revolution and the eastern European ghettoes. For the authentic details about prize-fighting and the merchant navy in *Magnolia Street* he talked with boxers and sailors. His characters were drawn, initially, from life. Later, as he said, they developed their own existence. His interest in clothes, mannerisms, smells and social nuances was obsessive.

During the Second World War, he was heavily involved in propaganda for the war effort, following the success of his latest 'Doomington' novel, *Mr. Emmanuel*, which appeared just before the outbreak of war. The book began movingly with an account of Jewish refugee boys from Germany staying in the British countryside. This was drawn partly from Louis' friend Dick Blaker's expe-

7

rience — the Blakers took in two such boys, one of whom later went to Canada. The rest of the book, though based on diligent research, was less rooted in probability — but good to read in those tense days. It had both the charm and humour but also some of the glibness of one of the old Ealing comedy films — thoroughly English in fact, and despite the tragic circumstances of the book, in a curious way it, too, had elements of a comedy; but that seemingly was the mood of the time and what the public wanted. He followed this up with an enthusiastically received film version of the book, starring Felix Aylmer and the glamorous blonde Norwegian Greta Gynt — then one of the foremost actresses of the British screen. He scored a further hit with a script he wrote for a film on the Arnhem campaign, *This is the Glory*.

Quite apart from the overwhelming catastrophe of the Holocaust, the war years brought particular personal heartache for him. Thanks to his tendency to draw his characters from the life, he quarrelled — greatly to his regret — with his 'adopted mother' Mrs Whymant (though not with her children). Having seen one of his novels, *No News from Helen*, in the making, from an early stage and discussed it thoroughly and apparently having given her approval, she and her husband decided that it was libellous and tried to get the publishers to suppress it. Louis already felt bitter against them because they had not in his view done enough to help Dick Blaker, who was a close friend of theirs, and had married Mrs Whymant's daughter May. Blaker had died in 1940, penniless, in Hollywood, of drink and the long-term effects of First World War gas, having failed to earn a living as a screen-writer. The loss of his great friend, after great efforts to get him adequate hospital care, hit Louis hard.

After the war was over, he continued to enjoy a fan club among a now middle-aged readership, but his baroque style of writing was no longer in fashion and like most popular writers he gradually found himself overshadowed. By the time of his death, the name Golding, for the next generation of readers, had come to mean William Golding and *The Lord of the Flies*. In addition, he now encountered visa restrictions to the U.S.A., because of having written the film script for *The Proud Valley* (1940) starring the black, left-wing singer, Paul Robeson. However, perhaps on account of such radical contacts, he was not altogether out of touch with the younger literary world, and among his friends were the poets Dannie Abse and Emmanuel Litvinoff.

In the 1950s he went to live at Hamilton Terrace, St. John's Wood. As with all his houses, his new home was stylish. His study, the walls decorated in 1930s eau-de-nil, was on the second floor and had a bathroom attached to it. He slept on a divan in a corner of the room. As a host he kept an excellent table, with meals provided by his housekeeper, Mrs Kastner, a middle-class German-Jewish refugee, who had been in Teresianstadt concentration camp. He enjoyed, as ever, a reputation as a brilliant and hilarious raconteur.

His output never flagged, but now, as an older man, he settled to an established routine: at 10 o'clock in the morning he would dictate his correspondence from his bath to his secretary in the other room. At 10.30 he wrote at his big maplewood art deco desk or in his eau-de-nil armchair, until lunchtime. Lunch was his main meal, followed by coffee in the sitting room and a short walk. In the afternoon he slept in bed with a black mask over his eyes. From 4 to 5 he resumed writing. This was followed by supper, unless he was going out to dinner or, less frequently, giving a formal dinner party. Usually, he would end the evening at the cinema or theatre, invite friends round informally, or go to 'Fitzrovia' — in the form of the cheerful Fitzroy Tavern, an artists', left-wing politicians' and actors' favourite. Annie and Charlie Allchild, the good-hearted Jewish couple who ran it, invited patrons such as Louis to contribute to their fund, 'Pennies from Heaven', for poor East End children.

For his servants and his secretaries and assistants who typed his manuscripts and arranged his travel, the regime at Louis's house was dictatorial. From his study he would issue commands, using a buzzer. Everybody had to be exactly where he wanted them to be when he wanted them, and he easily felt let down if they failed to obey promptly. Nonetheless he enjoyed their devotion — as among his friends — on account of his *joie de vivre* and wide-ranging curiosity about people and their lives, which lay at the root of his writing. Not least, he was capable of considerable generosity to those he appreciated. Among his beneficiaries in his later years were the cultivated Adair sisters to whom he lent money, seemingly without expectation of repayment, to start a literary club in Soho.

Surprisingly, late in his life, he married, a relationship based on affection and admiration. His wife, Annie Wintrobe, was a childhood friend, a widow from the same Manchester roots, who in her youth had been partly the model for Bella Winberg in *Magnolia Street*. She was sweet-natured, charming and a wonderful cook. Their marriage came too late for them to have a close life together for long. She made him comfortable, but he was still a busy writer distracted by his commitments, travelling abroad as ever, and within two years he was dead, of cancer of the pancreas. He lived to see his novel, *The Little Old Admiral*, appear in that year, 1958, signing off, typically, 'Motor-Yacht *Di-Ell II*, August 9th 1957.' A final, unfinished novel of his, which was completed by a neighbour and fellow writer, Rupert Croft-Brooke, was published long afterwards.

Like the work of most prolific writers, Louis's books are uneven. *Magnolia Street* was not his favourite book. He preferred *Five Silver Daughters,* which takes a deeper look at the Russian antecedents of the characters in the book and the postwar Russian and German scene. *Magnolia Street*'s faults are evident to the modern reader. It is sometimes repetitive, because of the need to reintroduce characters who have appeared and disappeared a hundred pages before. It can be unashamedly sentimental after the manner of Arnold Bennett.

Its spectacular success, however, was well deserved. It is a book on a grand scale, appealing to Jews and non-Jews alike. Its message, for all the unhappiness it encompasses, is joyous and positive, and it is full of humorous incident. It is also an important document of social life in northern Britain before and during the First World War. More memorably than any other English Great War writer, save possibly Henry Williamson, on suburban South London, in his *Chronicle of Ancient Sunlight*, Louis Golding draws a picture of how that war affected a particular district from a home front angle, with his vignettes of grief, anti-German hatred, local heroes, jealous soldier husbands and military charlatans. In *Magnolia Street* he does not set out to denigrate loyalty and patriotism, though writing at a time when this was fashionable. Nor does he question *why* the war was fought: he concentrates on its ironies and tragedies. One irony of the book is that the First World War, that terrible effort of mutual destruction, brought people together, integrating immigrants with their English neighbours.

Above all *Magnolia Street* is a classic account of the life of Russian-Jewish refugees in Manchester, doing for that city what Israel Zangwill (1864-1926), for example, did for Bethnal Green with his novel, *Children of the Ghetto*. There is a Dickensian quality about the boldly sketched players and the author's unconcealed contempt or affection for them. Like the works of Arnold Bennett, *Magnolia Street* has a profound sense of place and period. A vivid evocation of a world already disappearing by the time it was published, Louis Golding's 'Doomington' epic still makes compelling reading.

Hugh Cecil
October 2005

Note: Throughout this edition, the word "nigger" has been changed to "negro", "black man" and (the Yiddish) "schvartzer". As used in the 1930s, the word was not so outrightly offensive as it has become in modern times. Otherwise, the original text, complete with some archaic spellings and punctuation, is unaltered.

Book I

Chapter 1

I

This is a tale of a small street in the Longton district of Doomington, in the North Country. Its name is Magnolia Street, and the streets that run parallel with it, right and left across the central thoroughfare of Blenheim Road, are called after the mimosa, the acacia, the laburnum, the oleander, and several other blossoming shrubs that never blossomed in this neighbourhood since the Romans were hereabouts.

It is the street of the magnolia which will occupy the whole of our attention during the course of this history. We shall not attempt to deal with the arbutus, or with the rosemary. Heaven knows that the Winbergs, the Derrickses, the Shulmans, the Coopers, the Bermans, will keep us busy enough over the crowded years which extend between 1910 and 1930 when we take a last glimpse of them.

But let this be clear at once. We do not hope to render the tale of the small street from year to year over a score of years. Merely to record what was thought and said and done in Malkeh Poyser's grocery-shop or Steve Tawnie's public-house during so long a period would be a task which might appal the grimmest chronicler. But it may be possible to present some sort of picture of what was happening before the war, in 1910, and during the war, and to indicate where, in 1930, it all led to. And the task seems worth undertaking because, of those of our fellows who live in cities, the greater number live in just such a small street.

But we must get hold of the special quality of Magnolia Street, in virtue of which it is so much more adapted to our purpose than the streets of the oleander or laburnum. For the street itself plays a role at least as important as any of the humans in this chronicle. Its main configuration was the same in 1910, when Benny Edelman so comically saved little Tommie Wright's life, as it was in 1930. The Jews lived in the odd-numbered houses on the south side of the street; the gentiles lived opposite in the even-numbered houses. So it is to this day. The Jewish working-folk have infiltrated into the streets north of Magnolia Street; the gentiles have seeped back, again south of it. But generally speaking, in the even houses of Magnolia Street only the gentiles live, and in the odd houses the Jews.

Now the space that divides the two sides of the small street is a matter of thirty feet or so. But during the greater part of the time covered by this history, that space might have been a broad sea, so strange to each other did those folk seem. But there were moments or periods or passions, in which they were as one folk, either all of them publicly or few of them secretly. There was Benny Edelman, for instance, saving the life of little Tommie Wright, and causing as much excitement as a cup-tie. There was a great war that broke out, and for a time, at least, there was no division between the odd and even pavements. There was the death of a young man who had survived all the hazards of the War to have his skull smashed after a football-match. And all night long, on both sides of the street, there was weeping among the women, the Jews and the gentiles equally, for the youth was much loved. There was the love of Rose Berman and John Cooper. She was a shop-assistant. He was a merchant-sailor and came back to Magnolia Street from time to time. But no-one knew of this love, though, for a time, it was suspected. These things will be told in their place; but they were exceptional.

By the spring-time of 1910, the greater part of the district of Longton south of Magnolia Street had hauled its flag down before the advance of Jewish immigration. And Magnolia Street had not. It was hard to say why. Acacia Street gave up the gentile cause without showing fight at all. Mimosa Street and Lavender Street resisted the movement for a greater or a lesser period. There was positively a pitched battle in Oleander Street, but the Levinsky family, which captained the Jewish division, was acclaimed victor in the end. And Magnolia Street, as we said, stood firm.

It was not that its architecture was more in the nature of a medieval fortress than the architecture of Acacia Street. Nothing could be demurer than its five-roomed houses and tiny front gardens (they soon ceased to be gardens on the Jewish side of the street). A likely interpretation of the mystery is Miss Tregunter, of the upstairs front-room in number twelve, an ancient maiden lady of genteel manners and inflexible will-power. Early one morning Miss Tregunter rose from her bed to draw the curtains aside and shoo the cats away from the dusty

16

little box-hedge of her garden. And looking across to the opposite side of Magnolia Street, the overwhelming fact fell upon her that it had wholly lapsed into Jewish occupation.

"This must stop!" said Miss Tregunter to herself. (So it might be figured out.) "This must stop!" And it did.

You never saw her conducting an actual propaganda. Nor did she ever stand at the front door of number twelve and call names, as Mrs Derricks of number eight used to, at any hour of the day or night, after one of her son's famous theatrical parties. No. Miss Tregunter merely drew her curtains aside and shooed the cats away from the garden, and snipped the dead leaves from the geraniums in her window-boxes; or at most, she shook her bony finger at some swarthy little Jewish boys who had the effrontery to play piggy-and-stick within twenty yards of her window. Whereon the little boys with sinking hearts realised they were already late for *chayder*, Hebrew school. And they crept away guiltily, and Miss Tregunter settled back again upon her stiff arm-chair to keep watch through her steel-rimmed glasses and lace curtains over the gentile privileges of Magnolia Street. She was the insuperable nucleus of resistance, which saved a half of Magnolia Street for gentiledom.

Nothing so vulgar as street brawls took place in Magnolia Street, though sometimes the Derrickses and their friends, the "Boys," gathered at the front door, being very drunk, and shouted with all their lungs when one of the old Jews came by! "If yer vant to buy a vatch, buy a vatch! If not, get away from my vinder!" It was a vulgar exhibition, and it displeased Miss Tregunter, sitting behind her window-boxes.

But if the old Jew who came by happened to be Rabbi Shulman, with his greasy coat, his dinted silk-hat, his long black beard, his wild eyes, he was not displeased. Though the Derrickses cheered and jeered and cried "Old Clo'es!" till the tears ran from their eyes, he was not displeased. He was not aware of them. He was not aware of Miss Tregunter, however frigidly she stared down at him from between her lace curtains. It was as if he walked at the centre of a pillar of flame, and he heard only the sound of that flame whistling and the voices of creatures compounded out of a similar substance. There was a smile on his face, and he muttered, as if in reply to some spiritual being who had addressed him.

17

Chapter 2

I

There were four institutions in Magnolia Street which fulfilled the functions of clubs in a more leisurely order of society. They stood at the four corners of the street. The two gentile clubs were Steve Tawnie's public-house, the Lamb and Lion, at the Blenheim Road corner, and Mrs Durbin's barber-saloon, at the corner of Aubrey Street. The adults assembled at the Lamb and Lion, the youths at the saloon. The conversation in the public-house was rather more philosophical than the conversation at Mrs Durbin's.

It faced up to the problems of the universe. At the saloon the conversation moved along the two channels of girls and sport.

At the opposite corners were the two Jewish clubs. Facing the saloon was the synagogue, called the Lithuanian Brotherhood. The worshippers included babes in arms and mummy-like old women, but as a club it was the rendezvous for the greybeards. The Jewish women met socially in Mrs Poyser's grocery-shop, facing the Lamb and Lion. There they foregathered in between the washing-up after one meal and the preparation for the next; or they called in on their way from the market, to show what a fat chicken they had picked up or how fine a silver hake for chopping and frying.

On a certain Sunday morning in May, in the year 1910, there was news, and news of the Mrs Poyser sort. News was, in a sense, Mrs Poyser's prerogative. She weighed it, she sorted it out into bags, she handed it over the counter, along with a pair of kippers or a pound of sultanas.

The sort of news, that is to say, which concerned a young man and a young woman, and was it really serious, and how much dowry did she have, and how much did the engagement ring cost him. They went in for another sort of news at the Lamb and Lion and the barber-saloon: such and such an outsider was a dead certainty for the Derby; Doomington United had arranged to buy from Sheffield Wednesday the full-back who had so distinguished himself last season. As for the Lithuanian Brotherhood, news travelled slowly there. You might have thought they had heard only yesterday that Titus had destroyed the Temple, so sadly they shook their heads and beat their breasts.

It was Mrs Seipel, the cabinet-maker's wife, who brought the news in to the grocery-shop that morning. The news she brought was of such a nature that it quite put out of her head the fact that she had had another letter last night from her rich brother, Adolf, in New York. It was one of the loveliest letters she had had from him for a long time. It was an exciting letter. She, and her husband, and her grandfather, and her children, might as well start packing up for New York this very day. But the news she brought in to Mrs Poyser's shop was exciting, too, more immediately exciting. She forgot to tell the women about Adolf's letter. They forgot to ask her had she heard from him. She told her tale. She wrung her hands. "Can you believe it?" she asked miserably.

It was clear she herself did not wish to believe it. Mrs Poyser suspended judgment. She patted into shape smartly the lump of butter on the scales. The other women conferred among each other with dismay and incredulity on their faces. The door-bell tinkled. Old Mrs Edelman entered.

"Good morning!" she said.

"Good morning!" answered the assembled women.

"It's not true!" Mrs Poyser determined.

"What is not true?" asked old Mrs Edelman.

"Nothing! Nothing!" said Mrs Seipel hurriedly.

It was not the sort of news to retail to old Mrs Edelman.

"Her boy, Sam, said he saw Rose Berman walking out with a gentile yesterday!" narrated Mrs Poyser coldly. Then a flush of colour mounted suddenly to her high cheek-bones. She turned on Mrs Seipel. "I hope you gave him a good box on the ear, he should not tell such lies again!"

"A Jewish girl? With a *goy*? Yesterday? *But it was the Sabbath!*" Old Mrs Edelman enunciated the clauses slowly and terribly. They called her old though she was only about forty. Her hair was grey, her chin was hard. She had hard grey eyes. She looked older than many women twenty years her senior.

"A Jewish girl from this street!" added Mrs Poyser, as if it were the high point of the infamy that the girl came from Mrs Poyser's street.

19

"Rose Berman it was!" announced Mrs Seipel hurriedly. After all it was *her* story. It was *her* son, Sam, who had seen them walking out together in a park in South Doomington.

"A gentile from this street!" supplemented Mrs Poyser. "Would you believe it?" She looked at Mrs Seipel with a glance that suggested it must all be a malicious invention on somebody's part.

Mrs Seipel's stock was not high this morning. You might think she had no rich brother, Adolf, in New York, from the way they all looked at her. The little woman was wretched. She wondered was it not somehow her fault. She had not boxed little Sam on the ear. But then she was never unkind to anybody, not even her own children. She determined next time Sam said he saw a Jewish girl walking out with a gentile boy, she would be very stern about it.

"Maybe he did *not* see her!" she suggested lamely.

But Mrs Poyser now, for the time being, transferred her weight to the other side of the balance. "He did! Of course he did! Why else should he say such a thing?"

"God would prevent it!" benevolently suggested Mrs Emmanuel, the wife to the clerk of the Jewish Board of Guardians.

"What?" Mrs Shulman rapped out. She was the wife of the Rabbi, who lived two doors away, at number five. She felt that God was her husband's prerogative and Mrs Emmanuel had no right to be deciding what God would or would not do. "If God wills a thing it is so!" she pronounced. The dictum admitted of no argument. "But He would not will such a thing! No, He would not!" she conceded.

There was silence for half a minute. A pound of rice slipped from Mrs Poyser's shovel into a bag, down to the last punctilious grain. Mrs Seipel fumbled with the handles of the shopping-bag. Her eyes wandered to the heaped groceries in the window on her left hand. Between the pyramids of salmon tins and the mound of loaves, she suddenly caught sight of him descending the steps of number six. It was the young man whom Sam had said he saw walking out with Rose Berman yesterday. It was the young man who was going to be captain of a ship some day. His name was John Cooper. He walked with a slight swing in the shoulders and hips as if the pavement of Magnolia Street lifted slowly to the pull of the moon. His face came into view, bronzed and firm. A handsome young man...

Mrs Seipel turned away, blushing to the roots of her hair. She had a poignant vision of Rose Berman's mother only next door, a few yards away, sitting in her scrupulous kitchen under the brass trays and candlesticks. Or she might be cutting into rhomboids the *ingber*, the cooked ginger sweetmeat, she sold in her little parlour-shop. She was chirping away like the kettle on the hob. Her face was pink as a doll's. She stopped chirping, as the cough bubbled out slowly from the depth of her lungs. The cough eased. Then she took up the note again, her eyes shining just a little brighter than before.

"Rose Berman! Oh Rose Berman!" protested the inner voice of Mrs Seipel. "How could you be so cruel to your poor mother? And you always so wonderful to her! Oh Rose, Rose!"

"A gentile from this street!" repeated Mrs Poyser. It was almost as if it might have been tolerable had it happened in anyone else's street.

"What?" asked Mrs Billig, the latest arrival. "This street? What number?" Mrs Billig did not ask out of idle curiosity. It was her duty to acquire all data regarding Jewish maidens and Jewish youths, their comings and goings and hand them over to her husband, the kind Mr Billig. For Mr Billig arranged weddings. There were some who called him outright a marriage-broker. But that was not just. He brought young people together because it did him good to see them happy, not merely because he made a commission out of it from both sides. It made his blue eyes twinkle with joy. He purred and stroked his stomach and said "Ram-bam-bam!"

"What does it matter who?" Mrs Edelman twisted herself round so sharply that you seemed to hear the bones creak. "A gentile is a gentile!" She herself had two sons. She knew that the moon would go up in flame like a newspaper before anyone might say of either of them he had been seen walking out with a gentile girl.

"Yes! Yes! So I say too!" cooed Mrs Billig. "I'm sure it's as you say, Mrs Shulman. God would not will such a thing. A little boy. He walks a long way. No, Mrs Seipel, a little boy like your Sam, he should not walk such a long way. He gets tired. He sees things that are not there."

Mrs Seipel hung her head. She was beginning to feel it *was* her fault, definitely. She should have kept Sam in yesterday afternoon, to say the week's portion out of the Pentateuch, to do his soul good. She turned her head from side to side, embarrassed. The other women seemed to look at her with blame in their eyes, only sister though she might be of the rich Uncle Adolf, who lived in New York.

Then, happily, the door-bell clanged again. It was Rose Berman herself who came in, none other. Naturally it was Rose who came in when there was shopping to do at the Bermans'. It would not be Rose's mother, who was quite busy enough these days in her little home-made-sweets shop. Nor would it be Ada, Rose's younger sister. Ada was no doubt too busy cleaning her fingernails and brushing her fine pale hair.

"Good morning, everyone!" said Rose Berman. She smiled. The women smiled and nodded. The suspicion within them melted in the warmth and odour she brought in with her. "My mother's quite run out of ginger, Mrs Poyser," said Rose. "And cinnamon. I ask you, can you make *ingber* without ginger and cinnamon? How much can you let me have?" she asked briskly. "I'm going to make her a good stock of *ingber* this afternoon. How's Becky?" she wanted to know. Becky was Mrs Poyser's daughter. "I thought she looked sweet in her green dress yesterday."

Mr Poyser had appeared behind the counter a minute or two ago, after some mysterious trafficking with sugar-bags at the rear of the premises. He appeared, but no-one had taken note of his existence. One talked of Mrs Poyser's shop, not Mr Poyser's, though he was in evidence as much as his wife. He was visible but not audible. He merely did the weighing and the packing, while Mrs Poyser attended to the spiritual part of the business. He was a thin man, with hollow cheeks overgrown with a short stubble and, when he used it, a secret sepulchral voice. But when he talked with his daughter, Becky, his voice had a fluting fullness in it. When he heard praise of her, which was rare, a blush held his hollow cheeks.

"You liked her green dress, yes, Rose?" he said eagerly. "I chose the stuff for her!"

"Absolutely the right shade!" said Rose, smiling at him. He smiled back humbly.

"Thank you, Mrs Poyser, thank you so much. I must be getting back. mother will start polishing the *samovar*, or the candlesticks, or something, if I'm away any longer. You know what she is!"

The other women knew what she was. "Go, Rose, go!" they said. Their eyes beamed, as they followed her out of the shop and past the window.

"It is a shame, a scandal!" Mrs Poyser decided suddenly, "To say such a thing of such a girl!"

The voices of Mrs Shulman, Mrs Billig, Mrs Edelman, two or three other ladies from neighbouring streets were lifted in affirmation of Mrs Poyser's decision.

The word had gone forth. Rose Berman had *not* gone out walking yesterday with John Cooper, the merchant sailor, who came up from the sea from time to time, and went back again. She was a good girl, a Jewish girl. She loved her mother dearly. How should she go out walking with a gentile sailor? How should she? *But she had.* Little Mrs Seipel knew. She was younger than the other women. There was something in the quiver of Rose's lip that morning, there was a light all about her. A wicked light it might be, but it flickered and sparkled on her hair and cheeks. And the young man, he was so quiet and handsome. It would be a hard thing for any girl, if he looked at her from under his eyebrows, to say to him: "No, no, you must go... what will the neighbours say?"

"But your mother, Rose, your mother!" Mrs Seipel implored. "She is so weak. She hangs on a hair. If she finds out...."

It was about time she made Mrs Berman one of those light egg-cakes she liked so much, Mrs Seipel realised. She remembered with a twinge of conscience that it was many weeks now since she had brought in some little home-made dainty for Mrs Berman.

"Good morning, all!" she said. She felt guilty and unhappy. She hurried off down the street, to number nineteen, home. She remembered suddenly the lovely letter that had come last night from Uncle Adolf. He was her brother, but she always thought of him as uncle, just as her own children did, and all the children in the street did. The thought of the letter eased her heart. In a month, or two, at latest, all their worries would be over. They would be sailing off to New York, with a trunk full of English linen and cutlery.

In the meanwhile she must get that egg-cake made quickly for Mrs Berman.

She must take the egg-cake over as soon as possible, to serve as buffer between the delicate little woman and the harsh news that threatened her, that was probably even now on its way to her. Little Mrs Seipel shook her head.

"Rose, Rose!" she sighed.

II

There was a glory about number nineteen, where the Seipels lived. When the front-door was opened an elfin music fell upon the spiritual ear. Uncle Adolf was the name of that glory and the notes of that music.

The stranger, as he passed by the front-door that May morning, would not have realised how glorious that house was. He would have been unaware of Uncle Adolf, the celebrated New York business-man. As he saw Mrs Seipel approaching,he would not have suspected she had so glorious a brother. If he had seen Mr Seipel come in a few minutes earlier from his melancholy little cabinet-maker's workshop away across the town, he would not have been tempted to accredit Mr Seipel with so heavenly a brother-in-law.

Heavenly... that was the sort of language you were driven to regarding Uncle Adolf. In a sense he really belonged rather to Heaven than this earth, and you do not bother the angels with tales about the children needing boots and the cabinet-making has been so bad during the last six months it has been necessary to pawn the sewing-machine.

Of course Uncle Adolf understood things were not any too well with his sister in Magnolia Street. He had already promised a number of times to send over an enormous money-order to pay the family's fare to America and settle all their debts. But this time it was quite certain. The letter in the clock said so. Yet if Uncle Adolf could only understand that sometimes it was a matter of not being able to lay out the money for butter, and Mrs Seipel didn't hold by margarine, he would certainly have sent along a few dollars just to get along with. There wasn't any doubt of that.

On the other hand, how could you expect so big a business-man to think in terms of a pound of butter or a new pair of shoes for little Janey? So once, when things had been very black for months, and the weather seemed to be getting colder instead of warmer and there wasn't a shovelful of coal in the house, Mrs

Seipel *did* bring herself to write him a letter. She hated doing it, though he was her own born brother by both parents. She could give away to a poor man, Jew or non-Jew, the one little slice of fried fish she had kept back for herself, and her face quite pinched for want of food. But she could not bring herself to ask anybody for anything, not even Adolf, though he was rich enough to have all the fish in Loch Lomond caught and fried for his guests at a single dinner party.

However, things had been very bad of late, with all these strikes and lock-outs in the cabinet-making world. So she bit her lip and sat down to the sewing-machine, which was not then in pawn, and wrote to Uncle Adolf. And then she cried for shame.

"Mammy," her small daughter, Janey, exclaimed. "What are you crying for?"

"I'm not crying!" said Mrs Seipel.

"But you are, you are!" insisted Janey. Her own mouth trembled too.

"Crying? Am I? So I am!" realised Mrs Seipel. "Don't you know, Janey? Didn't I tell you? Next week it is the anniversary of the death of my poor mother, peace be upon her! She died so young, it always makes me cry!" Janey was not convinced.

And then, about four weeks later, a letter came from Uncle Adolf. He had written almost the very moment he got his sister's letter; which just showed the sort of man he was. Pure gold. Any other brother with a tenth part of the business that Adolf had to deal with would have left his sister waiting for months before he got down to an answer. There was no money in the letter. But in a way the letter was sweeter than if it had contained five one-hundred-dollar notes, all crisp and shining and boot-buying and wallpaper-providing. It was a fine letter. He let Hannah, his sister, know how much he loved her, and Reuben, his brother-in-law, and Janey, his niece, and Sam, Eli and Berel, his nephews, and old Reb Feivel, his grandfather, who lived with them. He loved them all. And quite soon he hoped to send over the money for all their tickets and their outfits; they had as good as got it on the mantelpiece already.

But as for Ready Money, it was like this. In a way it would have been more convenient if the sum that had been asked for had been a really big sum. It was so much more awkward when you were in business to deal in small sums. Small sums were much more difficult to get hold of. The point was, that if once the clerks started talking about the boss dealing in small sums, it would do no end of damage. The next stage was that your rivals in the business got wind of what was happening.

"Ha!" they said to themselves. "So this is the sort of shyster business that poor old Adolf has been forced to come down to! Ha!"

And they smiled and winked when you came into the club, and they tapped the sides of their noses. And before you knew where you were.... The whole Seipel family in Magnolia Street on the other side of the ocean recoiled with horror from the brink of the abyss which Uncle Adolf hinted at. And to think that they themselves had very nearly pushed Uncle Adolf over! Old Reb Feivel, and Hannah and Reuben Seipel, and Janey aged twelve, and Sam aged eight, and Eli aged four, and Berel, aged two, sighed and shook their heads. But there was salt herring with the potatoes that night; for Reuben had got an order for two wash-stands. And Berel could get through as many salt herrings as a seal. He thrived on them. He was a bonny baby.

That was one of the noblest things about Uncle Adolf. He never lost patience with his poor old relations in Doomington, though what with the company he kept these days in New York, judges and magnates and managers and heaven knows what else, he might have been forgiven if he had written far less frequently.

He always kept them posted as to the developments of his business, which was Real Estate. Even as a boy in Russia, he had had grand ideas. Of course you couldn't expect anything to come of them, in a small village on the Dnieper. But New York was giving him his chance — as it would give them all their chance, he reminded them, in a month or two, please God, as soon as he had the Ready Money.

Ready Money. That was the keystone of the arch, the *leit motif* of his almost operatic letters. The whole difference between the Old World and the New lay in this very matter of Ready Money. The American idea was that you shouldn't have any Ready Money. It was all wrong. It was wasteful. In a sense the very fact that he had never had any Ready Money, was the source from which the golden waters of his success flowed.

Now when Reb Feivel, his own grandfather and Hannah's, came over from Russia to Doomington, at the express suggestion of Adolf, the idea had been that he should send over a little money annually to keep the old man in comfort. But just at the time he arrived in England, some five or six years earlier, Ready Money had been just a little tighter than usual; so, of course, Adolf hadn't been able to send it. And since that time it had slipped his mind.

Not that Reb Feivel was in the way. He ate about as much as a sparrow, was gentle as a dove, was wise as an owl, and in his love for his Lord splendid as an eagle. There was so much benignity in his seamed cheeks and so soft a light in his old eyes that he took peace with him wherever he went; and if he appeared at a moment when Mrs Derricks stood upon the opposite pavement, jeering in her drunkenness at the smoggy van Jews and demanding who killed Christ — even Mrs Derricks was checked at the height of her anathema and her voice broke, and she tottered back into her own kitchen unsteadily.

For though you might have said of the other Jews in Magnolia Street that they nourished a spark within their bosoms which, fanned into flame, might have agitated them into nailing Christ upon a cross, somehow it seemed flatly impossible that Reb Feivel could have done so cruel a thing. He would, with that streak of sweet cunning there was in him, have had himself strung up first upon that same cross, and there would have been no place that evening for the hanging up of Jesus, that evening or ever again. And that would have been a poor thing for the race of theologians. But Reb Feivel was not there. Even Mrs Derricks confessed as much. So they hung up Christ, after all, between the thieves.

No, Mrs Seipel did not mind having her grandfather, that rare old man, under her roof. Though she remembered him from her girlhood days in Russia, sometimes she was not quite certain whether this old one she cherished now was quite the same. She remembered the celestial Visitors who had come to Abraham and had put Sarah to the test, and Sarah had laughed. But Hannah Seipel did not laugh. She looked at him when he bent his head over the holy books with a sort of awe. Was he a Visitor or merely a grandfather? She wondered if she heard voices round about his head. Perhaps she was hungry, sometimes, and got a little light-headed.

She would have liked it greatly if dear Adolf had managed to get hold of a little of that elusive Ready Money which he had promised for the maintenance of the old man. She and her husband, Reuben, God be praised, could do all the maintaining that was necessary. But how fine it would be to buy him a new silk praying-shawl instead of his old cotton one, which was so threadbare! And a stick, an ebony walking-stick, with a bone handle and a collar of stamped silver!

There hadn't been any Ready Money, unfortunately, for Reb Feivel. And it was the same when Passover came round each year, and when the children were born.

The claims of Real Estate, alas, were always too exigent.

Yet they were all very happy, thank God. And last night, only last night, a letter had come from Uncle Adolf, in which he told them he had thought of a way of getting hold of a little Ready Money without letting his clerks know. It would be with them in a few weeks. And then good-bye to cabinet-making, goodbye to the long trudge to the market to save threepence on the Sabbath chicken. When they joined Uncle Adolf in New York, poulterers would come round to their own door and offer them fat geese and ducks, like those that waddled in the old home in Russia, among the creeks of the Dnieper!

Mrs Seipel passed through the lobby into the kitchen of her house.

The pot of broad beans for her husband's dinner was spluttering on the hearth. Janey must have put them on for him. Janey often had to look after the family while Mrs Seipel was doing this and that for other people. Mr Seipel sat at the table before his pile of Yiddish newspapers. He had a superstitious reverence for the printed word in Yiddish. Janey sat on the sofa reading melancholy poems about ladies named Oriana and Mariana in a penny selection from the poems of Lord Tennyson. The two elder boys, Sam and Eli, were at Reb Aryeh's Hebrew-school at the corner of the street, next door to the synagogue. The baby Berel, sat on the floor, wondering what his big thumb was about.

"Well?" asked Mr Seipel as his wife entered. "What did they say? There was a fine noise, eh?"

"I don't care what they all say," Mrs Seipel said defiantly. "It's poor Mrs Berman I'm thinking of."

"What is it, mamma?" asked Janey quietly.

"Weren't you here when Sam came back yesterday?"

"No. What is it?"

"Rose Berman from our street. Sam saw her arm in arm with that sailor from across the street. Cooper, *you* know. He's got a sister in your school, hasn't he?"

Mrs Seipel did not notice the deep flush that spread over her daughter's cheeks. She did not notice the way Janey buried her face in her book again.

She did not know that the lovely melancholy maidens were no longer called Oriana, Mariana.... Enid, Enid, was their name.

"Oi!" a disappointed sound came from the scullery. "No eggs!" deplored Mrs Seipel. "And I *did* so want to make an egg-cake for Mrs Berman." She came back into the kitchen again. "Janey darling," she begged. "I don't want to go back into Mrs Poyser's. Go and get me half a dozen of the very best eggs. Take the shopping-book with you."

Janey put Lord Tennyson down on the sofa.

"Did you pay anything off the amount this morning?" she asked.

"No, darling, no." Mrs Seipel looked round helplessly to her husband. He was deep in his Yiddish newspaper. "There's only one-and-threepence in the house. And we owe Mrs Poyser four pounds five and six. So I thought I'd give the one and threepence to the butcher. But then I thought the children would like some pink-cream chocolate." Her voice lacked conviction. Janey knew very well who the pink-cream chocolate was for. Pink-cream chocolate was Mrs Seipel's one extravagance.

"Give me the book, mamma," said Janey. "I'll go. And the rest of the one-and-threepence to pay off Mrs Poyser."

"Uncle Adolf —" Mrs Seipel started off. Janey said nothing. Her mouth twisted a little wryly. She put Oriana and Mariana out of her small brother's reach and went off for the eggs.

The Seipels were always getting into debt. The sewing-machine, Mrs Seipel's fur stole, Mr Seipel's large microscope (which he had won in a raffle) led a vagrant existence between the pawnshop and number nineteen Magnolia Street. (It was always the gentile woman who put in the fires on the Sabbath who did the pawning. Mrs Seipel would have died with shame to be seen entering a pawnshop.)

It was not because the Seipels were improvident or had expensive tastes that they were always in debt. The children were neat but never gaudy. Mrs Seipel liked her bar of pink-cream chocolate once a week, if possible, but apart from that, did not eat enough. Mr Seipel loved his broad beans to distraction. But that was not reason enough to keep the family so chronically in debt.

It was, of course, partly Uncle Adolf. The whole street knew about Uncle Adolf, what a great business he had in New York, and how generous he was.

How far that little candle threw its beams! The light fell faint and golden on the faces of the whole Seipel family. Tradesmen insisted on the Seipels taking out credit accounts with them. And the fact is, that a bill for three-and-six for the week's milk is not hard to pay, but after two months the milk bill is a lump in the throat. You can't swallow it.

But it wasn't only Uncle Adolf. It wasn't all these lock-outs and strikes in the cabinet-making trade, either.

After all, there were other cabinet-makers, and they managed to keep going. It was the incurable habit of the whole Seipel family, from old Reb Feivel to his great-grandson, Berel, of helping lame dogs over stiles. Janey was as bad as any of them. It was significant that when she first received an autograph album, the first verse to be inscribed in its lemon-yellow pages was the celebrated injunction regarding lame dogs:

Do the work that's nearest
Though it's dull at whiles
Helping when you meet them
Lame dogs over stiles.

You would not have found it hard to believe that on the occasion of the birth of each of the Seipels, a choir of angels gathered about his crib chanting that madrigal. Doubtless they sang a Hebrew version over Reb Feivel's cradle in Kravno and he, where he lay beside his mother's breast, overheard them, and having but lately left their company, understood every word they said.

They must have been a company of angels oddly unlike the imaginings of Fra Angelico, with their wings tucked in under their caftans and the ringlets of their ear-locks tumbling down against their ethereal cheeks.

The Seipel children were all just as quixotic as their parents and grandfather. No sooner had the boys received their allowance of nuts for the Passover than they were out in the street distributing them to boys less lucky than themselves. The baby, Berel, found it more than he could do not to give away his rattle or his sponge-biscuit to any baby that turned up. (The sponge-biscuit was not such a sacrifice, for he preferred salt herrings.) As for Janey, her generosity was morbid. This very morning she was in a state of pitiable sniffle because she had given away her last and loveliest handkerchief to Rachel, the daughter of Rabbi Shulman, whose need was greater than hers. She thrust upon her her hair-ribbons, her day's lunch, her story-books, because she looked so shabby and wretched. But Rachel Shulman was not wretched. She was merely too vacuous to refuse to accept these things, which she made no use of. Her family had lived on irregular contributions from many sources ever since she could remember. So she accepted Janey Seipel's handkerchiefs and hair-ribbons as the church accepts its tithes. She dropped them behind the kitchen-sofa, where there was already a great accumulation of odds and ends. A day or two later Rachel added another handkerchief to the heap, and, lifting the hem of her skirt, wiped her running nose. It was no joy to Janey Seipel to make these offerings to Rachel Shulman. For the true joy of giving is when we give to those who are richer than ourselves. And, in truth, there was one human creature who seemed to Janey so much richer than herself that she would willingly have added to the heap of her wealth, her autograph-album, her best shoes, her life itself, all, all.

It was not a man. Janey Seipel, who was nearly twelve years old, had no illusions about men. She was the only member of the family who entertained any doubts about the magnificence of Uncle Adolf, though she never breathed a word of her doubts to anyone. She knew that her father was a great darling, she loved him dearly; but she knew that if he were not just a little bit silly they would have prospered more. All men to her seemed either somewhat silly or somewhat cruel. Always they were somewhat coarse. She was a child, but she had learned much in her few years that it would take her many years to unlearn.

It was not a man she was in love with. It was a girl of the gentiles, who lived on the opposite pavement, Enid, the sister of that John Cooper, the seaman, who was also beloved by another Jewish girl.

It was a strange thing that the Cooper family should have provided for two Jewish girls, their heart's secret delight, their own private and divine possessions. They provided also, in the person of little Dick Cooper, a gold-haired lad of eleven, a creature whom the whole street loved, Jews and gentiles, but quite openly. The child had the sort of beauty and innocence which a meadow has, with lambs skipping in it. He was too lovely not to be loved. Perhaps these Coopers were either secretly or publicly beloved, because their breed was finer than any other among the gentiles of the small street. There was gentleness in them, and it was impossible for it not to assert itself in subtle ways among the commoner creatures that hemmed them in.

That may be true or not. But it was true that Rose Berman and John Cooper loved each other, and no-one had suspected it till now; and that little Janey Seipel loved Enid Cooper, and no soul in the world had an inkling of it, least of all the divine Enid. For Janey did not merely love her. She adored her. She was her idol. She dreamed of Enid all night, and smiled, thinking she heard Enid say: "Yes, Janey darling, that would be sweet. Let's go away to Layton Park together for the whole day. And we'll take lunch and buy a glass of milk when we get there. And ice-cream."

Enid was not pretty, her features were too thin. But to Janey she seemed the most exquisite, the most gracious, of human creatures. As she walked along the Jewish pavement to buy eggs at Mrs Poyser's, she saw Enid on the other side of the street. Again she bent her head, she blushed so fiercely. But Enid had, she knew, no more consciousness of her, than of the paving-blocks she trod on with such airy feet.

Not for years would little Janey know what it was she so loved in the gentile girl from across the street. It was something that was always to escape her, but she was to love always, as she was always to love Enid. The name of it was, simply, England. Enid was England. She was a grace, a humour, a method, a world infinitely removed from her own feckless world of top-heavy benevolences and avuncular chimeras.

She was still many years indeed from understanding these things. But even now, as she looked upon Enid, she looked upon landscapes she was never to see, green midland dales by quiet rivers, the shoulders of huge white downs, rolling acres of sunset heather. If she could but hold Enid's hand in her two hands one day, and sit at her feet and look up into her grey eyes, and talk with her.... Oh then, Uncle Adolf could go and chew his head, and all New York come tumbling down, for all she cared... if only she and Enid went out into a meadow some day, and they listened to birds and looked at flowers and Enid would tell her what their names were.

III

It is about four o'clock this same day. Mrs Seipel has finished baking the egg-cake for Mrs Berman. She judges that it is set enough to take over to her without damage. She knows that it has been decided at Mrs Poyser's shop that Rose Berman was not seen walking out yesterday with the *goy* sailor. But she has been pretty sure all day long that if they got any chance that day, the women would make at once for Mrs Berman to smell out the land.

At two o'clock Mrs Seipel was brought to the front door to pay the collector the weekly penny for the Jewish Hospital. She saw Rose Berman going off looking very sweet in a high-waisted mauve frock, white gloves, and a huge hat. Rose Berman may not have been going off to meet that sailor. But Mrs Seipel did not remember the time when Rose left her mother at two o'clock on a Sunday before.

At two-thirty Mrs Seipel was brought to the front door to pay the collector the weekly penny for the privilege of being buried by him — herself or any member of her household. She looked up the street and saw Mrs Billig passing the Berman door. Between two-thirty and four there had been ample time for Mrs Emmanuel, Mrs Shulman, Mrs Poyser herself, to pay Mrs Berman a visit. At four o'clock she set out with the egg-cake on her brief journey. A few seconds before she arrived, old Mrs Edelman descended Mrs Berman's steps. Her eyes were, if anything, harder, her chin starker, than usual. She made no sign to Mrs Seipel, but stumped past her to the synagogue, where she spent many hours at odd times of the day and night.

Who then was this Mrs Berman concerning whom the women of Magnolia Street were so solicitous? Who was this Rose, her daughter, concerning whom it was so grossly incredible that she should break her mother's heart by gazing out, secretly, to the far end of the town, with a gentile lad? We must halt a moment here to say who they are.

It was about ten years ago that Mr Berman was run over by a horse tram in Bridgeways, down the hill, where the family lived at that time. He was returning from the morning service at the synagogue when someone jostled him in the road, and the phylacteries he was carrying under his arm slipped into a puddle. In the moment's confusion, all that he remembered was the fact that the cord of the bag which contained his phylacteries had almost worn through. He had intended to talk to his wife about it that very day. The moment the bag slipped he had a dreadful vision of the phylacteries soiled in the mud. At once he bent down to retrieve them. There was a loud shout, the clash of the horse-bells as the driver pulled at the horses' heads, the screech of a brake. But it was too late. The horses were on him. He was a strong man and it was odd that the injuries proved fatal, but he died two or three days later. He was much comforted that the cord of the bag of the phylacteries had held, after all, and the sacred things remained cosy in their plush nest.

He left his wife with two daughters to bring up. Rose, the elder, was fourteen and already working. She served in a stationer's shop. Ada was only eight. It was a hard struggle, but Mrs Berman tackled it bravely. She went about travelling with table-cloths and towels tied up in a big black bundle. She was also very proud of her little house. They moved up into Magnolia Street quite soon after the accident; Rose insisted on it. For in the other house Mrs Berman used to brood so in the evenings over her dead husband. They had been very fond of each other.

After her long day's trudging with her black bundle, she did too much in the house. She would have everything spick-and-span. It wasn't because she was a lonely woman. All the neighbours liked her, she was so small and kind and pretty. Her two daughters, more particularly Rose, the elder, adored her. No, Mrs Berman had to be up and doing something. If it wasn't the brasses that needed polishing (though, to be sure, they shone like mirrors) then she would be preparing the samples for next day; or Mrs Emmanuel was in bed with a cold and wouldn't it be nice to make a few *blintsies* for Mr Emmanuel and his three boys.

She hadn't always been such a busy little woman, not before her husband was run over. She showed tendencies that way even then, but he discouraged her.

"Sit!" he commanded her gruffly. "Sit! I am stuffed full. Why should you bake more cake for me? Am I King Solomon?"

And she sat on the sofa and played with her hands. And if the children were not there, he would come over to her and lift her bodily to his knee and hold her arms fast to her side and kiss her till she gasped for breath.

She didn't marry again, though she was only in the middle thirties when he died and the marriage-brokers got busy. Two small step-daughters, and pretty ones, would not have stood in the way of a dozen anxious widowers.

But she would have none of them. She remembered the other too vividly, so she was up and about all day long, doing things. She did far too much, and she was by no means strong.

She hid her exhaustion cleverly under her chirrupings and behind the glint of her gold-rimmed spectacles. Rose, her daughter could not forgive herself for not having realised earlier how delicate her mother was. But Sorrah Berman was clever enough in that sort of way to take in a dozen Roses.

Her rather sad and rather dry little cough dated from a certain wretched winter when she would go about in all weathers, lugging her bundle of cloths. For two or three years Rose tried vainly to get her to give up her business. But the mother pooh-poohed her.

"And what shall we live on, daughter? Shall the ravens feed us also, as they fed the prophet?"

It was a sound argument, for the family could hardly live on Rose's earnings as an assistant in a stationer's shop, and Ada was still at school. They might have moved into two rooms instead of having a house of their own; but Rose realised that that would break her mother's heart, to be reduced to living in two rooms, after having had such a house and such a husband — a husband who treated her more like a highborn lady than a mere wife.

And then, a year or so later, a fine thing happened. There was a vacancy at Messrs. Saunders, the big music-dealers in Deansgate; and in a fit of amazing self-confidence, Rose applied for it. She was so gentle and neat that they took her at once. No Jewess had been known to serve in so "classical" a shop before.

They did not ask her if she was Jewish or not; and when she absented herself on the Feast of the New Year and the Day of Atonement, the understanding was she had a cold. She attended on Saturday mornings and less august feast-days, for she had not as much feeling about that sort of thing as most of her neighbours. If she had been any other sort of girl than the sort she was, the folk might have made it awkward for her, one way or another. But she was so gentle and worked so hard that it was impossible to treat her unkindly. Besides, everything she did was for her mother. Everyone knew that. Her mother was not getting any better, and she needed delicacies. And in such a case to break some of the less severe laws is almost accounted a *mitzvah*, a pious duty. In that way they tried to appease their consciences at the sight of Rose Berman going off to work upon the Sabbath morning.

And then, in a few months, Ada left school and got a job at once as a buttonhole-hand in Mr Winberg's small rainproof-factory at number nine Magnolia Street. She hadn't got the brains of Rose, or her manners, and you couldn't expect her to get such a "classical" job as to help Messrs. Saunders sell music in Deansgate. But she would make her way in the world. She was much prettier than Rose. At least you stopped to look at Ada when she passed you in the street. It wouldn't occur to you to stop and look at Rose. (Except on a day like this day in May, when something seemed to have happened to her, her feet were so light and her eyes shone so.)

Really everything ought to have gone quite nicely now in the Berman household, if only Mrs Berman had got a little better. At first she only had her cough in the winter; then it stayed on the whole year. So Rose definitely forbade her mother to do all that scrubbing and polishing she used to do. She did it herself, when she came back in the evenings. Ada was no good at that sort of thing. And besides Ada was only young. She would only be young once. (Rose was apt to forget that she was very few and twenty herself.)

But Mrs Berman wasn't happy. Rose quite well knew what was wrong. She was fretting. She hadn't enough to do. She couldn't sit still and do nothing. Sometimes she had an orgy. She took down all the brasses, including the samovar, and polished them. Sometimes she even washed the floor, and crowning infamy, scrubbed the front steps. And there she sat on the edge of the sofa, waiting for her daughter to come in. She trembled all over, she felt so frightened of what Rose might say.

And then Rose had a brilliant idea. She converted the parlour into a little home-made-sweets shop, for her mother to handle all by herself. She knew that there would be a little unhappiness about giving up the parlour, which was one of the prettiest in Magnolia Street. But in a few weeks, her mother was so pleased and excited about her little shop that she quite forgot about the parlour. (The furniture went to pay for the counter and the shelves, and the scales.) It was not hard work, like trudging through slushy streets with a black bundle of cloths. She made the sweet called *ingber* out of ginger and cinnamon, with a sprinkling of burnt almond; she dipped apples in treacle and impaled them on sticks; she stuffed dates with Brazil nuts; and she sold these things and felt herself a queen, no less, ruling over her little shop.

She was not aware that the gentiles on the other side of the street took this to be another instance of the innate commercialism of the Jews. She was not aware that her new enterprise caused Miss Tregunter acute displeasure, Miss Tregunter who could remember the time when every house in Magnolia Street had its little front garden with shrubs in it, and some of them even had flower-beds. And at that time there was not a parlour window which lacked its aspidistra in a plant-pot, lifted upon a bamboo table.

It was enough to have made Miss Tregunter's hair grey, if it were not grey already. There were moments in which Miss Tregunter even had the idea of removing to some nice street in the north end of Longton, where only gentiles lived, such a street as Magnolia Street used to be. But no. Her jaw set grimly. She would not be turned out of house and home by any Jews. Let them all set up shops in their parlours. "Shoo! Shoo!" she said. Why couldn't those cats — Jewish cats they were, chiefly — leave her hedge alone.

The only person whom Mrs Berman was afraid of displeasing with her venture was Mrs Poyser, of the grocery-shop, where sweets were already on sale. But those sweets were boiled in factories. They were not home-made. There was no real competition.

Mrs Poyser was quite amiable, however. She wished Mrs Berman much luck, and insisted on all her customers sampling her neighbour's *ingber*. "As good as sagrada for the stomach," she said, "closed *and* open".

So Mrs Berman chirruped softly over the preparation and selling of her sweets. It seemed to keep her together for quite a long time. But in the winter her cough was really troublesome. As time went on she began to lose her vitality. She was listless, sometimes, for hours at a time, which wasn't in the least like her. So that she hardly noticed it, and Rose herself hardly noticed it, when Rose took the sweet-shop into her charge, as well as the housework. She already spent the greater part of the day down in Deansgate, looking after the interests of Messrs Saunders, the music-dealers. So altogether Rose had a good deal on her hands.

And that was why it was so surprising to see Rose go off this Sunday afternoon all dressed up in her mauve frock. Almost as if she were going off to see a young man, a long way off; secretly.

Mrs Seipel hesitated a moment outside the Berman front door. Then she summoned up her courage. She knew how Mrs Berman appreciated her egg-cakes. Light as goose-feathers, Mrs Berman always said. She was in the parlour-shop, of course, on the right hand of the lobby. She sat perched on a high chair, for Rose wouldn't have her standing about behind the counter, in between customers. She was weighing out little packet of *ingber*, trilling to herself merrily.

"Good afternoon!" said Mrs Seipel.

"Ah, good afternoon!" said Mrs Berman. "Why didn't you bring your Berel with you? You know he always gives his *ingber* away unless I make him eat it in the shop!"

"Yes, of course!" stammered Mrs Seipel.

It was clear that Mrs Berman imagined she had only come in to place her regular order for sweets for the children — the one order she always paid for in cash. "Please! Give me a quarter!" Thank Heaven! Janey had after all forgotten to confiscate the remnant of her one-and-threepence. "And see," she said, "what I've brought you!"

"Oh really, really!" Mrs Berman crowed. "Really, you shouldn't!" She almost clapped her hands, like a small child.

"How beautiful! See! If I blow on it, will it go up like a balloon? We must have some at once, you and I, Mrs Seipel! 'Ada!' she called out to her younger daughter. 'Ada! Put the kettle on!' Mrs Seipel and I are going to have a cup of tea! You will, won't you, Mrs Seipel?"

That was exactly the opportunity Mrs Seipel had been hoping for. "Come, Mrs Berman, come!" she said. "Let Ada serve in the shop! I'll make the tea, yes?" She helped the frail little woman down from her high stool. Together they went down into the kitchen.

"Ada!" cried Mrs Berman. "Didn't you hear me say put the kettle on?"

"What, mother?" asked Ada vaguely.

"Let it be! Let it be!" begged Mrs Seipel. "What for should a girl like Ada put kettles on? With such pretty hands, too! The time will come when she will have one servant to put the kettle on for her and another to pour the tea out for her and another to give it her on a silver tray!"

Ada looked up prettily from under her long lashes. At first glance she was a much prettier girl than Rose. People who were not capable of seeing beyond that first glance, though they looked a hundred times, would have gone on saying there was no comparison between them. Ada's hair clustered very charmingly over her eyes and around her temples. She had large grey eyes, with flecks of green that danced about in them, when she smiled. Her lips were soft and alluring, though a severe judge would have found the mouth somewhat nerveless. She had a dainty throat, and the most charming little hands, and it was her great grief that working on the button-holes of Mr Winberg's rain-proofs did her hands no good at all. But as she spent almost as much time attending to her hands as she spent on Mr Winberg's button-holes, she still managed to have them look very nice indeed. She was polishing her nails at this moment, making pretty little pink shells out of them. No wonder she had not been able to put on the kettle yet. She was a pleasant girl, and with the assistance of her mother and sister, dressed as attractively as anyone in Magnolia Street; not *rich*, like the aristocratic Miss Winberg, but attractively, without a doubt.

Next to looking after her hands, she liked to have herself photographed. She photographed very well, and professionals were ready to do her for nothing, or dirt-cheap at least, she looked so good in their windows. The house was full of her photographs. As Mrs Seipel descended the two steps into the kitchen, she paused a moment, to see Ada standing dauntless against a raging sea, and on the terrace of a medieval castle, and on the deck of a luxury yacht. And in a picture on the mantelpiece, she was showing her smooth shoulders, wearing nothing at all so far as Mrs Seipel could see, where she rose, a photographer's Aphrodite, out of a sea of chiffon.

"Go, Ada, go!" said Mrs Berman. "It will do your hands no harm if you serve a little *ingber* with them!"

Ada went. It was all Mrs Seipel could do to prevent Mrs Berman getting busy with cups and spoons. "No, please!" begged Mrs Seipel. "And if Rose should come in and see you doing things for me? She would throw me out, no?"

Mrs Berman made a gesture of surrender. "Go, go!" she said. She sat on her rocking-chair and rocked, humming to herself. She reached behind her head for a pile of knitting and got to work, for it was clear she could not bear to be inactive for one moment. She was knitting a dainty little openwork bed-jacket for Ada. It would look very pretty on Ada's white shoulders.

The spectacle was very pretty and it would have afforded Mrs Seipel a great deal of pleasure on any other occasion. But this afternoon it only deepened her misery. She could not remember when Mrs Berman had looked happier or frailer. It was quite clear that the other women had shirked telling her what had been said about Rose and the sailor, in the grocery-shop that morning. They had not been able to bring themselves to it. "Not even old Mrs Edelman," she muttered to herself lugubriously, Mrs Edelman who had never been known to spare man, woman or child before.

The tea was ready. Mrs Seipel could not trust her voice to announce it. Mrs Berman was involved in some deep computation of purl and plain. Suddenly she looked up.

"What is it, Mrs Seipel? " she asked. " Why are you so silent?"

"Nothing, nothing!" swallowed Mrs Seipel. It was ridiculous in a way. As if it was she, not Rose, who had been seen out in a park with a gentile youth.

"Tell me!" insisted Mrs Berman. "Haven't you heard from Uncle Adolf lately? Isn't his business going well?"

"Oh, Adolf is all right, long life on him!" said Mrs Seipel. Her gesture indicated that if Messrs. Rockefeller and Vanderbilt, long life on them, were half as all right as Uncle Adolf, they had nothing to worry about.

"What is it then?" Mrs Berman gently insisted.

"Nothing, just nothing!"

"Really nothing?"

"Nothing!"

"Ah well then! A slice like this? Oh yes, Mrs Seipel. I know. It melts in the mouth like foam! How's your little Janey?"

Mrs Seipel pulled herself together. She had come in not to be asked about little Janey, but to see what was to be done about Rose. She *had* to get it off her chest. If she did not, the tale was bound to get round to Mrs Berman in some crueller and uglier fashion. The report was possibly not true. On the other hand it very possibly might be. She got down to it.

"About your Rose..." she started.

"Yes," said Mrs Berman. "My little Ada. You might think she was going to be an actress some day, the way they all want to take her photograph."

But Mrs Seipel was positive she had uttered the name of Rose, not Ada. Could she possibly have been mistaken? Mrs Berman was going on about Ada and the people who wanted to take her photograph.

"Have you seen that handsome one with the black eyes who's been here two or three times? Hummel his name is. He's a photographer, too. If my Ada marries a photographer, she'll save herself —".

Mrs Seipel was not interested in the latest young man who had fallen victim to Ada's pale charms. "That lovely frock your Rose went out in" she started.

"A picture, no?" said Mrs Berman. "And did you see my Ada's new green frock. With all the flounces?" She went on for a little time more about Ada's frock and how sweet she looked in it. Mr Hummel, the photographer, had approved of it, too. Then she insisted on getting some chocolate biscuits for Mrs Seipel. She knew her guest had a sweet tooth. Once more Mrs Seipel introduced the name of Rose. Once more Mrs Berman behaved precisely as if it had been Ada's name that had been mentioned.

It was odd. It was very odd. Mrs Seipel could not remember that Mrs Berman had ever before deliberately avoided talking about Rose. Ada was her baby, and she spoiled Ada. But Rose was her strong right hand, her husband. She venerated Rose.

41

"I see Rose has gone out this afternoon," Mrs Seipel plunged desperately. "I wonder where she's gone to on a Sunday afternoon?"

"And poor little Ada staying indoors. A shame, no? There should be a society for bad mothers."

"Of course Rose hasn't gone out to meet anybody? I didn't know that they were already talking a match for her." Mrs Seipel was behaving with a shamelessness entirely foreign to her. Her cheeks burned. But it was as if the last few words had not been uttered at all.

"Yes, yes, Mrs Seipel," her hostess insisted. "Another cup of tea? Of course you can!"

And then for one dreadful moment a dreadful idea occurred to Mrs Seipel. Mrs Berman knew that Rose, her daughter, her darling, was walking out with a sailor, a gentile, *and she did not mind*. Rose Berman, the daughter of a man who had, in a manner of speaking, died for phylacteries. *And Mrs Berman did not mind.*

Mrs Seipel looked up quickly. She looked up to the brass candlesticks that held the lit candles on the Sabbath evenings. She saw the brass plate on which she placed a beaker of wine each Sabbath, as punctiliously as her husband had done through all the long years. She saw on a ledge an open copy of the Pentateuch, with the skewer with which Mrs Berman marked her place while she read out the holy words. She looked into Mrs Berman's eyes, so full of Jewish gentleness. She kicked her own shin under the table with the worn heel of her shoe.

"Well now, look at the time!" Mrs Seipel cried. "What will my husband think of me? And my boys, they must be out of Hebrew-school by now! Give my love to Rose, yes, when she comes in!"

"The little doveling!" sighed Mrs Berman. "Come, you must take a treacle apple for your Berel! Please, Mrs Seipel!"

Mrs Seipel walked up Magnolia Street carrying the impaled treacle apple before her. Her head was buzzing frightfully. "Does she know? Does she know? Of course she doesn't know! There isn't anything to know! I'll give it my Sam next time he comes home with tales!"

She was about to turn into the little garden before her house, which had long since been cemented over, like all the other little gardens on the Jewish pavement, when she saw Mrs Briggs crossing the road with an — "I say, Mrs Seipel! I say! Just one moment!"

But Mrs Briggs didn't merely come half way across the road that separated the two pavements. She came the whole way across the road. A queer pang of premonition touched the heart of Mrs Seipel. There was something symbolic about that crossing of the road. Mrs Seipel's heart dropped a beat. She looked almost scared.

Mrs Briggs was the wife of an odd-job-man who lived across the street from Mrs Seipel. She was as decent a woman as anyone could wish for. She was not merely ready to lend a hand to all the women who lived on her own side of the street. It distressed her that there was this feeling between themselves, the gentiles, and the folk on the other side of the street, the Jews. It was not a feeling exactly. She knew that. Really there was no feeling. It was just as if the two lots lived in different cities. To her it was all nonsense. They went to church and the others went to synagogue; it didn't seem to matter to her more than if she went to a Whist Drive, while her next-door neighbour went to a Fancy Dress Ball.

Mrs Seipel was like that too, on the whole. If there had been a few more like them on both sides of the street, it might have been as neighbourly a street as any in Longton. But perhaps it would have taken a lot of Briggses and Seipels to make up for one Miss Tregunter.

The two sides of the street, as we have said, had practically nothing to do with each other. But that didn't prevent Mrs Briggs and Mrs Seipel nodding their heads friendlily when they both stood at their front-doors, engaged with some tradesman. Now and again they would actually advance to the middle of the roadway and exchange a few words. But they felt a little uncomfortable about it, which was ridiculous, as if they were doing something wrong. And when Mrs Briggs went to have a gill at the Lamb and Lion and Mrs Seipel went to get her groceries, they both felt that the other women were eyeing them rather strangely. Perhaps they weren't really, and it only felt like that; but it amounted to the same thing. So for quite a long time after that they didn't go out to the middle of the roadway to have a chat; but they would still call out "Good morning" to each other shamelessly from their front door-steps.

It was different when they met in the tramcar, for instance. There they felt themselves quite free from all the restraints of Magnolia Street and chattered away nineteen to the dozen.

"And how's your little Tony getting on, Mrs Briggs? Does he still have those swollen glands? Believe me or believe me not, but if you will only wrap his neck up in his own left stocking after he's worn it for a week, with a hot potato inside it, believe me... well, I ask you. Just look at my little Eli. Swollen glands he had, like duck's eggs...."

"And have you been hearing lately from your rich brother, Mrs Seipel? Only yesterday? So you'll be leaving us any day now! It won't be the same street, Mrs Seipel, with you gone. On my word it won't!"

It certainly would not have been the same street with a few more Mrs Briggses and Mrs Seipels scattered about. But it was a good thing that pleasant and simple folk like these should recognise their kinship, even if they had to get into a tramcar before they could do it freely. It would be a good thing to feel that it would remain so. But there was a war coming. And nothing would remain so. Excepting perhaps, the generous letters of Uncle Adolf. Probably the first thing Uncle Adolf would do when the Last Trump awakened him would be to call for pen and paper to write his dear sister a lovely long letter. He'd be sending her the fare for a ticket to paradise, the very moment he could lay his hands on a little Ready Money. A little Ready Money that was all he was waiting for....

"Just one moment, Mrs Seipel!" cried out Mrs Briggs, coming the whole way across to the Jewish pavement. "Have you heard?" Her eyes twinkled with pleasure.

There was just a trace of crossness in Mrs Seipel's voice as she replied. Had *she* heard? Wasn't she responsible for the whole thing? For it was clearly the Berman-Cooper business that had brought Mrs Briggs venturing across the whole width of Magnolia Street. Wasn't it she who, with her own eyes, had seen the two young people... or her son Sam, to be exact?

"Have I heard?" said Mrs Seipel. "It was my son Sam saw them together yesterday and came and told me!"

How quickly, Mrs Seipel reflected, news of this sort travels! Who could have told Mrs Briggs, who? Old Mrs Edelman was no friend of hers, nor Mrs Billig, nor any of them.

"Do you think there is anything in it?" asked Mrs Briggs eagerly. "I hear they've been going out reg'lar. She isn't the sort just to go out larking for a box of chocolates. Of course *him* — he's different. He's younger than she is. She'd probably settle him down a bit. A fine good-looking pair they'd make, I must say!"

For a moment Mrs Seipel was bewitched out of herself. She saw the lad and the girl with Mrs Briggs's eyes. She saw his firm chin with the cleft in it, she saw her small firm mouth. She saw his great hand close round her fingers. She saw him take her into his arms....

"I wonder," Mrs Briggs was prattling away, "what that sister of his would say? Mary, they call her. You know, that one who never smiles and never talks, like a image. There she is, sitting in the parlour window, now. Do you see her? A monument in a cemetery, I call her. Quite high up people the Coopers were — you've heard say, haven't you? — before they had to come and live down Magnolia Street. You never know how people like them will take things. 'What, a Jew-girl!' they might say — what? What were you saying, Mrs Seipel? I didn't catch!"

"I was only saying it's all only nonsense. My Sam, he's so naughty sometimes, the tales he comes back with! I gave him a big smack," lied Mrs Seipel stoutly, "and sent him to bed at once! Don't you know, Mrs Briggs, it would kill Rose's mother if any tales like that got round to her! I've just been in to see her! It's wonderful the way that girl does everything for her mother, everything! And do you think she'd just push her into her coffin by going out with a Christian? The scandal, Mrs Briggs! You know how it is, don't you, with those old-fashioned people?"

Chapter 3

Let us cross the roadway with Mrs Briggs to the gentile pavement of Magnolia Street. We make a long journey, all the way from the ghettoes of Russia, the walled towns of Judea, the black camel-hair tents of the wilderness beyond Jordan, for the dwellings of the Jewish pavement have something of the quality of all those. Here, on the other side of the street, in the place of the Tawnies, the Briggses, the Coopers, the Derrickses, here is England; or here, at least, is the North Country. The Lamb and Lion, the public-house at the corner, is a fortress of the spirit of the North Country. It concerns us especially because it is one of the four clubs of Magnolia Street, and certainly the gayest.

Or we should say that the private bar was one of the Magnolia Street clubs.

The Lamb and Lion was no hole-and-corner affair. Its main frontage stood on Blenheim Road in the world's eye; it was only its meeker side, where the private bar was, that faced on Magnolia Street. The saloon bar faced the main road, a noble expanse of tiles bloomed over with a purple glaze, that looked like the interior of a royal bathroom. There were cornices of golden tiles and blue tiles, and a pagoda and one or two gothic gables. It was a beautiful public-house, and nobody begrudged the way Steve Tawnie would walk down towards it along the opposite side of the road, as if it were not his own at all, and pause to look at it, and wink at it, till all the tiles winked back.

The public bar, nothing like so grand as the saloon bar, nothing like so cosy as the private bar, was a triangular room wedged in between its neighbours. It had no *cachet*. It gave you no status to drink in the public bar. You drank, and sometimes you got drunk. If there were any small children hanging about the Lamb and Lion waiting for their mothers, you saw them only at the door of the public bar. If there was any *al fresco* drinking on the pavement during bank holidays and cup final days, it was the patrons of the public bar who did it, ladies and gentlemen without substance or tradition, the peaks of their caps at the back of their heads, their bonnets a little askew.

The saloon bar was somewhat frigid and aristocratic; its patrons hailed from the flourishing establishments on the main road.

There was a shield on the wall that faced you as you entered, with the painted text;

LET CONVIVIALITY BE MODERATE AND TEMPERATE.

The two pink-and-white elderly maiden sisters who ran the post office were never immoderate. The Curate of St. Lukes-in-Longton sometimes came in to have a drink and nobody could have been less intemperate. He beamed friendlily through his glasses. He believed in mixing with his people and subjecting himself to their temptations. "A whisky-and-soda!" he demanded. "Without the whisky, ha! ha!" Everybody laughed a little nervously.

In the saloon and private bars there were tables for you to put your glasses down on, though the chairs in the first were upholstered in plush, in the other they were plain wood.

In the public bar you put your glasses down on ledges along the wall. Those were the main distinctions in the furniture. A sequence of superior barmaids looked after the saloon bar whilst Mrs Tawnie herself looked after Magnolia Street in the private bar. But the private bar looked after itself, in a manner of speaking; it was a club, almost a family sitting-room. In the public bar, in addition to Mr Tawnie, there was a "chucker-out." There was really no need of a "chucker-out," with a Steve Tawnie about the place. But it would have been deemed rather niggardly not to employ one, as if the Lamb and Lion couldn't rise to it. A "chucker-out" was a feature in all the best public-houses. In any case, there was a lot for him to do in the way of collecting empty glasses and shouting, "Time, gentlemen, please!"

The "chucker-out" was a small man with a pointed nose and skimpy hair. His name was Sim Watkins. It is hard to know what would have happened if some stout patron of the public bar had become obstreperous and there had been no-one there to deal with him except Sim Watkins. He might have gone a long way by shouting "Time, gentlemen, please!" at him in the explosive way he had. He wore a celluloid collar and a tie as thin as a shoelace, a red tie with blue and brown stripes. He often changed his

47

collar during his tenure of office at the Lamb and Lion, but he never wore any other tie. When the war came he put that tie aside. When it was over he put it on again. But he had managed to put some money away during his war-service. Out of that money he bought himself a Sunday tie, as thin as the other one, a blue tie, with brown and pink stripes. So it was not wholly without profit he went to the war. He also picked up a dose of malaria. He survived it in Basra, but it put him out in Doomington, some years later. He was shouting "Time, gentlemen, please!" very loud and important, when the sweats got hold of him. A few days afterwards he died, whispering "Time, gentlemen, please!" soft as a bat. Nobody knew what happened to his two ties. They never got so steady a "chucker-out" again in the Lamb and Lion, not forward in any manner of speaking, but able to hold his own, respectful-like, with the most awkward customer.

It is not to be denied that even in the Lamb and Lion, respectable house though it was, there was occasional chucking-out to do in real earnest; and Steve Tawnie, the proprietor, did it then. And even he wasn't often forced to do it in the vulgar way familiar in lesser public-houses that have no purple tiles and gothic gables, He just roared at the offender, who subsided.

If the offender was not amenable to being roared at, Steve lifted him by the back of his coat and deposited him on the pavement, quite gently, and as if he belonged to another animal species, somewhat as a dog places a kitten that has wambled into danger back in its mother's basket.

The Lamb and Lion was full of Steve's roaring. He roared with laughter day and night. His sense of laughter was a sort of infinitely sensitive jelly, which did not merely react to actual contact but to the faintest threat or hint of contact. You could not say to him "Fine day for the time of year" without setting him off hallooing till all the glasses danced on the shelves. And if you told him a real joke, the consequences were disastrous.

He was not tall, but so broad that, when he stood in the public bar, he gave you the impression he could stretch an arm for a glass in the private bar and fill it at one of the handles in the saloon bar. He was not merely a publican. He was Steve Tawnie. He was, that is to say, one of the most famous goalkeepers that Doomington United ever put on the field, even in those brave days of Billy Meredith, the toothpick-chewer. It was sometimes said it wasn't quite fair to play him, for all he had to do was to stand in the goalmouth with his eyes shut and no ball could get by him. That was an exaggeration. He left a little space on both sides of him, and if a ball threatened it, he would hurl himself at it, roaring, as if it were the best joke in the repertoire of George Robey.

He used to play for Sunderland, and they sold him, one chilly season. When Steve heard how much transfer money had been paid for him, he stood up against a wall and shouted. The tears ran down his cheeks. He had bought the Lamb and Lion out of the gate money earned on his benefit match. People left the ground when that match was over feeling that football would henceforth be a melancholy thing now that Steve Tawnie was out of it, a game played by deaf mutes for the delectation of undertakers. It was a measure of the haunted silence that fell upon Magnolia Street a few years later, when the war came, that the street did not seem notably more silent, even though Steve Tawnie left it, to see if he couldn't do a bit of chucking-out in the country round Longueval and Ginchy. Only one feature in Steve Tawnie's universe was no joke, and that was Maggie Tawnie, his wife. If she passed across his line of vision, he stopped roaring. He merely looked at her and worshipped, his mouth open. It had happened when he first set eyes on her, clattering on her clogs out of the yard-gates of Ormerod's mill at Blackburn. That was about ten years ago now, when United went up to play their famous second replay with the Rovers. The suspension of the roaring, the open-mouthed adoration, still went on. She was to him all that there is of fragile and precious, though she was nearly as large as he was. She had coppery-red hair piled up magnificently, in a style of coiffure a little suggestive of the pagoda and gables which glorified the facade of the Lamb and Lion. She had a clear high-tinted complexion and a bust like the mother of all living. She had grand legs and calves, which did not lose their shapeliness as the years went on, possibly because she refused to discard her clogs, excepting for outdoor wear. She wore dresses of stout ribbed silk and lace collars fastened at the throat with enormous brooches that looked like tombstones on the graves of favourite dogs.

It is not without our scope to go back so many years and tell how cunningly Steve tracked her down from Ormerod's yard-gates to her own home, how adroit a suitor the burly fellow was, how splendidly he won her, what sort of a honeymoon that was under the shadow of the Big Wheel at Blackpool, a honeymoon which combined the sweet secrecies of love with a tumultuous publicity that made the yellow sands black as a load of coal the moment the happy pair set foot out of their hotel. But we can say so much at least that now, a decade later, they sometimes still gave the impression of being a honeymoon couple, the way they billed and cooed behind the handles of the private bar, where the Magnolia Street folk gathered to sip their nightly pints.

The Tawnies had a little daughter whose name was Nellie. It was impossible to see how she could be anything else but Nellie, with her blue eyes and her gold hair bound up on the side of the head with a pink ribbon. Her Granny used to come up from Blackburn to see her. She swore that she was the spitten image of Maggie at her age. It seemed incredible. It seemed beyond the farthest boundaries of biological elasticity that such a little gold-haired Nellie should grow up into such a big red-haired Maggie. But you could not stand up against Granny's vigorous prophecies. That was the way it was going to be. And as a matter of fact, when you saw her up against Dick Cooper, who was a few years her senior and lived a few doors away, you saw what Granny meant. For Dick's hair was a refined gold, his eyes were blue as periwinkles. You saw the red sheen on Nellie's hair which some day would blaze up in it till it was all as tawny as copper dahlias. You saw that the blue of her eyes was thinly painted over a green glaze.

Nellie was a little ray of sunshine and a Tinker-bell and a put-your-head-on-my-shoulder-daddy. She was going to marry Dick Cooper some day. She was quite decided about that. So was everybody else except Dick Cooper. He did not suspect Nellie Tawnie's designs, being eleven and therefore much younger than Nellie, who was seven.

But she did not lack admirers. The Lamb and Lion was her slave as one man. Perhaps, in the vexed question of the "chucker-out," she ought to be given some consideration. For the bluntest-mouthed navvy with a few quarts inside him would keep a check on himself with so innocent a ray of sunshine dancing among the beer-handles. Her father hugged her so voluminously to his bosom that it was a great surprise to see her emerge unscathed. But she did like the rugby ball after a ravening scrimmage has done its worst at it. Her nose and gold locks and pink bow came out just as they had been.

Her mother, too, would as soon have slapped the Vicar as her little gold-haired daughter. It was a good thing that Granny sometimes came up from Blackburn. She yielded to none in her adoration of little Nellie, but it did not prevent her from putting the idol over her knee and pulling down its panties and slapping it good and hard. It was then Nellie made it quite clear she was Steve Tawnie's daughter. What lungs little Nellie had! She roared loud enough to call the police and the fire-engines. But the firemen and the policemen knew it was only little Nellie getting a bit of what might be good for her. They smiled to each other across their tears.

II

When Mrs Briggs conveyed the news to her neighbours that evening, in the private bar of the Lamb and Lion, it was hardly news at all. Somehow they all seemed to know already, and they were not very excited. It was odd how phlegmatic they were about it in the Lamb and Lion and what heart-burnings it had caused in Mrs Poyser's shop. "Oh, aye!" was about all they said. They lifted their glasses and drank and put them down again. The women, of course, may have felt differently, but they didn't say any more. John Cooper was the sort of young man concerning whom women, even the most virtuous, do not learn without indifference that he has been making love to some other woman than themselves. He could not kiss a girl in Rio de Janeiro, without making a girl, and more than one, feel lonely in Magnolia Street.

Steve Tawnie, on the other hand, didn't merely say "Oh, aye!" He leaned back against his shelves and roared with laughter. Perhaps, with Steve Tawnie, that was about the same thing as saying "Oh, aye!" "Hoo-hoo-hoo!" he boomed. The bottles behind him danced, precariously. "Hoo-hoo-hoo! The young rascal! So he's got himself a bit of skirt at last in Magnolia Street! I wondered which one it was going to be!"

Walter Hubbard, the tram-conductor, flushed. He was sitting quietly in a corner, with his pretty wife, Dolly. He was the good young man of the gentile pavement, but he wasn't quite a teetotaller. They would have liked him to take the pledge at the

Primitive Methodist Chapel, but he hadn't gone the whole way. He took Dolly, somewhat rarely, into the Lamb and Lion and they had a half-pint apiece and everybody looked at them sideways and sighed a little. He came in rarely because he was very jealous of Dolly and he didn't like to have other men looking her up and down. They were such a devoted couple and they sat holding each other's hands and they never took their eyes off each other.

That was why Walter Hubbard flushed up so darkly when Steve Tawnie hurled out his remark about John Cooper finding himself a bit of skirt in Magnolia Street. He squeezed Dolly's little hand in his own till she went quite pale. But neither of them said a word.

When Jessie Wright came in a minute or two later, she, on the other hand, was quite eloquent about it. The subject might quite likely have dropped if not for her. The patrons of the private bar really hadn't much use for the Cooper family. They recognised that the Coopers belonged to another class than their own, and they had long stopped being curious about them. They were stuck up, and it was left at that. The old man Cooper, who died early in 1910, had never as much as shown his nose in the private bar. Not that he was a teetotaller. By no means. Hour after hour he'd sit in his corner in the saloon bar before a glass-topped table, getting more and more fuddled.

It was whisky *he* drank. He never had a word for anyone, good or bad. He was dead now, anyhow.

So now the Coopers consisted, first, of that dark block of a woman, who was as silent as the old man and never left the house, if she could help it. Mary her name was, she looked after the others. The next member of the family, the merchant-seaman, John, was away most of the time. He, too, had never been known to drop in for a friendly one in the private bar, any more than his father. Sometimes he'd have a quick one in the saloon bar, but even that wasn't good enough for him, more than once in a way. Then there was a younger sister, Enid, a hoity-toity chit of a girl. And Dick... Dick of course, was different, little Dick with the gold hair and blue eyes. Everyone approved whole-heartedly of the marriage arranged by Nellie Tawnie between herself and Dick Cooper. Nice kid was Dick. So quite likely there wouldn't have been any more heard about the Cooper-Berman business at the

Lamb and Lion for a long time to come, if Jessie Wright hadn't come in. She was in a fair state about it.

"A perfect disgrace I call it!" she proclaimed. "Never heard of such a thing! He calls himself a gentleman! He'll be the captain of an English ship some day! Going off like that with a dirty Jew girl!"

Mrs Briggs looked rather uncomfortable and embarrassed. So did Sally Carter. So did Bill Carter himself, if one could properly fix any expression at all upon that large nebulous face. Mrs Stanley, the shoemaker's wife, who was born in Germany and had blonde plaits, tried to look non-committal.

"A little sheeny!" repeated Mrs Wright. She brought out the words with a great deal of venom. You had to look twice to make sure it was really she who uttered them, and in such a tone. There was no getting away from it, she was very attractive. She had rosy-red cheeks and a small plump figure, a delightful handful. Her eyes were a bright grey-green. But the mouth was hard. That's where it was. The line of the mouth was hard and cruel; there was something lewd about it, too.

"It ought to be stopped!" she rapped out. She looked significantly at Bill Carter. But Bill Carter had only been a policeman. They had had to get rid of him. He was far too vague and gentle to go on being a policeman. He was nothing but a night-watchman, now.

The way Jessie Wright talked about Jews was a more sinister thing than the booings of the Derrickses. The Derrickses just got drunk and booed. They had to have something to boo at and the Jews were handy. Later, during the war, they booed in another direction. But Jessie Wright's rosy cheeks got rather sick and yellow when the question of the Jews came up. She embarrassed the other people in the private bar. To them the Jews were foreigners and they took little more notice of them, than if they were really living in Russia, and not just across the street. They were English, particularly Elsa Stanley, who came from Germany, and wore a shawl and even tried to wear clogs, to show how English she was. They looked the other way when Mrs Wright started talking about Jews. Jessie Wright was a queer woman, though she was so good to look at.

When the Derrickses started jeering, it didn't distress them at all. It appealed to the simple savage in them, which once had been tickled with bear-baitings and cock-fightings and had nothing more bloody to satisfy it these days than an occasional smashed rib at a football match or a streaming nose at a prize-fight. Only Mrs Stanley turned away her watery German eyes from the sight of the Derrickses booing across the pavement.

It plucked a forlorn and desperate string of premonition in her heart. She went in to Otto, her elder son, and they talked German together, and he twanged a guitar to the strains of *Drei Lilien*. Then she felt a little better.

The private bar was not Steve Tawnie's proper place by rights. He went off soon to the saloon bar, and his wife, Maggie, came in to take his place, with a great creak of stays and jangling of earrings. She knew every word that had been said. All the three Tawnies always knew every word that was said in all departments of the Lamb and Lion. She didn't like to see the folk looking so serious. She got to work, and not even Jessie Wright in a tantrum could stand up for long against the bluff cajolings of Maggie Tawnie. "Coom now, coom!" urged Maggie. "Get a drop down thee, lass! Don't take on so! Or people will start thinkin' tha wanted 'im for thaself!"

"Not me!" said Mrs Wright, subsiding. "Once married, twice shy! No! I'm going to remain a widow! My little Tommie's man enough for me to have hanging about the place!"

There were a few present who had a distinct impression of older men than Tommie having hung about the place now and again; quite late at night, too.

But it was none of their business. Take 'em as you find 'em, was their motto.

"Yes, yes," agreed Mrs Stanley. "These men, it is dreadful the mess they make!" She looked into Mrs Wright's eyes earnestly, with her pale-blue eyes.

She shook her head and one of her plaits slipped. She spoke with feeling and in a guttural accent. Her husband was by profession a shoemaker, but he spent most of his time calculating which horses would win which races and bring him a large fortune. His calculations were worked out on countless scraps of paper that littered his shoemaking-cellar, and got stuck in the butter at home, or buttered into the bread-jar, and gathered like pigeons about his feet when he sat in the Lamb and Lion. He was busy with them at this moment, as much aware of John Cooper or Widow Wright as he was aware of the herpetology of the Grand Duchy of Baden.

54

"Frank, Frank!" his wife commanded. "Put away those dirty beets of paper!" But her voice lacked authority. "Now if Fly-by-night ran second to Heartache at Doncaster and Hieroglyph was third at Newbury to Bucentaur —" he muttered.

"What would you do mit such a man?" enquired Mrs Stanley with a pale smile. She addressed Mrs Wright, who was felt to be an authority on men.

The company did not learn what Mrs Wright would have done with such a man, for at that moment there was a rapping at the frosted-glass window let into the wall which was the facade of the Jug and Bottle department. Mrs Tawnie slid the window along in its groove. The face of Kate Ritchie was revealed, a lady who lived at number fourteen.

"Oh good evening, Mrs Tawnie! Good evening, all!" said Kate Ritchie, poking her face into the bar. She smiled a little haggardly.

"Good evening, Mrs Ritchie!" replied Maggie. After all, Kate Ritchie's money was as good as the next one's *whosoever* she might be married to. Maggie did not take sides.

But the others did not say good evening. There was a certain amount of chilly grunting. That was about all. They looked at the wall or up at the ceiling glassily. All except Mrs Briggs. She could not help thinking that on a night like this, bygones might be bygones; excepting that it wasn't bygones exactly, not by any manner of means. But what was she against so many? "The usual pint!" Kate Ritchie demanded, trying to keep her voice from shaking. But she did not succeed. Maggie filled her jug for her. She waited and looked about her, hoping against hope. But no-one said: "Oh won't you come in, Mrs Ritchie? There isn't no need to be standing outside like that, as if you was a stranger!" So "Good night, all!" she said huskily, and went off with her pint.

"I wonder what *she* was waiting about for?" said Mrs Wright.

"He's pretty nearly due, I should think," ventured Dolly Hubbard. "Her husband."

"Her *husband*!" snorted Mrs Carter. "If I had my way —"

But the conversation was once more interrupted by a rapping at the Jug and Bottle window.

There was a certain quality about that rapping which indicated immediately who it was that rapped. It was a timid rapping, a defiant rapping, the rapping of one who has been sent forth to fetch beer which other people than himself will drink, the rapping of one to whom beer is poison. Henry Briggs, the odd-job man, winked at Walter Hubbard. Walter Hubbard, relieved to find that Henry Briggs had winked at himself and not at Dolly, his wife, winked back. Jessie Wright winked at Sally Carter, Elsa Stanley joined in all the winking, and Frank Stanley went on muttering over his cabbalistic bits of paper.

"Good evening, Henry!" proclaimed Maggie Tawnie, even before she slid the panel aside.

"Good evening, Mrs Tawnie!" said Mr Derricks. He reached forth one large jug and another large jug over the ledge. "Two quarts of old, please!" he said.

"Good evening, Henry!" said Jessie Wright. "Another party tonight?"

"Yes," said Mr Derricks. "They've all come. All the Boys. We're going to have a grand party tonight!"

It was all Maggie Tawnie could do to prevent herself from sniffing. *We* indeed! She knew where Henry Derricks would be while the party was going on. He would be upstairs in the back bedroom, doing fretwork.

"Hallo, Henry!" said one voice, and another voice. "Hallo, Henry!" came the shrill voice of little Nellie, from her far place on the counter of the saloon bar, against the beer-handles.

Everybody called Mr Derricks Henry. His own children had always called him Henry. He was the sort of father whom children in their cradle do not seek to call "da-da!" with a lifting of the little hands and a dribbling at the corners of the mouth. They seek to call him by his first name, and never use any other. His position in the Derricks household was that of a rather meek stepchild. He had worked for many years at a brewery not far off in Begley Hill. He had always had a weak digestion, and the smell of malt and hops made him sick. Every morning as he entered the yard of the brewery, his stomach heaved a little as the lush warm smell assailed him. Even on Sundays and Bank Holidays, when he did not go to work, his stomach heaved a little at exactly the same moment, as if it were a duty.

"Hallo, all!" said Henry, pushing his face forward, and screwing it up a little with the spasm the beery gust had caused him.

"Hope you have a nice time, Henry!"

"Henry, don't go to bed too late!"

"So long, all!" said Henry, smiling wanly at their humour.

"See you again soon, Henry!"

They saw him again quite soon. It was astonishing how quickly Mrs Derricks and her son, Wilfred, the Longton Nightingale, and their friends, the Boys, all of them colleagues of Wilfred in the music-hall profession, got through those two quarts of beer. And another two quarts of beer. And another two. It was obviously being a very good party. The Derrickses lived only three doors away, and the noises became quite merry even before closing-time. It was a good thing Henry managed to slip into the Jug and Bottle Department just a couple of seconds before Steve locked the side door, for anything might have happened to Henry coming back with two empty jugs.

Less than an hour later the party had become really jolly. The Boys (a term which included the hostess, Mrs Derricks, and any lady that might be present) never bothered their heads about their neighbours. But they were fast getting to the point at which they became morbidly sensitive to the existence of the hook-nosed ones opposite, the point at which with a sudden rush of anger, they remembered that the Jews had crucified their Saviour. They surged out, all except Wilfred the Nightingale, to the front door. "Who killed Christ?" they wanted to know. "Who killed Christ?"

Wilfred did not join in these manifestations. He was afraid of the small Jewish boys, who seemed at eleven or twelve to attain a pitch of virility which he would not attain if he lived to be a hundred. There was already a faint down on their upper lips, whilst his own would always be smooth as any girl's. He was thirty at this time, in 1910, but he looked fourteen. He still looked fourteen in 1930. He was a case of arrested physical development, a pathologist's specimen. He never exceeded a height of four-feet-six or reached the age of puberty. The wiseacres of a later date would have argued whether the thymus gland had persisted too long in him or whether his condition was due to a deficiency of the pituitary gland. But the subject never arose for discussion at the Derricks' parties.

Wilfred was perfectly formed; his hands were pearly, and in a distressing manner, exquisite. His hair fell about his brow in blonde clusters, though by the time his King and Country called him to alleviate the lot of his fighting brothers, both the blondeness and the clustering of his hair needed a little artificial manoeuvring. He wore an Eton collar, an Eton coat or 'bum-freezer', as they termed it in Magnolia Street, and long herring-bone trousers. His feet looked very dainty and small even for his height of four-foot-six. In 1910 he had just begun to use the paint and powder which were necessary for the maintenance of the bloom of his professional boyhood.

But he was a boy in a very tragic sense, too, the weak shell of a boy. So he did not venture to join the others, when they stood on the pavement, jeering. "Smoggy van Jew!" they cried. The Jewish women were awake in their beds. "A cholera should take them!" they muttered. Miss Tregunter behind her lace curtains disapproved icily. The rosy-cheeked little widow, Jessie Wright, sat in her parlour, darkly gloating. She had put her small boy to bed long ago, but she could not bring herself to go to bed, she was too happy. The widow of a highly respected insurance agent, she was far too much of a lady to indulge in such common goings-on. But she enjoyed them. She sat hunched up on her deep plush arm-chair and purred.

Sometimes these carousals went on for long hours after midnight, until the milkman deposited the dawn on the doorstep with a can of milk. But tonight it did not last so long. It happened that John Cooper of next door, who was second mate on an oil-tanker, was home between voyages. He was a sturdy young man with broad shoulders, a heavy jaw and huge fists. He could sleep through the most howling gale in mid-Atlantic but the drunken bawlings on the pavement disturbed him.

Or it may be that, being in love with a girl of the Jews, and that girl being the daughter of a sick woman, he determined he wasn't going to stand for this foolery. He came out. He looked very unpleasant as he covered the few yards between himself and the Boys.

"Look here, all of you!" he said quite quietly. "If you are not all back again in ten minutes I'll knock your heads together, see?"

He went back into number six again. There was silence for a few seconds among the Boys. Mrs Wright in the armchair in her dark parlour winced with anger. "Can't he mind his own bloody business, now he's got hold of a stinking Yiddisher?"

The silence lasted only a few seconds among the Boys. They were too drunk for it to last any longer. "Who killed Christ?" Mrs Derricks began again shrilly. The others followed. Nine and a half minutes later John Cooper came out a second time. He knocked all their heads together, grimly. None of them showed any signs of fight. He did not lay hands on Mrs Derricks, of course. She sat down on the edge of the pavement and whimpered. She opened her mouth just once more; but there was something about the set of John Cooper's jaw which checked her eloquence. There was no more fun at the party that night.

Chapter 4

I

Who were these Coopers? Whence came they? Alien alike to the gentile and the Jewish pavement, by what catastrophe did they find themselves in this place?

They knew little more at the Lamb and Lion than that Mr Cooper had once been wealthy and his wife had once been a grand lady. Perhaps they exaggerated his wealth and his gentility. They never saw Mrs Cooper. She died several years before the collapse of the Coopers into Magnolia Street. The Coopers were reticent people and the frequenters of the Lamb and Lion never got any small change out of them to pass to and fro across the beery counter. But it was known, or pieced together, that Mrs Cooper had married 'beneath herself'. She lived in the country, in Cheshire. It was said there was a Baronet Sir somewhere in her family. Herbert Cooper dealt in manicure-sets when she married him, and his hands looked like it. His son, John, who went to sea, inherited his father's carefulness about his hands. Mr Cooper must have been good-looking, too, for John was handsome and Dick, the small boy, a queerly beautiful creature; the two daughters, Mary and Enid, were not plain either.

It was not a happy marriage. She was a country-woman and she looked for stability; but Mr Cooper was an unstable business-man. If he had confined his attentions to manicure-sets, Magnolia Street would never have happened to him. He had too many irons in the fire. He speculated a good deal and consigned the manicure-sets to a manager who, after he disappeared, was found to have pledged the manicure-sets for a good deal more than they were worth.

His disappearance coincided with the crash of the De Hoeg Silver Mine in Nicaragua. Actually, the mine was sounder than some of Mr Cooper's speculations. But there is no guarantee against the convulsions of nature, and the whole mountain which was being disembowelled for that silver, slipped in an earthquake and overwhelmed the plant, the borings, the water-supply. The silver was still there. But it required as much capital as had already been expended to hack a way through to it and get things started again. The capital might some day be forthcoming. Herbert Cooper was not the only ruined investor who lived in the hope that it might be. But the others carried their hope and despair to a less doleful limbo than Magnolia Street. They even found Mayfair a more convenient place to hope and despair in. It was a matter of temperament.

The silver mine and the manicure-sets crashed within the space of a week or two. Mr Cooper was forced to realise all his assets. They included a number of slum houses in the streets of the flowering shrubs in Longton. A kindly lawyer arranged that he should keep one item of the property so that he should have somewhere to lay his head till things cleared a little. The item was number six Magnolia Street. Mr Cooper seized desperately at the straw. He must wait somewhere, he told himself in his anguish, till the capital was found to restart the De Hoeg mines. The foreman of his manicure-sets might also be traced and something recovered from that source.

He had never seen Magnolia Street when he went to live in it. He was so shattered that, perhaps, had he seen it, he would not have known what he saw. It seemed always, till the day he died, there was a film over his eyes. If John had been about, he might have prevented the move, though he was only a boy of twelve at the time. But John was away at a nautical training college, having said from an early age that he was going to be a merchant seaman. He was away when the crash came. He finished the term; then he had to leave and continue to learn his job on a training-ship.

If his elder daughter, Mary, had seen it, it was quite certain the Coopers would not have gone to live in Magnolia Street. She would have had just strength enough to prevent the move, but she had not enough to overturn the *fait accompli*. She had not been well or happy in her father's house. Soon after her mother died, she went to live in Shropshire with her mother's sister. She had been devoted to her mother, and the place was intolerable without her. Ostensibly she was away till she got strong again, but it was likely she would have stayed away permanently. Her father had an efficient housekeeper. She herself was as happy as she knew how to be in the country. Her aunt was not wealthy but they had similar tastes. They bred dogs. Her brothers and sister came to stay with them for the holidays. She hoped, in course of time, to be allowed to keep

Dick, the youngest, with her, for she loved him as much as she had loved her mother.

When the crash came she was bed-bound. She had a broken leg. She knew it was her duty to join her father now, to look after the youngsters. There would be no housekeeper in Magnolia Street, But she first wrote to her father suggesting that he should come and take a tiny house near her aunt in the country. Could he not watch developments there, too? She got so incoherent a reply that it did not seem to be the man she knew who wrote it. She left Shropshire for Doomington. When she first entered Magnolia Street, and turned in at number six, she felt as if she installed herself in a coffin and someone must soon come to close up her eyes and bind her jaw.

In one sultry moment she saw the street revealed as in a flare of lightning. She saw on the one pavement the shabby-genteel and slatternly-genteel Christians, on the other the swarming, pushing, successful slum-Jews. It was as if they had fallen, all but John, down a steep funnel and they lay at the bottom looking up at the high blue air, but no rope would be lowered to lift them out again. She knew that the spinal cord of her father's spirit was broken. Because he lived rent-free in this hovel he would cling to it more fiercely than he had ever done to the thousands of pounds he had played with so foolishly. He would wait and wait for that capital to be forthcoming which would tear the flesh and bone from the mountain till its silver heart was exposed. But she knew that capital would not be forthcoming. Her father would drink and drink more, and get more morose, and the soot would gather upon them all upon all — but John sailing the broad seas. Her small sister, Enid, might become a shop-assistant or a school-teacher and think what a lady she was and how superior she was to all those common people living in that common street. And little Dick? He was two years old, then, at the time of the disaster. Even then you felt almost sick to look at him, he was so lovely. What would become of him? Their aunt had already suggested he should live with her in Shropshire. She was a poor woman but a lady. His wife's people had always snubbed Herbert Cooper. Now that one of them offered to help him in the time of his humiliation, he replied with a letter of such hysterical abuse that any connection henceforth between him and his wife's people was out of the question.

What then would Dick become? A mechanic? A clerk?

So the Coopers went to live in Magnolia Street. They had just a few shillings a week, in addition to the house they lived in. It was as much as Mary Cooper could manage, to look after her father and young Dick and keep Enid as smart as she liked to be. John was getting a few pounds a month nowadays; he sent home a little money, so there was just enough for Enid to go to the Layton Park Higher Grade School. *Quite* the little lady was Enid. Her elder smiled wryly. She looked so genteel in her straw hat and her blue gymnasium skirt and knickers and long stockinged legs.

And Dick. He was ten now. His hair was gold, a ridiculously pure gold. He had dark blue eyes and dark lashes. But he was no little sissy-boy. John had bought him boxing-gloves, and they boxed together when John was home. He was a sturdy little devil. He was not quick or clever, but he was a stonewaller. He could stand any amount of punishment — John didn't spare him — and hove in with one or two to the solar plexus the moment John dropped his guard. He was good-natured and simple. He was so beautiful that Mary would have gone down on her knees and done scrubbing for him in the Jews' houses. With Dick about and his gold hair and blue eyes she did not regret the roses she didn't prune or the dogs she didn't breed. He was so beautiful that he carried a sort of light about with him, as if he were not a little human creature, but the incarnation of some aesthetic principle. But she didn't let him know how she felt about him. She would put him over her knees and slap him when he deserved it. The old man wasn't capable of it.

But when Dick went off to school or was out with the lads, playing, she felt once more the taste of soot on her tongue and the smell of it in her nostrils. She was practical in a sort of way, she had to be; but she had this faculty for generalisations, in virtue of which, for instance, she saw Dick, whom she idolised, not only as her small brother but as an aesthetic principle embodied.

She would look across the street to the Jews. She saw them not merely as families but as agents of certain racial principles. She saw her own family as specimens of social deterioration. Miss Tregunter, she said to herself, who lived further down the street, was just such another instance. 'She herself' was Miss Tregunter. She would never marry. She would step some day into Miss Tregunter's shoes and shoo the cats away from the little front garden hedge. As for her neighbours, the other gentile families on the even pavement, they were in their own land. Their type, their status, were fixed, though now and again one of them, by chance, might depart from it or exceed it. But the Jews opposite were not in their own place. There was an unquiet heaving in that sallow and swarthy paste. The gentiles, the small artisans, to whose level her folk had fallen, earned just so much money and were content with it. It was enough for the elder folk to buy their nightly pint at the Lamb and Lion. Sometimes, but not often, there was enough for the whole family to go for a week's holiday at Blackpool.

But the Jews were not content with that. Their eyes looked beyond the dark fringes of this town, beyond the shores of this small land, to the shores of a land richer and further. They heard the surf beating and the crackling of the dollar-bills beyond the surf. But they were not content to wait, as her father was content to wait, till the capital came; or to seek it, as Mr Stanley, the shoemaker did, in the hazards of racing and football-prophecy. They started as work-folk, working for others. Then they made factories, shops, in their own little houses. Then they went further afield. They took over derelict factories by the black river and brought forth gold out of their corruption.

So Mary Cooper saw it, as she stood a moment upon her doorstep, looking across the narrow roadway to the Jews. She did not see it all quite clearly or truthfully; for she was a sad woman, somewhat embittered. But there was truth in what she saw.

II

John Cooper, second mate of the oil tanker, *Greyhound*, had an eye for a pretty face and a trim ankle. There was just a slight pulling away of the lower lip towards the cleft in that firm jaw of his, which might indicate a too concentrated interest in pretty faces. He was only twenty-four, but there was nobody on board the *Greyhound* who had a better-looking visiting-list, from Yokohama to Bilbao and Buenos Ayres than John Cooper.

Yet if you were to reflect upon that slight pulling away of the lower lip, it might occur to you that in the shadow it made lurked some other secret than his interest in young women.

And that, after all, was not a secret. He had a strong face and, quite frankly, a sensual one. It was part of its charm for many women.

The secret in the shadow of that lower lip was the girl named Rose Berman, who lived opposite, in Magnolia Street. At least it was a secret until that Saturday early in May, when little Sam Seipel saw Rose Berman and John Cooper walking arm-in-arm through the naked daylight in a park in South Doomington. It was the first time that the lovers had walked together within so few miles of home. It was the first time that the small legs of Sam Seipel had carried him so many miles from home. But there it was. The secret was a secret no longer. All next day they talked of it in the grocery-shop, and in the evening the private bar took up the tale. Next day they talked of it in the barber-saloon, until, as it chanced, John Cooper, coming in to have his hair-cut, heard the name of Rose Berman in the air. He pushed forth his jaw so unpleasantly that the subject was avoided with great circumspection for fear John Cooper might come in to be shampooed. On the Sabbath day, after the morning service, the old men in the synagogue talked of the matter.

John Cooper had a sensual face, it is not to be doubted; but the quiet line of the lip indicated something more than, and outside of, his sensuality. It spoke of a restraint he imposed upon himself such as he was not accustomed to tolerate; it exposed some sort of exasperation and, perhaps, of bewilderment, the sense of having come up against something stronger than himself, and itself so frail a thing.

John Cooper was a first-class navigator, and he knew quite a lot about machinery. But he had always been a specialist in women, a long time before Rose Berman came into his life. He knew what to expect from Argentine girls that the Italians had no inkling of. The Germans, he considered, had never left school. He could distinguish between the Southampton and the Newcastle technique. He came back to Doomington, too, from time to time, though he disliked it. The old man was all shot to pieces and he felt he ought to put in an appearance for Mary's sake. He had already suggested once or twice that they should move into a less sordid neighbourhood, but the old man could not be moved. He had fallen into a sort of torpor. As soon as he understood what was being suggested, he was terrified. Mary, too, seemed to have grown into the place. It gave Enid pleasure to have a handful of girls to look down on. As for Dick, he had not known anything else.

So John came to Magnolia Street from time to time. Here, too, he was spontaneously aware of what girls lived there, even the small ones, with whom he was a great favourite, though they kept their distance. He knew that little blue-eyed Nellie from the Lamb and Lion would some day be a luscious mouthful. He was rather interested in the young widow, Jessie Wright of next door, though there was something in her face that put him off. Some day, he conceded, she might be a good week-end's fun. He was pretty sure he could bring her round to that way of thinking any time he wanted to. There was not much doing, else.

The other side of the street, where the Jews lived, was more exciting. He was used to exotic material and there was no meaning for him in such a distinction as Jew and non-Jew, a distinction to which Mrs Derricks, the mother of the Nightingale, was so sensitive, at least when she was drunk. They were Jew girls, instead of being French or Russian. There were more people per house living on the other side of the street, and there were therefore more girls. The daughter of the big black Rabbi fellow might be agreeable if you could only see her face through her hair. Why didn't she use a comb sometimes? There was a nice well-dressed girl at the place they'd made into some sort of waterproof factory. A little too fat, perhaps, and rather la-di-da. He didn't much care for the daughter of the people who kept the grocer's shop. Her bones were too big.

And then there was a girl at number three, nearly opposite their own house. The deuce of a pretty girl! What a neat figure, what jolly little hands! Her mother sold sweets in the front room. What dodges these Jew people were up to to bring in another penny! The mother too was pleasant enough, when the daughter wasn't about to throw her in the shade. Such pretty colour in her cheeks, as if she were years younger than she could possibly be! He wondered if there'd ever be a chance of scraping up acquaintance with the daughter. He sighed. There were quite a lot of young fellows hanging round her, and if ever he got a look in, he'd get his sailing-orders next day.

But it was not Rose Berman, the elder girl, that the young fellows came down to Magnolia Street to see. It was Ada, her sister. And it was Ada who caused these early mild distresses in John Cooper's bosom. He was aware there was another sister, for he was unable constitutionally to be unaware of a girl, if she was there to be aware of. Nor was it in Magnolia Street he first became aware of Rose.

She, for her part, had long since become aware of him. Rose Berman could not remember the time when she was not in love with him since she first set eyes on him, that is to say. And yet in a sense she had loved him before then, she used to tell herself, in her darkness and her loneliness; in those times when she feared that, despite all she did, she had not the strength to hold her mother much longer on this earth. He had seemed to her a young man, and something more than that, a strength, a force, a resting-place, something that could embrace you like the sea, or something against which to lean your tired body, like a hillside.

Of course, there was no single soul in the world to whom she ever breathed a word of such nonsense; not even her mother; nobody. She did not often indulge in it herself. But even when the words or the image did not form themselves in her brain, he was a state of her blood. She knew the way he walked, when he came back with a new double-breasted suit, what girl was taking his fancy. His eyes were more beautiful than anything she knew. Of course, his small brother, the one with golden hair, was more beautiful, as a picture might be. But that was cold, it was almost frightening. But the sailor-man was flesh and blood. What fine firm hands he had, and there was a sort of bow-shape to his mouth, though it was so strong.

Some of the singers and teachers who came to buy music at Messrs. Saunders were handsome. They knew it, the way they trained their hair and carried a handkerchief in their sleeves, with a faint dash of scent. And they carried on an ever so respectful and correct flirtation with the girl-assistants. Messrs. Saunders rather expected it from their girls, so long as it was all nice and respectful. After all, theirs was a clientele of artists. It was not chops that were on sale at Messrs. Saunders. And when you and the clients had advanced to a certain recognised stage of intimacy, you were allowed to ask them to write their artistic names in your autograph-album and they were allowed to write something beside their names, a few bars of music, a few lines of verse, all correct yet a trifle gallant.

That was, of course, as far as it went; and Rose Berman prized her autograph-album highly. She prized the signatures more than the gentlemen themselves. They were gentlemen, not men. Not as the sailor-man was a man. She loved him. He was as much a hero to her as to little blue-eyed Nellie from the Lamb and Lion. But he was much further away. It was not so much her sense of the intervening pavement that put him so far off. She thought that business all rather silly, so did her mother, even. As if it mattered about people being Jews and not being Jews, as if the heart wasn't just the same heart, and being born or marrying or dying was Jewish or not Jewish.

Her mother's cough made him seem far away, but it made all men and all things seem equally far away. It was the one thing that was near to her.

There was another reason why he was so far away — the reason why a mountain you can never get to is far — or the moon, if you like. There he was, a young man who now and again stayed for a day or two just across the street. But he might as well be in China. He might as well be the Emperor of China.

And then, upon a certain Bank Holiday, four summers ago, Rose went out alone one afternoon to Layton Park. Her mother had insisted she should have an outing. She seemed quite well and cheerful that day. So Rose left her behind, busy over her ginger and her apples, with all the windows open, and the warm air coming in.

She was sitting on the top of a hill-side shaped like a horseshoe. At the bottom of the horseshoe the Besses o' th' Barn band, a famous band of those parts, was playing. They were skillful, and were playing very gently, like a breeze wandering about. She lay back on the slope of the hill, with her head in her hands. Her eyes were half-closed. There was an image behind her eyes, of that young man who lived in Magnolia Street, and went to sea and came home from time to time. He had come home a day or two ago. She had seen him last evening. She thought he must be like that music in the bandstand below; that he could hold himself and be so gentle that you could hardly hear him and that suddenly he could come into a splendour like brass and bronze, like all those instruments. He could throw back his chest, he could open out his arms, he could call like the wind on the great seas he sailed.

She smiled. Her lips were parted a little, showing the even teeth. There was a shadow across her eyelids. The shadow stayed. It did not move. She opened her eyes. They looked straight into the eyes of John Cooper, who stood over her, bent towards her slightly. He did not move. He seemed like the figure-head of a ship in harbour.

The smile went from her face. A pallor came into her cheeks. Her heart seemed to cease beating, then took up its task again, and beat like a hammer. And then he spoke.

"I know you," he said. He seemed somewhat puzzled, the way he screwed his eyes up. He seemed also as if he were not quite certain he spoke the truth. "I know you," he repeated, as if to assure himself.

"Yes," she breathed.

He still looked down on her, bending towards her.

"It *is* you," he said again, "from Magnolia Street?"

"Yes," she answered. "I live there." There was hardly any force in her voice. Surely he could not hear her. But he was not listening. He looked into her eyes, he saw the way her lips moved, the perfect teeth behind them.

"Your sister —" he started. Then he stopped. He knew that he had never seen eyes so beautiful as these before and would never see any again. He did not know how it happened, but in the instant during which he made that realisation, he suddenly saw himself in his cabin on board ship; not the *Greyhound*, nor the *Adamantor*, from which they had transferred him; any ship. He was in his cabin. He had a book open, propped up against his knees.

It was not a book that many officers in the merchant service carried in their kit. He picked up in the ports the usual Oppenheims and Nat Goulds, like the other men, and left them about when he had finished them. But there were times when these authors did not satisfy him. It was for those times that two or three volumes went with him, rather secretly, wherever he went. They were De Quincy's *Opium-Eater*, the *Republic* of Plato, the *Morte d'Arthur* of Sir Thomas Malory.

He looked down into the eyes of the girl on the grass slope of Layton Park and it seemed as if he were looking into the pages of the last of these books, propped up against his knees. The ship was lurching somewhat. He heard the slap of the uneasy water against the sides.

"My God!" he said. "You are beautiful!" It seemed to her that soon, quite soon, she must get up out of this dream. But she would not do anything herself to break it. She smiled up at him. His eyes were sombre.

"I'm so glad you think so," she breathed. "I'm so happy!"

"What shall we do?" he said.

"Do?" she echoed him. "Do?" Perhaps this was not a dream after all. "I must be going home soon."

He put his arms across his chest. "I mean you no harm," he said shortly.

"I know!" Her heart fluttered a little. Had she offended him? Had she shown that she mistrusted him?

"I must talk to you," he said. "We're not strangers!"

"No," she admitted. "We're not strangers." Indeed they were not, or he was not to her. He had been to her at once a familiar spirit, and something as remote from her as a star. But even the star that is hidden for long seasons is no stranger.

And then she went on quickly. "You see, my mother —"

It was not the last time in the history of John Cooper and Rose Berman that that word or its idea came between them.

"Your mother —" he started impatiently. He was not used with women that they should interpose other things or people between themselves and him. He saw at once that his tone was an error. He saw her small, delicately formed lips tighten. "I'm sorry!" he said. "I'm sorry I spoke like that!"

"Oh please!" she insisted. She smiled again, as she looked up into his eyes. It was, after all, a fine day. The breeze was so warm. Look at all those other people enjoying themselves! Might she not too just once? Perhaps she might stay away from her mother just half an hour longer.

"It *is*," she admitted plaintively "a fine day!"

He was down on one knee a few feet away from her. She raised herself. She looked squarely into his eyes, astonished at her own temerity. He looked straight back into hers. The queer sombre look had not gone out of his face.

"Let's have a cup of tea somewhere!" he said.

Was it *he*, was it truly *he*, who addressed her, in words so casual? The words might be casual but the tone was not. Wasn't it as if a cloud spoke to her, or a voice spoke to her out of a tree? How was it it had not happened long ago? They were not strangers.

"Are you alone?" she asked. "My small brother, Dick, is with me."

She looked alarmed.

"He's at the bottom there, playing with some other boys."

She peered through the crowds that sprawled all the way down to the bandstand like squat clumps of foliage.

"Yes," she said. "I think I see him." She thought she saw his small head moving about like a nimbus.

"It's all right," he informed her. "We'll leave him to it."

Immediately her acute sense of maternal responsibility was aroused.

"You can't —" she started.

"Oh yes I can!" he said firmly. "I intended to lose him. That's why I brought him. There's nothing like teaching them young how to find their own way home again."

This was a method of treating one's dependents diametrically opposed to hers. But she could see there was something in it. "Yes, I see!" she said meekly.

"You'll come?" he asked.

"I'll come!"

"Oh that's grand!" he said. He smiled, for the first time. She observed the wrinkles that formed at the corners of his eyes. She almost clapped her hands.

"I knew! I knew!" she sang out in her own heart. "I knew his eyes would go like that when he smiled!" She was rising.

"Let me give you a hand!" he said. She put her small firm hand into his. He took his other hand to it as if she were too great a weight for him to lift with one hand only. His fingertips lay along both sides of her forearm. A tingling ran along to her shoulders and darted inward to her heart. It was like that moment when a swing attains its highest elevation and then seems to pause in mid-air before it swoops.

"O-o-o-oh!" the sound came long-drawn from deep within her. She suddenly tore her hand from his and hid her face in her palms.

"Never mind!" he whispered into her ear. "You lovely, lovely kid."

The blushes raced after each other over her face like waves on a beach. "No, no!" she whispered. She could not bear it. "Oh no! Please don't!"

He looked away from her. "I'm not looking!" he said. Her blushing ceased. "I should like some tea!" she whispered. He still did not look at her. They set off. He knew she was at his side. Then he was aware she had stopped. He turned towards her. Her eyes were shining.

"Oh!" she cried. "You're a sailor! You must be able to row! Will you take me for a row on the lake?"

"I will take you," he said, "anywhere in the world!"

But she had not heard that. A doleful thought had struck her. "Oh no! Oh no! We can't go."

"Why not?"

"Somebody would be sure to see us, somebody from Magnolia Street!"

He grimaced. But he did not say a word. He was more careful now.

"Nobody," she went on, "nobody from Magnolia Street must *ever* see us!"

She did not, as she uttered the words, realise how shameless they were. Was she not boldly assuming that they would be together again, often and often, for people to see them if they were not careful?

"If you don't want them to see you," he said, "they shan't!" He did not multiply words. "What's your name?" he asked.

But she had of a sudden realised how brazen she had been.

"Oh I'm so sorry!" she said piteously." I don't know what I'm saying!"

"We'll both feel fit as fiddles when we've had a cup of tea," he assured her. "What is your name? Mine's John!"

"I know!"

"You know? What do you mean you know?" He looked at her.

"We're neighbours!" she reminded him. "You can't help knowing!"

"Fool that I've been!" he swore to himself softly. "She's been there all these years!"

"Rose is my name!" she told him.

III

This had happened four years ago now. The sense of wonder never went out of it for both of them. When they were together again after his absences, and he took her off to some remote café at the other end of the town, where nobody they knew might see them, and they sat for hours in some snug alcove — it might strike them both at the same moment that the other was not real.

"John! John!" she would cry out. "It can't be you!"

"Oh no!" he replied grimly. "It's not me! It's little Lord Fauntleroy!" and with his arm about her shoulder, he crushed her against himself so fiercely that she had to set her teeth to prevent herself crying out.

He did not forswear his attentions to the ladies he knew in Rio de Janeiro or Cape Town. They existed not merely across far lands and seas, but in another state of his mind. If sometimes she lifted her mouth to his face and with her lips smoothed his eyelids down, it was a bliss for which he would willingly see all the gilded apartments of all the pretty ladies in all the world's ports burn down about their ears.

No word regarding those charmers ever passed between them. She was shrewd, not in the least sentimental. He hardly doubted that she guessed their existence. If one word had crossed her lips implying: "John, I need you more than they! Won't you wait? It may be a month... a year?" if such a word had crossed her lips — despite the heavy turbulence of his impulses he would have controlled them.

But she uttered no such word. Her duty lay by her mother's side, who, but for her, would have gone out like a smoke, long ago. To have put into words such a thought, or to allow it even to come forward into the front part of her mind, was a disloyalty of which her nature was incapable. No sort of a casuist in any other direction, she would have converted that thought into such terms as this: "Wait, John, just you wait till we've packed mother off the scene! Then we'll get to it! What a grand time we'll have!"

But the truth remained that this was the essence of the situation. She said no such word. For years, though he sometimes ached for her like a child, he too said no such word. Excepting once.

It was on the visit to Doomington that came after his first meeting with her in Layton Park. He had been away for ten months. He had learned during that period that his life, which till now had been a formless thing, a mere going to and fro, a woman here with a white skin like a lily, a woman there with a tooth like a snake — he had learned that there was a point round which henceforth all his life revolved, and the name of it was Rose Berman, the little Jew girl from Magnolia Street. He said this to her, in quite few words. He said she must marry him. When she was silent for so long, and in the dimness of the wooded place they were in, he peered into her face to see why she did not reply — he feared for a moment she was dead, so white she was, and her eyes were closed, and her bosom was still as the tree-trunk against which they leaned.

"Rose!" he called out. It was like a child in the darkness, who fears suddenly that it has been left alone.

She opened her eyes. "John," she said. "I love you! I love you so much! But I can't! You know why I can't!"

"But let her be with you!" he insisted. "Why shouldn't she be with you, always? Till —" He did not conclude the thought.

"It wouldn't be right for you. It wouldn't be right for her, either. I've got to be with her altogether. I know she'd mind nothing — nothing at all — if she saw me happy. But the others — all the neighbours and friends and relatives, they'd be dreadful. We'd have to go away. She'd have to cut herself off from everything she's always known. The strain would be too much. She's not strong enough to stand it."

"So I — so you —" he started incoherently. It would have been hard to recognise in that distraught youth the firm-jawed hulk of a young man whose single word could galvanise into deference a gang of lurching stevedores.

"So you must leave me," she said, "if you want to. You see how it is."

He knew that, like himself, she was a person who did not multiply words. She meant she would not marry him while her mother was alive. He must go, if he chose.

But he did not choose. He loved her not only because she was beautiful, with a shy sort of beauty that you did not suspect, until in a moment it flooded you. He loved her because at the centre of her small body was a core of strength, the sort of strength that the saints had. She was beautiful and she was saintly. No compound so strange as that existed in the world as he had known it till then.

"Leave *you*, Rose? Me? I know a good thing when I see it! We've got time, I suppose! We're not doddering yet! Kiss me, Rose, and don't talk such a lot!"

IV

They had waited. It was four years now they had waited. Their love was the hidden melody of their lives, like the noise of a tiny

74

spring hidden deep in greenery which only they can hear who know of it, and they must put their ear close to the ground before they are sensible to that elfin music.

It was part of its very quality for John that it should be love in secret; for in his dealings with all other women it did not matter who knew of them, from the captain to the galley-boy, or any beachcomber in the water-front tap-rooms.

Sometimes, after being separated from her for many months, when his ship was nearing its English harbour, he determined he would get her to come down to meet him, to Southampton or Hull, or wherever it was, and stay with him there till he went off again. If he asked her to come, she would come. He knew that.

But when he landed, he could not bring himself to act so. It seemed villainous to treat her as if she were some girl you bought with a swell weekend and a new frock. He went to Doomington, letting her know, care of Messrs. Saunders, that he was coming. If it were her half-day off she might go with him so far away from her mother as some village in the Derbyshire hills. If not, again they sat together in the alcove of their café, each reaching suddenly for the hands, the mouth, of the other, as if the next moment it might prove to be a shadow.

"When?" he asked of himself. "When will we be free?" But he could not utter the question aloud.

He had a feeling that his elder sister, Mary, knew of the situation. He had not said a word himself, for the understanding with Rose was that neither of them should speak, till they were free to act. In any case the Coopers did not discuss their affairs with each other. They had retained, Mary reflected bitterly, at least the sense of reticence out of the ruin of their former quality. Of course she knew that John, her brother, loved the Jewish girl from across the street. She found in herself no trace of distress that the girl was a Jewess, a shop-assistant. No instinct of fight had ever stirred in her, from the first moment of her family's collapse. She saw no more in the love of John and Rose than the culminating biological expedient of that force, or that inertia, which was impressing the body and spirit of her fallen family into the mean fabric of Magnolia Street.

There was, it is almost certain, one other woman in the street who knew of the love of these young people. She was the mother of Rose Berman. What else can she have meant when she called Rose to her one evening, when Ada was out with one of her boys, and said: "Rose, my daughter! Ha, don't look into my eyes so, you sly one!"

"What, mother, what? What is it you're saying?"

"Rose, my child. I am so strong. I have not felt so strong for years. Look at my cheeks, would one not say a farmer's daughter?"

"Of course you are strong, mother! Like a horse! Your cough hasn't been troubling you of late — not so much, oh not half so much!"

"Yes, that's true!" the mother said, coughing. For she coughed so frequently that they hardly noticed it, except when it was hard for her to catch her breath. "That's why I wanted to speak to you, Rose!"

"Yes?" A moment's silence. Rose looked up into her mother's eyes, rather frightened, a tiny sense of guilt tapping away at her heart.

"If it should ever occur to you... You see, Rose, how strong I am, how I can look after myself? And then there is Ada always —"

"Ada, Ada! Shall it be in two weeks or two months that Ada shall be married? And which boy shall it be?"

"Yes, yes, she is a pretty child. I was like Ada when I was a girl in the homeland. You would not believe it, Rose!"

"You? Ten Adas and a hundred Roses!"

"Nonsense, child! You must not flatter me so! But yes — you may be right about Ada. Who knows how soon she will be married. That photographer, he gives her no peace! I think he means it!"

"Hummel, you mean? Johnnie Hummel? No, mother, no! He's only playing with her! As soon as he finds he can't get what he wants out of her, he'll go somewhere else. The sooner the better!"

"You don't like him?"

"I hate him! If he'd only stop talking sometimes! Ugh! Forget about him, mamma darling!" She made the gesture of someone sweeping a filthy cobweb from her face. "What was it you were saying? Should it ever occur to me — should *what* ever occur to me?"

"Yes, yes, Rose. Should it ever occur to you to wed, Rose, no matter with whom, you would not let me stand in your way? How strong I am these days. You have said it yourself. Could I not look after myself? *No matter with whom, Rose!* What? You silly child. What is wrong with you? There now, Rose! Ah come now, Rose! Rosy-Posy! Why do you weep, Rose? What have I said? Ah my baby, my baby, I shall not say it again!"

"Never, never again, mother! Say you will never say such a thing again!"

"My darling, if you bid me to! Was there ever a mother before with a daughter like you? What do you say? Time for my glass of milk with the egg beaten up in it? Sweet Rose, let me not have the egg beaten up in it tonight! You know how I dislike that egg beaten up! Let it be a holiday!"

"What, *mutterel*? No egg? Who ever heard of such a thing! How shall you keep up your strength to serve behind your counter? All business-woman eat eggs beaten up in milk. Mr Saunders told me that Mrs Saunders will not go night or morning without her egg beaten up in milk, and she so rich she could have them beaten up in champagne, if she wished to."

"If you will have it so, daughter!"

Rose did not fail to perceive the significance of her mother's "no matter with whom." Her heart was almost mild with pride in her mother, for being so wise and so free. It was indeed a wiser and a freer thing than it is easy to say, for a Jewish mother who lived in Magnolia Street, to bid her daughter marry a *goy*; and to do that under the very shadow of their august neighbour, Rabbi Shulman, whose long loose frock-coat flapped about him like the wings of some dark protecting bird of Israel.

She told John of this. She was beside herself with her pride in her mother.

"And your answer was?" asked John.

"You know what my answer was," she said quietly.

"Yes, I know what your answer was," he repeated. He was silent after that. He looked away from her, as if the wall of the café were the bows of his ship, and the grey waters swung beyond.

"John," she whispered, pressing his hand. "John! Are you cross?"

He turned round as gently to her as an animal to a hurt cub. He smiled, and shook his head.

"You grand John," she whispered, "to have waited for me all these years!"

Then he broke his silence. "Stuff! Rubbish!" he stormed. "All these years! You're only a kid! You've not started growing up yet!

77

Wait till I take you in hand!" he threatened her. "I'll knock all the nonsense out of your head!"

"Only a kid yet?" she asked. She was nearly twenty-five. Her neighbours in Magnolia Street had long since given her up as an old maid. That's often the way it is, reflected the women at the grocery-shop, when a girl has had the bad luck to have a younger sister at home so much prettier than she is. "Only a kid yet?" she went on. "And me old enough to be your mother!"

She was, in point of fact, about a year and a half his senior. He looked at her hard. "Why, you're not even born yet!"

He would wait. If he must, he must. Some day she'd call him and he'd go. He'd go back to her from the furthest sea in the world. It could be managed somehow. He was well up in his company's good books.

"Get some tea down you!" he said gruffly.

She got some tea down her. Then they rose and went for a walk.

It was the walk that was their undoing. It had been their custom to take a bus immediately outside the café to a village a few miles away, where they walked through meadows alongside the Mersey, sniffing the meadowsweet, hurling stones into the water, or suddenly kissing each other as if they had never done so in all their lives before. But Rose was not happy about her mother that afternoon. She wanted to get back immediately to Longton. John pleaded for a compromise. There was a park a few minutes' walk away. It was not much of a park. But it was a good deal better than giving up Rose immediately. Besides, they both had always felt there was something a little sacred about all parks, even those which consisted mainly of asphalt and iron railings, since a certain day in summer four years ago.

"Let's go for an hour's stroll in the park, then," John pleaded.

"Forty minutes!" she conceded, but she entered the park with misgiving.

"John!" she cried out suddenly, not more than five minutes later. "John! There's Sam!"

"Sam?" he asked. She seemed so frightened that he looked round fiercely for some man who might at some time have molested her. "Sam who?"

"Sam Seipel! From our street!" she said. Her eyes filled with tears. "I knew it would come! Sooner or later it had to!" She put her head upon his shoulder in the public park, with the gesture of one who has nothing more to lose, and cares no more, therefore, for the niceties of decorum.

"Where?" he cried. "Where?"

"Down those trees! Don't you see him? That small boy!"

He started off in pursuit, aware that a shilling will often prove a useful silencer with small boys.

But the small boy had disappeared. The small boy, seeing the fierce sailor running after him, ran more quickly and doubled more dexterously than any other small boy did that day in Doomington.

"And now," said Rose, her bosom heaving, "they'll all get to know! Oh John, John!"

"To Hell with them all!" said John. But he scratched his head ruefully. "Come on, Rose, old girl, we've got another thirty-two minutes!"

Chapter 5

I

It was the following Saturday. The beards were gathered in the Lithuanian Brotherhood. The beards had heard a rumour of a Jewish maiden who lived in Magnolia Street and had been seen out walking with a gentile youth. The beards were wagging.

It was the custom of the beards to come together on the Sabbath afternoon in the women's section of the synagogue. There they regaled themselves upon a feast of salt herrings, black bread, boiled potatoes and subtle scholarship. The beard of Reb Berel, the beadle, was in attendance. It was a humble beard, yellowy-grey, for he took snuff. He did not often eat or drink, he did not love or hate. He took snuff instead of these things. He blew his nose into a great red handkerchief which on week-days he extracted from the rear pocket of his antique frock-coat. On Saturdays he blew his nose into that same handkerchief, having unwound it from around his waist. The beard was not large and the edges of it were dim and blear.

The beard of the beadle was in a state of great uncertainty this afternoon. In the matter of Rose Berman and John Cooper it had at last found something outside its competence. Otherwise it was kept busy all day long. It provided wine for the prayer which lets out the Sabbath. It was on the spot for each of the three services of the week-day, to see that the full quorum of ten should not be lacking. If one lacked it went forth into the highways and byways to bring in the tenth, however pressing his business be. When a mourner entered the synagogue, it was there to bid the world turn round and grieve with him in his mourning. When a death occurred it arranged that there should be psalm-singers: it went about among the crowd gathered to hear the funeral-eulogy, shaking a box, and dripped tears among the pennies of the well-wishers. It sent over the marriage-canopy when it was asked for, and the poles to support it. It arranged, on the eighth day after the birth of a male child, that the circumciser was there, and the plate and napkin and all to hand. It was a familiar of death and marriage and birth, but it had itself forgotten how to die. It was there when the synagogue was founded. The War did no more to unloosen it than a storm does to unloosen the seaweed that has

80

grown into the sunken piles of a pier. It was known that it had a wife. It must have frequented her company, for they had children. But nobody knew, or nobody remembered, where it lived. No one ever visited the synagogue so late or so early as not to find it there.

And on this Sabbath day in May it looked more dim and blear than it had ever done before. All the other beards gathered there that day lacked something of their quality. Excepting, perhaps, the beard of Rabbi Shulman. That existed in an ether rapt out of circumstance. It swept a long way down his breast like a black water. It had little volume, for the habit he had of drawing his thumb down the one side of his chin and his finger down the other, seemed to have kept it sparse under the cheek-bones. But each separate hair of the beard had its own wild splendour, as if it caught a gleam from his coal-black eyes. He was the arbitrator in all matters of faith and custom, when he could be brought down from the high places where he walked. He rarely ascended the pulpit to deliver an oration, and when he did he spoke in such cloudy symbols of matters so occult, that there were not many who understood more than a few words. But the more enigmatic he became, rapt away from all present like the Burning Bush in its own flame, the louder grew the wailing of the women behind their wooden partition; and to all it seemed that their cheeks were scorched as in a great heat.

It is not certain that he had become aware of this reported treason in the lowlands. But Reb Aryeh Lipwitz, who kept a small Hebrew-school next door, was aware. Today his beard was sterner, its angles sharper than usual. It was he who had ascended the pulpit at the morning service. His voice was always loud. His message was always simple.

"Thou must not carry money upon the Sabbath! Thou must not ride the tramcar upon the Sabbath!" But today some more pertinent message was expected from him, some comment on the rumour that drifted like a miasma through Magnolia Street. It was clear he intended some comment, for his hand shook, his eyes were a little glassy. Once or twice he cleared his throat. He beat his breast. He shook his head. But no sound came. "Thou shalt not," he said at length, "carry money upon the Sabbath! Thou shalt not ride the tramcar upon the Sabbath!" The thing had defeated him. There could be no such thing. It was only a nightmare.

The beard of Reb Feivel, the grandfather of Mrs Seipel, was gathered among the beards. You could not doubt from the sight of it that he was the kindest of old men born, his beard was so soft and woolly and lamb-like. It was a somewhat tousled and distressed beard this afternoon.

The beard of Mr Emmanuel was there, the clerk to the Jewish Board of Guardians. It was a short pointed French beard, hardly a beard at all if you compared it with its neighbours; a beard which did not exclude Mr Emmanuel from being considered a man of the great world, yet at the same time was a public recognition of his tenure of an important Jewish post. The short beard of Mr Emmanuel was perplexed. Its single arrow-head was divided this afternoon into two thinner arrow-heads that intersected each other. It was a real grief to Mr Emmanuel that the two pavements of Magnolia Street looked so coldly on each other. It puzzled him, too, because he loved his fellows, and he did not understand why they, too, should not love each other.

And now when a young man from the one pavement and a young woman from the other *did*, it was alleged, actually love each other... he should have gone about dancing on air all day. But he did not. He tugged hard at the two sections of his little beard, trying to get them to stick. But they kept apart, obstinately.

The short stubble of Mr Poyser was there, but you could hardly call it a beard. Other beards were there from the neighbouring streets. But all beards were turned as one upon the beard of the kind Mr Billig.

The eyes of Mr Gershon Billig were blue and bland. His hair was flax white. His cheeks were pink and chubby, his forehead unwrinkled. But when your eye fell upon his beard, the words came to your lips immediately. "What a dear old man!" He had a beard like sterling silver. You were convinced he would have readily converted it into silver shillings, if there had been a recipe for such a conversion, and given one to every child he met, till the supply ran out.

But it was not because Mr Billig was so kind that all the beards were turned upon him. It was because Mr Billig arranged matches. He wasn't what you might call a *regular* marriage-broker. He had only to smile on the boy and girl and sit himself between them and bring their hands together and stroke them with one hand where they lay in the palm of the other. That was about all he needed to do, and the marriage was as good as fixed. The regular marriage-brokers had to do about as much intriguing as a court-chamberlain in a renaissance palace, and to combine that with so much eloquence that they got hoarse, and even then, the marriage frequently did not come off.

When Mr Billig took a hand, however, the young people were so fluttered and embarrassed, they did not know where to look. He had few failures to his account. When, however, on the morning of the marriage ceremony, the two fathers pressed a little acknowledgment into his hands, it was his turn to be fluttered and embarrassed. He turned his eyes away, and his pink cheeks became quite rosy.

"*Nu*, Reb Gershon?" muttered the beards that afternoon in the synagogue. They did not say any more, but what they meant was quite clear. "*Nu*, Reb Gershon? What about it? Haven't you got a nice young man on your books for her? Well, yes, she's not so young herself any more. Then why not a nice widower, with a nice business? A young man might make trouble about her mother, no? But if it was a widower, with perhaps two or three little children, then *she* might look after the children, and he wouldn't make any trouble about the mother. And the old woman, no harm befall her, she's not long for this world anyway! She shouldn't stand in the way too much!"

Mr Billig passed his fingers through his silky beard. His fingers drummed upon his stomach, which he could only just accommodate between the form he sat on and the table. "Ram-bam-bam!" he mused. "Ram-bam-bam!"

"For the honour of the street!" continued the silent appeal. "What? Shall it be said in Lavender Street and Mimosa Street that a Jewish girl from Magnolia Street went off with a *goy*, a street with a Rabbi Shulman, a Reb Feivel, a Reb Aryeh, living in it? *And* a Reb Gershon? God should prevent!"

The last salt herring had been stripped to its skeleton, the peel removed from the last boiled potato. Mr Billig stroked his stomach. His blue eyes beamed like forget-me-nots touched by the sun after a shower.

"You can rely on me!" he said out, quite loud. A sigh of relief soughed amongst the thickets of beard. Mr Billig looked at the clock over the door. "Yes," he said to himself, as he rose to go. "It is time. She will be waiting for me."

83

Mr Billig had no great distance to go, only so far as number nine, where he had an appointment with the aristocratic Miss Winberg. Number nine Magnolia Street was not only the Winberg residence, but the Winberg factory. A few months later Mr Winberg had obtained possession of the house next door, and had knocked the two houses into one. A year or so after that Mr Winberg was in negotiation for the purchase of two or three houses in Oleander Street, that backed against his factory in Magnolia Street. But that rate of progress was a snail's pace compared with the developments forced upon him by the Great War. During the dizziest boom periods he kept his feet planted on solid earth, however the comets of speculation might whistle about his mousy hair. Post-war slumps meant something to him, but not much, at a time when many of his competitors were wiped clean off the slate like a little smudge.

Mr Billig rolled benignly along Magnolia Street that warm evening in middle May. He was not fifty; quite young, in a manner of speaking. He looked old, but he had the heart of a little child. A woman was wheeling towards him a real little child in a perambulator. Mr Billig stopped and squeezed the baby in its belly and said "Goo-goo!" at it. Mr Billig had not looked a year younger when he came to live in Magnolia Street. He looked exactly the same twenty years later, his eyes as blue, his cheeks as pink. You might almost say of him he was an old man by profession, as Wilfred Derricks was a boy by profession. Of course there was a difference. It was a matter of glands and secretions with the poor Nightingale. With Mr Billig it was a matter of a kind heart. Abou Ben Adhem must have looked a lot like Mr Billig.

He had an appointment with Miss Winberg this afternoon. He stroked his stomach happily. Mr Ivor Lionel, the son of a client of his, was in love with Bella Winberg. He stopped in mid-street and corrected himself. Not a client, a friend. He would fix up this little business of Bella and Ivor Lionel, and then turn his attention to Rose Berman. Rose Berman could wait a day or two. He did not expect much in the way of a *bonté* from the Bermans. But what did that matter? That wasn't his motive in fixing up these things. Love was his motive.

Mr Billig believed in love. He thought there was nothing quite so touching and delicate as love. And when he busied himself about the introduction of a young man to a young woman and getting them handcuffed together under the marriage-canopy before either of them had time to find out if the other had warts, he did it because he knew the young people were going to love each other. Like Ivor Lionel, for instance, and Bella Winberg.

He knocked at the Winberg door. Mr Winberg had conveyed a special message to him that morning at the synagogue to the effect that Bella would see him at half-past five. He was not to come before, for one of her admirers was having tea with her in the lounge. He must not be late, as she was going out to dinner with one of her admirers.

At half-past five Mr Billig knocked. He was admitted by a maid. She was the only example of her species in Magnolia Street and had caused much scandal on her first appearance. He was admitted into the house. The smell of the work-rooms with their rotten floors and great swathes of wallpaper flapping over the benches and machines, assailed his nostrils. He was led immediately into the lounge, which the less aristocratic inhabitants of Magnolia Street called more modestly the parlour.

Bella Winberg was lying disposed upon an enormous red plush sofa, as alluring and opulent as herself. Immediately above her head was a black-and-white enlargement of her charms at the stage to which the first fourteen months of her existence had carried them. She wore no clothes and was lying on her plump little stomach. One leg was lifted coyly into the air. It was easy to deduce from the facts presented by that enlargement of the infant Bella, the eighteen-year-old maiden who, as Mr Billig entered the room, half sat and half lay on the red plush sofa. There was an air of lazy calculation in her infant eye as she contemplated the rattle or whatnot enticingly held up by the photographer to woo her complacency. The swelling lines, fold upon fold of flesh, were there, the thick rose-bud mouth, the dense tropical luxuriance of her hair.

The enlargement of Mr Julius Winberg, the father, hung on the left side of the baby Bella. It did no justice at all to his beady sapient eyes, but it represented correctly his hollow cheeks and long, lean, pointed nose. He seemed a sapless little man, and it was not to be wondered at, if the picture on the further side of Bella represented his wife, her mother — as it did; such frills and flouncings were there, such solid flaps of well-nourished flesh, such a billowing of hip and bosom. No wonder that Mr Winberg's nose seemed sharp as a pelican's beak, as if he too, to maintain his offspring, were compelled to tear at his breast to feed them. On the wall facing these three enlargements, was a smaller enlargement of Bella's brother, Eric, somewhat aloof, in his lace collar and velvet coat and buckled shoes, somewhat patrician, a sort of Romney of Magnolia Street portraiture. Eric's name on his birth certificate was Isaac, but he had called himself Eric from an early age. He lived in his own world. He did not have much traffic with his family, who were Jews.

Near Eric's photograph hung a mere cabinet-size photograph of Dora, the baby, at the age of two. It was almost as if her parents were not quite sure whether Dora's photograph was worth enlarging, so sickly and unconvincing a child she was, and she might not last much longer, and the least said the soonest mended. But they were wrong. Little Dora was a sticker. There was to come a day when very refined voices indeed might tell them how wrong they were, in discreet boudoirs in Hanover Square and over afternoon tea in pleasant country-houses near Godalming and Petworth.

The lounge had a sense about it of a hot jungle breaking on a steamy beach. Myriads of little coloured ornaments hung on shelves and tables and overmantels, like humming birds arrested in mid-flight. Plumes and tufts and feathers nodded everywhere. In picture-frames and plush-padded boxes as many shells were cluttered together as the steamy tide uncovers on a Polynesian beach. And fat and friendly, with plump fingers and sweet eyes, Bella Winberg sat at the centre of all this, very indolent, but very much aware of what was what.

There arose about her an odour of cinnamon and frankincense and nutmeg. The smell of Araby was in her bath-salts. Even at the age of eighteen, which Bella attained in Igro, she had many suitors, many more in a month, alas, than Becky Poyser of the grocery shop, four years her senior, had in a whole year. Bella's parents did not need to summon the aid of any marriage-broker to get their daughter married. It was Bella herself who had insisted that Mr Billig should be allowed to pay her a visit, and that she herself should tackle him. Catch Mr Winberg paying a commission to any marriage-broker, when dozens of young men were tumbling over each other's heels to pay *him* a commission for the mere privilege of being allowed to pay court to Bella. Or not exactly a commission. They were willing to put fifty or a hundred pounds into the business as a token of good faith. Quite a few did, and though they did not win Bella, who was destined for more handpainted oil pictures than any of them could offer her, none of them regretted the little investment. For quite a few of those young men had almost as keen a nose for business as Mr Winberg himself; and it was to the father, as much as to the daughter, that their smell of money directed them. But many loved Bella for herself alone. They would have been just as willing to marry her, if she had been as poor as the tousled Rachel, Rabbi Shulman's daughter, for she would be an ornament to any man's parlour and a joy between his bedsheets.

Bella Winberg was as obviously destined to a future of wealth and brilliance as Mary Cooper across the street was destined to a future of shabby penury. It was clear, even in 1910, that Miss Winberg would, not many years hence, be living in a super-de-luxe apartment on Riverside Drive in New York, or whatsoever avenue in that fickle city would, not many years hence, house those Jews who do not live in *quite* the best places though they pay quite the highest rents. It was just as clear that Mary Cooper, a good many years hence, would still be living in Magnolia Street, if Magnolia Street were still extant.

There was this in common between Miss Winberg and Miss Cooper, that the spirits of both were steeped in a divine inertia, though the odours that rose about the nostrils of Miss Winberg were the odours of scent, shut windows, flowers, plush furniture, chocolate-wrappings; and the odours in the nostrils of Miss Cooper were dust and grate-blacking and bacon-rind. Miss Winberg would sit still in one place and young men, as by a natural law, would gather about her, attended by platinum bracelets and caviar and the presidency of women's leagues for providing woollies for poor babies. Miss Cooper would sit still in one place and nothing would gather about her but the evening shadows and the smell of tomorrow's porridge, which she had allowed to catch in the saucepan.

All the Jewish girls used the word "aristocratic" regarding Miss Winberg. Becky Poyser from the grocery-shop used it with a slight sniff. The Rabbi's untidy daughter, Rachel Shulman, used it with a sigh of adoration, as of a being whose perfumed flesh was made out of a different substance from her own. There was only one creature in the world more radiant in Rachel Shulman's eyes, and he was a Winberg, too — Eric, the ducal one. The men, as well as the women, on the Jewish pavement, used the word "aristocratic" regarding her quite naturally, which indicated the essentially Oriental nature of their ideals.

To the gentiles opposite them she seemed nothing but a fat little Jewess, only differing from the other little Jewesses in the quality of her clothes and the amount of her jewellery. But to the Jews she embodied an ideal that harked back atavistically to a far earlier set of values than those which had evolved in the pale of Eastern Europe. She was the sort of female that their Asian forebears cherished, a sheikh's darling. Though she looked smart enough in 1910 in Doomington versions of London versions of Paris models, and though she looked still smarter in 1930 when she went for her models straight to Lanvin and Poiret, the ethnologically-minded observer would always have suspected that she would have looked most completely at home in the baggy breeches, silken headwear and voluminous over-gowns of the Oriental Jewess. He would have said that in Tunis, for instance, her parents would have sold her by weight to her suitor, and they would not have made a bad thing out of it.

"Ah, good evening, Mr Billig!" came the sweet gurgle of Bella's voice. She looked up at him as he came in, just as she had looked up at the photographer who took the picture of her seventeen years earlier, just as she looked up at the young men who came to pay court to her, just so adorably and with just the same air of lazy calculation.

"Ah, good evening, good evening, Miss Winberg!" His stomach moved a little from side to side as he advanced. She reached forth her hand to him languidly.

"Do sit down in that arm-chair, just at the foot there. That's right! I want to look at you!"

Mr Billig's self-assurance became less assured. He was not frightened of Bella. A fly would not be frightened by a creature so sweet and indolent. But he was fluttered by her, his kind old heart began beating like anything. She made eyes at him. There is no doubt about that. Lazy as she was, she gave herself a few minutes practice every night and morning in making eyes at her mirror. And Mr Billig would do as well as a mirror; and better, for after the worst had been said about the fat old fraud, he was a man, anyhow. So she made eyes at him. And he blinked back at her, and stroked his benevolent beard and purred and said "Ram-bam-bam!"

But he kept hold of himself. He was too downy a bird to be caught napping. He merely purred and blinked and said "Ram-bam-bam!" and with the tact and cordiality for which he was famous, led the conversation round to the subject of Mr Ivor Lionel.

"Such a wonderful young man!" breathed Mr Billig. He lifted the palms of both hands. "And so loving a disposition! You would think him a dove not a young man! But arms he's got! I tell you, Miss Winberg. He got the prize for boxing at his school. He was at one of those big schools, where they all live together. A public school they call it, no? He was in a Yiddisher house and he won the prize for boxing, and yet such a dove! I know —"

"He hasn't any money, I believe!" interrupted Miss Winberg.

"Money? What are you talking about money? His family came over to England with Oliver Cromwell. He goes back a long time before that, a long time. They used to live in a town in Spain hundreds of years ago he told me where, where the oranges come from. Oh yes, Seville, no? And you talk about money?"

"No, I just asked."

But Mr Billig was launched on Mr Ivor Lionel's chief claim to exalted matrimony. If his blue blood did not get him there, nothing else would. He had no intrinsic distinctions, excepting his prowess as a boxer, which had not survived his fifteenth year. "His mother was burned up with Isaac of York, a few hundred years before that," Mr Billig continued with enthusiasm.

"His mother?" Bella enquired.

His voice rasped a little. "No, of course not. On his mother's side."

"Oh Mr Billig. I'm so sorry. Am I being stupid?" She touched lightly with her middle finger the stretched trouser above his knee. The tiny sensation went straight up his thigh and along to his arm-pit. "And besides," she went on, "I've met Mr Lionel. I don't like him much. And my parents don't like him at all."

Which was true. Miss Winberg was already quite well aware of the young genealogist, though she lived in a slum and he lived in a house on Baxter's Moor, with a grand piano and an upright piano and a conservatory. She had already excluded him from the sphere of her calculations. She had an easy prescience that her future was bound up with New York rather than old York.

Mr Billig thought hard. What fresh tack might he pursue to recommend to this highly disturbing young lady the scion of the antique houses of York and Seville? Then suddenly it struck him that it was the last word in magnanimity to be handing over to another the juicy peach which swelled and sunned itself within so few feet of his own mouth. He sighed. He was an old man. He knew it. Perhaps he had not had out of life everything it had to offer. He sighed again.

"Why do you sigh?" she asked.

"Did I sigh?" he said. "This is no time for sighing. Shall there not be instead a merry-making?"

"No," she said decisively. "With that one, no! I don't like him!"

"Oh!"

"With me it must be a question of love!" she said. Love! That was a word which Mr Billig had been waiting for, a subject concerning which he had a scholarship at once subtle and generous. He had a good deal, in fact, to say on the matter of love.

But somehow today his eloquence lacked sparkle. He was not convincing, even to himself. He was aware she was not listening. He was aware she looked into his blue eyes, his frankly attractive blue eyes, with a long scrutiny. He was aware she spoke.

"Such eyes!" she said.

No owls rested in Mr Billig's hair. He was not born yesterday. He knew the tale of Samson and Delilah as well as the next man. So, hurriedly he went on with his pleading, his flute-like praise of love.

"Such eyes!" she said again. And then, in a lower voice: "But I don't like beards!"

He whipped round to her, as well as his rolling stomach would permit him to engage in a process of whipping round. He was not aware of what he said. "For you," he cried, "for one kiss, I would cut off my beard!"

The next moment he was aware. A bright spot of scarlet thickened in the centre of his pink cheeks. He tried to speak, but could find nothing at all to say. She had not heard him. Or had she perhaps heard him? She gave him her hand again, like the Queen of Sheba being gracious to a somewhat inferior nabob.

"So you see how it is, Mr Billig?" she said. He rose uncertainly. He tried to purr and say "Ram-bam-bam!" at her. But the proper noises would not come. And so he left her.

"Rosie mine," said Mrs Berman to her daughter two or three evenings later. "Are you going out tonight? You can. I've got everything ready for tomorrow."

Rose looked steadily into her mother's eyes. Her love seemed to spurt up from her heart through a thousand small channels till it gathered in the throat and beat tumultuously, in a single pulse. It sounded an innocent enough question: "Are you going out tonight?" But Rose knew how much more it meant. It meant: "Are you going out to meet your lover? Then go, my sweet, go! And he is a *goy*? Then go none the less, my dear sweet! And will the women gather round us and show their teeth, because you, a Jewish daughter wed a gentile, and I, a Jewish mother, urge you? And will the old men thunder in their beards? We care a fig for them, don't we, Rose?"

"No, mother," said Rose. "I'm not going out tonight. I'm going to be with you." But she said to her, more silently: "You lovely, you heroic one: do you think I'd leave you to the thunder of the old men and the sharp teeth of the women? Oh no, oh no! That's not the stuff I'm made of! Nor he, either!"

"Well, Rose. Mrs Billig was in today. She said her husband would so like to see you, at half-past eight. I promised you'd go if you were free. Will you go in?"

"What can he want to see me about?" asked Rose. Mother and daughter looked at each other. There was, of course, only one thing he could want to see her about. Mrs Berman knew just as well as Rose how fatuous it was for Mr Billig to want to see John Cooper's sweetheart.

"You see," pleaded Mrs Berman. "She asked very special. So what could I do?"

Rose smiled. She knew it was impossible for her mother to deny anything that was asked of her. "All right, mother, I'll go." But her mouth looked grim. It was odd how grim so gentle a mouth might look. "What fun it would be," she said to herself, "if John could come too!"

"What are you thinking about, Rose?" It was a note of alarm. "You'll be nice to the old man?"

"Darling!" She went up and kissed her mother on the centre of her forehead.

Rose knocked at Mr Billig's door at half-past eight. It was typical of Rose she should put on her whole going-out costume to walk the few yards, just as if she were going all the way to business in Deansgate.

"Come in, come in!" welcomed Mrs Billig. "Straight into the parlour! He's not come in yet! But he'll be in soon, any moment!" She talked as if the Lord Mayor had called him into a private consultation on the future of the Infirmary Site, but he would not let even that make him more than a few minutes late for his appointment.

Rose followed Mrs Billig into the parlour. The parlour smelled of walnut sideboard. It consisted almost exclusively of walnut sideboard. Mrs Billig was very proud of it. She polished it and rubbed it as she might have polished and rubbed a baby if the Lord had been so kind as to endow her with one. She didn't like people to think they were rich, so she was careful to point out what a struggle it was to pay off the installments on the pink plush suite of parlour furniture which was huddled up in the part of the room not occupied by walnut sideboard. Sometimes she and her husband went without bread for days, she said, to pay off the installment on the parlour furniture. But the walnut sideboard meant so much to her, she claimed it quite fearlessly for her own. Yet she would always make one stipulation about it. The walnut sideboard was hers, yes. But it didn't mean anything. "People think," she would remonstrate, "that because I've got a walnut sideboard, I'm rich." But she wasn't. They weren't. They were poor people, but, thank God, their wants were few and frugal. It made it all the more admirable to see them always getting about with a smile on their faces, and ready to do a good turn for anybody.

"Beautiful, isn't it, no?" asked Mrs Billig. She thought she detected a mark on the polished surface of the sideboard. She breathed on it, then polished away reverently with her apron.

"Beautiful!" said Rose."

"You will take your things off, Rose, yes?"

"I think I won't, thank you!"

Rose was not very communicative. She did not like Mr Billig to imagine he could keep her waiting ten minutes, fifteen minutes. She drummed with her fingers on the pink plush arms of her arm-chair. Mrs Billig had intended to have a tactful word or two with her about this business of the gentile sailor.

Some people said it was true. Some said it wasn't. For her own part, if it was just a matter of a nice box of chocolates and a gold brooch well, why not? She was broad-minded. She knew quite well what she wanted to say. But Rose's face was not encouraging, somehow. She was quite relieved when she heard the key turn in the front door and knew at last that her Gershon had come.

"Ah!" she said. "He is here!" She blushed like a young bride. They were a very devoted couple.

"So I gather!" said Rose.

Mr Billig entered. "Ah, Rose!" he cried. "What a pleasure! What a pretty pleasure!" He held out both arms to her. Rose went on drumming with the fingers on the arms of the chair.

Mrs Billig had his skull-cap ready. She took his silk-hat off and put the skull-cap on his head. Mrs Billig looked at Rose. It really shouldn't be at all difficult to get her off with that widower. Of course, as they had perceived at the synagogue, it could hardly be anything much better than a widower when a girl gets to that age... He had been busy on her account the last two days. Having had no luck with Bella Winberg, he felt it all the more important to fix up something satisfactory for Rose Berman. If it was really serious about her and the sailor from across the street — not only was it a dreadful scandal, but where did *he* come in? He would merely have let another chance of turning an honest penny slip through his fingers.

Mr Billig had found his widower — or Rose Berman's widower — to be exact.

"My mother told me you wanted to speak to me," said Rose. Rose was conscious that she was not being nice, exactly, to Mr Billig, as her mother had requested of her. But her mother hadn't said that Mr Billig would sit stroking his stomach and saying "Ram-bam-bam!" at her for minutes at a stretch. It seemed like minutes. Perhaps it was not so long.

"First," said Mr Billig, "just let's have a talk."

"About what?"

"About what? Just a talk!"

"I'm dreadfully sorry. I've got a lot to do at home tonight!"

"Ah!" he said slyly. "So you're not going out? You're not going to meet anybody?" He tapped the side of his nose with his finger.

"Will you please tell me what you wanted to see me about?" she said shortly.

"Yetta," he called to his wife. "Make us both some tea. And bring some cake." His voice was very magnanimous. Rose got up from her chair.

"I'm afraid I'll have to go unless you tell me what you want me for."

Mr Billig's eyes twinkled a little nastily. He didn't like to have his hand forced. "My dear Rose," he said, "what for you are in such a hurry? Sit down, let's be friendly."

"I'm sorry, Mr Billig. You don't seem able to get to the point." She was still standing. "Have you got a match for me?"

"Yes, yes!" he said hopefully. She was a sensible girl, after all. "But such a match! Sit down! Sit down!"

"No thanks! A widower, I take it?"

Mr Billig gurgled a moment. "Well, it's like this, Rose. If you can call it a widower, when a wife dies with the first child —"

"It's very kind of you," said Rose, without heat. "If I ever want a widower, I think I'll be able to find him for myself. No tea for me, thank you, Mrs Billig," she called out into the kitchen. "Good night, Mr Billig!" She was out in the passage. She was aware that, after all, she had obeyed her mother. She had been nice to the old man, fantastically nice. The thought was suddenly more than she could bear. She put her head back round the parlour door.

"Oh you unpleasant old man!" she said. Then she left the house.

IV

Mr Billig had not been having a good time of it. First there had been Bella Winberg. Then Rose Berman. But that wasn't the end of it. The next day was the day of the two detectives.

The Billigs had no children and their tastes were simple, so that Mr Billig fortunately needed to do nothing in the way of a regular job, and what regular job was he capable of doing, other than running a Hebrew-school, like his neighbour next door but one, Reb Aryeh? And wouldn't that be taking the money out of poor Reb Aryeh's mouth? And besides, what with Mr Billig's headaches, how could he bear to have a crowd of noisy boys running in and out of the house, God bless them? And what would become of the walnut sideboard?

They managed to live, the Lord be praised. Money came in this way and that. He sometimes arranged love-matches. He arranged passports for people who wished to go to America, he knew how to procure birth-certificates and to arrange divorces with the minimum of scandal. He was really a capable business-man, though he would have repudiated with blushes any such compliment. "Nothing but an old Hebrew teacher," was the way in which he spoke of himself. But business-men were quite pleased to ask him down to their houses — not to their offices — to drink a glass of tea with lemon and eat a lump of cake. And various matters came up, including the matter of business, and how bad business was, and there seemed only one way out of it — here they lowered their voices — and that was to "make a bankrupt."

And in course of time they did. And Mr Billig paid off another installment on his phonograph with its mahogany case of records. But he was not rich. Rich? Because with the sweat of his brow he bought a phonograph to comfort the old age of his wife and himself. Others had children. Children were more expensive than phonographs.

It must have been in connection with one of these informal consultations with his business friends that the two gentlemen paid their visit to Mr Billig the very day after Rose Berman came and thrust herself on him and behaved so badly.

The two gentlemen wore bowler-hats. They were detectives. They were sent down to interview Mr Billig on behalf of the Atlantic Fire Insurance Company. It was some business about a man named Levine, and he had a cellar in which he sorted "jobs and fents," by which is meant the waste ends of made-up pieces of cloth. Many a Mr Levine was sorting "jobs and fents" in 1910 who in 1930 was educating his boys at the best public schools. But only a minority of them had fires in their cellars, like the Mr Levine concerning whom the detectives called on Mr Billig. There was some question of Mr Billig having received some money from Mr Levine, shortly after Mr Levine received a great deal of money from the Atlantic Fire Insurance Company.

The matter had to be cleared up. And it was. As if Mr Billig wasn't always receiving money in this way and that, as thank-offerings for recovery from sickness, for safe crossing of the Atlantic, for making up a nice Hebrew inscription for a tombstone; the same money to be expended on the Jewish poor, of whom, the Lord be praised, there were enough and plenty. Naturally there were working expenses.

The old men were gathering in the synagogue for the midday service at the time the detectives called on Reb Gershon. There was a handful of women at Mrs Poyser's shop, holding eggs up to the light and squeezing loaves, to see if they were fresh. It was as if an angel breathed it into their ear, so quickly they all heard of this preposterous visitation. There was such indignation in both places, such a hissing through the beards and such a cackling over barrels of herrings, that there might almost have been a detective pogrom in Magnolia Street that day, with a little encouragement.

But it is believed that even the detectives were heartily ashamed of their suspicions and the suspicions of the Atlantic Fire Insurance Company, after half an hour of the troubled innocent eyes of Reb Gershon, and the pitiful bird-like protests of his wife. They crawled back again down Magnolia Street, with their bowler-hats well down over their eyes, and their ox-like shoulders drooping, as if it were they, and not Mr Billig, who had been suspected of arson.

For some days after this episode, Reb Gershon looked like a real old man, instead of a pink doll of an old man. The colour went out of his cheeks; the flesh of them seemed to be puffed and goosey. When he met a baby in a perambulator and it howled into his face suddenly — as babies sometimes did when he passed them in their perambulators — he didn't go over and shine over them like a moon, and say "Ram-bam-bam!" His face twitched, and he hurried away from them, shuffling.

And then he took to his bed. Really, what with one thing and another, life had been too much for Mr Billig lately. But the neighbours were so nice to him and his wife while he was laid up, it almost made the visit of the detectives worth while. There didn't seem much point in getting up too soon, either. Poor little Mrs Seipel, who had not received the promised money order from Uncle Adolf, managed, none the less, to get a chicken on credit and brought it in beautifully roasted. "So tender a chicken, like a banana!" sighed Mr Billig gratefully. Mrs Berman crept in with some cakes when Rose was out at business. Mrs Poyser sent in some smoked salmon and a bag of Bourbon biscuits. Mrs Emmanuel brought in some fish cooked in sweet and sour sauce.

"They are not neighbours," said Mr Billig weakly from his pillow, "but brothers and sisters." And the way Mrs Billig sat by her husband's bed, holding his hand — "It is an Art Gallery picture," voted the women at Mrs Poyser's shop.

He didn't worry his head any more about finding a nice Jewish widower for Rose Berman. By the time he got out of bed, the face of things was so radically altered in Magnolia Street, that no one worried about Rose Berman any more. There were other things to think about.

Chapter 6

While Mr Billig was still in bed, an engagement was announced in the Berman household. It was not, needless to say, the engagement of Rose Berman and John Cooper. The feeling was gaining ground that the whole Berman-Cooper idea was ridiculous. A girl who devoted her whole life to her sick mother could not be carrying on in secret an intrigue which would kill her mother the moment she got to know about it. Pah! Foolishness!

The engagement was announced of Ada, the younger sister, and Johnnie Hummel, the photographer. A satisfactory match. It was known that Mr Hummel had a good connection in the country districts. There were quite a number of young men who retreated with hang-dog looks from Magnolia Street, when they heard the news. Some of them had been moping round for a year or two. The younger Miss Berman had not been impressed by them. She went on polishing her finger-nails.

And then Johnnie Hummel turned up. It could hardly he two months ago. He had gone straight in and won. They were going to be married in a couple of months.

Ada was having her photograph taken when her destined husband first set eyes on her. She was posing against the Falls of Niagara in the establishment of one of Johnnie's friends, when Johnnie himself appeared. He had learned downstairs that his friend had a pretty girl sitting at that moment. He saw no reason why he shouldn't help with the lighting and the screens and so on; moreover there was nothing like getting the sitter engaged in a nice animated conversation if you wanted really natural results. So he came up. The girl was not merely pretty. She was stunning. She really had got herself up to look quite her best for this photograph.

"She's for me," Johnnie Hummel said to himself, "even if I've got to marry her!"

So he started talking. He did not stop talking until he led her under the marriage-canopy. If she was to be for him, he found, he had to marry her; for she was not loose, she belonged to a respectable family. He started talking. His black eyes flashed.

His waxed moustaches glistened. His hands moved as freely as flowing water. And he talked.

He was a photographer, but talk was far the greater part of his profession. He described himself on his cards as 'Artist and Enlarger to the Trade.' He did not have his own studio, like his less persuasive friends. He handed over to them on a large commission the work which his tongue had wagged out for him. He carried a camera about on his journeys, it is true. But all that was donkey-work. He did not care for it greatly. He was not much of an Artist in that sense. Most of his work came into the category of 'Enlarging to the Trade'. He would travel about the countryside, extract from his victims either their own photographs or the photographs of those nearest to them, and send them off to Doomington, where his collaborators would enlarge them and send back again in great garish frames.

His speciality was the commemoration of the dead. Whenever and wherever a farmer died in the counties within a radius of fifty miles from Doomington, his widow would find Johnnie Hummel at her ear, almost before the corpse had been taken off. He would talk and talk and talk. There would be no escape from him. If she sought to escape, he would make her feel she was guilty of gross disrespect to her dead. A week or two later her husband's image, an 'Enlargement to the Trade', would hang on her parlour wall, a series of grey blurs, slipped eyesockets, thickened lips. She would be poorer by anything between ten shillings and three pounds, according to the amount of gold in the frame and the impotence into which her grief had thrown her.

There was something vulture-like about Johnnie Hummel. For not only would he appear on the scene when someone was dead already. He had an uneasy instinct for finding out when a death might be hoped for in a day or two. He would put up at the village pub until the moment to pounce was due; in the meanwhile he could pick up an honest penny with his camera, though you never could expect anything like such good results from the direct photography of the living as from the indirect photography of the dead.

But Johnnie displayed his real genius at the times when the papers announced 'Five Hundred Miners Buried in a Mine near Bolton'; or, 'Terrible Tragedy in Blackburn Sunday-School Treat, Three Hundred Children in Blazing Hall'; or, 'Isle of Man

Pleasure Steamer Sunk, No Survivors'. Then Johnnie got busy. Then Johnnie flew like lightning to Bolton, to Blackburn, to the Isle of Man. Then Johnnie talked. He talked like the wind, the river, the forest, like something elemental, the sound of which cannot be subjugated. Then Johnnie reaped his golden harvest. The goods trains groaned with the crates in which he despatched to Bolton, to Blackburn, to the Isle of Man, the 'Enlargements to the Trade' of the dead and dying.

Or sometimes he reaped another sort of harvest, a couple of black eyes and one or two missing teeth. But that was not often. The most ferocious fist fell limp in the blast of that talking.

And there were times when he talked to win more delicate prizes than gold sovereigns. He talked to win a wink here, a body there. And in the studio of his collaborator, he met a girl standing up against Niagara Falls. In all his travels he had never met a girl so pretty. She was so pretty that she took his breath away, and stopped him talking; but only for one moment.

He met the sister and the mother of the girl. They were slum Jews. They lived in a dreadful hole called Magnolia Street. They were not, like himself, the sort of Jew whom any right-minded person would take for an Italian. But he did not let them see how low he thought them. On the contrary he was very charming to them. His talk was better than a couple of stalls at the theatre. He didn't seem to get much forrader with the elder sister; she was the old-maidish type he didn't care for particularly, but he treated her to his talk quite as generously as he did the others. The mother was not hard work at all. As for Ada, she was a plum, a peach, a little red apple; a lovely bit of goods to get back to after a gruelling week among the widows and orphans of the miners; and a real economy, too. Sometimes you had to pay the women you slept with; always you had to pay landladies.

He was so charming that it was strange that the setts of Magnolia Street did not open up to swallow him as he walked to the house of his fiancée one evening towards the end of May, in 1910. Ada was by his side. He twirled his waxed moustaches. He waved his hands. He talked and talked. Ada looked, and listened, and worshipped.

And John Cooper, the seaman, who also happened to be walking down Magnolia Street at that moment, on the opposite pavement, saw him and heard him. He went up into his own house. His heart was heavy with foreboding.

"I'm a damn fool!" he said. "What has that louse to do with Rose or me?"

He was to discover that that louse had a lot to do with him and Rose.

"To hell!" he said to himself. "Only one day more! I must get a move on, or Rose'll get there before me!"

II

"Rose," said Ada. "I want you to congratulate me." (This was the evening before.) Mrs Berman had closed her home-made-sweets shop. Rose had reckoned up the day's takings. Rose had made the evening meal. Rose had cleared it away.

"What's that?" asked Rose.

"I want you to congratulate me," Ada repeated. She lifted her chin with a gesture of defiance, but her fingers were fluttering nervously. "And you, too, mother."

"What is it, my child?"

"I got engaged to be married an hour ago."

"Ada, Ada, my child!" The colour went out of Rose's cheeks. Her breath faltered. "With whom, Ada, darling?"

"Who do you think?" said Ada, with a forlorn attempt at roguishness.

"Not — not —" Rose brought out.

" Who do you think? Johnnie, of course!"

"Oh, Ada, Ada!" Her mother's arms were round her. Her mother's tears were falling on her face.

"What are you crying for, mother?" asked Ada.

"Do not all mothers cry when their daughters tell them news like this?"

"Ada!" cried Rose sharply. "I won't hear of it!"

"What? I beg your pardon?"

"I'm sorry, darling. I'm sorry, forgive me." Her cheeks were death-pale. "I mean, Ada dear, I don't think he'll make you a good husband. I didn't really think it was so serious as all this!"

"Well, it *is* serious. I love him. And he loves me. And we're going to get married quite soon. He said, now he's made up *his* mind, he's not one for waiting around."

"Indeed!" cried Rose. Her eyes flashed. "He's made up his mind, has he? Well we've not made up ours!"

"But we have!" said Ada.

"Oh, no, we have not!" said Rose.

Then Ada lost her temper. "What do you mean, *we* have not? Who's getting married, me or you? You've bossed me and mother and everything else long enough. I'm tired of it."

"Listen, Ada, my dear!" said Rose, regaining control of herself. "Don't talk like that. You know it does mother no good."

"It wasn't me, it was you!" said Ada. Her lip trembled.

"My dear, you know how much I love you. If I thought he was the right man for you, I'd be so happy, I'd not know what to do with myself. I'd buy your wedding-dress for you tomorrow. But Hummel's not the right man. Ada, Ada, he's *not* the right man. He's just talked you deaf and dumb and silly. You mustn't dream of it, Ada dear! Do you hear what I say?"

Ada had put up her hands to her face. Her bosom heaved. Mrs Berman went over to her and put one hand on her shoulder. The touch seemed to set in motion forces which no one had suspected in her. Her hands fell from her face. Her cheeks were fiery-red. Her mouth was working uglily.

"How dare you? How dare you poke your nose into my business? Haven't I told you I love him? Do I poke my nose into your business when you go sneaking off into the country with your *goy* sailor? Do you think I don't know? Do you think —"

"Ada! Ada!" cried Rose. But it was not of herself she thought. It was of her mother. Mrs Berman was crying, crying, like a small child. Then a cough came and choked her crying. It was the soft wet cough which brings blood from the lungs. "Ada! Look! Mother!"

Then the demon in Ada sank as quickly as it had arisen. She threw herself at her mother's knee. "Mother, mother, forgive me! Don't cry, mother darling! Oh Rose, Rose, will you ever forgive me? Rose dear! I *must* marry him! I love him so much!"

III

Rose told all this to John next day, in the café. John put both hands on her shoulders. He looked her straight into the eyes for a full minute. Then with the tip of each middle finger he delicately smoothed her hair away from her brows. Then he bent towards her and kissed her.

102

"Never mind, kid," he said. "We'll see it through."

She placed her head up against him. "So you're going tomorrow?"

"Six weeks. Seven at most. I'll be back before you know where you are."

"What would I do without you, John? Hold me close!"

"Rose!"

"Yes?"

"Don't you sometimes feel it's all just too much for you? You're only a bit of a thing, after all. Does it never occur to you to cut and run?"

She drew away from him and looked carefully into his eyes. "You're not tired, are you, John? Of waiting?"

"I didn't mean that," he said shortly.

"No, John, of course you didn't! No, it doesn't occur to me to cut and run."

"I mean, even for *her* sake. To take her with you — to me. Away from it all."

"She'd come if I asked her. Oh yes. She'd do even that for me. She'd do anything. But she'd just — oh she'd just fade, go to nothing. I've twice tried to send her to a nursing-home in the country. It was cruel. She's got to have all the neighbours round her, and her candlesticks, and wine-beakers on the mantelpiece. She's got to say the prayer over the Sabbath evening candles in her own kitchen. I don't know what it is. I suppose like that she still feels she's with *him* — my father, I mean. She couldn't stand being away from him. When she was away in the country, she used to look at me with such big eyes every time I went to see her, it broke my heart. She didn't say anything. She just looked at me. I had to bring her back home. It would be worse if she went off... with us. She'd be cut off much more completely, without any hope of getting back at all. You see, don't you?"

"Yes, I see."

"This last couple of weeks, John — ever since that small Seipel saw us — everybody's known. Of course they have. But they just won't let themselves believe." She sighed. "And now —"

"Yes?"

"There's this new complication. She's afraid — of Ada, what's going to happen to Ada. She tries not to let me see it, but I can read her like a book. I don't suppose you could move her now — not till she sees how it's going to turn out with Ada. Oh it's all so mixed up. John, John, why did you ever come up to me... that day... in the park?"

"Are you sorry I did?"

"Are you?"

"Enough of this chatter! Shut your eyes and take things easy! Like this! You look tired!"

Chapter 7

I

It was a Thursday afternoon about a month later than the convention in the grocery-shop with which this tale of Magnolia Street began. John Cooper's ship was away wallowing on the high seas somewhere. Rose Berman was selling Sinding's *Frühlingsrauschen* to music-teachers over Messrs. Saunders's counter. Mrs Poyser and her customers were satisfied that their instinct regarding the rumour that had coupled the names of these two was correct. There was nothing in it.

They were more interested in Ada Berman's catch. They thought she was cleverer than they had given her credit for to book so presentable a young man, with such fine eyes and waxed black moustaches and such a fund of bright conversation.

Mr Johnnie Hummel was occupying their attention at the moment when a young man named Tommie Wright was toddling down Magnolia Street and turning right-handed into Aubrey Street. He is an insignificant young man; his age is not more than four, and he has inherited his father's looks rather than his mother's. He had not her green eyes, her rosy cheeks, but it is a nice little face. We must regard him carefully, for within less than half an hour, with the assistance of one Benny Edelman, he is to be responsible for such excitement as has not been known for years in Magnolia Street. He is to annul that sea, that prairie, which, according to the convention, faces the windows of each side of the street, when its inhabitants look out through them. Not until the first weeks of the Great War was such an oneness again achieved. The latter, of course, was a more terrific thing. In the incandescence of those first war weeks, gentile pavement fused with Jewish pavement, house melted into house, Magnolia Street almost became one single organic creature, in which opposites were caught up, flaring roof-high, fear and daring, dismay and rapture, pride and hate.

But those weeks in June and July of 1910 were exciting enough to be going on with. And young Tommie Wright gives no indication at all that he realises himself to be a potent agent of destiny, as he continues toddling down Aubrey Street and crosses Victoria Street, where the tram-lines run. He gives the

105

tram-driver in Victoria Street the fright of his life, for he is so small the driver hardly notices him till he has very nearly run him over. The tram-conductor, whose name is Walter Hubbard and who is a neighbour of the young man, recognises him.

"I suppose that mother of his has got another of her men friends in today," he mutters. "It would serve her right if the kid got run over or drowned or something, one of these days."

"Town Hall, please," says a lady.

"One penny, please. Thank you. If only Dolly and me could bring it off sometime," the reflections of Walter Hubbard continue, "she wouldn't let the little beggar go wandering off like this on his lonesome. So help us God!" he vowed.

The invocation of God by Walter Hubbard may have had something to do with it. For the next thing little Tommie Wright did, having managed not to get run over, was to try hard to get himself drowned.

Beyond Victoria Street a slushy expanse of clay-croft weltered between Longton and Bridgeways Gaol. The Longton District Council had no right to leave ungirdled by railings the twelve-foot-deep pool of muddy water at the centre of that croft. It was impossible to expect Tommie Wright to walk within a hundred yards of any pool, however noisome, without falling in. So Tommie Wright fell into that one. The clay-croft was sometimes as crowded as Epsom Downs on Derby Day, but that Friday afternoon it was as deserted as an Arctic floe.

However, just as one isolated walrus might be lounging about an ice-floe, it so happened that one young man was lounging about that croft. His name was Benny Edelman. He was the elder son of the dour lady we have met once or twice. He was a cabinet-maker by trade. Another strike, or lockout, had just begun in the cabinet-making so there was nothing much for him to do but lounge about. He did not pick his feet up as he walked. He was a bit of a lout. But he was a well-made, good-looking young man, none the less, with an amiable face. Unlike the walrus, he could not swim.

It was, therefore, with a horrible sinking of the heart that he heard gurgles proceeding from the pool and made his way thither. There was no doubt about it; a small boy, Tommie Wright from number four, was drowning. Benny Edelman looked round anxiously, but not a soul appeared on the horizon to assist Tommie Wright or himself. It is just possible, also, that it occurred to him that strictly he did not know the small boy. The small boy came from the gentile pavement of Magnolia Street, which, as his mother had grimly enjoined upon him, did not exist.

But Tommie was getting yellower and yellower. Benny could not quite make up his mind whom at that moment he loathed more, himself or the spluttering object in the water. But he jumped in. A minute or two followed which seemed to him in later years more concentratedly unpleasant than the whole of the Great War; for though he lost a leg in the Somme campaign, he knew much less about it at the time than he knew about saving Tommie Wright, and, in that Somme excitement, it would not have worried him if they had taken away both arms and his head, as well.

And then he was aware that he and Tommie lay panting on the bank like a couple of newly landed trout. It is probable that a few minutes wholly devoted to panting ensued, but it seemed to him that the air around him filled at once with a noise, a loud noise. He realised that the noise was produced by the crowds that came flocking in from Magnolia Street, Jewish and gentile Magnolia Street indiscriminately. In English, Yiddish, and Yiddish-English he heard himself compared with Judas Maccabeus and Florence Nightingale.

So quickly had they arrived on the scene, the old and infirm as well as the young and hearty, that you could have thought they had got the news of the rescue a minute or two before Benny Edelman himself became aware that a rescue might be necessary.

All the small boys were there. That was natural. They had just finished afternoon school, and the little Jewish boys were on their way for a further scholastic session at the Hebrew-school of Reb Aryeh. But a Jewish young man does not rescue a gentile small boy with incomparable bravery from drowning every day of the week, so they ran about on the clay-croft, shrieking. Reb Aryeh in Magnolia Street sat in his alpaca-coat and skull-cap gnawing his finger-nails, with his walking-stick on the table before him, awaiting the arrival of the truants. Then it occurred to him he had waited long enough and he set out to fetch them.

On the edge of the pool the hair of young Dick Cooper flickered like a gold kingfisher. The little Briggs boys and the little Poyser boys played tig with each other, and nearly gave Benny Edelman another chance to show his mettle.

Old Mrs Edelman was there, quite still and impassive. The news had come to her that her son had been drowned. She had not said a word but set out for the croft immediately. When she discovered the very different truth, she still said not a word. But the hard line of her lips relaxed slightly. Deep in her heart, she was proud of her son. He would come to some good yet, idle though he was and entirely incapable of acquiring an atom of Hebrew scholarship.

Mrs Poyser was there, with her red-haired daughter, Becky. She supposed the business would not go to pieces if she left her husband in charge for a few minutes, to see if she approved of what had happened. She approved, evidently, for she was engaged in animated conversation with Maggie Tawnie, whose earrings clanged, like bells in a steeple.

Kate Ritchie of the gentiles and Leah Winter of the Jews were there. Nobody took much notice of them. So they shook hands with each other and cried, so happy they were that little Tommie Wright had not been drowned.

Young George Derricks, too, mingled with the crowd. He was not a very ostentatious boy, and he was not about for more than a few minutes. But when Mr Emmanuel, the clerk to the Jewish Board of Guardians, and Mr Stanley; the shoemaker and racing expert, compared notes that evening, and both found that they had lost their watches that afternoon, presumably on the Longton clay-croft — it was felt that the presence of young George Derricks had something to do with it. Not that you could bring up the matter at a joyful time like this; and George Derricks had such an innocent, clean face, too. And he had a mother; no less a mother than the eloquent, the large-bosomed Mrs Derricks. Mr Emmanuel had another drink at Mr Stanley's urgent recommendation. But he did not like it. Really, he did not like it. Mr Stanley, on the other hand, did.

The barber-saloon was well represented. Mrs Durbin was there, the leading spirit of the business, with a cap pinned tight on her hair, and the clogs and shawl she wore in all weathers. She always smoked a small pipe, and she took a tug at it on the clay-croft, but found that it had gone out in the excitement. Her son, Albert, who did the actual shaving along with his brother, Arthur — their mother did the lathering — was by her side. He was a great expert on sociology. He had forgotten to put down his hair-clippers. He twinkled amiably through his pince-nez.

Dolly Hubbard was there, the wife of the tram-conductor. She was sure Walter wouldn't mind if she, too, went down to see what had happened. A man tried to speak to her, but she blushed and turned away. Walter did not like men to try and speak to her.

Bill Carter, the night-watchman, was there. He had just got up, for he slept by day. No one noticed him, though he was as big a man as any in Magnolia Street. He somehow never managed to take the attention, even in the days when he wore a policeman's helmet. He stood about vaguely and beamed. His wife and the Rabbi's wife were talking to each other energetically though neither understood much what the other was saying.

And now the mother of the rescued child appeared, Jessie Wright herself, with her red cheeks a little rosier than usual and her hair disordered. Her dress, too, was not properly buttoned up at the back. But one could forgive more than that to the mother of a child just snatched from a clayey grave... The festival of the clay-croft was approaching its climax.

Other citizens from both sides of the street were there, whom we have met or are to meet shortly. Admirers were also present from Oleander Street and Lavender Street and Mimosa Street. But these, as knowing this was an affair which went closest to the bosoms of the dwellers in Magnolia Street, kept decently in the background. And now Reb Aryeh, too, was approaching, his dreadful walking-stick in his hand. The benign Reb Feivel seemed to be expostulating with him.... But it were wiser at this moment not to blur the central picture that emerges out of all this glad confusion.

Benny Edelman has just sat up. He is panting less. He is sluicing muddy water out of his hair. Tommie has just sighted his mother. He utters a sudden loud yell of fear, for he realises suddenly he should not have gone crossing tramlines and falling into brick-ponds. He throws both his arms round his rescuer and howls into his soaked shirt. And Jessie Wright, devoted mother as she is, seems for the moment to forget the existence of her small boy. Her eyes shine. She, too, like her son, throws her arms around Benny Edelman's neck, and, transported, kisses him on both cheeks.

Whether this proceeding would have frozen Miss Tregunter to the marrow, had she been there, whether Reb Aryeh, who arrived just at that moment, turned his head away from the spectacle abruptly, and spat, it is not necessary to decide now. The fact is that that kiss, so sexless, so impassioned, set fire to Magnolia Street. For weeks and weeks the fires of innocent love blazed. There was no gentile pavement, no Jewish pavement, worth speaking of. There was only Magnolia Street.

II

It is impossible to describe as less than a triumph the procession which set forth from the Longton clay-croft, marched up Aubrey Street, passed one street after another of the flowering shrubs, and then turned at length into Magnolia Street. Many of the folk who had not had time to get to the joyful company on the croft, joined the procession *en route*. Benny Edelman led it, with little Tommie curled up in his arms. He was flanked on one side by his mother, on the other by the pretty widow. Immediately behind him walked Mrs Shulman, the Rabbi's wife, though she ought to have been lying down, seeing the condition she was in. "Mad Moisheh," as they called him, the eldest son of Mr Emmanuel, drew up the rear with the milk-cart he drove for his living. "Hup! Hup! Hup!" he shouted, and cracked his whip. The old horse roared between the shafts. The milk-cans thundered an *obbligato*.

The procession swarmed over the gentile pavement, the Miss Tregunter pavement, as if all alike were descended from Hengist and Horsa. They made as one man for number four, where Mrs Wright lived. The few people (always excepting the diehards) who had not yet added themselves to the triumph, added themselves now. They flooded into the parlour, the kitchen, the scullery, the upstairs bedrooms. Then Benny Edelman sneezed. Then Mrs Wright took the situation in hand. "Get out of the kitchen, everybody!" she commanded. "Can't you see they're sopping wet? They'll catch their deaths of cold!" She bundled everybody out. "There now, there!" she said, addressing herself to her son and his rescuer. "Take those things off at once. Put them up over the fire-guard to dry! I'll go up and get you some things to change into!"

Mrs Wright went upstairs. She went to her late husband's wardrobe and got down a nice suit he had hardly worn. She picked up some underthings from a chest of drawers. Mrs Wright was not the sort of widow who sells her late husband's things the moment he dies. She is aware they may come in useful some day. She got a change for Tommie, too, and went downstairs, with a heap of clothes over each arm. She forgot to knock at the kitchen door. With such crowds of people laughing and crying and chattering all over the place, it was not to be wondered at that she forgot to knock at the door. She walked straight in. Both the men had removed all their clothes. Tommie lay on his back on the rag mat, crowing and kicking his feet up in the air. Benny stood over him, balanced on his shapely legs, both arms stretched out.

Benny looked a bit of a lout with his clothes on. That was his tailor's fault, chiefly. And not even that; for he had never worn a suit which was not reach-me-downs. Without his clothes he looked a bit of an Apollo. His head stood well on his neck. He had broad shoulders and a fine chest and narrow hips. The white skin stretched over the muscles was touched by the flickering fire-light.

For one moment Mrs Wright stood and took in all there was to see, a very quiet and expert moment. Then, having strayed in upon a strange man in his nakedness, she shrieked, as in duty bound. She turned tail, blushing like a schoolgirl.

"Oh! Oh!" she cried. Then she thrust the two heaps of clothes into Mr Emmanuel's arms. "Take these!" she demanded, not daring to look into his eyes, she was so embarrassed. "Tell them to put these on at once!"

She fell with her load of embarrassment giggling into Mrs Tawnie's arms. But she had made up her mind. She knew what she wanted. She knew she was going to get it.

Chapter 8

I

It is not easy to offer an explanation of the affectionate and uproarious good humour that prevailed in Magnolia Street during the next few weeks. Of course nothing can have been more winning to simple and decent people than the episode out of which it all arose — the saving of Tommie Wright by Benny Edelman. But it would not have been quite the same thing if it had been any other small boy and any other young man. First, Tommie was an orphan. It wasn't at all certain that Mrs Wright was quite as devoted a mother as she might be; she had other hobbies. (But nobody allowed himself to think such a thought during these weeks.) Second, when people came to think of it, Benny was an orphan, too. In some ways he was worse off than an orphan, for, with all respect to the old lady, it was no bank holiday to have Mrs Edelman for a parent. Tommie was a nice quiet lad. So was Benny. Now and again they just seemed about as old as each other. Everybody knew things had been going rather badly with Benny of late in this miserable cabinet-making business. But he had kept his end up somehow. There was always a pleasing grin on his face.

It was also very touching to see the way Tommie just idolised Benny. He refused to be separated from him. People stood at their doorsteps and smiled with a tear in their eye to see Benny trudging up the street, with Tommie's little hand in his big one. Even Mrs Edelman was touched by the sight. She smiled down at the small boy. The first time that happened Tommie cried. But after that he realised she meant well, and he would go up to her and kiss her. She didn't quite know what to do about that; after all he was male, and gentile.

Mrs Wright was extremely charming. Nobody remembered the queer hatred she had always had for the Jews. She had obviously forgotten it herself. She often had Benny in for a cup of tea, and some biscuits and iced cakes, specially brought in from Mrs Poyser's, so that he should have no qualms about them. It was all proper and respectable. People hadn't been quite so sure about that once or twice previously, when Mrs Wright entertained some of her men friends. But they were sure enough about it now. There was always a chaperone in the house when Benny came to tea. It might be Benny's own younger brother, Norman. And if Norman came, as like as not Mrs Wright would ask him to bring his best girl, Fanny. Sometimes it would be quite a tea party, with Mrs Carter coming in, too, and Mrs Emmanuel or Mrs Seipel. It wasn't any strain upon Mrs Wright. Her late husband had been an insurance agent of substance, and she had compounded the endowment policies he had left her into a small annuity. One of these days she wanted to pick up a small tobacconist business. In fact she had had her eye on one at the corner of Laburnum Street for some time. But she was in no hurry. "Time enough for that," she said, laughing, "when Mr Right comes along." Everybody laughed merrily at the pun.

And then Mrs Wright behaved so prettily towards old Mrs Edelman. She used to bring her flowers. Mrs Edelman was puzzled by them at first. She had a dim memory of flowers growing by the riverside in Russia when she was a girl and between the stalks of corn. But she didn't quite know what you did with these pagan lumps of colour tied up in bundles. Then Fanny, her Norman's best girl, told her. "Like this," she said. "You cut the straw here. See, Mrs Edelman? Then you put them in vases, with water. What, you have no vases? Of course, you have. That's what these ornaments are for, on the parlour overmantel."

Still Mrs Edelman had qualms. Then she gave way. She lifted them to her nose awkwardly. "Thank you," she said to the gentile lady. She made a dish of potato-cakes for Mrs Wright. "Take!" she commanded her. Mrs Wright took, and dropped them into her slop-bucket.

So the people on both pavements laughed and joked and invested each other's doorsteps. The gentiles found that the Jews were not so outlandish, after all. You certainly couldn't say about them, as you had always been taught to believe, that they counted each penny as they spent it. They were just simple folk, like themselves, some more pleasant, some less. The Jews made corresponding discoveries about the gentiles. But there was one element in their enthusiasm which was probably lacking from that of their friends across the road — a certain element of relief.

It relieved them to feel, as they all felt now, that the rumour which had spread in the street regarding a Jewish girl and a gentile lad had nothing in it, almost certainly had nothing in it.

113

They threw themselves with gusto into all the jolly fraternisings that went on during these weeks. They were proud of their hero. It was lovely to see how grateful the mother of the small boy was. It was all just a little like the Kingdom of Heaven.

II

It was a grand time, those few weeks in Magnolia Street during June and early July, in 1910. It has been said before that there were four institutions which might be called clubs, in Magnolia Street, two for the Jews and two for the gentiles. The doors of all four were cordially thrown open to both sides of the street during that period.

The sense in which the portals of the synagogue were thrown open was, of course, only a moral one. It would acutely have embarrassed its usual denizens, if Mr Briggs, the odd-job-man, or the brothers Durbin, the barbers, had marched in that Sabbath morning two days after the rescue, at the time of morning prayer. It would also have embarrassed Messrs. Briggs and Durbin. They would have obeyed a natural instinct, this being a place of worship, to take their hats off. A moment later, they would have perceived that Rabbi Shulman, Reb Feivel and the others kept their silk hats glued tight on their heads. Other features of the ceremonial might have seemed anomalous to them. No, they would not have been happy in the synagogue. Even the Jewish womenfolk were not quite at their ease there, excepting a few pious bodies, like Mrs Edelman, to whom the thick odour of the synagogue was more than food and drink.

But when Benny Edelman came in that morning, the whole synagogue got up and stared, as one man. He shambled in, blushing to the rims of his ears. He was not much the worse for his dangerous adventure, excepting for a slight sniffle. The sniffle would have been much more formidable if Mrs Wright had not promptly tackled it the day before with a glass of hot whisky-cordial, several aspirins, and a suit that had belonged to her late husband.

None of the small boys paid any attention to their prayers that morning, with the consequence that there was more nose-tweaking and arm-pinching than usual on the part of parents anxious for their sons' souls. But the parents themselves were almost as bad. During the part of the service when the weekly portion of the Pentateuch is read out from the unrolled scroll, Benny's gallantry received, as it were, divine recognition. He was called up by name to the pulpit, there permitted to endow a charity with half-a-crown, and to stand and shake and blush for a few minutes in the hot glare of public acclamation. Benny rather felt that the experience was as unpleasant as dragging small boys from brick-ponds.

The ceremony would have been really complete and official if it had been possible for Mrs Wright to be present, too, on the further side of the women's partition. But somehow, it had not occurred to anybody to have her there, and Mrs Wright would have been too shy to attend, in any case. It was reserved for Mr Emmanuel, about a month later, to organise the really complete and official ceremony in celebration of the Wright-Edelman rescue.

But if Benny Edelman in the synagogue voted half-a-crown to the Home for Aged Jews, Jessie Wright went to church next day and put half-a-crown in the plate for the Mission to the Chinese. That evened things up. There was quite a church-parade that morning in Magnolia Street. A number of people who hadn't seen the inside of St. Luke's for some months joined Jessie Wright. The excursion was, in a sense, a thanks-offering for the rescue of little Tommie. The vicar was delighted. He had not seen so strong a Magnolia Street contingent for a long time. He was beginning to despair of Magnolia Street. He wondered if the close vicinity of the Jews infected them with a virus of free thinking.

Most of the Magnolia Street gentiles were members of the Established Church of England. They all contributed handsomely that morning to the fund for the Mission to the Chinese, though, in point of fact, they were not conscious of any fiery missionary ambition to propagate the principles of their Church among Chinese or Jews or Catholics or anybody. They had been born like that and would die like that.

St. Luke's was at the top of Blenheim Road, where it ran into Begley Hill Road, a thoroughfare which at that stage of its existence completely lost its Jewish character. The spire of St. Luke's cast no deep shadow over Magnolia Street. The vicar was a scholarly gentleman and something of an authority on Plotinus. Plotinus and his own six unmarried daughters between them took up most of his time; so that the care of the souls of Myrtle Street, Acacia Street, Magnolia Street and the other streets of the flowering shrubs, which made up the poorest section of his parish, devolved more and more into the hands of Mr Tressider, his curate. Mr Tressider was muscular and socialistic, but found it impossible to shed his Oxford-cum-Cuddesdon accent, to which his parishioners listened and refused flatly to believe that such sounds actually existed, though with their own ears they heard them. He did not succeed, as he had hoped, in setting up St. Luke's as a dangerous rival to the Crown and Anchor and the Lamb and Lion.

Miss Tregunter, who was a patron of neither, never failed of a Sunday morning to go forth to St. Luke's in her black bonnet and her black lace shawl, with her black red-edged prayer-book in one hand and her black reticule in the other. But you felt she undertook the journey not only because she desired to enter into communion with her Maker but because it was inestimably the correct, the genteel, thing to do. She was present this Sunday morning, too. But she would have been present in any case; so that her appearance was not to be construed as an endorsement of the shameless merry-making that had been going on in Magnolia Street since Friday afternoon.

Bill Carter and his wife, Sally, joined Mrs Wright's church party that morning. Strictly speaking, Bill was a Baptist, but, so long as he remained a policeman, he took his wife to church regularly. It seemed only right and proper to him that a state servant should support the state religion. His presence, large as he was, and policeman as he was, did not seem, however, to add largely to the moral prestige of St. Luke's. Since they had turned him out of the police force, he saw no alternative but to become a Dissenter again. And then Jessie Wright, with the small Tommie, went to offer up thanks that morning in the Anglican mode. So Bill went, too, with his wife, Sally.

Mary Cooper did not go, but her young sister, Enid, went, with Dick beside her. Janey Seipel saw her go off; prayer-book in hand. How willingly, that morning, would she have accepted Jesus, if it meant she could kneel down by Enid's side. There was a missionary to the Jews who lived in Magnolia Street, at the home of the Carters. He did not know how close opportunity was that morning. But opportunity came so rarely; how should he know?

Both Tawnies were at church, and Nellie Tawnie, too. Mr Derricks went, with his son, George. So did the Briggses. The two barber Durbins went, though Albert was not sure that sociology and Christianity were quite compatible. Kate Ritchie, too, went to church. They could shut her out of everything else, from the private bar to the Christmas Clubs, because they did not approve of her husband. She tossed defiantly the lovely feather in the lovely hat her husband had bought her, when he came home after his last voyage. Her husband, too, like John Cooper, was a sailor, but of less exalted rank.

The vicar and the curate smiled with pleasure, when they saw the large detachment from Magnolia Street enter the church that morning. Mr Tressider came round afterwards to Mrs Wright, and congratulated her, and pinched Tommie on the cheeks. Tommie didn't like that. Tommie kicked Mr Tressider on the shin and shouted at the top of his voice: "Where's Uncle Benny? I don't like that Uncle! I want Uncle Benny!"

Miss Tregunter heard. She was horrified. But she said not a word. Grim and gaunt she turned her nose toward Magnolia Street and her window-boxes.

III

If the synagogue, like the church, kept apart, the other clubs brought together. During these amiable weeks the gentile women often dropped in of a morning at the grocery-shop to be friendly, and to buy, perhaps, some non-committal item of food, like a tin of mustard or a packet of self-raising flour. It was not their habit; for Mrs Poyser's shop was almost as specifically Jewish and ecclesiastical as the synagogue itself. The dairy foods were rigidly segregated from all others. There was not a particle of food on sale which was not sacramentally wholesome. On Fridays the special bread sprinkled with poppy-seed for the Sabbath repast made its strict appearance. The foods or properties associated with each festival came round as regularly as the seasons, the three-cornered tarts for Purim, the small candles for the Feast of the Maccabees. For the Passover every vestige of the regular stock disappeared and a new stock loaded the shelves, from the large sacks of unleavened meal to the least grain of sugar.

117

What sort of pious application could Mrs Drew, who kept the nearest gentile grocery-shop over in Aubrey Street, show to compare with this? She sold some hot cross buns for Good Friday, ordered a few dozen chocolate eggs for Easter and laid in an extra case of real eggs for Pancake Tuesday. She sold crackers, too, for Christmas. But she did this, which was not much, without enthusiasm. Mrs Poyser attended to the ritual aspect of her calling not merely with enthusiasm but with an inquisitorial fire.

Mrs Drew began to get a little nervous when she saw the way her customers started dropping in at Mrs Poyser's. It might be Mrs Tawnie herself, from the Lamb and Lion, in her shawl and clogs like the old mill-lass she was; and though it was rumoured of her she might wear cloth-of-gold dancing shoes all day, if she wanted to, that rich she was now, clogs were good enough for her Steve when he first saw her, and good enough for Steve they were now, or for the Pope of Rome, for that matter. Or it might be the rather meek and serious Mrs Stanley who came over, the *deutsche* woman, wife of the shoemaker. She found it a real convenience to be able to drop in across the street and buy a few such delicacies as she had enjoyed of old time in some *Feinkost* establishment on the Lange Reihe in Hamburg, a few *Böcklinge* or a bismarck herring.

She even went so far as to give a German party one evening. "For fun," she exclaimed. It didn't mean she was one jot less English at heart. Her elder son, Otto, was there playing the guitar. He was a baker and never got the flour out of his eyebrows. *Es war ein Mal ein treuer Husar*, he sang. Mrs Seipel wept, she found the tune so touching. She and Mrs Emmanuel drank lemonade and ate a bismarck herring piece. Even Mrs Winberg was there, although she was so rich. She too ate a bismarck herring. The gentile guests drank beer and ate *Bratwurst*. It was a real German party.

The Derrickses next door heard there was a German party afoot. The Derrickses looked at each other uneasily. They didn't like the sound of it.

IV

It was in the private bar of the Lamb and Lion, however, the club specifically devoted to good cheer, that the rescue was most gaily celebrated. On the actual evening, Benny Edelman wasn't there. With any other host than Steve Tawnie, the evening might have been a Hamlet without a Prince of Denmark; but Steve could be relied on to see that it wasn't. Steve could make you split your sides laughing at your own mother's funeral, and this was no funeral, by any means.

Benny Edelman wasn't there, because Mrs Wright had packed him off to bed. It was perfectly delightful to see the way Mrs Wright took him in hand and saw that no harm came to him; almost as if she wanted to keep him intact for her own use some time. But there was no lack of company in the private bar. The habitués from the gentile pavement, male and female, were there in full force, very nearly. And Steve stood outside the pub roping in the Jewish gentlemen, just as if he were Reb Berel, the beadle of the synagogue, scouting round for odd Jews to make up the quorum. There was no question about the Jewish ladies entering a public-house. It was as unthinkable as the sight of a lot of Moslem women in Mecca, without veils, holding a public meeting.

Leah Winter, of course, did push her way into the private bar. She lived on the Jewish pavement, and was, in fact, Jewish. But what could you expect of Leah Winter? Strange men slept in her house. It would be less painful to ignore Leah Winter for the time being.

The young men who worked at the Winberg's rainproof factory, and were on their way home, needed no roping in. Neither did Mr Emmanuel and Mr Seipel and a few others who lived on the Jewish pavement, whom we do not name, for their history is not part and parcel of the history of Magnolia Street during the twenty years in which it occupies our attention. Norman Edelman, Benny's younger brother, was there by right patent. Mr Poyser needed a little lassoing. He was not certain how his wife would take it, if he entered a public-house. But she was quite pleasant about it. The spirit of camaraderie had got hold of her.

The Jewish men did not really fit into the atmosphere of the Lamb and Lion. Liquor was to them not so much a nightly routine as a ceremonial occasion. And then it would be sweet wine from Palestine to bless the Sabbath board, drunk not out of a glass mug, but a silver beaker. Or it might be a glass of brandy, at an engagement or a wedding. Beer they did not drink.

But they all made the effort that night. Poor Mr Seipel did; with the consequence that he completely spoiled an overmantel at his cabinet-works next day, and had to begin it all over again.

Mr Emmanuel was walking on air, even before he had one with Mr Tawnie, Mrs Stanley, Mr Briggs, Mr Seipel, with almost everybody. He did not like the taste of the stuff, but he drank it in the spirit of one who endures much for the sake of a cause. He disliked the taste less as he went on drinking, and as he went on drinking, glorified the cause more. The cause was love. His eyes twinkled. He made speeches; or they might all have been the same speech. Slight, except for his broad shoulders, pale and tall, with a big head poised insecurely on a high neck, Mr Emmanuel stood swaying among the gentiles and the Jews who, at length, loved each other. Punctuating his periods with his pince-nez, he urged the complete elimination of races, though races, *qua* races, were to be retained in their entirety. He had not yet reached his peroration; for indeed, he had never yet been known to reach a peroration, when his pale face became paler and a wild light flickered in his eyes. The gentle Mr Briggs took him in hand and he was not seen again that night in the Lamb and Lion.

One or two other Jewish gentlemen and Mr Albert Durbin were counted out. The rest stayed on. It was a grand night.

"And now we'll sing: 'He's a jolly good fellow!'" thundered Steve, meaning the absent Benny, and also meaning that it was getting near closing time. But no sooner had they sung 'jolly good fellow', than somebody started off 'Rule, Britannia!' and 'God Bless the Prince of Wales'.

The Jewish guests thought it would balance things nicely if they sang the Jewish anthem, 'Hatikvah'. But the whole company did not know it, not even all of themselves. The international note, however, was struck with: 'I've got diamonds in Amsterdam'. Then somebody wanted Obadiah, to swing her up a little bit higher, Obadiah, do. Then Steve Tawnie shouted "Time, gentlemen, please!" and got hold of one or two gentlemen who did not agree with him, and laid them delicately down on the pavement. So the love-festival came to an end for that night, though there was a lot of chattering at front doors for still another hour or two.

V

Benny never went into the Durbin barber-saloon, for the simple reason that the Jewish youths all seemed to find their way to Mr

120

Cohen's saloon on Blenheim Road. But he often used to cast envious eyes on Mrs Durbin's shop. Chaps went in for a three-halfpenny shave and sat about for hours talking and joking and smoking cigarettes. It was a go-easy place.

The morning after the Tommie Wright business, he got up without a trace of a cold, thanks to Mrs Wright's whisky cordial. But he had by no means got all the clay out of his hair. It occurred to him it would be nice to have a shampoo at Mrs Durbin's. No doubt he slyly reckoned they would not be displeased to have him there. The more he thought of the episode on the brick-croft, the more he realised what a stout fellow he had been.

But he certainly had no idea what fuss they were going to make of him. He sat in his chair, and blinked and gaped and the other Jewish youths from round about came in, and talked girls and sport, and the Durbins would not let him pay a penny for days and days. They anointed his head with free oil, till his cup ran over.

The satisfaction that Benny got as he leaned back in his chair while Mrs Durbin lathered him, was akin to the satisfaction a schoolboy feels when he, too, is at last allowed to sit in the prefects' room. It was not a matter of marble and plush, but of privilege. There was a horsehair sofa against the long wall that faced the shaving-chairs. This was for the use of the more honoured clients, who were shaved more than twice a week and sometimes had a shampoo, even a friction with hair-singe. Small boys (in the shell, as it were) sat on a rickety wooden form, when they came to have their hair cut. They were not allowed to come at all on Saturdays, when there was far too much doing to get the young men nice and clean for the girls they were going to take out that evening.

Reflected in the mirror before him were two pictures that Benny contemplated with approval. They were one picture, to be exact, for they displayed precisely the same subject, namely the Bride of Abydos. The lady wore a red cap from which a blue veil fluttered against the nape of her white neck. Her shoulders were bare, and so was a great deal of her bosom.

"I always smoke Gilligan's Cigarettes," the Bride of Abydos hinted. "Do you?"

She, or she and her twin sister, were the sole decoration of the room, unless the noble array of fifty shaving-mugs inserted in a

121

nest of pigeon-holes on the wall facing the door ought to be listed as a decoration. For certainly they were not used, though the numbers up to fifty, painted boldly on the face of the mugs, invited fifty fastidious gentlemen to reserve for their sole use their private brush and soap. The gentlemen of Magnolia Street were not so fastidious. Between the two large mirrors, on the wall facing the Bride of Abydos, hung a mysterious framed text, which announced simply:

DR. GAEL'S ELECTROLYTIC SCALP TREATMENT:
ONE-AND-SIX.

It hypnotised Benny. It hypnotised the other clients, and the Durbins themselves, probably. The time could not be remembered when that text had not hung between the mirrors, or when the treatment it recommended had been tried. Who was Dr Gael? In what house of learning had they conferred their diploma on him? And Electrolytic? Why Electrolytic? Yet obviously the word implied subtleties of dermatological research beyond the boundaries of the merely electric.

In 1930, Benny once more sat on a chair, a more sumptuous chair, in that saloon, and was still recommended to try Dr Gael's Electrolytic Treatment, though the place had ceased to be the Durbin's Barber-Saloon, and had become Clausen's Pompeian Rooms. No one in those intervening years had dared to give Dr Gael his chance. The elder Durbin, Albert by name, who shaved Benny Edelman that June morning in 1910, still hung about the place in 1930; but if at last, after all these years, someone should have conceived the desire to have Albert Durbin and Dr Gael collaborate in the electrolytical treatment of his scalp, it was now too late. Albert Durbin no longer wielded the razor or clipped the clippers. A shell exploded near him in 1915 somewhere in Flanders and took out both his eyes.

But in 1930 as in 1910, he still prattled about sociology. He always had red hair and his eyes, before they were poked out by pieces of shrapnel, were a yellow-grey. He considered himself an intellectual. He was not a socialist, he was careful to inform Benny that morning, as he held his razor suspended over the taut tendons of his neck. Socialism was unscientific. He was a sociologist. His pronunciation of the word was a little unsteady, and would have indicated to a scholar that his knowledge of the subject was unsteady, too.

But it was less than that, to be honest. It was based on a section of a fortnightly encyclopaedia of human wisdom which he had once read in a lavatory. He had retained some of the simpler jargon, the Omnipotence of the State, the Law of Natural Selection. One or two names also adhered in his memory from that session, Locke, Comte, John Stuart Mill.

"A little off the top?" he asked Benny, but only because it seemed to him that John Stuart Mill saw eye to eye with the manoeuvre. He expounded the principles of sociology with a sort of murky garrulity, and could go on permuting and combining his stock phrases over the length of time required for four shaves, three haircuts and a couple of shampoos.

There were times when the sheer impetus of his talking made him utter words of sociological or economic wisdom without the least consciousness that some of the first thinkers of the day were arguing along precisely those lines.

"Say what you like," he insisted. Benny really hadn't much chance of saying anything. "There can't be any war between nations any more. Sociology says so. Victory would be just as bad for the winners as for the losers. That's sociology, that is!"

"I see!" said Benny dimly. Really it *was* a high class saloon when the barber talked like that at you. They never talked like that at Cohen's.

The other customers had heard it all before. They weren't taking much notice. It was hoped that Doomington City would do better next year with the new centre forward they had bought just before the end of the season.

A moment later young Charles Stanley came in. Albert Durbin welcomed him with a tiny scream and an alarming sweep of the razor. Charles Stanley, the younger son of the shoemaker, had a hare lip, but a forehead of great beauty. He was in the Sixth at Doomington School, and read Aristotle, Spinoza, Hegel, in the original languages, and permitted himself to read Pindar and Catullus in his spare time. Albert assumed him to know even more sociology than he did himself. The son of an English father and a German mother, the youth seemed to Albert an incidental corroboration of his views, in so far as they touched upon a war between Germany and England, for instance. There could be no war between Germany and England. Sociology forbade it.

123

Albert gave tone to the Durbins' saloon. But nobody listened to him, not even himself. His younger brother, Arthur, a great expert on league football, was taken more seriously. He could tell you who had been top and bottom of the various divisions, and finalists in the Cup Finals, for years and years. He knew the names of all the Derby winners, their jockeys and their owners. He was organising a sweep this very morning, when Benny made his first bow to the Bride of Abydos. He insisted shyly on buying Benny's ticket for him, and Benny countered by buying one for little Tommie. Arthur had a light touch with his razor and was a more satisfactory barber than Albert, though he was one of the few people who respected Albert's intellectual attainments. He did a little boxing, too, and could deliver a good straight left.

He was, in fact, exactly the sort of young man for whom the wars which were so unthinkable were waiting. He had the proper gentleness and decency and bearing. He was not the sort of young man whom the wars would appoint to a nice safe coast-battery or a wooden barrack in the cindery desolation of Le Havre. He was not even the sort of young man who would get a kick from a mule in the belly or a shell-splinter in the wrist, so that he might keep high and dry till the business was over. He was the sort of young man who was just blown into teeth and eyelashes and broken bits of bone.

So, from season to season, Arthur estimated the chances of the Football Cup coming back to Doomington and Albert scraped a ghostly razor along the ghostly chins of Locke and Comte and John Stuart Mill. But the Durbin business was a flourishing one, and it is clear that neither Albert nor Arthur was the stuff out of which good business-men are made. The leading spirit of the business was their mother, a small black lady, Eliza by name. She was wearing her cap, of course, as she bent over Benny, lathering him. The black head of her hatpin was as small and black as her eyes. She had a faint moustache on her upper lip. Her pipe was going pleasantly. The smoke struck rank against Benny's nostrils, as she rubbed his chin with her hand.

She was the firm's lather-boy. She used the brush less than most members of her profession. She had a great belief in that rubbing of the chin with the palm of the hand. She applied it so vigorously that the hairs crept out of the chin of their own accord and slunk away. She did not bully the clients, but she let them know about it if they were allowing too big an interval to go by without shaving, or if the hair was beginning to grow untidy at the back of the neck. Blackheads were her especial enemy. She pounced upon them and the most inveterate gave up the ghost before her onslaught. You paid for her zeal sometimes by the sharp sting of a coal of tobacco falling from her pipe upon your cheek. But you said nothing about it, lest she should so maul you with the edge of her palm that your jawbone ached for days.

But her hand was unusually gentle with Benny that morning. She allowed no hot spark to fall on his fresh cheeks. Her black eyes beamed down on him, but she said no word. Albert did all the talking necessary for one family.

After business-hours Mrs Durbin retired, as her custom was, into the Lamb and Lion, where she drank two glasses of stout, as black as the head of her hatpin. The excitement had by no means died down. Benny Edelman had been brought in, and Mrs Wright was there, of course. But Mrs Durbin did not join in the conversation. She merely listened, tugging away at her pipe, and ramming the tobacco down sometimes with her leathery thumb. At closing time she went out into Blenheim Road and towards the freer country beyond St. Luke's. She was already in her walking-out costume, for her cap and shawl never came off. She walked for miles and did not come back for hours.

No-one knew where she went on these excursions. In an earlier age her neighbours would have said of her she went forth to ride upon broomsticks and to join her sister witches at their Sabbath. They would not, in the end, have burned or drowned her. She was not of the sort who would have sat down tamely while they tied a stone round her neck, to see if it would keep her afloat when they threw her into the millpond. She would have sent them packing pretty quickly, with a buzzing in their ears, for she had a sharp tongue, when she cared to use it.

Her neighbours had the instinct that she was, eminently, a sensible woman. Otherwise it would have been impossible, even in an epoch so enlightened as the first decade of the twentieth century, for them to see her going off late at night and staying away so long without inventing odd explanations of her absences. The children were not so sure. They never got quite used to that pipe and that hatpin. And certain harassed mothers of Magnolia Street, on both pavements, were not slow to take advantage of the fear the children had of her. "Be quiet!" they threatened. "Stop crying, or I'll lock you up in the cellar with Mrs Durbin!" Mrs Durbin was only ousted from the cellar during the periods when a Dr Crippen came into public prominence.

So that, sometimes, if a child came home late from playing in some neighbour's house and he found Mrs Durbin bearing down upon him, he gave a loud yell, and took to his heels; or stood still and frozen, awaiting what was to happen.

But nothing happened. She merely went off into the night, no-one knowing where. She did no more than walk and walk, for in her small bony limbs flowed the sap of an unquenchable vitality. At a later stage in the development of the possibilities open to women of energy, she might have managed a firm or gone into Parliament; now there was no more for her to do than to be her sons' lather-boy. The type of success open throughout all ages to women of charm was not open to her. She felt more of a man than most of the men she knew. Only one man in all her history had made her conscious that she was in truth a woman, with a weak woman's mouth for a man's to strengthen.

But he died long ago, leaving her with their two sons. Albert might have been fathered by some other man, so unlike was he to that stocky fellow with a chest like an ape's and hair tough and red as a basket of carrots. Albert's hair was red, too, but it was a miserable apologetic red, that you might snuff out if you breathed on it. All other men since had seemed poor stuff to her, no more fit to lie with than a yard broom.

He died long ago. It may have been of him she thought as she trod the midnight streets, with the bowl of her pipe clutched in her left hand. Or she may have thought of nothing at all but the towels that were to be washed and the firm was running out of bay rum.

On the night that followed Tommie Wright's rescue, she was out later and fared further than usual. She got as far as the moors that heave darkly beyond Layton Park. It was a warm night with a moon that rose late and travelled slowly through banks of cloud. On such nights as this young men and young women make love to each other under sandy shelves and tussocks of gorse, and cannot bring themselves to leave each other, it is so warm and the moon seems rather to help than hinder their love-making.

The moon came out of a thicket of cloud. Mrs Durbin heard a voice. She had heard that voice in her saloon that morning, and again that evening, in the Lamb and Lion. She saw a face. She knew those rosy cheeks and those green eyes. But the cheeks, too, looked green in this light. Perhaps she was mistaken. She withdrew silently, being fairly sure that the young man and young woman had not been aware of her. She smiled. Once, long ago, she, too, had lain under these sandy ledges, and a man's arms were about her.

It had not been very comfortable, but fierce enough. That was the way Albert, her son, came about. Albert liked bloaters for his breakfast and she had none in. She turned back and reached Magnolia Street and a tom-cat rubbed himself against her leg in an ecstasy. The tom-cats of Magnolia Street loved her, as if they deemed her as male and wild and lonely as themselves.

Chapter 9

I

So in one way and another, in one language and another, in the four clubs, in the private houses, Magnolia Street celebrated the heroism of B. Edelman and the well-being of T. Wright. But there were certain individuals who, for several reasons, all very different from each other, remained outside the merry-making.

Reb Aryeh, for instance who kept the Hebrew-school, was not propitious. He quoted the examples of Rehoboam and Jeroboam and the other wicked kings, and pinched the brachial muscles of his pupils till they were blue. The boys had competitions later, to see whose muscles were bluest.

As for Rabbi Shulman, he lived so completely in a cloud of talmudic metaphysics that he might not have noticed it if his house had been burning about his ears and some creature, Jew or gentile, had carried out himself and his whole family in a series of incomparably brilliant rescues. Among his manifold duties was to decide whether a given fowl, whose interior had excited anxious suspicions, was ritually pure, or not. The problem would so promptly and so passionately absorb the whole attention of Rabbi Shulman, that he would not have noticed whether it was a Jew who had posed it, or a blue-eyed Norwegian, or a pig-tailed Chinese. It was not to be wondered, therefore, that Rabbi Shulman was not aware of all these doings in Magnolia Street when night and day he was not aware of treading other pavements than those of Jabneh and Babylon and Tiberias, where the holy colleges had been.

His wife gave birth to another male child three or four days after the rescue, and it was said he was hardly aware even of that. Mrs Shulman was bitterly disappointed. Things always went against her. The Rabbi's wife though she was, she would have liked to be in at all this pleasantness, along with the other Jewish women. And then she went and had a baby. The doctor said it was brought on by the excitement of that famous Thursday afternoon. She should have been lying down instead of walking in a procession. The baby was a good month before its time. And another boy at that.

Mrs Shulman was by nature a disappointed woman. Her first husband, a parchment-maker, had disappointed her by dying a year after the marriage. So she led Chaim Shulman under the canopy, a Rabbi whose learning and piety were a byword twenty-five years earlier in their Russian village.

She had tried to console herself after her first husband died by setting up a small general store, but it did not come up to expectations. So she married the Rabbi and hoped the whole village would flock to her. It did; but it went straight through the shop without pausing to look at her goods, and sought out the Rabbi, to consult him either on the state of their own liver or the liver of the chicken they had bought for the Sabbath. They had often known a prayer from the Rabbi to be far more efficient than a dose from the doctor. And it was cheaper. If anyone ever thought of some *quid pro quo* for his services, it was not the Rabbi.

He did real harm to his wife's business. In so holy a house it was considered almost blasphemous to think of buying common onions or handkerchiefs. So the shop failed. And the Rabbi and his wife came to England.

Mrs Shulman had a child by her first husband. It died, just to spite her. Years went by and Mrs Shulman did not bear another child. It was as if the Rabbi, being so spiritual a person, had not got the knack of it. A perpetual querulousness settled on her face. There was shame as well as disappointment in her barrenness.

Then it seemed that the Rabbi accidentally stumbled on the way of it. Mrs Shulman gave birth to Rachel. It *would* be a girl, of course. Her chagrin was profound. She was certain there would be no more children, so they would have no-one, after all, to say the Kaddish after them, the Prayer-for-the-Dead, when they lay in the cold ground. They would have to have bought mourners interceding for them at the seat of the Most High. She sighed wretchedly.

But her grief was premature. Less than a year later, Solly was born. Less than a year after that Benjamin was born. Less than a year after that Yossel was born. It was as if Rabbi Shulman had now lost the knack of not producing children, and sons, moreover. It would have been so nice for Rachel if she could have a little sister to keep her company. But there weren't any little sisters. Yankel followed Yossel, and Issy followed Yankel. Then came Mick. Now came another male child, just when Mrs Poyser's shop was humming all day long like a happy beehive. Mrs Shulman cried for disappointment.

And where was the money to come from to feed so many mouths? Rabbi Shulman had as much instinct for money as for Ming china. People came. Sometimes they left money, sometimes they did not. Sometimes a fat chicken would turn up from nowhere, dead or alive. Sometimes there would be nothing in the house for days on end but a few raw herrings. Sometimes the house, all of a sudden, was as full of clucking as a farmyard. There might even be a puzzled quacking at the scullery sink. It was all very strange and very disappointing.

But Magnolia Street was delighted that Mrs Shulman had another baby. The baby added the one touch that had been lacking. It was almost as if, in a very mystical way, Benny Edelman and Jessie Wright had had a baby. Magnolia Street saw to it there was a good deal more than raw herrings in the Shulman larder during Mrs Shulman's absence from their midst. Maggie Tawnie brought in with her own hands half a bottle of brandy. Mrs Seipel contributed one of her famous egg-cakes. Jessie Wright, with her instinct for the delicate thing, sent a bunch of roses. Poor Rachel Shulman had so much to do that the roses fell out of her hand behind the kitchen-sofa.

"What can I have done with those roses?" she asked herself wearily. She thrust back with her thumbs her lank black hair. "Oh, they'll turn up somewhere!" But the roses were pot pourri a long time before they turned up.

II

Kate Ritchie, of number fourteen, did not join in the celebrations, either. It was not because she had a baby, but because she had a husband. He was away at sea now. "He should be back any day," muttered Kate forlornly. She wiped a tear from her eye with the edge of her apron. "I'm that lonely!" she moaned, "that lonely! If it was only him getting off the tram and coming up the street and knocking at the door!" What a knock that would be! Enough to set her wonderful parlour candelabra jingling, with its gongs and crystals, that he had bought for her on his last leave. But he did not knock at the door.

Last night she had intended to walk, straight into the private bar without a with your leave or by your leave. She knew they would all be there gathered together nice and cosy sipping their pints, and talking about the Jew fellow who had saved Jessie Wright's boy; and what harm would it do them if she came in, too? She could pay for herself, she asked nothing from nobody, *and* stand a pint to the next one, if she had a mind to. And the mess they had made of her scrubbed steps as they went tumbling up the street to Jessie Wright's — enough to break your heart after scrubbing like that for a good hour and more.

But at the last moment her courage failed her. So she took her jug under her shawl as usual and went into the Jug and Bottle Department, and would you believe it, it took minutes and minutes before anyone heard her knocking, there was such a noise going on. Songs and speech-making and that. All the Jews were there, too. She heard the tall one, with the pince-nez, his name was Emmanuel, carrying on like the private bar was the Free Trade Hall.

She had never felt lonelier in all her life before, than she felt in the dark lobby of the Jug and Bottle Department, knocking at the glass panel and no one hearing. At last she got her jug filled. Then she carried it away and sat by her white hearth. But she could not drink it. And when she tried her tears fell into the beer.

She looked around her, trying to find solace where she so often had found it before, in the beauty and cleanliness of her home. It was, indeed, a model of a small house. She changed all her curtains each week, and the curtains in the back rooms were just as full and white and elaborate as the front-room curtains. Every morning she scrubbed her doorsteps with brown stone, giving their edges a fine artistic finish with a slab of blue; and there was so little traffic up and down her steps that twice a week would have been quite ample. Before her parlour-window she had not merely one bamboo-table with an aspidistra in a plant-pot, but three separate bamboo-tables, each with an aspidistra in a plant-pot. Above her mantelpieces she had mirrors flanked with classical panels. Her kitchen-hearth was scrubbed like fine linen and a great fireguard hemmed it round. This was no precaution against injury to children. No children ever visited Kate Ritchie. Its purpose was to keep sparks away from the fluffy mat, compounded out of a thousand pieces of coloured rag, which lay in the centre of the polished linoleum.

She occupied herself about the house all next day in the effort to forget how miserable she was. She polished the stair-rods, though she had done them all two days ago, did up the kitchen grate, put new paper frills on the shelves, whatever she could think of. She desperately wanted someone to come in and say how lovely it all was, particularly the astounding tapestry table-cloth she had received from Alexandria not long ago, in which were traced in gilt thread, a camel, Lord Kitchener, the Sphinx and a handful of pyramids. It was not the day for the 'landlord,' unfortunately, the day when he called for his nine shillings, and she could ask him into the kitchen and would he like a cigarette? (There were always cigarettes about, in case *he* turned up suddenly, as he usually did.) The postman came, but of course you couldn't ask the postman in, and take him away from His Majesty's service.

The baker had not been very pleasant to her last time, so she didn't ask him in. But it *was* the dustman's day, and although she'd never done it before, she couldn't help asking him wouldn't he like to look at her new aspidistra; and hadn't she done well with the new coat of whitewash she had given the scullery, and done it all with her own hands?

"Very fine indeed, mum!" said the dustman. He called her 'mum.' She gave him threepence, as well as a packet of Woodbines, for that.

And then the dustman, too, left her; left her to the kettle singing on the hob rather mournfully; the tom-cat yowling on the hearth-mat rather grossly. Had she not already given him a pint of milk today? She went and filled his basin for him again.

Later that evening she went out. She got her pint from the Jug and Bottle Department and brought it back into the kitchen and set it beside her feet. She sat back in the arm-chair and rocked to and fro. The tom-cat was away courting. She couldn't bear a night like last night again.

And then it was the idea came to her that it might be nice to go over and have a word or two with Mrs Winter. She hadn't seen a thing of her for a week or two — Mrs Winter, who lived on the other side of the street. Jews, of course, are Jews, taking them by and large, and the things they do say about Mrs Winter...

A knock at the door. Not a great uproarious knocking like a fire-engine; a mild dubious knocking.

That was Mrs Winter. It couldn't be anyone else. She went to the door. "Come in, Mrs Winter! Come straight in!"

III

Strange men used to come and visit Leah Winter. Sometimes they stayed all night. That was what was wrong with Leah Winter.

She kept lodgers. It was not to be expected that she should keep Jewish lodgers, being a lady whom strange men used to come and visit. Her lodgers were the *fire-goyahs* of that region of Longton, that is to say, the elderly gentile women who tended the fires and turned the gas on and out, on Friday evenings and Sabbaths, in the Jewish houses of those parts. Like Kate Ritchie, like Leah Winter, they were outsiders. For though Magnolia Street was a small community — or two small communities, to be exact — no community is small enough not to contain Outsiders. The *fire-goyahs* did not belong to the odd pavement of the Jews, they had no place in the even pavement of the gentiles, excepting in the public bar of the Lamb and Lion. There was always an odd handful of *fire-goyahs* under Leah Winter's roof; sleeping on the kitchen sofa, in odd passages and cupboards.

They had an extreme devotion to Mrs Winter. There was nothing they would not do for her. They admitted that strange men came and visited Mrs Winter, but they swore fiercely there was nothing in it. Mrs Winter and the strange men just spent the time together in the kitchen, chatting. Who should know, if they, the *fire-goyahs*, didn't? They could come in and boil a kettle for themselves on the kitchen fire whenever they wanted a drop of tea.

"Innocent, the poor dear," they agreed, "as the babe unborn!"

But was it true, or was it not true, that the strange men sometimes stayed the whole night? The *fire-goyahs* did not flinch. They knew that their own innocence did not come into question. Certain of them had been what they had been, and many a married lady with gold rings and gold necklaces in Magnolia Street, may have been a good deal worse. Certain of them had always been frozen monuments of chastity. But by the time that ladies became *fire-goyahs*, all of them alike were further from the breath of suspicion than any chapter of nuns in a convent.

It was true. The strange men sometimes spent the night. But always in the back bedroom. Winter spent the night in the front bedroom with the key turned in the lock.

It may have been true that Mrs Winter's relations with the strange men were strictly proper. But it was generally assumed that the shrill defence the *fire-goyahs* undertook of Mrs Winter's good name, had something to do with her slackness about the rent. She was slack about everything, down to her hair and her corsets.

On the Friday afternoon following the golden Thursday, she sat on the doorsteps of her house, number eleven, doing nothing, thinking nothing, just feeling miserable in a slack way. She had had a feeling, even before she did it, that it was a mistake to go into the Lamb and Lion last night. Everybody seemed so jolly, surely there could be no harm in her going in, too. Lots of the Jewish men were there already. But that was different. She realised from the big eyes they made the moment they saw her, she had made a mistake. Apart from that, no one had taken any notice of her.

And then, as usual, she had gone in that morning to get her groceries from Mrs Poyser. Mrs Poyser always gave her what she asked for in the ordinary way of business; though of course, she was not encouraged to stay on and chat, like the other customers and go behind the scenes to inspect the piano which Mrs Poyser had just bought for her daughter, Becky.

But for some time now Mrs Poyser had realised that any intending son-in-law who saw Leah Winter about the place would be so discouraged at the thought that any human female could look like that with the lapse of years, that it might make a bachelor out of him for life. Yet she did not like turning away good money, whether strange men did or did not leave it on the mantelpiece. And she went on serving Leah Winter.

And then Leah Winter went into the public-house — a Jewish daughter. The other women were murmuring and complaining. How could they expect to go shopping in the same shop where a Jewish woman is served who goes into public-houses?

So that Friday morning Mrs Poyser spoke to Leah Winter. It had to be done. She informed her she must get her groceries elsewhere.

Mrs Winter was rather stupid. It took Mrs Poyser quite a long time to convey her meaning. Then at length Leah understood. Her lips trembled just a little, a comb slid out of her back hair; then she went off with her basket to another grocery-shop lower down Blenheim Road. She sighed heavily as she clopped along in her loose slippers.

That was why Leah sat about on her doorstep so blankly that Friday afternoon. Then she suddenly remembered that she had not made her Friday evening dinner. She rushed back into her kitchen, with her hair streaming out of its combs and slides, of which she used about ten more than necessary, for once she started putting combs and slides into her hair, she forgot about it and kept on putting them in automatically. The combs and slides fell in showers about her as she moved. Her progress was a welter of loose strings and slipping skirts. She seized her fishboard and her chopper and her fish, and returned to the doorstep and sat down and proceeded to chop up the stuff and roll it into balls and flavour it, as if number eleven Magnolia Street were a solitary hut in the heart of the Gobi desert. And she had not yet plucked her Sabbath chicken; so she sat down and plucked, till the air about her was a small snowstorm.

And the other Jewish ladies going about their business on the Jewish pavement, crept into their own houses, mortified that the gentiles should have so shameful a sight to see. And sure enough, Mrs Derricks passed at that moment, and paused, and snorted and passed on.

But nothing disturbed Mrs Winter as she sat plucking her fowl or rolling her fish-balls. For the time being she had forgotten her mortifications. Shall not a Jewish woman prepare the board for the Sabbath? For Mrs Winter was a pious woman in her way, and never, on Sabbaths and holidays, failed from taking up her place in the women's section of the synagogue. For she knew that in the sight of the God of Israel she had as much right to her place there as Bella Winberg or Lady Rothschild. She knew also that in the same just sight, she and Miss Winberg and Lady Rothschild were so much dirt weighed in the balance with men, their masters, and she chanted with particular satisfaction the prayer: "Blessed art Thou, oh Lord our God, Who hast made me what I am."

She ate her Friday evening dinner all by herself that evening. None of the strange men came in to share it with her. Her loneliness came back to her. Strange men were all right in their way, but they could not be relied on. Sometimes no strange man came for weeks. And though her *fire-goyahs* were so staunchly attached to her, they were only *fire-goyahs*, after all. She yearned to exchange a word with someone nearer to her own social level.

She wondered how Mrs Ritchie might be this evening. Had he sent her a present lately, like that scarf worked with metal threads? Or that tortoise with hammered brass plates in its shell, you never saw such a beautiful thing?

"Yes," she muttered. "I'll go over. Why not? I'll wash my hands and put my hair straight. And Mrs Ritchie's that particular about her oilcloth, shall I put on my best pair of shoes?"

She washed and put on her new shoes. She crossed the gulf between the two pavements, where Benny Edelman and Tommie Wright had thrown a bridge yesterday for other feet than hers. She knocked.

Kate Ritchie came to the door.

"Come in, Mrs Winter! Come straight in!" So Kate and Leah sat together chatting for an hour, two hours. It was a strange thing how much they had to talk about, one being a Jewish lady and the other a gentile. Or perhaps it was not so strange.

And then the *fire-goyahs* began to drop in. Fortunately there was still just time to get in some beer from the Jug and Bottle. It was really quite a social evening. The *fire-goyahs* had discharged their duties at the houses of their clients and, finding their landlady not at home, they knew there was only one place where she could be. So they dropped in, too. Mrs Ritchie treated them very nicely; there was a little of the *grande dame* in her manner, perhaps, but she was regular glad to have company that evening.

A word or two must be said about these *fire-goyahs*, for the picture of Magnolia Street, or the Jewish pavement, at least, is incomplete without them. What they did all week was not quite clear. Some did a little charing, some received small money orders from time to time from the antipodes. It was not for the gentiles they did their charing. They had cut themselves off from their own world. But on Friday evenings they came into their own. There was always a certain pride in their demeanour when they entered the Jewish houses to turn out the gas and leave the place dim and cosy in the last inch of candlelight. And they disintegrated the fire with real virtuosity, redeeming with their naked hands those lumps of coal which still had mischief in them, and placing them in a neat heap in the corner of the grate to be the foundation of the morning's fire. Whether they carried their pride patent on their foreheads or concealed it beneath a mask of heartiness, there was no doubt they were aware of the privilege of their condition.

They had not become Jews, of course; but they were not purely Christians. Indeed, they sometimes developed a type almost as duplex as the Christo-Mohammedanism of some Albanians or the Buddhistic Confucianism of some Chinese. There are Muslim Albanians who give each other eggs at Easter and pay pilgrimage to the eikons of Christian saints. There are Confucian Chinese, who, among the memorial tablets of their Confucian ancestry, give obeisance also to Buddhists who have crossed their family. So certain of the *fire-goyahs* developed a punctiliousness with regard to the mixing of meat and milk foods; there was a Roman Catholic *fire-goyah* who added without warrant from the Vatican the saints Abraham and Isaac to her litany; and when once, on the feast of Passover, she saw Max Emmanuel, the little painting-boy who lived next door, nibbling leavened Eccles cake in complete oblivion of how wicked a thing that was in the Passover season, she nearly fainted with horror; but not before she had boxed his ears and dropped the impious thing through the bars of a street-grid.

The last *fire-goyah* to come in that evening was May Agnes Hartley. She is the only one of that company to whom a name is given, because, while the others came and went, she stayed. She was there still in 1930.

It was odd that room could still be found for her in Kate Ritchie's neat little kitchen. But she merely flowed into those parts of the room which were not already occupied. And as she flowed, she sang. It seemed hardly believable that such incoherent masses of *fire-goyah* should be as instinct with song as Shelley or his sky-lark. Hour after hour she sat before the sooted window of her attic, looking out upon the backs of the Oleander Street houses, singing. She sang as she made her fires. She sang that evening in Kate Ritchie's kitchen.

She sang no music-hall catches. Her themes were the iniquity of Mrs Billig, who had tried to reduce her *fire-goyah's* fee from twopence-halfpenny to twopence in virtue of the cup of tea she had drunk (and the water not even boiling); or the glory of Isrol Poyser, the grocer, who had given her a newlaid egg when Mrs Poyser wasn't looking; her acute doubt that Mrs Poyser's daughter, Becky, would ever achieve a husband, despite the new piano and the singing lessons. She sang the glory with which some day Bella Winberg would come back to the house she was born in. She announced that Max Emmanuel would some day have traffic with ladies who wore tiaras, that old Billig was no good man, despite his bright blue eyes and his beard of white silk; she foresaw the greatness that was to come to the small Mick Shulman, and much blood must flow from his snub nose...

For May Agnes Hartley had powers, it seems impossible to doubt, though to have stated such a thing in Magnolia Street would have brought the whitewash in great flakes from the ceiling, it would have evoked such gales of laughter. And if there had been one to listen to her well, it may have been possible to write down in 1910 the whole history of Magnolia Street in 1916 and 1930. She had no acute sense of proportion, for the big war she sang of, that was to cloak the lands with blood, occupied no greater space in her descants than the red beard of Mrs Edelman's new lodger and Mrs Seipel's sewing-machine that had gone to be pawned. But it is remembered that on a few occasions, setting eyes on little David Emmanuel, she stopped as if she saw not him, but the doom that waited for him. For that death, and a few more, and a leg, and a pair of eyes, were the offerings required by the Great War from the small street.

So she came over that evening into Kate Ritchie's kitchen and sang of the Jews, but plaintively, in a minor key. Her songs were only of the Jews. No one listened to her. It was of Benny Edelman and Jessie Wright and Tommie, that Kate Ritchie and her guests spoke.

"But won't you have just one more glass?" insisted Kate Ritchie.

"I don't mind if I do!" said Leah Winter. Her head was already swimming, but she knew that the *fire-goyahs* would help her across the road when it was time to go home. And drinking beer was no sin. Where did it say in the Bible that drinking beer was a sin?

"I'll have one with you!" said Kate. Her hand was a little unsteady. She even spilled a little on the polished linoleum. That drew her up. She went and mopped it up sternly, a little too sternly, perhaps.

And then May Agnes Hartley in her singing said she saw Benny Edelman putting a gold ring on a lady's wedding-ring finger. She could not see whose face it was. The lady was no Jew. No one took any notice at all.

"Another one for you, Maggie?"

" Yes, mum!" said Maggie.

Kate smiled. She liked the lower orders to be respectful.

"Here you are, Maggie!" It was really a very social evening.

IV

And only next day Pete came; Kate Ritchie's husband, that is to say. A great shameless childish roaring black man he was, with the arms of a gorilla and a mouthful of gold teeth. He hallooed greetings from pavement to pavement, and whether it was that people were afraid to put any affront upon him, or whether his colossal vitality made them reply despite themselves, they nodded back and muttered "Good morning!" and then hurried indoors rather fearfully.

She told him about Benny Edelman, how brave he had been. He hurled himself across the road and slapped Benny's back so heartily that Benny nearly bit off an inch of tongue. Benny was no weakling, but his back felt sore all day. Spotting Tommie Wright immediately after, Pete threw him high in the air and caught him as if he were a threepenny ball. He also gave him a shilling. Tommie announced that he liked that uncle. Later in the day Kate and Pete went off to the Doomington Zoo, they went off somewhere every day. Naturally Kate did not devote anything like so much time to house matters, while Pete was with her. The next day they went to the Layton Park Gallery, where there was a picture of a baby afloat in its cradle in a flooded countryside. The baby lifted its chubby little fist and opened wide its blue eyes, and Pete and Kate both mopped their eyes before the picture, it so affected them. But there was an enormous canvas of a landscape near it, consisting chiefly of cabbages and beehives; and they mopped their eyes before that picture, too.

So it is probable that it wasn't so much the subject-matter of the pictures which affected them, as the fact that they were together and so happy, that crashing negro from Trinidad and the neat little woman from Blackburn — or Bacup, as some said. And they walked home again to Magnolia Street, he holding in his hand a brown paper parcel containing her old hat, and she holding on her head a new hat, a very jaunty one, that Pete had just bought for her in Deansgate. And she tossed her chin in the air with a queer mixture of timidity and defiance, when she saw a knot of women gathered at Jessie Wright's doorstep, very obviously discussing herself and her new hat and her big buck blackie. And that night, and all the five nights he was with her, they either went to a theatre or sat about, as large as life, in the private bar. And, of course, nobody dared say a word, or they would soon have had Pete Ritchie's fist smashing down on their skull. As for the house, she couldn't keep it in *quite* such apple-pie order while Pete was with her. She couldn't clean the steps *every* morning and polish up the linoleum till it looked like old mahogany. But she could make him so many ginger suet-puddings that the whites of his eyes rolled in his head; for he had always been a one for ginger suet-puddings. And then, on the sixth day, he had to go back to sea. And then, perhaps, in some ways, it was a good thing that the house *had* been a bit neglected. For it took your mind off things like, if you had to buckle down to the yard flags, which needed a good scouring. And goodness gracious, if there wasn't a worm somewhere eating at the roots of this new aspidistra, the way its leaves were all curling and growing yellow. She took the small trowel in hand with which she loosened the earth about the roots of her aspidistras, and found that worm. It glistened like a streak of mercury across the prism of the tear that hung on her eyelashes. "I'll give it you!" she said fiercely. "I'll give it you!"

V

Kate Ritchie and Leah Winter did not join in the Edelman-Wright celebrations, because they were not asked to. Eric (né Isaac) Winberg, did not join in because he was not aware of them. He was not aware of anything that happened in Magnolia Street. He was not aware of Magnolia Street at all, excepting in the gross sense that he had his meals in it and slept there.

If the Pytchley and the Quorn Hunts, if Brooks's Club and the Beefsteak Club, are outside Magnolia Street (and it would be futile to argue that in any sense they are not) then Isaac Winberg was also outside Magnolia Street. He was not, of course, inside the Pytchley Hunt or Brooks's Club; but then he was only fifteen, and with a Winberg there was no saying what might not happen.

Eric Winberg was svelte and elegant, with a smooth pale oval face and quiet dark eyes. You could not deduce from them how fantastic was the world he lived in. He was an aristocrat. His ancestors had crossed the Channel with William the Conqueror. He would some day inherit large lands. He was the darling of the West End. Peeress-mothers asked him to their parties to meet their little peeress-daughters. He shot. He rode to hounds. He came in first in the most dashing point-to-point of the season.

On Saturday morning when Benny Edelman went to the synagogue to receive the commendations of God and man upon his recent heroic behaviour, his shoulders brushed the shoulders of Eric Winberg. But to Eric Winberg the hero might have been a fly or a lamp-post. He took no notice of him. He twirled his little cane. He wore his top-hat at a slightly jaunty angle. His Eton suit was immaculately well-brushed. He, too, wore an Eton suit. Wilfred Derricks, the Longton Nightingale, was not the only dweller in Magnolia Street who wore an Eton suit. But the Nightingale wore it to let the world see he was the world's Boy. Eric wore it in a sort of secret understanding with his Norman ancestors. The spirits had bewitched him. They had made him the son of Jews and to live in a mean street. But he would not let them down — the Fitzeustaces and the Fitzgeralds, who were his own people.

He never nowadays uttered a word to any human being in Magnolia Street which betrayed the nature of his obsessions. But there had been a time when he permitted himself one queer confidante. This was none other than Rachel Shulman, the Rabbi's daughter. He was aware she adored him then. She adored him still, but he had ceased to be aware of her.

In the days before he attained his tenth year and she her eleventh, he would request her to come out walking with him to Baxter's Moor, a region where, as he imagined, other members of the Norman aristocracy lived. He would say nothing at all to her for minutes at a stretch, while one member of the working-classes and another passed by. Then at length some lady or gentleman of the patrician kind approached them. Then he gave tongue. Bending towards Rachel's ear, just loudly enough for the stranger to overhear him, he declared: "So when Lord Henry offered me the goblet, I simply couldn't refuse." He said no more than that.

Rachel's heart beat joyfully. She was aware that, literally, no Lord Henry could have been offering Isaac Winberg any goblet. But in a deep, *deep* sense, she knew it was true. Some minutes later, once more a stranger approached who seemed to the boy to have the patrician manner. Once more he leaned towards her. He twirled his little cane. "So when Lord Henry offered me the goblet, I simply couldn't refuse." It seemed to him that was the manner in which earls and the sons of earls conversed with each other.

He had taken Rachel Shulman with him, because he knew she loved him. He knew that he could not impart the news about Lord Henry and the goblet to anyone else than her without unpleasant consequences. Anyone else would think he was mad or joking. Rachel, who loved him, knew the truth.

But when he attained his tenth year, he realised it was a grave error to be seen by the Normans in the company of such a slut. He did not speak to her again. A year later he went to Doomington School, where he became a notable athlete, despite his lean frame. He got his second team colours for cricket and was a useful outside-left. He was now a highly respected private in the OTC. At his first OTC camp the quartermaster-sergeant took such a fancy to the quiet and aristocratic youth that he arranged for him to mount the transport-horses whenever he was free. He rode as easily and instinctively as a cygnet takes to water.

It was just about this period that he stopped attending Jewish prayers. He was duly observed by Mr Furniss the Head Master, seated among the other boys of his form at the Christian prayers. But Mr Furniss did not know how he could take any action in the matter if the lad had a feeling for Jesus. Was it the duty of a Christian head master to remonstrate with a Jewish parent that his son showed a feeling for Jesus? The matter puzzled and slightly distressed him for some days; but seeing with what decorum the boy sang the hymn of the Christian soldiers marching as to war, he allowed the matter to drop from his mind.

But Eric Winberg had heard no call from Golgotha. He had had no more traffic with Mr Benjamin Stern, the red-bearded missionary who lived on the opposite pavement of Magnolia Street, than with Rabbi Shulman, who lived next door but one. Jesus was a more correct prophet than Moses. There was nothing more to it than that. You could count on the fingers of one hand the peers who made their protestations by Moses; and most of those were mere German Jews, who had made money.

The news found its way to Mr Benjamin Stern that a Jewish lad from across the street sat among the redeemed singing the hymns of the Redeemer. It travelled by way of Charles Stanley, who was in the Sixth. He told his mother. She told Mrs Carter, who was Mr Stern's landlady. Mr Stern's mission was to the Jews. He had once lived several streets north of Magnolia Street, where no Jews lived. But when he saw that the half of Magnolia Street had become Jewish, he felt that nothing could serve him more usefully than to take up his place on the side of the street that faced the Jews. He peered round with his screwed-up eyes in all directions for some breach into the thicket of thorns which was opposed to him. Sometimes, in his despair, with his hands held before him and his head high, he walked full into the thicket, thinking, it may be, that the Lord would decree a miracle and he might walk straight through as through a veil of mist, and tell them on the other side of the peace passing all understanding that he brought them. But the thicket was impenetrable. The thorns were like steel spikes. They stuck out all about his forehead, ringing it with a crown.

And then, in the grace of Christ Jesus, it was given to a Jewish young man to save a Christian child from drowning. Another Jewish young man had saved all children from drowning, long ago, by being nailed up on a cross. It seemed to Mr Stern that there was a thinning in the darkness all about him, that the thicket of thorns would not always remain so deep and sharp. And then the news came to him of the Jewish boy singing among his Christian brothers, for Christ's sake Who loved them all.

His heart leaped within him. Upon the Sunday morning that followed he saw the youth in his best clothes walking up Blenheim Road, clearly to attend service at St. Luke's. He did not know how to refrain from going up to the youth, from giving him a word of welcome, a word of warning. The Way was steep. The steepness would not defeat him, if he kept firm hold of the one true Staff; which was also bread and wine for that long journey.

"Excuse me, excuse me!" He touched Eric's shoulder. His touch was too light, his voice too low. He touched and spoke again. "Excuse me, excuse me!"

Eric Winberg turned round. He perceived that the missionary who lived opposite him, in Magnolia Street, had something to say to him. He looked with distaste on the missionary's shabby broad-brimmed hat, his thick-lensed glasses, his bushy red beard, his black frock-coat, the pockets bulging with gospels and pamphlets. The Jews said of him that he was an apostate Jew. They said he was receiving a large annual salary from the Society for the Conversion of the Jews, and that he would retire any day with some woman to enjoy his nest-egg.

"I've no time!" said Eric curtly.

"But — I beg of you. Only one moment. I believe the service doesn't begin for —"

"What service? What do you want?"

"I wished to speak to you of Christ Jesus, my child. I have heard that only lately —" The look that came into Eric's eye was not one of patrician hauteur. Mr Stern knew that look too well — the loathing of the Jew for the Jew who has gone to Christ. "Pah!" said Eric. "You filthy man, go away! You make me sick!"

VI

And finally there was Miss Tregunter, who lived in the Hubbard first-floor front-room. If anyone had nothing to do with the Edelman-Wright celebrations, she hadn't. She disapproved of all gaiety, she thought it unrefined. She had a lot to do with the refined reputation of the Hubbards. But if Miss Tregunter had occupied the first-floor front-room of the Borgia palace, the Borgias would have had a different reputation.

Miss Tregunter was not an interfering old lady. She rarely descended from her upstairs room, for she had had the tiniest of kitchenettes installed on the landing, and she asked help from nobody. It would not, of course, have been genteel for Miss Tregunter to go out and do her own shopping. The tradesmen were only too proud to deliver their wares to Miss Tregunter, and Dolly carried them upstairs with care, for Miss Tregunter liked everything just so. She ate very little, but all she ate was genteel. The grocer provided her with rashers as thin as tissue-paper and woe upon the greengrocer if there were any eyes in his potatoes. She ate asparagus in the season, about two or three stalks, and made herself a dish of strawberries dainty enough for a bird or a princess to feed from.

It can be imagined how icily she disapproved of the habit the gentile ladies formed at this time of dropping in to make a small purchase now and again at the Jewish grocery-shop. From her watch-tower window she saw Dolly creep in one morning, for poor Dolly didn't want her friends to think her high and mighty, and what was good enough for them wasn't good enough for her, and what difference is there, after all, between Jewish candles and Christian candles? Miss Tregunter spoke to Dolly quite briefly about her dreadful lapse. It did not occur again.

Miss Tregunter hardly ever came downstairs, except to snip away a withered flower from the little beds in the front-garden or shave off a projecting leaf from the level surface of the box hedge. And yet she imposed her gentility on every corner of the house. A new wallpaper was not chosen till she was consulted. Walter paid for Dolly's clothes, but Miss Tregunter saw they were quiet and proper. She appointed what flowers should be planted, and presided over their growth, though Walter did the labouring. That was in the front garden and in the neat borders she had got him to construct round the four sides of the tiny back-yard. But no soul but herself laid a finger on the flower-boxes on her own window-sills; she and no other prepared the soil and enriched it with a little manure and watered the plants and tended their leaves and flowers. No wonder she shooed the little Jew boys away when they started playing ball or piggy-and-stick within hurtful distance of her boxes. The wicked little Jew boys, to whom a lily and a turnip were alike vegetables, and they did not wipe their noses and their stockings came down over their boots.

During this period, it must be confessed, the little Jew boys lost their sense of proportion completely. So did the little gentile boys. They played together on each other's pavements as if Jews and gentiles were as good as each other. More than once the little Jew boys had the audacity to play directly under her windows. They included one or two of the lads who had lately been elected

145

to scholarships at Doomington School and therefore thought themselves cock of the world. She motioned to them to go away at once. They, positively, did not go. She opened the window, and opened her mouth. A queer over-articulated voice came out of it, her lower jaw fell and rose like that of a ventriloquist's doll.

"Go away! Go away! "she cried. "I know Mr Furniss, the High Master. If you don't go away I'll tell him!"

The awe invoked was not enough. They did not go away.

"Go away!" she cried again. "I'll tell the Chief Constable!" A few days later she invoked the Bishop. For she was genteel and had genteel friends.

Yet no-one knew where Miss Tregunter came from and from what sort of a family. She had come to live in Magnolia Street some years towards the end of the last century, while Walter's mother was still alive and a long time before his sister got married. There had been no Jews for many streets south of Magnolia Street for some years after. When the old Mrs Hubbard died, Walter and his sister would have liked to move into a smaller house, for he was still a very junior tram-conductor with small wages, and his sister earned less. But it was quite impossible to suggest to Miss Tregunter that the house was going to be given up and she must make arrangements to carry her window-boxes elsewhere. And besides, entirely of her own accord, Miss Tregunter offered to pay two shillings a week extra for her room.

So they stayed on. And then Walter's sister was going to get married. And then there seemed a very real danger of Miss Tregunter being forced to go, for, of course, she could not stay on in the house with only a young man about the place. And once more the danger was averted. Walter and Dolly met each other. And they got married. And Walter kept his sister in the house a full month after the marriage. So everything was very proper, and Miss Tregunter stayed on behind her window-boxes.

The Coopers were, no doubt, the best-born family in Magnolia Street. But it is possible that Miss Tregunter had more exalted blood in her veins. It is also possible that in her actual origin she was humbler than Mrs Tawnie, or Kate Ritchie, neither of whom was a lady in the ordinary sense of the word. But Miss Tregunter stood completely outside such categories of blood, lofty or base. It was only by a real exercise of the imagination you remembered that blood of any quality flowed in her veins at all. The sharpness of her features, the angularity of her movements, made her seem rather a marionette than a human being; and that illusion was heightened by the faculty she had of sitting behind her curtains for many hours at a stretch, and looking down through her geraniums on to the street below. Such a person as she, might have been a duchess or a bargee's bastard daughter. If the invincible demon of gentility had seized either of these, after eliminating every circumstance of tradition and association, it would have made of her Miss Tregunter.

Yes, she was genteel. It was a good thing for both Miss Tregunter and the Hubbards, that they lived in each other's house. Their house was a credit to Magnolia Street and the whole neighbourhood. If it was not for that house there wouldn't have been a single gentile or a single garden left in Magnolia Street, or the whole region, perhaps. But the day was to come when the house of Walter Hubbard was not so genteel as all that. It was a very unrefined day and it was a good thing that Miss Tregunter did not outlive it.

Chapter 10

I

Kate Ritchie, Leah Winter, Rabbi Shulman, Eric Winberg — for one reason or another they did not join in the fun. Rachel, the Rabbi's daughter did, and in a very special sense. In that sense she was herself the mistress of the ceremonies.

She didn't have time to go to the ordinary parties. She had too much to do. Her mother gave birth to a baby a few days after the rescue; and really, short of actually having it, it was on Rachel that all the trouble fell. And then she had all the looking after the boys to do. Her father mixed them all up. Her mother, even when she was up and about, left them to themselves, she was always so busy worrying about those of them that were not there.

All the children looked exactly like each other. Rachel looked exactly like the boys, excepting that she was a girl and they were boys. Solly looked exactly like Benjamin, one year his junior, and Benjamin exactly like Yossel. The only way of giving them their right names was to see them all together and work downward from the eldest or upward from the baby.

Even now, a few days after he was born, Abey showed himself a Shulman of the Shulmans. Perhaps Mick, who was three years old, was the least Shulman of them all. There was something about that snub nose, those sturdy little fists, the way the ears lay up against the head, which was clearly not Shulman. But who, excepting the *fire-goyah* who had second sight, foresaw that it was Madison Square Garden? Rachel was the only member of the household who could say their names straight off. Her own stockings were always falling down, she spent so much time lifting up the stockings of her brothers. She had a heart of gold. It is possible there was some beauty in her face, if you could ever have seen it clear through her hair. John Cooper, who lived almost opposite when he was in Doomington, was smart; enough to realise there was something to the girl if she only got busy with herself. But she was too busy with her father and her mother and Solly and Benjamin and Yossel and all of them. And Eric Winberg. She loved Eric Winberg. He had not cast a single glance at her for five years, but she loved him. She would have laid down her neck in the gutter for him to tread on it.

But when Benny Edelman rescued Tommie Wright and for some weeks reigned in glory, she fell in love with Benny Edelman and wanted him to be the guest of honour at her garden-party. At least she persuaded herself she was in love with Benny, as many another lady in Magnolia Street, young and old, did. It was really Eric she loved always, always, even later on, in the War, when he climbed high on to a white horse and fell off again, down, down.

She wanted Benny to be the guest of honour at her garden-party. Of course, she never gave a garden-party. She never even went to one. The fact was that it had happened once that the aristocratic Miss Winberg had come in from the aristocratic suburb of Didsbury, and she was all pink like a pink fat little rose-bud; and she had a pink parasol; and she did not smell so much of bath-salts, as she waddled down the street, as of petals falling from a pink tree, and of pink ice-cream; and the word went about she had just come from a garden-party.

Somehow, for Rachel Shulman, the word was less like a pink petal than a pink burr. It stuck. It stuck in her blouse, her hair, her soul. She too wanted to go to a garden-party. A garden-party would be so different from the kitchen of their house, with all her brothers sitting about everywhere, on the sofa, on the kitchen step, on the yard step, all with their noses buried in books, and her mother complaining that there weren't any boiled potatoes when she hadn't bought any potatoes for a fortnight. She saw pink parasols all over a green lawn and there was music and tennis and ice-cream which tall gentlemen with shining hair and princely manners offered languid ladies in pink deck-chairs. The daisies had pink edges to their whiteness and there was pink raspberry pop and pink icing on the cakes. Oh what bliss it would be to go to a garden-party!

And then, when everybody was exerting themselves to do honour to Benny, the breathless idea struck her: not merely to *go* to a garden-party, but to *give* one! To give one for Benny's sake! She would have Benny on her right hand and Eric on her left. (Even now she could not keep Eric quite out of it.) Benny was wearing a top-hat and frock-coat, while Eric was wearing a top-hat and his Eton suit. Practically everybody was in top-hats. She herself wore a pale pink dress with a blue sash, and a large floppy straw-hat sheltering her face from the supernal sunshine. It was, indeed, Heaven! The blaze and beauty were too much for her weak eyes. She turned round from Heaven. The pink ices melted in the strong sun because there was no-one to eat them. There were no pink ices for them to eat. There was no garden-party. Her father was sitting in the corner bent nearly double over the great yellow volume on the table before him. Had he had anything to eat to-day? Or yesterday?

She knew he wouldn't notice it if he didn't get anything to eat for a fortnight. Or perhaps longer; until his spirit slid gently out of his enfeebled and enormous body, still bowed over the page of Zohar in which he still read, with glazing eyes, of the light that shone in the Cave of Machpelah whilst Jacob dwelt in Canaan, but ceased when he went forth to Egypt, and did not shine again till his body was brought back to his own land.

"Father!" she cried. "Father! Will you have something to eat now?"

He made no reply.

"Solly! Benjamin! Yossel!" she whimpered.

They did not lift their faces from their books. They gestured at her vaguely.

She knew that they had been induced to go off that night with the Briggs boys and the Poyser boys and George Derricks and some others to a roller-skating-rink. Benny himself had consented to accompany them. Her brothers wanted to get through as much work as possible before the others came. There was no time to eat.

They hadn't eaten anything at all, though they had come in from school two hours ago. She remembered she hadn't even given them any food that morning to put in their pockets to eat at lunchtime, as they sat on the hot-water pipes in the school basement.

Why, there they were, still on the table — the bagels that she had brought in for them from Mrs Poyser's that morning. Bagels are like large wooden curtain-rings to look at. They now were like curtain-rings to eat. She cut them and buttered them and handed them over to the three boys. They reached their hands out but did not look at the stuff they were eating. They just lifted it into their mouths and nibbled at it and kept their eyes glued on the *Via Latina* and the *Anabasis* of Xenophon. *They* were not dreaming of pink pop and ices in celestial garden-parties. Rachel felt a sharp sense of guilt. She went into the scullery to wash up, and smashed three plates.

The Shulman boys were going to a roller-skating-rink party. It would be impossible to indicate more forcibly how bacchanalian the spirit was that had taken possession of Magnolia Street.

Yossel Shulman was twelve. He had won a scholarship at Doomington School and had entered on his first term. Solly, the eldest, had won his two years ago, Benjamin last year, There was no reason to believe Yankel would not win one next year. None of the boys had inherited their father's passion for holy learning, but all of them were studious to their finger-tips. They did not love scholarship for itself, but because it was the road to a professional career. Solly had gone on the Classical Side. He was going to be a doctor. Benjamin had gone on the Modern Side. He was going to be a research chemist. Yossel was going to be a solicitor.

These determinations were crystal-clear on the day they first crossed the threshold of the school as elected scholars. They announced them to Mr Furniss, the headmaster, with a simplicity and directness that almost terrified him, accustomed as he was to young men announcing ambitions that ranged from the unlikely glory of the Poet Laureateship to the naive modesty of becoming an engine-driver or a cowboy. In almost every important quality the young Shulmans were already the thing they had severally decided to be, a doctor, a solicitor, a chemist. There was still a certain amount of actual knowledge to acquire, but that was purely a matter of time. There was just one aspect in which the young Shulmans failed to look the professional man in the chrysalis stage. They were so busy acquiring Greek verbs, the rivers of South America and Henry the Eighth's wives, that they did not remember to wash themselves. They did not even forget. They just did not wash themselves. They did not tie their shoelaces. They forgot to put ties into their collars. At number five Magnolia Street they had not been trained in these arts.

But Doomington School was taking them in hand. There was an appreciable difference between the ears and neck of Solly and Benjamin, Benjamin and Yossel. It was not that the other boys persecuted them. The Shulman boys were not the stuff of which martyrs are made. They were merely ducked so frequently in the washbasins in the school basement that they slowly acquired the habit of ducking themselves.

There was practically no attitude or occupation which prevented them from acquiring another and still another morsel of that learning in virtue of which they would some day deliver babies, and present statistics about the by-products of coal, and help Messrs. Cohen & Robinson draw up a contract of partnership. They had their noses in their books as they walked to school and from school; it was only a ray from the halo of their mystic father that prevented them from being run over a hundred times as they crossed the road among a hurtle of lorries and trams, swallowing French irregular verbs with a slight motion at the throat, such as a frog makes swallowing flies. When they sat down they stayed down, till there weren't any more battles to learn off in the Wars of the Roses.

They were never top of the form in school, like the brilliant Charles Stanley, the shoemaker's younger son, whom his mother had brought back from Germany only two years ago. He was top of the Sixth. He had already contributed an essay on Neo-Platonism to the *Hibbert Journal*.

The Shulman boys lacked his genius. But in their own forms they were never lower than the first five. Solly would make a good doctor some day. He would be married and he would never dream of going out to a patient without both of his shoelaces being tied properly. There'd be little about coal-gas Benjamin would not know. Yossel, Yankel, Issy, they would be good husbands and decent members of their professions. And no nonsense about pink ice-cream at garden-parties....

"Some tea?" asked Rachel. "You've had no tea all day!" But nobody answered. There was no sound except the tap leaking in the scullery and the leaves of the textbooks, turning, turning.

An hour went by, an hour and a half. Then at last there was a loud knock at the door. The Briggs boys were there, the Poysers, George Derricks, Benny Edelman. Tommie Wright was with Benny Edelman. He refused to be separated from him. Nellie Tawnie was with him, too. She had given up the idea, for the time being, of marrying Dick Cooper. She was going to marry Benny Edelman. Nellie Tawnie's grandmother was away in Blackburn. So there was no way of persuading Nellie that this was purely a bachelor party.

"All right!" Benny had promised benignly. "I'll look after her!"

"See she comes to no harm!" roared Steve.

"Right, Steve!" said Benny.

The party knocked loudly at the Shulmans' door. "What's that?" cried Rachel. The boys kept their noses in the books.

"Of course!" cried Rachel. "You're going to the skating-rink to-night, with all the boys! Have you forgotten?"

The Shulmans lifted their studious eyes. Slowly awareness came back into their faces.

"Oh yes, of course!" they said. "Oh yes, of course!"

"And you've not had a drop of tea since this morning," she wailed.

"Oh that doesn't matter!" they said. They picked up a handful of books each and stuffed them into their satchels. "So long!" they said.

"I hope you have a nice time!" she ventured. She sighed. She would have liked to go with them but there was too much to do at home. So far as she was concerned, she would rather give a party herself by day, in a garden. There was so much dust flying about in roller-skating-rinks. There would be none on the soft grass, under the trees, with a band playing somewhere beyond the shrubbery, and pigeons cooing in the tree-tops, and Benny and Eric in their top-hats, and Bella in a wonderful creation from Paris.

"Won't you have a little strawberry ice, Bella? Do. I can personally recommend it."

"I don't mind if I do."

"That's right. And a little wafer to go with it?"

Her father made some slight movement in his corner. "It's about time poor father had *something*!" Rachel realised. "Really it is!"

"Rachel! Rachel!" her mother cried from upstairs. "Have you forgotten those napkins?"

"Coming! Coming!" shouted Rachel.

They all had a lovely time at the roller-skating-rink. Frankie Briggs could skate quite nicely. He took Benny in hand. It was too funny watching Benny trying to learn to skate. He tumbled about like a rhinoceros. At first Tommie was terribly alarmed and his yells punctuated the steady grind and thunder of the skates. Then he realised it was funny, and he insisted on learning to skate himself.

The Poyser boys were looking their best. There were three of them, Joe, who was shortly leaving school, and twins, Harry and

153

Jack, aged ten. The twins were great experts at piggy-and-stick, and were famous for having smashed Miss Tregunter's window once.

It had been a dreadful time. An icy silence hung over Magnolia Street, like the silence that might hang over the synagogue if someone should drop the Scroll of the Law in the moment of extracting it from the Ark. They carried groceries in the morning before they went to school and in the evening after they returned and before and after their attendance at Reb Aryeh's Hebrew-school. So it was understandable that the young blood should rise in them occasionally and induce them to play piggy-and-stick in the gutters. But nothing at all could be said for them in extenuation of the Miss Tregunter blasphemy. That was a bad day's work.

They behaved very decently at the skating-rink. You could tell which was Joe. He was bigger than the twins. As for the twins, one was wearing a big brown bow and the other was wearing a big blue bow. So you could tell which was Harry and which was Jack.

All the boys tried to skate with varying degrees of success and Benny kept a father's eye on them. But the Shulman boys did not try to skate. They sat together on a form at the edge of the rink, with their books balanced on the padded railings. "*Quadrupedante putrem sonitu quatit ungula campum*," murmured Solly. "*Amo, amas, amat*," murmured Yossel. Benjamin was muttering a chemical formula to himself over and over again.

George Derricks did not spend all his time skating, though he skated quite creditably. He spent some of it seeing if the Shulman boys had anything worthwhile in their pockets. All he found was a pocket-knife. It was not a good one, but he thought he might as well have it as not.

II

Yes, George Derricks was present, too, at the roller-skating-rink party. He was present at all the parties, though he was the only member of his family who was. He was always slipping in and out from one house to the other at this time. He produced a vague sense of discomfort whenever he appeared, but you really could not *say* anything. You never by any chance found him with

154

his hand where it shouldn't be. It was only later, when it all died down, that Mrs Carter saw that her long silver pickle-fork was missing and Mr Poyser couldn't find his fountain-pen anywhere. Other things were missing, too. But the fact was that people were rather fatalistic about George. If he wanted a thing he got it; if he didn't get it one day he got it the next day. So what was the good of regretting it?

What he did with the things he appropriated was a profound mystery. During the days that succeeded the triumph on the brick-croft, when both Mr Emmanuel and Mr Stanley lost their watches, you did not see him study the time on the dials of two watches, or of one, even. He did not cut his pencils with two separate knives, all equipped with cork-screws and nail-files and awls and tin-openers, or with one, even. It was never reported that he dived for pickles in his mother's pickle-jar with a long silver pickle-fork. It was very puzzling.

In his demeanour and appearance George was a model. He was much the nicest-looking boy at the parties. His waterproof collar was always sponged quite clean, both its stud holes were in good condition. The way he raised his hat to Jessie Wright and old Mrs Edelman indiscriminately was a treat. But he never looked better than at the great reception Mr Emmanuel staged a couple of weeks later in Unity Hall. His hair was flawlessly parted in the middle. He had a flower in his button-hole. And when Becky Poyser sang Tosti's *Goodbye*, he was seen to dab his eye with a handkerchief, for the sad sweet song had got the better of him.

How little did George, or anyone else, suspect that treacherous piece of soap which lay in wait for him round the corner? For the imp of the grotesque was too much for him. After so brief but brilliant a career, it would have been fitting if they had caught him on the point of successfully appropriating a grand piano. But it was a twopenny piece of carbolic soap that was his undoing. As his hand dived down upon a tray of pieces of soap exposed outside a hardware shop in Blenheim Road, his own bootlace tripped him up, this being the first occasion for years that his boots were not tied properly. It was, perhaps, rather the bootlace than the soap that undid him.

So that George disappears from our tale quite soon after we make his acquaintance. They took him away to a Reformatory School for some time. He reappears for a brief moment in 1916, in a blaze of glory and a Distinguished Conduct Medal.

Yet people didn't blame George; they blamed his mother. Virtually he had no mother, she was so completely wrapped up in his brother, Wilfred. His father was like that, too; he virtually had no wife. But the old man did not fall into evil ways. He went on with his fretwork.

"Just unnatural, I call it!" declared Mrs Briggs at the Lamb and Lion, a lady who did not usually pronounce harsh judgments. "Not the poor boy's fault at all, *I* don't think!"

"And of course the poor father, what with his indigestion and that, never able to do nothing with him, neether!" affirmed the slightly querulous voice of Sally Carter.

"Father, indeed!" snorted Mrs Tawnie among her ivory beer-handles. "As much 'is father as I'm Queen Alexandra!"

"You don't say!" murmured Mr Briggs.

Mrs Tawnie suspended her pump-handle in its pumping for a brief moment, as if she wasn't at all sure she wasn't going to interpret Mr Briggs's remark as a contradiction.

"O dawn't I," she contented herself by saying, "dawn't I!" And she shook her head till the great mass of her red hair tottered.

III

Perhaps the Edelman-Wright merry-makings reached their peak on the second Sunday after that good Thursday. One or two independent streams of joy happened to be flowing, but they were all caught up in the main river before the night was over. In addition to everything else, there was a lot of unaccustomed money about. Mr Stanley, the shoemaker, was responsible for that, but not, of course, in his shoemaking capacity.

That was the strange thing about Mr Stanley. He could sometimes put other people in the way of making an odd pound or two, but the more he studied, the more difficult he found it to make an odd pound or two for himself. He was a shoemaker, but his heart wasn't in it. Perhaps, if he had only taken shoemaking seriously for just a few years, he might really have managed to get away from it. But he didn't. He knocked the nails into the soles as if he hated them, and that isn't the way to knock them in straight. They often go in sideways and poke a hole into the socks of your customers and then they go elsewhere with their next pair of shoes.

His heart was in racing and football; but not in the sense that nearly all the lads and men on the gentile pavement were keen on those things. He never, or rarely, went to see the actual horses race in the Doomington Handicap, or to see a needle contest between Doomington United and Sheffield Wednesday, who had only a point between them, and if Huddersfield only got one point out of Everton, the winner at Old Trafford was sure of the League honours.

He did not care for horses or footballers as flesh-and-blood propositions but as units in a game of possibilities. All in all, Mr Stanley had been forced to spend a good many hours over his last, and there he had developed a peculiarly abstract type of mind. Perhaps he brought it with him to his shoemaking. But if you were to study any of the countless scraps of paper which foamed about his feet wherever he went, you would say that those hieroglyphics represented the efforts of some modern necromancer to discover the Elixir of Life, or of some abstruse mathematician to plunge into a new dimension. You would hardly have guessed that it was merely Mr Stanley's effort to establish whether Golightly would beat Angel's Kiss in the two o'clock next Friday at Doncaster. But to judge from the decades that Mr Stanley had been doomed, and was still doomed, to spend at his shoemaking, you would have concluded that there was not much to choose among these various occupations in the way of hopelessness.

Now and again Mr Stanley fell upon hours of deep gloom. His most infallible systems of divination seemed as fallible as all the others. It was in times like these that a demon of doubt assailed him. Perhaps there *was* no such thing as a system. Perhaps it was *all* a combination of chance and crookedness. His whole edifice of abstruse calculation tottered about him. With a sudden spasm of fury he lunged forward with his fist and sent it scattering.

It did not occur to him at such a time to abandon his betting and apply himself with more zeal to his shoemaking. Had not Johnnie Grey, who now owned half a dozen theatres in London, started off his fortune at a horse's bridle, and him nobbut a trolley-boy on the Oldham trams? He did not give up his betting. Instead, having trusted so vainly to his honourable, elaborate and ill-starred systems, he became the blindest devotee of chance and dreams. He would run after a scrap of paper caught in an eddy and allow his eye to catch a word upon it. If the two initial letters of the word were contained in the name of one of the day's starters, he backed it. He slept with a pencil by his bedside to jot down some promising image that his dreams might present to him. Or he consulted his wife anxiously and shamefacedly to see if she had dreamed anything useful. But his wife was a stolid woman and she did not dream often, and when she dreamed, it was in German. She was not of much use.

Normally speaking the Jews on the opposite pavement had no place at all in the universe of Mr Stanley. He did not mend their shoes for them. They had no data to offer on the subject of the Cesarewitch or United's match next week, away, against Aston Villa. They did not exist for him.

Excepting only during those periods of totemism. Then, really, Mr Stanley presented as edifying a spectacle as some equatorial savage, necklaced with cowrie shells, all of a flutter with taboos and mutterings and eyeball-rollings. He became alertly conscious of the little Jewish boys with their brown eyes and their curly hair, playing on their own pavement. He became conscious of them as people do of the gypsies who congregate on the downs and meadows round race-tracks on big days. And somewhat in the same manner he approached them, feeling at once desperate and silly. He would give them pennies and bid them close their eyes and circle with a pin over the day's list of probable starters. He could scarcely breathe with the suspense of it as the pin circled and then swooped, upon some fifty-to-one outsider, it may be. He sweated with excitement. Next day he put his shirt upon it, smiling to himself darkly. He tried to persuade the clients of the Lamb and Lion to stake their shirts too. But they were sceptical. Sometimes the little Jew boys picked a winner for him. Much more frequently they did not. It was a difficult business.

But it was all very different during the Edelman-Wright epoch. Somehow he couldn't go wrong. He kept buzzing about from pavement to pavement, just giving tips, in the way Jessie Wright gave flowers and Mrs Seipel gave egg-cakes. He emerged from the twilight of his laboratory into the easy sunlight. He consulted no oracles. He gave tips, and they were lucky ones. He had given tips for ages in the Lamb and Lion, so they didn't do anything about it, most of them. But the Jews put five shillings on each way, just because it seemed unfriendly not to. And for a week or two outsider after outsider that Mr Stanley had recommended came romping home. Mr Stanley didn't say: "I told you so!" Although he himself did not happen to back any winner, he went about with his head in the air. At one and the same time he decided that his success was the fine flower of his studies, and that absolutely all you had to do to succeed was to name the first horse that came into your head, before you had time to think of another one.

Mr Emmanuel, for instance, found himself ridiculously richer by five pounds ten, and all he remembered doing was to say yes, he would, when Mr Stanley asked him would he. It had something to do with a two shilling piece, and he was certain he had not even handed it over to Mr Stanley. He had been spending his winnings violently, yet he still had a lot left. He was Clerk to the Jewish Board of Guardians, who looked after the interests of the Jewish poor of Doomington; and though he was not fated to be of much practical use to humanity in the millennial schemes he expounded from public platforms, from his swivel-chair in his office he performed countless acts of unrecorded benevolence. In that small arena, he had a gimlet eye to distinguish the false from the true. The false had short shrift from him; the true received the benefit of prolonged and devoted hours, spent either at his desk or tramping about the countryside among the houses of rich people.

He often did not see eye to eye with the Board over the merits of the applicants for their help. So when he won five pounds ten he bought Mrs Levitsky a load of coal, for it was cheaper in the summer, and her bronchitis always came on that bad in the winter months. He also bought a chicken and two dozen eggs for Mrs Braunstein, who had had a baby. He had recently sold his album of foreign stamps to keep Mr Finestone in the country a week longer. Mr Emmanuel was a keen collector of foreign stamps, it was such an international hobby. So now, having won five pounds ten, he started his collection again humbly, with cheap packets of Forty Assorted, Price One Shilling.

But Mr Emmanuel had not only won five pounds ten. His son, Max, who painted, had just won a prize in an art competition organised by the Art Gallery authorities. A writer in a newspaper had said: "That young man will go far. If he is really fifteen, he is a genius. If he is fifty, he is still a genius." One or two old women, and a journalist or two, had already used this same word, "genius," regarding young Max. To Max it was no more than if they had said "turnip" or "Saskatchewan." He hadn't any feeling for words. He just went on thrusting away with his paint-brushes or tracing a long curve with his charcoal, delicately, almost lewdly.

Mr Emmanuel didn't like the painting which won the Art Gallery prize. It represented a fat lady in blue tights sitting on a low flight of doorsteps. They were, in fact, the doorsteps of his own house in Magnolia Street, and the fat lady had a face suspiciously like Bella Winberg. Mr Emmanuel did not think painting much of a career, it was too self-centred. Of course, he was not old-fashioned and stupid about it. He knew there was good money in certain forms of art, and that the artists who drew the frocks in the women's magazines could earn ten pounds a week at it, and more. But the boy was not shaping that way at all. He hadn't any interest in people. Above all, he had no interest in Love.

Yet Mr Emmanuel couldn't pretend he wasn't proud of his son for winning the prize, even if paintings of fat ladies in blue tights don't help people to love each other. And there was still quite a lot of the five pounds ten left that Mr Stanley's wizardry had conjured out of the void for him. And he was happy, he was terribly happy. The reign of Love, as between the Jews and gentiles, was beginning. He didn't delude himself. Magnolia Street was only a small street and an obscure one. But it was a beginning. The good word would go like the odour of lime-blossom from street to street, from district to district. From Doomington to Liverpool, from Liverpool to Birmingham...

He stopped. He found he was pacing up and down the parlour delivering a speech. His wife, Slatta, looked on with adoring eyes.

"Tell them, Slatta," he bade her, "tell them all to come in on Sunday afternoon. We shall have a party."

"Yes," she whispered, "of course I'll tell them. Go on," she urged him. "Yes? From Liverpool to Birmingham...?"

So the Emmanuels had a party that Sunday afternoon and nearly the whole street came in. It was a good thing that the party looked after itself. There was a lot to eat and drink and everybody knew everybody and there was a good deal of joking and even a little kissing and things went on merrily. The Emmanuels were not good hosts, really. It was the small boy, David, who did all the fetching and opening that was necessary. Mr Emmanuel could not resist treating the party as a public meeting and addressing speeches at it. Max was rather surly. He sat behind a plant-pot, dabbing at his sketch-book — the curve of a nose, the way an eyebrow went.

He sat there for quite a long time, not saying a word to anybody. He did not like to have Magnolia Street bang up against him. He did not notice the two small girls who came in, the one about twelve, small and dark and Jewish, the other, only a year or so older, but fair, tall, gentile. He was not aware of the adoration with which the eyes of the younger rested on the face, the not thrillingly beautiful face, of the elder girl. Only when the elder girl, finding something that the younger had said incredibly funny, threw back her head and laughed, only then did Max Emmanuel lift his head from his sketch-book.

It was not a noise that belonged to these noises nor by any means a cruel noise. It was a clear pleasant tinkle, like spring water. It was not a face that belonged to these faces, with its fine hair, thin nose, its suspicion of a cleft in the chin. He knew who she was. She was Enid Cooper from across the street. The small girl was Jane Seipel. His pencil dropped from his hand. His sketch-book slid from his knee. It was very rarely indeed that his pencil and sketch-book behaved so. Enid Cooper stopped laughing. Max made no effort to retrieve his things, so she bent down for them. He bent too. Their hands met. She smiled. He smiled back, with a queer promptness, a sense of recognition. Jane Seipel noticed nothing. She would not have noticed it much if the wall had sagged a bit. Her hand lay warm in the cool hand of her adored.

For this bliss, too, Benny Edelman was responsible. Redoubtable Benny! Enid Cooper had come walking up to Jane at school, during the recess, just as if she were any ordinary mortal.

"I live in your street," she said.

Jane blushed a peony-red.

"Isn't it fun," Enid continued, "the way that great big clumsy fellow rescued the little boy?"

Janey's eyes shone. It was true. It was true. The goddess *had* stepped out of a cloud. The goddess *was* addressing her with her own lips.

"Yes," whispered Jane, "isn't it fun!"

Then came Saturday, two days later. They spent the afternoon in Layton Park. Enid told her the names of flowers. Enid said: "We'll take lunch together and buy a glass of milk when we get there. And ice-cream," said Enid.

And to-day it had occurred to Jane that Enid might like to come to the Emmanuel party. And it had occurred to Enid that this might be fun, too. So it was that Max Emmanuel met Enid Cooper, and did not for a long time meet her again.

"I hope," said Max, "you're not being bored."

"It's perfectly lovely," said Enid.

Jane went on staring, round-eyed.

"They're *good* faces," Enid continued.

"You mean," said Max excitedly, "good to draw? They are. How clever you are!"

"You must do Jane's some day," she insisted. Both their faces turned round towards Jane. She had not moved. With the eye that was invisible to Jane, Enid winked. It was a tolerant good-humoured wink. Max winked back.

"I will!" he said. "Shall I draw you some day, Jane?"

"No! Do Enid!"

He looked at Enid. "I shan't be able to," he said slowly. "I don't know why."

"I wonder," Enid murmured. A small boy was offering her cakes. "This is your brother, isn't it?" she asked "Thank you, so much."

"Yes, that's David."

"He's a genius," said David shyly. "The paper said so!"

"You go and look after mamma," said Max. "She looks thirsty."

"Mamma, mamma!" David tugged at her skirt. "Do have somethink, won't you, mamma?"

Jane sat on, holding Enid's hand. Enid and Max talked, they did not quite know what about, but they talked easily, as if they had met often and talked much. Max's mother listened — but it was to her husband she listened. Her husband had rehearsed his speeches before her for twenty years, so she had got the habit of

162

listening. Whether she definitely bent her mind to them or not, it is certain that something of their general purport must have seeped in. She was a lady of two minds. She could never quite decide whether her first duty lay by humanity at large, or by her husband and their children. The other women in Magnolia Street voted for their husbands and children. But then they were not married to Isaac Emmanuel. She was tremendously proud of him, and her pride was not abated by the fact that he hurt her feelings all the time by omitting her from his schemes and organisings. His family, somehow, did not seem to belong to that humanity which was to be welded together in a seccotine of universal love. Slatta was only his wife. Moisheh, Max, David, were only his children.

But Slatta Emmanuel, also, had utopian and millennial leanings. How could she not, after being married so long to such a husband? She did not think she could address a crowd as eloquently as Isaac. But she felt that Isaac ought to give her a chance. Did not Edith Zangwill accompany Israel Zangwill on platforms and hold her own very creditably indeed? She had recently spoken just after her husband at the Doomington Hippodrome and had brought the house down. Slatta Emmanuel figured herself, too, in a picture hat, like Edith Zangwill, holding a small posy of flowers in her hand, and enchanting a multitude.

Or she might at least be allowed to come on the platform, like the less eloquent wives of other public personages, and sit at Isaac's right hand, and smile all the time, and nod pleasantly to an acquaintance from Magnolia Street occasionally, and show the world an example of what universal love did for you.

But Isaac Emmanuel did not see it like that. Isaac knew best. She sat and listened and worshipped that evening at the party, while little David went round quietly, asking people to have another slice of cake.

It was David who found out that the Seipels hadn't come yet. He plucked at his mother's skirt again: "Mamma, mamma," he whispered. "The Seipels! They've not come yet!"

"Yes, yes," his mother murmured, but he knew she had not taken in what he said. She was unable to switch her mind away from his father's eloquence, and there was no chance of that stopping for some time yet. So he slipped off on his own accord and went to the Seipels and asked them why they had not come. The whole party was held up waiting for them. So the Seipels came, and brought the Reczniks with them, and the Recznik gladness was incorporated in the Emmanuel gladness which was part and parcel of the Edelman-Wright gladness which made Magnolia Street sweeter than Eden during those early summer weeks in 1910.

Mrs Recznik emerges only briefly out of the obscurity of Lavender Street, and disappears almost at once. She had been deserted by her temperamental husband about a week earlier. She was aware, like all unhappy wives in Longton, that number nineteen Magnolia Street was sanctuary, particularly for ill-treated or deserted wives. So she came, as by the operation of a law of nature, to number nineteen with her three children and occupied the parlour and the best bedroom. Then, this Sunday afternoon, Mr Recznik returned, found out where his wife was, and came along weeping and wailing and strewing his hair with ashes. He was so wild with joy at being reunited with his family, that he kissed Mrs Recznik, the small Reczniks, Reb Feivel, Mr and Mrs Seipel, and Sam, Eli and Berel Seipel, with fury all over their faces. The fury was such that they were sore for days after. For Mr Recznik had a beard like barbed wire and had not shaved all week, the lady from Babylon had kept him so busy.

And then David Emmanuel came along with his message. So the Seipels went to the party and took the Reczniks with them. Mr Recznik had by no means calmed down. He had hardly entered the Emmanuels' parlour when he started the kissing all over again. He spared nobody. It wasn't pleasant, but it certainly helped things to go with a swing. The girl Seipel, Janey, came in a little time later with a girl friend.

And then Mr Poyser the grocer was there, and his daughter, Becky; Mr Poyser looked less secret and sepulchral than usual. He always did, as soon as he got away from Mrs Poyser. He did not have much joy out of his wife. She was too much of an institution for that, like the Board of Shechita or Trial by Jury.

But there were dark undeclared places where Mr Poyser was alone. In those places other ones reckoned with him, he had attained Heaven knew what degree of cabalistic efficiency. He wore tiny badges in his lapel from which initiated eyes might learn what degree of efficiency it was. It was said of him that he was not only a Freemason and a member of the Independent Order of B'nei Brith, but a Rechabite, a Buffalo, an Oddfellow and a Zionist. That must have been an exaggeration and an overlapping. He was certainly a member of the Independent Order of B'nei Brith and a Zionist. In those days people still spoke of Zionists as if they constituted a secret murder society. There were large photographs of Mr Poyser on Mrs Poyser's walls, wearing sashes and chains and medals and other insignia. There were framed testimonials to his incomparable worth as an Hon. Treasurer to this or that society over so many years. Sometimes he went forth in strange headgear and strange garments, concealed under an overcoat, to incredible conventions. Not even Mrs Poyser asked for information about these. She stood aside and watched him disappear into the night to fulfil those mysterious assignations.

He was not wearing any of his robes at the Emmanuel party, and he would have liked to. They would have made him look a little more imposing. But they could not have made him happier. Becky sat beside him, looking very happy, too. Each of them was still happier because the other one was happy. And the reason was not a monumental one. It was merely that Mrs Poyser was not there. A cold in the nose kept her at home.

Becky looked almost pretty. Perhaps it is too much to say that. With her pale grey eyes, her very red hair, her freckles, her big bones, she could never look that. But she knew she was her father's love and solace, as she was her mother's love and tribulation. She was not of a type which appeals to the Jewish young man. She was already twenty-two, and there was no young man, not even a nibble of a young man. Mrs Poyser felt it an implied criticism of herself that Becky had no young man. She wanted Becky to provide her with a race of grandchildren, so that when all her own children were married, and herself retired from the grocery-shop, she might still have an audience upon whom to lavish her intelligence and eloquence.

But Becky was very shy, because her bones were so big and her hair so red... She didn't dislike young men, but she was incapable of taking the initiative with them, and that seemed the only way in which she was likely to provide her mother with grandchildren. Mrs Poyser put a piano into the living-room, though it was already so chock-full of sacks of sugar and flour that you would have thought it impossible to introduce a foot-stool. Becky Poyser had piano lessons, but her scales and arpeggios did not tempt the passing young man to loiter. Becky Poyser had singing-lessons, but this produced no result either.

So Becky turned to her father, and her father to Becky. They were more like lovers than father and daughter. And Mr Poyser sat on Mr Emmanuel's sofa squeezing his daughter's hand, and both gaped with happiness, because Mrs Poyser was at home, and of late her eloquence had been almost too much to bear. Mr Poyser did not care a damn if the line cast by all this piano-playing and voice-training did not ever land a young man. He was selfish. He knew it. In the privacy of his own heart he stamped his foot defiantly. He wanted to keep his daughter all to himself for ever, to the last red hair on her head and her last freckle.

He didn't do any foot-stamping at the Emmanuel party. Nor did Becky have to sing or play the piano. That was another reason for their being so happy. They could just sit still, no parlour-tricks were expected from them. But one thing was quite definitely going on that afternoon. A young man, a gentile, was flirting, actually flirting, with Becky. He was a friend of the barber, Arthur Durbin. "Won't you try just this once?" he kept on urging her. "It's good for you!" He thrust a glass of beer under her nose. "No!" she said, of course. "I never take anything stronger than lemonade." It was a reply, uttered in a tone which would have numbed most young men. But it seemed to encourage Arthur Durbin's friend. He kept on cracking nuts for her, and then, as bold as brass, he came and sat down on the sofa beside her, though there was really no room at all. His thigh lay plumb along hers.

Undoubtedly Arthur Durbin's friend was one reason why Becky was looking almost pretty that evening. But friendly is friendly, and when a gentile gentleman positively pushes his knee into your leg, a decent Jewish girl can only squeeze her father's hand tighter and turn her back on such impudence. But the way she turned her head once or twice, and threw a coy look over her shoulder, was like a play. You would hardly have thought Becky Poyser capable of it.

Benny Edelman was in good form that evening. His jokes were simple but hearty. He removed chairs from under people just when they were going to sit down and poured lemonade down

166

people's backs. He was really just a great boy. As was only right and proper, he too, had come in handsomely on the Stanley stakes. He had put five shillings on a couple of rank outsiders which brought off the most breath-taking double of the season. He was up a good eleven pounds.

"And what," asked Arthur Durbin, friendly like, "are you going to do with all that money, Benny?"

Benny's mind at the moment was somewhere else. He was trying to arrange for Albert Durbin to sit down on a drawing pin.

"Oh, I suppose it'll have to go into the business!" he replied, off-hand.

"Business? What business?" asked a chorus of voices. No one till then had connected Benny with any opening-up of businesses. Benny suddenly realised he had said what he had no intention of saying. He blushed. "I was only joking!" he said. It was said later by Mrs Carter that she quite clearly saw Jessie Wright kick Benny hard under the table. But that may have been just wisdom after the event. Further enquiries were drowned in the howl emitted by Albert Durbin as he sat down on the drawing-pin prepared for him. The howl was drowned in roars of laughter. The roars of laughter were trebled when Arthur Durbin's friend suddenly pounced forward in a practised manner and kissed Becky Poyser full on the cheek. The party went on from strength to strength. It went on late enough for both the Tawnies to come across from the Lamb and Lion after closing time. It really became almost noisy enough to challenge comparison with a Derricks party. But for the Derricks hate, it substituted the Emmanuel love. That was the keynote of it. Mr Emmanuel was hoarse, he had done so much orating. His head tottered on his long neck, as if a sudden draught would snap it off.

Yet it must be admitted that after the Hubbard episode, though the noise still went on, it was only noise, an automatic backwash of noise. The more Mr Emmanuel reflected on that during the next few days, the clearer he saw it was so.

Dolly Hubbard had come in to the party almost last of all. Her husband, Walter, the tram-conductor, didn't like her to go into other people's houses, Jews or no Jews. It wasn't that he wasn't pleased with Benny Edelman for saving Tommie Wright. He was, like everyone else in Magnolia Street. He stood him more than one pint, several nights running in the private bar. But he didn't like Dolly to go to any houses where young men were. He didn't like them to come into his own house. He didn't even like young women to come in, though all other women than Dolly were just shadows to him, not flesh and blood. He was relieved when they left.

But young men, men of any age, never came at all; not even the local secretary of the YMCA, nor the lay preachers from the Primitive Methodist Chapel in Upper Longton, where the Hubbards regularly attended. If, by any chance, some man did come into the house — the gasman, for instance — the odd film did not come down over Hubbard's eyes through which he saw women as shadows. A light seemed to spurt up behind his eyeballs. He saw them with a devastating clearness, not so much as men, but as creatures with questing hands and dangerous loins. He shuffled and twisted about on his chair, a faint dampness on his brow; and then, when the visitor left, he raced over to Dolly with a beating heart and held her so close to him that she cried out, and kissed her mouth so long that she was forced to break free for breath.

To the neighbours it seemed that the Hubbards were the sweetest couple for miles around. They knew that Walter was by way of being jealous, but quite a few of the wives would have liked their own husbands to be a lot more jealous. They envied Dolly that her husband loved her so fiercely after four years of married life, and no children either.

And as a matter of fact, apart from this one embarrassing trait in Walter's character, there wasn't a man in all Doomington Dolly would rather have for a husband. It was a good thing to know that you meant more to a man than his food and drink; lots of the women round about couldn't say any such thing. She blushed happily to think how much he loved her; she had rosy cheeks and they were like poppies now. You couldn't deny it was nice to know that, wherever Walter went, there wasn't a bit of skirt in the kingdom, however toffed up it was, whatever sort of goo-goo eyes it made at him, could make him stop thinking of her for one single moment.

He was always bringing her in little presents, and it was that rather more than any natural distaste that made him into a virtual teetotaller and a non-smoker. As a trolley-boy, to tell the truth, he had got into rather bad company. The trolley-boys of

Longton were rather a fast lot and some of them drank and smoked like any full-blown inspector. He still had a bit of a craving for his pint and his packet of Woodbines, but you couldn't spend money on such things often and bring in a pound-box of chocolates for Dolly on pay day, or a pot of freesias, perhaps, or half a dozen little hankies, hemmed with lace.

But the fact remained. He did not want her to go into houses where young men were. It so happened, however, that on this particular Emmanuel Sunday, Walter had to go off to a meeting of YMCA secretaries; and time lay very heavy on Dolly's hands. So she thought she would slip over to the Emmanuels for a few minutes. What harm could it do? All the street was there to look after her, anyway. She therefore waited till Miss Tregunter's bedtime had come and gone a full half-hour, and then she went across.

But she reckoned without Miss Tregunter. Even from her bed, like a ship's captain on his bridge, she seemed to remain on guard over the decencies of the gentile pavement. Miss Tregunter knew she had gone to a house where Jews, young men, moreover, were. And certainly Dolly stayed longer than she intended, it was such a nice break.

A knock came at the door. David Emmanuel opened it and came back into the parlour looking rather scared. Before he had time to say anything, Walter Hubbard showed up in the door behind him. His face looked almost green. His eyes were staring out of his head.

"Hello, Walter boy!" shouted Steve Tawnie.

But it might have been a cat whimpering for all the notice Walter took of him. Dolly said not a word. In an instant her face became as green as her husband's. She rose to her feet. He turned round. She followed him. The others tried to laugh it off; but it was not easy.

Walter still said not a word to Dolly as they crossed the roadway and entered the house. He was not angry. It was not anger that came upon him at these times. She busied herself with a kettle and tea things. Walter could always do with a strong cup of tea at night. He sat down at the table and opened his Bible. But the Bible said nothing to him tonight. He opened his photograph-album, for he was a talented photographer, but he paid little attention to his prints, either. He watched her out of the corner of his eye, as if she might have smuggled a young man in with her as they opened the door, and she were only awaiting the moment when he was thoroughly absorbed, to slip up into the bedroom, and sink into his arms.

No. The back of the Emmanuel party was broken after Walter Hubbard came and took Dolly off with him. The noise went on for a good hour perhaps. Then it subsided. The guests began to go. Albert Durbin was the last of them. He wanted to talk sociology to Mr Emmanuel, and Mr Emmanuel was far too gentle to tell him how tired he was. So they stood at least five minutes on the doorstep, while Albert went on about John Stuart Mill, on and on. Then Albert stopped at length, and said good night.

And all this time Mr Emmanuel was conscious of a figure standing in the darkness on the pavement opposite. He made out the broad-brimmed hat, the bulging overcoat, the thick walking-stick, of Ben Stern, the missionary. A phantom ray of light twinkled on the thick lenses of his spectacles.

He stood there, a few yards away, as if the distance interposed between the pavements were broad as a sea, as a prairie. He stood there hesitating during all the long minutes that Albert Durbin went on sociologising. At last, when Albert left, he seemed to make up his mind to cross the road. His body lunged forward. A thrill of loathing crept up Mr Emmanuel's spine. Quickly he went into his own house and closed the door behind him.

Chapter 11

I

Mr Emmanuel stood upon his doorstep, the tip of his nose twitching slightly. A scent of soot drifted down upon his nostrils. A lustre was going out of the air, so palpably, it seemed to him, that if he lifted his hands and held hard, he might prevent it from going. From day to day the Edelman-Wright festivities continued, but the heart was going out of them. It was not only Walter Hubbard who, in his jealousy, had carried his wife away from a house where young men were. It was Miss Tregunter who had stretched forth a skinny claw. It was the gentile pavement claiming its own again. It was the beginning of the end of Love, which had seemed likely out of this small seed to grow into a tree that would spread branches cool and far.

Mr Emmanuel was, like most idealists, a lonely man. If he was aware of his wife's pathetic anxiety to identify herself with his causes, he was egotist enough to regard her with little more than good-humoured contempt. Or it may have been the atavistic contempt of the oriental for his female chattel. He had hoped for discipleship in one or the other of his three sons, but he had not found it. The eldest, Moisheh, was the pure essence of lout, so far as he could see. There was nothing to be hoped for from Moisheh. In Max, the painter, however, he was bitterly disappointed. He hardly expected in his own life-time to see masters and workmen kissing each other and the nations strewing each other with rose petals. He had sometimes hoped that in Max a son was born to him who would take the torch from his dying hand and jump on to the platform he had vacated, and in shriller, sweeter, more coherent language cry: "Love one another!"

But the boy was not like that. He was completely wrapped up in himself and his paint-box. Isaac Emmanuel sometimes felt so hostile towards him that he wanted to gather up his blocks and brushes and tubes and hurl them into the fire. But he did not, of course. He was too gentle for that. It was true he could behave disastrously when aroused, excepting with Moisheh, who intimidated him. But both the younger boys often bore for days a blue weal on the arm-muscle where their father had screwed it between finger and thumb in a sudden access of fury. These rages terrified him as much as they terrified them. But he could not manufacture them. He could not go up of set purpose to the boys' room and destroy Max's blocks and tubes, as he was often tempted to.

There remained the small boy, David. David was not clever. He would certainly never be able to mount platforms and proclaim the gospel. He had a religion, it was true. Mr Emmanuel was the only person who was aware of David's religion. Its name was Max. It sometimes made Mr Emmanuel white with anger to observe the deep and quiet adoration of the younger for the elder brother. The anger had a deal of jealousy in it. Nobody adored *him* in that dumb blind manner. Excepting his wife, of course; but he did not count her. So, in a manner of speaking, Mr Emmanuel was quite alone in his house in Magnolia Street. He was a busy man. He had a great deal to do at the Board of Guardians, and he imposed a great deal on himself outside of that. But it was only with the top of his brain he did that work. Lower down it was concerned with deeper problems. On platform after platform he stood swaying, expounding love to all men. He demanded that masters and workmen should love each other, and proved how they did; till a lock-out or a strike occurred, and his face flared up as if someone had struck it. He also proved, like Albert Durbin the barber, but on ethnical rather than sociological grounds, that wars were unthinkable, till the Great War broke out. Then his big head lunged and lolled about as loosely on his high neck as a child's balloon on its string mooring.

Throughout he saw Magnolia Street as an epitome, sharing with one other person in the same street the faculty of standing away from it, of seeing in it something greater than itself. That other person was Mary Cooper. It is to be confessed that their two names are a strange collocation; but if they had had an opportunity to meet and talk together quietly for some hours, it would have been a precious thing for both of them. Only once, only briefly, do they utter a few words to each other, and that is at the very end of our tale.

These two saw in Magnolia Street the working folk of the Jews and the English reduced to their quintessence. But whereas for her, impotent and embittered, there was nothing but melancholy in that spectacle, to him, impotent and sanguine, it was a perpetual excitement. He was aware, as she was, of the stability that reigned upon the gentile pavement and the unquiet heaving among the Jews. The stability that was to her stagnation, was to him a state of contentedness. These *goyim* lived in their own land, in the unconscious enjoyment of antique traditions and present pleasures. They streamed out upon Saturday afternoons to football matches, they streamed in upon Saturday evenings to public-houses. They so loved Vesta Tilley, that when they heard her announce that all the nice girls love a sailor, they seemed ready to eat her. When the cricket matches were played against their kinsmen in the antipodes, they could neither eat nor drink till they learned how the score stood at the close of play.

As for the Jews, every element in their confusion thrilled him. The elder ones did not feel themselves to be in their own land. They looked backward to Poland and Russia, they looked forward to America. But he saw the hearts of the younger Jews divided in another way. Not all of them wanted to 'get on.' In these few years of their boyhood and girlhood they had become more impregnated with England than other foreigners might in two generations. He saw the small boys conforming to the type of the small boys opposite. They played football and cricket and studied the team-scores with, if anything, more passion. They became, or yearned to be, 'sports' and 'decent chaps.' Just as successfully the little Jewish girls were becoming English 'misses'.

He was also aware of one more element in the heaving and seething. There was a type of Jew, both among the younger and the older folk, who had not known felicity in Russia, and would not in America, and were not at ease in England, though this was the gentlest of the lands. They looked forward to Zion. Each year with resonance they declared: *'Leshonoh Habo Berusholayim* — Next Year in Jerusalem!' To some it seemed a heartbreaking dream. Some said: 'Let us only get down to it, acquiring a *dunam* here and a *dunam* there, whilst our politicians do what they can in the Chancelleries of Europe!' None guessed how amazingly, in how few years, something of their dream would be accomplished.

But not these were the thoughts that eddied in the unlucid waters of Mr Emmanuel's mind as he came to his doorstep once and again and looked out upon the street, in the days that followed his party. His face had something of the expression of a child who has convinced himself that he is building a sand-castle in which he will really be able to live, and ask his friends to come and stay with him; and then he sees that the tide has turned, and is coming closer minute by minute, and that the foundations of his house will soon be brown slush.

The parties actually were still going on, though a little spectrally. Some of the lads, however, henceforth totally disregarded the fact that a cleft had been set down between the odd and even pavements. They were of the generation that a few years hence were to fight in the same trenches and be lousy with the same lice and mute with the same glory. So the lads went off again to Doomington Zoo and the roller-skating rink. And Jane Seipel still went out walking in Layton Park with her divinity, Enid Cooper. But that was hardly a party, of course.

The gentile women still dropped in to Mrs Poyser's, but not so regularly. The Jewish youths for some reason felt themselves not quite at ease in the Durbin barber-saloon and resumed their patronage of Mr Cohen, the Jewish barber in Blenheim Road.

Mr Emmanuel blamed himself partly. He had hardly been into the private bar since the first great night of the merry-making. If he had kept on going in, Mr Seipel and the others would doubtless have kept on going in, too. But the beer he had drunk that night really had made him feel ill. He provided it at his own party, naturally, but he tried to keep his nose away from it. And then he had a lot of extra work to do lately, and his ordinary work had been disorganised by all these excitements. So he had not been in to the private bar for a number of days now.

He stood on his doorstep feeling very dejected, a Canute bidding the tide turn. But the tide kept on sliding forward.

"No!" he thought. "I won't have it! It mustn't all go to pieces! Such a wonderful beginning! It may not come again in my whole lifetime!"

His head swayed and swung. He wondered what he could do. What can I do? What can I do?

"Oh well!" he sighed. "I'll go in and have a pint with them anyhow, at the Lamb and Lion to-night!"

He knew it was not much. But he had a dim memory of a little Dutch boy he had read about. The little Dutch boy put his thumb into the hole which the sea made in a dyke and held the breach for hours and hours against the whole force of the sea, till it turned at length, defeated, and he saved Holland.

He, too, would put his thumb into the hole. It might be given to him, too, to save Holland. So he went in that night to the Lamb and Lion.

"Good evening, all!" exclaimed Mr Emmanuel as he entered the private bar, doing his best not to make it sound like "Mr Chairman, Ladies and Gentlemen!"

"Well I never!" exclaimed Maggie Tawnie heartily.

"If it isn't Mr Emmanuel! What a stranger!"

Mr Emmanuel winced. What a stranger! He would rather have been greeted with any words than those.

"What's yours, Mr Emmanuel?" asked one or two voices. He would like to have answered a lemonade. "Oh thanks very much, Mr Stanley. A bitter, I think! Oh but it's on me! You mustn't forget that five pounds ten!"

"Don't mention it! But if you'd backed Daffodil last Tuesday and put it all on Dragoman, same as I told Steve —"

"And did you back 'em yourself, Frank?"

"That's got nothing to do with it! What I say is this here —" he began rather shrilly.

"Now quiet, quiet!" requested his wife. She looked at her husband affectionately. His dark eyes, bright mouth, swinging hips, had all the enchantment for her which made her forswear her country nearly a score of years ago.

"All right, Elsa old lady!" He loved her, too, in the time he had to spare from his figures and scraps of paper.

"A wonderful innings!" Mr Briggs was saying. Mr Briggs was reviewing the week-end cricket. "He carried his bat right through. I never saw anything like it. How many sixes did he knock up, did you say?"

Mr Emmanuel had not backed Daffodil last Tuesday and put it all on Dragoman. He did not know how many sixes he had knocked up, and who had knocked them up. They had already forgotten he was here, most of them. They were not hostile in the least, they were kindly people. They had merely forgotten he was here. He looked round for Benny Edelman. He too, had stopped coming, apparently. He was not here. Neither was Jessie Wright. She would come soon, he thought. She did not come.

He tried hard to think of a little billiards or cricket small-talk. He had been reading of a big boxing match in Paris, but he could not remember the names. He could only think of one celebrity in the sport world.

"Talking about Hackenschmidt —" he started uncertainly.

But nobody had been talking about Hackenschmidt. They all stopped for a moment, politely. But Mr Emmanuel could not think of anything to say about Hackenschmidt, either. "Strong man!" he muttered. "Oh yes," someone else muttered, "Very strong man!" Then the conversation resumed its former courses.

There was the usual traffic every now and again at the Jug and Bottle Department, and Kate Ritchie came and asked for her pint. One or two of Leah Winter's *fire-goyahs* came and asked for theirs. So did a few other men and women strangers. Then came a rapping which everybody recognised, except Mr Emmanuel, who was no expert. It was a timid and defiant rapping — the rapping of Henry Derricks, which had not been heard much the last two or three weeks.

"Good evening, Henry!" proclaimed Maggie Tawnie, as always, before she had slid the panel aside.

"Good evening, all!" said Henry.

"Evening, Henry!"

He placed two enormous jugs on the ledge before him.

"Haven't you got nothing bigger at home, Henry?"

"Only the bathtub!" replied Henry with spirit.

"Big party tonight?"

"All the old gang!"

"Mind you don't get tiddly, Henry!"

"Don't cuddle the red-haired ones! They're the dangerous sort!"

Henry promised he wouldn't. "Thank you, Maggie!" He blinked nervously all round. "Goodnight, all!"

"Goodnight, Henry!"

He withdrew. At the moment that he withdrew from the Jug and Bottle, Mr Emmanuel withdrew from the private bar. He remembered he had a long journey to make to get some money out of a rich manufacturer for the baby-crèche he was trying to get up in Longton, for gentile and Jewish babies. He was aware that no-one noticed his going. There was a taste of dust on his tongue and the rims of his eyelids were smarting, as if there had been pepper in the air.

There had not been what you might call a party at the Derrickses for some time, not since the beginning of the Edelman-Wright business, in fact. The Boys had dropped in at Mother Derricks's now and again, but they had never felt the atmosphere propitious for the starting up of a party. They were not a brave company. They felt their sort of party wouldn't be popular for the time being. So they waited. More discreet than brave, they were accurate judges of the psychological moment. They felt now, that if they had a party, they would not need to cramp their style. So they sent Henry out with a couple of large jugs. Mrs Derricks got busy with a great steaming dish of faggots.

Henry brought in the beer duly, but the Boys did not ask him to stay, nor did he want to. He knew that before the evening was over, all the photo-frames he had fretted, and the cigarette boxes, and the menu-card-holders, would be smashed like eggshells between the fingers of the Pocket Samson. He couldn't bear the sight of that, or the smell of the beer, so he was much better up in his room, fretworking.

It was really no tribute to the Pocket Samson's powers to be able to smash all those fretwork 'novelties,' as they were called, any child could do it. But perhaps it was a good thing. It gave Henry something to set his mind on, while the high jinks went on downstairs. He turned himself assiduously to the manufacture of more menu-card-holders. It may have been his own secret and tender dream that some day someone would put menu-cards in those menu-card-holders. But the menu at Mrs Derricks's parties did not vary sufficiently to justify the use of them. There was beer and faggots, or tripe and beer, or beer and black puddings. Sometimes there were winkles, too, or pigs' trotters, or cow-heels.

In the meanwhile, downstairs, his son, the Nightingale, was sending forth his voice.

It was as a Nightingale, a boy-singer, that Wilfred made his appearance in all the shoddy little variety theatres from Bradford to Runcorn. He had one or two engagements as the cheeky little boy in pantomime; but they did not re-engage him. His joking sent a shudder round the audience. It made them cough uncomfortably, they felt so awkward. It was exactly so with his military audiences at a later date. He returned, therefore, to sing songs of Araby and tales of fair Kashmir and to wish that those lips could only speak, those eyes could only see, those beautiful golden tresses were there in reality. It was a fairly pretty voice, though he had to twist his mouth grotesquely before he could use it. In order to fill even a small theatre he had to pull his face into such frightful contortions, that you thought he must snap those delicate jaw-bones.

Bridget Derricks was his mother and he was the apple of her eye. He stood to her in a double relationship. She petted him and coaxed him and kissed him as if he were truly the small boy he seemed at first glance to be. He was also her friend, her confidant, the mature son of thirty, almost everything a husband might have been.

Also, she was afraid of him. If anything crossed him, a demon seemed to get hold of him. Only the day before he had gone to the tin trunk under her bed where she kept her new hat. Spitting like some small beast, he dug his even teeth into it, and tore it into shreds and danced on it. Some days earlier he had filled her shoes with treacle, and pulled the kitchen tablecloth from the table with its load of cups and plates. It was as if the wretched spirit inside him, which had kept growing from decade to decade within the monstrous little body which had not kept pace with it, at length found too much for it its accumulated exacerbation. It was always his mother he treated so, as if in some obscure manner it was she whom he blamed for his misfortune. If he did not ignore his father, he treated him kindly. He bought him some three-ply wood or a new fret-saw.

That was another reason why both mother and son wanted to have a party. After destroying the new hat, he went off to bed and stuffed the pillow into his mouth, and kicked the eiderdown beneath him in his misery and moaned for hours. Until, when Mrs Derricks thought it safe, she crept up to him and, with extraordinary delicacy, seeing she was so robust a woman, she twined his hair about her fingers and breathed into his ear: "Never mind, duck; never mind. I 'ated that 'at! It looked a fair sight on me, it did! Like a bloody plant-pot! 'Adn't you better be gettin' up, lad? 'Adn't we better 'ave t' Boys along to-morrow evenin'?"

She was an uproarious woman, though some of the uproar may have been due to her fear of Wilfred going off into one of his fits, and the idea that if she shouted loud enough, she might stave it off for both of them. But she would have been a cheery soul if Wilfred had been a placid coalheaver and not a queer little stunted Nightingale. Otherwise she wouldn't have been so popular with the Boys. She was a great favourite with them. The Boys were variety artistes, like Wilfred, who did turns in the smaller theatres in the northern area. The Boys were usually males, though now and again they included a girl or two. But somehow the parties never went quite so well when there were girls about. That was partly because Mrs Derricks hated not being the centre of attraction and if there was to be any prodding in the corsets and wicked nibblings at the lobe of the ear, she liked it to be her own ear and her own corsets. She must have turned the half-century, but she could still behave as skittishly as a twenty-year-old without looking silly.

Wilfred, too, wasn't keen on having girls around. They made his forehead prickly and his hands damp. He became smaller. He went inside himself. He heard his own voice, more pipe-like than usual, as if it came from some distance off. He glowered at them, his lower lip protruding sullenly. It was as if they made him conscious of the functions which were lacking in him, though he had so acute an intellectual realisation of them.

But that night, as he sat among the Boys, he was a Boy, too, in another sense than that which was his livelihood and his tragedy. His hand looked absurdly tiny clasped round his beer-tumbler, but not one of the Boys had it filled more often than Wilfred. He could not get drunk. He merely twittered more and more excitedly, like a mouse in a cage over which a terrier stands with cocked head, looking down at it. There was no limit to the faggots he put away. He did not touch the black puddings. They were a little too gross for him.

He had an astounding range of dirty stories; but when the Ventriloquist told a new and good one, he greeted it with a series of short and sharp yelps of delight. Having one woman there, gave the telling of dirty stories a quality it could never achieve in unmixed male society. Quite early in the evening, Mrs Derricks got very drunk and rosy, and started hanging her head, and being coy and girlish. Which only stimulated the Boys to more and more shocking tales and feats of daring. They smacked her behind and squeezed her bosom. She warded off the danger and had at them with a story which took the breath out of even such brassy lungs as theirs.

All the favourite Boys were there that evening. One or two newcomers had been present last time, but they had not been asked again. The Nightingale had had no pleasure in them. There was in them a certain quality which reproached Wilfred for his shortcomings, a certain quiet but excessive maleness he could not bear. But the old gang was present in full force tonight. It was lucky that their bookings permitted them all to turn up. The Baritone was there, whose posters announced him to have come hotfoot from Covent Garden. Cynics declared that it was the market, rather than the Opera House, which was indicated, for he did not sing well. But he sang often. The Prologue from *Pagliacci* was his favourite, and he sang it five or six times over that evening, without seeming to be conscious he had already sung it four or five times. But there was so much noise the whole time it didn't matter if he sang it a seventh time.

The Pocket Samson, was there, too, of course. He never slipped out of favour. He was small, but not like his host, abnormal. Not, at least, when his host was there, did he seem abnormal. He had a fine set of muscles and it was always expected of him at the parties that he should show them, the way the muscles about his shoulder-blades touched and all the unusual undulations and stiffenings he was capable of producing between the elbows and the wrists. He always wore a pair of slips around his loins, so when they asked him to show the muscles he kept about his legs and thighs, he slipped his clothes off and it was all very respectable. He agitated them without pride. He was modest and could lift great weights.

The Ventriloquist sat beside the Pocket Samson. It was a strange profession for him to have adopted, because his mouth seemed to move even more feverishly when he snapped the jaws of his doll than when he talked in his own person. His consonants were doubtful when he produced them from his mouth, but when he sought to lift them out of his belly, they became converted into a standard 'nnyu' sound, which made you feel he kept his nose there. He was a bad ventriloquist, and his bookings rarely prevented him from turning up in Magnolia Street.

The Conjurer had managed to turn up, though he was booked up more often than the others, He did his famous trick of balancing a lighted lamp on a stair-rod during the course of the evening, but not so dexterously as usual, for he set fire to Mrs Derricks's hair. With great presence of mind the Baritone quenched it with the contents of the beer jug. The company howled with laughter, except Wilfred, who looked on vigilantly, out of his sharp eyes. The quenching with the beer-jug did not make Mrs Derricks look much more damp and dishevelled than she was before. She howled louder than the rest and gave the Conjurer a resounding kiss.

After the accident, the party took its usual military turn. That came on, as a rule, just after closing time. The Boys did not look very military when they were sober, or even when they were drunk. But they were a very war-like crowd, none the less. It is not clear whether they were all born equally infected with a lust for war, or whether one of them infected the others. But it is certain they were all conscious of one element lacking from their parties which prevented them from being actual Heaven. There was no war on anywhere, no English war, at least.

It was rather wretched for them to have to put up with the Boer War, which had been over a long time now. But as the party went on, it seemed to go back in time nearer and nearer to the Boer War or the Boer War to advance in time towards it. The names of De Wet and Cronje arose amid a hissing and booing, and the relief of Ladysmith aroused such thunder that you might have thought it was relieved only last week.

Goodbye, Dolly, I must leave you
though it breaks my heart to go,

the Baritone announced thickly. "We don't want to fight," threatened Mrs Derricks, "but by jingo if we do..." But it was clear she *did* want to fight. Her lip curled so that you could see two of her large upper teeth. The Nightingale also bade farewell to his true love.

Goodbye, my Bluebell, he sang,

Farewell to you,
One fond last look into
Your eyes of blue.
'Mid camp-fires gleaming

'Mid shot and shell
I shall be dreaming
Of my own Bluebell.

His mouth gaped and twisted like a hole in an old boot.

But tonight the Boers didn't seem quite enough. They itched for more excitement than the embers of spent wars offered them. The Conjurer and Wilfred were convinced there was going to be a war with Germany. "This 'ere bloody kayser," they muttered. The Baritone was inclined to a war with them Frenchies, despite the *entent cordial*, which he distrusted anyway.

"But it's pretty clear, any bloody old 'ow," grumbled the Conjurer, "that the country's lousy with spies." Then he stopped suddenly. "Ush!" He put his finger to his mouth. "I shouldn't put it past that there *Deutsche Frau*," he breathed darkly. "Tha knows, t'shoemaker's wife next door. She's probably listenin' to us this very moment with 'er ear clapped up against that wall!"

Everybody looked at everybody else anxiously. It was later remembered to the Conjurer's undying glory that he had unmasked Mrs Frank Stanley, as she called herself, four years before she came out in her true colours. It was a comfort, anyhow, that the Boys were keeping watch over the safe being of the Union Jack, however sedulously the generals and the statesmen, the Kayser's tools to a man, held their eyes turned from the little black cloud on the edge of the North Sea.

For the time being, however, there wasn't anything doing in that line, Germans or Frenchies, or Dagoes generally. But there was always the enemy within the gate. Like one man, the whole party rose and made for the front-door; except, of course, Wilfred. He always stayed behind to supervise the proceedings from behind the parlour curtains. They swarmed out to the pavement, and looked across to the houses of the Jews. Mrs Derricks was the choir-leader. "Who killed Christ?" she asked. The others followed, chanting. They booed louder and longer than usual that night; for last time, the seaman, John Cooper, had come and knocked their heads together and stopped them booing. They knew that John Cooper was now away at sea. They booed as if Benny Edelman had not saved little Tommie Wright from drowning, as if Mrs Carter had never bought a tin of mustard from Mrs Poyser, as if Mrs Berman had not stuffed with sweeties the pockets of Nellie Tawnie.

Mr Emmanuel heard the booing as he came in late from his distant excursion in aid of the babies. He heard it the moment he descended from the tram quite a distance away, in the main road. He felt his cheeks burn as if a hand had slapped them. He lost his footing and almost fell in the slushy roadway. He turned his steps towards Oleander Street so as to go round by way of Aubrey Street into Magnolia Street at its other end. It was not pleasant to run the gauntlet of that booing. But he thought better of it. His heart was filled with bitterness as he walked down the street, past the booers. It seemed as if twilight was come while dawn was still flushing the heavens.

His head tottered on his neck. "Something must be done!" he muttered. "Something must be done!"

At that moment a thick-set figure was moving parallel with him down the opposite pavement. He too, walked as if a great weariness were upon him. He seemed hardly able to lift from the ground those queer elastic-sided boots.

"Something must be done!" this one muttered, too. "In the name of the Lord Jesus!" he added.

Chapter 12

I

Ben Stern, the missionary, took his key out of his pocket and let himself into the house of Mr Carter, the night-watchman, where he lodged. He went straight into his own room, for he never troubled Mrs Carter in any way, not even to boil a kettle. That was a good thing too, for Sally was a delicate woman, and if Mr Stern had required any attention at all, she would not have been able to have him. She herself had not been at all well since she had that baby — and then it went and died. But Mr Stern was a gentleman who looked after himself, and she was glad to get two of her rooms off her hands. A woman came in and scrubbed his floors and took away his washing, and the rest he did himself.

He was very faint when he came in that Monday night of the Derricks party. So, very quietly, so as not to awake Sally, for he knew she was delicate, he prepared his spirit-stove and made himself some tea; then he got a loaf out of a tin, and with his spectacles pushed up against his forehead, and his pale grey eyes close against the loaf, he proceeded to cut away at it with slow regular sawings. And then, in the middle of his cutting, he remembered that the exact wording of a passage in Daniel had eluded him all day long, so forgetting all about his faintness, the knife still embedded in the loaf, he went across to his little table under the window, where his Bible always stood open. Hour after hour he sat there, now turning the pages rapidly, now held up by a single word for thirty or forty minutes. To him there was no such thing as time. There was only the eternity of Jesus Christ.

When Sally Carter came down next morning to let her husband in after his night-duty at the factory, Mr Stern's door was open. She caught sight of the knife embedded in the loaf and the cup of tea untasted. Mr Stern sat at the small table before the window, having fallen asleep with his cheek down against the sacred page.

She wondered whether she ought to wake him, and give him a hot cup of tea out of the pot she was brewing for her husband. But it was the essence of the understanding between them that Mr Stern was to be no nuisance, and if she started taking notice of his goings-on, a nuisance was exactly what he would be. Then she remembered the business of the pork chop, which had happened only last Thursday. He had had an attack of his rheumatism and Sally was aware that he had brought in no supplies for a day or two. She thought it might be nice for him to eat a little pork chop, seeing that she was cooking some for Bill, so she brought one to him, where he lay on the sofa in the parlour with a rug over him. But when he saw what she had brought him, a sort of spasm came on his face, she couldn't tell whether it was the rheumatism or the sight of the pork chop. "No, no, please!" he implored her, in his guttural foreign voice. His Adam's apple rose up and down, quivering. So she took it away again, none too pleased that she'd gone to the trouble of preparing a special tray for him, and carrying it herself, too. It was odd how little he managed to exist on — tea, and fruit, and bread, and he would chew raw vegetables — for he was a big man, bigger than he seemed, the way his shoulders stooped and his head lay forward on his neck, as if the vertebrae there were weak.

To the others the affair of Edelman and the small boy was a break in the monotony, a comic excitement, an opportunity to increase the business. To him it was a finger of light fallen from Heaven. He saw the barriers crumbling between the people of Christ and the baptised of Christ. Again and again he had been disappointed and mocked and stabbed to the heart, as, not long ago, the youth, Winberg, had stabbed him. But now, surely, surely, the dawn was coming. He looked through his window to the houses of the Jews opposite. Not one of them till now had allowed him to penetrate beyond the *mezuzah*, the little casket of holy script nailed up upon the lintel. Till now the humblest presser, the dullest slattern, earth of this poor earth, had been as remote from the agonised yearning of his finger-tips as Rabbi Shulman, who was like a column of flame as he moved, rotating upon the axis of his unspeakable assurance. There was, indeed, much in common between these two men; this most of all, that they were less human than spirits cloaked so loosely in flesh, that a heat and a wind seemed to come out from the imperfect places of the fabric.

The flesh of two creatures in spiritual essence so alike, could hardly have been more dissimilar. Benjamin Stern was loose and red and vapourous, with short fat fingers stubbed out upon

185

chubby palms. His eyebrows, his beard, faded into a smoke, into nothing at all. The pupils of his eyes could not be distinguished from the whites they were set in. Rabbi Shulman was lean, tall, powerful, angular. His thick hair, his long beard, were black as the blue sheen of coal. His face was yellow, like a Mongol's; he had high cheek bones. His huge nose was curved like a blade. His fingers were long and gnarled like the roots of olive trees. Their joints cracked uninterruptedly like noises in the fire, as he turned the pages of the Commentaries. His eyes were dead-black as the fur of a black cat.

The two men were both profound scholars, both slaves and masters of an idea. Benjamin Stern knew well that in the sight of those stricken eyes which, from their elevation upon a Cross, had besought him to go forth on the path he had chosen, all these lost Jewish souls were equal. The salvation of a shambling, handsome, good-humoured lout, like Benny Edelman, of so simple and unkempt a Magdalene as Leah Winter, was as great a thing as the salvation of any keen intellectual or moneyed prince. But it seemed to him that if once he might secure, in a silent place, for a day and a night, this tall Rabbi, a success as glorious might come to him in this late end of time as came to those poor men from Galilee who went forth with a message. Did they not speak the same language? Did they not go a long way together along the same road, until it forked, and in his blindness, the Rabbi moved away into profitless undergrowth, starred by flowers so curious and desolate?

The thought that he might some day secure the Rabbi's attention was, perhaps, an instance of that madness which one or two kind Jews, and many of the gentiles, imputed to Benjamin Stern. But he did not entertain it often or long. Secure that man? How shall you secure the wind walking or the flame soaring?

So, in the days of the fraternisation between the two pavements, he turned his mind towards less preposterous prizes. But the thicket was not less impenetrable than before. The ease, the comradeship, were not for him. He was made to understand even in the gentile houses that they preferred him to keep away; for when their guests, the Jewish men or women, entered and saw he was there, they turned back with hatred and nausea in their faces.

He knew well why they hated him so, apart from the loathing they had, as all humble Jews have, for the perverts of their race.

186

If they would but let him speak, he could have shown them that there, in the thing they accused him of, at least, he was guiltless. But they would not let him speak. It was the matter of one Eli, a carpenter. About fifteen years ago this Eli had come out of a village in Russia where there had been a pogrom, and Leah, his wife, with him. He had been a great scholar, though so young a man, and a carpenter. And a madness had come to him. He had become a Christian and preached at the street corners.

The Jews of the streets of the flowering shrubs blamed Benjamin Stern for this, but he was not to blame. The young man, Eli, did not meet Benjamin Stern till some months before his death. He visited him in Magnolia Street two or three times, and he seemed already like a dead man walking, his cheeks were so grey and his eyes so hollow. And then, on the Day of Atonement, he had done a sacrilege which men could not speak of, having burst wild-eyed into the synagogue and held up the Cross before the open Ark. That night, deeming that the Lord commanded her, his wife went to the room where her husband lived, and killed him, having loved him greatly. They had a small son, Reuben his name was; the same night he disappeared, and no-one knew what became of him.

"At least," Ben Stern said to himself, "I could tell the truth of it to the clerk to the Guardians. A man of a Christian heart, he would not treat me so." For he had often been present at meetings addressed by Mr Emmanuel to promulgate the doctrine of Love. And that was his own doctrine, though he gave Love a human shape and a divine substance. He determined more than once to cross the pavement and have a word with Mr Emmanuel. Some nights ago, after the whole street had gathered in Mr Emmanuel's house and had gone away again, he saw the host left on his doorstep alone. He made forward as if to speak to him. But Mr Emmanuel, like all the others, closed the door in his face.

It was a few nights later that the Derrickses and their friends assembled and came out upon the pavement, and stood blaspheming.

"Who killed Christ?" they asked.

"You! You, O my children!" a voice tolled in the hollow heart of Benjamin Stern. "You hang him on a Cross, and pierce His hands and feet with nails and His side with a spear, again and again and again!"

The jeering went on loud and long. Two men walked slowly down the street. "Something must be done!" they said, both of them, and tears were in their eyes.

But what could Mr Stern do? He stood in his doorway, wondering. What could he do? The spikes in the thicket were steel spikes.

And then he remembered the little children, and how they should go to him. He smiled sadly into his beard. Into those eyes myopic with much study, came a glint of cunning. So he went forth into Blenheim Road and bought sweets for the little ones, and stuffed them into the back pocket of his frock-coat, among the gospels and pamphlets. He waited till the evening came, and timidly stepped down into the cobbled roadway between the two pavements. He called the children to him, seeing the small Poysers and Seipels playing together. They came closer, hypnotised by the horror of this summons. He put his hand into his pocket and brought out a fistful of sweets and offered it to them. Whereas, as one animal, they fled from him, screaming, and kicked at the doors of their houses, as if a devil pursued them. Not one of them stopped howling for ten minutes.

There was much dark and angry talk that evening among the women at the grocery-shop, and among the men in the synagogue, after the evening service. And when they asked Rabbi Shulman what he judged should be done, he swivelled his mind away with difficulty from the text he was studying, and said: "If it were fruit that a kind man offers them, let the children take. But let them remember to make the blessing, should it be a fruit they taste for the first time this year. But as for sweets bought from a gentile shop, who knows with what impurity they were put together? Let them not eat such sweets!"

Then, at last, something broke in the heart of Ben Stern. He felt that his Cross was more than he could bear. As he went in and out of his house, the Jews muttered, the women called the children to them and held their hands tight. It occurred to him that now he would leave this street. He had failed. And then no, he said to himself, no. It seemed to him it would be to abandon a last and solitary fortress. He stayed on in the house of Mr Carter, and sat down to his food, cutting at the loaf with right and left sawings. It was poor food, but it sustained him. All bread to him was the flesh of his Lord.

The whole street was shocked by the Derricks' goings-on, though the two pavements took it differently. The Jews shrugged their shoulders fatalistically. As it had been, so it would be. How had the prophet Hosea said? "It is in my desire that I should chastise them; and the people shall be gathered against them." But the gentiles, notably the Carters and the Briggses, were furious. They wanted to do something about it, but they did not.

They did not do anything at all spectacular, the Carters and the Briggses, during the whole span of their history with which we are concerned. They were simple folk, like many millions of others, living in a poor street. Yet when the span of their history is considered as a single entity, something of grandeur emerges. And that must be, not because there was anything grand in any of them, but because they were human beings. The archangels, who are neither born, nor die, may be ready to admit more cordially than we human beings might, that any career subject to birth and growth, struggle and love, sickness and death, has a certain splendour.

Sally Carter had not given a party, as most of her neighbours had done, and she determined she would have to do something about it, really she would, just to show them Derrickses, the tikes. She had not quite felt up to giving a party, she was that delicate. For she had had a baby, and it had died. It did not occur to her that that seemed to indicate that it was the baby who was delicate, rather than she. But she said she had never got over it. She was becoming a rather querulous woman as time went on, and doubtless it was because she had nothing to complain about. It is likely that if Bill had just taken hold of her by the shoulders and given her a good shaking, when she first started saying how delicate she was, she would have forgotten about it. And if only he could have induced himself to give her a black eye, she might have turned out the toughest and happiest little woman in Magnolia Street.

She needed, so to speak, something to get her teeth into, but she never got it, not for a long time. She was neither tough nor happy now. It was a good thing that Mr Stern gave her so little trouble, or life would have been altogether too much for her.

But this latest Derrick's party, coming when it did, gave her a nasty shaking-up. "Really!" she said. She went in and out between her kitchen and the scullery saying "Really!" in a tone of great indignation. She forgot completely to nag old Bill, her husband. On the contrary, it made her realise, for a reason she could not guess, and in a way she was not accustomed to, just how large and sweet he was, sitting under the window there, wondering what it was all about. She forgot the pain in her side she'd been complaining about. Or was it in her back? She'd brought in a pound of tripe for his supper, or his breakfast, that is to say. One gets that mixed up with a husband who works by night and sleeps by day. He liked his tripe boiled in milk, with onions, but not too much pepper. (Bill Carter *wouldn't* like pepper.) She went into the scullery to get it ready for him. He sat on in his chair under the window, the vast pillars of his legs stretched out before him. He smiled like a small boy, who knows his mother is preparing something nice; his thick thumbs revolved round each other steadily. His dog, Bucky, sat crouched with her face between her paws, looking up at him steadily, and adoring him.

Bucky was predominantly a rough-haired terrier, though there was something of greyhound in her slim hips. She had brown and gentle eyes like a gazelle. She loved rats. The sight of a rat made her go clammy all over with playfulness and affection. At first the rats misunderstood her when she came scorching up to them and turned them over with her paws and pushed them along humourously with her nose. They were paralysed with horror. But when they found that nothing serious was happening to them they swiftly unparalysed themselves. They fled with extreme speed, and on attaining a rat-hole, found it impossible not to turn round to see what sort of a strange dog it was that turned them over as if they were not rats, but dog-babies.

They perceived the expression of pained surprise on Bucky's face and realised they had misjudged her. They were still a little shy, but that wore off after a day or two. They and Bucky became great friends.

When Bill Carter was still a policeman, he was rather like that with burglars. He didn't want to play with them quite so earnestly as Bucky wanted to play with rats, but they loved playing with him. On Bill Carter's beat the burglars lolloped about like rabbits in a spinney.

It was no wonder that one or two of the inspectors felt unfriendly towards Bill Carter. But that was only in his professional capacity. As a man no-one disliked him. In fact everybody liked him, when they could remember he was about somewhere. He was the sort of person who was always left behind on police sprees, when the Force went off on holiday in big char-à-bancs. It was not because he had had a drop too much. It was merely because it was possible to look at Bill Carter without seeing him. It was just like that when there was a round of cards on. It was said he often had an ace and ten at Pontoon and gleaned no profit from it, merely because the next player to him forgot he was there, and just played on, as if he wasn't.

He was always just as invisible, even as a policeman. Wits used to say that if ever his professional duties brought him into the same room as a forger forging a bank-note, the forger would as likely as not get on with the job, without noticing he was there. He never got a stripe, and from the beginning there was an unfriendly inspector or two at C Division Headquarters who wanted him out of the way. But he was guilty of absolutely no slackness in dress or duty for the most fastidious critic to put a finger on. The unfriendly inspectors did not unload him till 1909 and he did not get a job for many months, because a discharged policeman was a more uncomfortable object in some ways than a discharged convict. Then at last they took him on as a night-watchman in Rawlinson's engine-works.

As a youth he had been a miner in a Northumberland pit. He then enlisted in the army, saw varied service in India and came home to enlist in the police force. Such a career might have provided a skeleton on which to build up an exciting personality. But Bill Carter was neither excited nor exciting. As a policeman he had been an early witness of not a few garish spectacles, including a murder or two. But his presence robbed them of all appearance of melodrama. When you saw the lady under the sink with her head hanging on by one tendon, and Bill Carter was in the near neighbourhood, you just felt it was bound to be like that and you cleared your throat and wiped your nose. When he took his notebook out of his back pocket, it was as if he were going to take down an order for a few pounds of potatoes.

Bill Carter finished his dish of tripe. "Thank you, Sally!" he said, wiping his mouth on his sleeve. "That was champion!" He looked shyly at her. "You are looking pink and pretty to-night!" he said. He said it in a voice that made her fair flush up.

"All right," she said, "you can, if you want to." He wanted to, and did.

"Not so wet, Bill," she objected. "You are a caution!"

Bill went out into his little back garden with Bucky adoring at his heels. He pottered about among his roses and asters for a few minutes. But the flowers seemed to know it was only Bill Carter, so they were not particular.

"Listen, Sal!" he said. "Look here!" His face was serious. She knew what was on his mind. She had told him about these Derrickses and the way they bade fair to break up the harmony which had grown up in Magnolia Street. It had upset him a lot.

"Yes, Bill?"

"Do you think, if I asked Benny Edelman or Mr Emmanuel or some of them Jew fellers if they'd like a game of bowls, how do you think they'd take it?"

Bill Carter played bowls quite well. He had once won a silver vase for bowls in a police tournament, and it stood in the middle of the kitchen mantelpiece. He was rather shy about it.

"Bill," she exclaimed a little mockingly, "you are a one! The ideas you *do* get! They'd love it! And what's more, Bill, really we can't go on going into all them houses and never asking no-one back again. So what I say is this here —"

But at that moment there was a knock at the front-door. They heard it quite plainly, for the intervening doors were open.

"Who can that be?" said Sally.

"I'll go!" said Bill.

"No!" said Sally, for the first time since she had had a baby. "You've got to go off soon! You take it easy!" She went and opened the front-door.

"Oh, good evening, Mrs Carter!" said a small fair boy.

"Gracious me! If it isn't David! Isn't that right?"

"Yes, that's right," smiled the small boy. It was David, the youngest of the Emmanuels. Bill had come up out of the back garden by this time. "Good evening, Mr Carter! Hello, Bucky, good dog! My father's sent me over to you. Will you please take one of these?"

He held a small pile of leaflets in his hand. They still smelt damp and inky, as if they had only just come off the press.

192

"Why, what's this?" asked Mrs Carter. At that moment Benjamin Stern appeared at his door, with his hat and frock-coat and walking-stick, all ready to go out. He saw there was a visitor on the doorstep, and screwing up his eyes, he recognised who it was. He made a movement as if to return into his room, and then it occurred to him that it would look very cowardly in the eyes of Mr and Mrs Carter, if he turned tail and fled from a small boy, merely because he was a Jew.

"Good night, Mr Carter, Mrs Carter!" he said. He tried to pass through the doorway without brushing up against the boy, for he knew well how the Jews shrank from contact with him, in a tram, a shop, wherever it might be forced upon them.

And then he heard the quiet pleasant voice of the small boy. "Oh, Mr Stern, won't you take one? You must come, too, won't you?" He smiled up into the desolate eyes of the old man, as he handed over a leaflet to him.

Never before, since he came to live in Magnolia Street, had any Jew smiled at him, man, woman or child. He felt he would faint with happiness. He had a wild impulse to lift the boy to his bosom and crush his face up against his beard and cover it with kisses.

But he did no such thing. "Thank you!" he said, gruffly, it seemed, but there was a lump in his throat; it was as much as he could do to say even so little. The leaflet shook like an aspen-leaf between his fingers, as he stumbled back with it into his own room.

"Well I never!" Sally was exclaiming as she brandished the leaflet. "Look at this here, Bill!"

"Bah goom!" said Bill.

III

Mr Stern's knees felt so weak he was not certain he would be able to reach a chair. His head was swimming. He pushed his spectacles up against his forehead and brought the leaflet close to his eyes. But what he read impinged against only a small portion of his mind... great presentation ceremony... Unity Hall, Longton... entertainment by well-known theatrical stars... Wilfred Derricks, the Longton Nightingale... local talent... Miss Poyser... prizes for Great Raffle invited, in aid of the Longton

193

Crèche... Mr Isaac Emmanuel in the chair... your co-operation and presence cordially invited...

Now one phrase, now another, detached itself. Now the phrases ran meaninglessly into each other. Now he could see nothing at all, for the leaflet fluttered so and a mist slid before his eyes.

So something was to be done, after all. The old divisions were not to be re-established. Wilfred Derricks, none other than Wilfred Derricks, to be chairman of the entertainment committee!... He saw the friends and the mother of Wilfred Derricks standing on the pavement, flushed with drink. He heard them jeering.

His heart skipped with joy like a foal. Assuredly the Lord was among them, not in might but in gentleness.

"But the fruit of the Spirit is love, joy, peace, long-suffering, gentleness, goodness, faith," he chanted. The words were out of the new dispensation of Jesus, but the tone was the tone of the old men that sing in synagogues on the darkening Sabbath evenings.

And the crèche for children that the good man, Emmanuel, had at heart; he had heard of this already. They were to be the Longton children, immaterial whether Jewish or Christian. He had more than once determined to speak to Mr Emmanuel on the matter, but he had not dared, at the last moment. He could be of use. He could direct that the collections in certain churches should be earmarked for the Longton Crèche some Sunday....

"And not for that one nation only, but that also he should gather together in one the children of God that were scattered abroad."

Joy carolled in him like skylarks on a fresh morning. It came from the thought of the house in which the children of the Jews and the gentiles would be harboured together; and from the thought of the gathering in which all these folks were soon to be assembled in love and charity. It seemed to him the hand of God was quite palpable in the knitting together of those ideas; there was something even of miracle in the way in which the obstinate rancour of the Derrickses had been dispelled.

But his joy chiefly arose out of the smile the little Jewish lad had given him. He thought that in that way the little Jewish lads, who were the friends of the boy Jesus, must have smiled when they splashed the water in the trough of Mary's well in Nazareth.

Of course the boy had been sent over by his father to give a leaflet to him, too. David his name was. How lovely and apt a name! So small a boy would not have taken it on himself to ask him to come. How did he say it? "Oh, Mr Stern, won't you take one? You must come, too, won't you?" He held the syllables apart like beads of music and then allowed them to come together, tinkling sweetly.

Why had he been of so little faith? He should have spoken to the father long ago; or the other night, at latest. So much of their dearest dreaming was identical. Must his faith remain weak of backbone to the end?

Contributions to the raffle were asked for, in aid of the Longton Crèche. He took the heavy gold signet ring from his finger, which his father had given him. He had no earthly possession he cared for more. He fumbled about among his papers and found an envelope, dropped the ring into it, and closed it. Then he rose. He was quite giddy.

He heard the Carters discussing the new development in their kitchen. As he came down the doorsteps into the street, he saw that groups were gathered in front of many of the houses. The leaflet was in their hands. The air was full of pleasant excitement. He crossed over to the house where the Emmanuels lived and knocked at the door.

It was Mr Emmanuel himself who opened it. Mr Stern's heart beat so rapidly he was afraid he would not be able to speak. He remained silent a moment or two until his heart stilled a little.

Then cold and incisive came the voice of Mr Emmanuel. "I beg your pardon. What do you want here?"

Mr Stern's throat drew in a sharp gust of breath. "I have just got a copy of your leaflet, Mr Emmanuel. I wanted to congratulate you. You ask for contributions. I've come to say that anything in my power —"

"Excuse me, Mr Stern," said Isaac Emmanuel. His voice was so raw and harsh that Mr Stern looked up with quick terror in his eyes. He well knew the expression that had invested them. He had seen it in the eyes of the youth, Winberg, not many weeks ago, when he spoke to him one Sunday morning in the road near St. Luke's Church.

195

The two men looked into each other's eyes. Both were silent for some seconds. A spot of colour rose on Mr Emmanuel's cheek-bones and deepened and burned. With hideous clairvoyance Mr Stern perceived the passions working behind Mr Emmanuel's skull, as a man sees the works of a clock through the glass walls of its case. He saw the detestation. He saw the intention arise to say whatsoever he could say of most damnable, however false it was, however false he knew it was. He saw the words like points of green light shoot from the brain to the vocal organs.

"I don't need your help," said Mr Emmanuel. "My name is not Eli."

Mr Stern's jaw dropped. His head fell further forward upon his chest. He turned round and shuffled away heavily. He did not see the points of fire dwindle and die upon Mr Emmanuel's cheek-bones. He did not see him bite down so fiercely on his lower lip that the blood started from it. He did not hear him call after him: "Oh Mr Stern, please —"

Mr Stern heard and saw nothing. He went back to his own room.

Chapter 18

I

Isaac Emmanuel lay tossing on his bed for hours during the night that followed the Derricks party.

"Isaac, what is with you?" his wife enquired at uneasy intervals. "Shall I get you some brandy? Is that cramp coming again?"

"No, nothing!" he replied irritably. "Go to sleep!"

Something must be done! Something must be done! drubbed the refrain. Of course, he muttered, nothing was easier than to say "Something must be done." He could think of only one thing to do, and that was to poison the Derrickses. He would not have thought of so extreme a measure, if he were not feeling so wretchedly disappointed. And he was tired. He was aching to go off to sleep. He knew he was keeping Slatta awake, too. Poor woman, it wasn't her fault, anyhow.

"Sleep, Slatta!" he whispered. He stroked the back of her neck with two fingers. She smiled and went to sleep instantly.

Dawn was creeping round the blinds before he had himself dropped off. His head sloped backward down the receding slope of the pillow! His little beard pointed into the air forlornly. A snore shook gustily in the caverns behind his Adam's apple. It was music to Slatta Emmanuel. Silent as a ghost she rose up from beside him, and crept downstairs to make the fire and the breakfasts.

It was ten o'clock before Isaac rose. He came down looking haggard, with dark circles round his eyes. He mumbled through his prayers as if it were the Lord's fault that he had not slept. Then thrusting the phylacteries viciously into their bag, "Tea!" he said. It was not a gracious voice. The kettle was havering on the hob. The teapot was warming on the fender. She made his tea for him swiftly, and put his breakfast cake on a plate before him. He never took a larger breakfast than that. He drank tea in the Russian manner, out of a glass, sucking it through a cube of sugar. He drank up one tumbler and a second. He did not touch his cake. He wedged still another cube of sugar between his teeth. "More tea!" he said. Then suddenly the cube of sugar dropped from between his teeth and rattled down on the plate in front of him.

"I've got it!" he cried exultantly. "I've got it!"

"Got what?" his wife exclaimed. He *was* ill, after all, as she had feared.

"Quick!" he cried.. "Give me my tie and collar!" He ran over into the scullery, filled a basin with cold water and plunged his face in it. He passed a comb through the tangles of his hair.

"Isaac, what is it?" his wife cried.

"My tie and collar!" he threw at her. He clipped the studs into the collar and made a clumsy bulb out of his tie. Then he rushed to the front door. Slatta ran after him.

"You've eaten no breakfast!" she wailed. "You've not touched a thing!"

But he was already racing down the street. He crossed the roadway. He knocked at a front door; of all the front doors in all the world it was the Derricks's front door.

"*Gottenu!*" exclaimed Mrs Emmanuel, throwing her hands into the air. "A madness has fallen on him! I have always known what it would come to!"

She wondered was it her duty to go and protect him from the harm that might befall him at that gross house. She remembered what had happened on one or two previous occasions when such an idea had occurred to her, so she held back. Mrs Derricks came to the door.

There was speech between Mrs Derricks and Mr Emmanuel. It lasted a minute, two minutes. Then Mr Emmanuel passed out of sight through the gates of the enemy. Mrs Emmanuel turned back into her kitchen, her heart a-twitter with apprehension.

II

Mrs Derricks got up that morning an hour or two after her husband and her younger son went off to work. They had done an hour or two's work already. It always fell to them to clear up the place after there had been a party. Mrs Derricks had a bad head. Her tongue was furry. That was also part of the routine of the morning after a party. Wilfred, who, on the other hand, to keep himself young, never got up before noon, got up half an hour earlier than usual, carolling blithely. He was more skylark than nightingale this morning.

Mrs Derricks shuffled between kitchen and scullery, groaning from time to time, and holding her forehead. "Oh my poor 'ead.

Oh my poor 'ead!"

"You naughty old woman!" Wilfred teased her. "I told you you were taking too much! Get on with those kippers now! I feel I could do with 'em!" He rubbed the surplus rouge off his cheeks with his towel, then took out his lipstick. Daintily he pursed his mouth up into a bow and traced the lipstick round it.

"How's it look, mother?"

"Bonny!" she said, as he expected her to. "Oh my poor 'ead! All rackin' and achin' —"

There was a knock at the front door.

"Who's that?" Wilfred said sharply.

"Ah dunno! Maybe the landlord!"

"No!" said Wilfred. "Tuesday's not his day! Go and see!" He gathered up his rouge and lipstick and powder and, agile as a monkey, stepped over to a cupboard and hid them away. He took from a nail a beautiful flowered-silk dressing gown. It went very nicely with his gilded hair. Then he stepped back into his chair again, and absorbed himself in the *Era*.

Mrs Derricks staggered along to the door and fumbled about with the handle for a moment or two. Then it yielded. A tall gentleman was standing on the doorstep; he was smiling so energetically that his head swung about and looked as if it might drop off.

"Oh, good morning, Mrs Derricks," said the gentleman. Then he stuttered a little, as if he did not quite know what to say next. Then, "How are you?" he said, and laughed nervously.

Then Mrs Derricks saw who it was — Mr Emmanuel, his name was, one of the Jew-men from across the street. She remembered at the same time that he was something more than that. He had some sort of official position. Town Councillors had been known to call at his house.

Her immediate instinct was to close the door in his face; not out of rudeness, but out of sheer fright. Tied up with Town Councillors as he was, he had come to arrest her, and Wilfred, too, and all of them. The neighbours had threatened to complain, and they had gone and done it. Her lower lip started quivering. She peered over Mr Emmanuel's shoulder, but there was no policeman there. And the way Mr Emmanuel was grinning at her — no, it was clear he had not come to lock them all up. What? Lock them up? She planted her feet wide apart to steady herself, and folded her arms across her bosom.

199

"Well?" she asked truculently, "And what may you be wantin'?"

"The fact is," replied Mr Emmanuel, "I've come for your help. And your son's. Sings beautifully, Mrs Derricks. I've never heard such a voice. I want —"

"What if you 'aven't?" Mrs Derricks interrupted.

"It should be wider known, Mrs Derricks. Nightingale. No wonder they call him the Longton Nightingale."

"Look 'ere," started Mrs Derricks. Then she screwed her head round. Her son had come up behind her. He was tugging at her dress.

"All right, Wilfred!" she said. "All right!"

"Oh do step in," twittered Wilfred politely. "I take it you've come to see me? Won't you come this way?" He opened the parlour door and showed Mr Emmanuel in, like a tiny page-boy in a hotel.

"Hummm!" rumbled Mrs Derricks. Jew-men in the parlour! What would Wilfred be up to next?

"Thank you, Mr Derricks. So kind of you," said Mr Emmanuel. "I'm not disturbing you in any way?"

"No, no!" insisted Wilfred. "Please! Won't you sit down?"

They were bowing and scraping and nodding at each other with all the complicated punctilio of two elderly counts at a court of the Pretender to the throne of France. Then before Mr Emmanuel really quite knew that he was not still sucking tea through a cube of sugar in his own kitchen, he had started off. He got up almost immediately from his arm-chair. He strode up and down the floor. He stabbed the air with his pince-nez.

"I wouldn't be troubling you like this, Mr Derricks, but I want to feel I have not only the wealth but the genius of the street behind me. Yes, Mr Derricks, I mean genius. And when I say wealth, I mean wealth. I have already been promised the support of the Winbergs in the matter. They are most enthusiastic."

He had, of course, been promised no support by anybody. His whole scheme had only been in his head a minute or two. He was clarifying the details as he went along.

"But, of course, money is not everything, as you and I well know, Mr Derricks. You and I live in the art world. You may have read in the newspaper, about my son, Max? *The Chronicle* had a half-column interview, with a portrait. He won the Art Gallery

200

prize a week or two ago. He has promised to do a little lightning-sketch work on the night. That is to say, if you are agreeable. That side of the arrangements will be left entirely in your hands."

"Excuse me, Mr Emmanuel. But I'm afraid I haven't got the hang of the thing at all. On the night? What night? What arrangements?"

"Oh, how absurd of me, Mr Derricks; of course, of course! It's all about this young man, Edelman, you know. The way he saved Mrs Wright's small boy from drowning! I thought it a capital piece of work. Didn't you? And — I'm sure you'll agree with me — something ought to be done about it."

Wilfred didn't look quite so sure. "I should have thought," he said, "if you'll excuse me, quite a lot has been done about it."

"Yes, yes, quite so," Mr Emmanuel caught up hurriedly. "Bravery is its own reward, too. But one or two of us have been thinking that if we could organise a presentation, if you know what I mean — well, wouldn't it?"

Wilfred looked a little confused. But before he had time to ask Mr Emmanuel to straighten things out a bit, Mr Emmanuel was plucking at the second string. "That would be very nice, of course. But then there's this matter of the Longton Crèche for Babies!"

"What? What's that?" Mrs Derricks enquired. "Babies?" The conversation was evidently entering a province where she had a right to show up and have a word.

"Ah!" said Mr Emmanuel, beaming, and opening wide his two arms. "A mother's heart! See how it opens up to the magic touch of the word baby!"

He realised he had, perhaps, not paid enough attention to the old woman. It was as important, or very nearly, to win the mother over as the son. The Crèche should settle her.

"Indeed, my dear Mrs Derricks. You have said it yourself many times. 'What we need in Longton here,' you said, 'is a Crèche for the babies.' And I go further than you. I think we should have a playroom for the elder children, too. In that way the mothers will not only feel free to go out and do a day's work, when they have to. They'll feel free to go off with their husbands, or their friends, of an evening, to a park, or a music-hall. How often has a poor mother been prevented from going off to hear your son sing — and that is what I call singing —

201

by the fact that she hadn't anywhere to plant out her children?"

Mrs Derricks was a little surprised to find what a humanitarian heart she had harboured all these years. "Yes," she agreed. "Them poor workin' women as 'aven't got nowhere to put their poor children when they go out to 'ave a pint of an evenin'! It's a cryin' shame!" She fumbled for her handkerchief, couldn't find it, and dried her eyes with her sleeve.

"But, please, Mrs Derricks, I don't want you to distress yourself. It's not for that I've come in this morning! Oh no! Oh no!" He paused. He forgot for a moment what he *had* come in for. Then he went on: "Just think of it, a little white house, where all the children of this neighbourhood, irrespective whether —" hastily he drew the words back in time. It would be extremely tactless, he realised, under these special circumstances, to stress the inter-racial hospitality of the projected Longton Crèche. The mistake he had been about to make put him off his stroke for a moment. "The babies," he dithered, "think of them, Mrs Derricks, counting their little toes, one, two, three, four —"

Wilfred broke in. It was lucky, perhaps. For Mr Emmanuel was stumped, and might have gone on counting to eleven. "What has all that to do with me, Mr Emmanuel?" he asked shortly.

"Oh, my dear sir, that's exactly what I was coming to. I want to feel that the drive is coming from Magnolia Street. In my official capacity, I have contacts with influential people. Perhaps you know that? Well then. I felt that this presentation ceremony to young Edelman will give us just the opportunity we want. He will receive the present. The whole street will subscribe to it. People from neighbouring streets will ask to subscribe, too. But we will not let them. This is *our* affair, Mr Derricks. They will be able to subscribe to the raffle in aid of the Crèche, as much as they like. As I said, Edelman will come on the platform to receive the present. The child whom he rescued will be led on by his mother at the same moment. The notability — we must decide later who to invite — will hand the present over to the child. The child will hand it over to the man who saved him. There will be applause. There will not be a dry eye in the place.

"And then — and then — the lesson will be read, the moral will be pointed out. What was the child doing on the croft all alone? Why was there no little play-room for the child to go and play in? Toy trains and teddy bears and —"

202

"And bunny-rabbits," suggested Mrs Derricks enthusiastically.

"Of course. Bunny-rabbits. But Mr Derricks, where do you come in? This is where you come in! We want the people of the neighbourhood to subscribe heavily. We want to ask some rich people along, to see what we can get out of them. Yes, we're quite frank about that. We want to put them all in a good humour, so that they dip their hands in their pockets as deep as they'll go. We want to give them an entertainment worthy of the Doomington Palace itself. And you can do it, Mr Derricks. You're the man we need. We can't move a foot without you! I appeal to you!"

Wilfred's fingers were drumming restlessly on the table before him. Mr Emmanuel's excitement had at last communicated itself to him. His eyes were scurrying about hurriedly. He tried to keep his voice from going up into his shrillest treble.

"Who d'you think you'll be having down to see the show, Mr Emmanuel?"

"I have people on my books who have more money than they know what to do with."

"People in the theatre-line? Managers?" shrilled Wilfred.

"Managers?" said Mr Emmanuel lightly. "I was asked to dinner last week in Didsbury and the General Manager of the Oak Theatre Circuit was there. 'Mr Emmanuel,' he says to me, 'It's my belief that London's played out. There's no more variety talent in London. We've got to go to the Provinces for variety talent these days. In fact, don't let it get about, that's what I'm here for.'"

Mr Emmanuel heard himself lying with astonishment. It was not that he was lying, exactly, as that he was lying so serenely, so masterfully. Wilfred Derricks was yelping with excitement.

"I think it's a wonderful idea, Mr Emmanuel. I congratulate you. It's a pity we haven't met earlier. I should have loved the chance to have a word with you. I've got an engagement in Bury for three nights and Saturday matinée, at the end of the week. Won't you let me give you a couple of tickets? Perhaps you could bring your friend along with you?"

"What?" said Mr Emmanuel. "When did you say? What nights are you playing in Bury?"

Wilfred saw Mr Emmanuel and the Manager in the centre of the third row of the stalls. They were smoking large cigars. Of course, they only put in an appearance for his turn, and immediately it was over, drove off in a large motor car. Mr Emmanuel was keeping time to his song with his pince-nez. The manager took out a little notebook and made a little note....

"Thursday, Friday, Saturday," he said. "Of course it's not much of a theatre. They can only put up three nights and a matinée. Still, if you can make it convenient —"

Mr Emmanuel's eyes were far away. He was wondering if it was possible to do without Wilfred Derricks, after all. He had got the idea into his head that the presentation ceremony must take place on Saturday night of this same week, at the latest. He wanted it to take place tomorrow night, tonight. But that, he realised, was impossible. Exactly in the same way he wanted the millennium to happen not a month later than a year next October. His impatience frustrated a good many of his schemes.

"We must have the presentation next Saturday night at latest," he said to himself. But he said it aloud.

Then Wilfred stopped twittering. He showed his teeth like a little rat. "Oh must we?" he said. "Must we, Mr Emmanuel?"

It was a grim tone, a tone of warning. It pitched-forked the ludicrous idea that had taken possession of Mr Emmanuel out of his skull.

"Oh," he said, chastened. "When do you think it would be convenient, Mr Derricks? As early as possible, don't you think? I'm sure it should be as early as possible."

"It's *got* to be a Saturday night!" Wilfred decided.

"Yes. I suppose it has. Of course it has."

"Then, a week come Saturday night! Saturday, July the ninth! How's that?"

"We'll have to wait, of course, till the — till the synagogue service is well over!"

"But of course!" cooed Wilfred, his voice as smooth as honey. "And there's something else I'd like to tell you, while we're about it. We want this to be a regular slap-up show, real professional talent. Oh yes, I quite agree with you, a little amateur talent won't do any harm. On the contrary it'll show the other stuff up all the better. I have a number of friends in the profession, naturally. They're devoted to me and to mother. Aren't they, mother? There's Bob Gatling, for instance. He's a Baritone. Straight from Covent Garden. I'll see if I can't get him to give a turn. I'm sure he will, to oblige us!"

"Of course 'e will!" Mrs Derricks confirmed.

"That would be excellent!" agreed Mr Emmanuel, with a slight sinking of the heart. But a moment's thought comforted him. Naturally one would not get the Nightingale without the Baritone, and the Baritone without the Ventriloquist. But they *were* professionals, anyhow, however disgracefully they behaved when they got drunk. Their names would look well on the leaflets.

The leaflets....

"Mr Derricks," he started off again impetuously, "I'm going to get the leaflets out this very day. I can't tell you how delighted I am we're in this together!"

"I won't have anyone's name in bigger type than mine, Mr Emmanuel!"

"I wouldn't dream of it." Mr Emmanuel was dancing with impatience. "I must be going at once. Oh goodbye, Mrs Derricks! and you, Mr Derricks!" He pumped energetically away at their hands. "I'll be in again this afternoon!"

"Mother, won't you ask Mr Emmanuel would he like a cup of tea?"

"No, thanks, really not! I haven't a moment to spare!"

III

Mr Emmanuel hadn't a moment to spare. He hurried out of the Derricks's house as if he had just learned his own house was on fire. Then he stopped short at the garden gate. What was the next thing to do? What? The leaflets? That really seemed a bit precipitate.

Mr Emmanuel hurrying out of the Derricks's front door was the phenomenon that first drew the attention of Magnolia Street to the fact that momentous things were afoot. They were buzzing the news to each other a few moments later at Mrs Poyser's shop. The beards wagged at the synagogue.

Then Mr Emmanuel caught sight of an errand boy leaving the Winberg factory with an object a little like a corpse hanging limply over his arm. The Winbergs! Ah, of course! They had promised him their help. He had best see about that. The Winbergs meant Bella. He hoped she would be down already.

She was. Mr Emmanuel was forgetting the day was getting on. She was lying on the red plush sofa in a silk peignoir. She might have been expecting him, so carefully was she disposed on the sofa and the peignoir on her. There was a little Moroccan inlaid table beside her, with a cup of coffee on it and a plate of Turkish Delight.

"Mr Emmanuel," her buttery voice gurgled. "How delighted I am to see you!" She held forth her white arm. He took the fingertips and kissed them. He didn't know what had come over him this morning, the way he was strutting and cavaliering all over the place. The Cause, he remembered, the Cause!

He told her of the idea, or of the twofold idea, that he had given birth to this morning. He told her of the ineffable ideal upon which it was based. He forgot where he was, who he was talking to, what he was talking about.

"Won't you sit down, please, Mr Emmanuel?" came the voice of Bella Winberg, quite firmly. It was odd to find that padded voice had a skeleton of hardness underlying it. It brought him up sharp. "It will make it much easier," said Bella, "if you sit down. Exactly where are we now?" He told her. He related his signal diplomatic triumph over the Derricks contingent. She smiled her approval. But she requested him to perceive that it was only a negative victory. He had assured the cessation of their hostility. That was all, and only for the time being. She talked good common sense. He was astonished, and delighted. Now and again she varied her tactics, as if to show that she was a female, too, not merely a person of intelligence. She smiled, showing her pretty teeth. She dropped her handkerchief, revealed her ankle. She revolved her charms, as it were, as a cook rotates a grill on a spit. Then she became the sensible woman again.

"And by the way," she wanted to know, "what are you going to present Benny Edelman with?"

He had not had time to think out the problem. "A set of ivory fish-servers," he said, haphazard. The rich houses he went to in Didsbury all had ivory fish-servers. He had longed for some himself, for years, vainly.

Her delicious laughter tinkled among the pampas grass tufts as if the throat of one of the stuffed humming birds had started vibrating suddenly.

"No, no!" she said. "Can you see the Lord Mayor handing a set of fish-servers to Tommie Wright and Tommie Wright handing them to Benny Edelman? It can't be fish-servers! No, it must be a gold watch, with a nice little inscription!"

Mr Emmanuel glowed. "But of course. What else could it possibly be?"

"And who's going to do the presenting? Have you made up your mind?"

"I had an idea," he said, "that if we asked the Chief Rabbi —"

"No!" she said. "Nor the Bishop! Don't you see the complications it would lead to?"

"Yes," he said humbly. "You are quite right!" His jaw dropped. He did not seem to be going the proper way about things at all. He was making a fool of himself before this girl. One would think that it was she who had had the idea in the first place, not himself. He pouted, he tapped the floor with his foot a little sulkily.

Through her lowered eye-lashes she saw phase succeed phase transparently round the edges of Mr Emmanuel's boyish mouth.

"Mr Emmanuel," she said, "have I given you any idea how proud I am you've come to me first with this beautiful, beautiful scheme of yours?" Her voice was like maroon velvet. "I count myself first, because the other thing... it was mere diplomacy, wasn't it, Mr Emmanuel? You and I between us, we'll get things *done!*"

His bosom heaved. He didn't know whether he was going to cry or not.

"We can't possibly ask the people in the street for more than a shilling per house. But we must get that shilling. And then — of course, we'll be a long way from being able to buy a handsome gold watch. You'll let my father make up the rest? I know he will. I can guarantee that. We'll be so proud," she whispered, "so proud. Do you know, I've sometimes felt that you've rather neglected us," she reproved him with melancholy delicacy. "Do you think we weren't as proud as the rest of you that Benny was such a brave, brave boy? Why did nobody ask us to come and join in, while all the rest of you got together in this house and that house, and were so friendly and jolly? I love parties, Mr Emmanuel. Just because my poor father is making a little money... Oh, it's hard, hard!" The suspicion of a tear glistened in her eye

Mr Emmanuel threw himself upon her sofa impulsively and clasped her hand between his own two hands.

"I had no idea you were so interested, Bella." He had not called her Bella for some years. "I'm so happy I've got your help, happier than I can say. You must certainly sit on the Crèche Committee. And there's a new vacancy on the Hospitals Collection Fund Committee. I must see at once about getting you nominated. Then —"

She changed the subject.

"So we'll get out the leaflets today?"

"Yes, I think that if we get down to it at once —"

"Have you got a pen on you? Get me that writing-block, please. We'll draw it up at once."

The rich black flowing hair caressed the sparse pale broken hair. The fountain-pen scratched away industriously.

IV

Mr Emmanuel was well in with the printers. One way and another he gave them a lot of work. Within a few hour's the leaflet was set up, printed and delivered. Mr Emmanuel was waiting in the parlour impatiently, looking out through the curtains. Then the boy came, trundling his hand-cart. Mr Emmanuel uttered a glad cry and sprang from his chair. He did not need more than a few dozen leaflets, but printers do not set leaflets up in few dozens. The boy came staggering up the path with a large bundle. Mr Emmanuel grabbed it out of his arms and retired jubilantly to the parlour.

"Slatta!" he called, "Slatta!" She wouldn't understand much about it, but he was so excited, he could not resist dragging her into it.

"Yes, Isaac, yes?" She came running out of the scullery, with an egg-beater in her hand. Her husband was slashing away at the coarse rope that bound the bundle. He savaged his way through the packing. Then he saw them, green ones and pink ones and yellow ones, the lovely leaflets.

"Listen, Slatta!" he bade her. He read out the concoction which Bella and he had composed only a few minutes ago, it seemed. The reading was tremulous with joy and anxiety. He read out the leaflet again in a voice given up to pure appreciation.

"What do you think of that now, Slatta?"

"It's like a Psalm!" she said.

At that moment Max passed by the open door. "Max!" his father shouted suddenly. "One moment, before you go upstairs!"

The boy came in. "Yes, father?" His flat fringe lay over his eyes. He flung it out of the way. His servant, David, stood behind him.

"Max, listen here!" He started to read his masterpiece, went on for a heading or two, then stopped suspiciously. He knew the way Max's attention wandered. It fastened like a fly on your nostril and stayed there. "Are you listening?"

"Aren't I just!" said Max. There was no doubt of the sincerity of that tone.

"What do you think of that?" said his father.

"I think we all ought to have a jolly good time!"

"What do you mean, a good time? Oh, of course, of course! Naturally we'll have a good time! Now, Max, do you see what it says here about local talent?"

"Yes, father," said Max, just a trifle acidly. "That means the people who are not like... like Mr Derricks and his friends, professional, *local* talent. You see?"

"I see!"

"I've already been in to Mrs Poyser. You know her daughter, Becky, she's been taking piano and singing lessons for a long time. She should be able to put up a good show by now."

"Well? You got her to play and sing?"

"I did. She didn't want to. That girl's too shy. She'll never come to anything if she stays so shy. I think it's her father's fault. He makes her worse."

"But her mother made her think better of it?"

"Yes," said Mr Emmanuel curtly. "But I'm sure *you're* not going to be shy and silly, Max." A note of wheedling came into his voice.

"Why, father?" The voice was very innocent now.

"I was only thinking it would be so nice and interesting if you'd do a bit of lightning-sketching on the Night." (He already talked of it with a capital N and a slight upturning of the eyes.) "You're so quick with that charcoal pencil, aren't you, Max?" he explained.

"Oh, yes," said Max sweetly. "I'd love to do a little lightning-sketching on the Night." He imitated the slight upturning of his father's eyes. The voice was far too sweet to be true. "On my own conditions," he added.

"What do you mean, your own conditions?"

"I'm interested in behinds. I've been doing them for the last fortnight. If they'll only let me do behinds —"

Mr Emmanuel's face was livid with anger. "Get out of here, you apostate!" he yelled. "Get out or I'll —" He rose. His thumb and finger twitched venomously towards Max's arm. Max got out of there.

Mr Emmanuel looked the other way. David remained unobtrusively on the threshold. The others allowed two or three minutes to pass while Mr Emmanuel's flame of anger flickered down.

Then — "Father," said David gently.

Mr Emmanuel could not yet trust himself to speak. David waited another minute. Then, once more, "Father!" he said.

"Yes, David?" Mr Emmanuel answered, without looking at him.

"As soon as you'd like anyone to go round with the leaflets, shall I?"

"You're a good boy, David," his father said heavily. He was feeling a little helpless. "Shall he take them now or later, Slatta?"

Slatta hesitated a moment or two. "I wanted to say, Isaac —"

"Yes, what did you want to say?"

"Wouldn't it be a good thing if you went in to see Benny Edelman, first? Just to make sure. He ought to know as soon as anyone, oughtn't he?"

There was silence for a little. Of course. The woman was right. After all, Benny had a lot to do with the whole thing, and it had not yet occurred to him to have a word with the hero. He rose from his chair. The sight of the great bundle of virginal leaflets, so many seeds, as it were, to be sown in the furrows of his own ploughing, brought back something of his enthusiasm.

"I'll go at once, Slatta — I won't be long. Don't go till I come back, David. As for *him*" his thumb pointed up to the attic and Max — "I forbid you to go near him again this evening!"

Benny Edelman was quite rosy with embarrassment. "No, really, Mr Emmanuel," he insisted. "No, I can't have that now! What? Me getting up on a platform in front of all those people —"

It had been quite pleasant to be made a fuss of for a week or two; but he wasn't at all sorry it had been dying down a bit of late. He didn't want to be so conspicuous. Why, there had even been something in the paper about him.

"I ask you, Mr Emmanuel —"

But it was not really difficult to overrule his objections. The gold watch helped, too. And then, of course, there was the Baby Crèche. Benny was not going to pull the nice antiseptic dummy-teats out of the mouths of the babies, was he? He was not going to condemn the babies to roll in the Longton gutters, was he? All because he felt just a little awkward-like, and more credit to him for that, too.

"Well, Mr Emmanuel, seeing that you put it like that now —" His good-looking face was all troubled by the picture Mr Emmanuel had evoked of the babies deprived by him of their pretty cots, their pretty white curtains...

Then he turned round to Mr Emmanuel suddenly. "What date did you say this was fixed for?"

"A week next Saturday night. Saturday, July the ninth!"

"I'm sorry," said Benny a little unsteadily. "I'll not be able to come!"

"What do you mean you won't be able to come! Now, now, Benny! Don't talk nonsense!"

"What I meant was... You see, I'd arranged to go and watch Lancashire play at Old Trafford. A whole party of us."

"But that's ridiculous. They don't play cricket at night. The presentation will be at night, after *shool*."

"Of course," said Benny. "How stupid of me! I mean — I was thinking about getting back from the cricket match in time. I'm sure it'll be all right," he went on unsteadily.

Mr Emmanuel was relieved he had carried his point. He could not have stood any further postponement. He did not know now how he was going to survive at such a pitch of excitement during the next twelve days.

"You'd best not tell your mother!" he said, wagging his finger at Benny. Benny turned large eyes on him. "Tell my mother what? What do you mean?"

"That you're going to watch a cricket match on a Saturday afternoon! You're a bad boy, Benny! You'll come to a bad end!"

"I say," said Benny. "Hadn't you best go and see Mrs Wright, too? I mean if you're going to have Tommie up on the platform, hadn't you best make sure that Mrs Wright —"

"Benny, you'll make a town councillor one of these days. You mark my words. I think you're quite right. I'll just slip along and have a word with her. I'll be back immediately. Then it'll be all fixed up."

Mrs Wright was almost ecstatic. "I think it's such a *sweet* idea! However did it come to you? Often have I sat back in this chair, looking at my little Tommie there, and thinking that if it hadn't been for his dear, kind, brave uncle — where would he be now, Mr Emmanuel, where would he be now?"

"That's not a question for minds like ours to worry about, Mrs Wright! But he's not there, is he? He's here! Aren't you, Tommie?"

"And often as I've sat back I've said to myself: 'Wouldn't it be wonderful if there'd be some way of showing Mr Edelman what we all think of him! But what can I do, a lonely widow like me? It's for bigger people than me to see to it,' I've said to myself. And here you come along, Mr Emmanuel — Oh, Mr Emmanuel, may I kiss you?"

He blushed. "And on the presentation night, too!" he stipulated.

"You lovely man!" she said. She put her two hands on his cheeks and kissed him chastely on the left temple. Mr Emmanuel looked in for the promised moment at Benny Edelman's. He smiled.

"That'll be all right, Benny!"

"That'll be fine, Mr Emmanuel!"

He continued along the street. People were eyeing him with approval and profound respect from doorsteps, from windows. Excepting Miss Tregunter, perhaps. She sat like a stone image behind her curtains.

"A couple of figs for Miss Tregunter!" he said to himself. He could have danced the rest of the journey.

"Go, David!" he said. "You can go and give out the leaflets. Everybody in Magnolia Street is to have a leaflet. You can do the other streets tomorrow night. I must go along and see Mr Derricks and tell him what's happened."

Chapter 14

I

That Tuesday was a hectic day, but it was only a beginning. Mr Emmanuel was almost too busy to be happy, even. The business and the happiness extended themselves to the whole street. There were difficulties, of course, as was to be expected with so much to be done in so short a time. There was some trouble about getting the hall for the great night, for one of the secret societies to which Mr Poyser belonged had already earmarked it for their summer soirée. But Unity Hall was in the heart of the region of the flowering shrubs, and none other would have been of the slightest use. Besides, the name was an omen which Mr Emmanuel refused to relinquish on any terms. Theologically, too, the name had a reassuring ring about it. Messrs. Poyser and Winberg overrode *that* difficulty. There was a certain amount of trouble over the order in which Wilfred Derricks's friends would consent to give their indispensable performances. Bella was called in. Semitic as her charms were, the Boys could not withstand them. Old Mrs Edelman was, for some quite cryptic reason, troublesome. The assistance of Reb Feivel and Mr Billig was called in to prove to her that there was nothing stated in the Jewish scriptures against the presentation of gold watches to gentlemen who save their kind from drowning.

There was a little trouble about the raffle, but not in the matter of selling the tickets: for the streets of the flowering shrubs responded to the call magnificently. A fresh block of tickets had to be printed, with the consequence that a fresh supply of presents had to be admitted. That was where the difficulty came in. So many gifts were volunteered which it would have been tactless to allow anyone to win. The cast-off wardrobes of Leah Winter's *fire-goyahs* stood high in that category. Who wanted Agnes Malone's moth-eaten boa? But it was impossible to hurt Agnes Malone's feelings. Bella was called in. Bella performed miracles of tact.

Mr Emmanuel had three lieutenants: Wilfred Derricks, who had the entertainment side of things in hand; Bella, who had the tact end to look after; then David. David did almost everything else. It was he who kept the communications open, when the vanguard was engaged in a sortie. It was he who collected the presents, and, with wizard cunning, allowed one or two to get broken or lost *en route*. It was he who collected the Magnolia Street shillings for the presentation gold watch.

It is likely that nothing would have got itself done at all if not for the three lieutenants. Mr Emmanuel was so busy and happy there was hardly any chance for him to get down to actual details. But there was one detail he had to take in hand; the matter of the notability who was to hand over the watch. David could not arrange that for him, nor Wilfred, nor Bella, even. A believer in high aiming, Mr Emmanuel aimed at the Lord Mayor, but missed. The Lord Mayor would be out of town. He then aimed at Mr Furniss, the High Master of Doomington School; but Mr Furniss was presiding that night at a National Congress of Headmasters. He aimed at one or two prominent business people, civic leaders, lawyers. For one reason or another they declined the honour. It was not the first time Mr Emmanuel had asked them to preside over one or another of his schemes. The distinguished gentlemen were all too busy.

In the meanwhile the day, or the night, was approaching. There was still a lot to do, and everything else was going smoothly; everything but this matter of the magnate. Mr Emmanuel began to look more and more worried. His head began to sway more dangerously on his neck. On Monday he had nothing but two glasses of tea and some cake, he was so busy harrying the magnates. But they were firm. On Tuesday he did not even eat any cake.

He was still busy, still happy in a sense. Had he not got the whole street on the *qui vive* with love and excitement? But he was losing flesh. Mrs Emmanuel burst into tears quite suddenly in Mrs Poyser's shop. The strain was telling on her as much as on him.

And then Wednesday morning came, Wednesday afternoon. His two latest efforts had been turned down with impoliteness. He would not even take his tea. When Slatta at length induced him to, it took the skin off his palate, it was so hot. It was Wednesday evening. The presentation was on Saturday. He lurched miserably over to the front door. He stood on his doorstep, and looked up the street.

And then a figure that had been absent from Magnolia Street for six weeks or more, hove to round the corner, with a slight

214

swing in the shoulders and hips as if the pavement lifted slowly to the pull of the moon.

Then a wild and lucid certainty leapt full-born into Mr Emmanuel's brain.

"Slatta!" cried Mr Emmanuel. "Slatta! We must get that young fellow! Do you see? Cooper! He's just back from sea! Don't you see, Slatta? It would be perfect! perfect! Better than twenty Lord Mayors! Why are you looking at me like that? Do you think I'm mad?"

Slatta thought he was. She went over tearfully to Mrs Poyser's shop and told them all so. Mr Emmanuel, his hair and beard all disordered, a light burning in his eyes, went over to the house of John Cooper. Ten minutes later he returned, his hair and beard as disordered as before, the light in his eyes quenched.

II

It was not long after Rose Berman came back from her duties at Messrs. Saunders, the music-sellers, in Deansgate, that she had to go in to Mrs Poyser's to do a little shopping. As she stood there, waiting for the weighing of her butter, Mrs Emmanuel entered. In a moment the air twittered and thrilled with the name of John Cooper.

Rose Berman put a hand on the counter to steady herself. She went pale. She waited for the women to turn their heads and stare at her. They did no such thing. She might, in their minds, have as little connection with John Cooper as they had with the Conclave of Cardinals at the Vatican. In their minds existed nothing but Benny Edelman and Tommie Wright and a gold watch, huge and mellow as a harvest moon, that was even now slipping up over the edge of the horizon and would shortly blaze full in the centre of the night heavens.

Rose Berman stealthily withdrew her hand from the counter. The colour came back into her cheeks. She accepted her packages from Mr Poyser. "Well, I think I'll be getting along now. So long, everybody!"

"Good evening, Rose! Good evening! Your mother's looking better today, a blessing on her!"

The love of John Cooper and Rose Berman is not of the Emmanuel variety, a love with bands and banners and gold

215

watches and 'Mr Chairman, Ladies and Gentlemen'. It is strong enough, deep enough, and still love in secret.

They are in their secret café there, at the other end of Doomington. It is this same evening, two hours later. They have already been there half-an-hour or so. Something of the sweet routine has been already accomplished.

"John, your shoulders are bigger than ever. Look, the seams of your sleeves are coming undone!"

"Rose, you look tinier than ever! I could put you in a waistcoat pocket now. It used to be a coat pocket!"

"Have you shaved?"

"Till I bled, you little devil, and that's all the thanks I get! What stuff do you put on your hair?"

"None! How dare you?"

"I like it! I want you to use lots more! Pints!"

"Do you love me?"

"I hate you!"

"I hate *you*!"

"Oh hell! Oh you darling! Darling! Darling!"

"John! Don't! You're hurting!"

"Do you no harm!"

So it went on. That sort of conversation repeated itself at intervals without reference to content suspended in the air like a bright cloud. But they had got on to a matter which concerned others than themselves now.

"So he's been over to you?" she said. "I thought he would. What did you say, darling?"

"What did I say? What d'you think I said?"

"I'm asking *you*, John!"

"I told him not to be a blamed fool!"

"In so many words?"

"In just so many words!" His lower lip protruded in the unpleasant way it had. She said nothing for some seconds. He thought the matter was over and done with. He put his hands on her cheeks to draw her mouth to his. She removed them, and still holding them, said, very quietly:

"John!"

"Yes, old girl?"

"Don't get angry!"

"What on earth for?"

"I'm going to ask you something!"

"Any damn thing in the whole damn world!"

"Don't swear!"

"Anything in the whole world! Well, what is it?"

"Am I in the habit of asking you for things?"

"I wish I could get you to say what you *would* like me to bring you from those places! And when I do have a brainwave, you lock the stuff up in a chest!"

"That's not the sort of thing I'm going to ask for!"

"What on earth is it, then?"

"John! I want you to do what Mr Emmanuel asked you!"

"Rose! Have you gone crazy?"

"Oh no! Will you?"

"Will I? I'll be damned first!"

"Be quiet, John! I'll never ask you anything again!"

"But Rose, I don't understand! *You* don't either! What? Me get up on a platform like a little Queen of the May? Me? What do you take me for, Rose? What on earth's bitten you? Me? If the chaps ever got to know of it... Me handing a watch to a little boy and a little boy handing on the watch... Jesus Christ! I beg your pardon! Honestly, you don't know what you're asking. Besides, what the hell for? No, I can't help it! I've got to swear, or break the furniture! What the hell for?"

"Can I say a word?"

"Will you tie my hair up in pale blue ribbon, Rose? Shall I wear a little velvet suit? No, Rose, don't turn away like that! For God's sake don't let's quarrel over something so piffling as this. There's never been any sort of a breeze between us before. And there won't be again! We're not that sort, you and me! You're joking, Rose! Good old girl! You're pulling my leg! Aren't you, Rose? Rose, turn round!"

She turned round. "John," she said. "I'm not joking. I'm awfully serious about it."

His manner changed completely. "What d'you want me to make such a darned fool of myself for?" he said quietly. "Apart from what I feel myself, I'm not the sort of person for the job. He wants an alderman or an MP."

"He's tried," she said.

"Yes," he admitted glumly. "He was quite frank about that. Flattering, isn't it, to come in at the last moment when everyone with guts has said no, not at any price. And not guts only. It's a sense of humour. A cockeyed slum tea party."

"No, I don't think you should talk like that about it. It's not kind to me, or yourself, for that matter. And it's not true. It's a lot more than that. As for your coming in at the last moment, he hadn't the ghost of an idea you were coming back. Even if he had, I don't suppose he'd have asked you first. But coming when you did, he suddenly realised how absolutely marvellous it would be for you, just you, no-one else, to take on the job."

"And can you begin to explain why?" with a slight note of bitterness in his patience.

"It's not easy," she said. She had not straightened out her ideas on the matter; but she felt, exactly as Mr Emmanuel had done, the justice and poetry, the brilliance, of his inspiration. She felt it even more forcibly than he, but for a reason which she only dimly admitted to herself, which she would not for the wealth of China have avowed to John.

A Lord Mayor? An MP? An eminent barrister? What miserable scarecrows of men were they to be invited to any honour, whatever it might be, when John Cooper, prince among men, was on hand to receive and confer it?

She knew it would make her feel sick with pride to see her lover go up on the platform before all these people, though they were people he despised. It was an assertion of how much the bravest, the strongest, the handsomest, he was, the chief among them all. And that young man, so chosen, was her lover, hers, and he came back to her from all the seas and would come back to her again and again, till their day dawned for them.

She felt all this, but breathed not a word of it. "I'll try to explain why," she said. "Because the whole business will fizzle out if you don't come to his rescue. It's all built up round the presentation and it'll go to pieces without you. At least he thinks so. He's got the idea into his head, and it won't be driven out.

"And I don't want it to go to pieces. I think this idea of a crèche for the Longton babies is a beautiful one, and the concert, or whatever it is, will start it off beautifully. And I think his other idea of bringing together the Jews and the Christians is beautiful, too. It's all so silly, the way they look at each other as if the other people were animals in a cage. And he's fighting it down. He's simply splendid about it. This idea of love one another —"

"And that's why you and I must go skulking off to a café halfway to Chester, I take it?"

"I know it's all very muddle-headed. He's very muddle-headed, too. But he's a very lovely person. Besides —"

"Besides what?"

"I don't go skulking off, as you call it, because of him, or any of them. I don't care a snap of the fingers for *them*. You know why I drag you out here."

"Yes, Rose. I'm sorry. Kiss me, so I'll know you know I'm sorry. Thank you."

"Not at all. *I* like it, too. Where *was* I? Oh Mr Emmanuel. I don't want him let down. Everybody lets him down all along the line, his wife, his sons, the working classes, Germany, France. That's the way he feels about it all. Yet he comes to the top always, always, like a cork. You should hear the way he goes on."

"He's a windbag. He should talk less and do more."

"That's where you're wrong. He does an awful lot, too, on the quiet, an awful lot. He's amazingly kind. One keeps on finding out in odd sorts of ways. That's why I don't want him let down."

"But me, Rose, darling, *me*! Where do I come in?"

"Where do you come in? I'll tell you. Oh by the way, it's just occurred to me. Do you think he could ever have found out about that business in the Bay of Biscay. I mean, during that storm, when you jumped in after that sailor —"

He stopped her short. "Look here. Nobody in this town knows, not even Mary. You wouldn't have known if not for that damn letter slipping out of my wallet. If you've been telling anybody —"

"No, darling, no. I *never* talk about you. You know that. It just occurred to me that he might have seen something rather appropriate in this meeting of the heroes —"

"Stow that!" he said crustily.

"All right! Well then, to go on again. Why do you fill the bill? Oh yes, there's one thing I hadn't realised. He probably hasn't realised it, too. You remember that night when the Boys had a party and you went out and banged their heads for them?"

"Yes."

"Well, the Boys have got a lot to do with this show. That's part of his triumph. You should see the way that Nightingale goes chirruping in and out of Mr Emmanuel's house. As if Mr Emmanuel kept him in a cage, and he let him out for an airing now and again."

"The little bag of poison! He gives me the creeps!"

"Well, there they are, strong men and baritones and conjurers, the whole lot of them. They're rather a handful. He feels a bit nervous about them. Suppose something went wrong? Suppose they cut up nasty? They could easily wreck the whole thing. With you being there, he'll feel different about it. Moral support and all that!"

"I see," said John," a sort of unpaid chucker-out when the toughs get unpleasant?"

"No, no! You don't understand! What I meant was —" But she determined to give up that line of attack. Judging from his face, it was not profitable. "The fact is, John, he knows, like they all know — how shall I put it? — that you're — er, a gentleman!"

John started growling.

"Well, there it is. You are. He's quite man of the world enough to know you're more of a gentleman than most of the big-wigs who've cold-shouldered him, although you live in Magnolia Street. And there you are!" She suddenly cried out delightedly, like someone suddenly coming up against clear sky after blundering in a thick wood. "That's exactly where you *are*! Where we *all* are! You're Magnolia Street. It's become a sort of obsession with him. All in the family — our own Jews and Christians, our own hero, our own Nightingale, our own gold watch, our own gentleman!"

"Oh you clever little devil, aren't you? Aren't you a clever little devil?"

"Kiss me, our gentleman!"

"God almighty, so I suppose I've got to!"

"Got to kiss me? All right, if —"

"No, vampire! I mean I've got to hand over that potato?"

"Yes, please, John!"

"I shall loathe it, Rose!"

"Yes, John, only town councillors don't!"

"Absolutely, absolutely, absolutely no chance of being let off?"

"No, please, John!"

"All right," he growled. "I'll slip in tonight and tell him! Yah! Yah!" — he made fierce faces at her.

"Yah to you!" she said.

The next evening was Thursday evening. One more evening, then only the next after that. Mr Emmanuel rotated through the streets of Longton like a small sandstorm.

But when he saw Rose Berman, coming up Magnolia Street after her day's work, he stopped rotating.

"Thank you, Rose, you're an angel!" he said to her, like a conspirator, out of the corner of his mouth.

"What for?" she said.

"I didn't know before. At least I did. And then I thought not. That's your affair. Good luck! I just want to thank you, Rose."

She blushed. She put a finger on her mouth.

"Hush!" she whispered.

"Like the grave, Rose darling!"

Chapter 15

I

It is Unity Hall. It is Saturday night. The air is so thick with smoke you can hardly see. It is so full of noise you cannot hear yourself speak. You certainly cannot hear Mr Emmanuel speak. He is making speeches between every turn. He will never get such an opportunity in his life again.

Who is here? Everybody is here, even Eric Winberg, stooping for a moment to consider how the commoners amuse themselves. It would be easier to say who is not here. Miss Tregunter is not here. She is sitting behind her curtains biding her time. Mr Benjamin Stern is not here. Mrs Berman is not here. She very much wanted to come. With a hint of tears in her eyes she begged to come. But Rose was firm. And a very good thing, thought Rose, with all this smoke about.

All the rest of Magnolia Street is here. The people who keep shops have turned Doomington upside down to get people to take over for them during the great night. A number of people in the street whom we have not met are here, for we have not been able to meet all of them. Some we might have met have gone already. There are already a number of new Magnolia Street faces since the May morning when we first came here. A street waxes and wanes, glows and darkens. It is a living thing.

Other folk are here, from all the streets of the flowering shrubs, from streets further afield, in Begley Hill and Bridgeways. But the Magnolia Street folk are up in the front part of the hall, naturally. For while the Longton Crèche belongs to them all, Benny Edelman is their own and none other's.

The very front row of all has been reserved for the notabilities. Six or seven of the right-hand seats of the front row are occupied by ladies who are interested in the Longton Crèche. You could see from a mile off that they are the sort of ladies who are interested in crèches. There are no gentlemen amongst them.

The rest of the front row is empty, excepting for John Cooper. He looks dreadfully isolated and conspicuous with twelve empty seats on each side of him. But he will not remain alone for more than another minute or two. It is only an accident that he has been alone so long. The ceremony has been in progress for a good half-hour. It has seemed a lot more than half-an-hour to John.

The fact is that Benny Edelman and Jessie Wright and Tommie Wright have not turned up yet. Naturally, it would have been only right and proper if they had turned up half-an-hour early, rather than half-an-hour late. But there has been some accident somewhere. They will turn up any moment now.

It is odd, of course, that they should both of them, all three of them, that is to say, be late. But there you are. Coincidences *will* happen.

It cannot be said that John Cooper looks happy in that front row, like a solitary tooth in a jaw. It cannot be said that he looks unhappy, either. The fact is that he looks like a carved statue. His face is entirely expressionless. A slightly grim statue, perhaps.

Rose Berman has placed herself in a position where she has his profile in view while she looks towards the stage, or pretends to. She cannot believe that that incredibly handsome and distinguished young man is her lover, her own very own for keeps. She asks herself now and again if she is dreaming it. She pinches herself to convince herself she is not. Or a gentleman behind her passes a bottle of beer to a lady, and the gurgling down the lady's throat sounds real enough.

For it is hot. Some of the members of the audience have taken the precaution to bring in a little liquid refreshment with them. Others, inspired by their example, send out their sons or younger brothers to the jug and bottle department of the nearest hostelry. The Lamb and Lion is not the nearest, by two or three.

Benny Edelman and the Wrights have not turned up yet.

The Boys have. Of course they have. What would the great night have been without the Boys? The whole point of the proceedings from their point of view was to have the Boys right bang in the public eye; more particularly in the eye of the General Manager of the Oak Variety Theatre Circuit, who has promised to turn up this evening.

So Mr Emmanuel has said. And it is clear Mr Emmanuel could not tell a lie. Is he not Clerk to the Jewish Board of Guardians?

No gentleman in a fur coat, with a large diamond pin in his tie, and a large cigar in his mouth, has turned up yet. It does not occur to the Boys that on such a night he would not turn up in a fur coat. Or if it does, they are certain about the diamond and

223

the cigar. No gentleman equipped with any of these has turned up yet. Neither have the Wrights nor Benny Edelman.

It was the idea of the Boys that they should sit on the platform all the time, a proceeding not without precedent, for so do pierrots and black minstrels. But the Boys did not go in for comic back-chat like pierrots. When it came to doing their turns, the Boys were solitary stars revolving each in his private Space. The idea was that when the General Manager came, he would be able to have a good look at them. He would be able to recognise them next time. It did not occur to any of them that that would prejudice their chances.

It was, perhaps, unfortunate that the inhabitants of the Jewish pavement of Magnolia Street had to sit facing the Boys all evening, and the Boys had to sit facing them. They could not help getting on each other's nerves a bit. They had not the most amiable memories of each other. But Mrs Emmanuel made up for it to a certain extent.

Mrs Emmanuel had, in fact, achieved her life's main ambition. She, too, at length, was sitting on a platform beside her husband. Not beside him exactly, for he was up and down, in and out, the whole time, from the dressing-room to the platform, from the platform to the dressing-room; then off and away thrusting through the crowd to the main entrance of the hall.

For really, he was getting disturbed, very visibly. Concerts, raffles, love speeches, crèches, were all very well in their way. But there was no doubt at all that the keystone of the arch of the evening was the presentation to Benny Edelman of the gold watch.

The gold watch. His heart dropped a beat. He forced his way back desperately to the dressing-room, where, surrounded by the principal prizes in the raffle, the gold watch burned on the table. He breathed again. He returned to the platform. He sat down for a moment at his wife's side. She smiled proudly. She nodded to her friends in the audience. They nodded back, not displeased to be nodded to from the platform. Mrs Poyser nodded back a little less vigorously than the others.

It was not that Mrs Poyser herself wanted to sit on the platform, though why *she* couldn't, if Mrs Emmanuel could, she could not quite see. But it was plain and simple justice that she should have sat at least vicariously on the platform, in the shape of her daughter, Becky. Becky was the star turn of the programme, she considered, or, at least, the only lady performer. And when the Boys heard that there simply was nothing for it, and they would have to put up with Mrs Emmanuel at one end of the row, they wanted to make things even by having the other female at the other end. But Becky Poyser said no. And when they insisted, she just bluntly said no again. And when her mother insisted, she threatened to get hysterical. She wouldn't give the best of herself, her mother decided, if she got hysterical. She hadn't much volume of voice at the best of times. It was the quality that Mrs Poyser pointed to. So the point was waived.

There had been a little trouble about Becky. They had put her down as the first turn on the programme, on the approved professional principle of starting a show with a dud. When Becky heard this she said she would not come; for she certainly would have died of shyness if she had been compelled to lead off the performance. Her father stood up for her. It was very astonishing, the way the meek man roared like a tiger. So that point was waived, too.

And taking it all in all, she had done credit to herself and her mother and her music and her singing mistress. She had come on second. The Boys having drawn lots, the Baritone from Covent Garden came on first and sang the Prologue from *Pagliacci* resentfully. The singing might have been worse, but the audience was in a state of great good humour to lead off with, and they would not have noticed it if it had been a great deal better.

Then Mr Emmanuel made another speech. He had, of course, led off with one. Then Becky played a piece on the piano. Here it was a matter of volume rather than quality. She had big feet to pound on the pedals with and big hands to pound on the notes with, and she scored a great success. It went round the hall that Mark Hambourg played just like that, and everyone was so impressed that an encore was urgently demanded. She gave it. The applause was uproarious. Becky became redder than ever with the excitement of her success. At the side of the second row sat Bella Winberg, in a marvellous pale green satin frock, all scollops and flounces and bare fat pale shoulder. Nobody asked Bella to play on the piano. Nobody asked Bella to sing. Becky flung her head back and sniffed her triumph across the footlights. Then she sang. She sang Tosti's *Goodbye*. That did not add to her laurels, but it stole none.

Jessie Wright would be coming in any moment now. What could she be doing keeping a small boy away so late? Wasn't that Benny lurching in now? No, it was not.

The Boys were getting a bit restive. They weren't sitting up on that platform in order that that horse of a Yiddisher girl should gather in the nosegays. And where was that General Manager? Mr Emmanuel saw through a corner of his eye that the Boys were getting restive. Through the other corner he saw John Cooper sitting like a rock in the middle of the front row. Or like a beacon in waters that threaten to grow a little murky.

He motioned Becky to her seat. But Becky was transfigured. She kept on bowing radiantly to the applause. The Jewish pavement shouted as if she were not only Hambourg, but Liszt, too, and Paderewsky. They felt the more Becky there was, the less Boys. But Mr Emmanuel whispered in her ear. Then he shouted in her ear. Then she sat down.

He made a small speech and called on Mr Wilfred Derricks, the Longton Nightingale. Wilfred looked a full year younger than usual. He started off with *Songs of Araby*, which went down well. And then, for his encore, he sang a comic song about a young man from Peckham Rye, which went on for a good many verses. He always believed mistakenly that he had a comic talent, and this seemed to him an appropriate occasion to exercise it. He wouldn't give them all that classical stuff, a bit above their heads, he thought. The comic song did not go down well. There was much applause.

Mr Emmanuel wondered anxiously whether there was a tendency for the gentile members and the Jewish members of the audience, respectively, to applaud a performance less in regard to its merit than to the racial origin of the performer. He put the uncomfortable thought out of his head swiftly. No, that wasn't Jessie Wright coming in at the door.

The Conjurer did his turn. He balanced a lighted lamp at the end of a stair-rod and Mrs Emmanuel's hair emerged from the danger unscathed. The Ventriloquist was not in good form. So far as the non-moving of his visible vocal organs went, he was never in good form. He would certainly have done himself more credit if the General Manager of the Oak Theatre Circuit had turned up. But he had not turned up yet.

And also it was a little tactless on Mr Emmanuel's part to stand at the door looking anxiously out into the street, during the whole time that the Ventriloquist was doing his turn.

Slatta Emmanuel, on the other hand, smiled blissfully. She was in Heaven. Half the audience might have been carried off in a dead faint, and she would not have stopped smiling. A girl from Acacia Street was, in fact, carried off in a dead faint. She did it regularly, even in her friends' houses.

The keystone, or stones, of the arch, were still lacking. John Cooper looked like Gibraltar. The Pocket Samson lifted cross-bells and dumb-bells and cracked jokes. Then he showed his muscles. The applause was polite from all sections.

Mr Emmanuel tugged so hard at his hair that it nearly came away in his hand.

It had been arranged that the Nightingale should wind up this section of the proceedings with another song. Then, as the programme stated, came an address from Mr Emmanuel. Then the presentation by Mr John Cooper, second officer of the SS *Greyhound*, to Mr Benjamin Edelman, of a handsome eighteen-carat gold watch, suitably inscribed, in commemoration of his heroism in rescuing Master T. Wright from drowning in the Longton clay-croft pool on the afternoon of Thursday, June the 9th. That was, from every point of view excepting the purely philanthropic, admittedly the climax of the evening's proceedings. But if, by any chance, anyone should feel tempted to go at this stage, there remained the raffle. After Mr Emmanuel had briefly summed up the general and particular benefits that would accrue to Longton old and young from the establishment of a Baby Crèche, he was to read out the numbers that had won the principal prizes; these would be presented on the platform there and then. The numerous other prizes might be collected immediately after the close of the performance.

That was the way it was to go, according to the programme. But they could not go like that till Mr Edelman and Master Wright, at least, had made their appearance. Mrs Wright, strictly, could be dispensed with.

It was quite clear in the auditorium that things were not going so well as they might, up on the platform. Nobody, except Mrs Emmanuel, looked happy. Mr Derricks was down to give another song, but apparently he was making trouble about it. Above all the noise, John Cooper heard quite clearly what was being said. So did the ladies who were interested in crèches.

227

"I beg of you, Mr Derricks, I beg of you. If *you* won't, the others won't."

"Why did you promise he'd be here?"

"He will. I swear it. He will. They'll all come together, all three of them."

"I'm talking about your friend, the General Manager. Your *friend*!"

"Please, Mr Derricks. I appeal to you. Don't let me down. I promise you. I'll make it right with you."

Wilfred Derricks rose to his feet. He nodded curtly to the Baritone, who was accompanying him, to take his seat at the piano. He launched his voice into the sticky skies of Mr FE Weatherley.

Mr Emmanuel signalled to the dressing-room, where David had been left in charge of the gold watch and the raffle prizes. David ran round the curtains at the back of the platform, parted them and waited for his father's word.

"David, my love, run for all you're worth and find out if either Benny Edelman or Mrs Wright is at home. Find out if there's anything wrong. Run!"

David wriggled his way through legs and thighs and raced off to Magnolia Street. Wilfred finished his song; the Baritone, accompanying himself, sang another. A large section of the audience felt that it had had enough, even more than enough, of professional entertainers, for the time being. The Conjurer rose to his feet with a pack of cards in his hand. Card-tricks are always rather exasperating to all but the three front rows, even when the air is not opaque with smoke.

"Becky!" a cry arose. "Becky!"

With amazing aplomb Becky sprang out of her chair without waiting for a signal from Mr Derricks. She should certainly have waited. She sat herself down at the piano and got down to it again. There is no doubt her massive performance shored up the collapsing fabric of the evening, for the time being. Mr Emmanuel felt things, miraculously, were safe with her for at least ten minutes. She would not stop till she was asked to. Once more he thrust his way through the audience to the main entrance.

David, what could have happened to David? Would the child never come? The child had, in point of fact, only been away two minutes. Mr Emmanuel returned to the platform. No David, no Benny, no Tommie, nobody.

Then the crowd found that it had had enough of Becky, too. A certain restiveness had been noticeable for some time. "We want Benny!" cried a voice. Other voices took it up. "We want Benny! We want Benny!" Feet started pounding on the floor. There was a whistle or two. "We want Benny! We want Benny!"

Not a muscle moved in John Cooper's face. Rose Berman's heart ached with anguish that she had inflicted this humiliation on her lover. Mr Emmanuel rose weakly to his feet, and with a weak gesture commanded silence.

"Ladies and gentlemen," he started. "I want Benny, too. We all want Benny. He's on his way now. He'll be here at any moment. And while we're waiting I propose asking Miss Bella Winberg to step up on the platform" — he was shrieking in the effort to make himself heard — "and announce the numbers of the winning prizes in the raffle! Miss Bella Winberg!" He made a gesture towards her, inviting her to step up. Miss Bella Winberg was far too downy a creature to take chances of that sort. She shook her head, emphatically. "No!" she went with her lips. Again he appealed to her. She went "No!" with her lips again.

He smiled sickly. "Under the circumstances," he howled, "I will myself read out the winning numbers. I have the list here." As he was drawing it out of his pocket, he saw that David stood panting on the floor of the hall below him, immediately under his feet. He bent down. "Well?"

"Nothing!" the child panted. "Both houses locked! Not a single light in them!"

"We want Benny! We want Benny!" came the refrain steady and formidable.

Mr Emmanuel's throat quivered. He straightened himself slowly. In so doing, his eye fell on a member of the audience sitting at the end of the fourth row from the front, on the lefthand. It was the side of the hall nearest to the dressing-room. In the dressing-room was the gold watch. The member of the audience on whom his eye had fallen was George Derricks. His hair was beautifully plastered down on both sides of a perfect parting. His cheeks shone like apples. A smile sat upon the cherubic face.

Instantly a wild fear and a wild certainty possessed themselves of Mr Emmanuel. He hurled himself along the platform and down the three steps that led into the dressing-room. The snug nest of blue velvet and padded pink silk was gone. The gold watch that had rested there was gone. *Someone had stolen the gold watch.*

"We want Benny! We want Benny!" The refrain lost all cohesion now. There were whistles and boos and catcalls. "We want Benny! We want Benny! We want Benny! We want Benny! We'll *have* Benny!"

But they could not have Benny. Benny at that moment was lying in the arms of Jessie Wright in a hotel bedroom in Blackpool. How could they have Benny?

II

It was much more comfortable lying that way in a soft bed, between cool sheets, than getting aches and pains all over, lying under bushes and thickets on Doomington commons.

But Benny's heart was heavy within him, though the woman in his arms was as light as a feather and the green eyes hidden under those eyelids were like a wine in all his veins. He had a vision of another woman who would shortly mourn him as dead, and sit on a low stool seven days as she mourned.

And there was a pounding upon his ear-drums, as if he heard from a long way off feet that thundered upon the floor and grim voices that shouted in chorus: "We want Benny! We want Benny! We want Benny!" His heart was heavy. He could not fall off to sleep.

But Jessie Wright slept extremely well. The flush on her cheeks was not lust only. It was triumph, too. She had scored. How gloriously she had scored over them all!

Her small son, also, slept well, in an adjoining room.

"Uncle Benny is going to be your daddy now," she said, as she kissed him good night. He was pleased about that. He had had enough sporadic daddies.

"My always daddy?" he asked.

"Yes," she said, and left him.

230

Chapter 16

I

Benny was not clever, but he was not a fool altogether. The degree of a man's sexual sagacity is not to be measured in terms of his talent for general conversation or playing eighteenth-century instruments. He had not gone through the world with that well-featured face and pleasant shambling indolence without being aware that women looked at him, even when they thought they were doing something else.

Then, Benny had a mother who treated him as a small boy. That is always dangerous. For when a pretty woman appears who conveys instantly that that mother's son is everything that a man can be, that he is exactly *her* sort of man in fact, he will go up in flame at once. Particularly if he has been out of work for one reason or another for some months, and time has been hanging heavy on his hands. Who knows what sort of adventure Benny Edelman went in quest of on the Longton clay-croft? Anyhow, he found it.

So when Jessie Wright intruded upon him that Thursday afternoon of the rescue, and him standing naked before the fire, both arms stretched out — a demon of audacity surged up in him which till then he had not known he harboured. He did not drop his arms to cover his nakedness. He held them stretched out. He was conscious of the firelight flickering on his stretched skin, of his good muscles, of the easy way his head sat upon his neck. He was conscious of her moment of expert scrutiny. Then she shrieked. He smiled. He knew what a fake it was.

She gave him hot whisky-cordial and aspirins, and said quite openly — why should she not? — "You'll come in as soon as you can, won't you, to see how your little boy is? That is if your cold doesn't keep you in bed. He's your little boy now as much as mine, you dear brave Mr Edelman. Aren't you, Tommie?" Tommie agreed. The public wiped its eye with its handkerchief.

He was feeling as right as rain next morning, particularly after the Durbins had shaved him and shampooed him and massaged him and put hot towels round him and made him feel generally as lewd as a late Roman Emperor.

He went into Jessie Wright's patently. Not even his mother could say at this juncture "— Jezebel, Delilah." Jessie's kitchen was full, as it was for days and days after. But she found the opportunity to whisper: "Tonight? Shall we go out?" She managed, for she was a practised woman, to invest her words, her mouth as she shaped them, her hand as she hid her mouth, with such promise of pleasure that Benny Edelman's virgin body rocked in the gust of desire that smote it.

"Yes!" The word issued between his teeth in a sudden sharp hiss. "At the clock where the road goes up to Layton Park. At nine."

"Yes!"

Then he remembered it was the eve of the Sabbath. His mother would preside over the white tablecloth and make the Sabbath prayer over the candles. He and his brother would make the prayer over the squat beakers of wine their father had left to them. It would fall to him to cut the plaited loaf spotted with poppy-seed. The candles burned steadily in their candle-sticks. The fish came, and the roast chicken, the sweet made out of carrots and raisins. The blessing followed now....

"No!" he said. "I can't!"

She turned on him the fatal green lamps of her eyes. All that she possessed of female cunning glowed in them. She pouted. She thrust the scarlet tip of her tongue through her bright lips. It pierced to his loins like an adder's fang.

"It must be later!" he said huskily. "Eleven? Is that too late?"

He had a desperate fear that it might be; that he might be condemned again to sterility, the futile expense of his youth. He waited, hardly breathing.

With deft eyes she saw it all. She kept him dangling for some seconds over the gulf.

"All right!" she said. "We'll make it eleven!" She would have been quite content to make it two or three next morning.

They met at the clock-corner where the road goes north to Layton Park. He was a few minutes early. Five minutes after the hour she had not come, nor ten minutes after the hour. He sweated with anxiety. A sickening doubt began to torment him. She was only making a fool of him. What an idiot he was to think a woman like that could fall for him — a pretty woman, as you could see a mile off, a well-dressed woman, a woman with her own little nest-egg in the bank! He looked at himself. He had his best suit on, but it looked like a sack. He was all hands and feet. He was —

She kept him waiting only twenty minutes. She knew exactly how to start off these affairs. Twenty minutes would do. "Oh God!" he said. "I thought you were never coming!"

"Well," she said, smiling sweetly, and with no effort at explanation, "I'm here, aren't I?"

They walked off up Layton Road, their fingers clasped. They did not say much to each other; they had not much to say to each other from beginning to end of their relationship. But there was something almost pathetic in the spectacle, reduced to smallness as they were in the darkness and silence into which they moved — the spectacle of a young man and a young woman devoted naively and completely to the celebration of the simple godling of lust.

The devotion was naive and complete, but not the vows themselves. With her five fingers she made him conscious of each of his own five fingers as a separate vehicle and organ of pleasure. And when they lay down at length somewhere in the moors that heave northward beyond Layton Park, she continued his initiation from finger to arm and breast and thigh, down to the last arcanum of his body.

It was a warm night. A moon rose late and travelled slowly through banks of cloud. "Jessie," he murmured. "If it's like this here, on this hard ground — what will it be like some day? In a soft bed, Jessie, with sheets? I love you, Jessie, I love you!"

"There'll be a soft bed some day, with sheets, Benny! Benny!" she cried. "Hold me closer! closer!" She held him to her as if to drain him of all the youth his dark dour mother had kept virginal for one-and-twenty years. "Kiss me! No! Open your mouth! Like this! See?"

The moon went into a thicket of cloud, and came out again. A figure came wandering among the sandy shelves and tussocks of gorse. It was a woman. She wore a cap on her head, stuck on with a hat-pin, the head of which gleamed like an ivy-berry in the moon's pallor.

Benny was not aware of her. Jessie was. The figure moved off again. "I don't suppose she spotted us," thought Jessie. "And what if she did? She can go to Hell! They can all go to Hell!"

They would both have liked the soft bed and the sheets sooner than they got them. But there was nothing for it. They saw quite clearly that though Benny could quite safely go across to her house for a few minutes now and again, it could only be for a few minutes, and then with Tommie very much in evidence and, preferably, a handful of neighbours in addition.

"No!" said Benny. "I'm not going to have people talking!" He was quite firm about that. "It was bad enough the fuss they made about Rose Berman and that sailor fellow next door to you. And I don't suppose there was anything in it, at that. Do you?"

Jessie was not interested.

"But I won't have people talking!" He meant, of course, that he wouldn't have his mother talking. He was still very much mother's boy. Jessie set her jaw firmly. He was not going to be mother's boy very much longer. But she wasn't going to stampede him. She could take her time, though not too much of it.

After a night meeting from which he had arisen more than usually thrilled and unsatisfied, he asked her heavily what about her backyard wall — she asked him to go and investigate it. No, the wall above the door would not bear his weight. It would look a little odd to go repairing the wall just at this moment, as if to make it bear the weight of a man climbing over it.

"Or the door itself," he said, "What on earth need I climb the wall for?"

"No!" she said, Her jaws snapped. He knew when she spoke like that she meant it.

"Too many people are interested in that back door."

And it was not her intention to grant him the soft bed a moment before its due time. It was harder for her than for him to bear this perpetual insatiety. She knew what satiety meant. They were like strong swimmers condemned to swim in an enormous stretch of waist-deep water. But she knew that the longer she deferred the immersion into the deep water the more tightly she bound herself to him.

The sharpening of his physical appetites sharpened many other attributes in him, though he still seemed from day to day the same lazy shambling Benny. She found him capable of prodigies of duplicity. It was only rarely that his fundamental unintelligence betrayed him. As, for instance, on the occasion when he backed one of Mr Stanley's doubles and brought off a sweet eleven pounds.

"And what," asked Arthur Durbin, "are you going to do with all that money?"

Benny's mind was elsewhere at the moment.

"Oh I suppose it'll have to go into the business," he said.

It was a mistake, the mistake was duly remembered when the news came through that Benny Edelman and Jessie Wright had got married in a registry office in Blackpool, they they were coming back to Doomington, that they were going to run a small tobacconist's shop at the corner of Laburnum Street.

So *that* was the business that Benny was going to put his winnings into: it was so long ago as that they had been planning it...

It took Jessie only a week, in fact, to decide that in Benny she had found not only her man, but her husband. She immediately got her lawyer to work on the matter of the tobacconist's shop. It would be pleasant to live in Laburnum Street. No Jews lived there.

III

Jessie Wright was a perverse woman. She suffered from the unsatisfactory embracings on the draughty moor, but it was a new type of experience, and it kept them both in a state of excitement such as she had never known in her affairs flanked by every modern convenience. Benny Edelman was a simpleton in sex, compared with many of her acquaintance. But his simplicity impassioned her far more than all their sophistication. Benny Edelman was a Jew. She hated Jews. She hated them all the more violently when her Jew crushed her in his arms till she was breathless with ecstasy. She hated Jews.

She never asked herself why. Her late husband, the insurance agent, had not instilled the toxin of Jew-hatred in her. He had been elderly, bland and generous, with nice manners, and no particular ideas about Jews. Nor had she herself had any unusually unpleasant experience at the hands of Jewish pawnbrokers or moneylenders. She was not a religious-minded woman either. Her hatred was not theological in origin. She merely hated Jews. It was a condition of her blood. It was something almost metaphysical.

As her passion for Benny grew upon her, her Jew-hatred concentrated itself upon that person who alone disputed with her the possession of his heart, his mother. She convinced herself that she had always hated Mrs Edelman with an especial hatred. It may have been true. It was possible that she had sometimes felt her own lewdness rebuked by that craggy purity. So it was that she was now able to construe her affair with Benny into a duel with the old woman for the soul and the body of her son. But she could play her game in the dark, secretly. The old woman had no weapons to counter hers.

No, her late husband had had no particular ideas about Jews. If he had, he would not have come to live in Magnolia Street. When he led her to his bed, there were still not many Jews on the opposite pavement, or she would not have come. The flood-tide of Jews came later. But Tommie was born soon. Mr Wright died soon after. It was not easy to move while events of such importance in her life were taking place. So she waited. She felt a man would come sooner or later who would take her away to a street where there were no Jews.

And then Benny Edelman rose to the surface of the brick-pond with Tommie in his arms, and so, by way of Blackpool, all three migrated to Laburnum Street.

IV

They arranged to elope to Blackpool on the afternoon of Saturday, the ninth of July. Benny was to go to a cricket match, as he and some of his friends had arranged, and to meet her in the station that evening. There was no reason for him to take any of his own equipment. Jessie had been steadily buying a new outfit for him; and for herself, too, the softest and sweetest of honeymoon undies that she could lay hands on. After her spartan austerities on the commons, she was determined that Saturday night was to be a gala night — everything that oysters and stout and hot baths and scents and silks could add to the soft bed, the cool sheets, that had begun to tyrannise over their abject and disordered imaginations. Indeed, she felt it was high time. If she did not soon, and very soon, involve herself and her

236

lover in the fury and languor of such an encounter as they planned, she felt she would break down. She would call him in from the street from her bedroom window. The whole cunning edifice would fall in soot and scandal about their ears.

Benny Edelman was now as one possessed. He had forgotten the dark lonely woman, his mother, and his pleasant brother, his dead father, whom he had cared for greatly, his relatives, his friends. He was aware only of the hounding torment of his passion. It was only when Isaac Emmanuel came in one day and told him of the great plan he had devised for the handing over to him of a gold watch before the assembly of all the people he knew, that a sense of shame arose in him. He was not deluded when Mr Emmanuel came back and reported how happy Mrs Wright had been made by his plans. When he met her that night he made a last stand. He appealed to her to postpone their elopement, for his mother's sake, for poor Mr Emmanuel's sake, for the sake of all those people, for their own sakes.

Suddenly he found she was fallen to nothing in his arms. Her face was cold and pale, there were no tears in her eyes. Her bosom was heaving wildly.

"Darling!" he cried. "My love! Jessie! Wake up! I'll come with you anywhere! Any time! Tonight if you like! Jessie! What have I done! Oh my God! Wake up!"

Her bosom heaved more softly. Her heart took on its ordinary measure. She sighed once or twice. Then she turned over towards him.

"My darling!" she whispered. "Kiss me!" Only the winking stars knew if she winked back at them.

Chapter 17

I

John Cooper was a fairly equable young man. He was not over-talkative whether it was his first day home from sea or his last day home before sailing. Rose Berman was not garrulous, either, but she always found enough to say to John in their Paphian café; particularly when he was off next day. Then she became a regular little rattle, she was so anxious he should not see how miserable she felt.

Today was one of these last days, but Rose was sitting in her alcove quiet as a mouse. John shook her by the shoulders.

"Pipe up, old girl! What's all this strong silent stuff about?"

She said nothing. She merely rested her head on his shoulder and let it stay there.

"All right," he said, "we'll have a competition."

They both said nothing for a little time.

Then: "Quite happy?" he asked.

"Quite!" she whispered.

"We'll leave it at that!" he said. He looked down into her eyes. He made tendrils out of her dark hair with his fingers.

"You little sweet!" he breathed some minutes later.

"John!" she said.

"You mustn't speak during the service!" he warned her.

"John! You know how rotten I feel about that Emmanuel business!"

"I know, my pet, I know!"

"It was all my fault. If I hadn't bullied you —"

"No, darling, we're not going through all that again. It was awful, and I've never enjoyed anything so much. I wouldn't have missed it for worlds!"

"It's very nice of you to take it like that!" she said plaintively.

"It's true!" There was a slight brusqueness in his tone.

"All I wanted to say is this. I'm sorry, and whatever you may say, I'm still sorry. Well. I want to say something else. I want you to understand that there's no connection between my being sorry and the something else I want to say. I mean — you *do* see what I mean, don't you?"

"Don't stop for breath!"

"No! Don't talk like that! It's serious! It's the most awfully serious thing I've ever said to you!"

"Oh I'm sorry! Is anything wrong?"

"No, no! Not serious like that, I mean!"

"What is it, Rose?"

"John! I've been thinking!"

"Yes?"

"I've not treated you properly. All these years."

"Haven't you? I haven't noticed it?"

"You might make it easier for me!"

"But I haven't the ghost of an idea what you want to say!"

"Let me get up. I can't talk like that. Take your fingers out of my hair!"

"There you are!"

"Well, John —"

"Yes?"

"Don't look at me! Look the other way!"

"I say! This is pretty bad!"

"John, when you come home after your next voyage — is it true, John, you'd often not come back to Doomington at all if it wasn't for me?"

"You bet!"

"You'd go to London, I suppose?"

"Oh I suppose so. Anywhere. I've not thought about it. There's always been you."

"I've not been fair to you, John!"

"How?"

"I'm making *you* pay for my mother being ill."

"You mean — we'd have got married long ago if — if she'd been all right?"

"Yes, I mean that."

"Don't worry, darling. I'm hanging on."

"When you next come back, John, would you like me to try and join you in London — or somewhere?"

John gave a long low whistle.

"I see, now. I see what you're driving at."

She stared intensely down at the spoon and fork against her plate. She drummed with her fingers on the edge of the table.

He had a vision of her at the window of some high room, looking out on trees, and the sweep of the river, perhaps. She looked down on the moving barges and the broken lights. He was lying back in bed, his head lying against the hollow of his clasped hands.

"Come away from that window!" he cried. "You'll catch cold in those thin silk things. Come away at once!"

"Yes, John!" she said meekly. She came over to him and climbed into bed beside him.

He had a vision of a French girl in a brothel in Tunis, all red plush and gilt. The girl wore a pair of open-work stockings, nothing else. The *patronne* came in with a bottle of cognac and three glasses. She stayed a little while, chatting as if John was an old friend of hers.

He had a vision of a Russian girl in Riga, in a brothel that looked like a convent. She mumbled words to the eikon in the corner before she got in beside him.

He said nothing for some moments. He was aware of a sick drumming in his pulses.

"Rose," he said at length. "You're saying this because you're thinking of me?"

"Yes, yes!"

"And of yourself? Are you thinking of yourself?"

"Yes, of course!"

"Rose, I've always been straight with you. Be straight with me now! And of yourself?"

"No, John!"

"You love me as much as I do you, don't you. Rose?"

"I love you more than anything and everything in the world. But I'm not like you."

"How? Why?"

"I can't answer." She stopped for some seconds, and pondered. "My father — he was a holy man, in his way. My mother, on the other hand — she's not. Not in *his* sort of way. I'm more like him than her. I'm saying something dreadful, am I? No, please, darling, I don't mean I'm holy or religious or anything. Do try and understand me, John. You see — that's how I am. If I hadn't been like that, I'd have been in London with you years ago. Or in a room in a hotel in Doomington. And you'd have forgotten all about me. But I'd not have forgotten about you."

"Isn't it because you're like that, I love you? Isn't that the reason? Because you are you?"

"You've not answered, John! What I asked you... just now..."

"My dear, my dear. Not if the world looked like coming to an end."

"Darling, the time will come, my lovely patient John!"

"I say!"

"What?"

"Look here! If the world *does* look like coming to an end —"

"Well!"

"You'll get a wire!"

"I'll pack up straight away."

"There's a train arrives at Euston, let me see now — I'll look it up for you!"

Chapter 18

Old Mrs Edelman's family consisted now only of herself and her younger son, Norman. Her elder son, Benny, was dead. The survivors duly sat mourning. They sat on low stools for seven days, and Norman did not shave, and Norman slit his waistcoat; just as if they had taken Benny off to the cemetery and put him in the wet ground and heaped sods on his coffin.

It might have been otherwise (now that the damage was irretrievable and what was wed could not be unwed) if there had been any chance of bringing Benny's wife into the Jewish fold. A Jewish lad from Oleander Street had married a gentile girl a few years ago and had made her a Jewess; so that you had the strange spectacle of that big-boned blonde daughter of the Picts and Scots smothering the meat in ritual salt, and wiping the noses of her little boys, preparatory to sending them off to Hebrew-school.

But there was no chance at all of bringing Jessie Edelman into the Jewish fold. She was not that sort of a daughter of the Picts and Scots.

The defection of Benny hit his mother hard. She had just managed to keep house for her two sons on the money they brought in, though Benny had been out of work a lot lately. And she kept lodgers. But lodgers, if they were not *fire-goyahs*, were not stickers. Here today gone tomorrow, they just served to buy in an occasional hundredweight of coal or a new pillow-case.

Benny knew how hard it would be for his mother to manage. So, though his wife wasn't any too free with the money, as he soon learned, he scraped a pound or two together out of his pocket-money, and sent it over to her. She sent it back. He tried again. But she was not going to accept money from any corpse. She sent it back again. There was nothing more he could do.

Benny did not remain long the light-hearted youth he had been. He had lost his mother. His wife was not all honey and peaches. He tugged fiercely at his pipe. He smoked a pipe, now that he was a tobacconist's husband, like a real Christian. He longed for a dish of fried fish, as his mother had fried it, with a good helping of red horse-radish sauce and a pickled cucumber, perhaps. And then there would be the leg of the Sabbath chicken to follow. He had always preferred the nobbly leg to the breast or wing.

"You'd best come and unpack these fifties," called out Jessie Edelman, "mooning about like an old sheep."

"Yes!" said Benny meekly, "I was just coming!"

There was only one way, the elder Mrs Edelman realised, to wipe out the disgrace. It could not wipe out the disgrace exactly; nothing could ever do that, even if the apostate pair had gone to live in Australia, instead of just a few streets away.

Only one way. Norman must marry. There must be a nice Jewish wedding. There would be, in course of time, a nice Jewish baby, a circumcision, it might be hoped. The Lord would surely do something to make up for what had happened by allowing it to be a circumcision.

As she dreamed, as she commanded, so it came about. If there had been no nice Jewish girl on the spot, Mrs Edelman would have gone off to Mr Billig, who lived lower down, at number seventeen. He sometimes arranged these things, although he always saw to it that the young folks loved each other. He would not countenance it, unless they loved each other. But Mr Billig's kind services were not required. Norman, although he was only nineteen, was in love with a nice Jewish girl, aged eighteen. Her name was Fanny Gustav. Her father was a learned man, an orator, who made orations in synagogues on Sabbaths and festivals. She was quite good-looking, with her grey eyes and her coils of fair hair; she was a good housewife, too. She could pluck a chicken with the best of them. It was all very suitable.

Of course it would mean a fresh mouth to feed at number seven Magnolia Street. (It did not occur to Mrs Edelman that the young people might go and live elsewhere. She was a strong woman, determined to live down the disgrace her elder son had put upon her, so far as it might be humanly done. And she was going to live on in Magnolia Street to do it.) It would mean a fresh mouth to feed, and, blessed be the Lord, still another fresh mouth to feed, as soon as it could possibly be delivered.

That was what Mrs Edelman wanted. She wanted more than anything in the world another little Edelman boy to make up for the big one that had gone out into the wilderness. As for the money side of it, there would be more lodgers and steadier lodgers. The Lord would see to that. Fanny would help with the lodgers.

So before 1910 was over, there was a merry-making at the house where earlier in the year there had been a mourning. A canopy was lifted, a wine glass sipped from, a ring slipped on a finger, a wine glass broken. But it was two or three years before Fanny, the youngest Mrs Edelman, gave birth to her first baby.

It is possible that it would have been born a year or two earlier, if Fanny had stood out against the ministrations of the Jewish mothers in Magnolia Street. But Mrs Edelman senior and Mrs Shulman and Mrs Seipel and Mrs Billig were so anxious about what had happened, or what had not happened, when Fanny gave no indication that she was going to be a mother; and there was such a terrible flutter among the dove-cots, and such a laying of heads together, and an urging of this and that, that, if a tenth part of their simples had been effective, Fanny would have produced five at a birth.

But everything comes in God's good time. And so did Fanny's baby, Jacky. For it *was* a boy. Old Mrs Edelman looked up to Heaven with streaming eyes. She dandled the brick-red little object in her arms, and laughed, and cried. It seemed to her in that moment as if her eldest-born had never been born at all. Here he was, born only this very moment, "A *babele*, a *kindele*!" she crooned.

"I say!" breathed the youngest Mrs Edelman weakly from her pillow, "Who's got my baby?"

Chapter 19

Our tale of Magnolia Street in 1910 draws to an end. Indeed, we have already trespassed on the years to come, in announcing the birth of Jacky Edelman. The years to come are not so golden that we must race to meet them. Perhaps Jacky was not unlucky that he did not collect many of them.

Our pre-war tale ends, then; and it ends in the household of Isaac Emmanuel. From Isaac Emmanuel himself, however, we think it is decent to turn our eyes away for the time being. The fiasco of Unity Hall hurt and humiliated him profoundly. For weeks it was as much as he could do to open his front door and step down into the street. He knew that there was a gentile pavement again, and a Jewish pavement.

He knew that the party with which the Boys celebrated the fiasco of Unity Hall was more virulent than any that had gone before. He knew that Miss Tregunter behind her geraniums smiled, and showed her grey teeth.

Gradually his old optimism returned to him, as blood flows back into a limb from which it has been excluded by a tourniquet. But even in his wildest optimism he did not suspect that within few years a flood would flow in Magnolia Street, or a fire burn. And in the roaring of that water or that flame, it was a matter of not the very least importance what pavement you walked on. With or without glory, you might, or you might not, survive that indifferent holocaust.

Mr Emmanuel need not have been so diffident about stepping down into the street. His fiasco was more of a success, in some ways, than it might have been if it had succeeded. For people looked on him with much more affection, and curiously enough, respect, than they had ever done before. They went and listened to his speeches, too. These began again soon.

Even his son, Max, took more notice of him than he used to. He used to be aware that his father's eyes were upon him, but not that they looked at him with pain and disappointment. He knew only they were a shade of bluey-grey with a yellow rim. He was fascinated by the way the light struck on the blonde small hairs about his cheek-bones. He wondered if there was any way of getting it down in paint. He remembered again the blue thighs of Dora Pettigrew as Aladdin. He remembered the way Rabbi

Shulman's face went back in a series of ridges. He did not think of people as people, or think of them at all; he merely felt them, as flesh, as surfaces.

But now, after the night of Unity Hall, when his father spoke to him and their eyes met, Max saw deeper than the bluey-grey irises with the yellow rim. He became for Max the only resident of Magnolia Street that was a person, not a thing. He listened when his father spoke. He derived from him the vision of Magnolia Street. That was why Magnolia Street never ceased to be for him his most aesthetically thrilling experience. Its shapes and colours still dominated his painting, even at the Baronne Edmonde de Millavray's villa in Beaulieu, even in his little Arab courtyard in Djerba. He could not see how Portland Place or Curzon Street could begin to compare with it in tone, in variety, in drama, in character, in colour.

It is wrong to say that his father was the only resident in Magnolia Street who lived for him beyond the boundaries of his preoccupation with the paintable. There was also the girl, Enid Cooper, with whom he had talked briefly at the party his father gave to celebrate the catastrophic rescue of Tommie Wright. Her voice haunted him. It did not translate itself into an emotion which he needed to convert into paint applied upon canvas. Her nose troubled him. It was not a beautiful nose. He did not want to paint it. It turned up at the tip slightly. It was not a Magnolia Street nose. Her eyes were grey and intelligent. They were outside the scope of his fierce devotions. She lacked colour, or the sort of colour, rather, which sent his paint-brush careering. She was not, in fact, Magnolia Street. He put her out of his mind.

Colour had already become his passion, before he could speak, before his mother conducted his toddling limbs to the Elementary School round the corner. When he cried, it was not the shaking of a rattle that wiped away his tears, or some elderly gentleman making comic contortions over his cradle. Such activities only infuriated him. His mother found by accident one day, that when she flapped a large scarlet shawl with yellow fringes before his eyes, his crying stopped in mid-air. And while the big tears of his spent ill temper still rolled down his face, his eyes shone, enchanted. She imagined that it was a sort of hypnotism, the mere flapping of the big shawl, and she did not for many months understand why, when she flapped before him her week-day shawl, a nondescript grey thing, a thing of no delight at all, it produced no effect upon him.

It dawned on her at length; she discovered with joy that she had found an unfailing recipe for the establishment of silence, when the small Max opened out his lungs. She appreciated her discovery all the more, as Moisheh, her eldest, had been not merely a noisy child, but a bellower, a hallooer, of an obstinacy unparalleled in infant history. At the most tender age, if that adjective could be used in any connection regarding Moisheh, he had had lungs like brass. His favourite time for giving them an airing was three in the morning. The entertainment proceeded till three in the afternoon, with little variation of tone or diminution of volume.

So she flapped her scarlet shawl with yellow fringes industriously before Max's eyes. The child looked on, enchanted. A sheet of coloured paper, a dish of red apples, produced the same effect. As he grew up and his eyes sharpened, he saw colour in Magnolia Street heaped in dazzling profusion — the colour of the cherries in Mrs Derricks's bonnet, the odd greeny-blackness of Reb Feivel's frock-coat, the gold hair of Dick Cooper, the brown-scrubbed steps with blue edgings of Kate Ritchie, the yellow citrons that the Jews carried on the Festival of Tabernacles between their homes and the synagogue, the blue thighs of the Principal Boy in *Aladdin*!

The blue thighs of Dora Pettigrew! It was several years ago now since he had seen those tubular flowers blooming out of those monumental knees. They had bloomed to the undoing of many hapless young men, including the young Earl who shortly married her. They made a painter of little Max Emmanuel.

No. He would have become a painter in any case. But they gave him an impulse and a direction, the full force of which asserted itself some years later. They implanted in him that *sens des fesses* which Renoir deemed indispensable to the healthy painter. His breath came short under the ribs as Dora Pettigrew marched, like a field of bluebells, like a parade of policemen, upon the stage. Her tights were so tight that her flesh and they were one. He imbibed a truth which he expounded later, while it was still a shocking thing, that there is no such thing as a flesh colour, or a necessary colour attaching to any object at all. There is no colour outside the colour imposed from within by the pattern. Hence those green faces, yellow faces, gamboge breasts, that so distressed his critics. Dora's blue thighs gave him a sense of the joy of the third dimension, their fatness, their sleekness, their sloping away, their piling up, the darkness on the inner sides of them, their high lights.

He sat back in the threepenny gallery, his eyes shining. Many another young man sat back in that theatre, all the way down from the gallery to the front row of the stalls, their eyes shining. But the discomfort the other young men felt was not in the fingers. The fingers of Max Emmanuel ached for a brush, a paint-brush, and gallons of blue paint... to paint those blue thighs, nothing else, to paint those blue thighs, for ever and for ever.

And in a sense he never painted anything else. Hence those candid breasts in his painting, those folded buttocks, the voluminous hips, the nothing at all concealed or diminished, in the whole state of the female body. Hence the reputation he won of being the wildest of the libertines, when he was a young man to whom sex, in its merely carnal aspect, meant less than it does to most churchwardens. Hence the outcries of provincial museums when the work of Max Emmanuel accompanied the work of his colleagues for exhibition in Lowestoft and Dumfries, hence the anathema with bell, book and candle, hence the town councillors who would rather pour a phial of strychnine into their daughters' salad than let them gaze upon so lewd a spectacle as the paintings of Max Emmanuel, as the blue thighs of Dora Pettigrew.

Dora Pettigrew had blue thighs. But she sat on the doorstep of Isaac Emmanuel. She had the face of Bella Winberg. She smiled like Rose Berman. She was the flesh of Magnolia Street rendered into paint.

It took a long time for Max to realise what a lot his younger brother, David, had to do with it all — had to do, that is to say, with the lordly serenity in which his genius flowered. Only three years separated Max from David, but the three years might have been thirteen for all the notice Max took of him; excepting when he wanted this or that done. Then David did it. In fact he did it before Max said he wanted it done; with the consequence that Max never realised he did it.

It was not that David was a ninny. He was a sturdy lad with an almost morbid appetite for fair play. If there was a fight between the small boys of Magnolia Street and Oleander Street, and David's opponent fell and hit the ground, he would lift him to his feet and give him a suck at his stickjaw and wait till he was quite recovered, before he hit him on the nose again. Sometimes Moisheh in sheer absent-mindedness gave David, or some other small boy, a kick from behind or a tweak in the ear. Whereon David flung at him so promptly tooth and nail that it was quite a long time before Moisheh was so absent-minded again.

But you wouldn't suspect David's prowess when he sat hunched up in a corner in the room where Max was painting. Max didn't like to have people about when he worked, but he took no notice of David. He might not be there. So David sat on, quiet as any mouse.

The small boy was nearly twelve. He didn't understand much about painting or about Max. But he had a feeling for what they meant when the old women and the journalists said 'genius' about his brother. He didn't show what he felt. He was a boy who showed little and said little. But he walked about for days as if he heard a lovely music. For he loved Max consumedly. No-one else much existed for him. The child was aware that he could die for Max. In a sense, when the war came, he did. Max went on painting and David died.

Book II

Chapter 1

I

Regarding the effect of the Great War upon them, or their effect upon the Great War, the others have been vocal — the misunderstood generals, the sensitive city clerks, the rhapsodists, the objectors, the equestrian lesbian ladies, the bull-dogged submarine-chasers, the nurses stern or flighty, the politicians, the financiers, the batmen, the clergymen. But the dwellers in the hundreds of thousands of small streets, the Magnolia Streets of Dijon, Doomington, Leipzig, Bologna, Minneapolis, Vilna — these have not been so eloquent. Their tale has not been told.

The tale of the soldiers, on the other hand, and all those direct participators, even so soon, so few years after the Great War is ended, has darkened more paper than any theme in human history, saving the Bible, perhaps. There is something of futility in all that monumental writing and reading. It is as if a man were to lift a bucket and another bucket and another bucket out of the ocean, to show how deep it is. It will never be computed to what heights men soared and to what depths they sank, what woe they endured, during those years.

But here the endeavour is a humble one. What, in our small street, did they feel when the soldiers went from their sides, the women, the old men, the children? With little music or none the soldiers turned the corner out of Magnolia Street into Blenheim Road, and already they were phantoms. No peering into the darkness which was about them could make their lineaments clear. But now and again, when some wife or mother stood over her scullery-sink, washing the plates, or ironing the linen at the kitchen table, in a moment when she might not even be consciously thinking how her husband or her son fared, suddenly there would be a gnat-like singing in her ears and a mist before her eyes; and one moment later, the singing would cease, the mist be there no more. In stark silence and acute clarity she saw her man playing Pontoon, it might be, in the canteen at Etaples, turning his head to wink at her, because of the good cards he held; or all tied up in a hank of barbed wire in a shell-hole under Beaumont Hamel. He seemed to be not more than a few feet away from her, as if there were no scullery-wall.

Then the singing came back again, and the mist rolled up. But perhaps she had seen him as truly then as ever she had done when he came in to the house and kicked his boots off and demanded a mug of tea. Perhaps, too, she would never see him again.

In that sense only, in this narrative, will it be our business to tell how the soldiers of Magnolia Street fared. Many pens have already engaged themselves with the action before Eaucourt l'Abbaye in which Benny Edelman lost a leg. Many another than he lost a leg or two legs that day, when Morval and Geudecourt were carried. Many lost more. Mr Henry Briggs, the odd-job-man, was doing odd jobs in the Carency valley amid the bursting of the shells and the singing of the nightingales, at the time of the German assault on Vimy Ridge in May 1916, when one of those shells interrupted his odd job and one of those nightingales sang his threnody. But the threnody we must listen to was sung by Martha Briggs, in the private bar of the Lamb and Lion, and her voice was not so low and kind as it had been of old.

Little David Emmanuel, as we have said, died too. But we shall not bend our ears to listen to the words he said, as he lay dying. He may have said no word at all, because Death came so quickly, or because, even in his extreme moment, he kept his habit of silence. But we shall take our place in the kitchen of the Emmanuels on a certain Friday evening. The women sway to and fro in their black shawls. The *fire-goyah* has been and gone. She has turned out the gas, and the Sabbath candles are almost burned down to their sockets. The fire is nearly out. The first candle goes out, and the second. All the candles go out. The spent cinders whisper as they sift through the bars into the grate below. There is no other sound.

II

It is 1916. Some that went out of Magnolia Street are dead already, others are to die. We have been far afield, and when we now return, let us not too hastily cross the thresholds of the houses. We might by some precise and ridiculous irony enter at a moment when some wife or mother holds in her hand a slip of paper just received from London, and it would be no happiness to us or to her if we caught sight of the expression in her eyes, and of her dropped jaw. Or we might enter at a moment when some gentleman closeted with himself in secret meditation, winks his eye at his own reflection in the mirror, as who should say: "Bit of all right, this bloody War."

We can with more seemliness enter Magnolia Street through the portals of one or another of its four clubs, for who can say no to us, if we wish to join in at the morning service of the Lithuanian Brotherhood? And if the Lamb and Lion has opened for the first session, Mrs Tawnie will serve us a pint of ale. As for Mrs Poyser, so long as we do not ask for anything so luxurious as a jar of jam, she will oblige us. So will Mrs Durbin at the barber-shop. She will lather our jaw-bone till it aches. The energy with which she rubs the soap in with the edge of her palm has not slackened, though one of her sons has had his eyes poked out by shell splinters in France, and the other is in France, too, and she has not heard from him for weeks. Her small black eyes are not dimmed. They still shine like the beads of two hatpins.

The congregation at the Lithuanian Brotherhood this morning is as small as it can be. The quorum of ten is there, and not one soul more. If only one of the ten had been lacking, Reb Berel, the beadle, might have been hard put to it to find a tenth. We enter during the recitation of the Eighteen Prayers, so there is little chance of distracting the worshippers, who stand facing Jerusalem, swaying to and fro rapidly, with their praying-shawls drawn down over their foreheads. Do not move. Stand in the corner there, in the shadow under the women's partition.

Whence have you, for your part, come, who have this morning slipped into the dark synagogue? From the black mud of Loos, from the feverish lowlands of the Struma, from the swilling seas? From the War? You have come from the War, you say?

Look at those old men. There is no War. Is this the year of the Christian Era, 1916? Those old men, uttering those same words, prayed so three centuries ago and ten centuries ago. They will pray so ten centuries hence. If it was your fancy to absent yourself for a moment from the visions that go by your side, where you might for so brief a time not hear the phantom bullets whining nor see the flares soar and break, you did well to enter here. This evening you will, no doubt, go into a music-hall, but you will not leave your ghostly ones outside. They will come in with you, and sit down beside you, whether the seats are occupied or empty. They will make jolly jokes on the stage about the plum-and-apple and the lice and the sergeant-major and Kaiser Bill. None of you will be able not to laugh, neither you nor the ghostly ones. You will just be able to catch their windy titter and see the glint of their teeth. For they are very funny, those funny men; they go about from city to city, being funny, and sometimes they go to be funny in the base camps. The girls, too, are lively, and generous. Because you are soldier-boys, they will let you see far more for half-a-crown than they would have dreamed of, before the War.

But tonight, in the music-hall, you will not forget. Here, now, during the recitation of the Eighteen Prayers, you may. As the old men sway and shake and mutter, and sometimes their voices fall again, till it is like a trouble among the reeds on the edge of a lake, you will say there is no War. These old men, these same old men, Rabbi Shulman and Reb Aryeh and Reb Feivel and the others, have prayed in this same place, for decades, for centuries... before the Prussians encompassed Sedan, before Napoleon marched down from the high Alps, before the wars of Wallenstein and Gustav Adolphus ravaged the German coastlands. Nor, if the rumour came to them that this or the other general with his army of mercenaries was marching down on them; he was at the city gates now; he was at the gate of the ghetto now; his troops had now ignited the brands for the burning of the walls of synagogues... were they perturbed. They did not recite one prayer the less, or omit a single syllable out of a single prayer.

So it was at this time, whether Nicholas of Russia or Mackensen of Germany swept the great tides of his armies upon Lemberg or Cracow, in ruinous flow or ruinous ebb, Rabbi Shulman still leaned up against the Holy Ark as he prayed, and Reb Feivel stroked his beard and Reb Aryeh beat his breast. Or if, at this very moment in Doomington here, or in Dusseldorf there, the alarms were sounding and the enemy aircraft dropping their bombs, it would be as if flies were buzzing until the prayer was ended duly. For these were old men and they feared God more than they feared their fellow men, and in their ways they loved Him.

They were old men. You did not often see young men at the week-day services of the Lithuanian Brotherhood. A Great War had taken them away.

256

Chapter 2

If Malkeh Poyser, who kept the grocery-shop, had been a person of importance on the Jewish pavement in pre-war days, she was now both a Pharaoh who had dreamed dreams and a Joseph who had interpreted them, so that all her granaries were full though dearth was elsewhere. This was the season of the plenitude of her power, for as the rationing of food came in, the sources of her plenty dried up, and it was much less easy for her to express her pleasure by conferring here a pound of white flour, there a quarter of real butter.

But at this time the sole Poyser sitting-room, the cellar, the bedrooms, were still stacked with sacks of provisions. In the evening, before the lights were put on, the house looked like some eastern caravanserai, where Ali Baba had ensconced in those sticky sacks not merely his forty thieves but any number of their children and grandchildren. That was how it looked when you were nervy, what with expecting the Zeppelins to come along any night, and no news from Egypt for a month now. But the genii of those sacks were not so malignant as that.

Malkeh Poyser had really been rather clever. She had guessed from the beginning how scarce things like coal, white flour, jam, tinned fruit and sugar, above all, were going to be. Her competitors in the neighbourhood had missed their chances, but Malkeh had turned no salesman down. There was one salesman, in particular, who swelled her stock. He was extremely anxious to get to Ireland, an anxiety which may have had something to do with the likelihood of compulsory military service. Mrs Poyser relieved him of his stock. He duly went to Ireland.

She bought and she bought. There was no room to eat or work or sleep, the place was so crammed with sacks. And then the house immediately behind hers, at the corner of Oleander Street, fell empty. She promptly rented it and the sacks lurched across the narrow entry that separated the two streets and trundled up to the top beam of the attic and down to the lowest pit of the cellar. She rented it. She might have bought it. But there her courage stopped short. Many a time, for many a long year after it, when houses were so short in Doomington that

257

couples couldn't get married, and when they did, they paid a pound a week for a little back bedroom, she bitterly repented her pusillanimity.

But now, in 1916, that dreadful mistake cast no shadow before it. She had other things to think of. Her eldest boy, Joe, was in Egypt. Two or three months later he was in Macedonia collecting fat out of mess tins against the shore of Lake Doiran. He gained a great reputation as a fat-collector along that section of the front. Sometimes he also went out to collect Bulgars.

As for her daughter, Becky, she was doing war-work in London. So that left only Mr and Mrs Poyser to look after the shop, and the twins, Jack and Harry. They were bright young men. By day they stood in the market-places selling embroidered pillow-slips to gentile ladies. Gentile ladies had a lot of money to spend these days and they were beginning to buy silk stockings, too. So Jack and Harry sold them silk stockings. By night they slept in the house in Oleander Street, where all the sacks were. A sack of sugar at their head and flour at their feet, the twins slept soundly, and got up betimes to attend to the gentile ladies in the market-places.

Sometimes they called in at a small tobacconist's in Pendleton for letters. They thought it better if Mrs Poyser did not see their personal letters. They were big boys now, seventeen years old, and sometimes they made appointments to meet after business hours the gentile ladies to whom they sold embroidered pillow-cases. The two boys and two gentile ladies might even have a party and use those pillow-cases. Boys got old quickly nowadays, and before you knew where they were, there they were marching off to the station with pack and rifle. And there were no pillow-cases where they went to, then.

Also, sometimes, the boys got letters at that shop from Becky, who was on war-work in London. But her letters did not bear the London postmark. And she was not really on war-work. At least, she had done her war-work, already, if it might be put like that. She was expecting her baby in about two months now.

Babies are objects you cannot make light of, even in war-time. If you lived in a palace as big as the Doomington Town Hall, with as many rooms in it as the Bridgeways Gaol, it would get about sooner or later that you were going to have a baby. And if you lived in number one Magnolia Street, with just one living-room for a whole family, in which all the cooking and quite a lot of the washing were done, a great deal of grocery was stored, in which the suitors for your hand were entertained, where you indulged in the piano-playing and singing lessons which were going to lure those suitors if you lived in such a house, people would find out sooner rather than later that you were going to have a baby.

Not that any suitors for your hand had been entertained in number one Magnolia Street for quite a long time, or that you'd done much in the way of piano-playing or singing. You knew it was hopeless. So did your dad and your brothers and all the girls in Magnolia Street and the women and the babies, and the Jews and the Christians, anybody, everybody. Only your mother didn't know it was hopeless. Bitterly, implacably, your mother refused to admit it was hopeless. You remembered a night long ago, six years ago, it might have been six centuries ago; a night in Unity Hall when there should have been a presentation of a gold watch to Benny Edelman. Only there was no gold watch and no Benny Edelman. And something had got hold of you. You had gone quite mad. You had played and played and played till the roof rattled. You had stood in front of all those faces, and opened your mouth and sung. But it was a long time ago now. You had remained quite sane since then.

"Well, Becky, won't you let us have a tune on the piano? Like you did that time at Unity Hall?" Mrs Poyser would ask grimly. Or with her eagle eye she might notice some youth strolling up Blenheim Road who came in from time to time to buy a packet of Gold Flake.

"Sing us a song, won't you, Becky dear? That nice song, darling, about the Long Long Trail? What, you're hoarse, Becky dear? No, no, you're not hoarse. I think it'll be better for you if you're not hoarse."

The door opened. The bell above the lintel clanged. "A packet of Gold Flake," said the young man.

"There's a long long trail a-winding
Into the land of my dreams"

the sad unpleasing voice of Becky Poyser announced.

The young man was not excited by the information. "Thank you, Mrs Poyser. Good evening," he said.

Who would marry Becky Poyser, with her red hair and her big hands and her freckles? And whom would Becky Poyser marry, for that matter? She was quite happy, quite happy, if only her mother would let her alone. One hair of her daddy's beard was worth all the boys in Doomington. Her brothers, too, were nice to her, always bringing her in little things... If only her mother would leave her alone, if only she wouldn't perch her at the piano between the sacks of sugar, as soon as some wretched pair of trousers came into sight....

And now Becky Poyser was going to have a baby. Oh it was sure enough. She'd seen enough babies coming into Magnolia Street to be in no doubt about it. She'd been to the doctor, too. She'd been again. It was queer that her mother hadn't spotted anything yet. She hadn't the slightest suspicion. She'd as soon have believed that a shark was in hiding under the scullery-sink.

A shark would have been more welcome to Mrs Poyser than a baby. It would not have been a shame to her, to paralyse her eloquent lips, to pierce through to her proud heart.

But it was going to be a baby. She was bound to spot it soon, if not tomorrow then next week.

So one Friday evening, after supper, after the *fire-goyah* had turned the gas out and the candles still had an inch or two to go, Becky told her mother. The twins were out. Her father had gone to bed, for he had a headache. Her mother was reading a Yiddish version of the Pentateuch. She looked very tall and black and stiff on her chair. Her shadow shook slightly on the wall on her left hand, where a photograph of her husband in all his masonic regalia hung. Becky knew that such an opportunity could not come again. She was glad her father was out of the way. He would learn soon enough, but it was easier for him and herself if he were not to be there.

"Mother," she said. She distinctly felt herself make the word, but she did not hear it. Obviously she had not made the word properly, for her mother did not hear it either.

"Mother," she said again.

Her mother did not lift her eyes from the page. She was a little annoyed at being interrupted. "Yes?" she asked sharply.

Becky's courage failed her. "Nothing," she muttered. "Nothing."

"Yes?" her mother repeated. She lifted her eyes and rested them on Becky, where she sat on the metal stool over against the fire.

But Becky could bring out no sound. She looked mournfully and idiotically back into her mother's eyes. Her jaw dropped.

"What's the matter with you?" said Mrs Poyser. "What are you sitting like that for, like a dummy?"

She felt a damp line gather along the bony rib of her forehead. She was damp, too, under the arms.

"Mother," she said. "I've got something to tell you."

"Well, tell it," said the other. "Can't you see I'm reading the Torah?"

"Mother, mother." But she could say no more. Mrs Poyser's eyes opened wider. She seized the corners of the table. "Becky," she said — her voice was lower now — "What is it?"

"I'm going —" she started... "I'm going... I'm going to have a baby."

Her mother said nothing. She sat and stared and gripped the corners of the table till her knuckles were pale as dough. She said nothing for a long time, many minutes. Then she brought out: "Are you mad?"

The other hung her head. "It's true," she breathed.

Again there was a long silence. Then Mrs Poyser spoke again. "You're mad. Of course you're mad. You don't know any men. How should *you* have babies. *You!*" she flung out savagely. Her voice was bitter with all her accumulated humiliation.

Then the daughter broke down at length. "It's true! It's true!" she sobbed. "It's true! It's true!" She beat her forehead with her clenched fist. Her mother ran towards her like a fury. She lifted her head by the ropes of that red hair which the young men of Longton had found so little to their taste. She pulled at her daughter's hair till it seemed she must pluck it out.

"True, is it?" she shrieked. "True, is it? Is it for this I've brought you up like a true Jewish daughter? Is it for this I've got a marriage policy out in your name for the day —" Then she stopped. "It's not true!" she said. "You don't know any men!" Then she lifted her voice and called to her husband. "Isrol! Isrol!" she cried, as if she would rip out her throat.

But Isrol Poyser was already coming down the stairs. He was in his vest and pants. His hair was disordered. His face was like a dirty cloth.

"What is it?" he cried. "What is it? Malkeh, Becky, what is it?" He rubbed together in regular circles the thumb and forefinger of each hand.

261

The tears were streaming down Mrs Poyser's cheeks. She clapped her hands together like one demented. "Your daughter," she cried. "Your daughter... such a year upon her. Ask her. Such a shame —"

"Becky!" he said. His voice was very mild. "You poor girl! I've been thinking for a week or two now... Oh you poor girl!"

His daughter threw herself down at his feet and the great ropes of her red hair streamed over his red slippers. He comforted her, as if he and she were quite alone. His wife might not have been in the same room with them.

"Go to bed, Malkeh!" he urged his wife. "Go to bed!" She went.

She did not say a word. She did not get up for some days. "Another attack of her colic!" said Mr Poyser and Miss Poyser, in answer to the anxious enquiries of the customers. "She'll be up in a day or two!"

From that night, till the day a month or two later when Becky Poyser went off to do war-work in London, there was only one occasion on which direct speech passed between the mother and daughter. Apart from that time, Mrs Poyser only addressed Becky through her husband or the twins. The twins, of course, guessed pretty quickly what the trouble was, and the secret was safe enough with them. If Becky addressed her mother directly (excepting behind the counter, where appearances were kept up) Mrs Poyser took as much notice of her as if a cat mewed.

The one occasion on which Mrs Poyser spoke to her daughter was the evening she got up after her collapse. She asked the twins to go out. They recognised the tone and made no bones about it. They went out. Then Mrs Poyser turned to her daughter and without any sort of preamble went straight at her.

"Who's the man?" she asked.

"Father's already asked me," she replied.

"Who is he?"

"She won't tell me!" This from Isrol Poyser.

"What do you mean she won't tell you? Who's the man?" she demanded, turning round on her daughter again.

Becky pushed forth her lower lip sullenly. She was silent.

"Well?"

The girl turned round. She picked up the poker and rattled it between the bars.

262

"Drop that poker! Who was he?"

Becky dropped the poker. She turned round.

"Do you know how old I am?" she asked.

"Old enough," her mother said, "not to act like a tart on Oxford Street!"

"Now-now-now!" her husband said nervously.

Becky sat down on the metal stool against the fire. It was very hot.

"I ask you for the last time. Will you tell me?"

"I won't tell you!"

"*Gottenu!*" Mrs Poyser shrilly appealed to Heaven. "Why have I deserved this thing? What have I done? Have I not given charity?" She stopped a moment as if she waited for a reply. Then she tried another tack. "Don't you see?" she implored. "We must get him to marry you! Don't you see, you fool?" Then she stopped short suddenly as a hideous thought struck her for the first time.

"Is he a Jew or a Christian?"

"I won't say!"

"Becky, Becky, tell me! Only that! Is he a Jew or a Christian?"

"I won't say!"

"Ask her!" she shrieked. "Isrol, ask her! Make her say!"

"Of course," said Isrol, "of course he's a Jew! How can you ask such a thing? Is he?" He turned to Becky plaintively. The girl's jaw now was like a lump of lead.

"I won't say!" she replied.

"Of course, he's a Jew!" repeated Isrol. "You mustn't ask it, Malkeh! Come now! What's his name, Becky? It's me! It's your daddy asking! Have I been a bad daddy to you? Perhaps, after all, it'll be a good match. There will be a *simchah*. In war-time... well, war-time is war-time. But if you only tell us his name, perhaps we can send Mr Billig down to his house tonight to arrange a match. Eh, Becky? Come, be a good girl! You'll tell your daddy, yes? You'll tell me his name, yes?"

"I won't!" said Becky.

And indeed, how could she? She did not know his name herself. She did not know whether he was a Jew or Christian. She only knew that he had looked on her that evening in the sandy road under the moor. He looked on her with the eyes of one to whom she was lovely, though she had big hands and freckles and coarse red hair. He was a soldier. He did not look happy. She knew she was not. But that night they were less unhappy in that dark place padded with last year's leaves. How should she tell them his name?

So it was arranged she should go to London on war-work. It was a real sacrifice on the part of Mr and Mrs Poyser, for business was increasing all the time by leaps and bounds. But nobody could say that the Poysers didn't do their bit for their King and Country, with Joe in Egypt and Becky on war-work. Not even Mrs Derricks, mother and champion of redoubtable patriots.

II

When we said of you, who slipped into the Lithuanian Brotherhood during the morning service, that you are a ghost, we did not mean it literally, of course. No literal ghost ever knocked back a couple of pints the way you did at the Lamb and Lion, an hour or two later. In a way, whoever you are, you've never been quite so substantial before. Once you couldn't bear anything heftier on your feet than box-calf, and look at those boots now. And whatever rough work your hands did in the old time, the work they've been doing lately is rougher. Your face, too — it was a Doomington face at the best of times, your skin had something of the grime and pallor of cities. It's now as chopped and red and scarred as Adam's.

And one thing more. You may have been, it's not impossible, one of those lads who felt about women they should be treated respectful. Oh doubtless you and your pals made lewd jokes about them. But it didn't come to anything — or once or twice, at most, and you so loved her you felt you could die of glory or it was so casual your stomach heaved for shame. No, let's say it didn't come to anything at all. And then you became a soldier. And the women were here and there, and the medical officers looked after you like fathers. And when you mightn't ever come back at all from your next spell up the line, it didn't seem to you there was much point in spending your last night and your last few francs on needles and knitting. So you're a man who knows what women are about now. There's a sign of your knowledge on your face, too.

But the odd thing is that in some queer way you look more innocent now than you did before you went away. It may be that you've been brought up against certain general ideas since then, like God and Death and Eternity, which once were no more than highfalutin' words to you. Of course, you've not had time to chew the rag about them. But there they've been, if only for a minute or two, and there they weren't before.

That odd innocence has got something to do with it; for somehow, you look a little ghostly, as if you didn't really belong to this world you've come back to. And you don't quite belong, you never will, to the world you've just come from for a few days. Perhaps, that's what one means by a ghost, somebody who doesn't belong to either of two worlds, and hovers about uneasily between them.

At all events, seeing it was into the Lithuanian Brotherhood you slipped for a moment and not into St. Luke's, the presumption is you're a Jewish ghost. But in the matter of ghosts, there's not really much Jewish or Christian one way or the other. When you're blown up by a high-explosive shell, they might find a disc with the letters 'C of E' on, or 'Jew' or 'RC.' There's little more to it than that. But you want a shave, ghost — a most unghostly thing. And you needn't lather your chin this morning in a can of warm grease. Let's see what Mrs Durbin can do for us, in her famous saloon at the corner.

She can do what she's been able to do for years, rub the chin with the edge of her palm till the bone feels like cracking. If anything, she puts more into it than she used to. It's not so gay a place as it was. Really, you can hardly call it a club in the way that you can still say it of the Lithuanian Brotherhood and the Lamb and Lion and Mrs Poyser's shop. It's Mrs Durbin's clientele that has been hit hardest; the young men have other things to do than to sit about talking League prospects and smoking Woodbines by the hour. Or they do it in other places, when Jerry eases off for a bit.

The fellows come in when they're on leave. They want to get toffed up for their girls. But they don't hang about. They're restless. Mrs Durbin is the only member of the old staff still on active duty. Her two sons have had another job for a year or so now. It was an odd thing about the sociologist — Albert, that was, the elder. He had always said the War couldn't happen. And when it came off; he still couldn't get the idea out of his head. The War couldn't happen, could it? Therefore it wasn't happening. He had always been a half-baked creature. He'd been a sociologist on one plane, and on another he became a metaphysician.

There wasn't any War, he said. It only seemed like a War. He'd spent all his life prattling in his mother's shop, and he went on prattling in a military hut on Winnall Down near Winchester and in the Harfleur Valley in France. Wipers didn't dry him up. The fellows first laughed, then they jeered, then they got cross, then they took no notice of him.

When the chunks of shrapnel poked out his eyes, it was hard for them not to be funny. They were. They told each other he wasn't really blind, it only seemed like that. He could see a blighty one when it was coming, so he kept his eyes open. He was back in Magnolia Street now, you could see him in the saloon any hour of the day. He wanted to talk sociology and metaphysics to the customers. Perhaps that was one reason why they didn't stay about so long as they used to. His big dark blue glasses made you feel a little miserable if this was your draft leave. He was learning to read Braille. A big Braille volume was always open on his knees, but his fingers were still a little tough and clumsy. When he heard a footstep approaching, he cocked his ears anxiously, for he liked to have a good talk. But more often than not, the footstep passed on. He sighed, and went on with his fingering.

He was a little anxious about his younger brother, Arthur. Arthur was about the only object that entirely eluded the grasp of his metaphysics. In this War, which, because it couldn't happen, wasn't happening; or if, in a manner of speaking, it was happening, that was only because it so strenuously *seemed* to be happening — in this War, in this metaphysics, there was just no monkeying about with Arthur. He was at the front. But he was in a very cushy sector, according to the last news of him. He'd be all right. He put his Braille volume on the form beside him and tapped in his pockets for his pipe and baccy. Arthur would be all right. Mother said so. There was no getting past mother. She knew. She had ways of knowing.

There was less trade at Ma Durbin's than there used to be, so she and the new man got through it quite nicely between them. Albert was beginning to be quite a hand at washing the towels, too. The new man was named Bill Stephens. He had been invalided out of the army, where they'd called him up in the early

266

days as a Territorial. A shell exploded against his back collar-stud and knocked his nerve to bits. He'd always been a barber so he came back to civil life to be a barber again. Perhaps that was the last thing he should have gone in for, after having his nerve knocked up like that. The way the razor trembled up against your stretched throat now and again was something cruel. He had a weakness for the lobe of the ear, and on his bad days you were pretty sure to lose a piece of lobe.

But barbers in civil life were nowadays not to be picked up out of the hedgerows, or the small advertisements in the *Daily Chronicle*. So Mrs Durbin kept him on. What was more notable, she kept on her customers, too, those who were still available. She kept them on by the sheer strength of her personality. If one of her old clients was unfaithful to her with another barber, her eyes so blazed when she next saw him, that he'd slink back the same day, even if he didn't want any attention, hoping bygones would be bygones.

She didn't wander about late at night in the highways and byways so much as she used to. In the first place, it was pitch-dark, you couldn't see a yard or two in front of you. And then it wasn't her own old man she kept on meeting out in the deserted streets, as she used to. It was Arthur. At least she kept on thinking about him, and imagining all sorts of things, which was silly. She knew he'd come back. And when she knew a thing, she knew it. The neighbours made that clear. So did Albert. So did Bill Stephens. She was clever, she was. There weren't so many young men about in the shop by day, but the women often slipped in of an evening worriting about with their tea-leaves and their cards. A pack of geese, that's what they were. But in war-time it's funny how you clutch hold of a couple of wet tea-leaves, even, to help you along a bit.

You couldn't exactly say whose fault it was — the children's most likely. The children had always taken her for a bogey-woman. But now the women, too, had all got it into their heads that she had second sight. You couldn't knock it out of them, either, such stuff and nonsense. She could play about with tea-leaves and aces and knaves, of course she could. She'd picked up all the rigmarole when she was quite a girl. But it might as well be cherry stones or tram tickets. It was just a game. As a girl she'd often played it with other girls. And who couldn't play it? In the little town in the north of Lancashire where she was born quite as many people read tea-leaves as read their ABC.

And then, as the war went on, the women started worrying her to read their cups and shuffle packs of cards for them. As a matter of fact, it became quite an industry, all this fortune-telling. One or two old dames in Rosemary Street and Myrtle Street were making a good thing out of it. Would Johnnie come home? Was Tom in danger? And of course it didn't stop there. If Johnnie never came home, then they'd try and have a word with him, across the veil, as they called it. The women had money to spend, nowadays, and even if they hadn't there was always the separation allowance or the pension. Many of them spent more on fortune-telling than on beer. It was the old dames who told fortunes that bought the beer. Some of them wouldn't dream of opening their mouths without a big jug of beer under the table, to refresh themselves like, when the spirits had been a bit rough.

But Mrs Durbin put her foot down on that sort of thing; that is to say, she wasn't going to trouble no spirits, and no spirits were going to trouble her. She'd go so far as reading tea-leaves or cards for the women, though she'd told them straight out it was all stuff and rubbish. But you had to be neighbourly these days, and they seemed to set a great deal of store by her fortune-tellings; all the more because she herself 'skitted' at it, as they said. And, of course, there was no question of leaving a shilling under *her* doily. That made them all the more trustful.

So she did it. No harm could come from it. If she saw in the cards that a big man with a red beard was coming across the sea, Mrs Briggs could tell herself till she was blue in the face that that meant her husband was coming home on leave, even though Mr Briggs was a small man and had no beard. If she said she saw something happening, and then it didn't happen, they couldn't turn round on her. She'd said all the time it was all stuff and rubbish.

And yet, sometimes, she couldn't help wondering if there wasn't something in it, after all. She sat and wondered, seeing Arthur in the tea-leaves and the cards come back to her again and again. That was the way they made witches in the Middle Ages. They told harmless old ladies that they had powers. The harmless old ladies were certain they hadn't. Then they were less certain. Then they were drowned in a pond or burned at a stake. But that was in the Middle Ages. Anything so barbarous couldn't happen in a kind up-to-date year like 1916.

III

We're very fine and large, thank you, at the Lamb and Lion; us women that are left, that is to say. Steve's gone. He wanted to go off quite soon after the War broke out, but Mr Asquith and Lord Kitchener didn't see the need of taking on such elderly gentlemen for quite a long time. One fine day, soon after the appeal was issued for the second hundred thousand, he disappeared. At least it wasn't a fine day. It rained cats and dogs. And when the doors of the recruiting station closed that evening, there were still a few hundred men waiting for someone to take notice of them and wondering if the trenches were much wetter. So Steve came home and didn't say anything more about it. Neither did Maggie, his wife, nor Nellie, his daughter. They all knew it would come, sooner or later.

He didn't like the way the Huns bombarded Scarborough in December, 1914. He got very surly about that. A few months later they raised the age limit; even then he had to do a little sharp lying about his age. He'd got on very quick, since then. He was a sergeant-major now, and the life and soul of any mess, waiting-room, trench or cattle-truck which included him. The bombardment of Scarborough didn't do his temper any permanent harm. He roared with laughter all the way from Salisbury Plain to Béthune. Once or twice he made such an uproar in his dugout when someone made a joke, that the enemy thought trouble was brewing and indulged themselves in a little earnest 'strafe' to show they were still knocking about. He went through the battle of Loos without a scratch, but, as a battle, taking it by and large, it didn't carry him far.

He had a rather prolonged spell in the trenches under Hulluch, and was on his way back when a sniper lodged a bullet in his rump. It was not serious, but it was painful enough. None the less, Steve thought it so funny that the nurses had to gag him. He'd had leave since then, and told them about it in the Lamb and Lion, winking and nudging and guffawing till the tears ran down their cheeks. There were more women than men there these days, women who drove trams, who turned shells, who cleaned windows, who posted bills, who knitted stockings. Their laughter boomed among the handles and glasses. There was a deep note in their laughter these days.

Mrs Tawnie and Nellie knitted stockings. They were far too busy to go knitting stockings, but they knitted them. They had both realised long ago that neither of them would ever finish knitting a pair, and if they ever finished it, no one would ever be able to wear it. Their hands seemed somehow less adapted to the labour than the delicate hands of many a born lady, that hadn't seemed quite up to the job of stirring their own teaspoons. But the Tawnie women remained faithful to stockings till late in the War, except for a brief flirtation with gasmasks. Fragments of heel and instep hung over handles and dribbled into pints of ale. But the ale was getting that bad, a little taste of stocking could do it no harm.

Little blue-eyed Nellie was almost officially 'chucker-out' at the Lamb and Lion, since Lord Derby had called up Sim Watkins, her predecessor. He thought for his part that his profession was as essential as his neighbour's, and was rather hurt that they did not 'star' him. But they did not. He used to wear a tie, a thin red tie with blue and brown stripes. Before he knew where he was, he was wearing no tie at all, but a pith helmet, to protect his pointed little head from the ardent suns of Mesopotamy. He was a long way from Doomington. Nobody loved Sim Watkins. Sometimes, at night, when the bull-frogs clanged in the ditches like glass gongs, he cried.

And little Nellie, tripping in from school and standing up on a chair behind the bar, did his work for him. "Time, gentlemen, please!" she called out like a two-year-old. Mamma beamed. She was keeping the nest cosy for Steve.

Despite the shortened hours, and no treating soldiers and sailors, and you couldn't get a nip of brandy without writing to King George about it, business had never been so good before. It was a bit hard to get help, perhaps. Girls could earn big money on munitions, or toff themselves up among high ladies in canteens and hospitals. But they did their part on the other side of the bar, anyhow, the poor dears.

And no wonder, when any moment the boy might come rat-tat at the door with the telegram in his hand... no wonder they wanted a bit of bucking-up, like.

"A Guinness, my dear? Certainly, my dear! 'Ere, Nellie, 'ere! Catch 'old of these 'ere stockin's!"

She was a lion of a woman, that Maggie Tawnie. It didn't matter how busy she was, but if bad news came to any of the neighbours, she'd be one of the first to see could she do anything, Jews or not Jews. The stranger might think that her own husband was away goal-keeping on a foreign tour, the way Maggie kept her head up and her colours flying. But sometimes, big woman though she was, she'd come over funny all of a sudden. Once or twice it happened when she was filling a glass of beer. She just went on pulling the handle and in a moment or two the floor was swilling.

"Mother!" cried little Nellie sharply. "You *are* gormless!"

Maggie Tawnie blinked. A high spot of colour came out of the high colour in her cheeks. "Lizzie!" she cried, glaring at the barmaid, as if *she'd* done it. "Wipe up that slop!"

IV

And then, when it happened a second time that she went on tugging like daft at that beer-handle till her clogs were all swimming, she thought she'd go and have a word with Mrs Durbin. She didn't believe in this fortune-telling any more than Mrs Durbin herself; but if there was any encouragement to be got that way, why shouldn't she have a drop, too? It would do her no harm if Mrs Durbin said she saw a big broad man in the tea-leaves, all safe and sound, in some nice quiet base camp. Even though she knew it was all a lark.

She was rather ashamed of herself, acting like one of these silly chits of factory girls; so she went out quite late that night, and passed by Mrs Durbin's door more than once, before she could bring herself to knock. And then, just as she was about to lift her hand to the knocker, the door opened of itself, a tall woman put a foot forward as if to descend; then, perceiving the presence of another visitor, the woman withdrew into the lobby, wrapping her shawl round her face so as to hide who she was.

It was too much for Maggie Tawnie's humorous common sense. She burst into laughter, and pulled apart the two edges of the woman's shawl.

"Coom, coom, Mrs Poyser," she said, "there's nowt to be ashamed on! I know you 'aven't been visitin' your fancy lad 'ere! Well, 'as she good news for ye?"

"Yes she has!" declared Mrs Poyser a little violently, as if she feared Mrs Tawnie would belittle it. "She saw a letter, a fat one. It's in the post now."

271

"She did, did she?"

"Yes, she said I ought to be getting it some time this week; tomorrow perhaps."

"Good luck," said Maggie warmly. "Egypt, that's where 'e is, isn't 'e? There's nowt to be a-feared of out there, lass! Well, good night! P'raps there's a letter in the post for me, too!"

Mrs Poyser didn't mind who got a letter now, so long as she was getting one. "I'm sure there's a letter for you, too, Mrs Tawnie!" she said generously. "Good night!" She went.

And she was right. "See, Maggie," said Mrs Durbin. "'Ere's a letter for thee! See 'im? This wun 'ere!" Her left eye sketched the ghost of a wink. Maggie winked back. It was all great fun. They weren't taken in, either of them.

"There's wun 'ere for me, too!" Mrs Durbin continued.

"It's a bit overdue, now, the bad lad!"

"Well, never mind, Mrs Durbin. Somethin' tells me it'll be 'ere within the week."

"For sure," said Mrs Durbin. "The tea-leaves never lie. I'm just brewin' a cup of tea, Maggie. *Do* stay and 'ave a drop!"

Mrs Poyser and Mrs Tawnie got their letters, if not the next day, then the next week, or the week after. But no letter came for Mrs Durbin, not even the week after that. Then she got a printed letter from the War Office, saying that Arthur was missing, believed killed. But *she* did not believe him killed, not for one moment. She got down to her tea-leaves and cards again, though she wasn't in the least worried, really. She saw him large as life again and again, coming back to Magnolia Street. That was what made her feel there might be something in all this fortune telling, after all. For it was so clear, even without the tea-leaves and cards, that he *was* coming back.

The cards and tea-leaves lied, alas. He did *not* come back.

Chapter 3

I

There were two or three men in Magnolia Street who, on the fourth day of August, 1914, walked about like men in whom something has broken. It was a dismay without any reference at all to the hurt that the War might inflict on them and theirs. Their eyes were vague and piteous, like the eyes of small beasts or children. They could not walk straight. Their feet dragged behind them like lumps of lead.

One of these was Reb Feivel, the grandfather of Mrs Seipel, the cabinet-maker's wife. He could bear much pain for himself, though an old man; as when his grand-daughter spilled a saucepan of hot oil on his foot or a dentist extracted an oak tree of a tooth. He smiled. He said not a word. But he could not bear other people's pain. His lips went white and his hands shook like leaves. He heard the rumour of the feet of the armies going to meet each other, and felt on the delicate plasm of his own heart the griefs they were preparing to inflict and endure, those hundreds of thousands of guiltless lads. If he had guessed what millions there were to be of dead men and men dying horribly, of men that horribly could not die, he would not have borne it. He would have died years before his time. But as the tragic months went by, he was not blind to what there was of solace even in so desperate a war. He saw how godlike simple men might be. It helped him to breathe and to live for some years more.

It was somewhat similar with that rosy milleniarist, Mr Emmanuel, the Clerk to the Jewish Board of Guardians. He was not so balanced a thinker as Reb Feivel, and there were moments of exacerbation in which he believed that the Great War was deliberately organised in order to flout those theories he had expounded publicly from many a platform; a slap in the face, quite simply. But he, too, as time went on, found that the War was not merely an argument for his theories more eloquent than any that any pacifist could conceive, but an agent for their realisation more efficient than any pacifist dared have hoped for.

There was a woman, too, whom it broke. But she was broken already, it may be. This was Mary Cooper. She knew that all men were fools, like her father. That was why they had made this

War. That was why they kept on making this War, when if they had been women, they would just have said no, and turned back to their homes. Let the million fools gouge out all their eyes! But let them not hurt one gold hair of the head of her young brother, Dick. For the love of Jesus Christ, let not one gold hair come to harm.

And the last of these, whom the War broke, was Benjamin Stern, the missionary. His head seemed to float loose from the cracked vertebrae of his neck. Perhaps he too, like Mary Cooper, had been dead and broken for a long time now. But now he admitted it, in the bitter stillness of his own heart.

Six years have passed since we met him first, looking mournfully through his window upon the houses of the Jews opposite, and shaking his head, and turning back to his book again. No success has come his way, for he cannot count it as a success that he had led a youth and his sister, who lived some streets away, to Christ, and he knows now their father died raving, and he sees now the signs of madness gathering in their eyes, too.

He has been waylaid more than once by louts jumping out on him from dark entries. But he would have welcomed it if they had ill-treated him more desperately. Blows so feeble were too little atonement to repay his Master for the hours upon Calvary. Sometimes in his unhappiness, he prayed that when they should attack him again they might put an end to him. Then he prayed for forgiveness for that weakness... In Thy Time, O Lord, In Thine Own Time. ... He took out of a drawer a bundle of leaflets — the proceedings and achievements of the various societies for the conversion of the Jews. He put them back again, sighing deeply.

He was a wanderer into many devious by-ways of scholarship, and had, for instance, studied deeply the question of the prophecies and calculations men in all ages have engaged on, regarding the end of the world. The subject had such a fascination for him that he feared it might be unholy, and sometimes put it aside for years at a time. But he always returned to it. He was aware how often, with what precision, men had foretold the end, as for the year 195 and the year 365 and supremely the year 1000, and they had always been shown fools. But it seemed to him that the numberless failures might have been only numberless miscalculations. Somewhere, in stars or Scripture, the principle of exact foretelling might be embedded. He pondered the matter deeply, and covered countless sheets of paper with symbols and formulas. But his speculations were controlled by one consideration which was to him a certainty. The end of the world was tied up with the Jews and their final acceptance or final rejection of the Jew, Jesus Christ.

He always came back to that point, however tortuously the path might have led from it, into however abstract an ether of pure numbers he had been launched. He could no more extract himself from that preoccupation with the Jews and Jesus Christ Who had died for them, than he could walk away out of his own bones and skin. He knew that in this world there are more gentiles than Jews; but they had accepted Him or not accepted Him. Those who had not, possessed his mind no more than all those myriads who had died in the ages before Christ was born. But the structure of the universe, it seemed to him, was bound up with Christ and the Jews, and their dealings with each other. He had few friends, and these were educated men and Christian priests, of one sort or another. Even to these, Benjamin Stern's view of the universe seemed as likely as that Brahmin account, according to which the world is made out of the mangled limbs of Purusha, who was destroyed by the gods.

When the War came, he knew this was Armageddon, the end was come. He knew that his Master Christ, and he, had failed. The War was fallen upon all the nations, because the Jews had not accepted Him.

Benjamin Stern was a Christian, and the old Mrs Edelman who lived opposite, at number seven, was Jewish. He was a man of great learning, and she, though she was a pious old body, was ignorant. But she led a small school of opinion, of which the other adherents were ignorant old women like herself; and the main tenet of their philosophy regarding this Great War was precisely the same as that of Benjamin Stern. They and he held equally that the War had come because of the Jews. There were others, of course, and there were more when the War ended, chiefly among the defeated powers, who said the same thing. But they merely meant that the War was due to the machinations of Jewish financiers. There was nothing mystical about that idea. But Mrs Edelman and Mr Stern meant the War was caused, not by the Jews, but because of them, and that God had caused it.

Mrs Edelman maintained that because the Jews rode on the tram-cars on Sabbath in these bad days, and mixed meat and milk foods, and did not say the blessings before and after meals, therefore God had determined to punish them. It was true that the punishment involved some suffering for several hundreds of millions of people who were not Jews. But that could not be helped. The remissness of the Jews, according to Mr Stern, was of another nature. So the War came; but it did not seem to him a punishment; it seemed the final collapse of the moral fabric of the universe.

As the War went on, he left the house less and less frequently. He made no effort now to bring the Jews over to his Master. It was too late. The end was appointed, and imminent. So far as his landlady, Mrs Carter, was concerned, he almost threatened to become what she was so thankful he had never yet been, a nuisance. But he needed so little to eat and moved so rarely from his table, that the threat did not materialise. The Bible was, of course, always on the table; but he had a number of mathematical and mystical treatises, too. The table and floor were littered with sheets of paper on which he made infinite computations. As the months went by the fine edge of his intelligence blunted. He accepted, on grounds that he would once have scorned, the prophecy that the world would cease in 1917. But he did not live to ascertain that this prophecy was also false, like those that had preceded it. He died in the last days of 1916, no tears being shed for him. The weeping was for men younger and lustier than he, who did not die among a spilth of logarithms and algebraic formulae.

And now, too, having avoided it so long, he was a nuisance. It was really quite unpleasant for Mrs Carter to have all the trouble of it and her husband away in France. And then, two or three days later, he was not even a nuisance. He was nothing at all.

II

It was not so with one old man in Magnolia Street, poring with wild eyes over the holy books. The War did not break him. To him the War was a ghost; to him and many of the young men who came back from fighting in the War. To these young men, too, in the extremity of their bewilderment, in the insensateness

276

of the long assault upon their nerves, the War sometimes became a ghost. Sometimes the spectral mood lasted only a moment, sometimes it extended over days and weeks. They performed all their duties perfectly, but it was not they who performed them so much as a demon that had taken control of them. They themselves stood apart and witnessed the coming together of armies of shadows. The big guns became mere problems in mathematics, the bullets that sped by — malignant thoughts upon a journey.

The War was another sort of ghost to Rabbi Shulman. The things apprehensible to the senses and time measurable by the clock had never seemed to him to be real in themselves, for which reason his grasp upon them had never been strong. Even the angels and the patriarchs and the kings and the wise men, of whom he read in his books, partook of the unreality. They were but methods towards the comprehension of Jehovah, the truth.

So that now, as the war years went on, the history of mankind as the holy men had written it and the young men were fighting it, overlapped and became indistinguishable. Across the gulf of his remoteness he might hear from his wife or his sons or the greybeards at the synagogue, of the atrocious deeds of enemies; but the image presented to his mind was of the cruelty of the Ishmaelites, when eighty thousand young priests, all bearing golden shields upon their breasts, broke through the armies of Nebuchadnezzar at the sack of Jerusalem, and demanded water and food from them. "First eat and then you may drink," commanded the Ishmaelites, and they gave them salt food and increased their thirst greatly. After which the Ishmaelites gave them leather bags, filled, not with water, but with air, which the priests raised to their mouths, and the air entered their bodies, and so they died.

He might hear of young men, prodigies of strength and valour... But they had the lineaments of that Akiba who bade defiance to the Babylonians for three long years, and when their catapults hurled stones from outside the city to break down the inner wall, he was wont to catch them on his feet and throw them back again.

As for the deciding of this War, was not the decision inscribed long ago? Nor shall angels prevail, though another Hanamel arise, and conjure the angels and arm them and station them along the long ramparts between Switzerland and the sea.

277

"Hast thou not read, Reb Feivel," he asked, "how, when Hanamel conjured the angels, the Chaldaens retreated in terror at that sight? But it availed naught, for Jehovah had appointed the defeat and the victory. And even though Hanamel at the end called upon the Prince of the world to raise Jerusalem high in the air, Jehovah set the city down upon the earth again, so that the enemy might enter and fulfil the doom."

"Yes, yes," breathed Reb Feivel fearfully, "that was long ago. And now our children are fighting in another War. But neither angels nor devils fight, only the great guns... Or dost thou think, perhaps...?"

But the Rabbi uttered no reply. The sight of his long lean fingers on the yellow page before him recalled to him the courage of the Levites, who, when the Babylonians demanded of them that they should pluck their harps and sing, bit off their fingers and asked: "How may we pluck the harps of Zion in a strange land?"

Chapter 4

I

When we first met Mrs Stanley it was only a matter of secondary importance that she came from Germany, that she had been back to Germany, that she had returned from Germany only two years previously. It is true that it seemed to matter now and again to the Boys, but they were beings of exceptional prescience.

But it is all very different now, in 1916. It is not good enough to say that Mrs Stanley married an Englishman and is therefore a fully-qualified English citizen by marriage. Where did she come from? How did she get to Magnolia Street? We want to know all about her.

Mrs Stanley's name was once Elsa Kohlenberg. Her people kept a small *pension* in a side street that led down to the Alster, a large urban sheet of water in Hamburg, that is sluiced down through canals to the Elbe. This was a long time ago now, in the later years of the last century. It occurred to her and her parents that a knowledge of English would be useful in a *pension*. She therefore accepted the opportunity which presented itself to become *kinder fraülein* for two or three years to an English family in a suburb of Doomington.

Nobody could have been safer than *Fraülein* Kohlenberg in a foreign city. Not because she was plain. She was not plain. But she had a sober head on her shoulders. A year or so after she arrived she took her shoes to be mended to a young shoemaker named Stanley. Perhaps the springtime that year was more upsetting than it usually is in the Doomington area. He must have been quite attractive to look at, with his dark eyes and bright mouth and swinging hips. He compared favourably, no doubt, with the stolid young Hamburgers who went out rowing on Sundays on the Alster and took their girls to beer-gardens after, to drink a couple of pints of beer and devour two small sausages apiece with potato salad. Perhaps she would not have married him if he had not assured her he would not be a shoemaker much longer, three months at most. For she was not an impulsive person. Perhaps she would have married him in any case, for it is given to the most level-headed people to do something rash once in their lives. In the unruly heaving of her bosom, she must have thought herself very intelligent and far-sighted to have got so explicit a promise from him that he would give up the shoemaking and start in on a small retail business in three months. The trusted only daughter of a retired customs official who keeps a small *pension* in a side street leading to the Alster, cannot easily write and tell her father that she has married a shoemaker.

But Frank's courting was so vigorous that before long she found it advisable to marry him, even if he was to remain a shoemaker six months longer. Elsa Kohlenberg had been, in fact, indiscreet. She had never been indiscreet before and would never again be indiscreet; but she paid for that one indiscretion with much heartbreak for many years, and when the Great War came, she found she hadn't really started paying till then.

Frank Stanley did not give up the shoemaking after three months, nor three years. He was too busy with the ghosts of the horses and the ghosts of the footballers. Elsa bore it all without complaint. She loved him, with a love that was all inside herself. She was not demonstrative. He could keep her and their two boys starving for half a week and she said nothing. She knew he loved her, too, in the time he had to spare from his scraps of paper.

He was faithful to her now, in 1916, and had been for years. It had not always been so. A few years after her marriage she found he went with other women. He was very attractive and the other women thought his wife was a fool, and they made him think so, too, so he went with them.

She did nothing rash. She knew what he had been up to when he came back a little flushed and festive, and smelling of drink. She thought the situation over carefully. She was in a state of anguish, but she did not show it. Her elder boy, Arthur, was about three years old, the other one, Charles, not quite twelve months. Frank, himself, forced action upon her. He did not come home one night. When he returned next morning, she told him quietly that he must not spend the night away from home. She did not wish him to go with other women at all, but if he spent the night away again, she would take the children and go back home to Hamburg, where her father had died lately, and her mother was ready to take her in, for it was hard to keep the *pension* going single-handed.

He saw she meant it. He did not really care for the other women. Then a big win at Doncaster, some months later, went to his head. He got very drunk and determined that he'd show her, the *Deutsche*, and he wasn't going to let anybody, wife or no wife, dictate to him. So he spent the night away from her, with a lady who was as excited about the big win at Doncaster as he was himself. Elsa, without making a fuss about it, had kept a little money on one side; it would have gone into the satchels of the bookmakers long ago if she had not. With that money she went home to Hamburg, taking her small boys with her.

She helped her mother with the *pension*, and the boys grew up as little German boys. Arthur, the elder, whom they called Otto, was not clever. He became a baker. The younger, Charles, was an astonishing scholar. Her husband wrote to her a few times to return, but she did not. Her mother was an invalid and the whole work of the *pension* fell on her shoulders. It was not successful, because people who lived in that part of Hamburg wanted to be able to look out on the Alster. They might as well live in a cheaper part of the town, if they were going to be cooped up in a side street.

As for Frank, it was fortunate he had so much to occupy his head, or he would have been miserable. It was not the women. He hadn't really cared for them at all, and he dropped them and they dropped him, as soon as he had a long spell of bad luck. It was the racing, of course, and the competitions and the football, that kept him busy. He had all the greater impetus to press on to that fortune which was lying in wait for him just round the corner. She would come back to him, then, if only for the sake of the boys — Charles, particularly, who was so good a scholar, it seemed (for she wrote to him sometimes).

Elsa's mother died after an expensive operation. A few days earlier another letter had come from her husband, rather more mournful than usual. Things were going badly with him. She sold up the furniture of the *pension*, and it was surprising how little it brought considering how large it was. She was just about able to pay the passage for herself and the two boys. This was a couple of years before we met them. The family came to live in Magnolia Street.

Otto — who had left the country as Arthur — got a job as a baker. He was a very stolid lad. Even during the War he never got the flour quite out of his eyebrows. He played a guitar and sang German soldier songs to it, *Strasburg* and *Drei Lilien*, and *Waldeslust*.

His brother, Charles, had a hare-lip, but a forehead of great beauty. It was as white as marble and finely moulded. They granted him a special scholarship at Doomington School, and in two years, at sixteen, he was in the sixth form, having learned not only English during these two years, but Latin and Greek and the Romance languages, though he had learned the rudiments of some of these in the Gymnasium. He read Aristotle, Spinoza, Hegel, in the original languages and permitted himself to read Pindar and Catullus in his spare time. To him it was the same thing if he lived in the Gurlittstrasse in Hamburg or Magnolia Street in Doomington. When, shortly, he went to Cambridge he was only conscious that he took a train journey instead of a tram journey, and on a train you can read more Descartes than on a tram, before you must close your book and get out. Now, some years after that, he had left Cambridge for the defence of a munition dump near Shoeburyness. But that dump meant less to him than the dump over in Egypt where they had been finding new fragments from Sappho, whole lines at a time.

II

For a long time after the War broke out, Elsa Stanley was Mrs Derricks's chief topic of conversation at the Lamb and Lion. You might have thought the War had deliberately brought itself about in order to establish Mrs Derricks's contentions. To begin with the woman had always looked and talked like a German spy, all the more because she tried so hard to look and talk like an Englishwoman. She often had things to eat in the house which nobody but a German spy could have eaten. She and her elder son, Otto, used often to sit down to a dish of pig's-knuckle and sauerkraut, and they had been overheard talking German together frequently.

Moreover, it was well known that she had returned to Germany a few years after her marriage, while her two sons were still babies. What had she gone back to Germany for if it was not to hand over to her employers the results of her researches into the naval and military dispositions of the United Kingdom? That was artful, if you like, to take her children with her, so that it should all look innocent and above board. And what was the place she had gone to? Hamburg, no less. The postman could be brought in to testify that she kept on receiving letters from Hamburg every few months, till the very outbreak of the war. *Hamburg*! A port, that is to say! A place where ships went to and came back from, as black a piece of evidence as you could ask for.

The Boys, of course, echoed Mrs Derricks's conclusions vociferously. It was, in point of fact, the Conjurer who had first given tongue to these dark doubts regarding the German *Frau* next door.

"I shouldn't put it past that there *Deutsche Frau*," he had announced at one of the parties. "She may be listenin' to us at this very moment with 'er ear clapped up against t'wall."

It was really rather difficult for the patrons of the Lamb and Lion to resist the arguments of the Derricks party, even if they were disposed to.

On the very day the War broke out, Mrs Stanley tried to make light of it. She came into the private bar, as usual. Mrs Derricks was there, and she didn't say anything. Nothing like that about Mrs Derricks. She just planted her feet square, crossed her arms across her bosom, and stared the *Frau* straight in the face. Mrs Stanley coloured up to the eyebrows. Everyone noticed it. Mrs Briggs and both the Carters and the negro's wife (who had slipped in that day) and Mrs Tawnie herself. And instead of just asking for her beer and sitting down to it, as she would have done if her mind was easy, she dithered about for a few seconds, and then went out again.

Her husband, Frank Stanley, the shoemaker, was English all right. It was generally agreed that he wasn't a partner in the woman's espionage, only her decoy duck and her tool. He kept on coming into the private bar for some weeks, and tried to induce his wife to come in, too. But she didn't. She shut herself up in her kitchen and didn't go out into the street a moment more than was necessary. He tried to bring up the subject of his wife and these ideas which were growing up about her and choking her. But the effort produced so immediate and grim a silence, that he had not the courage to persevere. The atmosphere of the place wasn't pleasant for him either, so after some weeks he, too, kept away from the Lamb and Lion altogether.

283

He still fiddled about with little bits of paper, though it was hard to say what images of what dooms he was trying to conjure, for football and racing were not the golden mysteries they had once been. English League Football had stopped altogether, and the Scottish wasn't much to write home about. Football had become a mere week-end by-product of munition-making. As for racing — there was nothing worth the name outside Newmarket. Sometimes his little bits of paper came fluttering out of his front door on a through-draught, and they excited the liveliest suspicions. On one or two occasions they were forwarded as likely evidence to the Chief Constable, along with urgent requests signed by several of the neighbours that prompt action must be taken in the matter of Elsa Stanley.

The Chief Constable was not convinced, though he *did* go so far as to send down a couple of officers to make enquiries. It seemed necessary, therefore, to Mrs Derricks and the Boys that they must themselves take action. Their resolve was strengthened on the day after an air-raid night in April, 1916. It was only discovered next day that it had been an air-raid night, for the raiders had not managed to get nearer than a few hundred miles from Doomington; but by the grace of God the Boys had been staring up at Mrs Stanley's front bedroom window just about the time when, it was discovered later, the raiders had been discharging their bombs. They saw Mrs Stanley light the gas and *then* pull down the blind; she did not, they observed, pull down the blind and then light the gas. Nor did she pull the blind firmly, so that it stayed down. It sprang up again, then she pulled it down again, after a calculated interval. It was clear to the most rabbit-headed that the woman must be signalling to her countrymen. Next day their suspicious were triumphantly confirmed. There had been an air-raid over the Thames estuary.

This time the Boys did not address themselves to the Chief Constable. The Chief Constable might be in *Frau* Stanley's pay for all they knew. So they set forth on their own accord to let the spy know what they thought of her.

III

It was an opportunity the Boys had long been waiting for. It brought back to them something of the hectic rapture with which they had greeted the outbreak of the War. For days they walked about as if they didn't know where to put themselves, they were so happy. They couldn't understand how on earth they had ever got any punch out of so snivelling a back-entry squabble as the Boer War. The parties with which they celebrated the early glorious days exceeded anything that Magnolia Street had known for years, and were only to be equalled again on a great day in 1916 when George Derricks came home with the DCM.

The War effected in them an important moral improvement, so far as it can be deemed a moral improvement not to stand on the pavement and shout "Who killed Christ?" when a Jew makes his appearance. It seemed, indeed, to alter the whole character of their theological convictions. They felt they had been in error about the Jews and Jesus. It was the Germans who had crucified Him, or, more specifically, Elsa Stanley rather than Rabbi Shulman. The patriotism of the Boys was a thing of the spirit rather than of the mere body. That applied particularly to Mrs Derricks and Wilfred. For biological reasons they were neither of them acceptable to the military authorities. The Pocket Samson, also, was too small for the most bantam regiment to have any use for him. But the Baritone, the Conjurer, the Ventriloquist — they would have been welcome at any recruiting office. Yet they were convinced that they were of more use to their country out of the army than in it. It was not merely because they felt that such talents as theirs must be economised. Would there not be peace some day, and what sort of a place would post-war England be without baritones, conjurers and ventriloquists? But they felt, too, that wherever they moved they were like a flame to kindle the doubting spirits of civilian and soldier alike.

The Boys very properly, then, did not join up of their own accord. A certain amount of misguided pressure was brought to bear on them later, but the Baritone, at least, managed to convince tribunal after tribunal that it would be a mistake to put him into khaki, like any mechanic or professor or ploughman. Not that the Baritone did not assume khaki at all at any time. He did, twice nightly and at matinées, whenever he got an engagement. And soon after the Tanks made their first memorable appearance, he toured the country in a revue which, with dance and song, displayed the full splendour of war and the fearfulness of its new engine. A caterpillar bevy of chorus girls assisted him, poking their arms and legs through holes in a painted canvas, and crying "Boom-boom!" realistically. And then they all joined in the chorus:

We are the tanks
That broke the ranks
Out in Picardy.

It was a successful item and a good imitation of the real thing. In some respects it was a notable improvement on it.

The tribunals were not so intelligent about the Ventriloquist. It took them a long time before he gave them the opportunity of a heart-to-heart talk with him, he was so busy flitting up and down the country, encouraging folk. At last, in February of 1916, he was informed, wherever he might be, he was 'deemed to have enlisted.' It was not till several months later he accepted that interpretation of the matter; but when he did, he made no bones about it. He became an efficient soldier and was always ready to lend his talents to any concert-party free of charge.

The Conjurer's career followed somewhat similar lines, excepting that instead of waiting till they made a conscript of him, he was foolhardy enough to enlist as a married man under the Derby scheme. His wife was one of those mysterious ladies who suddenly appeared out of nowhere at this time, to convert gentlemen who had always seemed incurable celibates into married men with all the responsibilities which the state of marriage implies. Mrs Derricks and her entourage had known nothing about the lady. She gave the impression of having emerged like a rabbit from the Conjurer's top-hat. She was a slightly lachrymose creature but soon became cheerful in the company of Mrs Derricks and her Boys. Both she and her husband drew much satisfaction from the promise of the authorities that the married men would not be called up till the single men were combed out; but the authorities were not very punctilious and the Conjurer was called up while many a carefree bachelor lay skulking in factory and office. The Conjurer was very vocal about it, but he had to go. His wife went, too. It was stated that she had been enlisted to be his spouse by a sergeant-major, on behalf of whom she would receive a more substantial separation allowance than from any mere private, however cunning a Conjurer he might be.

There was never any question about Mrs Derricks doing her bit. If a few more thousand Englishwomen had done their bit as conscientiously as Mrs Derricks, the War would not have come to so premature an end. Post-war history has not yet done her the credit due to her. Whatsoever certain vainglorious claimants from Putney and Peebles might say, it was she, it was none other, who initiated the practice of presenting young men in civilian clothing with white feathers. There were occasions on which, being a little fuddled, she presented white feathers not merely to young men with inconspicuous disabilities, like being blind or minus a few fingers; sometimes the recipients lacked a limb or two. But the risk of piquing a few heroes was little price to pay for the privilege of inspiring some pasty-faced "conchy" with a sense of decency.

The frustration of the spy, Elsa Stanley, who lived next door must also be reckoned as part of her war-service. Without receiving a penny for it she followed Mrs Stanley from pillar to post, bidding unsuspecting passers-by take care what they were saying in the presence of so sinister a person.

If she had not been a woman, she would have done even more. Brandishing a sword in one hand and a rifle in the other, she would have stormed the enemy's front-line trenches, none more impetuously. But she was a woman. Was it not enough, apart from her other services, that she was the mother of two such doughty ones as George and Wilfred? George, whom she had always nourished as the apple of her eye, over whose infant slumbers she had crooned the tale of his country's heroes, did he not get the DCM? And Wilfred, her little Nightingale, did he not also serve in France?

Yes, Wilfred also served in France. From Calais to Boulogne, from Boulogne to Le Havre, from Le Havre to Rouen, there was no base camp so dangerous but that Wilfred would intrepidly visit it. He was no more merely a Longton Nightingale. He was the British Army's Nightingale. Wherever there was a hut where Woodbine Cigarettes and Horlick's Malted Milk were sold, whether Roman Catholics or Evangelists or Anglicans sold them, he sang them the old favourites, like *The Temple Bells Were Ringing* and the new favourites, like *Keep the Home Fires Burning*. He opened his arms to the dear soldiers, as if he would clasp them to his bosom, which was neither a man's nor a woman's, neither a girl's nor a boy's. The black hole of his mouth gaped and twisted. The soldiers who were near enough to see his face shuffled awkwardly on the benches, but even those at the back felt it all a little eerie. Yet it was not so eerie as the place they had come from and were going back to. They listened to the Nightingale politely, and were not sorry when he stopped singing.

"And now, dear boys," said the minister in charge, "Let's sing *Lead, Kindly Light*! All together boys!"

How the boys went to it! The Horlick's mugs danced on the trestle tables and the lamps swung from the beams. That was always the effect of the Nightingale's singing. It was no wonder he was so popular with the hut leaders, Catholics or Evangelists or Anglicans, whatever they were.

IV

But on the day after the air-raid over the Thames estuary which *Frau* Stanley had so cunningly manipulated with her arrangement of window-blinds and incandescent gas mantles, Wilfred had not yet been invited to undertake his triumphant tour in France, though he had done doughty home-service with the YMCA. The Conjurer and the Baritone were there, but the Ventriloquist was somewhere else, exerting his influence among the more bashful of his countrymen. The Pocket Samson was, fortunately, on the spot.

So the Boys went forth to express their disapproval of Mrs Stanley. They had already done it on previous occasions to the extent of throwing ordure and bricks over the yard wall which separated the Derricks and Stanley houses. They had also smashed Stanley windows. But they had felt a certain sense of hesitation about an armed frontal attack, so long as Mrs Stanley's two sons, Otto and Charles, were still about the place. Otto and Charles were now, however, away in the army, seeking to undermine the discipline of the troops with the aid of German gold. Mr Stanley too, was out of the way. The Boys had waited till they had seen him go off for the morning to his shoemaker's cellar in Aubrey Street.

Then they sallied forth. Mrs Derricks armed herself with a flat-iron. The war cost her a great deal in flat-irons. The others had broomsticks, chunks of brick and other material. They addressed themselves to the Stanley home. They smashed in the parlour windows, they uprooted the few sad little box shrubs in the garden, they hurled themselves at the door. Then the Pocket Samson climbed up through the ruined window, took his stand on a table just beyond the curtains, and then with loud cries of pleasure hurled out plants, plant-pots, ornaments, family albums.

Miss Tregunter looked on white and impassive from her upstairs room. She did not approve of such ungenteel proceedings, but neither did she approve Mrs Stanley's secret activities on behalf of the German War Office. The older Jewish women gathered in Mrs Poyser's shop huddled together like sheep among the sacks of sugar. They had seen with their own eyes in their native countries somewhat similar proceedings, and their skin tingled with dismay, for when fires broke out they did not know how soon the wind might blow the flame in their own direction. A small group of women stood in the roadway and cheered in a not wholly convinced manner. They included, oddly enough, no other lady than Mrs Shulman, the Rabbi's wife. She was the only one who cheered with any conviction.

"Dirty Sherman!" she cried out. "You dirty Sherman!"

A young woman turned in from Blenheim Road at that moment, and saw what was afoot. Rose Berman looked tired and anxious, years older, but the childish sweetness still lay on her lips. Her eyes darkened. She clenched her fists.

"The skunks!" she muttered. "God almighty! If only John were here!"

She saw the face of Elsa Stanley at the upstairs window, surrounded by its coils of straw-blonde hair. It looked pale and empty like the moon. Her arms waved about her vaguely. Then she retreated to the further wall of the room; then came back again to the window.

Rose Berman started across the street, her mouth twitching. Then she stopped. It was as if she felt a warm weak breath upon the back of her neck. She turned round and saw her mother's face against the window. She saw quite clearly through the glass the large tears coursing down her cheeks.

"No! No! I must go in to her at once!" muttered Rose. She looked round desperately and spotted Berel, the youngest of the Seipels. She called him.

"Go, Berel!" she bade him. "Go at once to Mr Stanley in his cellar in Aubrey Street! Tell him what's happening!"

He fled.

The face of Mrs Stanley reappeared at the upstairs window.

"Yah! Yer dirty bloody spy!" cried the Boys. "We'll show yer!"

Then the front door opened and Mr Stanley appeared, his shoemaker's apron round him. He still had a nail or two in his mouth and a hammer in one hand. For it had taken him no time to come over from Aubrey Street, to enter his house through the back door, to come out again by the front door; not time enough to drop the hammer and spit out the nails. He strode forward to the Boys with his dark eyes fixed only on one of them. It was as if Mrs Derricks and the others were not there at all.

He lifted Wilfred, the Nightingale, by the back of his coat, as you lift a cat by its neck, and carried him into the house with his four limbs hanging loose. He closed the door behind him and entered the parlour, upon which the Pocket Samson promptly left it. He seated himself on a stuffed chair and tore Wilfred's trousers with one tug from their braces. With his other hand he pulled the leather belt that held up his own trousers out of its buckle. He then proceeded to beat the small bare buttocks of the Nightingale so long and so fiercely that the blood ran on to the threadbare carpet. For a long time the Nightingale uttered no sound, his teeth sewing his lips together. Then he broke. He howled and screamed, this man of thirty-six, like the small boy he seemed. It was as if fate, which treated him all along so grotesquely, had said: "You want to be a small boy? Here's your chance!"

Then the shoemaker stopped. He carried him over to the window and dropped him, like a kitten in which the life is just barely twitching, into the mess of broken plants and china.

"I want my Wilfred, my poor poor duck!" a voice was saying. He heard it faintly above the roar of humiliation which beat like a millrace in his ear.

"Take your little bag of poison!" cried another voice. "There 'e is, the stinking puppy! And you, yer bitch! Are yer gettin' out of it? Are yer gettin' out of it, I say?"

"I want my Wilfred! My poor poor duck!" the voice said again. It was his mother's voice. He felt himself lifted into her bosomy warmth. Her large hands covered his bleeding buttocks. Her tears fell in a soft shower on to his gilded hair. She took him into their own house again. The Boys had gone. They were too tender-hearted to stay on, whilst poor Wilfred was being treated so and Mrs Derricks was being abused by that common woman. They could not bear it. The Boys had all gone.

But wheresoever they betook themselves all that day and many a day after, the Pocket Samson, and the Conjurer and the Baritone, they still heard the voice of Mrs Briggs shrilling in their ears. Mrs Briggs of all women, the wife of the odd-job-man. Such a nice refined woman, they had always thought. Just at the moment when the shoemaker had swept poor little Wilfred off his feet, she had come storming up like a tornado.

"Don't yer know," she had screamed, "Yer dirty bitch, don't yer know the poor woman's goin' to 'ave a baby?"

Such awful language, you couldn't have thought the gentle Mrs Briggs capable of it!

"Yer fat sow, get back into your sty again! The poor little woman up there, goin' to 'ave a baby an' all! D'y'ear what I say? I'll tear every 'air out of yer lousy 'ead!"

And there in the parlour was little Wilfred being flayed alive and screaming his lungs out, and here was Mrs Briggs clawing at poor Mrs Derricks's hair like a harpy. No wonder Mrs Derricks couldn't stand it. No wonder she broke down and sobbed.

"I want my Wilfred!" said she. "My poor poor duck!" So she lifted him up and took him into her house again. And Mrs Briggs went up to Elsa Stanley in the front room, and comforted her and made some tea. Rose Berman, too, came over from the opposite pavement. Her mother had baked some home-made cakes yesterday, so she brought a few over with her. But Elsa Stanley couldn't eat any of the cakes, her lips were trembling so funny. It was all she could do to swallow a drop of tea.

"Never mind now, never mind!" crooned Mrs Briggs, while Rose Berman held her hands and chafed them tenderly. "Never mind, 'oney, we'll look after yer!"

V

The Boys made no bones about it. In the engagement just described, the forces of virtue had been routed. They realised that against so insidious an enemy, you cannot proceed in full daylight and unfortified with a little alcoholic stimulus. Was not a tot of rum issued to their comrades-in-arms in the trenches when an assault was intended to the enemy? Instead of running their heads against a brick wall they would henceforth counter subtlety with subtlety. So henceforth they ran out singly on dark nights and smashed a Stanley window or thrust a note under the door and withdrew at once to the base of operations and slammed the door.

Mrs Derricks was more foolhardy. Whenever she saw Mrs Stanley in the street she had no hesitation in letting her know she had her eye on her — excepting, of course, if Mrs Briggs was anywhere about. Mrs Briggs was about half Mrs Derricks's size and weight, but she was so *common*, you couldn't possibly try issues with such a creature.

The child that had aroused Mrs Briggs's apprehensions was born a month or two later, a not quite seven-months-old boy. He only lived a few days, though Mrs Briggs and Mrs Seipel lent all their skill and twenty hours a day to tide him over. Mrs Derricks had no ill feeling against the little creature, but she wasn't quite certain it wasn't the best thing after all. For if the Lord had spared him, what was more likely than that he'd become a spy to spy out the land for the Germans in preparation for the next war, assuming that this one was over by then?

About Elsa Stanley, once of Hamburg, there was a touch of rather wistful beauty these days, particularly in the months following the death of the small baby. It managed to touch a chord in Mr Stanley which had not vibrated for a long time. When he sat over his last, her brow haunted him queerly. She had a fine brow, the skin over it almost pale blue, it was so delicate. Their younger son, Charles, had inherited it, but his hare-lip spoiled it. There was no flaw in her face. He rose from his stool to go to his meal and her brow was before him in a pale glow as he moved along. He kissed it somewhat shyly before he sat down to his place.

So that he listened to her now, when she asked him could they not move into a new house. It was not easy. You had to pay enormous premiums these days, to landlords, agents, outgoing tenants, a whole race of vultures. If only that horse had come in first in that wretched race at Newmarket, as by all the signs it should have done! He sighed bitterly.

None the less, in the June of 1916, they moved. The removal was carefully supervised by Mrs Derricks from her upstairs window, who was on the lookout for bombs and dossiers and tins of explosive and the other furniture of espionage. But either Mrs Stanley was too cunning to have any about the place or she had stuffed it away in drawers and chair-padding. The flight was a complete endorsement of Mrs Derricks's assertions, for why would Mrs Stanley have found it necessary to move if she had not realised that the game was up, so far as Magnolia Street was concerned? In a way Mrs Derricks and the Boys, the remnant of the Boys that was left, missed Mrs Stanley. They felt that life had lost something of its savour.

So it was it happened that when Lance-Corporal Arthur Stanley and Private Charles Stanley came back to Doomington after the War was over, they did not return to Magnolia Street. Charles, the younger, returned to the city in the Midlands where he had already enjoyed the appointment for one year of tutor in classical philosophy. He had had a brilliant career in Cambridge and was the most redoubtable philosopher they had known for years. He was so redoubtable that no college, not even the humblest, could be induced to offer him a fellowship. That was not because his hare-lip interfered with his worth as an expositor, it was rather because he could not help displaying his entirely valid belief that the other philosophers of the university were shallow demagogues or addle-pated mystics.

Later on in the War he was one of the guardians of the Severn Tunnel. It was perhaps fortunate that the enemy did not seriously challenge his vigilance. For he devoted less attention to the Severn Tunnel than to the question of the authorship of the Pseudo-Platonic letters, a nice problem in taste and scholarship which had much occupied his attention lately.

His brother, Otto, the baker, went further afield, so far as Mesopotamia. He enlisted, of course, under the name which appeared on his birth certificate, Arthur. But there were those in Magnolia Street who were not deceived by such a manoeuvre. He left his guitar behind him. It was the one really incriminating piece of evidence which Mrs Derricks sighted from her post of observation when the removers were transferring the Stanley furniture into their van. He marched with English soldiers and substituted for *Strasburg* and *Drei Lilien* such songs as:

All soldiers live on bread and jam,
All soldiers eat it instead of ham,
And every morning we hear the colonel say,
Form fours! Eyes right!
Jam for dinner today!

His voice was a little guttural, but he made up for that by the ingenuity with which he could piece together a musical instrument out of the most unlikely elements. It was a talent he greatly exercised during the unpleasant five months when the Sixth Division and the Thirtieth Brigade were beleaguered in Kut. He was by profession a baker, but there was increasingly less and less material for him to practise his gifts on in that line. The last weeks were the most unpleasant; nonetheless, Lance-Corporal Stanley still managed to pipe up a few notes on an old reed or a fragment of comb. Then he and General Townshend surrendered.

Mrs Derricks had always known about Lance-Corporal Stanley, of course. But it came as a great shock to her that General Townshend was a spy, too. Just about that time a sergeant from Rosemary Street was invalided home from Salonica and came into the Lamb and Lion. He knew nothing about Lance-Corporal Stanley. But he stated that in the sergeants' mess at Karaissi, a camp just above the ramparts of Salonica, evidence had been adduced after the fall of Kut which proved irrefutably that General Townshend was a spy.

Mrs Derricks mopped her eyes. Spies everywhere. In high places and low places, in the frontline trenches and the next-door kitchen, it was all the same. She pushed her glass a few inches forward on the counter. "Another 'alf, Mrs Tawnie!" she said mournfully.

VI

The War lost something of its savour for Mrs Derricks and the Boys when the Stanleys moved out of Magnolia Street. But Mr Derricks, the husband, never got any pleasure out of the War. He was too old to be a soldier, and wartime food conditions made his inside more squeamish than ever. During the few days his son George was home again in 1916 — all splendid with his DCM — poor Mr Derricks was doubled up with colitis. The Boys, or those of them that were still about, brought up a jug of beer to his bedroom and insisted on his celebrating the hero's homecoming. They had to force it down his mouth, for beer upset him at the best of times, and what with his colitis he would as soon have taken a drop of weedkiller and got out of it altogether. The Boys were shocked at his behaviour, which they held to be not merely unfatherly but treasonable. They forced the stuff down and left him to it. No, Mr Derricks got no fun out of the War at all.

It was always a matter of great regret to Mr Derricks that he saw so little of his son George the time he came home in glory in August 1916. He had seen nothing of him for some years, the greater part of which George had spent in a Reformatory, where he had filled the Governor and officials with affection and self-searchings. They could not help asking themselves whether the lad had not been the victim of some dreadful mistake, he was so courteous and quiet and his hair was plastered down so straight on both sides. His term of service came to an end a year or so before the War, and the Governor, who was a very gentle man despite his fierce exterior, called him to his room and gave him a fountain pen as a parting present. It was stated at the Lamb and Lion that when George had left and the Governor wanted to see what time it was, he couldn't, for his watch was missing. But that was the sort of thing they always said about George at the Lamb and Lion. Not that they said it with any ill feeling. The ill feeling, if any, was for Mrs Derricks, though she was such a good customer.

So George started life again with a fountain pen. He did not come back to Doomington, for he was a shy youth, and he felt he might be something of a public figure in Magnolia Street. He went to London, instead, without a single note of introduction, but his pleasing manners soon commended him to a large circle of friends. He joined the Army in the early days and went out to France quite soon. His peculiar talents made him the darling of his platoon and officers; for his own part, it gave him a quiet thrill of pleasure that for the first time in his career he was permitted to exercise his gifts openly and in a warm steam of public appreciation. There was nothing that George could not 'win' for you, if you expressed a desire for it, however fleeting. ('Win' was the expression in use at that time to describe the process 'to get possession of'.) He could have 'won' a church spire without the sacristan noticing it, if there were any church spires still standing on his section of the front and the sergeant-major had suggested that it might be a useful ornament. He 'won' jars of rum for his colleagues and cases of whisky for his officers. One of his greatest achievements was an arm-chair, which was much appreciated. He got his decoration for 'winning' a couple of machine guns, after disposing quietly of an officer and two men, all three of whom were snipers. He 'won' a large handful of prisoners in the same encounter, for his gift included animate as well as inanimate objects. He was inconsiderately prevented from achieving further 'winnings' by the barrage of his own artillery, which wounded him agreeably. It was a 'Blighty one', as it was termed, and the news of his decoration came to him whilst he was in hospital in Netley. Despite his innate modesty, he could not forgo the pleasure of seeing his dear parents again in Magnolia Street, however effusively they might welcome him after so long an absence and with so meritorious a ribbon over his breast.

So George came home. Wilfred had, unfortunately, left some weeks ago for his first French tour. Mr Derricks had colitis. The Stanleys had moved. So altogether Mrs Derricks and her stalwarts were rather down in the mouth. It was a God-send, this home-coming of George with his DCM.

As the train drew into the station, several of the Boys were there, and Mrs Derricks. She was magnificently there, with her great bosom and huge arms and her flaming face. When he got out of the train, she flung herself at him with so turbulent a pride and love that he fell back into the carriage, sweeping three or four of his companions with him. The ride home in a taxi was a Roman triumph. The taxi was waiting outside the station with a load of beer, and the Baritone in khaki. He could play a cornet as well as sing the Prologue from *Pagliacci*. He did both exuberantly all the way to Magnolia Street. Flags and decorations fluttered from windows Jewish and gentile. Streamers were suspended between front bedroom windows. 'Welcome Home To Our Hero' rolled and unrolled in the breeze. Blue-eyed Nellie Tawnie presented the hero with a bouquet of flowers.

It was a proud day in the annals of Magnolia Street, but George didn't like it much. He was a plant that wilted in the glare of excessive attention. He weakly suggested once or twice that he, too, like his father, had a touch of colitis. But it took him nowhere. He set his teeth and went through with it. The day was certainly Mrs Derricks's top day. She and the Boys had had gay times before, but nothing to touch this. It was in a sense a justification of all her life's philosophy. It proved the glory of War and indicated, though the process was not clear, how right she was in showing up Mrs Stanley for a German spy. She got a little hazy as the night wore on, and the stranger would have found it difficult to decide whether it was she or George who had 'won' those German machine-guns. She fondled them at her bosom and sang a beery lullaby over them. Then she got up suddenly with a fierce air of resolution. She picked up a flat-iron and staggered down the lobby into the street. The Boys were too busy to do anything about it. She stood swaying against the low wall of Mrs Stanley's garden, then hurled the iron against the parlour window. "Yah!" she cried. "Yer dirty German! Go 'ome to the bleeden Kayser!" She had forgotten that she had driven out Mrs Stanley a month ago now. Her neighbours were irreproachable patriots named Higgins. It cost Mrs Derricks quite a little sum in pane-glass before the War was over, as well as flat-irons.

George Derricks didn't enjoy his leave very much. He got away from Magnolia Street next morning and mooned about the streets a little wretchedly. He didn't quite know what was wrong with him. He felt empty somehow. It is just possible that George Derricks couldn't really feel happy unless he was 'winning' something. It was in the late afternoon that he saw his neighbour, Walter Hubbard, glued, so to speak, against the window of Furnival the Photographer.

Walter Hubbard was the exemplary young man who lived at number twelve. A soldier now, he was still a Sunday School official and the pillar of every YMCA hut he met on his military wanderings. Mr Hubbard, who was on leave from France, and might have been expected to show a little pleasure about it, looked wretched. His mouth quivered, there were pouches under his eyes. It was evident he was trying to expel some dark inhabitant from his mind. Partly for that reason, no doubt, he concentrated his gaze upon that magnificent camera which held the place of honour in Furnival's window. Partly also for the reason that he had once been a keen photographer. But he had given up photography for some years, now. He did not like to shut himself up in darkrooms, while his wife, Dolly, might be standing at the front door talking to strange young men. It was dangerous to leave a pretty little woman like Dolly to her own devices.

His wife worked at munitions during the day. There was nothing for Walter to do but to hang about till her shift was over.

It was with some feeling of sinful covetousness that he stood staring in at Furnival's window. He knew what a lordly camera it was, the sort of camera that takes the photograph of a daisy on the further side of a brick wall at midnight. He tried for several minutes to pull himself away from the spectacle, but it held him hypnotised. And then it was that he heard a voice in his ear announce pleasantly: "A bit of all right, Mr Hubbard, isn't it? A beauty I call it!"

Mr Hubbard flushed. He turned round and looked into the sleek and smiling face of George Derricks, the hero of Magnolia Street, whose welcome home had made the whole night hideous.

"Isn't what?" he asked sharply. It was as if the devil had marked him as he stood there lusting, and had become flesh by his side.

George Derricks winked. *"You know!"* he said. He pointed with his thumb over his shoulder to the camera.

"I congratulate you on your DCM!" said Hubbard hurriedly. "I heard about it! Good-bye!" he said. "I've got to go and meet my wife!" He strode off; feeling a queer spasm of fear and sickness. It was the first sensation he was aware of that night, the same fear and sickness, when a hand touched him upon the mouth, and a voice said, "Hush! It's only me, Mr Hubbard!" and a hooded torch-light flashed in a narrow beam to illuminate the smooth features of George Derricks.

"Hush!" repeated George. "Don't waken her! I've got it for you! That camera!"

A moment later there was no more George Derricks. He had disappeared through the window like a vapour. Walter Hubbard did not waken his wife, though he wondered how she could sleep so soundly by his side with his teeth knocking like castanets and a cold sweat pouring steadily from all his pores. The thief had placed the camera on the dressing table a few feet away from the bed. It squatted among the hair brushes like a great toad.

As soon as dawn broke he rose and emptied his kit bag and stuffed the wicked thing into it, and went over to the Derricks house. He felt that at any moment a posse of policemen must pounce on him out of an entry and march him off to gaol, triumphantly bearing before him the evidence of his guilt. For indeed he felt himself no less guilty, more guilty even, than George Derricks. He had sinned in his own deep heart. Derricks had been the mere agent of his sin.

It was George himself who opened the door. "So early?" asked George, rubbing his eyes. "Films? I didn't have time to get any films!"

"For God's sake," moaned Walter Hubbard, "take it back!" He thrust his kit bag into George's arms and fled as from a house of plague.

"*Take it back?*" called George gently after him "*Take it back? Well, you are a one! All right, then! I'll take it back!*" And he did. The camera that was missing one day from Furnival's window was not missing the next day, George Derricks had taken it back. Nobody knew, in fact, that it had been missing; excepting, of course, for the two thieves who had stolen it.

The episode, so far as George Derricks was concerned, relieved what might have been a tedious few days. It pleased him to realise that his stay in hospital had not affected the lightness of his touch. He went back to France with a happy song on his lips. Walter Hubbard went back less happily.

Chapter 5

I

Rose Berman was expecting a wire from John Cooper. She would have liked it to have come on the day when the Boys wrecked Mrs Stanley's parlour. She would have liked him to come lurching gently round into Magnolia Street just at the moment when they aimed the first brick; or perhaps, a few minutes later, after Mr Stanley had torn down Wilfred's trousers and told him with his belt what he thought of him. It would have been a shame to deprive Mr Stanley of the pleasure Wilfred had caused him.

And then she recalled that the wire she was expecting was not that sort of a wire. It would not announce John's arrival in Doomington. It would summon her to London. She had been awaiting that wire any morning now, for several hundreds of mornings.

For John had specified long ago that if ever the world looked like coming to an end, he would send her a wire, and ask her to go and be his sweetheart in London. (And even then, it was she who had asked first that she might be a London sweetheart.) For several hundreds of mornings the sick world had seemed as if it were on its last legs. But the sweet world still lived, and her mother still lived. It would be a dreadful thing if John died, though she loved the others dearly.

The wire arrived on a certain Saturday morning in late July. Rose opened it. She knew it was from John. She knew what it bade her do. She had had a letter from John only a few days ago. They had appointed him to the command of a mine-sweeper in the Channel. It was a job in which the end of the world might come just as you were about to light your cigarette. He had a right, after these years, and this year, to send that wire.

As she tore open the envelope, she felt as if she were with her own small hands pulling asunder the enormous shining gates of heaven, and she made a space for John and herself to pass through.

"Shall meet you," the wire said, *"Euston 2-40 Monday Afternoon From Doomington Three Days London"*
JOHN

There was no question about whether she could or could not, no address to send a yes or no. That was the way that wire would come, when it came at last.

She went up at once to her employer. "Mr Saunders," she said, "I have urgent domestic business in London. Might I have three days off?"

"By all means!" said Mr Saunders. She was a good conscientious girl. He had some idea, moreover, how urgent domestic business can be in war-time. He wanted to add "Have a good time now!" but he refrained.

Her mother, she realised, could not be left by herself. She was weak and got tired very easily. But her condition had been pretty much the same for the last two or three months. She could get her sister, Ada, to come in for the few days. It would not be for the first time...

It would not be for the first time. Only a few months ago, Ada had come in. Her husband, Johnnie the photographer, had been beating her again. It was a strange way he had of beating her.

"I don't like your face!" he said smiling. "It's too dolly! It's not really my kind of face!"

So, still smiling, he got hold of her by the hair and threw her down — still smiling and talking.

It was just in the same way he behaved on the fast of the Day of Atonement. Neither of the two Berman girls had been very particular in little matters of ritual. Rose still wasn't. Ada was now. She had become quite finicky since she had realised what a dreadful mistake her marriage was. It was as if she felt it would help her through her misery, to be a bit more careful about milk and meat foods and to say a prayer now and again.

She took the Day of Atonement really seriously. Everybody did, even Rose, as a matter of fact. And Johnnie came in on the eve of the Day of Atonement with a few slices of ham. He got a handful of plates and defiled them all by placing a little slice on each. He also brought in a pint of milk to swallow his ham with. Ada must have looked quite comic to Johnnie, so speechlessly shocked she was. Her eyes were round and large. Her mouth was a small black hole.

"Won't you have a little? No? Just a little? You won't? You're fasting? Of course! It's Bank Holiday! Come and kiss me then! Come here, you little bitch, come here!"

301

He seized her round the waist and kissed her with his abominable mouth full on the lips. "How's that darling? A bit hammy? You shouldn't be so particular on Bank Holiday! And now I'm off for a little rough-and-tumble with Elsie. You don't know Elsie, do you? That girl's got a mouth like a corkscrew —" and winking genially he left her.

That was one of the occasions when Ada came back to Magnolia Street, to be with her mother and sister. She brought her two children with her, Annie and Leo, aged four and two. It was not very good for the invalid to have her daughter staying with her for so sad a reason, looking so pale and silent and her fingers twitching. But Mrs Berman loved to have the children about. They were quiet, too — perhaps too quiet. But they were so sweet and pretty and loved their grannie greatly, she gave them such nice things to eat. And then Johnnie would come to Magnolia Street and look awfully hurt about Ada leaving him. He would talk so smooth and sad you would think his heart was breaking. So Ada went back to him again with the children.

"Yes," Rose determined that Saturday morning. "That'll be easy to arrange. Ada will come in for these three days. It will cheer mother up, too, to have the children about.

"Of course I must have a word with Mrs Seipel and get her to come in every now and again to see everything's all right. I couldn't *really* trust mother to Ada. Poor girl, just a bundle of nerves these days, no use for anything! She'll be there at night, anyhow, in case she's wanted.

"Dear Mrs Seipel — good as gold she is. You can always rely on Mrs Seipel..."

As for the home-made-sweets shop, that presented no problem. It had ceased to exist over a year ago; for though it had fallen to Rose's charge long since to do most of the housework when she came in of an evening and to make most of the sweets, it was impossible for her during the daytime both to sell music for Mr Saunders and sweets for her mother.

Mrs Berman's health had become too unsteady to permit her to do it for herself. So the fittings were sold and a little parlour furniture bought again, and sometimes Mrs Berman sat downstairs on the parlour sofa, knitting woollies for her grandchildren, and sometimes she did not come downstairs at all.

Rose went straight from the shop to Ada's house the day she received John's wire. Johnnie Hummel was there. He talked too much, as usual, but otherwise he was perfectly charming.

"Of course, my dear Rose. Of course she shall look after her mother for a few days. Should it always be on your shoulders? It's quite convenient for me, too. I have business in Glasgow and intended to go next Wednesday. But let it be Monday instead. The sooner I go the sooner I come back to her! Isn't that so, darling? What you blushing for? It's only your little husband, isn't it?"

"Thank you, Johnnie," said Rose. "I'm sure it's awfully kind of you!"

"What for do you thank me? Ah well, Rose dear! I must go now! One little kiss, yes?"

He went up to her and kissed her chastely. "And you, sweetheart? On both cheeks? So! Once! Twice!"

As he bent down towards Ada's face, his hair was black and shining like the back of a beetle.

"And here's something for you, children! Buy yourselves some sweets! Now just once more, Ada! Goodbye, Rose, dear!"

He was charming, perfectly charming. So it was all arranged, and Ada came in with the children on Monday morning. And Mrs Seipel would certainly be in and about. If Mrs Seipel was not doing something for somebody, her teeth would drop out. It was understood that Rose was going on business for Mr Saunders. Ada believed it, and so did Mrs Seipel. Everybody in Magnolia Street believed it.

But perhaps, if Mary Cooper knew that Rose Berman was going to London, she did not believe it. And perhaps Mrs Berman, too, didn't believe it. Almost certainly she didn't. She was in bed when Rose said goodbye. She looked at her daughter so roguishly, you would have said she knew beyond doubt her daughter was going to meet her lover after so many years, to lie in her lover's arms and to forget there were such things in this world as a sad little sister and a sick little mother and Doomington, so dark a city. "Goodbye, mamma!" said Rose.

"Goodbye, Rose!" said her mother. She winked. Indeed, indeed. The naughty woman winked.

Or did she not wink? Perhaps it was the draught made her blink her eyes.

"I should have remembered the window's always open," thought Rose. "I've no right to be leaving the door open too."

Rose turned and shut the door. She knew she was blushing. The wicked woman her mother was, innocent as the shorn lamb.

"And you'll be good, mamma?" she repeated again. "And take all your milk with the egg beaten up? You are looking so much better this morning!"

"Go, little daughter, go! You will miss the train! I will take all the milks! I will take twice as many!"

So Rose went. "You'll not forget what I told you," she reminded Ada, as she left her on the doorstep. If anything isn't all right, you'll just send that wire where I told you?" She had recalled, perchance, that there was a place in London called the Riviera Hotel. In a region called Bloomsbury it was. One of the music agents who came round to Messrs. Saunders had spoken of it.

"Of course," Ada said bravely.

"But I shan't bother you. Why should I? You'll send me a postcard yes, Rose? The Houses of Parliament, eh? No, the Albert Memorial, perhaps! And don't forget to send one to Mrs Seipel!"

Ada, too, looked quite fresh and young this morning, some shadow of her old self. It was still early, too early to waken the children to say goodbye to them. "Kiss Annie and Leo for me!" she bade. "Goodbye, Ada dear!"

"Goodbye, Rose!"

So she went out and caught the tram and took the train and got to London. And there he was waiting for her, her lover, John Cooper. She fell into his arms like a small stream falling over a bank into a lake. She seemed to be not there any longer at all, on that ringing platform at Euston Station.

II

Of course it was impossible that there had ever been love-making like this before. Now they had no bodies at all, neither he nor she. They were just voices. They were just ears in which the voices made music. They were just wind and flame and they went straight through the walls of solid stone buildings and came out on the other side. They did not need to avoid traffic. What harm could it do to two creatures who had no bodies? They did not walk the whole way along the Thames Embankment till they came to Westminster Bridge, before they crossed the river.

304

They must have crossed somewhere between Charing Cross and Westminster, where there isn't any bridge, for here they were manifestly, on the other side.

And a moment later they were aware they had bodies in a way that made them feel they had both been shadows all their lives before. It came because she laughed out aloud, suddenly, or because he squeezed her arm to his side just a little tighter than before. Here was she in her smart little hat tilted over her right eye and her fine sailor suit in gaberdine twill, her coat lined with rosy silk. Here was he spick and span in his uniform, with the sailor's rake in his legs, and his cap, to balance hers, tilted over his left eye. These were his firm fingers, and her soft fingers in their own way as firm as his. There was a man's chin for you, with a cleft in it! There was a girl's throat for you, with the tendrils of hair behind the ears!

They were so old and wise that day, so young and foolish. They said nothing about yesterday, nothing about tomorrow, breathed no word about the dark dear night that lay before them. It was all the lovelier now, that he had been so wise to exact and she so wise not for one instant to question.

"We will call," she had said, "tomorrow morning at the Riviera Hotel. Yes, John, please? That's in Bloomsbury," she added learnedly, as if she knew all London from Hammersmith to Bow.

"We will, of course we will! What for?"

"I gave an address. Just in case... in case they wanted to get in touch with me."

He halted for a moment. Surely, surely, they would not pursue her here? During these brief minutes? She did not let the thought stay with him. "It would be too funny," she said, "if that's where you're... we're... staying! We're not, of course?"

"We're not, of course! I want you to stand out on a balcony and be able to look out on the river. You can't, in Bloomsbury!"

"How lovely! On a balcony? We shall see the river?" She clapped her hands delightedly.

They gave the Riviera Hotel no other thought till they went there next morning, a hundred years later.

The evening came. They went to the hotel with a balcony. First there was a sitting room, with masses of flowers in it; then there was a bedroom, with masses of flowers in it. Then there was a door in the further wall of the bedroom. She went and opened it, wondering what fantastic place it might lead to. A

305

gymnasium? A library? It was more fantastic than she had believed.

"John!" she cried out. "A private bathroom! All to ourselves! How beautiful! How *expensive!*"

Yes, it was even illegally expensive. It had all needed a little manipulation... They had dinner in the sitting-room. A waiter wheeled in a table covered with fine linen and shining silver, with a vase of exquisite yellow roses at its centre.

"Oysters!" he ordered. "We'll start off with oysters!" She squeezed his hand under the table to show how apprehensive she was. "I don't know what to do with them!" she said behind her hand. "I'll show you!" he said behind his.

He ordered blue trout also, and pigeons, and two small châteaubriands.

"Have they," she whispered, "any pêche melba?"

"They'll bring them if they have to go to the lady's home town for them. And a savoury," he added. "Marrows on toast..."

"Thin and crisp!" she whispered.

"Thin and crisp!" he bade.

"Sir!" said the waiter.

And wine... A hock with the blue trout, with a happy Mumm following... A glass of brandy in a vessel big as the moon. "Brandy... we call it *branfen*... it's what we have at a *simchah!*"

"A what?"

"A merry-making!"

"How's this for a merry-making?"

"Kiss me! Before he comes back again!"

"Where — where the *hell* did you get those eyes from?" They went to the Alhambra to see *The Bing Boys are Here*. Violet Lorraine stretched out both her arms to them across the orchestra as if she would lift them from their seats in the front row of the stalls and plant them by her side and squeeze them both till they shouted, as if she would kiss them, him on the left eye, her on the right eye, because they were so happy and their cheeks were so flushed and they clapped their hands like children at a school treat. George Robey looked at them severely. "I don't mean," he said, "what *you* mean!"

They went back to the hotel and stood for a time on the balcony, looking out on the river, folded up in each other. Then she said: "My bath salts. I'll let you use half. I'm sure Bella Winberg never had such gorgeous bath salts!"

"Don't take more than your share!" he warned her. He went into the sitting room. Some time later, she called out to him. Her face was like a pink rosebud above the apple-green eiderdown.

"You've not used more than half of those bath salts?" he demanded sternly. As he looked at her, his knees were like straw.

She drew the sheet in confusion above her head. "I'm so sorry!" she stammered. "I've only left you a third!"

He set his chin fiercely. "Vampire!" he said.

"You're a man, you see... I thought..."

"Perhaps this time," he growled, "I might overlook it! Robber of widows and orphans!"

He passed through the magic door into the expensive bathroom. She heard him splashing like a walrus.

There were a few books on the table beside the right-hand pillow, where his pyjamas lay. She reached forward across his place to see what he had been reading. There were three or four volumes of murder and mystery. Under these there was a more modest book, its name was *Green Mansions*. She liked the name. It was cool and quiet. She took the book over to herself and turned the pages, humming softly. A printed card, with which he had doubtless kept his place, fell out. It lay in the small valley between her lifted knees. Tampico. The word stood out in big capitals. Her heart fluttered. The wild places across the seas where he went wandering. He was still splashing as if he had dived that moment from his dinghy into the waters that lie against Tampico. Her eyes followed the bold lines of the printed card:

TAMPICO
NEW CHANCRE HILL
SALOON AND DANCE HALL
OPEN DAY AND NIGHT
DRINKS OF ALL KINDS
A NICE BUNCH OF GIRLS CLOSE TO YOUR SHIP
WE SEE THAT YOU DON'T MISS YOUR SHIP
VISIT US AND HAVE A REAL GOOD TIME
FREE LAUNCH DAY AND NIGHT

She took the card up and placed it in the book again, the book called *Green Mansions*. She leaned over and laid the book down under the books of murder and mystery, so that he would not know she had seen it.

"The poor lad!" she murmured. "The shoddy stuff he's had to put up with!" She folded her arms across her shoulders, and felt how smooth and strong they were.

He was tugging at the door-handle on the further side of the door.

"I'm coming in, darling!" he said.

"Come in, darling!" she said faintly.

III

"Richmond Park!" said John to the taxi-driver. "As slowly as you like!"

"Yes, sir!" said the taxi-driver sympathetically. He approved of clients who wanted to go to remote destinations slowly, that is if they were not alone. If they were alone, it meant they were mad and intended to commit some special sort of suicide. If a pretty girl was with them, it meant a special sort of tip. This girl seemed younger than she actually was, this bright summer forenoon.

"But you won't forget —" Rose tugged at John's lapel — "just going round by way of that hotel... in case?"

"Of course, darling, I *was* forgetting! Go round by way of the Riviera Hotel, will you?"

"In Bloomsbury!" added Rose learnedly.

"Yes, m'm!" said the taxi-man.

They drove round by way of the hotel. "You might as well stay here," bade John. "There won't be anything!"

"I know there won't! I just wanted —"

"I'll be back in two twos!"

It took him no longer than that to return with the little buff envelope. It felt in his hand like a great mallet with which the frail sweet body of their delight was to be crushed into pulp.

"I'll lie to her," he said to himself. "I'll say the clerk said there was nothing in the place name of Berman. For her sake just as much as mine. Good Christ! Hasn't she denied herself everything all these years?"

He stood for one moment. His tanned face had gone grey and puffy. Was it just to shatter the crystal trance so hideously soon, when there were two days more in which to fortify herself, with the medicine of this felicity, against the sorrow that lay before her?

"After all, that other poor kid, Ada, is just hysterical. I know the state she's been reduced to by that rat of a husband. Probably, if it had been anybody but Ada, the wire wouldn't have been sent at all.

"She's got the wind up because Mrs Berman's temperature's gone up a degree or two, or she's had a bout of coughing. You've got to expect that sort of thing from people in that condition...

"I'll slip the damned thing into my pocket. Nothing for the name of Berman, old girl!... To hell! I'm not that sort! And she isn't!"

The decision was made and revoked in the few moments it took to walk from the desk to the door.

"I'm sorry, Rose darling!" he said quietly. He handed the wire over to her, as she leaned through the taxi window.

"Mother Dangerously Ill Come At Once," she read.

She looked older than her years now, on this autumnal morning which had suddenly become dark and cold.

"I'm so sorry, John," she said. "I must go."

"Rose, you poor kid!" He took the wire from her hand.

"It's been so lovely, John!"

"You poor kid!"

"It must be the first train I can catch. Will you tell him to go back at once, John?"

"Back to the hotel, will you, at once!"

"Yes, sir!" said the driver.

If they were people capable of altering their plans in this way, perhaps it was as well he had not taken them to Richmond Park as slowly as he liked. They did not look at this moment like lovers who sit enfolded in each other's arms the whole journey, so that when you got there you came back part of the way and then went back again, and round again, and back again, till the meter almost burst for excitement. They looked like young people who hand each other lozenges out of little bottles, and when they get to Richmond Park, they are all stiff and green.

He took them back to the hotel at once.

"Rose, old dear!" said John. He stroked her cold hand gently. "You're not thinking... I mean... how shall I say it... any old rot about this being a punishment and all that?"

She looked up with candid eyes. "No! I don't! I don't! I don't believe in that sort of thing, God or punishment or any stuff of that sort! I just believe that when things come your way, and there's no one else to do it, then you must. That's all I believe!"

"You're not sorry then?"

"Sorry? Whatever happens at all, I'm glad this day and night have been! Oh *so* glad, John, *so* glad!"

He opened his mouth to say something. He was not clear what he intended to say, what words he was to put it in. She knew what thing it was that had come into his mind. A silence fell between them. For, of course, if anything happened, then at last she should be free, free.

It was not a thought that either of them could find words for.

"Of course, I'll come up to Doomington with you," he said at length. "Perhaps if you want me, it would be good for me to be about!"

"Everything will be easier, if you are about!"

"Of course, I'll come, of course! And then, Rose, on my next leave —"

She threw herself at his mouth and stopped his words. It was as if she said: "Yes, John, the way will be clear! And you'll marry me, John! And the lands may be all smoking and the seas all tottering, and you and I will be together, for one moment or for all the moments that may ever be! But now, now, there's that poor sweet little one, up in Doomington! So brave she's been! She knew, she knew, the way she winked at me, that I was coming to be your sweetheart! What do you think of that, John?" But she did not say these things. Her mouth stayed on his. The tears from her eyes fell on his cheeks.

IV

Mrs Berman was still alive when John Cooper went back to his ship at Dover. She died a few days later. It had always seemed to Rose and himself that, whenever it came, her death was to be the solution of their problem. But this was not so. The problem took another name and a triple shape.

In the late afternoon of the day when Rose went to London, Ada found she had left her knitting at home. She and her mother were going to have a nice quiet evening together, knitting and chatting, after she had put the children to bed. The children were as good as gold. They never made a fuss however early they were put to bed.

Mrs Seipel was in with her mother. So Ada went off home to get her knitting. The small boy, Leo, was sleeping. She took little Annie with her. It was not the first time Ada had returned to an empty house. But this evening, the very moment she opened the door, she felt it was empty and quiet in a way it had not been before. Suddenly, out of nowhere, as if it had been too frightened to move earlier, the cat shot by her. The lobby was dark. It took her a few seconds to perceive that the bamboo clothes-stand on the left was awry and humped-up. Then her eyes got accustomed to the dimness and she became aware that the bamboo shoots it was composed of were all wrenched apart and the thin ones were snapped. Its mirror was smashed to fragments.

Her heart ran like a frightened mouse. She continued into the kitchen. The floor was littered with chair-legs, lumps of plates and cups and saucers, strips of oilcloth, pan-lids, broken junk. She did not relax her hold on the child's hand. With a spasm of terror she ran into the parlour, dragging the child after her. The ruin was just as complete there — smashed ornaments, padded chairs gashed, the rug slit, mirror broken. He had treated with especial malignance the enlarged photographs of Ada herself, posed against French châteaux, the Pyramids, Niagara Falls...

She let go of the child's hand. The child had till now been silent as a mute. But feeling her mother's hand go, the terror was released upon her like a high wall of water.

"Mummy! Mummy! Mummy!" the child shrieked. "Daddy's gone! Daddy never come back again!"

And Ada, seizing the little one in her arms, fled from the place not as if a demon had left it, but as if a demon had for the first time taken up its habitation there.

She knew that he was gone, that he would never come back again. She knew that he had gone about from room to room, to extinguish it in desolation. She saw him smiling, smiling, his white teeth showing between his vivid lips. She heard him say, as if he was at her ear: "Oh no, Ada darling! I'm not going to be a soldier! Why should I be a soldier? I shan't buy no headache powders from Mr Billig! We're going to America, you and me, Ada darling! As for the children, we'll drown them, yes?"

She did not stop running for the traffic in Blenheim Road. She ran, her hair flying behind her. She went so fast that now and again the child's feet were torn from under her and were dragged along the roadway.

311

She found herself outside her mother's door. She stopped. She remembered how weak her mother was. Her mother must not know. If only Rose were here.... But the child was shrieking at the top of her voice. She had not stopped shrieking all the way from the other house. A moment later Mrs Seipel came downstairs.

"What is it, Ada?" she cried. "What is it? We heard Annie all the way from the corner! What's happened? Hush, Annie, hush! Here's some stick-jaw! Ada, Ada, what is it?"

But Ada could bring out no word. Her jaws swivelled stiffly like the jaws of a doll. She lurched into Mrs Seipel's arms, her eyes grey as glass. Mrs Emmanuel and Mrs Edelman came hurrying up, Mrs Briggs also, from across the street. At this moment Mrs Berman herself appeared, frail as a wraith, with her hair falling loose over her pretty flushed face.

"What is it?" she moaned. "What is it with my Ada?"

It was the child who answered. "Grannie!" she cried, reaching out her hands to her. "Daddy's gone! Daddy not come back any more!"

"Come, come, Mrs Berman!" insisted Mrs Emmanuel. "Come, you mustn't stand out here in the cold! It'll be the death of you!"

"My Ada!" she moaned. "My little daughter! Annie, my baby, what have you seen then?"

But the women would not let her stand about any longer in her nightgown in the damp air. "Come!" they insisted. They led Ada and the child in with them. "To bed at once! All of you!"

It had been too much of a strain for Mrs Berman. She had a small haemorrhage in the early morning. One of the Seipel boys was sent off to the General Post Office, which was open all night, to send a wire for Rose at the Riviera Hotel. Mrs Berman lived a few days longer. When she died, Ada was almost as dead as she.

V

It was many months before John Cooper and Rose Berman met again. There had been correspondence between them. Here follows the gist of some of their notes.

Rose to John:

She died yesterday. Will you believe it when I say that just as she died, she tried to wink at me? It was to show she understood

312

about us two. If I hadn't got you I should like to die, too...

You know Ada's husband has left her. You were right about him from the beginning. It's clear he'll never come back. Ada and the children are here with us. That's going to make everything different — I daren't think about it....

John to Rose:

Your mother was as brave as you, and she helps me to understand you. If it weren't for what I know about her, you'd be altogether too much for me. You're the bravest girl God ever thought of.

It's filthy about Ada. Yes, I thought he was that sort of louse the moment I set eyes on him. It was in Magnolia Street. How many years ago was it? Too many is all I can say. But that's all over. We'll get married the moment I get away again, if my leave only lasts five minutes. Anywhere you like, synagogue, register-office, mosque, hygienic dairy....

Rose to John:

I said it was going to make everything different. I mean, Ada and the two children. John darling, don't try and forgive me. I know you can't. You must forget me. You've been so splendid, waiting and waiting all these years. You see, it's Ada. She's absolutely broken up. She's more like a baby than little Leo, who's two years old. He's such a fine kid. So's Annie, the elder one, too. They used to be so silent when their father was about. They weren't too young to understand how he was treating their mother. They were terrified and they hated him. Now he isn't there they're different children. Leo's going to be a boxing champion, I'm certain of that....

My pen's running away with me. It's not that, really. I'm so frightened of you. I've treated you so badly. What would you do to me if you met me in the street? I've got to look after Ada and the kids, John darling. They can't look after themselves. Some day, John, when she comes round... But I daren't, I daren't. I'm not going to tie you down any longer. Try and think gently of me, or try and not think of me at all. Isn't that the best thing?

John to Rose:

I suppose Ada isn't capable of going out to work? Are you going to be all the world's doormat all your life long? Are you ever going to think of yourself for one moment? Don't you see, you little idiot, what *you* want? You want an Annie and a Leo of your own. By hell, I know where you're going to get them from.

Rose to John:

You sound so angry, John dear. Please be kind to me. Of course Ada can't go out to work. She's suggested it, but I tell you she's in an awful state. I've only learned just now some of the things he used to do. You know I'm not a spooky person but I sometimes think he was the Devil. Do you think such an idea too silly for words? I don't see how he can have been an ordinary man. She can't go out to work, not possibly. She pretends she's looking after the house. But really she does less than my poor mother did even in the last year or two. She stops in the middle of drying a plate and just stands there crying. You should see the way the kids tug at her skirts and tell her to buck up. Leo looks awfully fierce.

So what else can I do, John? I can't let her down. So I let you down instead. I'm a bad woman. I can only say that both of us are stronger than she is. How you must hate me!

John to Rose:

How I hate you! You have no idea at all how I hate you! Wait till I come back to Doomington!

John to Rose:

I haven't heard from you for two months. What the devil do you mean by it?

Rose to John:

It isn't two months. It's one month. You see, I said to myself what right have I to keep it up? It isn't fair to him. I thought it would give you your chance. There must be such pretty girls when you put in at Dover. Ada's getting a little better. She can finish drying a plate without stopping to cry in the middle. Poor girl, she looks so pretty these days. If only she were free... I've been to a lawyer to see if there's any chance of finding out where he's gone to. But he's covered up his traces pretty completely. He used to talk about rich relations in Baltimore. He may have joined them.... It may take years before we find anything out or before she's fit for anything. Whatever you do, you can't expect me to stop loving you. I can't do without that.

314

Whoever the new girl is, I hope she'll make you as happy as I hoped to. She won't lead you such a dance, anyway. Whenever I think of the way I've treated you, my blood runs cold with fright. How patient you've been! But it's all over now. I'll always love you. I'll love her for your sake. At least I'll try....

John to Rose:

What you seem to forget is that you and I are married. George Robey married us. If you think you can treat me as that worm Hummel treated Ada, you're mistaken.

John to Rose (a month or two later):

By the way, we were blown up last week. Some of us got out all right. I did, as you see. They've not been able to find all the bits of the other tub, so I'll have another one in a week or two. Which means I'll be able to get to Doomington next week. I have a feeling it may be for the last time. Meet me at the usual place at seven on Thursday evening.

So they met duly at seven that Thursday in their favourite alcove in the café on the remote south fringe of Doomington.

"How are you?" he said.

"Very well, thank you," she replied. She fingered the knives and forks on the table before her rather nervously.

"Would you like some of these potato cakes?" he asked politely. "Favourites of yours, I believe!"

Her lip quivered a little. "Yes!" she whispered. "I'd love some!"

The waitress left to fulfil the order.

"You little devil!" he whispered at her between his teeth.

"I know!" she agreed. "I ought to have been drowned!"

"I was nearly, last week!" he said grimly.

"You poor old baby! Of course you were! How dreadful!"

"What a pretty little widow you'd have made!"

"John, John, why do you make fun of me like this!"

"I'm not making fun of you! I'm very much in earnest! We're married, see? Get that into your head!"

"But John, I've told you... don't make it so hard for me! I've told you... Ada..."

"Oh, Ada!" he snorted.

She looked at him sharply.

315

"I haven't got anything against Ada, you cuckoo! Sweet kid, Ada! What I mean is Ada's easily disposed of!"

She shook her head sadly. "You're wrong, John! It isn't easy! It isn't easy at all!"

"And what would Ada have done if there'd have been no you?"

"But there *is* a me! That settles it!" she said firmly.

"I know. I'm quite pleased there's a you, though I've never once heard you admit it in all your life before. And there's a me, too, don't you forget it!"

"I wasn't forgetting it!"

"All right! Don't hit me! But we're not the problem, it's Ada! And as I've said, she's no problem either. You mustn't think because I'm only a sailor, and a poor Christian, that I haven't got a business-head on my shoulders. I have!"

"John! What's happened to you? You've become a business-man? I can't bear it!"

"If you won't be quiet I'll gag you with potato cakes! Now listen! I understand about Ada. I agree with you. She's had a rotten time and she wouldn't be any use if she had to go out and forage for a living. Was your mother a very strong woman? She wasn't! But you wanted something to keep her going gently. So you fitted up that little sweets-shop! You've made a sitting room of it again, haven't you? Well, you'll just have to turn out the arm-chairs and the grand piano. It's going to be a sweets-shop again. I'm going to invest some capital in it and —"

"But John," she said delightedly. "Of course! How idiotic of me not to have thought of it! We can —"

"Don't interrupt! Oh well, you can interrupt. I don't know that I've got anything more to say. We'll be sleeping partners in the firm. Is that what they call it?"

"How soon, John? Not at once!"

"I'll go easy with you! How long will it be before you think she's fit enough? Of course there's a time limit!"

"I think if I tell her, it'll do her no end of good. Perhaps in a few months —"

"And we'll leave Magnolia Street, eh? Would you like to paddle round the Channel with me and do a little mine-sweeping? You'll fetch a yard broom? Or how about a little house down New Forest way, not too far from Southampton? With a swimming pool and a private golf course?"

316

She had never seen him so gay in all these years, with his eyes shining so brightly and the lights dancing in them! He looked more like a schoolboy than a fierce sea captain!

"She'd be so pleased," she said, "if she could see us together now!"

"You mean —" he said more softly.

"Yes, mother, I mean!"

"I think I might let Mary know, my sister."

"Will she be upset? Ought you to?"

"Perhaps she's known. Women are queer, I don't know if you've noticed it. They know things."

"Won't it be lovely, John? Oh, I'm dreaming all this!"

"Oh, no you're not! Are you dreaming this?" He tweaked her ear.

"Are you dreaming this?" She threw her arms round him and kissed him. Many minutes later he rang the bell as if the café were burning.

"These potato cakes are stone cold!" he said, staring sternly at the waitress. "Bring us some more!"

"Please!" Rose whispered into his ear.

"Please!" he called out after the waitress, as she retreated icily.

Chapter 6

The sweetheart of another sailor man lived in Magnolia Street, namely Kate Ritchie, whose husband was a negro. The day Rose Berman went to London to meet her sailor, Kate Ritchie went to Liverpool to try and find hers. Rose's eyes were shining like pansies with dew in them. The eyes of Kate Ritchie were like wet slack in a coal bucket.

They were not like that during the first few weeks of the War. All the women were so friendly and excited you might have thought Mrs Ritchie married to an admiral rather than to a buck negro. It made Kate look quite pretty the way she felt she was anybody's equal again. For the voodoo which had kept her out of the private bar was lifted. She drank her pint with the best of them. They were solicitous and sympathetic. They hoped Mr Ritchie's ship hadn't had the bad luck to be in an enemy port when the War broke out. They congratulated her fervently when the news came through he was merrily sailing the high seas, as merrily as them submarines were likely to let him. Kate became a knitter, perhaps the champion knitter of Magnolia Street. She even had a class to show some of the women how to knit body belts and trench helmets. She neglected her curtains and brass and aspidistras, she got so tied up in her knitting...

And then... and then what? It's impossible to say what exactly. Perhaps it was that the habit of feeling herself an outcast had eaten so deep into her marrow, that she didn't trust them, now they were being nice to her. The feeling of being an outcast isn't like a pair of old shoes that you can drop into the dust-bin, when you feel like it.

Perhaps it was because of Pete. That's more likely... her humiliation, her anger, her terror. After all, she *was* a white woman, and he *was* a black man. And hadn't she given him everything, everything? She's made herself lonely as a stone because of him. And now...

But no, it wasn't *his* fault. Poor dear! How could it be his fault? Perhaps little bits of Pete, bits of the black marble of his thighs, and his grand neck and his ribs, were floating somewhere on the cold seas, being cast up on rocks, were smashed to pulp weeks ago, months ago....

She had heard from him till early in 1916. He was going on to Valparaiso then, but he hoped to be back in a couple of months. He had not come back. Months went by. She did not get a word from him. She wrote to the Company. They had no record of Pete Ritchie on their books. She wrote again and again, telling them that there was some mistake. She had seen his papers frequently. Doubtless they thought she was some poor creature whom the loss of her husband had made crazy. They ignored her letters.

She did not let the women know that Pete had stopped writing, or that, perhaps, there wasn't any Pete at all any more. She gave up going into the Lamb and Lion, though at one time the mere thought of sitting about at her ease in the private bar would have gone to her head like a tumbler of port wine.

If she only knew... that was the worst of it... If there were only some way of finding out whether he was dead, or whether he'd just gone and found a new woman, and he was sending *her* presents and coming back and shining his gold teeth on *her* and filling *her* kitchen with peals of laughter. She was quite sure that the other woman didn't keep her kitchen so spotless as she had done against his coming back, nor the whitewash so fresh on the scullery walls.

There were times before the War when she hadn't heard from him for a couple of months at a stretch — when he went to Australia, say. Now it was war-time. It wouldn't look odd if the postman didn't call for three months, four months.

But if six months passed by, ten months, and the postman never came, the neighbours would start wondering.

"Where's that woman's blackie? It's just as I always told you, Maggie. When a white woman marries a blackie..."

She couldn't bear to let them think Pete had done her dirty, Pete that might be drowned or blown up many a long month ago now. She couldn't bear it. So late at night, when she came in from the munition work she was doing, with the blinds pulled down against Zeppelins, and her heart dark as her house, she wrote letters to herself, so that the postman should have something to deliver to her. She also made up parcels once or twice, for he had a habit of sending her parcels, and how should the neighbours know it wasn't Pete who'd sent them from a foreign country?

319

The neighbours did not know. But the postman did. Also, she was too zealous. It didn't take long before the neighbours knew exactly what was going on. Wilfred Derricks, in the flat few weeks that followed the departure of the Stanleys, joined in the game and sent her letters also, so that the postman should have something more to deliver to her. The envelope was usually empty. It often had no stamp.

Mrs Ritchie cried and cried in her kitchen. How she missed that nice Mrs Winter that used to come in and have a good talk with her sometimes! Her aspidistras decayed. The grease gathered on the sink. The curtains hung grey and tattered upon their rods.

II

No record exists of what Leah Winter was doing at this time. She was that lonely Jewish lady who sat on the doorstep plucking fowls, and sometimes got up of a morning (as the Jewish pavement alleged) to find that one or other of her gentlemen friends had crept into her room while she slept and placed a coin or two on her mantelpiece. She went long ago. Let us hope good fortune came her way. A great many fur coats and pianos and pairs of silk stockings went begging during the Great War, at least they went begging at the front doors of hospitable ladies. Let us hope they did not pass over hers.

It was Mr Winberg who had ousted Leah Winter, towards the end of 1910. She was an early victim of Mr Winberg's dazzling march to success and the ownership of that enormous rainproof factory which, like a black Versailles, extends for acres along the banks of the Mitchen. She was his next-door neighbour and stood in the way of his stripling factory; so, after some dubious negotiations with the owner of the property, he succeeded in evacuating her.

At one blow Mrs Winter and the meynie of *fire-goyahs* whom she had harboured for so long were turned out into the street. None of the streets of the flowering shrubs would accommodate Mrs Leah Winter, who was forced to betake herself and her clientele of strange men to those murky regions which slope downward from Begley Hill Road into the darkest of the Doomington limbos. Here and there in the vicinity of Magnolia Street, in an attic here or a converted cellar there, Mrs Winter's *fire-goyahs* found shelter. For they remained as indispensable to the Jewish community in their way as the Rabbi Shulman himself, or Mr Winberg, employer of labour. Still by gentile, and not by Jewish, hands must the gas be extinguished on Friday evenings and the fires lit on the mornings of the Sabbath.

But May Agnes Hartley, that sibylline *fire-goyah*, lived on in Magnolia Street to the end of her days; she rolled over to the attic of the Bermans at number three, where she put in the fire each morning in lieu of rent. It always tired Rose to put a fire in before going off for a day's work, and she wanted to keep her hands fresh and soft against the day that John should claim them. So there, in the Bermans' attic, May Agnes Hartley sat over her invisible tripod, and delivered her bosom of visions and prophecies, even to the Packard that Bella Winberg would one day transport from New York, even to the leg which Benny Edelman was to leave behind him in Flanders some day.

What then of May Agnes Hartley and her companions, what did they in the Great War? Perhaps there can be no clearer indication than this of how the work they had found to do was the only work they were capable of doing — that there were singularly few defections from their ranks, however hungrily the war-industries gaped for more and more women. It is known that a number of ladies, about as old as they, and with fewer attainments, became heads of canteens and auxiliary corps and funds and hospitals. But they had not been doing anything recognisable in the way of work before, so that it was easier for them. The *fire-goyahs*, on the other hand, had been engaged on work of real importance, and they knew it.

When the War came, it was as if the songwriter addressed himself specially to them, when he cried: "Keep the Home Fires Burning!" For indeed, it would have been unthinkable to them, whether or no the Germans reached the Channel Ports and battered Verdun down and swept in a grey tide along the Champs Elysées — it would have been unthinkable to them to let old Mrs Edelman turn out her own gas on the Sabbath evening.

But in the interests of historical accuracy one damaging admission must be made regarding them. They too, no less than the wholesale butchers, the coal merchants and other captains of industry, must be included among the profiteers. The charge for their services soared by 50% and then by 100%, from twopence, to threepence, to fourpence. It is true that in 1916 bottles of baby food had risen by $33^{1}/_{3}$%. and perambulators by 25%. But the *fire-goyahs* had no babies to look after, they needed no perambulators. Their behaviour in the matter seems to call for a little censure.

As the War went on they added to their duties another cognate occupation. In coal they moved and lived and had their being. They therefore by arrangement took the places of their patronesses in the coal queues, carrying away the family ration in the perambulator from which the family baby had been temporarily exiled. They had increasing opportunities to show their virtuosity, for as coal became scarcer, they managed to cozen fires out of exhausted cinders that seemed less inflammable than asbestos.

Though other *fire-goyahs* might come and go or die, the Delphic *fire-goyah*, May Agnes Hartley, lived on and sang on. She still spent the whole week singing, with the exception of the Sabbath hours, when she was professionally engaged, and the time required each morning for the putting in of the Berman fire. The time for standing in the coal queues was not yet, but when it came, the queues did not interfere with her leisure more than once. On that occasion one of her ladies duly armed her with a perambulator and bade her wait her turn. But after waiting for an hour or two in complete silence and immobility, and just as her turn was due, she suddenly trundled off the empty perambulator, singing over it as if a baby were there.

The song she sang was of the same nature as she sang week in, week out, in her attic. She still concerned herself mainly with the domestic detail of the Jewish pavement; with the grandeur of Mrs Poyser's store of sacks of sugar; with Fanny Edelman, how she had a hoard of tinned fruit and she fed her small boy on it, though four years old, and him with so delicate a stomach. She discussed with her muses the disappearance of Becky Poyser to do war-work in London and informed them she believed she was doing no such thing. And as of old, and as always, she sang of things that had not been and were still to be. She foresang the gathering on a Friday evening of the shawled women in the Emmanuels' kitchen; and how he that had two fine legs should now, shortly, have one leg only....

From one point of view, it is a sad thing that the church of her prophecies was so mean a place as the Bermans' attic in Magnolia Street, where none gave heed to her; or, if perchance they overheard her when windows were open in sultry weather; "*Meshuggene* May!" they might say; or more likely say nothing at all, for they were used to her.

But how different might not her fate have been, if she had been born into some small thriving Middle Western community. How they would have fluttered round her, the executives of the Women's Clubs, and surrounded her with dictaphones and stenographers, that no word of that arcane wisdom might evaporate into unrecording air! And they might have made a Church for her, the First Church of May Agnes Prophetess, and set up a Second Church and a Third Church in Boston, in Baltimore! Perhaps even they might have succeeded in convincing May Agnes herself, of her mission. And she would have sat in stiff robes of grey silk dispensing uplift among her chosen, and have died great in wealth and honour, having corrected the proofs of her testament on her death-bed.

But her fate was unlike this. She poked the fires out and built them up again, and went to her attic, and sat down, and sang.

III

The *fire-goyahs* used to go in now and again, as of old, to have a word with Kate Ritchie; but much less frequently, for even *fire-goyahs* had noses. The place smelled rancid, like flowers that have stood for weeks in a vase, and the petals have fallen, the stalks are rotten, the water is slimy.

So Kate Ritchie made up her mind to go in person to the shipping office in Liverpool, to find out about Pete. But she found out nothing at all, when she went one Monday morning in late July. The clerks tapped their heads and winked at each other. She came back to the office two or three times during the day, till finally the doorman refused to let her go past. She even came back at night, long after the doors were shut, for she could not bring herself to return to Doomington with no news of Pete at all.

She was still lingering about the docks at midnight, hoping against hope Pete might suddenly turn up round the next corner. Pete did not, but another negro did, nothing like so fine a negro as Pete was. But when he asked her to go to bed with him, she said yes, wearily, and shuffled along the street after him. She did not want to go back to Doomington, and she was afraid to spend the night alone in Liverpool. And she thought, because he was a negro, it might be something like it was with Pete. But it was not.

Kate Ritchie arrived back in Doomington on Tuesday evening, about the same time as Rose Berman, who also had spent that Monday night in a man's arms; but a wire had brought her back to her mother, who was dying.

Chapter 7

I

It was recorded that when the Derrickses raided Elsa Stanley's parlour, a small group of women stood in the roadway and cheered, and that she who cheered most loudly was Mrs Shulman, the Rabbi's wife. "Dirty Sherman!" she cried out. "You dirty Sherman!"

Her acute anti-Teutonism was a matter of recent growth, and was bound up with the activities of the strictly unteutonic Mr Billig. But she had been very war-conscious from the beginning, as opposed to her husband, who was conscious of the War only as a ghost. She had a large number of sons, the elder of whom were already of military age, and the others likely to be if things went on as they were now. Solly, the eldest, was doing medicine at the Doomington University. Benjamin was at the School of Technology studying the by-products of coal. Yossel, the third, had just won a scholarship to the University and was going to be a lawyer.

The enormous steel hand that swooped down out of the sky and seized young men by the scruff of the neck and landed them in camps, ships, aeroplanes, trenches, was no respecter of persons. Lawyers and shoemakers were all one to it, the sons of a tailor, the sons of a Rabbi. But Mrs Shulman just did not see why Solly should become a soldier. It was good enough for Norman Edelman. He was almost as much of a lout as his brother, Benny, the apostate. Young David Emmanuel might run off and enlist a full year before his time. He was a mere 'machiner'. But was not Solly the son of the Rabbi? Was he not studying to be a doctor? (The time had not yet come when medical students even in their first year were cherished as tenderly as rare orchids.) It seemed highly unreasonable that he should become a soldier.

So she consulted Mr Billig. Her husband was not aware she did so. He was aware of the Great War by now in a dim way, but no more than that. If he had had the faintest inkling that his wife meditated some sort of deception by which his Britannic Majesty was to be deprived of a soldier, he would have disapproved strongly on abstract moral grounds. But Mrs

Shulman did not consult him. Nor did she consult her daughter, Rachel. She had a feeling that however deeply Rachel loved her brother, the thought would excite her enormously if the Shulmans, too, had a khaki uniform going in and out of the house. She did not even consult Solly. She merely visited Mr Billig on the morning of Solly's examination and brought back a small packet of powder.

It will be remembered that the staple commodity of Mr Billig's pre-war commerce was Love. It should not be assumed, therefore, that the powder he supplied for Solly's use was a love-philtre. It was not. Mr Billig had much less to do with Love these days than in the old time. The young men who came to him, or were brought to him, sought help in a far different field. Some of these were, in fact, happily married. They were young men in whose bosoms military ardour did not burn. Some were Jews. Some were not. Mr Billig acquired an international practice as the War years went on. They did not want to be soldiers for various reasons. Some were frightened. Some had conscientious objections. A few had recently come from Eastern Europe, and had intended at the earliest possible opportunity to go westward, to America. They had no feeling about England one way or the other. They did not consider it their fatherland. Russia they abominated, and any faint impulse they were conscious of to shed their blood for England was effectively scotched by the fact that a blow for her was a blow for Russia.

One or two were Irish, even. These disliked England as much as those others disliked Russia. Mr Billig did not sympathise with all these points of view, but he understood them. He was a broad-minded man. When his clients desired to emigrate to Ireland, to Canada, to the United States, to Mexico, he helped them. It was not hard work in the early stages of the War, but later it called for a certain amount of ingenuity.

In fact, before long, to get away from England required not merely ingenuity, but a great deal of money, and even then it was often impossible. Mr Billig was forced to ask quite a lot for his services in this department; despite which, he was often out of pocket, for when his heart was touched he never let mere money stand in the way. So it was that, out of consideration for his poorer clients, he conceived a new scheme. It was a long and expensive business to go to America in order not to join the army. Could not something be done for his clients so that, though they stayed in Doomington, the army did not want them?

Mr Billig accordingly invented various specifics which produced various results, more or less convincing, according to the complacency or truculence of the medical tribunals before which his clients presented themselves. Now, Mr Billig was in all matters a scrupulous person. Before the medical examination he asked for very little more in return for his services than the actual cost price of his materials. If the examination was successful, and the client was either rejected or relegated to a low grade, he naturally received an additional *bonté*. If it was a failure, he did not ask for a single penny more.

It was sometimes stated that one of the specifics he most frequently administered was merely a well-known headache powder, to be taken in ten times the usual quantity. The effect of this, taken an hour or two before the examination, was to produce in the client certain alarming cardiac symptoms. If the well-known headache powder was, actually, the basis of this potion, it can hardly be imputed to Mr Billig as a deception, seeing that it produced the desired result on many occasions. Young men swallowed it on the morning of their examination by the military authorities; they (it was understood) became sick as dogs, and the authorities bade them be led away, they would have nothing to do with them.

It was this same potion, in fact, which Mrs Shulman, when she wanted to put Solly out of danger, chose, in preference to its various rivals, designed to produce frothings, twitchings, limpings and other discouraging phenomena. She brought it back, mixed it in a glass of water, and requested Solly to take it. Solly was doing the third-year course in medicine at the university and the table before him was piled up with manuals. He did not lift his eye from the notes before him, which neatly summarised the pathogenesis of bleeding in tumours of the kidney. He merely held out his hand for the drug and swallowed it.

It wasn't that Solly was a Hercules. He merely carried imperturbability to such a degree that if, by accident, he had swallowed a large dose of strychnine, he would not have noticed it. Mr Billig's powder no more accelerated his heartbeats than if he had been an engine in a siding. So he was duly enlisted in the army; he wasn't in the least upset about it. Neither was his

327

father. Rachel had visions, over her washing-up, of Solly storming fortresses single-handed and bringing back hundreds of prisoners at his horse's tail. He was enlisted into the Royal Army Medical Corps, in fact, in virtue of his medical training; but what he actually did was to cook meals for sergeants up and down the English countryside for the duration of the War. He was, however, less interested in cooking than urology. He became an early authority on Urea-Splitting Staphylococci in Urinary Tract Infections, and his roasts tasted like it.

But as for Mrs Shulman, words cannot express how angry she was at the failure of Mr Billig's drug. In her temper she broke nearly half the family crockery. Then she went outside to have a word with Mr Billig. It would be a happy thing for the chronicler if he were able to say she did not meet Mr Billig.

But she did. She met him descending from the sacred steps of the Lithuanian Brotherhood. Then occurred a moment as shameful as any in the whole history of Magnolia Street. Mrs Shulman smacked those pink cheeks and the noise of it rang from pavement to pavement. Mrs Derricks saw that thing take place, and Mrs Carter and Mrs Durbin. Miss Tregunter, seated behind her geraniums, was a witness of it, too.

Mr Billig's cheeks flared red and ugly like a cock's comb. His blue eyes, which were always as mild as a baby's, looked green and poisonous, like an adder's. But he said no word. Like a martyr whose bosom is bared to any hurt or indignity, he stood motionless for one moment on the steps of the synagogue. Mrs Shulman raised her hand to strike again, and then her hand fell nerveless. After Billig got on to the pavement level and covered the few yards between the synagogue and his own doorstep, unsteadily. Then, even at this moment of earthquake and ruin perceiving a small child waddling towards him, he put his hand into the pocket of his frock-coat and took out a penny. He gave it to the small child, crooned over it brokenly for one moment, then turned in to his own hearth.

Mrs Shulman did not do so grievous a thing again, it would have been too strong an assault upon the moral order of creation. But often, when he passed by, she cried out "Sherman, Sherman!" at him, for suddenly she became a very war-like lady, fit neighbour for Mrs Derricks, whose holy zeal in the rooting out of German spies has been praised elsewhere in these pages. It was a strange sistership, this of Mrs Shulman and Mrs Derricks; and as another and still another of her sons was taken from her side, she liked the enemy less and less.

But was that a reason why she should call out "Sherman, Sherman!" whenever Mr Billig walked down the street? Or why she should call every woman whose sons were not old enough to join the army a "Sherman!" Or why, whenever she was worsted in an argument in Mrs Poyser's shop, she should sniff fiercely and declare to the witnesses:

"Well, what do you egspect from a Sherman?"

The fact is that the khaki her sons wore went to her head like strong drink. They were all sallow, hollow-chested and wore big spectacles, with the consequence that they were all retained in England for home service. What the effect on her would have been if one or two of them had joined a fighting unit and been killed cannot be computed. Would her loss have added fuel to the strange fires of her pride, until she deemed all Magnolia Street to be Sherman except her family? Would the sharp point of her loss have pricked her pride like a bubble?

But Solly survived to be a doctor and Benjamin a research chemist and Yossel a lawyer, and Isaac, the next in order, who joined the army two years later, became a chartered accountant, and Issy, who was too young for khaki, started the tale again and became a doctor.

From the point of view of Mick, the second youngest brother, it was to be regretted that the War did not last another ten years. For if it had, the enemy would not long have survived his enlistment in the armies of the English. He was more warlike than his mother or than her associate, Mrs Derricks. He was more warlike than any of those old gentlemen in the clubs of Pall Mall whose blood-lust was deplored by the War poets in scathing quatrains.

For Mick, alone of all the Shulmans, had no ache to be a professional gentleman, a doctor, a research chemist, a lawyer, a chartered accountant. He yearned to be a soldier. His nostrils sniffed for the blood of Germans. He was a member of the Jewish Lads' Brigade, and because its members included no Germans, he was not permitted to attack them with swords or bayonets. So he boxed them instead. He had the eyes, the chin, the shoulders, the fists, the feet. Still only a lad of ten he had boxed big hulking fellows of fourteen who had left school, and drubbed them soundly. Under the young man's terrific inspiration, his brigade proceeded to the slaughter of schools, institutes, scout associations. He loaded the brigade shelves with cups and their breasts with medals. A fly-weight, he festooned the ropes with bantam-weights; a bantam-weight, light-weights quailed before his glove.

We are to see him contending for starry honours in 1930 and keeping far more exalted company, he a mere boxer, than any of his brothers, professional gentlemen though they were. But that is many years ahead. In 1916, a lad of ten, he is the most grim-jawed patriot in Magnolia Street. Woe upon Kaiser Wilhelm should he and Mick Shulman meet one dark night in the back-entry.

II

Rachel Shulman's mother was a patriot. Her brother, Mick the boxer, was a patriot. She was a patriot too. She did not hate the Germans, like the two others. She loved the English. Or to be more exact, she loved soldiers. She didn't really care whether they wore khaki or horizon blue or grey-green. She loved them all, because they were soldiers. Whenever she saw a soldier in the street, her heart thumped with affection and excitement. She wanted to hold all soldiers to her bosom and brush their pale brows with a kiss.

It grieved her profoundly that there was no chance of getting away from home in order to become a VAD or, later, to join the Women's Royal Naval Service or Auxiliary Army Corps. It wouldn't have mattered very much if those ladies had been mobilised to help the Germans. She would have joined them, just the same. It was the soldiers she loved. She wanted to be with them. Above all, she wanted to lift their bandaged heads to her knee during a battle and press a bottle of water to their parched lips. But failing that, she was quite reconciled to blacking their boots, cutting slices of bread and butter for them, anything, anything. Although in Doomington she frequently saw the costume worn by the ladies in their naval and army auxiliary corps, when she envisioned them in France, they wore another uniform — tall conical hats from which veils fluttered, long gauntlets, sweeping brocade gowns. They stood upon the parapets of towers and waved their hands, or threw down their kerchiefs, to curvetting horsemen.

She was still a little awkward with her stockings. They would keep on coming down. Her hair still hung about her face in wisps. Yet there were soldiers about the place, with smart little canes and leather grips to their breeches, and spurs, who called to her in the streets, particularly when they could not see faces clearly. Usually she squealed and ran away, she was so frightened and so proud that a soldier had spoken to her.

But perhaps once or twice she did not run away. Perhaps she went out for a walk with them once or twice, even though she was the Rabbi's daughter. Wouldn't that help to explain the little cigar-box full of military emblems she had hidden away in her tin trunk under her bed? Of course she could have got a few regimental emblems from her brothers. But she would not have been so secretive if it had been only from her brothers she received them. When her father was in the synagogue and her mother at the grocery-shop, and Isaac and Issy doing their home-work and Mick serving out straight lefts at brigade headquarters, she stole up to her room and opened her trunk and took out her cigar-box. Like a miser passing his gold pieces through his fingers, she dabbled among the exploding grenades of Grenadier Guardsmen, the serpent-twined caducei of the RAMC, the paschal lambs of the Queen's, the maple leaves of the Canadians. But over one of these emblems she lingered most lovingly, a stranger emblem than any of those others to have found its way into Rachel Shulman's tin trunk in Magnolia Street, in Doomington. It was the cap badge of the Inns of Court OTC — four quarterings crested by a crown and bound with a wreath, the whole fixed upon a silver bayonet.

What fantastic picture floated before her eyes as she knelt down upon one knee and gazed so fixedly upon that badge? Did she behold a legal gentleman in a wig, upon a white horse, his gown swinging out behind him, his sword clanking by his side?

Who then had given it to her? Or had no-one given it to her? Had she merely found it in the street? Here is one of the War's secrets and no-one will ever resolve it, least of all the Rabbi's daughter.

III

Rose Berman's mother was buried on the last day of July. They carried her away behind two slow black horses. Clop-clop! their hoofs went, along the cobbled roadway of Magnolia Street. Clop-clop! went the hoofs of the horses in the cabs of the mourners. Clop-clop! went the heart of Rachel Shulman miserably, for she had been very fond of Mrs Berman.

The whole street had been fond of Mrs Berman. It was only natural to expect that Mrs Poyser should close her doors during the funeral, but so did the Lamb and Lion, and Mrs Durbin's barber-saloon. The Magnolia Street branch of Mr Winberg's rainproof industry was shut, too, of course. And they let down the parlour window of the Bermans' house, and Rabbi Shulman stationed himself behind it, and delivered a funeral oration on the virtues of the deceased lady. He swayed to and fro, tugging at his long black beard. Reb Berel, the beadle of the Lithuanian Brotherhood, went about among the crowd, shaking his tin box for coppers, and weeping as loudly as any of the women. The gentile women wept, too, and dropped their pennies into Reb Berel's box. Miss Tregunter drew down her blind as a sign of deference to the undistinguishing potency of death. Mrs Derricks stood upon her doorstep and mopped her eyes, and sighed.

Clop-clop! went the funeral *cortège*, on its way to the cemetery across the hot July air.

Rachel Shulman had cried till she had no more tears to cry. Then she fell asleep on the sofa for an hour or two. Then she got up, feeling empty and disconsolate. So she went up to her attic bedroom, and pulled out the tin trunk from under her bed. Then she extracted her little cigar-box full of military emblems. She played with them, she ran them through her fingers, like a miser his pieces of gold. Slowly a water of peace welled up within her. The visions floated through her mind again.

She saw the ladies standing upon the parapets of towers, waving their hands to their lovers. The lovers galloped off to the field of battle. The air was full of swords flashing and sparks from the hoofs of thundering cavalry. The lovers were all one lover, the horsemen were all one horseman. He wore in his cap and on his shoulders all these emblems — the paschal lamb of the Queen's, the maple leaves of the Canadians, the four quarterings of the Inns of Court OTC. The name of the lover and the horseman was Eric Winberg, associate of peers.

"And when Lord Henry offered me the goblet, I simply couldn't refuse...."

The grenades, the stars, the guns, tinkled in the cigar-box. Her eyes were dull with dreams.

And then suddenly, as from a long way off, from those far impossible lands of faery, she heard the hard sound of hoofs. She had heard hoofs that day already in Magnolia Street, but these hoof-beats were not as those were. The hoof-beats came nearer and clearer. She ran to the window. A prince was seated upon a white horse. The sunlight glinted on his spurs. The hoofs made thunder. The prince wore the full equipment of a Captain in the Seventeenth Lancers. That Rachel Shulman did not know. But she knew the prince's name... Eric. Eric. Eric....

Captain Winberg drew rein a moment, and looked round. He was not aware there had been a funeral that afternoon in Magnolia Street, or clearly he would not have come riding this way. He looked round superbly. Then he made off toward Aubrey Street and disappeared.

Rachel Shulman's cheeks burned like red roses. The pupils were starting from her eyes in the wild incredible glory of it. She stayed at the window for ten minutes, twenty minutes, looking at the corner of Aubrey Street, where the prince had disappeared. Then she shuffled along to her cigar-box and lifted a handful of regimental emblems.

"It *was* a cavalry uniform!" she whispered. "It might have been Lancers, or it might have been Hussars! Now I shall have a cavalry badge, too!" she gloated. "Perhaps he'll give me a button, too! For old times sake!... And when Lord Henry offered me the goblet..."

She put the cigar-box back into the trunk half-an-hour later, and pushed the trunk under the bed.

The vision did not reappear for several days; and though the street could talk of nothing else at all, though Captain Eric Winberg displaced for the time being Haig and French, Joffre and Foch, in the public imagination, the fear began to grow upon Rachel Shulman that it had been a vision, after all. There had been no Eric Winberg riding on a white horse. It had been an angel, like those Mons angels.

Until, some days later, he reappeared in Magnolia Street. She had been on the look-out for him each day, and all day. There had been little eaten or drunk in the Shulman household since the first apparition of Captain Winberg.

333

Once again the horseman drew rein. This time he dismounted. He lifted his horse's hoof and examined the frog for a stone, which he may have thought to be there, or may not. He was about to swing into the saddle again, when he felt a hard pull at his tunic. He turned round to find himself gazing into the eyes of Rachel Shulman; or so much as he could see of them, through the untidy trellis of her hair. The eyes were a little dilated, as a peasant girl's might be, who thinks she has seen a Madonna move and smile in the dim chapel.

He tried impatiently to free his tunic.

"Excuse me, excuse me!" the girl stammered. "Eric, I mean — Captain Winberg! Please may I —"

"Let me go!" he broke in.

"Please, Captain," she implored. "I've got such a lovely collection of badges. And I was thinking, seeing we're old friends, like —"

A faint flush rose upon his dark smooth cheeks. He was conscious of people staring at him from doors, from windows... *him*, a Captain in the Seventeenth, being clawed by a little slut of an old Jew's daughter.

"How dare you?" he muttered between his teeth.

"How dare you lay hands on His Majesty's uniform? Let me go!"

She let him go. He swung into his saddle and cantered down the street, round the corner again, out of sight.

Chapter 8

I

When Captain Winberg of the Seventeenth rode into Magnolia Street for the first time, a few hours after the burial of Mrs Berman, the Magnolia Street branch of his father's rainproof industry was shut for the afternoon. But that did not hold up business very seriously. The establishment in Magnolia Street in 1916 was subsidiary to the main factory in Bridgeways on the bank of the Mitchen. There were two or three other small establishments in that region of Doomington, for it was considered advisable to split up the industry, as the danger from fire was serious, and it was wiser, if fire must come, that only a section should be destroyed at one time rather than the whole business. However advantageously the matter of insurance might be arranged, in war-time no Insurance Society could possibly arrange things as advantageously as the War Office.

So Mr Winberg had his rainproofed garments tailored in the smaller factories, like the parent house in Magnolia Street, and in the main factory set up those presses and rollers with which he coated his bales of textiles with rubber and sent them forth to be converted into overcoats and mackintosh groundsheets. Before the War the Germans had performed that operation and Mr Winberg had imported the proofed material for much less than his English collaborators were able to produce it. Now things had changed. There was a War on now. There had been for two years. Mr Winberg ministered to it with a zeal which he had never applied to the position he once occupied as president of the Lithuanian Brotherhood. It would be impossible to compute how many young men oozed out their last drop of blood in the rainproofs of Mr Winberg. They were not inferior to those produced by any of his rivals. The rain might sometimes come through. The blood did not. It flowed in a thick stream down Mr Winberg's rubber proofing.

Some of those same rainproof coats were tailored in Magnolia Street. The corporation authorities had made a little trouble about fire and fire escapes, but Mr Winberg dealt with them efficiently. He made them feel that if they pressed their scruples, they would be responsible for the pneumonias of whole battalions of their countrymen, whom their fastidiousness had deprived of the sure protection of a Winberg mackintosh.

In a sense those same mackintoshes were the spread palanquin upon which Bella Winberg reclined and greeted her suitors, stretching out her white hand to them indolently. She no longer greeted them in the plush lounge of Magnolia Street, where once the plumes and tufts and feathers nodded, and the myriads of little coloured ornaments hung like humming-birds arrested in mid-flight. Only two years after we met her first, she succeeded in convincing her father, entirely without violence, that Magnolia Street was far too shabby a frame for so rich a canvas as herself. They had moved to a house on the edge of Baxter's Moor. A year after the War started, the Winberg galleon, under the spread sail of the Winberg rainproofs, sailed statelily southward to a house in Didsbury.

"A mansion!" they called it in Magnolia Street. "What do I say, a mansion? A castle! A palace!"

"You don't say?"

"With its own tennis lawn, too!"

"And you should see those lawnmowers and garden-rollers! Standing about, you might think as cheap as yard brooms!"

"And those drying-cupboards, with big bath towels drying all the time, big as those screens they got for the living pictures!"

"You'd think it was a wedding every day with all the flowers in vases and tubs! How did you say they call those flowers, Becky?"

"Hydrangeas!"

They knew more about the drying-cupboards and the tubs of hydrangeas in the conservatory than Mrs Winberg herself, who was a little bewildered by all these bathrooms but put a brave face on it. Nothing happened at midday in that grand house in Didsbury that was not the subject for conversation that same evening in Mrs Poyser's shop in Longton. The grandeur of Didsbury enabled them to forget, for an hour or two, the terror of Ypres.

Most of all they kept careful tally of Bella Winberg's suitors.

"So he had to go straight back to Liverpool, by the next train. And what for? Because he stutters a bit. I ask you —"

"She liked him. Oh yes, he was that handsome how could she help liking him? But they couldn't agree about the marriage settlement!"

336

"It was fixed up, you might say. And then they found out his father had already done two bankrupts!"

"You know what I think? I don't care how much dowry she brings. You can't go on like this! The young men, they tell each other... and when once the young men start telling each other —"

The suitors gathered around her none-the-less, the fat sweet lady. They came in uniform and out of uniform, with diamonds in their tiepins only, or with diamonds both in their rings and tiepins. She took her time. She was twenty-one. She was twenty-two. She was even twenty-three. At any other time than this, it might have been said the gilt was beginning to tarnish off her gingerbread. Twenty-three and not yet married? But she knew the gilt was thickening, all the time that young men in a dozen countries thrust their arms into the sleeves of Winberg rainproofs.

She was a patriot like the other young ladies in Bidsbury who lived in houses with tennis lawns and conservatories. They became nurses or drove cars or knitted stockings. She knitted stockings. If there was the faintest suggestion of Berlin or Vienna in the ancestry of her suitors she turned her head away from them. She was pleasant to young Englishmen in uniform, but felt a certain instability in their prospects.

And then Mr Carlo P. Jonsen made his appearance. He was a Jew but he came from Sweden, and that made him more gentile, in a way, than any mere English or French gentile. For who had ever heard of a Swedish Jew? It was the last word in chic, and as though that were not enough, he was also an American citizen. In 1916 he seemed to be girt with the corselet of a twofold neutrality. He combined the Nordic with the Mediterranean advantages, for though he was blond, he had a keen sense of business.

He was wealthy, but not so wealthy as to despise the dowry that Mr Winberg provided with his daughter; and he was so charmed by her that he would have pressed his suit if the dowry had been half as much. He manufactured modern electric light effects and notions in Wooster Street, New York. And even so soon, with a little inspiration from Sweden, he was pioneering the adaptation to electric light uses of drains, chimney-cowls, gutterings and similar constructional items. It was cheap and smart, austerely Stockholm. Chandeliers were to look like bathroom basins. You switched them on by pulling plugs.

In the apartment on West End Avenue to which he brought his bride and the apartment on Riverside Drive to which they removed some years later, this Stockholm type of electric lighting was not adopted. That was confined to the showrooms. The plushy, velvety and brocade darkness was illuminated by hanging Moorish lamps. Soft waves of light welled inward from the cornices to light up the hand-painted pictures. Night and day unstintingly the thousand-dollar radio poured forth its music out of the three-thousand-dollar cabinet.

But that was some years later. In 1916 Mr Carlo P. Jonsen came to Doomington and to Didsbury, and there was led to the divan on which Bella Winberg reclined and she gave him her white hand; and soon she gave him her soft mouth; and there was as smart a wedding as there might be in wartime, and she went with him to the city which was to be her home, as appointed by the stars in their courses and prophesied by May Agnes Hartley, the *fire-goyah*, in her attic in Magnolia Street.

One of the bridesmaids at Bella's wedding was her little sister, Dora. She had falsified all expectations by surviving her measles, mumps and whooping-cough with ease. She was small, like her father. She had a pale square forehead and intense black hair and eyes that seemed only to be awaiting their opportunity. Her opportunity would come some day, you felt, through her faculty for dressmaking.

A Doomington newspaper that appealed specially to women requested them not to forget the lonely children.

"Their daddies are away fighting for their King and Country. Their mammies are away all day and night turning out shells for their daddies. Will the lonely children lift their hands to you in vain?"

"No!" decided the tender ladies of the southern suburbs. "They will not!"

So a group was organised to provide dolls for the lonely children, and the tender ladies with their own hands dressed the dolls. It was in this occupation that Dora Winberg, aged eleven, first displayed her talent as a dressmaker. Her photograph appeared in the newspapers. She showed an amazing skill and invention in her dolls' dresses, that subdued extravagance which one day were so powerfully to commend her establishment in Hanover Square to elderly ladies of title. With the quiet self-confidence with which she later compelled countesses to wear

338

gowns ten years too young for them, but without a trace of the bewitching foreign accent she developed, she besought her mother and sister to let her design their wedding dresses.

"You know perfectly well it would be much beautifuller than that old hag's stuff! And much cheaper!"

"Dora darling," said Bella, "of course it would! But we can't have people saying Bella Winberg had home-made dresses for her wedding day! You can do a frock or two for my honeymoon! There, darling!"

But when Bella's day came round, the day she had waited for in Magnolia Street on her red plush couch and among the Didsbury hydrangeas, the day that was like a gold carpet spread for her pretty feet between Doomington and New York, she and her mother and her father and her husband were only too happy to let the guests go on talking as long as they liked about little Dora and her dolls and her dressmaking. So were the guests. Anything to keep them from the subject of the bride's brother, Eric, born Isaac.

Really it was very awkward. It cast a cloud over the expensive presents and dresses and foods and wines — all so plentiful and expensive that you could never have guessed that mines floated and submarines lurked in the seas through which the ships tapped their way to bring them. It was awkward to have to be on the *qui-vive* all day long lest some blithe voice should pipe out:

"I say, Bella. What rotten luck Eric isn't here today! Leave up, I suppose? I'm sure I saw him only last week!"

Nobody would be such a fool. There was nobody who hadn't heard about Eric. Nobody would pipe out Eric's name aloud. But what was that name they were whispering behind their hands? What was that wink behind the wine-glass for?

"Eric, Eric, Eric..."

On the whole it was advisable for Eric *not* to turn up at his sister's wedding that day; even though he was only a few miles off and in the best of health. He was in his room at the Central Hotel during the ceremony. He stayed there all day long. He was wondering if another whisky would help things.

The Court Martial was fixed for tomorrow... Blast Lord Henry!

It was advisable for Eric not to turn up at his sister's wedding. Least of all on his white horse.

The whole point about Captain Eric Winberg was that he shouldn't have been on that white horse. And he wasn't a captain. A captain moreover, in the Seventeenth Lancers.

Wasn't it good enough for him to be a second-lieutenant in the Sussex Light Infantry?

No, it wasn't good enough. What were the chances of Lord Henry offering a goblet to a mere one-pipper in the Sussex Light Infantry? Pretty meagre.

It was odd how often Bella heard those words again with her mind's ear on her wedding day:

"And when Lord Henry offered me the goblet I simply couldn't refuse...."

She hadn't thought about them for ages, those mysterious words which, as Rachel Shulman once confided to her many years ago, he used to ejaculate, when he took Rachel out walking in the more refined suburbs. He waited till some member of the aristocracy approached them. Then out they came, as if he had never uttered them before. "And when Lord Henry offered me the goblet..."

Bella stood under the canopy. The expensive cantor who was conducting the ceremony made the blessing over a goblet of wine. Mr Carlo P. Jonsen, of Stockholm and New York, placed a gold ring on the second finger of her right hand. "Behold thou art consecrated to me," he said, "by this ring according to the law of Moses and of Israel."

At least he must have said so. But she didn't hear him. She stared at the cantor.

"Eric!" she wanted to cry out. "Eric! Here he is! What the hell did you want to get up on a white horse for? Here's Lord Henry! With a big black beard! He's offering *me* the goblet!"

She was a level-headed girl usually, but it wasn't to be wondered at if she was a bit on edge today,

II

This is how Eric got up on that white horse. He was on his way to America when the War broke out, to do something about the American end of his father's business.

He knew perfectly well that America and business weren't good enough for him. He should have gone to Oxford, as his birth and breeding entitled him to. He would have become secretary of the College Beagles in his first year. He didn't quite see how they could have avoided electing him to the Bullingdon.

But he wasn't good enough at his books to get a scholarship. Not even at Christ Church would they elect a fellow because he had a good seat on a horse. There were quite a few good horsemen at Christ Church, who knew a lot about Pindar, too. His old swine of a father wasn't going to pay to send him.

"I need the money! I can't take it out of my business!" said the old man.

Business! Pah! These Jews!

He stayed in America till the end of 1915. He was having a good time. They accepted him for what he was — a scion of the ancient English aristocracy. He stayed in some of the most baronial houses in Long Island.

But it wasn't quite what he wanted. An odd Vanderbilt and an occasional crusted Cabot had offered him the goblet. But he wanted Lord Henry to offer it.

And he wanted to ride about on a horse, on a white horse, issuing orders. The white horse had a tail like ostrich plumes. It pranced and curvetted, the pretty darling.

So he came back to England and tried to enlist in a cavalry regiment. But it was an extremely difficult thing to do. The cavalry was being reduced. It wasn't a cavalry War. And to get accepted on that much reduced cavalry establishment needed the backing of a score of Lord Henrys.

He had to be content with a commission in the Sussex Light Infantry. He was just about to go home on draft leave when he got a virulent dose of rheumatic fever. That kept him busy. He heard the white horse galloping through his dreams for weeks and weeks. They gave him long leave when he recovered. He had had a bad dose.

He went straight from hospital to Doomington, and to a military outfitters in St. Anne's Square, who provided him with the full equipment of a Captain in the Seventeenth Lancers. He arranged at a stables to hire a horse for an hour or two a day, for a cavalry captain on sick leave must keep himself in fettle. A white horse, insisted Captain Winberg of the Seventeenth.

He thought it beneath his dignity to stay with his family in Didsbury, a region inhabited by rich Jews. He installed himself comfortably in the Central Hotel, and went out hacking for an hour or two a day. In the Palm Lounge of the hotel he made the acquaintance of a second-lieutenant, Harding by name, who was stationed in the infantry training camp in Layton Park. It was

341

true Harding was only a second-lieutenant and in the infantry. But he was an Etonian.

He was not Lord Henry. But actually, and magnanimously, his uncle by marriage was. It was a very substantial step forward in Lord Henry's direction...

The young man was impressed and charmed by Captain Winberg's modest tales of the front. Young Harding was by no means a snob. "But really, Winberg old fellow, the mess at Layton Park's rather a scruffy show. However, if you'd care to drop in and have a drink some afternoon —?"

"Delighted!" said Captain Winberg, with a faint qualm of foreboding. "Delighted!" And he went on: "Look here, Harding, wouldn't the adjutant or someone lend you a horse? Or perhaps you could hire one? And we could hack about an hour or two! Layton Park's good going!"

"Damn good idea!" exclaimed Harding eagerly. "I'm sure I could fix it! How about tomorrow?"

So it was that Isaac Winberg came to realise within a hair's breadth his infantile fantasy; so it was that the nephew of Lord Henry, if not Lord Henry's self, offered him a tumbler of whisky and soda, if not a goblet; so Winberg of the Seventeenth went riding with Harding, once of Eton, now of the Second Fifth Doomingtons.

It was not only round the countryside at that edge of Doomington that Captain Winberg went riding so handsomely. He did not go so far afield as Didsbury. Rich Jews lived there. He ignored them. But he found it impossible, as we have seen, to resist the impulse to go prancing down the Blenheim Road into the region of the flowering shrubs. It was there he savoured his triumph even more exquisitely than at Layton Park, by the side of his Etonian, in the scruffy mess which treated him so politely.

He was surprised at himself. When he lived in Magnolia Street he had induced in himself a condition in which it did not exist. He slept there and ate there, but that did not make it real.

But now, as the hoofs of his horse struck fire from the cobbles of Magnolia Street, he felt he could cry Hosanna from his saddle. His nostrils smarted as if with the bursting of champagne bubbles.

But they were not aware of his exaltation, the Poysers and Tawnies and Emmanuels and the rest. He was aloof and impassive, as he had been of old time, with his smooth pale oval face and his dark eyes, the time when he came down the three steps into the street in his top-hat and Eton suit. Now he wore a more terrific panoply. The sunlight glinted on his spurs. The hoofs made thunder.

If Nellie Tawnie could have kissed his hand, she would have been content to go hungry all day long. If Rachel Shulman could have laid herself down in the roadway under his horse's hoofs, she would have forsworn any garden-party, though the Lord Mayor himself summoned her to be his hostess.

Indeed Captain Winberg on his white horse was to Magnolia Street all the apocalyptic four horsemen rolled into one. The most celebrated cavalry feat in the Great War had not yet been achieved — the advance of Allenby in Palestine; but it did not cause more excitement in its more spacious area, than the advance of Captain Winberg down Blenheim Road.

Captain Winberg was in the habit of going up to Layton Park every two or three days to pick up young Harding after lunch for their little constitutional. They sometimes had a whisky together in the mess before they went off. It is not known what trivial accident prevented him, some weeks after they met, from turning up for a period of half a week. The fact is clear that he was away at the time the General Officer Commanding intimated his intention to come some three days later to inspect the camp. It is certain that Captain Winberg would have kept away from Layton Park that day, if he had known.

He went straight to the mess, and waited about in the ante-room till Harding came along. He saw there was an inspection in progress, but it didn't concern him. Besides, it would look a little odd to clear off just because some big-wig had turned up. The inspection was over about ten minutes later. The scruffy ones returned to their mess like a pack of school prefects.

"Hallo, you here!" exclaimed Harding, the least scruffy of them. "Sorry to have kept you! I've not seen you or I'd have warned you! Come along and let's have a drink!"

"*I'd have warned you!*" Captain Winberg didn't like the sound of that.

They went to the bar in the next room and drank. A pleasant babble was going on. It stopped dead suddenly, as the Colonel and the GOC entered. The General beamed comprehensively and the babble started again a little uncertainly. Then he sighted Harding and came straight over to him.

"So it *is* you! I thought it was! How are you?"

"Fine, sir!" said Harding, very much at his ease. For the General was an old friend of his uncle, Lord Henry Harding had played cavalry on the General's shoulders not so very long ago.

"Excuse me, sir, may I?" he asked the Colonel. The Colonel nodded. "This is Captain Winberg, sir!" he said to the General, showing off his war-scarred specimen proudly.

"How do you do, how do you do?" said the General heartily. It did him good to set eyes on a cavalryman among all these foot-sloggers. Captain Winberg's appearance and bearing were quite impeccable.

"Oh, what?" said the General, peering closer. "Bless my heart, you're in the Seventeenth?"

"Yes, sir!" said Captain Winberg. He did not feel well.

"I've not heard from Richardson for months, the old scoundrel! I'd have heard, of course, if anything was wrong! How is he?"

"He was in fine form, sir, when they turfed me out!"

"What was it?"

"Shell-shock, chiefly, sir!"

"Bad luck! Let me see now, where did you leave 'em?" A minute pause, not more than half a second.

"In reserve with the horses at Albert, sir, waiting for that break through!"

He did not blink an eyelid. His whole nervous energy was concentrated on the task of not blinking an eyelid, He heard his own words 'with the horses' ring in his ears like a horrid bell. His heart stopped beating.

With the horses. But wasn't it twenty to one that the Seventeenth had been dismounted ages ago? There could be no retrieving the error.

"With the *horses*?" repeated the General. It was like a dreadful echo coming back at him. The General stopped. Again there was a minute pause. Then he turned round to Harding easily. "You've met Colonel Richardson of the Seventeenth, haven't you, Henry? Great pal of your uncle's! Stout fellow!"

He strolled on with the OC, leaving Harding with his friend. "Goodbye, young feller!" he said.

"Goodbye, sir!" said Winberg. The General and the Colonel had their heads together in the further end of the mess-room. It was too far and there was too much hubbub in the place for a single syllable to carry through to him; yet he heard what they said as loud and clear as if they bawled at each other through megaphones.

"I say, Williams, who's that fellow there?"

"You mean Winberg? Oh he comes up to do a bit of riding with Harding sometimes. Why?"

"Don't you know the Seventeenth were dismounted — when was it? February, last year, I think! Looks fishy, damn fishy! Will you look into it, Williams?"

"I will, sir!"

"Take your time! You might find something worth finding out!"

"Have another!" Harding was saying.

"Don't mind if I do!" agreed Winberg. "My throat's a little dry!"

The young men did their usual canter that afternoon. It was a pleasant day with a fresh wind blowing and white clouds sailing. But a little pulse beat above Winberg's eyes. The day seemed hot and close to him.

"Manage to get up tomorrow?" asked Harding.

"Rather!" the other replied. He knew that if he faltered he was lost — if he was not lost already. But he was lost already.

He had a very severe time at the Court Martial. He could not explain to them that he had mounted that white horse to make it easier for Lord Henry to offer him the goblet. It didn't make things easier that he had spent the first year of the War in America.

He served as a private for the rest of it, though he was an acting lance-corporal when the Armistice was declared. He rode no more horses, white or chestnut or grey, either in France or England. But he became a horseman again in America, when the War was over.

For early in 1919 his father gave him a lump sum of money and wiped him off his slate. He went to New York. He met his sister, Bella, from time to time, but their relations were not cordial. She never forgave him for being a scandal at her expensive wedding. He kept in touch through Bella with his poor old mother — who used to sell her jewels for him secretly, when he had a bad time on the Stock Exchange.

For he went on the Stock Exchange with his lump sum of money. He did well, but his heart wasn't in it. His heart was in fox hunting, of which he did a great deal in Virginia.

They adored him down there. They were much nearer his own type than the millionaires of Long Island. He was a great favourite in Virginia, though he was a little reserved, like most Englishmen. He could put away a pint of apple-jack with the best of them.

Chapter 9

I

A handful of women from the Jewish pavement were gathered in the grocery-shop. It was that half hour in the middle of the morning when the breakfast had all been cleared away but it was too soon to begin on the midday dinner; so there was time to slip over to Mrs Poyser's and do a little buying-in and have a chat about the day's news.

There had been news enough and to spare lately. Mrs Berman, peace be upon her, was dead. If she had not had such a miracle of a daughter as Rose, they would have seen the last of her long ago. But she had known something of what life was, at any rate. She had married. She had had children. You could not say the same thing, alas, about the poor lad from across the street, Frankie Briggs. Twenty years old, he was. He had just died in a hospital in York, his whole body one enormous blister, so that they placed him on an india-rubber water-bed, and he died, cursing and sobbing. And his father, the odd-job-man, had died earlier; he was killed during the German attack on Vimy, and the puffs of tear gas and the puffs of the song of the Carençy nightingales blew out over the broken woodlands.

No wonder Mrs Briggs was going to pieces before their eyes. It was a good thing that Mrs Seipel had moved out of Magnolia Street, for she and Mrs Briggs had always been the best of friends, and it would have distressed Mrs Seipel dreadfully to see the way Mrs Briggs was going downhill. Perhaps, if Mrs Seipel had not moved, she would have exerted a restraining influence on her friend. But how could you blame the poor woman, who had never in all the years gone by been known to have a drop too much, when she stood on the edge of the pavement, scowling and jeering, the beer slopping over from her jug into the gutter — how could you blame her, after all that had happened to her?

And then there was the great scandal of Captain Winberg. Apparently he should not have been riding on a white horse at all. He was not a captain, either. But he *was* an officer. And he wasn't any sort of officer at all now. It all seemed singularly foolish to the women in Mrs Poyser's shop. They could not make head or tail of it.

But the talk this morning was not of Briggs nor of Winberg. The news had come through of Benny Edelman's leg. They shook their heads and sighed, Mrs Billig, Mrs Shulman, Mrs Emmanuel, Mrs Hummel, and several women whom we do not know. Mrs Hummel was Rose Berman's sister, Ada, who had been deserted by her husband. She was accompanied by her two small children. She was afraid to leave them in the house alone. She was herself afraid to go out alone, even to the corner, in full daylight.

"How dreadful!" sighed Ada.

"Straight from God I call it!" pronounced Mrs Billig. Mrs Shulman snorted faintly. She and Mrs Billig did not recognise each other's existence since the assault upon Mr Billig. She snorted faintly because she felt, as ever, that this trafficking with God was a poaching on the preserves of her husband, the Rabbi.

Mrs Poyser nodded her head emphatically, thereby indicating that she, too, regarded the event to have been definitely contrived by the same high agent. That brought Mrs Billig and Mrs Poyser and God into the one camp, a redoubtable combination.

"That's what I always said, when a Jewish boy marries a gentile woman!" she summed up. "That's what always comes of it!"

She meant the remark to be taken generally. She did not mean that whenever a Jewish boy married a gentile woman, a Great War broke out that severed his leg above the knee. And this is what had happened to Benny Edelman, who had married Jessie Wright. This was the piece of news she had just conveyed from behind her weighing machine, as if she were the incarnate principle of Justice announcing her latest doom. She also did not mean to imply that she had always foretold this thing. It was *fire-goyah*, May Agnes Hartley, who had foretold it. But no-one remembered this. No-one listened to May Agnes Hartley, singing. Nor did she know herself what she sang.

"That's what always comes of it!" repeated Mrs Poyser. Her voice had a retrospective ring about it. She remembered, and they all remembered, how little joy the apostate had had out of his wedding from the very beginning. The lady had quite soon shown what a tartar she was. An errand boy by day and a bed partner by night, she had soon let him see that that was all he was fit for. He remained the sole errand boy, but within a year after the wedding, it was rumoured that he shared his other duty with one or two irregular competitors. It was a painful and unpleasant topic of conversation, but there were salutary lessons to be derived from it. Benny Edelman became the standing warning of his time. It only remained for him to lose a leg in the War. He did this, too.

"But what I can't see is this," began Mrs Emmanuel doubtfully. Being the wife of a celebrated philosopher, she felt that it was up to her to support the Larger Idea. "Suppose the shell that took off Benny Edelman's leg, suppose it killed the soldier standing next to him!"

"Well?" asked Mrs Poyser tersely.

"Now listen here," began Mrs Emmanuel. She was warming to it. Her husband had never let her make speeches on his platforms; but sometimes she used to try and make up for it in Mrs Poyser's shop, when Mrs Poyser was off colour. "Well, what I say is this. If the one who was killed was a Christian, did he have to die because Benny Edelman married a gentile woman? Did he?"

"Yes! Yes! Why should *he* have to die?" Ada Hummel enquired weakly.

Mrs Poyser felt the display of a little Biblical erudition would assist the cause of predestination. "When Samson the Giant pulled down the walls of the temple," she said, "were all the Philistines bad men and women? Sometimes the innocent must suffer for the guilty. When Joshua slew the Amalekites, even to the small babies —"

She stopped. She felt a sickness under the heart. She remembered Becky, her daughter, who had had a small baby. She remembered Joe, her eldest son, who was out across the sea, in a hot country among the snakes and fevers. She did not like the tendency of her exposition. Might she not be willing evil upon Joe? She was confused. She was, after all, a superstitious woman. "The Jebusites, also —" she went on lamely. At that moment she spotted through the tiers of grocery in the shop window on her right hand the eldest Mrs Edelman herself approaching.

"Quiet!" she said, "Here she is! His mother!"

The women fumbled about among their packages. Mrs Edelman came in. "Good morning, Mrs Poyser!" she said "Mrs Shulman, Mrs Emmanuel!" She enumerated the names rigidly. "And how is your Annie, Ada, a life on her?"

349

It was as if she had heard nothing graver that morning than the news that there were no chickens to buy in the market. What? Was there an apostate, Edelman by name, who had had his leg blown off in France? He was the husband of a *goy* woman. He had nothing to do with her. She had had a son, Benny, once. But he had died. She had sat a week's mourning for him on a low stool six years ago.

"Annie, thank you, she is much better, Mrs Edelman," said Ada Hummel bravely. "And your little grandson, Jacky — no evil eye befall him — is he well? How is his stomach?"

Mrs Edelman's hard mouth softened. Her eye beamed. "Oh such a child! God bless him! He already knows ten letters of the holy alphabet, and only just four years old, till over a hundred years."

"Till over a hundred years!" muttered the other women, like a congregation taking up a response from a priest. "Till over a hundred years!"

II

It was not strange that Mrs Edelman's eye beamed when she thought of Jacky, the son of her son, Norman. He was a delightful child. It seemed to her that she loved him more than she had ever loved her own children, Benny the apostate, or Norman, his younger brother, whom she had married off so urgently to Fanny Gustav that he might at once beget another Edelman to make up for the one that had gone into the darkness.

The child was so handsome, so clever. Mrs Edelman had a grim mouth and used it little, but when she repeated the bright things Jacky said, her mouth became beautiful and she chattered like a schoolgirl.

"Oh such a pity it is," she said often, "that his mother spoils him so, and gives him such rich things to eat no wonder he gets a stomach ache!" But the moment his mother's back was turned she would herself nip out of her pocket some stodgy chunk of sweetness that might tax the digestion of a ploughman.

Norman, the boy's father, didn't allow such womanly foolishness. He took his paternity very seriously. He used to take a public interest in football and a private interest in motor-bicycles and billiards. (His mother thought there was a suggestion of apostacy about billiards, so he never used to talk about it at home when he'd played a hundred or two at the Working Men's Club. Instead he applied himself to sparking-plugs and magnetos. He was a bit of a mechanic in his way.)

But when he became a father, Jacky became his sole hobby. He had an efficient touch as a father, as he had had an efficient touch with sparking-plugs. If Norman said Jacky should have no *strudel*, Jacky would have none, however loud he cried, till his father looked the other way, and then he would promptly find himself the owner of two pieces of surreptitious *strudel*, the secret gifts of his mother and grandmother.

There was nobody to control the number of pieces of *strudel* young Jacky devoured these days. His father was a soldier. Or he was something more propitious than a soldier, praise be to the Above One — a prisoner of War interned in Holland. For when the War came, and some months passed by, and it seemed unlikely that it should be fought to a successful finish without recourse to Norman Edelman, he enlisted. His touch with sparking-plugs was so efficient that he did not see how he could not enlist. The Air Force wanted recruits. He became an airman and a sergeant.

In the pursuit of a German 'plane he and his officer were brought down just off the Dutch coast. They managed to get ashore, and were regaled on a dish of cabbages and beetroot. If there was any food Norman disliked more than cabbage it was beetroot. He had existed on these vegetables for several months now. Apart from that he was happy. It might have been much worse. His mother and wife held their hands to their hearts when they remembered how much worse it might have been.

He was happy because he had Jacky to think of. There was nothing else in his letters but Jacky and what was his latest *bon mot* and Fanny must be sure to take the bones out of his fried fish.

"But it's better to boil it," he wrote, "for a small child, and don't let him eat too many sweets.... He can have an extra ration on Saturday evening. And then tell him his Daddy's sent them to him and some day soon I'll be coming back from Holland with a big big kit-bag stuffed with toys and chocolates."

Fanny's letters, too, were all Jacky. It was as if for both of them nothing else but Jacky existed, neither he nor she nor his mother nor Holland nor the Great War.

351

It was clearly something of a mistake. For when Jacky was drowned what else was there to write about? You must still write about Jacky, line by searing line, page by searing page, everything but the hideous truth about Jacky...

For Mrs Edelman had been walking across the Longton clay-croft with her small boy, in the middle of September. This was about two weeks after the news had come through that Jacky's uncle had had a leg blown off. The croft was a short cut to Begley Hill Road and friends from Begley Hill and Longton often met there in the neighbourhood of the brick-pond. It was not the first time in the history of the Edelman family that that brick-pond had played a part, for here Benny Edelman saved the life of Tommie Wright, whose mother he had married.

He was not at hand to rescue his nephew, Jacky, when he fell in some ten years later. He was having the stump of his thigh attended to at that time in France. His brother, Norman, father of the small boy, was eating cabbages and beetroot in Holland. And Fanny and a woman from Begley Hill met and had a few words with each other on the clay-croft. The woman had a baby in her arms. There was much goo-gooing and baby talk. So Jacky wandered away and was drowned.

How could she write and tell her man in Holland, how could she? The clouds enfolded her with morose blankets of guilt and soaked her with self-contempt to the marrow. Her mother-in-law walked in and out of the house with grey eyes like a dead woman; or walked by her as if she, the dead child's mother, were dead, as if she were not there.

The sparrows in the gutters of Magnolia Street twittered accusingly at her, till with a shudder of unutterable weariness, she would close the door and go into the kitchen and throw her head down on the table. She dared not pray for the relief of tears, or if she dared, the relief seldom came. Hour after hour she would look barrenly upon that high empty chair where Jacky used to sit, kicking tremendously against his foot-board.

So the letters came from Holland and went from Doomington, and Jacky, Jacky, was their burden always. Sometimes she would determine to tell him the truth. "Jacky is dead." The words danced devilishly across the paper. She would tear it into a hundred pieces, Fling them into the fire and break down and weep for hours. Mrs Edelman went in and out and took no more notice than if a tap dripped in the scullery.

He noticed her letters were now not so full of Jacky as they had been. Was he ill? he asked, demanding that nothing was to be withheld from him. He was not ill, she said. He was as well as he had ever been. But it was hard work housekeeping these days.

So it was the deception grew bigger and blacker. It was impossible to go back now. She sank deeper into the slough of this dishonesty for which neither she could forgive herself nor, assuredly, her husband when he came back. Every fresh letter she wrote was a fresh link in the heavy chain she forged. Week after week she heaped upon herself the exquisite agonies of inventing all the boy's adventures for retail in her letters. The pain of her wound was never left to go dull. She must always plunge a fresh knife into it and turn the blade round, till, after writing her letters, she lay back half swooning, a bundle of twitching nerves.

One day, some months later, she sat at the table writing to him. Her mother-in-law was not there. It was easier to write her lies when she was not there. It was not easy today. The pen lay like lead in her fingers. Her eyes, too, were like lead. She heard firm and heavy feet at the front doorsteps. They climbed the steps and strode down the dark lobby. There was something familiar in the stride. She started from the chair, her eyes round with apprehension. The door was flung open. With a bellow of joy Norman stood there, stretching out his arms to her, the father of her dead son.

"Fanny!" he shouted. "Fanny! I've come! They've let me come!" She started towards him, then an invisible rope seemed to be thrown round her. She drew up, still as a rock. He slipped his kit from his shoulders and flung it into a corner. He ran forward and clasped her.

"What's wrong, Fanny? What's up? Are you frightened? I thought it would be fine to surprise you... Where's the boy? Where's Jacky? I can't have missed him! He's not in the street playing! I looked out for him!"

"No!" she whispered.

"What's wrong, then? He's asleep, is he?"

"He's asleep!"

"Is he ill? Upstairs?"

"No! No! No!" she shrieked. "He's not upstairs!"

"Then where is he? Where?"

"He's not upstairs! He's dead!"

"God!" he shouted. His jaw stiffened. His eyes were bleak as stone. "Dead? When? How?"

"Six months ago! Drowned!" For a moment he swayed like one struck to the heart. His eyes lit on his kit in the corner, a wild instinct seemed to seize him to get hold of it and go. He opened the door. He looked out through the dark lobby into the dark street. He looked back towards the woman, who stood against the table, her whole body drooping.

In a flash he realised it all — the lying, the agony. His lips quivered. "Poor kid!" he said, and came towards her and lifted her from her feet.

Chapter 10

I

It was a night in late September in 1916, and the scene was the Jessamine YMCA hut in the base camp at Harfleur, near Le Havre. Magnolia Street was represented that evening by no fewer than three of its inhabitants. A conversation held between two of them was destined to produce consequences, of the utmost importance to Magnolia Street, by which Miss Tregunter herself was to be seriously inconvenienced.

One of the three was Max Emmanuel, the painter, the son of the humanitarian, Isaac Emmanuel. He occupied a little green hut just outside the kitchen of the main hut; in the intervals of whisking malted milk in thick white tumblers, he was engaged in a crusade to brighten the life of the soldiers with painting and poetry. The other two were only visitors to the Jessamine Hut. One of them was Wilfred Derricks, the Longton Nightingale, who was doing his second or third tour among the French base camps and was leaving for Rouen the next day. The other was Private Walter Hubbard, the tram-conductor. He was not, of course, conducting trams now. He was going up to the front, getting wounded, getting patched up again, and going back to the front. It was the sort of thing they do to cab-horses at bullfights at shorter intervals. He had this time been wounded rather sharply in the ankle, nothing serious, but he'd always have a slight limp if he ever got back again to the Doomington tram-cars. He'd been wounded so often, it was quite likely they'd hold him back for base duty.

Max Emmanuel was serving behind the counter when Wilfred Derricks arrived that evening. Max recognised the visitor, but he could not remember that a single word had ever passed between them; however, the little Nightingale danced about so excitedly on seeing him, that he concluded they must have had a happy hour together sometime, somewhere. He had always been a little absent-minded, excepting when he forgot to be. The people who bought his paintings preferred him like that. They felt they were getting value for their money.

The tall lady with red hair in charge of the hut's more earthly activities, seeing her colleague and the entertainer were friends, insisted on serving them tea in Max's hut, the headquarters of the Harfleur Valley Arts Club. Max didn't quite know what they were going to talk about, so he asked politely for Magnolia Street news. Wilfred at once tweeted up like a little sparrow on a roof.

"What," he said, "you've not heard about Captain Winberg on his white horse? Riding down Magnolia Street like Napoleon Bonaparte? And his sister — that fat tart, like a carthorse? She's been and got married to a Swede! Talking about Swedes —" he lowered his voice at this point as if the Jessamine Hut were swarming with them — "I don't put much faith in 'em, do you? Nor in the Swiss neether; nor the Pope of Rome, for that matter. I've heard it said by a fellow right in the know that the Swede that fat tart married was nothing more nor less than a German spy."

The Nightingale's note went up an octave. His eyes glittered. Talking of German spies recalled to him that dreadful episode in Magnolia Street when Frank Stanley had dropped him through his window like an old sack. He changed the subject abruptly.

"You *did* hear, didn't you, how my brother, George, got the DCM? Fine doings there was in Magnolia Street, when he came home! Wasn't it tough luck I couldn't be home same time?

"Talking about brothers, your kid brother's out here, too, isn't he? How's he been getting along?"

"Yes," said Max, "my brother David. He's getting on fine. He went and enlisted before he was seventeen."

"That's the stuff!" proclaimed Wilfred ardently. "Did you know that young Cooper has been and gone and done it, too? Them swank Coopers from number six. He wasn't seventeen neether. That's the stuff to give the troops!

"Oh by the way, how are you making out with this here painting? Do you still get time to do a little?"

"Precious little. It's not so much the time. You've got to feel like it. I suppose when once the War's over —"

"Now you look here," whispered Wilfred secretly. "I can put you in for a good thing any time you come home. Why not do the round of the halls with a bit of lightning sketching? That's art, that is! A word from me to old Milligan of the Pound Circuit and you're fixed up for a good three months. Not bad to begin with. You'd have to wear a bow and a velvet jacket, like a real artist. And the way you've got your hair would never do. Trust me. I'd make a good job out of you!"

He was shrilling away like a grasshopper. He jumped over to Max's hair and began arranging it in the way real artists wear it.

"You see? Like this! But you'll have to let it grow a good six inches longer!"

"I'll look into the matter," said Max. "It's terribly good of you. Hello, I think the concert's just about to begin! Old Buchanan, the hut leader, always starts off with *Nearer my God to Thee*. We'd best not miss it."

Wilfred Derricks began his repertoire that evening with a heart full of kindness towards his fellow humans, his neighbours from Magnolia Street, in particular. What was his delight, then, when a moment after Mr Buchanan had introduced him to the audience, he recognised, in the middle of the second row, still another of his neighbours from Longton, Walter Hubbard, in fact, the tram-conductor! It made no difference to him at all that Hubbard was only a private. He didn't believe in class distinctions in war-time. He winked at him and grimaced at him, till Hubbard sweated with discomfort. He flashed secret messages at him in between songs, till the soldiers on both sides of Hubbard stared and whispered. If he had not had the bad luck to instal himself in so conspicuous a place, Hubbard would have fled. His thoughts regarding the Derricks family in general were regrettably unchristian. Regarding George Derricks DCM, with whom he had connived at the stealing of a camera from a shop window in Deansgate, his thoughts were definitely hostile. He did not feel he had any affection for Wilfred.

It was clear, however, that Wilfred had conceived a real affection for him. Just before the last item, Wilfred made especially pointed gestures at him, of which the evident burden was: "Keep your seat, Hubbard, when the show's over. I've got something to tell you. Very urgent!"

The show came to an end. Mr Buchanan pronounced a long prayer and wound up with a couple of hymns. Wilfred's treble spiralled among the rafters. The soldiers threw themselves into the singing with the abandon which a Derricks' concert always produced in them. And then at length Wilfred was at Hubbard's side, shaking his hand warmly, and reaching up to pat him on the back, with a "Well I never! Isn't this grand! Good old Magnolia Street!"

"Delighted, to be sure!" said Hubbard awkwardly.

"There isn't anybody else in France I wanted to see more than you! Would you believe that now? You and me must have a talk!"

"Why? What for?" asked Hubbard. He looked up from under his somewhat heavy brows. "Have you been in Magnolia Street lately?"

"Now I'm not going to say a word till we can be proper quiet and have a good talk! I'll tell you what! You know there's a Jew-man from our street working in this hut? Cheek, I call it! The Christians going off to the trenches and these Jews staying back in the YM serving tea! He's busy now. See? At that tea-urn!"

"Yes, we've spoken to each other once or twice!"

"Well, he's got a little hut at the back there. I'll just have a word with him and Mr Buchanan and we'll go along at once, shall we?"

Wilfred had his word with Max and Mr Buchanan. Hubbard stood by, chewing at his lips.

"Come along with me!" said Wilfred. His voice dripped honey as they moved.

"Close the door, Hubbard. I've got something to tell you!"

Hubbard closed the door. He turned round, his chin thrust forward unpleasantly. "What's all this about?"

"You know I wouldn't take all this trouble, Hubbard, if I didn't like you. And the little woman as well. You've always been such a credit to the street, both of you."

"Look here, you get on with it, will you? You've got something to say about my wife. Have you or haven't you? What's Dolly been up to?"

"I don't say she's been up to anything at all. But when I saw you, I suddenly remembered that night, when I was back home last month... But if you're going to take it like that I'm not going to say anything. The last thing in the world I want to do is to make mischief between man and wife."

"You're not. I could trust Dolly with anybody in the world, if I was away for five years. Anybody, I say, if he offered her a thousand pounds. Well, what did you see? Who was it? I tell you I'll brain you if you don't tell me who it was?"

"Now look here, Hubbard. You must control yourself, or I'm off, see? I thought if I tipped you the wink, you could just let her know *you* know, and then it wouldn't go any further. I should be surprised if there's anything in it at all. But if you're going to carry on like this... Sit down, man! You make me frightened."

Hubbard strode up to the Nightingale and stood over him, darkling.

"Do you hear what I say? Will you talk or won't you? My God, I'll —"

His hands strained towards Wilfred's throat. The fingers trembled like leaves.

"Listen!" said Wilfred. "Open that door again. Come in and sit on this bunk. That's right!" He himself went over and stood within a foot or two of the open door. "If you think I like doing this, you're mistaken. But she's such a nice girl and you're such a nice clean-living chap —"

"Christ!" shouted Hubbard. "If you don't —"

"Ssh! Remember where you are! And this door's open! It's just this. I'd been out to a party with one of the Boys. I came back alone. It was very late. There were just a few people about, going home from the night-shift at Rawlinson's. At the corner of Magnolia Street, your Dolly passed me. She didn't notice me. I'm not that big. She was coming in from the night-shift too. She wasn't toffed up, you see, as if she'd been out anywhere."

"And who was with her? Who was it? Tell me, who was it?"

"Now just be quiet, or I'll quit, see? A chap was with her. A man in overalls. That's why I don't think there was anything in it. I'm sure there wasn't. He was just seeing her home, like."

"You mean... he went in with her?"

"Yes!" The little mannikin nodded. "Just for a brew of tea, that's all it was. They were both clemmed!"

The tram-conductor sat silent upon the bunk, his head fallen between his hands.

"And when" — his voice was thin and dry — "and when did the man in overalls come out again?"

"I don't know. It wasn't my business to go spying about on her, was it? I just turned in."

The tram-conductor was silent for a minute, two minutes. He did not lift his head from his hands.

"Now look here," objected Wilfred. "You mustn't take on like that, now. I'm telling you there's nothing in it. I thought it would be doing you both a favour, if I just dropped you the word. You see? Now you just send her a picture postcard, friendly-like —"

"Will you shut your blasted gob?" snarled Walter Hubbard. It was neither the language nor the tone of a trusted Bible Class Secretary. "When was this?"

"Oh, a few weeks ago!"

"What the hell do you mean a few weeks ago? When?"

Wilfred Derricks paused.

"Second week in August," he said.

"When? What day?"

"I can't tell you just what day."

"I'll brain you! Do you understand? You'll not get away from me! What day? Sunday, Monday, Tuesday? —"

"Oh, yes. I remember now. Ma and me had been to the Palace the night before. 'Rotten house, Wilfred!' Ma said. 'Yes, Ma,' said I. 'What d'you expect Mondays? Everyone spent up!' So it must have been Tuesday I saw her!"

"Tuesday, the second week of August," said Walter Hubbard, in a voice that seemed to come out of a cellar, so dank and sepulchral it was.

"That's how I figure it out," said Wilfred.

"What time?"

"Time? I should say about two-thirty. May have been three."

Hubbard added no word for another minute or two. Then he rose to his feet.

"Get away!" he brought out thickly through his teeth. "Get away!"

Wilfred retreated towards the kitchen-door of the main hut. Hubbard lurched round the corner, like a drunken man, and was gone. A few minutes later Max Emmanuel came over to his hut to send a book for one of his art-loving protégés. Wilfred had switched the light on. He sat perched up on a chair admiring his own raddled little face in a shaving mirror. He was smiling happily to himself, like a baby in a cradle.

Dolly Hubbard operated an automatic cartridge machine in Rawlinson's factory. She was happier now than she had been for some months, even though Walter was back again in France. He'd been wounded again, too, but only slightly, in the ankle — pretty quick work. He'd written to tell her it was quite likely they'd hold him back for base duty. He'd been that loving with her when he was home in August, that she smiled at the thought of it amid the hissing of the lathes and the grinding of the treadles.

Of course he still had it in his head that every fellow in the streets was winking at her on the sly; but when he forgot about it, he was like a lord, and herself a high-up lady, the way he'd open the door for her and not let her lift a finger for herself; and then, not a bit like a lord, he'd get hold of her and kiss her and hug her till he fair frightened her. She liked that more. It had been a treat. They wouldn't give her any time off at Rawlinson's to be with him. You couldn't hold up the supply of cartridges so as people could go off billing and cooing. But they'd had a grand time, just the same. He used to bite her ear when they turned the light out. What would Miss Tregunter say, she asked him. But he only bit the other one. It wasn't a bit like Walter to be so jolly and him always so serious-like. She smiled again and sighed.

And all that made it so queer, the letter she got from Walter, early in October. He couldn't stick it, he wrote, at the base. He'd insisted on getting passed for duty up the line again, and they'd passed him. What was the name of that man in overalls who saw her home, he asked, the night of Tuesday, the second week in August? What was he doing, seeing her home, and coming in with her about two-thirty in the morning?

But she hadn't been awake at that time for months now, since they'd taken her off the night shift. Surely he knew that himself. He'd been home on leave only two months ago, the time there was all that excitement about George Derricks and his DCM. She wrote and reminded him. And who'd been telling him such black lies? She hadn't been out with nobody. She loved him and she'd never love nobody else but him in all the world. So many fishes there are in the sea. So many kisses I send to thee.

The next letter he wrote was a very different one. Would she pray for him, he was a wicked jealous sinner? He knew she loved him and he loved her; he loved her so much he had to put his fist in his mouth to stop himself shouting out how much he loved her. He thought he'd washed himself clean in the Blood of the Lamb, but there were filthy stains all over him. She must pray for his soul or he was damned. But if ever he found out that a man in overalls had gone into his house at two-thirty in the morning of Tuesday, in the second week of August, and she, his wife, by that man's side — Jesus have mercy, he prayed, on all their souls!

"Walter darling," she wrote him, "dear old pal. Oh please, please. You upset me frightful your writing to me like that. So help me God I haven't been out with no other man, God should cut my throat before I die.

"And besides, dear loving Walter, I've got something to tell you. It will make you so happy. You've always wanted one. And you're going to have one. A baby I mean. I'll keep on here at Rawlinson's as long as I can, but not too long. You wouldn't want that. It was all different when you was here in July. That's why we're having one and didn't have none before. Please write and tell me at once how happy you are and if it's a boy shall we call him Walter...."

But it was a long time before her husband expressed any opinion regarding the name of his unborn child. A shell exploded within a few yards of him and buried him, the day his wife's letter came. They dug him out again. He was not dead. It was a sad thing for him, and for his wife, pink-cheeked Dolly, that he was not dead. Of course her cheeks were not so pink now she worked these long shifts, operating an automatic cartridge machine in Rawlinson's factory.

III

In later days, when they discussed the affair of Walter Hubbard in the Lamb and Lion, it was stated by one or two men who had served in the same battalion that he would have got a decoration if his nature hadn't been against him. He was so surly you couldn't get a word out of him. Even the toughest sergeant-major didn't like to rough-house him. He said nothing, but his upper lip drew away and let you see a couple of teeth and a small slice of gum. He looked the sort of customer who might put a bullet through your skull in an attack some time, among the confusion of shell-holes and barbed wire, if you'd fallen foul of him.

It was no good criming him. If you tied him up to a limber for a week, he still seemed to have something on his mind to keep it busy. In slack times, he would sit about hour after hour, thinking about it whatever it was. And all of a sudden, he'd shake his head and blink his eyes and reach in the pocket of his tunic for his Bible, for he was very religious. But his attention would keep on wandering, however hard he tried to keep his nose down to it. The Bible slipped out of his hand.

In an attack, he was the most dangerous devil in the company. He'd certainly have got a medal or two if anybody had liked him.

He was hot with the bayonet, particularly. The way he'd thrust his bayonet yard deep up Jerry's guts was enough to make you think Jerry was an old pal of his who'd tried to do the dirty on his wife when his back was turned. He was once seen thrusting and stabbing at a body for a full minute; it was clear he didn't know what he was doing; he thrust and stabbed away with his face green as grass and his eyes quite blind.

It seemed to Walter Hubbard that the man before him, propped up against the lip of a shell-hole, was wearing, not a grey-green uniform but a suit of overalls. The other people in the platoon did not know that. But the two men who, some time later, were wounded by the shell that buried Walter Hubbard, heard him go on jabbering for hours in his delirium about a man in overalls.

It was several months before Hubbard could lift a cup to his mouth without spilling it, and several more months before he was back again in Magnolia Street, where his wife, Dolly, and his son, Walter, awaited him at the station and Miss Tregunter awaited him in the front-room above her window-boxes. The geraniums were in full bloom, as red as bright blood. Miss Tregunter so far forgot herself as to lean forward through the open window and wave her scraggy arm to him in welcome, the brave soldier and the proud father who had come home again.

But he was not a proud father, not all the time. Sometimes he would tickle the small creature and take its clenched fists into his mouth and make sweet noises at it as if no man had ever fathered a baby before. Dolly stood by, her eyes shining, and the rose-pink back in her cheeks again, for she had given up her job at Rawlinson's for the present.

But there were times when he came, very softly, into the kitchen where the child lay in its cradle, as if he proposed to frighten some ghost there. He moved very softly, despite the wound in his ankle, which made him limp a little. Still as softly, he padded up to the cradle and looked down at it, and stared at it for half-an-hour at a stretch, seeking to surprise some mystery, to force it from its hiding places under those tiny eyelids.

"What is it, duck?" his wife would ask, her heart pounding. "Don't you think he's looking well? He's going on grand. All the women say so. He's put on a good half pound this week."

But he did not reply to her. He looked from the child's face into hers as if both of them were masks. Then he turned his sombre eyes again to the child and stood over him, staring. Then once more, very silently, he padded out of the room again and closed the door behind him without a sound.

She was frightened, not so much for herself, as for the child. It was his own child, why did he look at him as if he were some complete stranger? She thought it would do her good to talk to some of the neighbours, but it was difficult to explain to them. What could she say? That he stood staring down at the baby for long minutes at a stretch? Does not every father do that? She would have liked to have a good talk with Mrs Briggs; but Mrs Briggs herself had become so strange these days, since she lost Briggs in France.

Now and again, before opening-time, Mrs Tawnie used to drop in. She was quite crazy about the baby. Walter was away on one occasion when she came in, so before Dolly knew where she was, she was sobbing on Mrs Tawnie's bosom and opening out her frightened heart to her.

But "'Ush, 'ush, dear," Mrs Tawnie bade her. "What dost'a expect when t'lad's been blawn up like 'e 'as? Give 'im a bit of time, lass, to coom round. Go quiet and soft with 'im, and 'e'll be a different man in a month or two. 'E already looks much stronger and 'appier nor when 'e came. Cheer oop, lass, cheer oop!"

How should Mrs Tawnie suspect the ghost of a man in overalls that went slinking about the house, and sometimes crept up the stairs softly to the bedroom of Walter and Dolly Hubbard? (But however softly he went, the stairs sometimes creaked under his tread. Walter Hubbard heard it quite plain.) Had Mrs Tawnie suspected such a ghost she would have given Dolly Hubbard other advice. But she did not.

Sometimes the ghost hung over little Walter's cradle, so that the elder Walter turned back half-way across the kitchen, as if he had no right there. Sometimes it seemed that the shadowy arms were round Dolly's waist and her head was forced back in the violence with which the ghost's mouth pressed down on hers. With a snarl of fury Walter clenched his fists and strode forward towards them a pace or two. Then he saw there was only a frightened woman there, looking at him with large eyes, and a baby crowing and chuckling in his cradle in the corner. He sat down on the sofa and buried his head in his hands.

"Come to me, Dolly," he whispered... "Be kind to me."

She came over to him and rubbed his brows with the palms of her two hands; then she went over to the cradle and lifted out the child and placed him in his arms and together they talked baby language at him, till little Walter got tired of it and called for more nutritious entertainment.

IV

The whole street heard the crash of the cricket ball that smashed Miss Tregunter's window. It was as if horror went flying out through the jagged hole on whistling wings and opened its beak and hooted.

No other window would have crashed with so much noise — as if all decency and gentility and sanity were shattered into a thousand fragments. The small boys had been warned often enough not to play cricket on that particular pitch, least of all with a hard ball. But they noticed this morning that though Miss Tregunter sat as usual at her post of observation behind the curtains, her head had fallen forward on to her bosom so that they only saw the grey sparse hair. She was evidently asleep, though she had only risen an hour or two ago.

There was a lamp-post on the Jewish pavement almost opposite her windows, and the small boys were always using it as their wicket and Miss Tregunter was always warning them away from it. But she was asleep at her post this morning. And Berel Seipel had a brand new cricket ball. So the small boys determined to get in a swipe or two with it. And Berel lifted it over square leg's head. And so Miss Tregunter's window crashed with a noise like instruments announcing catastrophe.

In a moment or two half the street was at its doors. It was many years since this dreadful thing had happened, the smashing of Miss Tregunter's window. Only the small boys who had smashed it were nowhere to be seen. They emerged hours later, all white and shaking.

But Miss Tregunter was not to be seen, either. At least she did not push up the outraged window and thrust forth her skinny arm and cry vengeance in the names of the Chief Constable of Doomington and the Lord Lieutenant of the County. She sat impassive on her chair, her head fallen upon her bosom. The sparse grey hair moved slightly in the insolent draught.

You would have thought that one of the Hubbards would by now have made his appearance. It was their house. It was their front window. In the last analysis Miss Tregunter only leased the front window from them. But there was no sign of them. Neither had left the house that morning. What was this? Why was the house so strangely quiet? It was at the moment that people asked themselves that question that the air filled with the sense of a bird hooting and flapping its wings. They came and knocked at the door. There was no reply. They knocked louder. There was no reply. A youth went round into the entry between the Acacia and Magnolia Street houses and climbed over the backyard wall and tried the scullery door. But it had not yet been unbolted.

A policeman had come by this time. He and some men hurled themselves against the front door but it withstood them. Then Mrs Carter remembered that her key fitted the Hubbards' door. Dolly Hubbard had borrowed it more than once. The door was opened but the crowd held back, fearful of what might await it in this quiet house.

Then the policeman and some others entered. From the kitchen a trail of blood led through the kitchen door and up the stairs round by the doors of the back and middle bedrooms, along the passage to the front bedroom occupied by Miss Tregunter. The body of Dolly Hubbard lay across the threshold. She had just had strength enough to turn the handle and throw open Miss Tregunter's door. Whatever hideous sound there had been to hear, Miss Tregunter had not heard. She had been deaf for some years. But when Dolly threw her door open she screwed her head round. In the shock of that sight her old stiff heart had stopped beating at once. A series of gashes almost sundered Dolly's head from her neck. It was clear a razor had made them. Her hands and arms were criss-crossed with the cuts the razor had inflicted, in her efforts to keep it from her throat.

Walter Hubbard was found in the scullery with his head inside the gas-stove. There were several deep gashes in his throat, too, but he had evidently not been able to finish the job with the razor and so had tried to asphyxiate himself. He was still breathing when they pulled him out of the oven, but he died an hour later.

He was in his shirt sleeves. A shaving mug with soapy water, a brush and soap, stood on a table under a small looking-glass. He was finishing off his morning shave, his razor at his throat, when the movement of a dark shape caught his eye in the looking-glass, beyond the reflection of his own face. His wife was just clearing away the breakfast things. He saw her lift her face and smile at the man in overalls, as he advanced towards her. Then the heap of dynamite that had been stored so long in Walter Hubbard's skull exploded. He hurled himself at her, the eyeballs rolling in his head.

If she had had time to call for help with a voice loud enough to be heard, there was no-one to hear it. Mrs Higgins and Mrs Ritchie, her next-door neighbours on both sides, were out that morning. She managed to reach and to throw open Miss Tregunter's door. But she could do no more than that.

The baby was unharmed. When the people came into the kitchen, he was crooning to himself peacefully. But in a minute or two it occurred to him he was hungry. So he lifted up his slight voice and called to his mother, who did not hear him.

Chapter 11

I

It was a great misfortune for the Seipels that the Great War broke out when it did; for if it could only have delayed itself a few weeks, they would all have been safely on their way to America, to join Uncle Adolf. There was actually a letter from him in the clock on the mantelpiece telling them all to equip themselves with a couple of pairs of boots each, for no matter what you paid for leather in America it was not as good as English leather. Also, if Reuben brought a length of tweed suiting to be made up into a suit for Adolf; he would go round and show it to all his friends on Wall Street.

The actual passage money was to be expected in three weeks, at most. In the meanwhile the family was to make all arrangements at Garden's Travel Bureau. Uncle Adolf, over at his end, would look round for a lovely little bungalow for them somewhere in the neighbourhood of his own commodious dwelling on the board-walk in Far Rockaway.

And then the Archduke Ferdinand was assassinated in Sarajevo. In some weeks the World War broke out, with unfortunate effects on Uncle Adolf's supply of Ready Money, which was a tender nurseling, sensitive to the least breath of political disturbance. Uncle Adolf was forced to write and tell the Seipels that they must hold up the arrangements for crossing the Atlantic for a few months. So the Seipels stayed on in Doomington and it was 1916 now and the hope of joining dear Uncle Adolf before quite a long time had passed was dim.

Another tender nurseling in the Seipel garden that had suffered grievously was Reuben Seipel's melancholy little cabinet-maker's workshop away across the town in Ancoats. It had managed to carry on precariously from year to year; but the great gale that blew up in August 1914 which had whipped up other little industries, like Winberg's rainproofs till they roared like furnaces, was just too rude for Seipel's cabinet-making. It was snuffed out completely.

Reuben therefore did cabinet-making for somebody else. He was a good workman, though he was always hacking off pieces of his thumb with his chisel. It was a bad week when he did not make enough to have his nightly dish of broad beans and his Friday night stack of Yiddish newspapers. They made good reading in wartime and promulgated theories and reports which would have stupefied both *The Times* and the *Berliner Tageblatt*.

The Seipels in some ways were not anxious to go to America. If Adolf had not made such a brilliant success there and had not insisted so affectionately that they should go out to him, the idea probably would not have entered their heads. In fact the thought of America rather frightened them. And they loved England, in their own way. But it was certainly a hard job to make both ends meet in England; and in America Uncle Adolf would initiate all the children into Real Estate and before they knew where they were they would all be riding about in motor cars with silver fittings.

So they waited and waited for Uncle Adolf to send the money for the tickets. Yet they all knew that they would not be happy to leave England when it came to it. The whole family, from Reuben to Berel, remembered that a Jew had become Prime Minister of England. They could not think of it without a tear starting in their eyes. They thought of Queen Victoria, of blessed memory, as a Jewish matron. They had not seen Buckingham Palace, but in their visions it bore a somewhat oriental appearance, with its domes and cupolas, not unlike their vision of the Temple of Solomon.

Reuben Seipel loved England because of its political liberty. When he was a small boy in Russia, he once saw a gang of students being bundled off in chains to serve a sentence in Siberia, and he had never forgotten it. He had always had faintly socialistic leanings, but in Russia he had never allowed himself to talk of anything more compromising than boiled beans. Here in Doomington some of his fellow workmen talked openly of abolishing the monarchy. At first he sympathised with them, on general principles; but as the years went on, the thought of abolishing a monarchy which allowed its subjects to discuss its own abolition, became less attractive. He favoured a socialistic republic under the hereditary presidency of the royal line of Windsor, the new arrangement to begin on the conclusion of the reign of the present Prince of Wales, for whom he had an avuncular affection.

Mrs Hannah Seipel loved England because she loved her neighbours. She did not believe she would ever have such kind neighbours in Far Rockaway, in New York.

Jane Seipel, who was now an elementary school-teacher of eighteen loved England because she loved Enid Cooper, the most refined and distinguished of England's daughters.

Sam Seipel, aged thirteen, loved England because he had got a lot of bits together and made up a bicycle and he cycled over the English roads and loved them and the meadows on both sides of them and the hills they climbed to.

Eli and Berel Seipel, aged ten and eight, loved England because Izzy Cohen won the VC and George Derricks, one of their own neighbours, won the DCM and because there was such a lot of big red patches on the globe.

The consequence of all this loving England was that Reuben Seipel joined the army in 1915 with a vague feeling that when England won the War there would be no more students in Russia chained up in gangs. He also thought that Disraeli and Moses Montefiore would have approved the step. It was found he would not be much use storming trenches as he had a rupture, so he brushed out an Army Service Corps hut in Blandford for three years, and found with pleasure that boiled beans figured on the menu from time to time.

When Uncle Adolf heard that Reuben had joined the army, he said it was rather a pity. He had just arranged with a great friend of his who manufactured furniture, that Reuben should come over to become his manager at a princely salary. That would have to wait now, till the War was over. But when that happened, the first boat crossing from Liverpool to New York would carry the Seipels with it. Uncle Adolf would be waiting for them on the quayside with his hands stretched out to them.

II

Mrs Seipel's husband loved England and joined the army. Her cousin, Itzik Landsman, did not care about England one way or the other, so he did not join the army. He was a burly young man who pressed clothes for a living. He came over from Russia a year or two before the War in order to find a Doomington heiress and marry her. He belonged to the great pack of lame dogs whom the Seipels had helped over stiles at one time or another. In order to facilitate their efforts to help him over a stile, Itzik came and stayed with the Seipels when he first arrived; but he was so bulky that every time the Seipels strained and heaved to lift him over the poor man fell back again, straight on to the Seipel's best bed, where he remained for months.

He was not very comely. He had large cheeks, small eyes and two chins. Not a single Doomington heiress could be induced to marry him. So he resumed his ancient occupation of pressing gentlemen's clothes.

When the War came, nothing was further from his mind than joining any army; for he was a peaceful man by nature. To the appeals of soldiers and statesmen he turned a deaf ear; to the appeals of posters he turned a blind eye. He was not an Englishman. He was a Russian. And it had been his intention to become an American.

In a year or two he found himself faced with a repulsive dilemma. It was admitted by the authorities that he was no Englishman. But they proposed to waive the formality and enlist him in their historic armies; they even announced that they deemed him to have enlisted. If, on the other hand, Itzik Landsman repudiated that rendering of the situation, they would not force the matter. He was at liberty to return to Russia, where they would deal with him courteously.

Both these alternatives filled Itzik with loathing. He realised there was only one thing to do. (He had no confidence at all in the methods of Mr Billig.) He must address himself to his dear cousins, the Seipels, who had always been so kind to him. Reuben, the head of the family was away. He had enlisted in His Majesty's forces, and Itzik felt with a little heat that His Majesty ought to have been satisfied with one representative of the family; to demand a second was mere avarice.

"Vot I say is dis, Hannah," he proposed. "I'll come and be a lodger in your cellar, like it vos de front room. Do I need curtains?"

In that way only, so far as he read the situation, could he avoid the unpleasing alternatives which had been forced upon him.

Hannah Seipel remembered with dismay how inconvenient a guest her cousin had been when he quite patently occupied the best bedroom. She realised that that would be a bagatelle compared with the embarrassment of entertaining him in her cellar. Moreover, he had a prodigious appetite. It was uncanny the way the lame dogs who threw themselves on her kindness had prodigious appetites. Food was getting scarcer. Must she deprive Reb Feivel, her grandfather, and Jane, Sam, Eli and Berel, her children, of their ounce of butter per week, to fill the maw of her cousin, Itzik?

"It upsets me something dreadful, Itzik," she said. "You know what I wouldn't do for my cousin! But my cellar? No! Is it a large cellar? Where shall I keep my coal, Itzik, if I keep you in my cellar?"

"Coal?" said Itzik. "I vill sleep on de coal like it vos de bed from de Queen of Sheba!"

But Mrs Seipel had other scruples, She had a faint feeling that it wasn't fair to the shade of Queen Victoria and to her absent husband, Reuben. And why should young David Emmanuel and Dick Cooper from across the street join up a year before their time in order that Itzik should take his ease in her cellar.

"No, Itzik, it can't be!" she said again, and stamped her foot firmly.

"No, Itzik, it can't be!" echoed Reb Feivel and Jane and Sam and Eli and Berel. They were a very unanimous family.

Then poor Itzik Landsman broke down. It was awful to see the way the great mass of him quivered, the pouches under his eyes, the two chins, the paunch. Between his sobs he presented to them as horrifying a picture of conditions in the front-line trenches as any post-war novelist has succeeded in rendering. Yet even in the depth of his despair he besought them to believe that it was not these things as such that horrified him, the rats, the lice, the mud, the gas, the shells.

"No, Channah," he insisted. "Look at me! Do I look as if I care for shells? I spit on dem! But dey vill put guns in my hands and say 'Shoot! Shoot!' It vill not be tigers! It vill not be lions! Lions and tigers I spit on dem! I need no guns!

"It vill be living human beings, like me, like you. I cannot do such a ting. No! No! I shake! Ven I vos a small boy and I saw de oder small boys catch flies and tear de vings off — so! — I cry for hours! Today it is de same ting! I cannot set a trap for a mouse! A beetle — if I tread on it... I cannot eat for two days!

"So you must, Channah! You must let me be a lodger in your cellar! Am I not a Jew and a cousin?" He threw himself at Mrs Seipel's knees. "De coal it vill be to me like silk and satin. I vill

372

be quiet as a small dove! To eat — do not trouble about to eat. De Var has upset my appetite!" The tears rolled down his cheeks and were impaled on the stubbles of his chin.

It had always been the fault of the Seipels that they had such soft hearts. Before Itzik had gone half-way through the catalogue of the horrors of modern warfare, they were all sobbing together, softly.

"Come tonight, this very night!" wept Mrs Seipel. So Itzik Landsman wrapped up a few things in a bag and left his lodgings late that night and crept into the Seipel house through the back entry. Mrs Seipel had managed to clear away the coke and the debris and make up some sort of a shakedown out of a mattress and a feather-bed or two. It was not very comfortable and there was not much light and air. But a lot of people in dugouts between Nieuport and Switzerland had less, so Itzik Landsman had no cause to grumble. If he did, in fact, grumble now and again, it was because the cellar completely lacked the excitement which occasionally livened things up for the people in the dugouts.

Or almost completely. There were one or two alarms now and again. As, for instance when the inspector from the Gas Company came to read the meter. He had to go down into the cellar to do it and that was a little awkward. The boys rigged up a sort of screen out of sacking and Itzik crouched behind it, shivering and sweating. The dugout people can hardly have been much unhappier waiting for an attack. Then at last the 'All clear!' was sounded.

The three boys put their heads round the cellar door. "You can come now, Uncle Itzik!" they whispered. They enjoyed it quite a lot. Dr Crippen was sometimes stated by their mother to live down that cellar. It was much more fun having Uncle Itzik.

He crawled out from behind the screen.

"Oh my head!" he moaned.

"Bang, bang! Like a hammer! Have a pity on me, Channah! Maybe mit a bottle of stout I come trough!"

He developed quite a taste for stout in the cellar and Mrs Seipel had to let it be known that the doctor ordered it for her, because her blood was thin. It was all very inconvenient. The Seipel household was like a nest full of hedge-sparrows, all of whom had to go short because of the fat cuckoo hidden away in their midst.

373

III

In the spring of 1916 things were going rather badly with the Seipels. A nasty slice of Reuben's allowance had to be cut off weekly to pay a money-lender, to whom he and Reb Feivel had pledged themselves years ago on behalf of one of their lame dogs. Itzik Landsman took a lot of feeding and he made no contribution to the exchequer. It was impossible to provide him with gents' suitings to press down among the coal dust. Jane's wages as a school-teacher did not keep pace with the increases in the war-time cost of living. The three boys, Sam, Eli and Berel, were growing rapidly, but it was boots that were the trouble. They seemed to eat boots.

Mrs Seipel and Reb Feivel looked anxious. They each practised little economies when the other wasn't looking. Mrs Seipel ate her bread dry. Reb Feivel foreswore sugar with his tea. But that didn't seem to help balance the accounts.

The shop-keepers had stopped giving them credit for a year or two now. They were in debt to all of them, the grocer, the butcher, the milkman. It meant, in fact, that they didn't believe in Uncle Adolf, the Real Estate magnate, quite as much as they used to. It was an anxious time.

Yet it was the time the Lord of Hosts chose to prove to his servant, Reb Feivel, who had been so devoted to Him for three score years and ten, that, after all, His heart was in its right place. It might have been thought the Lord of Hosts had too much on hand at that time to bother about Reb Feivel. But this was not so. And, in any case, the armies in Europe had settled down to the comparative stagnation of winter warfare. The Lord could look round a bit.

It was true He had to sacrifice Cheikeh, Reb Feivel's elder sister, in order to vouchsafe His esteem for His servant. He could have performed a miracle, of course, but it was quite as simple to get old Cheikeh out of the way. For she was eighty years old and lived in Pittsburgh, and for those reasons would not much mind quitting the scene.

She had gone to America with her husband scores of years ago. She sent Reb Feivel annually a printed card of greeting for the high festivals. From that it was adduced each year that she was still alive and still lived in Pittsburgh. And then, when the need of the Seipels was sore, she died and left Reb Feivel three

374

hundred dollars. Reb Feivel promptly placed the money in the hands of his grand-daughter.

"No!" cried Mrs Seipel, "No! I should take your money? I am a robber?"

The old man was firm. "What shall I do with it? Do I need to buy dress suits to go to dances in?"

But he did need a new silk praying-shawl to go to synagogue in. Uncle Adolf had promised him one long ago and had forgotten it. So Mrs Seipel bought him one. She bought Jane a leather hand-bag. She also bought three pairs of boots for the three boys. Their toes were nearly poking out of the old ones. And she bought herself two bars of pink-cream chocolate. She bought them with many heart searchings, but it did not seem likely three hundred dollars would come their way again for a long time. What to do with the rest of the money? She and Jane and Sam and Eli and Berel sat sucking sections of the pink-cream chocolate, contemplating the matter. Reb Feivel sat sucking lemon tea through a cube of sugar.

To use the money to repay the grocer, the butcher, the milkman, was merely extravagant, it was agreed by everybody. It would leave them just where they were. So the idea came to them they would buy a little business with it. And that was how, in late June, they came to leave Magnolia Street, though it had never occurred to them that their next move would be anywhere in the world but New York. For a small sweets-shop business entered the market only a day or two later, and before they knew where they were the Seipels had bought it; the removal van was standing outside number nineteen Magnolia Street; it was lurching on its way towards number ten Wrigley Street, three miles across the city, in the gentile district of Hulme. That was the second removal from Magnolia Street within a fortnight, for the shoemaker, Stanley, and his German wife, had just moved, too.

The sewing-machine was not in pawn and therefore it went in the van. So did the hall-stand, the two wash-stands, the wringing-machine, the pictures of Beaconsfield, Herzl and Queen Victoria. So did Itzik Landsman. But it was a great job to get him away. He hugged his cellar till the last possible moment and then he made a dash for the van. It was a difficult thing to stow him away without attracting the attention of the van driver. Reb Feivel, Mrs Seipel, Jane, Sam, Eli and Berel made a lane to conceal him from the eyes of the neighbours and stood about laughing artificially while he dug his way between the wash-stands. As the cart drove off; one of his feet stuck out. Sam dropped a sack over it deftly.

It might be as well perhaps, at this point to finish off the story of Itzik Landsman. He never arrived at the sweets-shop in Wrigley Street, in Hulme. In the excitement, the Seipels and the vanman had unpacked quite a lot of the furniture before it was realised that Itzik was missing. And quite a lot more of the furniture was unpacked before the Seipels realised how convenient it was that he should be missing.

"If he turns up, mother, he turns up!" whispered Jane. "Don't look like that! He's not been kidnapped or eaten by a wild animal!"

"He is an orphan!" moaned Mrs Seipel.

"There's always a cellar for him in Wrigley Street, the moment he turns up! And if he doesn't we can't go to the police station and find out, can we? That's the last thing he'd want us to do!"

"Thank God!" breathed Sam.

"So come on, mother, let's get on with the unpacking!"

But the fact is that Itzik Landsman had not dropped out of the van. Of his own free will he extricated himself from the wash-stands and jumped out. For somehow, stowed away in the van there, he got the situation in perspective. He had not liked the Magnolia Street cellar. But he had got used to it. The thought of having to get used to a new cellar was just more than he could bear. He paraded before his mind's eye the reported horrors of dugout warfare. They seemed trivial to him compared with the horror of getting used to a new cellar. So he jumped out of the van. It was foggy. People did not notice that his face and his clothes were black with coal-dust; moreover, people often look like that in Doomington even when they have not spent several months in a cellar.

He walked. All afternoon and evening and all night long he walked. He had not known what an exquisite thing it can be just to move your legs and swing your arms. He walked next morning into a recruiting office in a small town north of Doomington. He could talk very little English; but when the authorities expressed a curiosity about his recent history, he managed to convey to them his mind was a blank excepting for the passion he had to enlist in the army. A full-blown private, he found his way some months later to his cousin's sweets-shop in Wrigley Street. Never were buttons more brightly polished, never was cane struck more smartly against thigh. In all his armies King George had no more fanatical servant than Private Itzik Landsman.

But to continue with the fortunes of Mrs Seipel's sweets-shop in Wrigley Street. Frankly, things did not look too rosy. She was the only Jew for miles round, and the gentiles were suspicious of her. They did not know what sinister incantations she uttered over her lemon-squash gums, and whether all was so innocent as it seemed with her caramels. Moreover Mrs Seipel herself could hardly distinguish a mint humbug from a fondant chip, and kali-suckers were a mystery to her. In this respect, it must be qualified, Sam and Eli and Berel were of material assistance. And on pink-cream chocolate she had herself long been an authority.

Nor must Reb Feivel be left out of account. As he shuffled in and out of the shop, his silk hat faintly tinged with green, his frock-coat a little undecided at the button-holes, his beard soft and woolly and lamb-like, his face like an amiable prophet's (if history has record of an amiable prophet) he drew excessive attention to the fact that Mrs Seipel's sweets-shop was not as other sweets-shops are; that it was, to put no fine point on it, a Jewish business, and to be left strictly alone, if not actively persecuted. Day after day Mrs Seipel stood pallidly behind her counter... but the bell above the shop door did not clang. She yearned for the goodly talk of Mrs Poyser's grocery-shop, for her friends coming back from the market, showing her how plump the Sabbath chicken was. So much was happening these days in Magnolia Street. The younger Derricks, the one with such a clean face, who had been in the reformatory — he had been on leave from France with medals all over him. The boys, Eli and Berel, had come home with excited tales of the great doings in Magnolia Street... almost like that time poor Mr Emmanuel arranged for Benny Edelman to get a present of a gold watch.

Of course, it was this same hero, namely George Derricks, who had got the gold watch, not Benny. Benny had gone off with that woman. Mrs Seipel tried to feel stern, but her heart ached for the poor fellow. He was off in France now, too.

And then there was all this confused business about the

Winberg boy riding about on a white horse. Why shouldn't he ride about on a white horse, if he wanted to? And Mrs Berman, peace be upon her! What a sweet little woman she had been! And what a jewel of a daughter! How silly they had all been! They had got it into their heads some years ago that she had been going out secretly with that sailor. If it had been true, and her mother had found out, it would have driven her into her grave long ago. It was her younger daughter's husband had done that. What a villain, a Haman, that man was!

And now God had shown Benny what for. He had taken his leg off above the knee. But was it quite so sure as that, she wondered, that God had had a hand in it? And what had his nephew, little Jacky, done, to go and get drowned in the clay-croft pool?

She wished she was over at the grocery-shop this morning. Mrs Poyser would help her to understand. From a distance Mrs Poyser began to assume almost Biblical proportions. She seemed like one of the great Hebrew women, Miriam, Deborah, Abigail, Hannah, born out of her time.

Three times a day Reb Feivel plodded away to a tram-car which would take him to the Lithuanian Brotherhood, in Magnolia Street; three times a day he plodded back, saving on Friday evenings, when he stayed with Reb Aryeh, who kept the Hebrew-school, so that he might be at hand for the Sabbath services.

A couple of weeks after the Seipels settled in Hulme, the small children invented a new game — who could first hit the old Jew-man's silk hat three times with screwed-up paper balls. But little Billy Hodge, who had a jolly red sweater and jolly red cheeks, introduced a refinement. He aimed at the old man's face. When Reb Feivel sat down at length before the fire, he chanted a little hymn of praise for his great-grandchildren, Eli and Berel, as they tenderly rubbed his face with towels, and combed his soft beard. It had been raining heavily for some days, and the paper balls were not clean. Mrs Seipel made him a tumbler of boiling lemon tea. She had ample time. There were no interruptions from the shop.

A few days later the sky cleared. As Reb Feivel came out that afternoon Billy's red face and red sweater struck his old heart like a shaft of the sun. He dived into a tail pocket and brought out a handful of caramels. Billy, suspecting poison, jeered.

Timeo, he sang, *Judaeos et dona ferentes*. Reb Feivel emptied his hand into the palms of Tommie Godden, who stood hard by, then moved away. Tommie Godden, sucking caramels and stroking his stomach with circular smoothings annoyed Billy acutely. Next afternoon Billy did not refuse.

It was characteristic of Reb Feivel that he chose, when a limited quantity of sweets made choice necessary, the ugly little boys and girls for his gifts — the little boys and girls whom teachers do not send on errands to the headmistress, who are not chosen to do recitations at Sunday School concerts. So it was that a whole section of Wrigley Street mothers, gratified that anyone, even a tumbledown old Jew, should at last recognise the virtues of their offspring, began to smile as he passed them standing, bare-armed and baby-laden, at their front doors. Billy and Reb Feivel speedily developed for each other a warm and equal affection. Billy once saw a young friend of his, by name Johnnie, holding taut a few inches above the ground a string tied by its other end to a lamp-post, the object being to trip up Reb Feivel at that moment shuffling abstractedly down Wrigley Street. Billy knocked Johnnie's head so hard against the lamp-post that Reb Feivel only separated the friends by hurrying into his grand-daughter's shop and hurrying out again with two sticks of barley sugar.

But Reb Feivel only began to occupy a really important position in the destinies of Wrigley Street after the satisfactory conclusion of the *affaire* Watkins. It was a tangled business. No one knew how it all started. But Mr and Mrs Watkins had quarrelled bitterly, that was indisputable. Mr Watkins worked at munitions and she worked in a steam laundry, and they both worked long hours, and the temper of neither was so sweet as it might be. But whether she called him something first or he her, what remark of hers it was he countered with an allegation which did not mean *that* but something else all the time, and the precise position occupied in the whole matter by Mrs Jenkins's jug of bitter left accidently on Mrs Watkins's doorstep it was now quite impossible to get to the bottom of it all. Yet there were two dominant facts. First, Mr and Mrs Watkins were, and always had been, very much in love with each other. Second, Mr Watkins and Mrs Watkins (née Smithson) had all the pride and all the obstinacy of the Hulme-Watkinses and the Miles-Platting-Smithsons respectively. Which was it to be? Separation or union

— police court or pints and kisses all round? For a long time the Separatists had it all their own way. The Unionists cast round in despair.

Then someone casually suggested: "The old Jew-man!" Two dozen despairing throats echoed "The old Jew-man!" And Reb Feivel, possessed of little English but more wisdom, was called in. The sequel was as blithe as any recorded in the annals of Magnolia Street. Mr and Mrs Watkins might have been celebrating a golden wedding or a funeral to judge from the profusion of liquor and ham sandwiches. It disappointed the welded Watkinses that Reb Feivel refused all refreshments; but when Mrs Watkins suddenly and loudly kissed him — Mrs Seipel was there and thought she would faint — Wrigley Street burst into delighted cheers. In a moment he became, not a benign shadow, but warm flesh and blood that once, long ago, had been young and loved a woman and had fathered children.

So the women no more called him, impersonally: "The old Jew-man!" They said to him: "Top of the morning, Mr Feivel!" or: "Mr Feivel, do take care of that there cough!" He had never attained such primacy in the parliaments of Magnolia Street; but then he was by no means the only old man of that calibre there. In Wrigley Street there was no competition.

Yet we must not linger in Wrigley Street, however we are tempted by the sophistry that the doorsteps and wringing-machines of Magnolia Street and Wrigley Street are the same doorsteps and the same wringing-machines. Our duty lies by our Longton Poysers and Briggses. It must be reported, however, that quite a number of their Magnolia Street friends took the trouble to visit the Seipels, isolated amongst the gentiles, all the way across the city in Hulme. As the months went on, the Seipels were not by any means so isolated, as we have seen. But the visitors still came, particularly the young men of the generation of Sam, Eli and Berel. These three, and their mother, were so delighted to see them that the visitors were rendered quite speechless by the amount of stick-jaw thrust upon them.

Jane Seipel also had a visitor now and again, no less a person than the beloved Enid Cooper herself. She came all the way from the small private school where she was a resident mistress, to bring flowers to Jane. The giving of flowers was not a frequent courtesy among the Magnolia Street folk, but it seemed instinctive in the two Cooper women. In the little parlour where

Mrs Berman had sold her home-made sweets, where they laid her out in her coffin, where Rabbi Shulman had pronounced her obsequies, a great bunch of red roses gave out their dark comfort for days after. It was Mary Cooper who had sent them over to Rose, by Dick, her brother. She sent white roses over to the mother of Frankie Briggs, when the lad died in York. But Mrs Briggs lurched up against the table where the vase stood which held them. The vase fell, and the roses withered on the floor.

It was a great bunch of yellow chrysanthemums that Enid Cooper brought to her friend, Jane Seipel, on a Sunday afternoon in mid October. Jane was small, somewhat chubby, and had dark timid eyes which made her look less than her years. She was eighteen. Enid was tall and fair and carried herself beautifully, quite a woman of the world. She was twenty. Enid brought flowers to Jane, and their pressed petals were to accompany her on long journeys. They were the most fragrant of her possessions.

The girls had been great friends since the days when the rescue of Tommie Wright by Benny Edelman had knotted the whole street together. Some of the knots came undone. But Jane and Enid remained great friends. To Jane it was more than friendship. She loved Enid with a shy and exquisite emotion. Enid was tactfully sympathetic. She had herself had a violent 'crush' on the History Mistress, not long ago, from which she learned how to tackle the situation. They went out for long walks and quoted Tennyson. Enid had a vague suspicion there was some slight similarity between herself and the Tennysonian heroines. Jane thought they were but pale foreshadowings of her.

Enid's 'crush' on the History Mistress was superseded in course of time by a refined love affair with a young amateur actor who wrote plays about Brahmin deities. It was a shade too refined, she realised, so she did not marry him. But Jane carried her love for Enid to Hulme and across the Atlantic and the broad plains of the Middle West. She had 'affairs' with boys, of course. But they were all creatures of a common texture, compared with her fair tall lady. Enid was Enid and she was England. She loved them with a devotion taller than the skyscrapers and broader than the prairies.

"Look who's come, Jane!" cried Mrs Seipel that Sunday afternoon.

"Enid!" cried Jane, springing from the sofa.

"Yes, Enid!" said Enid, entering.

"Darling, how are you?"

"Darling!" said Jane, and flung her arms round Enid's neck, and kissed her.

"And such lovely flowers!"

Eli, Sam, Berel, winked at each other. They always knew they were in the way when Enid came. "So long!" they cried, and went out.

"Give them each a penn'orth of caramels for me!" Jane called out to her mother in the shop.

"And another for me!" said Enid. "Well, my dear, what news?"

"One moment my dear, till I put these into a vase. But they're marvellous! How could you, Enid! In wartime, too! There! Aren't they lovely? What? What news? Oh the shop's all right! Everything's all right! Father's still in Havre! How sweet of you to come, Enid, and with these darling flowers! Have *you* any news? Oh tell me about the ultimatum!"

"Yes, that's what I've come to talk about!"

"Have you issued it?"

"I was going to!"

"Well?"

"Then Dick — oh please, Mrs Seipel! Do come in! You don't think I'm going to keep you out of your own sitting room?"

"I was just going to get a shawl," said Mrs Seipel, hesitating.

"I won't hear of it. Besides I wanted to tell you, too. You know, Dick, my young brother?"

"Yes?"

"He's gone and enlisted! Isn't he a young devil!"

"But he's not old enough," remonstrated Mrs Seipel. "What's he done it for?"

"He's not seventeen," said Enid.

"What on earth will Mary do?" wondered Jane.

"Exactly. That's why I didn't issue the ultimatum."

"What's that?" enquired Mrs Seipel nervously. She remembered the word from the early days of the War. Were more nations massing for the slaughter?

"Please, please, Mrs Seipel! Do sit down! Oh! There's the door bell! I'll wait for you, Mrs Seipel!"

Mrs Seipel returned after dealing with her customer. Jane was holding Enid's hand. Jane and Enid both were pretending she was not.

"You know, Mrs Seipel, I've long wanted Mary to remove from Magnolia Street. *You've* done it. *I've* done it. We're *all* doing it. Why shouldn't Mary?"

"Yes, why not?"

"Well, it's odd! I remember the time when John used to swear he wouldn't ever put his nose in that beastly slum again. Do forgive me, won't you? That's the way John talked. But he's quite different about Magnolia Street now. He seems quite pleased to be there. But of course we have our ideas why *that* is, haven't we, Jane?"

"Yes!" said Jane.

"Really?" said Mrs Seipel. She, of course, had no ideas on the subject at all.

"So that John's been no help in getting Mary to move. And he's away practically all the time. It doesn't concern him — or me, either, since I took this school on. But I *do* want to get Mary out of it. Do you know? Once or twice some of my mother's relations have suggested to her that she should sell out number six. I believe she could get quite a lot for it, comparatively, these days. Anyhow, quite enough to buy some small country cottage, big enough for her and Dick. Dick could get a job as a blacksmith in the country quite easily.

"But she won't hear of it. She's got her roots into the place. That's why I was going to issue an ultimatum. I was going to tell her that I'd never come and see her again if she didn't move. Dick could always come and see me, as he often does. Then Dick went and joined up last week. I suppose the example of that Emmanuel boy had something to do with it. I mean the younger one, David. He was also a lot under age. I've heard Dick talk about it once or twice. By the way, Jane —"

"Yes, Enid?"

"What's happened to the other Emmanuel — Max, the painter?"

"What do you want to know for?" asked Jane, not quite amiably.

"Janey, Janey!" remonstrated her mother.

"Nothing, my dear!" Enid laughed, and flung back her hair. "I really am interested in his painting. He's a very good painter indeed, I think."

"Yes, indeed he is!" admitted Jane, a little ashamed of herself.

"He's in France now, I think. He was in Salonica, you know."

"I know!" said Enid.

"Oh!" said Jane.

"Still in the YMCA?"

"I think so!"

"Well, I hope the War's over before he has time to serve any Horlick's milk to our Dick!"

"So do I! So do I!" breathed the two others piously.

"And you didn't issue the ultimatum?" asked Jane.

"Could I now?"

"You couldn't!"

"The place is bound up with Dick for her. You'd not get wild elephants to move her now. Well, I suppose now she'll stay there till the War's over, and I'll have to go down to Magnolia Street, whenever I want to see her."

"You don't mind, do you, Enid?"

"My dear, why should you say such a thing? I've a great affection for it in some ways. Like Max Emmanuel. And it hurts me, too, in some ways. I'll never be able to get it quite out of my mind."

"I see."

"I mean I've wanted to get out of it for ages!"

"I should jolly well think so!"

"And I want Mary to get out, too. She doesn't *belong*, does she?"

"No more than you!"

"And you don't either, Jane. You belong to America. You'll be an American girl, with a powder-puff in one hand and a lipstick in the other."

"Just let me catch her!" threatened Mrs Seipel. "There's that bell again!"

"I won't be an American girl!" said Jane rebelliously, and stamped her foot. "Don't talk about beastly America! Wait, Enid, I'll get chocolates and we'll read some poetry, shall we?"

"That'll be lovely!"

The poetry-reading was only interrupted by the shop door-bell tinkling every minute or two. Mrs Seipel came in and out, flushed and busy. She found time to make tea for the two girls. She admired the dainty way Enid balanced her cup on her knee. She was happy that Jane had a friend who was so much a lady. The reading of the smooth verses charmed her, though she had no clear notion of what they meant. Enid had a voice of silver brightness. She read and Jane listened. And then Enid left, and Jane read the same verses aloud again:

> "But when the third day from the hunting-morn
> Made a low splendour in the world, and wings
> Moved in her ivy, Enid, for she lay
> With her fair head in the dim-yellow light,
> Among the dancing shadows of the birds..."

"— with her fair head," Jane softly repeated, "in the dim-yellow light..."

"What's that, mamma, what's that? I'm sure I don't know where the Lemon Squash Gums are! *I* didn't put them away!"

Chapter 12

I

Mary Cooper's father died in 1910. Mary, in some senses, died a few years earlier, when she came to live in Magnolia Street. That was why she was incapable of making an effort to get out of it. A corpse does not trouble about the soil it is laid in.

But she was no corpse when Dick was about. He was seventeen now. To everything and everybody else in the world, she was less than half alive. She busied herself about John and Enid when they came to see her, she managed to read a certain amount of memoirs and biography. But if she had been deprived of all these, it would not have affected the tenor of her days. She would have gone on like a shade in a house of shades.

But it was not so when Dick was there. She breathed because of him and for him. When he came in after his day's work, she found there was sensation in the tips of her fingers where it had been lacking before. Where there had been twilight all day long, there was colour. It was strange that a youth so beautiful should be in no degree girlish. The purity of the gold in his hair had not been smirched by these twelve years of Doomington and three years of work in a smithy. He had no interest in schooling, and he wanted to bring in his few shillings a week at the earliest moment. So he had gone to work as a blacksmith's striker at the top of Blenheim Road. He liked horses and swinging hammers about. When he blew up the fire with the bellows, it was as if his whole head caught fire.

He was the darling of the girls and women in Magnolia Street, with that bright hair and his dark blue eyes; but he was serenely unconscious of it. He still remained unconscious of Nellie Tawnie's intention to marry him, though she had proposed to him explicitly more than once. He was a good footballer and played inside left for the local Begley Hill team. But it didn't seem enough for a strong lad like himself to be doing.

He was not seventeen, it was true. But he knew that David Emmanuel, one of the young chaps across the street, had joined up a year ago, when he too was not seventeen. So Dick Cooper went off in October and lied cheerfully about his age and was duly taken on. He went to the Flanders front in quite a few months.

It was a queer thing how his going darkened the street, already dark enough. When he left for the front the women moved about dejectedly and wrapped their shawls closer round their heads, as if they felt for the first time that year the nip of winter coming on. There was no difference to be observed in the demeanour of Mary Cooper. She always went about upright and pale, with no light in her eyes. They could not hear the fierce cry that rang in her head all day long:

"He must come back! I tell you, God, he must come back! It would be too foul a trick, even for you, God, if he did not come back! He must come back, I say! He must come back!"

Sometimes she saw him. Quite clearly she saw him. She could not make up her mind whether that meant she was out of her body, or he. She saw him playing 'House' on the floor of a hut in a big camp. His tunic hung on a nail behind him. His cap slanted down over one ear.

She saw him hunting for lice in the seams of his shirt. It was cold at night but he wore less than he did by day, thinking he might sleep through the cold but not the lice.

She saw him scramble over a parapet of sandbags, run so far as the barbed wire, then stoop to tear it out of his puttees. He was walking back out of the line. His eyes were shut as he moved. He was too tired to keep them open. Somebody pushed him out of the communication trench. They were shelling it with extreme accuracy. He staggered on among the shell-holes.

"But he'll come back, I tell you!" Mary Cooper said with grim white lips. For months she saw nothing at all, not even the table at which she was flattening out some dough with a rolling-pin. She seemed like one locked up in a concrete hut. She waited till the opaque stuff was disintegrated so that she might have sight of him again wherever he might be. Sometimes for a minute instant of time an image formed itself against and beyond the stubborn walls. He bent his head as he went down into a dugout. A point of corrugated iron caught his cap. She saw the glint of his hair, and at once the concrete imprisoned it.

Her sister, Enid, sought to withdraw her from this obsession, to put into her eyes some other aspect than that strained watching. She could not get her to visit her at the private school in Northenden where she taught. So she came back herself to Magnolia Street, though the journey distressed her. But she seemed to make no deeper impression on her sister than a coal

387

falling into the grate, even though they sat and talked for an hour or two and Mary made tea and toast like any sane efficient woman.

"He must come back!" the voice said, Mary's own voice, in the mournful catacomb of her brain.

Then she would again perceive the lad, in a sudden rush of visions that winked and twinkled like the lights of a train rushing at night by the edge of fretted water. He was back in the trench again. He had been working his way back on his belly since midnight, four hours ago. He was drinking beer in a brasserie with half-a-dozen other lance-corporals. There was a sergeant there, too. Had he already written to tell her he had got his first stripe? He was sewing a button on his trousers, sitting under a tree in spring leaf. The grass was cool under his thighs.

The visions came upon her all in the same few moments, though they rendered a real or unreal sight of him in widely removed times and places. It was as if they waited outside the doors of her spirit, till she became sensitive to them, and then they crowded in together in any order.

The lad was involved in some of the most formidable fighting in the War and came through without a scratch. Nothing more serious happened to him during the planetary combustions of April, 1918, than that he was forced to go sick with a poisoned hand. It recovered and he went back again to bullets pinging like mosquitoes and shells clattering like carts loaded with crockery. Bullets and shells seemed to be deflected from their orbits by an effluence that went about with him. Perhaps it was the demon obstinacy of a silent woman over in England, in Doomington, that fenced him about with a wall of ether from which shells slid away obliquely like flat stones ricochetting from water.

"He must come back! He must come back!" her voice went shrilling louder than sound across the land and the sea and the land. But there were other women who willed as obstinately as Mary Cooper that their loves should come back again, and they did not. And there were men who saw more fighting than Dick Cooper, and they, too, came back. It was chance, therefore, that the lad survived all those desperate hazards. But Mary Cooper did not believe this. She believed that, after all, there was a God, and a benevolent one, and that he heard her crying out in the little lightless street, and so her brother came back again.

Colour came into her cheeks, a brightness into her eyes, and stayed there. She had never known such happiness as was with her during the two years that followed. Dick went back to his smithy and swung his hammer lustily upon the anvil and flung his hair from his sweating forehead in the hot breath of the furnace. He met a girl and went out 'courting' with her and brought her home to Mary, who excelled herself in the scones and tea-cakes and cakes with marzipan and icing she prepared for the young lovers, for Dick, like his girl, had a sweet tooth.

He took up his football again for his local club and hardly a match went by in that second season after the War but he scored at least once. He was a peaceful lad and never quarrelled with anyone. But somehow, one Saturday afternoon, as the two teams came off the ground, a little breeze blew up between Dick and one of the opposing half-backs — Bill Staple, his name was. It had not been as clean a game as you might like.

"I tell you I wasn't off-side!" said Dick.

"And I bloody well tell you you was!" said Bill.

"Oh I was, was I!" said Dick. "Well how's this for off-side?"

The two lads were hard at it in half a minute.

"Give him one, Dick!"

"Downstairs, Bill!"

"Oo, that's a good 'un!"

Dick had an idea or two about boxing. His brother, John, used to put the gloves on with him from time to time. He got in one or two sound hooks to Bill's chin. They shook him up a bit. Then Bill came in again. Dick slipped. Bill's fist caught him full on the left temple. He slid to the ground without a word. He smiled a little. A small line of froth came up on the side of his mouth.

"Christ!" said Bill.

"Best take him to the Yiddisher hospital!" someone said. "It ain't far from 'ere!"

"Ain't nowt wrong with 'im!" someone else said. "'E's only just knocked a bit silly. 'E don't live far. Take 'im 'ome, I say!"

They took him off to Magnolia Street. He was mumbling a little. His girl was waiting for him. Mary had a steaming bath ready and as noble an assortment of cakes as a prince might fancy. He did not recognise his girl or his sister.

The women came running in. "Dr Shulman!" cried Mrs Carter. "He's just gone in to see his old man!"

Dr Shulman was paying his Sabbath visit to his father. He came in at once. He shook his head. He was mystified.

"This is beyond me," he said. "It's not an ordinary case of concussion. You must get another doctor in, at once."

But by the time the other doctor came, the lad whom all the embattled furies did not destroy, bombs and machine-gun bullets and shrapnel-shells, was dead.

There was an inquest. A small bruise was found on the side of his forehead and the rim of the upper jaw was fractured. The police surgeon recommended that the charge against the wretched Bill Staple should not be proceeded with. The blow on the cheek, he decided, had not caused death. Death was due to compression of the brain tissue due wholly to the continued lifting and swinging of his hammer at his work. He would have died the same death, but he agreed that death might not have taken place for some time yet.

So the women of Magnolia Street came in and mourned, all of them, with his sister, Mary. The Jewish women had had no dealings at all with the lad. How should they? But his simplicity and beauty were such that he seemed to all of them an incarnation of some dear and secret dream. The Jewish women lifted up their voices and wailed loudly, as was their custom, for they had come from the east at one time, where mourners show no restraint, but sway and moan and howl and tear their hair.

But loudest of them all, the Englishwoman, Mary Cooper, shrieked and clapped her hands and smote the wall with her forehead. The quiet tall woman had found a voice at length. The gentile women stole away. They were ashamed. Among them was the dead lad's sister, Enid, who had come over from the polite little private school in Northenden. She stole away, her heart cold with shame. But the Jewish women stayed all night long, wailing; their grief grew less at length and they tried to quiet Mary Cooper. But she would not be quieted.

Chapter 13

I

Mr Carter, the night-watchman and ex-policeman, was also an ex-soldier. He had belonged to section D of the Army Reserve, which meant that at the expiry of his twelve years' service he undertook a further four years' reserve liability. But that, too, had expired. He was getting on in years. However, they made no bones about accepting him when he enlisted early in the War. He was just the sort of man they were looking for.

He missed his wife a good deal, though she had a tendency to get a little shrill at times. In the period between his dismissal from the Police Force and his appointment as night-watchman in Rawlinson's Engine Works, she had quite dithered him, she nagged such a lot. But she had had to take in washing and that doesn't improve tempers.

Yet when he went to France he realised for the first time what a dear little woman she really was, and what a nice little backgarden he had, and how he could get on without his bitch terrier, Bucky, he didn't quite know.

In the trenches he missed his dog even more than his wife. Bucky was such a favourite with rats, and there were so many in the trenches that only a Bucky could cope with them. She would do it all with kindness, of course. She would point out to them that there wasn't room for quite so many soldiers and so many rats in the same dugout. And they would nod their heads and wipe their noses and go away. They would do anything for Bucky.

Sally Carter developed into a great sock-knitter during the early part of the War. Usually she made his socks much too small for him, for it was difficult to remember how big his feet were unless you had them under your eye. Sometimes she suddenly realised she had been underestimating his feet. In a panic she produced a pair of socks large enough to comfort the ankles of an elephant. Hannibal's army might have made some use of them.

In addition to knitting socks she wrote letters, lovely letters, all about everything. She wrote about their lodger, Mr. Stern, the missionary. He practically never left the house these days. She was just a little afraid he might develop into a nuisance, though she could never quite decide whether it was more or less of a nuisance if he stayed in all day. It was true he never trod on her scrubbed steps while they were still damp. But she couldn't let him go all day and all night and well into the next day without even a drop of tea to wet his lips. Do it for himself he simply wouldn't. He'd lost all interest in eating and drinking. So she had to make him a drop of tea and a bite of something to eat and stand over him till he got it down.

On the whole the balance tilted in favour of his being a nuisance, what with the awful state his floor was in, with books and rulers and scraps of paper everywhere. Always reckoning, he was, adding up and multiplying and subtracting till it made you fair dizzy to look at him.

"I beg you to understand, Mrs Carter," he said to her, "the Kingdom is at hand. You must prepare yourself. Write to your husband also. The year 1917 which is upon us is the year appointed by prophecy and calculated by logic. *In manus tuas, Domine.*"

She wrote and told Bill, her husband, what Mr, Stern said; not in the words he used, of course. She said if he weren't so weak and gentle she'd have been real scared. But if you asked her, the year 1917 wouldn't much concern *him*, and she didn't know how soon she'd have to get busy and look out for a new lodger. It was just as Sally said. He died on her at the end of October, 1916, and if it hadn't been for the neighbours, she didn't know how she'd have got through it.

Particularly as she was having a little trouble with Bucky. Bucky was pining for her master something dreadful, and it brought her all out in eczema. All she hoped was to keep Bucky alive till Bill got his next leave home. She got quite bad-tempered with the rats, she fretted so much; and she was all pink under her black nose. You mustn't forget Bucky's getting on in years, ten if she's a day she is, always sitting on the blue mat under the stairs thinking of her master.

Lovely letters... Bill Carter couldn't bear to destroy one. The pockets of his tunic bulged with them.

Then Bill Carter came back on leave, and Bucky, his terrier, was still alive when he came. She had a sense of situation and of type. She recalled how another dog had greeted another wanderer on his home-coming. So she wagged her tail like Argos, of whom Homer sang, and dropped both her ears. And Bill Carter, like Odysseus, looked aside and wiped away a tear that he hid from Sally. But upon Bucky came the fate of black death even in the hour that she beheld Bill Carter again, in her tenth year... or it may have been her twelfth, for no record was kept of her pedigree.

Though she wasn't any too strong, Sally was taking in a bit of washing these days, for the two lodgers who had followed Mr Stern were in the full sense of the word nuisances and with the aid of one or two of the neighbours home on leave she had turned them out. But of course she did no washing while Bill was home. It was lovely being together, like another honeymoon. Now they would weep a tear for Bucky, now bill and coo like a pair of turtle-doves. It was a little silly, they told themselves, for they were both over forty. But he looked as handsome in her eyes as on the day, long ago, when she first set eyes on him in his brave uniform. And he wondered if there was in all Doomington a woman with as fair a skin and as soft a voice as hers.

He went back to France again, and he came home in 1918. It was a strange thing that he did, for shortly before the War ended, he was sitting in a hut with a dozen other soldiers playing House, when a shell dropped through the corrugated iron roof. The shell put paid to the accounts of most of them. Two others were badly wounded. But when the smoke and the stink cleared away, there was Bill Carter sitting in the rubble, the pillars of his legs stretched out before him, his thick thumbs revolving round each other steadily. For despite his size, he was so easy a person to miss, that even the shell had not noticed him.

So he came back again to Magnolia Street. He arrived a day or two earlier than he expected, but he wanted to surprise her, so he did not send a wire. It was getting dark when he came, and Sally had not put the light on. There was a big fire behind her to boil her buckets of water, and she stood over a tub soaping a garment on a scrubbing board. The light flickered on the silver vase he had won for bowls, long ago. As Bill Carter advanced towards his wife, he seemed to sway and shake across a swirl of rosy mist. If Sally had read Homer, she would have thought how much he looked like the giant Polyphemus in his cavern, for he was so great in his simplicity that he evoked epical images.

But she did not say "Polyphemus!" at him. "Bill!" she cried, "My Bill!" and flung her soapy arms as high up him as she could reach and he bent down yards and yards and kissed her.

II

Mrs Carter had a bad time in the War, as a whole. After Mr Stern died, she had lodgers who robbed her. She had to take in washing. She fell ill. She was always writing letters to her husband, but he was bad at answering them. Sometimes she was without news for weeks at a stretch. But she went on mutely with her washing.

It was rather odd she was so silent, for she always used to say quite loud how ill she was, though there can have been nothing much wrong.

"Oh my poor liver!" she would say, holding her hand above her left kidney. "Catches me every time I breathe!" she complained, as if she breathed with her kidneys. But five minutes later she would be soothing her right kidney and complaining that her Bill didn't feel sorry for her, he was always pottering about in the back-garden, and she wished she were dead, and it would be better for everyone all round.

But her misfortunes in the War made her a different woman. So did the misfortunes of her neighbour, Mrs Briggs, the wife of the odd-job-man.

But could you blame Mrs Briggs? Can you blame a woman, when she loses her husband and her son in filthy War, that the wine in her turns to gall? That her voice that was so sweet once croaks like a corncrake across the stony stubble? You cannot blame her.

But it was a sad thing. Isaac Emmanuel perceived it and was much pained by it. Mary Cooper perceived it, but she was capable of feeling pain about no person or thing except her brother.

Henry Briggs did not come back from France, for he was killed during the attack on Vimy. Her elder son, Frankie, died in a hospital in York. No wonder Mrs Briggs went to pieces.

There were many people in the street who deplored the change, but none so keenly as Isaac Emmanuel. He had often stood at his doorstep twinkling happily through his glasses, at the sight of Mrs Briggs and Mrs Seipel advancing to meet each other in the middle of the roadway. He invested them with the rank of Delegate Extraordinary from their races. The secret agenda on their programme was the abolition of racial prejudice, though their ostensible topics of discussion were Sam's tonsils and Frankie's winter pants.

394

If there was one occasion during the whole of the War when Mr Emmanuel was unreservedly happy, it was the occasion of Mrs Briggs's onslaught on Mrs Derricks, when she and her Boys raided the house of Elsa Stanley, the German spy. He arrived on the scene at the end of the proceedings, in time to see Mr Stanley drop the little Nightingale through his window like a bag of rubbish and to hear Mrs Briggs screaming: "Yer fat sow, get back into your sty again! The poor little woman up there, goin' to 'ave a baby an' all! D'y'ear what I say? I'll tear every 'air out of yer lousy 'ead!"

Mr Emmanuel disapproved of such language and behaviour on principle. But he knew that the Derrickses were the supreme enemies of Love in those parts, and that if ever a doughty blow had been struck for Love, Mrs Briggs had struck it that day. He walked on air. He sang blithely to himself for days and days after.

Alas, poor gentleman! He was not aware how soon the poor woman would lose her husband and her son, and how swift and desperate a change it would work in her. By the time the earth had completed the half of one more revolution round its star, Mrs Briggs, too, had become a shouter from the pavement, an enemy of Love as besotted as Mrs Derricks. But whereas the second had transferred her odium from the Jews to the Germans, Mrs Briggs had become an uncompromising Jew-hater.

Magnolia Street was familiar with the sentiments she voiced; Mrs Derricks had proclaimed them often enough, but it was an odd thing that they should have seeped into Mrs Briggs's soul and lain there like a black mud all these years.

"'Oo killed Christ?" asked poor heart-broken Mrs Briggs. But that was only a formula. In the Lamb and Lion she accused the Jews of Magnolia Street of a later wickedness.

"It's all them Jews!" she hiccuped. "It's them wot made this War! My poor 'Enry and Frankie, alive and 'andsome this day they'd be if not for these 'ere Jews! Them and their fine 'ouses and motor-cars, while my poor boys — O 'Enry, 'Enry!"

The others sought to console her. But she merely lifted her bleary eyes to them, and shook her head, and did not understand a word.

And then one Friday evening in November, Mrs Seipel came back from Hulme on a sad duty to Magnolia Street. For news had come to the Emmanuels that their youngest son, David, had been killed in the War. And Mrs Seipel came down to sit with them and mourn.

And as she walked down the street she heard a voice she recognised lifted in derision. She had been told by folk that came to visit her of the dreadful change that had fallen on Mrs Briggs, her old friend. She had been back once or twice to Magnolia Street since her removal, but she had not set eyes on her until that evening. She stopped. Her blood froze in her dismay.

"Yah!" cried Mrs Briggs. "Get back to Germany! That's where you all belong! Spies and conchies the 'ole bloody lot of you! 'Oo killed Christ?" she added, as if the rest were not enough.

She was sitting on the edge of the pavement: with her feet in the gutter. Her hair lay loosely over her flushed face. She shook her fist at the door of the Emmanuels, behind which they mourned their dead.

And then a great anger and a great pity swept like a fire through Mrs Seipel's blood. She rushed across the roadway and seized Mrs Briggs's head between her two hands and shook it desperately as if she would shake out the poison that was clotted there.

"Shame on you, Mrs Briggs, shame on you!" she cried. "To be carrying on like that opposite that house! Do you know what you're saying? Do you know the news that's come to them today? Do you? Or don't you? Answer me, I say! I say answer me!"

"Lemme go! Lemme go!" complained Mrs Briggs. "Leggo of my 'ead!"

"I won't let you go! I won't! Don't you know they've heard only today that their boy was killed in France? Went out a year before he needed, the poor boy! Do you know? And you talk like that? Oh Mrs Briggs, shame on you!"

"Wot's that yer sayin'? 'Oo *are* you? Aren't you...?"

"Hold your head up! Yes, it's me! Mrs Seipel! Little did I ever think..."

"Wot's that yer was sayin'? Their boy, them people opposite, killed in France?"

"And you sitting here shouting and cursing! For shame, Mrs Briggs!"

"God forgive me, Mrs Seipel! I'm drunk! God forgive me! Them poor people with their boy killed... like Frankie, my Frankie! And 'is father, too! Did you know they'd killed my Frankie? My 'ead's that bad..."

"Get up now, Mrs Briggs, this very moment! Poor, poor Frankie! No, take this handkerchief! Come, let's go into your kitchen! Now, Mrs Briggs, now! Up! This way!"

And Mrs Seipel led Mrs Briggs into her own house and the two women sat there and wept for men who go to the Wars and die in them. And later, thinking Mrs Briggs asleep on the sofa where she had laid her, Mrs Seipel stole out and crossed the pavement to the house of the Emmanuels.

But Mrs Briggs was not asleep. She was more desolate than she had ever been since the moment she set eyes on the blistered body of her son lying dead in the hospital in York. She was half mad with shame. She lifted a jug from its hook and slunk through her back door to get it filled at the jug and bottle department of the Lamb and Lion.

Chapter 14

I

It may have been an accident that it was opposite the house of the Emmanuels that Mrs Briggs sat down and cursed, the day their sad news came to them. Or it may not have been an accident.

For a rather sinister report had been spreading round Magnolia Street for quite a long time. It was said that Mr Emmanuel wanted the War to stop. Perhaps Mrs Derricks had been more than usually indignant that day in the Lamb and Lion about Mr Emmanuel, and her indignation penetrated even the muddled wits of Mrs Briggs. So Mrs Briggs sat down with her feet in the gutter, shouting and shaking her fist.

It was precisely because Mrs Briggs had already lost her Henry and Frankie, and because he didn't want her to lose her Tony, who would be called up in a year or so, that Mr Emmanuel wanted the War to stop; also because Arthur Durbin was dead and Albert Durbin had lost his eyes and Benny Edelman had lost his leg, and there were lots of lives and eyes and legs still to be lost if the War did not stop.

But Mrs Briggs didn't see it like that; so she sat and raved while the women gathered in the dark kitchen of the Emmanuels and swayed to and fro in the unsteady candlelight, because news had come that David, the youngest, had been killed.

Mrs Derricks was very magnanimous about it. "That'll knock the nonsense out of 'im!" she said. "All this 'ere German propyganda about stoppin' the War and cetra! That'll learn 'im."

But David's death did not have that effect at all on Mr Emmanuel. He didn't want the War to go on till everybody else's David was knocked out, too. Before, when he wanted the War to stop, it was an emotion based on his general love for mankind. Now it was tied up with an acute personal anguish, and when he read that the Allies, or the Germans, had suffered so many thousand casualties, it was merely David dying so many thousand separate deaths.

Himself, Mr Emmanuel was a somewhat weedy specimen, despite his height and his broad shoulders, but his faith in humanity was a growth of extreme tenacity. He soon realised that the War was not a personal insult directed against his humanitarian convictions. He recovered something of his old jauntiness at the thought that War had become so unspeakable, quite clearly it would never happen again. The thought helped him, later, to recover from his grief at the death of his son, for he felt, in a way hitherto impossible to him, that he was buttressed by the grief or fear of a hundred million fathers.

He knew there was no chance of organising public meetings for the time being, so the most chimaerical projects for stopping the War whistled like comets across his brain, mischievously lashing their gassy tails. He would organise a women's crusade to sweep over the trenches from both sides to make the soldiers down guns. But he stood at his door and looked round at the women and turned his thoughts elsewhere.

He would invent a sort of sleeping-snuff, in collaboration with a chemist who would do the actual inventing. He and his associates would blow it into the air and it would enter the nostrils of all the generals, the admirals, the statesmen, the soldiers, the munition-makers. They would fall asleep at their posts for three days and nights and when they awakened, it would be impossible to resume the War, for everything would be completely disorganised. That scheme, too, seemed impracticable on reflection.

He wondered if a worldwide Prayer Week might be organised. He was very modern in his conception of prayer and considered that it was a type of etheric wave, like light or wireless.

But all these schemes required collaboration on a large scale and his efforts to enlist even two or three collaborators involved a lot of misrepresentation. It was bad enough for Mrs Derricks to shoulder him into the gutter when she passed him on Blenheim Road. It was worse for the Rabbi's wife to call "Sherman!" after him when he went off to his work at the Board of Guardians. It was worse when Mrs Briggs screamed filth at his house the day the news came that David was dead.

But the War must be over some day, he consoled himself. He blew his nose and wiped his glasses. It was clear that then at length Love would have its chance. He hoped he might take the chair at the meeting in the Longton Town Hall, at which the reign of Love would be officially inaugurated. He still collected foreign stamps, and was very defiant about his German and Austrian specimens.

The Emmanuels had three sons and only one of them seemed to be interested in the Emmanuel gospel of everybody loving everybody. This was Moisheh, the *meshuggene*, or mad one, as they called him, the one with a face like a horse. He never thought of seconding his father on public platforms, for he only had a small vocabulary, which consisted largely of "Hup! Hup! Hup!" That was the way he addressed his horse when they went clattering off together, doing their milk rounds. It was also the way he addressed his women. "Hup! Hup! Hup!" he said at them and they came up to him and kissed him obediently, or did anything else he wanted them to do. It made no difference to him at all whether they were gentile women or Jewish women, white or black ones, he loved them all equally, and in that sense he was a confirmed supporter of his father's doctrines.

Yet his parents did not welcome the practical support that Moisheh gave them. It was illogical of them. However, he went his own way, saying "Hup! Hup! Hup!" to his horse and his women. They too, like himself, had rather horse-like faces.

By the time the War started he had settled down a bit. He confined his attentions to one lady, a gentile she happened to be, but if she had struck his fancy, he wouldn't have minded her being a Parsee or a Jewess. They lived together and were quite happy. He had little ambition and less imagination. He was quite content to go on driving a milk cart all his days. For a long time it did not dawn on him that now that a War had broken out, he might be useful driving a limber instead.

But when at last it penetrated his skull he roared out "Hup!" fearfully and went off to the War and became a gunner. On the 24th of June 1916, he helped to fire off several of the fifty-two thousand tons of ammunition which were discharged behind the line between St. Pierre Divion and Maricourt.

The change in Moisheh Emmanuel that is to be recorded may have started then. Some convolutions in his brain may have been straightened out and a few straight surfaces convoluted, in all that noise and vibration. But most of the work was clearly done a year and a half later, in Palestine.

Moisheh Emmanuel was there. He bombarded Gaza, cleared the way to Ramleh and Ludd, and though he was not actually invited to enter Jerusalem with General Allenby, he cried "Hup! Hup!" in triumph till all the Turks that looked on from Moab and Gilead sweated with fear.

They sent him back again to France in the spring of 1918, but he had made up his mind to return to Palestine some day. When the War ended, he went back to Doomington, to the gentile lady with whom he had lived out of wedlock. He told her that she was going to be a Jewess and she looked frightened, for she thought it involved a surgical operation. He then presented her to Rabbi Shulman and stated that he desired the lady to be initiated into the mysteries of the Jewish faith, for he intended to wed her, and then to go forth with her to Palestine and till the ground there and have children there.

The lady was obedient, but not clever. It took her a long time to realise that rabbits and cockles had both passed out of her life for ever, and that a chicken was damned in death, as it had been in life, if a needle were found in its digestive organs.

And then Moisheh Emmanuel married her and took her to the land where Lord Balfour and the leagued nations had undertaken to assist them in the establishment of a National Home.

They were accepted on the roster of a colony in Esdraelon and Mrs Moisheh Emmanuel was a much more punctilious Jewess than many of her colleagues, who had had enough of meat-salting and prayer-intoning during their ghetto days by Dnieper and Danube.

As for Moisheh, none of the colonists was more lusty than he. He wore a white smock embroidered round the collar with forget-me-nots, and shorts also, and sandals. His face was brick-red, like the pimpernel in the stubble; it was still like a horse's face to look at, but a somewhat sanctified horse, a Biblical horse. And in the time of the gathering in of the sheaves he went up behind his team from the fields against Gideon's brook, cracking his whip and crying "Hup! Hup! Hup!" till the whole valley rang all the way to the hills of Gilboa.

III

Max Emmanuel, brother of Moisheh, was a painter. He had no other interest in the world than painting. He did not love Love or his father or his mother or his brothers or girls. He had a certain love of money, but that was because, if he disregarded money, he would have to go and press clothes or do ladies' fashion drawings or be a minor clerk in the Board of Guardians;

whereas if he made money, he could buy lots and lots of carbons, pastels, paints, brushes, the best linen for his canvases, lovely faded gold frames for his paintings.

He won a scholarship at the Doomington Art Academy, but he did not like it, so he went to London and became a Bohemian; and wore red shirts and black shirts and sombreros and lived in Fitzroy Square and slept on a divan and had lots of cushions but no chairs, and candles stuck in beer bottles but no gas mantles.

He went to parties in Charlotte Street, and to some even so far as Chelsea. They lasted all night and he drank at them, and sang and did solo dances. But he painted all day so long as the light lasted. He painted the blue thighs of Dora Pettigrew. He painted the faces of the maidens of Magnolia Street, Rachel Shulman with her black hair across her eyes, and Nellie Tawnie with a coppery sheen in the gold hair, the pursed bow of Rose Berman's lips, the chubby pale hand of Bella Winberg paddling over a red plush sofa.

Max Emmanuel was born into a household where Love clung like ivy to everything, and Love followed him to Fitzroy Square. For even in Fitzroy Square, in those libidinous back-bedrooms, the female breasts and buttocks he painted with such quivering carnality were misunderstood. They did not realise that those objects only fascinated him when they were transmuted into pigment. Otherwise they meant little more to him than door-knobs.

So a word went about among the painting women, of a corybantic stallion that had come up into the studios from Doomington. They heard him sing and saw him do solo dances at their parties, and the sallow women looked on him with pouchy eyes and lusted. They misunderstood him as completely as the church-wardens on provincial art gallery councils, who turned down his pictures because they were so lewd.

And when the painting women gave parties in their back bedrooms, they sought to get rid of the other men at dawn and to keep Max Emmanuel behind to entertain them. But he itched for his easel and when they turned round a moment to snuff out a fallen candle-end that threatened to set the cushions alight, he was gone.

That exacerbated them the more. They felt that when at last they had noosed him, the entertainment he would provide would be something to combine the fervour of a negro rape with the fastidious languor of a royalist vicomte. But they did not noose him at their parties. He slipped away. And that was why, when Max Emmanuel himself gave a party, Sarah Minnett wrapped herself in a rug and hid in a corner pretending to be a bolster.

When the other guests had gone, Sarah threw off the rug and informed Max she loved him. The word struck on Max's eardrum with an odious familiarity. His father used to utter it frequently, and it so embarrassed him, he blushed and choked. It sounded more intimate and repulsive on Sarah's lips.

She was a tall woman with a firm jaw and naked clavicles. She meant what she said. She took possession. She did not allow him to go out to parties as often as he used to, because of the designing women that lurked about at them, to entrap young painters. She reproached him frequently with not loving her; and he did not. So far as women made an impact upon him outside of their paintability, the curved sort gave him a mild pleasure, for it seemed to him the angular had the advantages of neither sex. But although he did not love her, said Sarah Minnett, she loved him. She threw her bony arms about him and punctured his cheek with her sharp nose.

It then occurred to Max Emmanuel a War was raging between the nations. It had been raging for nearly a year now but the painters of Charlotte Street and Fitzroy Square had not been much put out by it. The things they used to paint with and to eat and drink at parties went up in price steadily, and sometimes a patron who promised to buy a picture, did not buy it; for he had gone to the War. He might be dead, even. Apart from such embarrassments, the painters did not notice the War until unpleasant edicts were brought to their notice early in 1916 according to which they were deemed to have enlisted.

Some went to Ireland, some broke stones on Dartmoor, some painted pictures of soldiers in trenches, some elected to occupy the same. But Max Emmanuel had left Fitzroy Square months earlier. He had had so much love lately from Sarah Minnett, that the sudden realisation there was an enormous hate competition going on all over Europe intoxicated him.

He had not sold any pictures for some time, but he had a few shillings in his pocket, so he took the train back to Doomington, for he thought it would be agreeable, before joining the army, to see his young brother, David. He arrived at a Doomington quite void of brothers. It was extraordinary how many brothers had joined up in every direction.

He was a little chagrined to find that David was not there when he arrived. He felt rather lost without him. He always took David for granted, but things did not run at all so smoothly in his absence. Yes, he was rather angry that David had not written to him that he was going to join up. Why had he not written? Or had he?

David used to send him letters every couple of weeks, for it made him happy to feel he was still in touch with his brother, the genius, even if the genius was far too busy to send him an answer. Excepting, of course, if he wanted something. Then Max would write quite an amiable letter and David would get the thing done before a day had passed. Had David written to him to say he was going to join up?

Max couldn't remember. David's letters were illiterate, written in pencil as a rule, in a big boyish hand. He had left school at the age of fourteen in a low standard, for he was not clever. He was now a machiner of ladies' garments. Max wished that he hadn't crumpled up David's letters without even reading them. Suppose the poor kid got knocked on the head sometime. His heart stopped quite dead at the thought. Max suddenly realised that he cared for the lad a good deal more than he had known.

He knew that David loved him. He now also knew that he liked David quite a lot. The kid didn't make a song about loving him. Max appreciated that. It was a thing you couldn't help appreciating in the house of Isaac Emmanuel, where you had Love served up at all meals and at odd snacks in between.

A young man who had been suffering for months from the more exacting form of Love Sarah Minnett handed out, appreciated David's restraint all the more. He was really quite cross with David for going off like that.

And besides, the kid was only just seventeen, wasn't he? He was. Max was furious. It was absolutely unreasonable for him to go off and enlist a full year before his time just to make things uncomfortable for his brother. Mr and Mrs Emmanuel were both angry about it, too. Had they not already provided the army with a soldier in the person of their first-born, Moisheh? Could he not kill off enough Germans for one family?

As a matter of fact, David *had* written to Max to tell him that he couldn't stick it any longer not being in the army. He wanted Max not to write and tell them at home about it till he'd done it, and would Max wish him luck?

Max was obviously too busy in London painting the portraits of VCs and generals to have time to write to Magnolia Street. David gave Max a fortnight to write in, then another week, then another week. Every morning he waited for the postman's knock wistfully, but when he came he brought no word from Max.

He would have liked to take with him a nice cheery note from Max. It would have been a sort of talisman. He had a funny feeling about this War. He felt he had to go to it, but somehow, at the end of it... but there was no end of it... not for *him* at any rate.... He had the sensation of a sudden hot thrust on the left side of his chest and then of heaps of yellow clay pressing down on him all over. It was silly of him. He kicked himself. But he would have liked a note from old Max, just wishing him luck, only that. He'd have put it in a leather case and put the leather case in the pocket of his tunic over his heart. And that bullet might have glided off then. He could hear the sound of the deflected bullet striking against a petrol tin — a sound it would never make. For Max didn't send that note. And David never put it in a leather case over his heart. He just went off and lied about his age and they took him.

He had to go. He couldn't wait. Belgium had something to do with it. He was a credulous boy, and it may have been somewhat vain of him to feel that his going would help little Belgium get on its stocky little legs again. But that was precisely the effect all that Belgium propaganda aimed at. And with young David Emmanuel it registered a bull's eye.

It wasn't only Belgium. It was Max, too. He knew what a fool he was, but that's what it felt like and he just couldn't get away from it. He had to join up for Max's sake and for his painting. He was a rather superstitious youth and never walked under ladders and always threw salt over his left shoulder and touched wood. But if he touched all the timber in the forests of the Rockies there wasn't any turning that bullet aside that was coming for one of them. Or it might be a shell. Or a big torpedo coming through the water. He had a feeling it was a bullet. It was coming straight for him and Max, and he must get in its way.

Max must go on with that painting. He was a genius. He himself was a machiner of ladies' clothing and could be spared more easily. Not that he didn't enjoy life. Not half he didn't. He liked that little girl, Lily Weintrobe. They were getting on fine together. She was a bit shy, but he was, too; that is to say with girls. Not with fellows. They'd soon find how shy he was if they started taking liberties. When he came on leave in his khaki, he might kiss her, but he was not sure. Because if he kissed her some day, if everything was all right, he might marry her. And he wouldn't like to do that before Max saw her and said he liked her.

Oh yes, David enjoyed life. He went regularly to see Doomington City, he didn't care much for United. And he could skate a bit and sometimes the boys from his club went out for long walks in Derbyshire on Saturdays.

Well, there was lots of football in the army and certainly lots of nice long walks. So he joined up. He put the date down in the little shiny blue-backed exercise book he used as a diary. On the day Max came back from Le Havre and learned that David had been killed in France, he found that diary and read that entry. It was less a diary than a brief biographical record. "And then September tenth went to British Army," he read. That was all. As he read, Max's eyes were quite dry. But there was a hot pricking under his eyelids.

IV

It is unlikely that there was any collusion between David Emmanuel and the military authorities. He cannot have explained to them, that he had enlisted a year before his time in order that his brother Max, a genius, might be left to get on peacefully with his painting. But it looked like that.

The authorities didn't want Max at any price. He had patches on his lungs, fibroid growths on his tonsils and the valves of his heart revolted them. They wouldn't touch him with a bayonet.

Max envisioned with horror the prospect of keeping house again with Sarah Minnett in Fitzroy Square. What to do in order not to keep house again with Sarah Minnett? He thought with distaste of working at munitions. Besides, nothing would prevent Sarah Minnett working at the same munitions if she got to hear about them. He did not fancy himself as an agricultural labourer. By a process of elimination, he arrived at the YMCA which he joined a month or two later.

There was a chance of his meeting David in some YMCA hut. He did not worry whether or not he met Moisheh. It was very unlikely he would meet Sarah Minnett. Besides, in the intervals of whisking Horlick's, he thought he might do a little painting sometimes.

Max was destined never to throw Love quite off his traces. He found there was any amount of Love to be busy with in the YMCA, in addition to whisking Horlick's and selling packets of Woodbines. It was not a love which included the enemy within its scope, but apart from that, it was very comprehensive. And as he moved on from camp to camp, from Winchester to Aldershot, from Aldershot to Seaford, he found that he was less and less interested in painting and more and more interested in whisking Horlick's milk. Or in spreading the dusty floor with tea-leaves and sweeping them up again. Or in cutting vast monoliths of slab cake into slices. For it was for David he whisked the milk and cut the cake, and for David's nostrils he tried to sweeten the stale air with tea-leaves.

A torpor fell on that part of his brain — it was the greater part — with which he painted, and always ached to paint, the blue thighs of Dora Pettigrew. With the remaining part — he had hardly suspected it existed — he thought of David, loved David. He could not drive out of his mind the extra year which the lad had laid down on the altars of the army — as a propitiation, an intercession.

The fantastic words formed themselves in his mind. He did not evoke them. He hardly knew what they meant. He kicked himself earnestly. How many thousands of high spirited lads had gone off to the phantom sound of pipes and sight of banners — at sixteen, at fifteen! But he knew, he *knew*, it was not mere War-romance with David, though the child was quixotic enough and doubtless deplored Belgium as they asked him to, and was not insensitive to pipes and banners!

Twirling the wet broom into a bucket, Max asked himself quietly whether all the banded artistry of Fitzroy Square was worth a single hair of the head of his small brother, David. He received frequent letters from David, bearing the addresses of his various camps — Hexham Park Camp, Wangford, Suffolk; Number 7 Camp, Prees Heath, Whitechurch, Salop. Max did not crumple them up before he read them and throw them away as he used to. He took them with him wherever he went and cherished them as if a sweetheart had sent them. They were clumsy letters, about nothing at all, or very little. But to Max, they seemed lovelier than any of the canvases any of them had turned out in Fitzroy Square.

As for instance:

What I'm thinking of mostly at the present moment is when we both meet on leave what a ripping time we'll have. You know the time is getting on since we both saw each other in dear old Doomington. Won't it be great when both of us will be at home at the same time. Gee-whiz when I only think of it. I do so hope you are keeping on painting when you get the time. I would try and write much more to you, only at the present time I am in an extreme hurry and in a rather uncomfortable position for writing in. Any road, I leave you in the best of health, hoping you are no different and painting strong and here's the best of luck until we meet again. I am your truest ownest brother,

David.

X X X X

There was not much more in them than that, a wryly humorous note about the sergeant-major, a word of thanks for the gift of a safety razor:

a jolly good thing you done for me, seemingly small in size but priceless gift, to send me that safety razor because to get used to one of the army razors is jolly difficult and how painful, gee-whiz.

But one note, more artless than the others, affected Max most of all. There was little equity in the size of the slices of slab cake he cut that day, some being a good threepennyworth and others hardly a ha'porth:

Well, how are you keeping, I wonder, I am all right and quite cheerful. Tomorrow we go out, to France, I believe, just to see what the climate is like over there, I hear. Anyhow, thank God, I am feeling as confident as ever and going out with a jolly strong heart, to come back again soon. I don't suppose it is necessary for me to tell you not to worry or anything like that, as I know you now, but when you visit home next time tell them I was quite happy now and that I am now also.

Lots and lots of X X X X X X

David.

P.S. Don't forget to not stop painting.

V

Soon after David went to France, Max went off to Salonica, to pour out mugs of tea in a marquee under the black cypresses of the Besch Chinar Gardens, where once a Turkish pasha walked, attended by his twittering retinue of wives and now a British sergeant-major walked with a less voluble retinue.

He did not pour out many mugs of tea, for all the fibroid growths of his tonsils awoke into smouldering hostility and the valves of his heart began to murmur like sea-shells. They took him to the hospital on the plain by the Kalamarian sea-shore, which sweeps east from Salonica. They took him out on a Red Cross deckchair. He lay there and mused. To the north-east, Hortiac lifted its thousands of feet. Behind the hills lay Lake Lhangaza, where the aeroplanes squabbled and sank flaming into the water to hiss and drown. The whole compact ascent of Salonica met his head half-turned. The old Turkish walls staggered up to the Citadel of the Seven Towers. The minarets rose through the haze and the White Tower stood stoutly among its drinking gardens. Shipping came slowly into the harbour, misty-blue, and went out slowly again. The great cruisers, lying lean along the water, remained. The sails of the small Greek pinnaces flashed pearl and scarlet, where they rode at anchor, fishing, out in the dustless sea. The small butterflies fluttered round him, blue-white, brown-red, golden. A humming-bird hawk whizzed by. Beetles with great shells tottered over the baked earth. Brown lizards with the swift streak of green darted among the rocks. A tortoise crawled sulkily along.

"I'd paint this," said Max, " if David were here. He'd want me to."

Evening gathered. The sheep bells tinkled in the meadows and along the low hills. The Macedonian shepherds were folding in their flocks. The little shepherd boys plodded wearily along, thinking of the time when they should be men and abandon sheep for a man's game, knives and rifles among the mountains. Some soldier from Tyneside or Swansea took a shepherd's crook in hand and fed the sheep with crumbs of such brown bread as they were fed with in the idyllic days; the soldier, standing against the flushed sky, looked like a peasant out of Theocritus.

"That's just the way David stands," murmured Max dreamily. "His shoulders bent, just like that. That's what comes from being a machiner at ladies' tailoring. The kid mustn't go back to that when the War's over."

All day long Olympus had flashed hard with a white fire. Now Olympus softened through banks of rose-red and purple. The sun was almost set. There were green rifts in the western sky between layers of thin gold and against these rifts the rigging of ships showed marvellously delicate.

Magnolia Street was nearer to Max in Salonica than he had divined, as he found out a night or two before he left. They were sending him home again, for it had been decided that that malarial air was not propitious to his valves and fibroid growths.

As he walked along the water-front a little miserably, he was conscious of a desire to get into his blood some abiding memory of the city he was leaving soon. His hand had been so flaccid, he had not made a single note of all that strangeness and squalor and beauty. And David had written to him more than once saying how he was looking forward to seeing his sketches when they met in Blighty.

It was evening. The fishing boats were rocking against the breakwater and the half-naked fishermen were arranging their nets as pillows. But on the front, Floca's Café, the Hôtel Continental, the Hôtel d'Angleterre, were ablaze. The officers of five armies sat together talking a wonderful joint language. The tassels of fez caps drooped amorously a few inches from smart French toques that drew back archly. Fat proprietors loomed benignantly among the liqueur bottles, their eyes glowing golden as Grand Marnier, their souls as sea-green incorruptible as Crème de Menthe.

He loitered here a little, then turned along Venizelos Street to Ignatius Street. The drinking slums of the west side were awakening into life. Outside the doors of the cabarets, named modestly after Helicon, Olympus, Parnassus, ragged crowds were gathered, whose eyes glistened as they looked in on the red-clothed women singing and dancing on the platforms. He continued through the welter of the Monastir Road. Under the glare of the naphtha lamps gleamed heaps of melons, beside which the sellers counted their coppers into the folds of their sashes. Little boys fluttered lottery tickets on long poles. In every drinking den the shabby-booted little Greek infantrymen were showing their teeth over the greasy packs of cards which they had with them night and day. Here and there an Albanian shepherd, down from the hills, lay drunk under a table, with his dog mounted guard beside. From every corner came the thump of bronchial pianos, and the wail of consumptive violins, the insistent song of the women.

But you did not need to peer through half-open doors to see the women now. They stood on doorsteps or against their wide-flung windows. They wore a petticoat and knickers or perhaps only a short chemise. The rays of red lamps beat down on them. "This way, Johnny!" they sang. "This way! Very nice!"

The language changed according to the uniform that hove up out of the dusk. "*Eh viens-donc, mon petit!*" "*Ci piace, carino?*" As Max moved on from street to street the process of walking became almost mechanical. He lost the sense of his direction and identity, his eye became an automaton, registering the things it saw correctly but not intellectually. And then suddenly a sound broke across his trancedness. He heard a voice cry out: "Such oil he gave me to fry my fish in, a cholera should take him if it was *kosher*, even."

So amazed was he that he did not realise for some moments that the words were Yiddish words. He had been in Magnolia Street. It was not strange that a woman should cry out in Yiddish that the grocer had sold her some impure oil. The inflection was the same, the quality of the voice was the same. It might be Magnolia Street or the ghetto in a small town by the Dnieper.

Then he drew up like a reined-in horse. This was neither of them. This was Salonica the red lamp district there.

Then a voice replied to the first voice: "*Nu*, and what do you expect from such a low life? You know he's got a *shiksah* for his wife, a Greek woman?"

Max stood there. The women stopped. They saw the young man wore a version of the British khaki. "Jig-a-jig, Johnny? Very nice!" they said.

It might have been Becky Poyser, of the shop at the corner of Magnolia Street, commending the kippers that had come in from the market that day. Or Bella Winberg putting in a good word for the family rainproofs.

"No!" muttered Max Emmanuel. "I've no stomach for your other goods! But if you'd let me join you at a plate of your fried fish, even if the oil is not above suspicion..."

The women turned from him again to the discussion of their domestic troubles. They were fat and gentle creatures. He moved on a few paces. On the doorstep against the next lamp was a slightly larger group.

"Would that I had been burned before I came to Salonikki, should I so live!" said one woman. "You know how many drachmas he offered me? 'Such a year!' said I..."

"The thing to do is this," started one of her companions, evidently a woman of more experience. "When he comes in —"

But at that moment a French airman approached. He looked into the faces of the group on the doorstep. The woman who was about to offer counsel stopped. He and she recognised each other. "*Ah, c'est toi!*" she said indifferently. The two disappeared into the house. The group went on with their conversation as if no-one had come or gone.

Max walked on from doorstep to doorstep. All the women were Jewish, all talked Yiddish, except when a man came. Then it was Russian, French, Serbian, Greek, English, Italian, not many words of these, but enough to convey what they wished to convey. Then they resumed their Yiddish again.

"So Bash-shevva's got to America, yes? Such a madness that man had for her! I wonder how soon she'll collect the fare to send for Boruch, her husband?"

"Yes, in that shop in Venizelos Street, *such* stockings. Pure silk, I tell you! A *metzia*, a bargain!"

Max leaned up against the wall in a space between two lamps. He beat his temple with his fist. "Where am I, then, where am I?" he asked. "Has there been no War? I have never left Doomington. I'm in Doomington now. I'm in Magnolia Street. Isn't that Rachel, the Rabbi's daughter, with her hair across her eyes and her stockings falling down? No, it's not

412

Rachel. Her stockings are not falling down. She's wearing none...."

"Wasn't that Mr Winberg who just stole into that house? And Mr Billig, what *you*? With your rosy face and your blue eyes? Well, of course, you *live* here!

"But who's that shouting? Who's that woman standing on the opposite pavement shouting? There isn't any pavement, and it's too young for Mrs Derricks. Who is it then? It's not Yiddish! She's a *goyah*! Well, I'm damned! I'm dreaming this! Am I? What language is it? Who's she shaking her fist at?"

He crossed the roadway cautiously, skirting the yawning holes. Here too were red lamps and women at the doorsteps, in their chemises and knickers. The woman shook her fist. The woman opposite paid no heed to her. What language was it? He did not know. He thought it might be Serbian. She suspended her flow as Max moved by her. "Jig-a-jig, Johnny?" she asked. He shook his head. She took up her shouting again.

Some of the other women talked the same language, or something like it. Some talked Italian, some Greek. But they did not talk the Yiddish of the Eastern Pale nor the archaic Spanish of the Salonican ghetto. They were not Jewish. They took no more notice of the Jewish women opposite than the Jewish women did of them. As it was in Magnolia Street, world without end.

Excepting for that one woman, younger than Mrs Derricks, who stood on the edge of the pavement, shouting.

"This is very strange!" said Max weakly. "I shall get up soon!"

He found his way out of the red lamp region at length and went back to his quarters. "No! It was not there! I dreamt it all!" he said to himself an instant before his mind shut in sleep. An instant after it awoke, "No! It was not there!" he said.

He returned the next night, his last in the country, to find out whether it *had* been there, perhaps. It was with great difficulty he found the street again. But it was not the same street, though he had no doubt he had rightly remembered the name, painted clumsily on a wooden sign. It was not the same street. The Serbian ladies, the Greeks, the Italians, were still there at their doorsteps chatting under the red lamps, passing in and out of the doorways with their clients.

But the Jewish ladies — what had happened to them? The red lamps did not burn over their doorsteps. Their doors were locked, their windows fast. Where were they?

413

Bewildered, Max walked down the deserted pavement to the end of the street. He turned the corner and saw, at the end of another street as deserted, a large group gathered under a lamp. This lamp was not red. He walked down towards it. He saw that it hung on a nail driven into the wall of a wretched house. He heard the sound of an intoning as he drew near, from the group gathered round the wall. They sat on pillows and low stools. There were about thirty or forty of them. Directly under the lamp sat an old man with a parchment scroll between his hands, from which he read in a doleful monotone. Once and again he broke down for a moment or two, and the wailing of the people round him grew less restrained. The old man with the scroll looked like a woman fondling and crooning over her dead child.

There were women amongst these who had come from the street round the corner, the street of the red lamps. Max recognised two or three. Most did not belong there. One seized his mind, her pallid face standing abruptly out of the blackness. Her hair foamed round her forehead in black waves. There were small boys among them, less impressed by the solemnity. One ran a pin into his neighbour, and joined the weeping of the elders, to hide his guilt. There were old seamed women there, too old to weep almost; they wore the cap of the older Jewish women of Salonica, from which hang the cushioned pads of green silk, fringed with a pattern of pearls.

It was the fast of the Ninth of Ab, the day of wailing for the loss of the Temple. Often and long enough had Max heard that chanting, in the tiny synagogue at the corner of Magnolia Street. The little boys had begun to notice him: "British Johnny, British Johnny!" they whispered to each other excitedly. And Max still waited in the shadow and the old man went on with his reading. Then the word went round: "Israelite Johnny, Israelite Johnny!" The girls looked out of the corners of their eyes. The old women put their heads together and nodded and whispered. The old man looked up a moment, but he could not see, his eyes were wet with tears.

Then a youth rose from his stool and took Max by the arm and led him to his place in the circle under the lamp-light. He was a lad of eighteen, about David's age. He had David's eyes. He, too, stooped a little at the shoulders.

VI

Max did not stay more than a month in Magnolia Street on his return from Salonica. He tried to do a little painting, but it was flat, flat. Magnolia Street, which had once seemed to him a wild paint-box of colour, was drab and spiritless, like the eyes of Durbin, the barber, who had come back blind. He went to London and persuaded the YMCA authorities that though his growths were too fibroid for Macedonia, they were not fibroid enough to keep him out of France. He was sent to the base camp at Harfleur, near Le Havre, and he felt that if he stuck tight he might have a better chance here than elsewhere of coming up against David some day. He was attached to the Jessamine Hut and there organised an institution called 'The Harfleur Valley Arts Club.' He knew that there was a number of men passing through every base camp who would welcome the opportunity to dabble with paints, to strum some subtler instrument than the canteen piano, to read good books. He would consolidate his club, and sooner or later David might pass that way.

The lad was cheerful and wrote brisk letters.

Just one or two words to let you know all is well with me in every respect, hoping it is ditto with thee, compre, monsieur, trays been. I'm getting on in the French language fine. I've just had a lovely parcel sent to me by the Seipel family. Isn't it bong of them? How are you keeping? Won't it be fine some day to see what sketches you done in Salonica! Time is very quick out here and before long if all's well we'll be seeing each other in Blighty. Snuff said. I now finish my best regards to the boss of your Hut and my best love to you.

I am your loving young brother,

X X X

David

Max had come up against Magnolia Street in Salonica. He came up against it in Harfleur, too. He saw a certain amount of Walter Hubbard, the tram-conductor, of number twelve. Also the blithe Derricks, the Longton Nightingale, passed that way three times. But David did not pass that way.

And then a letter came from David saying he was pretty sure he was for a Blighty leave in November. Snuff said, he added, and not a word to no-one, because Max knew how things happened and also didn't. He'd been out a good year and he'd been unlucky to have missed it before. Any road, if Max could arrange to be back early in November...

Max managed to be back early in November, not quite so soon as he had hoped.

It was late one Friday evening when he arrived at Magnolia Street. There were more people about on the gentile than the Jewish pavement, for the Jews were in their houses, gathered about the Sabbath board, white cloth and glowing candlesticks. The *fire-goyahs* were already on their way to turn out the gas and to save those coals out of the fire which still had some life in them.

Had the kid managed that leave? Was he home, at this very moment, seven doors along? Was the old man holding forth, the candle flames glinting in his pince-nez, while David sat on the tumbledown horsehair sofa against the wall, squeezing his mother's hand? Or was she fussing about in the scullery, getting him some sweet dainty he liked and she mysteriously managed to concoct though sugar and butter and things were so short?

He reached the house door. It was open. He walked along the short dark lobby scraping against David's bicycle, which no-one had felt like moving, and where else was there for it to go? The light rayed out under the door where there was always a draught unless his mother stuffed the threshold with a rug.

He heard no sound. Had David come? Had he perhaps not come yet?

He opened the door and entered the kitchen. The *fire-goyah* had been and turned the gas out. The candles flickered a little unsteadily. The place was full of shawled women swaying. They sat upon the sofa and on chairs against the wall. His father sat against the window, between the wall and the table. His head lay on his chest slightly to one side, as if something were wrong with his neck. That was his mother, against the arm of the sofa, her knuckles clasped together so tight that they were pale as ivory.

He thought that must be Mrs Seipel by her side. And was that Mrs Poyser?

Why did they sit so quiet? Why did they not say a word as they swayed and clasped and unclasped their hands?

416

Why, seeing that David was dead, did they not shriek and tear their hair?

No-one said a word to him as he stood in the doorway. The women sat with their shawls drawn over their foreheads. His father's head did not move.

He suddenly felt very tired. He had been travelling a long time. He turned away from the swaying women and went up to the back bedroom which he and David used to share. The lights were still full on in the kitchen in Oleander Street upon which their house backed. They made a pallor in the room by which Max could see the bed he and David had slept in, the table, the mirror on the table which had a drawer.

The lad used to keep his papers and things in that drawer. Max reached forward and pulled at the drawer knob. His fingers fumbled about amongst the papers; it was like feeling the cloth of David's suit. "Do you like this cloth, Max? Isn't it posh?"

His fingers fell upon a book among the papers, a small exercise book. Max took it out. It had black smooth covers, or they might be blue. You could not tell in this light. He opened it. There was writing in it. It was like David speaking. He would never hear him speaking in any other way. He held the book up against the pale light and screwed up his eyes to read it. On the cover were David's initials reversed: ED.

The address also was reversed. You read: TEERTS AILONGAM NOTGNIMOOD.

It was to be a terribly secret little book. But the contents were not so desperate. 'Auntie Serra Golda died in Jerusalem,' he read, 'on August twenty-sixth otherwise second day of Elul.' On another page was a record of a cousin who had died and the number of his gravestone. On the next page the record took a more personal turn. 'I left School October 31st 1912 and started to work December 2nd at Waterproof, and a hand till January 15 and then I went to this trade for ladies tailoring for about seven months then back to Winberg for two months waterproof then Freedmans for about three weeks and then my dear brother Max got his scholarship for being a genius at the Doomington Academy then went on machine again for six months then my dear brother Max did a painting of Sir John Wegnel Big Doctor of Doomington Infirmary and sold it him....'

So the story continued. The whole history of the life of David Emmanuel was there, what firms he worked for at the waterproofs and the ladies' tailoring, the achievements in painting of Max his brother, who was a genius. And then the brief story came to an end. 'And then went on own at Bergmans and no word from Max. But he is so Busy And then September tenth went to British Army.'

No more. Max dug his teeth into his lip. His head sank upon his hands.

This was what the lad had left of song, of design, of marble. The instinct had been in him, too, to create; he too must have his monument when his young flesh was flattened under the damp heaps of clay.

Max sat on, he did not know how long, in the room where the bed was where David and he used to sleep. The small black book lay on the table under the palm of his hand. He stroked it as if he were stroking David's brows.

He went downstairs, he must be with his mother. His joints creaked, the stairs creaked as he descended them. His hand was on the knob of the door where the shawled women were, when he heard a rapping at the glass panels of the front door.

He went forward and opened it. A tall woman was there, he could not see her face.

"Are you Max Emmanuel?" she said. She spoke so low he could hardly hear her. "You must forgive me. My name is Mary Cooper. I live opposite. I have just heard."

"Won't you —"

"No, I want to say I'm so sorry. I felt I must say a word. I have a brother out there. I am so sorry. My heart aches for you. Goodbye."

She was gone again into the dark street, like a mere wraith of the sorrow of War. Max hurried back into the room where the women sat, swaying and silent. But his mother against the arm of the sofa was sobbing under her breath. Only one candle still burned, and that too would go out soon.

Book III

Chapter 1

I

The score of years between 1910 and 1930 were as tremendous as any in history; and they were tremendous not only in the theatres of War, not only during the four years the War englutted. A traveller who, in 1910, knew the lake-front of Chicago, or the country near Oxford, or the valley of Esdraelon in Palestine, and had not returned there till 1930, might well have said to himself: "Was it twenty years ago I was here? Was it fifty? It was a century!"

But a returner to Magnolia Street in Doomington, who had known it in 1910, might well have said to himself, as he looked round: "Is it twenty years since I was here? But it was yesterday!"

There were still box hedges trimming the little front gardens of the gentile pavement. There was still a home-made-sweets shop on the Jewish pavement, next door to the grocery-shop. There was still a little factory a few houses further down. You might still pray, or have a haircut, or drink a pint of old ale, at the corners of the street. You might meet one or two folks en route who looked so much the same as they did then, you would hardly give them a second glance.

You might meet Wilfred Derricks, for instance, the Longton Nightingale. Quite possibly Wilfred would be wearing his little Eton suit, though he did not wear it seven days a week now, as he used to. It would escape you on a casual passing-by how much paint and rouge, powder and peroxide, Wilfred had put on to keep him looking so youthful. And the poor Nightingale, who was fifty now, obviously needed quite a lot, for his living depended on looking not merely fifty but fifteen.

Or you might meet Rabbi Shulman. You would hardly have time to notice his eyes were a little softer than they had been and his bruised silk hat lay a little further down towards the back of his neck. But his beard was still as long and black; all his finger joints still cracked, as he beat his right palm with his gnarled left forefinger. It was probably the same frock-coat he was wearing, fastened together by one button. And these elastic-sided boots, surely he had brought them over from Russia with him, whenever that had been?

You would have seen the small boys of this later day playing in the street as they had played then. You would, for the moment, forget that the small boys of the earlier day were men now, and some of them had the roots of cow parsley tangled in their eye-sockets, in France, among the stubble of the fields.

You might, perchance, lift your eyes to the front bedroom window at number twelve and be a little put out to find there were no window-boxes on the sill and no curtains behind the window and no old lady in a lace cap keeping watch behind the curtains. You would, in fact, find that number twelve was empty. It would take you no time, of course, to find out that that house had been empty off and on for years, ever since the tram-conductor, Hubbard, had slit his wife's throat, and his own throat, and then put his head in a gas oven. The old lady, you would have learned, had died at the sight of the young woman, with her head hanging loose, throwing open her door.

But oddly enough, if you looked a little way up the street, to number six, where the Coopers lived, you would have found another woman sitting motionless behind her window curtains, in the way Miss Tregunter used to. You would almost have said it was Miss Tregunter herself who had moved a few houses further away, and had taken up her vigil behind the parlour window, as the steps were too much for her to manage now. But this woman was not so old, and she was more silent. Her name was Mary Cooper, in fact. The race of Cooper still endured in Magnolia Street.

Then you lifted your eyes higher than Miss Tregunter's window, as high as the roofs. A sort of rigging poked its way up from nearly every house-top. The melancholy of your evocation had stupefied you. For a moment you wondered what all those clothes-lines were doing slung up over the damp roofs of Doomington.

Then some indistinct figure bent down over a board and turned a switch. Then the air about you sagged at the knees, as the jazz music relayed from the Palasseum Cinema Café hurtled out through an open window. Then a great rip and roar hurtled between the pavements, as a business-like car drew up in its own length just near number five, where the Rabbi lived. A dark efficient-looking gentleman sat at the steering-wheel in a dark efficient-looking suit. The Rabbi at that moment was lifting the knocker of his door. It slipped through his fingers as he turned to the sound of the engine's snore.

"Ah, Solly!" he cried out.

"*Ah, Solly?*" you repeated. "This must be the Rabbi's eldest son! The one who was going to be a doctor! He *is* a doctor! He is on his round now! What year is this? It must be a score of years since I was last this way!"

Perhaps, O returner, if you can come back after a score of years and think you were here yesterday, you are a ghost. The street where Battling Kid Shulman was born, where Battling Kid Shulman will return a month or two from now with his honours thick upon him, is no place for you. Begone! Be absorbed into your own element!

II

Rabbi Shulman smiled beatifically as his eldest son drew up. So might Elijah have smiled when the mechanism which was to elevate him to Heaven came to rest beside him.

"Jump in, father!" cried Dr Shulman. "I've got a call to make in Begley Hill Road! The drive'll do you good!"

The Rabbi ran down the three steps like an excited boy, bent his long body over the side of the car and jerked the door open. Then he hesitated a moment. "But it soon will be time for the midday service, no?" he objected.

"That's all right! I'm coming straight back to Magnolia Street at once. I've got a call to make here, too! I'll get you back in time!"

The Rabbi still held the handle. Gripping it more firmly, he vaulted like an athlete over the running-board into the vacant seat.

"Go, Solly!" he commanded. Solly went. The Rabbi settled himself against the brown upholstery and smiled like the father of a Roman General assisting his son in a triumph. He had not smiled so the first time his son had invited him to sit down beside him, in that car.

A key turned in the lock of Bill Carter's front door.

"Sally! That was doctor's car, wasn't it?" inquired Bill Carter from his rocking-chair in the kitchen.

"Yes, Bill dear!" said Sally Carter, as she bustled along the passage. "Let me put my soap down, do!"

423

"He's coming today, isn't he, Sally?"

"Of course he is! He's only just gone to see another case! He'll be here at half-past twelve, like he said he would! What! You've not started on that gruel yet? What on earth will doctor say? Get it down you, Bill!"

The car snorted up Blenheim Road and into Begley Hill Road, still the main boulevard of Doomington Jewry. It stopped in front of a house with a garden, and a reception room on each side of the front door.

"Would you like to come in?" asked Dr Shulman. "You can have a word with Mr Billig. I've come to see his wife."

"I will stay here, no?" said Rabbi Shulman. There was a note of pleading in his voice. Perhaps his mind was engaged on some metaphysical problem which he did not wish to suspend. Perhaps it pleased him to be seen by all the passing people, where he sat in the fine motor-car of his son, the doctor.

Dr Shulman swung the gate open and rang the door-bell of the grand house of the Billigs. A maid opened the door and showed him into the parlour. That was grand, too; it seemed as big as the whole house the Billigs had once occupied in Magnolia Street, the Billigs and their walnut sideboard. Even in this big parlour the walnut sideboard seemed enormous. There was also a large walnut radio-cabinet, which could play gramophone records, too.

Mrs Billig was sitting in a velvet-cased arm-chair with her feet on a beaded mahogany footstool. Her cheeks were still as pink as a doll's, her eyes still as young and fresh as they had been of old time. Not old age, not even the operation she had had two or three months earlier, had made a perceptible difference in her appearance. She was a wonderful old woman. But Dr Shulman was a wonderful doctor. She swore by him, even though he was chiefly a doctor for poor people.

"So it goes well?" she asked him.

"Wonderful!" he assured her.

Then followed the brief flirtation which the older women insisted on as part of the treatment. He flirted methodically, scientifically, with his eye on his wrist-watch.

"Such a complexion!" he said. "If I could only tell my wife where to get such a complexion!" She kicked away her footstool in her pleasure. He replaced it gallantly. The minute hand had reached its appointed term. "And now, Mrs Billig, I must be getting on!"

"But tell me" — she suddenly remembered — "has your mother got that gold watch yet?"

"What gold watch?"

"Mick, the fighting one, that is in America, he sent her a big gold chain, yes?"

"Oh yes, so he did!"

"And he promised, soon he would send her a gold watch. With diamonds in the case. Has it come?"

"Did he?" asked Dr Shulman. He smiled. It struck him as amusing that an old lady recovering from an operation on the gall bladder should know more about his brother's presents to his mother than he did himself. The young beggar could afford it, anyhow, with those colossal purses they were paying him in America. "Oh it'll come along any day now!" He collected his things. Then he stopped a moment. "But he's got to win that big fight first," he muttered "Wasn't he going to send it her as a thank-offering?"

"What you say?" asked Mrs Billig.

"It'll come along any day now!" he repeated.

"In a good hour!" she hoped piously.

From the depths of the house a booming came closer. "Ram-bam-bam! Ram-bam-bam!" The door opened. Mr Billig appeared, in an alpaca frock-coat and skull-cap, and bright red carpet slippers.

"Ah, Solly!" the silver-haired ancient said warmly. He opened out his arms as if he would press the doctor to his bosom. "For me you are always Solly! Your father, how is he?"

"He is outside, waiting in the car!"

"No!" cried Mr Billig. "What? The Rabbi?"

He hurried out of the house, and across the pavement to the car. "Rabbi, Rabbi!" he called. "What an honour you should come all the way to my poor house! Will you come in, yes? Will you have a glass of brandy?"

"See, here is my son already!" said the Rabbi. "I must go back to *shool*. It is time for the service! He takes me back at once!"

"I will come with you!" declared Reb Billig magnanimously. "It will be like old time!" He rolled back into the house, his cheeks going rosy with boyish excitement. "My silk hat! My frock-coat! My walking-stick! My boots!" he hurled at the maid.

Dr Shulman tooted on his car. The two old men sat back against the brown upholstery. Rabbi Shulman drew his fingers through

425

his long black beard. Mr Billig purred like the engine of the car, Mr Billig bore no malice. He had once had his face slapped by the mother of that car, but neither he, nor Mrs Shulman, nor anyone else, believed nowadays that it had really happened.

It was not beneath Mr Billig's dignity to come back occasionally to the Lithuanian Brotherhood, least of all when a car, and a doctor's car, made it so convenient. He and his wife had all-the-year-round seats in the Old English Synagogue, the most fashionable synagogue in the town, as befitted their social position. But on the lesser festivals they liked coming back to attend service in Magnolia Street. They came back somewhat in the spirit of those magnates who, though they send their own sons to Eton, none the less come down on sports days and speech days to the minor public schools in which they themselves were educated. Mrs Billig in the female section preened herself in her thick purple satin among the women. For she always remembered how kind they had been, long ago, on the black day when the detectives came, such a year upon them. And how Mrs Seipel brought in a roast chicken, and Mrs Berman fine pastry and Mrs Emmanuel fish cooked in sweet-and-sour sauce.

It was years ago now since Mrs Berman died, and Mrs Seipel had at last managed to get to America to join her husband. But Mrs Emmanuel was still at hand.

"Good holiday, Mrs Emmanuel!" said Mrs Billig. "And your husband, he has got rid of his bronchitis yet?"

She looked about her and smiled tenderly upon her old friends. Beyond the partition, her husband passed his hands over his stomach happily. "Ram-bam-bam!" he boomed. "Ram-bam-bam!"

Mr Billig was right. It was exactly like old times during the midday service at the Lithuanian Brotherhood. Everything was as it had been twenty years earlier. It was like that two hundred years before that. It would be pretty much the same two hundred years hence.

Wasn't that Reb Feivel settling down in the corner against the partition? (No, Reb Feivel is in America. It is another Reb Feivel.)

Wasn't that Reb Aryeh, the Hebrew-teacher? (It is the Hebrew-teacher, but not Reb Aryeh. Reb Aryeh is dead.)

Wasn't that Reb Berel, the beadle? (Yes, world without end, that is Reb Berel, the beadle.)

It was a long time now that Bill Carter had been an invalid, and he was never likely to get much better. You couldn't say of him that he'd been a success in life. They didn't want him as a policeman. He had no luck as a soldier, for although his dropsy was due to the long amount of service he did in wet trenches, the medical board never admitted it. So he never got anything in the way of a pension from the army people, though Dr Shulman fought for him tooth and nail.

After the War, he went back to be a night-watchman in Rawlinson's factory. But when a burglary and a fire happened under his nose within a couple of weeks, he was dismissed. That was about the last thing of any importance that happened to him. Since then his dropsy got worse and worse. He was already a big man before the illness came on him; he now became bloated and enormous. For a number of months now the journey to the upstairs bedroom had been too much for him; so his wife made up his bed in the kitchen, where she did most of her washing. It meant she could keep an eye on him all the time.

We said you couldn't call Mr Carter a successful man. But that was not quite true. He did, after all, marry Mrs Carter. And if it isn't successful to have a wife like that, what is success? To the outsider, he was not a pleasing spectacle. A lot of little red veins showed in his cheeks. His speech had become a little defective, too. But Mrs Carter doted on him as if he were a Prince Charming. His voice was the whole of music to her, whether of birds or instruments. For her there was no other music in the world. If that voice should cease — and the graveyard dust seemed to have stopped his mouth half full already — it was hard to say what would happen to Mrs Carter.

The thought would come buzzing at her out of nowhere. She felt a sharp stab at her heart. It happened like this that autumn noon-time when she and Bill were waiting for the hoot of Dr Shulman's car. The shirt she was scrubbing dropped out of her hands. The pressure of her stomach against the scrubbing board relaxed. She clasped her side.

"Eh, what's that, Sally?" came Bill's voice thickly. His eyes were dull to everything and everybody else, but they were sharp to her least movement. "What's that, dear? Got them pains again?"

"No, dear, no! It's that kipper I ate for my dinner. I thought it would sit heavy on me, like. Has your pipe gone out, Bill? Would you like me to light it again?"

"Yes, Sally, please. I didn't want to bother you!"

"You know I like the smell of your baccy. It's nice and friendly with all this here carbolicky smell about! There, Bill, there! Your hands is quite steady today. That medicine doctor gave you is doing you good, isn't it, Bill?"

"Yes, Sally, it's a fine medicine!"

"He'll be here any moment now, Bill! Where did I put that scrubbing brush?"

You wouldn't think to look at him that Bill Carter got much pleasure out of life. And probably he didn't. For his contacts with life had now become so inefficient. Most people, though they never stop to think of it, get a lot of pleasure day by day, merely because they can put their feet firmly on the ground and grasp things firmly in their hands. But Bill Carter's hands and feet were flabby and insensitive. His eyesight wasn't good. He was a little deaf. He didn't get much pleasure out of life. But with all of his faculties that remained, he realised that he was everything that mattered to Sally, useless though he was to all the rest of mankind. Sally was the shape and substance of his will to be alive.

He never tried to rack his enfeebled wits to find out why such a fine woman as Sally should go on loving him. He had always taken things as they came. Once long ago — and he had long since forgotten it — when she had been a nagger, he accepted her nagging and did not question it. Now she worked herself to the bone washing for him, and he accepted that, too.

She seemed in his eyes still a fine figure of a woman. She seemed as beautiful as a spring day. But she had never been a fine figure of a woman and was not now. Yet beautiful she was, though she'd never been beautiful before. Her face was wrinkled, but it was of a delicate translucence; so were her hands, seamed as they were with a thousand wrinkles through their perpetual immersion in hot soapy water. But her eyes — you never saw in the old days how lovely they were. Perhaps they were not lovely. They were now. They were a sort of blue-grey, infinitely tender eyes. Her smile was tired, but it was so gentle that you felt the saints smiled like that when a vision came to them. Her hair was grey. It was a sort of smoke in the light of the fire which she had to keep burning in all weathers, so as to have hot water.

The shirt Sally was scrubbing dropped from her hands again.

"There!" she cried. "That's him! I'd best move the tub out of the way!"

"Shall I help you, Sally?" Bill said wistfully.

"Now then, naughty!" she reproved him. They were both as excited as if a bishop or a well-known actor or a lady-mayoress were coming to visit them. But it was only Dr Shulman, coming to pay his regular weekly visit. Their hearts went all warm when they thought of Dr Shulman. Of course, they were only panel patients, but the amount of trouble he took over Bill, you would think Bill was a baronet. He often came in between official visits, too, just to see how Bill was going on.

Sally leaned the scrubbing board against the rim of the tub, then moved the whole contraption nearer the window. She took a towel down from its rail, wiped her hands, then passed it delicately over Bill's face.

"There!" she said. "Now we're all nice and tidy!"

She bustled about for a minute or two, putting things straight. Then the expected knock came.

"Here he is!"

She went to the front door, blushing like a schoolgirl.

"Well, Mrs Carter, and how are *we* today?" enquired Dr Shulman.

"Fine!" she said. "He's not had such a good night for months now!" She led the way into the kitchen. "Don't you think he's looking fine?" she asked, a little anxiously.

"I'm very pleased with him indeed. How's the appetite, Mr Carter?" A few more questions of the medical sort followed.

"Would you believe it?" exclaimed Sally. "He was feeling so fit last night, there was nothing for it but we must go over to the Lamb and Lion. It was such a nice change and everybody so friendly, it was a rare treat!"

"By all means! By all means! If he feels up to it."

"And we had a glass of bitter each... You said he might, didn't you, doctor? It bucks up his appetite no end!"

"He's a credit to you, Mrs Carter!"

"Oh, and to *you*, Doctor!"

Bill grunted a few corroboratory syllables, "Not at all!" objected Dr Shulman.

"And now he says he feels that set up, he wants to start delivering the washing again. Shall I let him, Doctor? Do you think it's too much for him?"

"Not a bit!" he said. "Of course, you'll keep an eye on him," he whispered behind his hand.

"Of course, of course!" She was delighted the doctor had no objections; for those were Bill's great times, when he was fit to carry a bundle of washing where it belonged, to some of those fine people who lived in the big houses near St. Luke's. He had to take things very carefully, of course, and she always saw him safely across the road, and came back twenty minutes later to escort him back again. And she would naturally only send him with smaller bundles, for she didn't want to tax his strength.

But she always let him do it when it was at all possible. It made him feel he was holding his end up. He walked with such a proud smile on his face, pleased as Punch, like a messenger from the Queen of Sheba carrying gifts to Solomon. And when he returned to the kitchen in Magnolia Street, he sat down and took out his pipe and called for matches in such a commanding voice, that Sally Carter nearly cried for pleasure.

But she held back her tears. "Matches, Bill?" she said. "Here you are!" Then she pretended to be severe with him, "And if I catch you dropping any ashes on my rag mat, Bill Carter!" — she shook her finger at him. She was like a wraith in the rosy steam that hung above her washtub.

Or sometimes — of course it wasn't often — when she wasn't too tired of a Sunday morning, they would go along to church together, to St. Luke's. And when they thought of Jesus, he had a rather dark face and a bold nose and brown eyes, like Dr Shulman.

"He'd best keep on with that medicine," Dr Shulman resumed. "Well, I'm delighted to see how well he's doing. I'll be round again same time next week. Goodbye, Mrs Carter —"

"Excuse me, Doctor," started Mrs Carter shyly. "Aren't you getting a bit excited, like, about your young brother? If you don't mind my asking, of course!"

He stopped a moment and wrinkled up his brows. "Oh, *Mick*!" he said. "Doctors haven't got much time for that sort of thing, Mrs Carter! Well, I hope he pulls it off! He's a good lad!"

430

"He will, he will!" vowed Sally Carter.

"What's that, what's that?" Bill Carter wanted to know.

"Battling Kid Shulman!" she exclaimed.

"Oh, aye!" he said. "Tomorrow night!"

"Tomorrow night, is it?" asked Dr Shulman. "So it is!" The shadow of a smile passed across his face. How much more alive his patients were to the cosmic career of his brother, Mick, than he was himself — even a bloated relic of a man like Bill Carter.

"Good luck to him!" said the two Carters.

Dr Shulman thanked them on behalf of his absent brother. "And now, good afternoon, both!" he said.

"Good afternoon, Doctor!" they replied. "God bless you!" said Sally under her breath. She saw him to the door, and came back again. "Well, and what about a nice bit of dinner now?"

She moved the tub and scrubbing board into the scullery, and got busy with the tripe which had been soaking overnight. Bill had always been fond of tripe. She put out the plates and the forks and knives and tied a napkin round his neck.

"For what we are about to receive," she said, "may the Lord make us truly thankful! For Christ's sake, Amen!"

"Amen!" said Bill Carter.

They looked very happy, both of them, as they got down to their tripe. They had each other, and little else, but they wanted little else. They were happier than many a husband and wife who are well-to-do and have good health. After dinner she cleared away the things and they sat together for half an hour, he on his rocking-chair and she on a kitchen chair. He smoked his pipe, and she just sat, for she was tired after the morning's washing, and it must begin again soon. They couldn't remove all sight of the washing during these intervals, for there were always sheets and cloths and things hanging to dry from the clothes-horse. And Bill's bed took up a fair amount of room. Otherwise you couldn't tell the place from Buckingham Palace.

IV

As Dr Shulman's car turned from Blenheim Road into Magnolia Street, it was held up a moment by a van — long enough for both Mr and Mrs Poyser to become aware that it carried Mr Billig as a passenger. Neither made a comment; but about five minutes later Mr Poyser said: "I think, Dorah, I'll go over to *shool* for the midday service. I feel like it today."

If the spirit seized Mr Poyser to go and say his devotions in the synagogue rather than in the living room, Mrs Poyser could make no objection. But she knew, and he knew that she knew, that it was Mr Billig rather than the spirit that had seized him. She was grateful enough, in all conscience, for what he had done for their daughter, Becky. But she didn't disguise from herself that, after all, it had been a strict matter of business. Her husband, Isrol, however, carried gratitude to the point of a cult. Every year, at the Feast of the Maccabees, which is a season for the sending of presents, he sent Mr Billig chickens, fruits, cakes, as if Mr Billig were not a rich man who lived in a double-fronted house, but a children's ward in a hospital. Mrs Poyser couldn't raise any objections. The chickens and things came out of Mr Poyser's pocket money.

There were quite a lot of people — some even in Magnolia Street — who said openly that Mr Billig was a fraud, a hypocrite, a whited sepulchre. But they didn't say it in Mr Poyser's presence. He would get red in the neck. His eyes glittered dangerously.

For Becky was happy. She had a devoted husband. She had several children and would have more. And Mr Billig was at the bottom of it all. Mr Poyser was Mr Billig's slave for life.

We know, whether Magnolia Street has any suspicion or not, what sort of war-work Becky went to London for. But it was a lovely little girl, God bless her! Becky stayed on war-work quite a long time. Then her father went down to London to see how she was getting on. He took his sons, the twins, with him, for they were men of the world. They arranged to get the baby housed with a poor Jewish woman in Bethnal Green. They called the baby Rita.

Becky only returned to Doomington when her brother, Joe, got married. That was two or three years after he came back from Salonica, in 1918. Joe and his wife started a drapery business and Becky looked after the house for them. She seemed to have made good friends with some people in London during her war-work, for she went to Bethnal Green once a year, regularly. She'd have gone oftener if she could have been spared.

But after all, it was no life for Becky, a young, strong, vigorous woman. She was very miserable. She and her mother never met, for they had had a violent quarrel about something. Mr Poyser went to see his daughter as often as he dared, and she loved him as much as she ever did, but she was really fretting about her baby.

So Mr Poyser called in Mr Billig. For if there was one thing more than another you could say about Mr Billig, it was that he knew how to keep a secret. Mr Poyser laid all the cards on the table and told Mr Billig to provide a husband for Becky, and something more than a husband... a smoke-screen for the baby.

"Very difficult! Very difficult!" said Mr Billig. He played on the buttons of his waistcoat like an oboe player on the stops.

"If it's a matter of the commission —" started Mr Poyser.

"Me? Commission? Do I work for a commission?" asked Mr Billig.

"I beg your pardon!" stammered Mr Poyser.

"But it's *his* commission... the husband's!"

"No! No! No!" implored Mr Poyser, his weak eyes brimming. "It mustn't be that sort of husband! I don't mind how much commission I pay *you*, Reb Gershon, so long as I don't have to pay *him* any! A dowry is a dowry, but no commission!"

"That will make him much more expensive. A dowry for such a husband —"

"I have an insurance falling due. I will draw on that, my wife can say what she likes. But she, too, will be pleased to have it all settled with a nice husband. The only thing I say is this, Mr Billig —"

"*Yes?*" The blue eyes twinkled sharply.

"If he does not love her —"

"Ah *love!*" said Mr Billig. "Of course! It *shall* be a love match! Would I work if there should be no love?"

So Mr Billig set to work.

Really, it had been an extraordinary success, Mr Billig took no end of trouble over it. He realised from the beginning that he must make for a widower, and the more children the widower had of his own the better. He found a widower, a Mr Freesner, a mild little tobacconist in Leeds, with a paunch, a beard and four children. One more child imported from Bethnal Green didn't make much difference.

So Mr Freesner and Becky got married. The late Mrs Freesner had been a rather shrill and ailing woman, very dark and pasty-faced. All the children were dark and pasty-faced, too. He hadn't liked the first Mrs Freesner much, but he adored the new one. She was as strong as a horse. He thought her the loveliest woman he had ever set eyes on. He worshipped her plentiful red hair, her freckles, her large feet. He immediately set to work and had more children. Another two had already arrived on the scene and a third was on its way. It meant, at least, that there was still more shelter for the little lady from Bethnal Green.

Early in 1930 Becky brought her husband and a number of the children to Doomington, to stay with Uncle Joe. She couldn't bear to be parted from Rita, who was her favourite, so she brought Rita, too. The general understanding about Rita was that she was Mr Freesner's daughter by his first wife. What did one more child matter to Mr Freesner?

The only trouble was that Rita had flaming red hair and freckles and her feet were unusually large for a little girl of her age. On the whole it was felt that Becky had best not bring Rita to Doomington again, or people might start saying things. And as Becky refused to move an inch without Rita, Mr Poyser found that the only chance he had of seeing Becky was to take an excursion ticket to Leeds.

He liked Rita, too. She was such a big handsome clever girl. And as for his other two grandchildren — when he got them on his knee and danced them up and down, he grinned so happily his jaw looked as if it would fall off.

No wonder Mr Poyser was so anxious to go off to the Lithuanian Brotherhood and have a few words with Mr Billig. Mr Billig was the spiritual grandfather of Becky's children, so to speak. Mr Poyser was only their physical grandfather.

The service had already started when Mr Poyser entered. Mr Billig did not suspend his prayer, of course, but he smiled at Mr Poyser with extreme friendliness. Mr Poyser blushed and smiled back. The service came to an end.

"How are you? How are you?" exclaimed the old man, pressing Mr Poyser's two hands warmly. "What a pleasure! Why don't you come to see me some time?"

"I was hoping to come on Saturday. How well you look, Mr Billig! Every month you get one day younger!"

"Now, now!" warned Mr Billig, his finger at his nose. "You want me to stand security for some new business, yes?"

"A new business? I have enough with the old one! And your

wife? She has quite got over the operation yet?"

"Such an operation!" said Mr Billig tenderly, as if it were a baby in his arms. "Sixty-five pounds it cost me! Not one penny less! Sixty-five pounds! Didn't you hear what that operation cost? Sixty-five pounds, I tell you!"

Then he paused. He shrugged his shoulders. "But who talks about money?" he enquired.

"But she has got over from the operation?" Mr Poyser gently insisted.

"Yes, yes! She is much better! Dr Shulman is very satisfied with her!"

"And you are satisfied with Dr Shulman? In this street they swear by him, like he was one of God's angels!"

"I could have specialists, if I wanted!" Mr Billig specified. "But it's true. He is better than specialists. To think that the little boy should become one day so clever a doctor. You remember, Mr Poyser? If he ever had his shoelaces tied properly, it was a holiday!"

"Yes, yes!" said Mr Poyser. "But what about the other brother, Mick? Have you ever heard of such a thing? A little snotty-nose like that — excuse me, Mr Billig — and he's the champion from all the world!" Mr Billig's eyes narrowed.

"Not yet!" he snapped out. "Not yet?"

"The big fight — it is not till tomorrow night!"

"Yes," said Mr Poyser meekly. It seemed to him that Mr Billig was drawing very fine shades. The big fight hadn't been fought yet — but it was to be fought for the championship from all the world, and Mick Shulman was certain to win. Did he not know Mick from a small boy when he was not so high as his knee? How could Battling Kid Shulman lose?

Then he realised how astonishing it was — but that was too weak a word — that a blue-eyed old man, with a long silver beard, with a fat comfortable paunch, should be as well-informed about the imminent championship boxing match as his own twin sons were.

"How comes it —" he began. But Mr Billig interrupted him. There was a look in Mr Billig's eyes which he had seen there a few times already. It was there, for instance, all the time he was arranging with Mr Poyser and Mr Freesner what allowance was to be made to him in respect of Becky's transfer from father to husband.

435

"He gets a sum down whether he wins or loses?" Mr Billig enquired.

"So I think!"

"And so much more if he wins? Do you know how much?"

"I'm sure I don't know. It's in the papers. My boys could tell you."

"Money wants money. The more he gets the more he'll want. I have a girl for him, Mr Poyser. She is a rich girl, from West Hampstead, in London. From the best family — her father, and her mother and her mother's father, too, they were all born in England. Before that they came, on the father's side, from Frankfort."

Mr Poyser goggled a little at such illustrious social beginnings.

"She goes regular to Italy each year. I tell you, a girl for a prince, not for a box-fighter. But that's what she wants, what can you do? Jewish but rough, she wants him, and he should have a big name. And she can pay for it. You see, Mr Poyser?"

Mr Poyser did not see. His cheeks seemed to have fallen in a good half-inch. "But what —" he muttered.

"Whenever he comes back, Mr Poyser, I want you to bring him in to see me. If I come myself, it will be understood, perhaps. And who is he that I should run after *him*? A box-fighter! But you will bring him in, quite by accident, to see me in my house. Then you will go away. I will manage."

"But, Mr Billig —"

"You are a businessman, like me. If you bring him in I will give you two per cent."

"But, Mr Billig —"

"Let it be three per cent then! Are we not old friends? Did I not live in Magnolia Street once, too? Is it a disgrace?"

"But, Mr Billig don't you think, in America — there are so many rich girls there, too — perhaps a rich girl from America will get him?"

"Pah! Pish!" snorted Mr Billig. The suggestion made him quite cross.

Chapter 2

The news was first announced in a few syllables of blurred type in the stop-press column of the morning paper.

SHULMAN BEAT MARCUS. K.O. SIXTH ROUND.

It was amplified in a terse round by round summary in the first midday edition. The last edition had a full account from the vivid pen of a special eye-witness. There was a large photograph on the front page. The first installment of Battling Kid Shulman's autobiography appeared underneath: 'How I Became World's Light-weight Champion: Doomington Whirlwind Tells Own Life-story.'

No wonder they called Mick Shulman a whirlwind. In the certain assurance of imminent victory, he must have started dictating his story from his corner of the ring in Madison Square Garden, between the first round and the second, while they were flapping towels over him and massaging his thigh muscles.

He was not so much the Doomington whirlwind, as the Magnolia Street whirlwind; or rather, the special and peculiar whirlwind of the private bar of the Lamb and Lion. That was the impression you would have derived that evening while Steve Tawnie bellowed out the account of the fight to the assembled company. One or two members of the company had never set eyes on Mick Shulman, excepting, perhaps, as ordinary spectators at one of his fights. They had moved into Magnolia Street, that is to say, after the Kid left for America, comparatively unhonoured and unsung. But there were honour and song enough now, and the newcomers, too, were part of them. Certain other members of the company had been Mick's neighbours for years, but had not taken much notice of him till quite lately. Certain others had long been respectfully aware that he had picked up quite a name for himself among the 'fancy.' He had won his last thirty fights in first-class style. But even the fancy was divided about his prospects. Some of the experts said he had taken too much out of himself and was done for. Others said he had too much temperament. He should try a little boxing for a change.

But Mick Shulman set his jaw and went to America. He had his own ideas. He dropped overboard nearly everything he had learned about boxing at the brigade and the clubs, and landed, a compact whirlwind. He had pulverised every light-weight nose of importance throughout the continent. He drew more money to Madison Square Garden in the stupendous challenge bout against young Benny Marcus than any fighter since Dempsey, excluding two or three heavy-weights.

The people gathered that night in the private bar were gentiles. The people opposite were Jews. They lived their own lives, for the most part, though the distance between the pavements was now felt to be a matter of thirty feet or so. It was not now, as it had been in the pre-War years, as if a sea, a prairie, separated them. But the Kid was neither Jew nor Gentile. He was an Englishman, light-weight champion of the world. If you had mentioned casually that Mick Shulman was, as a matter of mere fact, a Jew, they would have looked up rather startled, as some Christians do when it is stated that the first Christian was also a Jew.

"'Round Two,'" Steve Tawnie thundered. "'Shulman landed with a left to the body, forced his opponent to the ropes and pummelled him in non-stop fashion, Marcus's body becoming red from Shulman's stinging punches. Easily the Kid's round.'"

"'Round Three. Marcus backed under whirlwind onslaught. He landed an occasional blow, but was taking much punishment and frequently holding. All the American could do was cover himself up. Shulman easily won the round.'"

"Yah!" muttered Mrs Derricks. "Bloody American!"

"Hush, mother, hush!" her son Wilfred, rebuked her.

"'Round Four. Shulman went hell-for-leather after his opponent, again forcing him to the ropes. Marcus tried to hold, but Shulman stalled him off and the round finished with Shulman well ahead on points.'"

The private bar listened like a school of novices at a reading from their secret books.

"Ah!" they said, entranced.

"'Sixth Round,'" concluded Steve. "'The Kid staggered Marcus with a left to the jaw and then jarred him again with a left and right to the body. Benny rose gamely and pierced the

Kid's defence with several good lefts. The Kid connected with another left to the jaw. Marcus made a feeble effort and landed low on Shulman's body, being warned by the referee. After Benny had gone to the canvas for a count of eight, the referee intervened, Shulman being awarded the fight on a technical knock-out.'"

Steve Tawnie lifted his eyes from the newspaper. They shone with triumph. He lifted his glass from the table.

"What I say is this 'ere, ladies and gentlemen — three cheers for Battling Kid Shulman!"

The cheers made the roof sing.

"From Magnolia Street!" he added.

"From Magnolia Street!" the crowd roared.

Mrs Derricks shook her head apprehensively. "Them Americans!" she muttered. She never had no use for them Americans.

There was an overflow in the private bar that evening from both the saloon and the public bars. The curate of St. Luke's-in-Longton, a later and more muscular curate than we met earlier, declared a little untruthfully that he had always prophesied the most dazzling success for the dear boy. The pink and chubby post-mistress who had succeeded her pink and chubby sisters would have liked a little more attention directed on herself and a little less on the prodigy.

The public bar had deserted as one man its darts and its shove-ha'penny board. It was symptomatic of the decadence of the times that Steve Tawnie felt himself compelled to offer the people bread and circuses. The saloon bar had its loud-speaker, though it still decently exhorted its clients to let conviviality be moderate and temperate. The public bar had its darts and shove-ha'penny. You had to be careful, these days, how you moved about the public bar, lest the darts transfixed you like a Sebastian. Only the private bar, the gentile pavement's club, was content with conversation, as it had been of old.

But tonight you could hardly call it conversation. It was tumult. It was rapture. There had been no faint trace of either of these during the last few weeks. A shadow had sat upon the open brows of Steve Tawnie and his gifted son-in-law, Andy Dexter, who played cricket for Lancashire. Their friends lurched about, shaking their heads despondently. Many of them had been engaged in a great War lately, and since then there had been much stagnation in cotton, the staple trade of their city. But it had been no matter of high politics that brought night after night from their bosoms a sigh vigorous enough to blow the froth from their glasses. The fact was that Doomington United, whose goal Steve Tawnie had once so immaculately protected, had won not one match, home or away, since the football season started. They had not acquired even the single point of a draw.

"I don't know," mourned Steve, "what things is coming to!"

It was high time that Battling Kid Shulman should bring to Magnolia Street the light-weight championship of the world.

There were many unfamiliar faces that night in the private bar. Several familiar faces were lacking. Where were the Stanleys now? Whither had Mr Briggs fled? The Hubbards? Let no shadow of the Hubbards fall tonight on this gay gathering!

They were all gone, and others that came here in the old days, they were gone, too! What has happened to the sparrows that twittered from those eaves yesterday? There are more sparrows.

But Steve was there. Maggie was there. What? Are there two Maggies? Here was one Maggie standing behind the counter. Her earrings rang like bells in a steeple. She winked at the curate her large bright eye. Here came another Maggie. She lifted the flap of the counter, and managed to find a place for herself between Bill and Sally Carter. She was a bit heavier than the first Maggie, and the chin drew on the neck a little; but they were both such magnificent women, for two pins you would call them sisters.

The first Maggie was Nellie, of course; Nellie Dexter she was now. It was odd to see how Nellie's gold hair had sprouted like a pot of cinnamon dahlias. She filled a glass for her mother.

"Here you are, mother; here's yours!" she exclaimed.

"Allow me!" said Wilfred Derricks, reaching for it, polite as a lord.

"Thank you!" said Maggie, like a duchess. Her eyes rested on her robust daughter. She smiled in the pleasure the sight gave her. As well she might. A little flighty Nellie might be, like all these here modern girls. She was fair crazed on dancing, big as she was. But she came in to lend a hand in the private bar a good four times a week. For after all, wasn't it going to be her own place, hers and Andy's, one of these days? Andy wouldn't have to spend *his* hard-earned benefit match money to buy himself any pub. But that was a long time ahead, please God. Time enough for Andy to hit up quite a few more centuries for Lancashire.

Yes, indeed, it was a nice long time ahead, if appearances counted for anything. Maggie's bust had dropped a little and her stomach risen a little, but her eyes were still as young as Nellie's. She still wore her dresses of stout ribbed silk and her vast cameo brooches. It was clear she had stuck to them all these years with the imperial contumacy of a Catherine of Russia, while the dresses of every other woman in the land rose from the ankle to the knee and descended to the ankle again.

"I'm that pleased," she said, turning to Bill Carter, "to see you about on your feet again! 'E's lookin' champion!" she informed Sally. "Like a two-year-old!"

Sally Carter's fingers trembled upon her glass. They were almost translucent, like the petals of a white flower. Some ladies have skin so white because they are of high birth; Sally's hands were so white because they were steeped in soap-suds day in, day out, year upon year.

"I couldn't keep him in no how," explained Sally. "As soon as he heard the news, he got that excited, like it might have been his own son!"

Bill looked a little sheepish. "Don't you believe her, Maggie!" he said. You needed some practice to catch his words accurately. Then he took a gulp at his beer and said assertively: "It isn't every day a kid from your own street becomes world champion, I'll bet it isn't!"

"That's right!" said Andy Dexter, tall, lissome, dark-jowled, fit mate for Nellie Tawnie. "Don't let her bully you, Bill!"

"Oo's bullyin' 'oo?" enquired Mrs Derricks out of her coma.

"Here!" cried Wilfred. "Nothing! Nobody! Come, mother! Take your beer and drink!" He closed her hands round her glass. She lifted it obediently to her lips and drank.

Mrs Tawnie heaved a sigh. She remembered a time when nobody needed to tell mother Derricks to take her beer and drink, before that sleepy sickness came and got hold of her. But it was a sight for sore eyes to see the way her boy, Wilfred, looked after her, as if she was his baby daughter.

"Oo's bullyin' oo!" she insisted. "I'll tell Mick! 'E was always my favourite!" she invented suddenly. Her malady had taken most of the vigour and sparkle out of her, but it had invested her with a new myth-making faculty no-one had observed in her previously. "I used to dandle 'im on my knee! I always said 'e was goin' to be the world champion. 'E'll show 'em — the 'ole bleedin' lot of 'em! Them Americans!"

She seemed to have transferred to them Americans some of the feeling she had once entertained for Jews and, some years later, for Germans. "Them Americans!" she repeated and shook her head violently till all the cherries tinkled. Nobody could remember that she had ever harboured friendly feelings for the tribe of Shulman, to the point of dandling its infants upon her knee. But they quite knew what she meant about them Americans. They had little use even for Young Benny Marcus, upon whose shoulders their hero had climbed to his present transcendent eminence. Marcus had informed the world that he was going to push the limey's nose where his back-collar-stud was. He said that he didn't like boxing with limeys, because they cried. Altogether the American had been very disrespectful towards the race of limeys in general (by which he meant Englishmen) and Mick Shulman in particular.

Albert Durbin, who had been a barber, from behind his dark blue glasses reeled off a list of figures. The American's reach exceeded the Englishman's by three inches, his biceps were an inch larger, he weighed-in a good two pounds heavier. His voice became shriller and shriller with triumph as he retailed the glorious disparities.

"Would you believe that now?" vaguely said Kate Ritchie. She was as excited as everyone else. "Would you believe that now?" she repeated, trying to inspire the gentleman who had escorted her into the Lamb and Lion with some of the universal excitement. But the gentleman said nothing. It did not seem to interest him that Magnolia Street had won the world championship. He did not seem to exult even for Doomington's sake, or England's sake. So blue and silent his face was, he might almost have been one of them Americans. He was no American, actually. An American face might be so blue but not so silent.

Half an hour of back-slapping and health-drinking went by, and an hour. The blue gentleman said not a word. He merely shoved his mug forward and slid it back again. A moment came when he deemed himself to have drunk enough. He inclined his head towards Kate Ritchie. She rose and followed his hulking

442

shoulders out of the private bar.

"Good riddance," exclaimed Nellie, "to bad rubbish!" The curate had been gone for some time. He had only called in for a few minutes to show that his heart rejoiced with his people's. The chubby post-mistress was gone, too. Now the fun really started. Everybody got so happy that the question was seriously considered whether the private bar should present itself as a body at the Shulman front-door. The least Magnolia Street could do, in the absence of the Kid, was to sing a hymn of praise to the Shulman parents. But closing time came on before the scheme could be carried out, and one or two of the intending carollers had been carried out already.

So Rabbi Shulman sat on an hour or two after midnight at his table in the kitchen with his book open before him, and no hymn of praise disturbed him. And he went to bed at length and lay down beside his wife. She wore a large gold cable chain around the neck of her nightgown. She smiled blissfully as she slept.

Chapter 3

Could it be said that the status of the street which Mick Shulman glorified in 1930 had advanced in status from the street which Benny Edelman had ravished in 1910?

The girls now wore artificial silk stockings and sometimes real silk stockings. In most of the houses gramophones were a rarity twenty years ago, and now there was a wireless set in almost all. The youths had little more to do in the evenings of the old days but to sit about yarning in the barber saloon. Or they played billiards. Now, for youths and girls, for old folk, for infants, there were three large cinemas within fifteen minutes walk and a great many more within fifteen minutes tram-ride. On the nights when the youths did not take their girls to the cinema, they took them scorching out into the countryside on the pillion seats of their motor-bicycles. Some of these young men had been out of work for a long time; had, perhaps, not known a full day's work since their boyhood. They were in receipt of weekly allowances from the state. They had no heels on their shoes, they were often hungry, but they managed to keep up their motor-bicycles.

But if Magnolia Street had advanced in status between 1910 and 1930, there was no clearer indication of the advance than the Clausens' Pompeian Rooms.

That was the name of the institution where Mrs Durbin and her two sons had once flourished. But it flourished now with a magnificence quite undreamed of by the simple-minded Durbins. The Clausens, a young Dutch couple on the lookout, had seen the advertisement Albert Durbin inserted in the *Hairdresser's Journal* soon after his mother died. The stock and goodwill were going very cheap. They snapped up the business at once.

They had a double window put in on the Aubrey Street front and that made it clear they hardly wanted to be considered a Magnolia Street concern at all. It certainly was a good thing that that double window did not face towards the synagogue. It would have been altogether too indecorous, for there were three wax women in it in a state of very exotic undress. It was a good thing, too, they stopped at the waist. From that point they became pedestals. If Doomington were not an English city, the three ladies would have given you the impression that the things the Clausens had to sell inside were much less innocent than permanent waves and shampoo powders. Yet that was all they were there for. They had diverse but very complicated coiffures, and the Clausens were prepared to do the same by you, if you were a lady. It was their strong suit.

In the Pompeian Rooms proper there was practically no space for men to have anything done to them — just a little cubbyhole with two shaving chairs and a small form. The rest was all partitioned off and took in the old living-room (where Mrs Durbin used to read tea-leaves) not to mention a fair part of the upstairs premises. It was hard to say where the Clausens themselves slept, unless they camped out among the three wax ladies.

There was a wooden partition in the Pompeian room to segregate the sexes, just as in the synagogue opposite. But its function was not the same. The purpose there was to make the sexes oblivious of each other before the footstool of Jehovah. The purpose here was to make them more attractive to each other on the couch of Aphrodite. Directly over the Pompeian partition, which stopped just below the frieze, was a large framed text, which, in 1910 and 1916, no less than now in 1930, exhorted you to try

DR. GAEL'S ELECTROLYTIC TREATMENT — 1/6.

It was queer that the Clausens, who were not merely hairdressers, but trichologists, had not removed the advertisement for so primordial and uncostly a treatment. Even in this season of acute trade depression the Clausens thought in terms of guinea, rather than shilling, treatments. It was like seeing a price list for cupping and leeching in a Harley Street surgery.

It can only be supposed that the Clausens felt, like every Durbin customer in the old time, that there was a voodoo attached to that text. If they removed it from the wall, Dr Gael would come round at night and nick pieces off their razors and clog the loose locks of their beautifully balanced waving irons.

Whatever Dr Gael's treatment was it must have been a poor

445

unsubtle thing compared with the trichological rites the Clausens had at their command. They were masters of the latest methods of permanent marcel, water and finger waving, and were enthusiastic corresponding members of the Beauticians' Book Club of America.

Truly the place had ceased to be a club for the poor youths of Magnolia Street. It gave the impression that it was rather inconsiderate of males generally to have hairs sprouting round their chins. Yet you could by no means say that it had become the club of the Magnolia Street ladies. Nothing was less club-like than those secret cubicles beyond the partition. They were so secret that sometimes you suspected the Clausens were not hairdressers but abortionists.

II

How far had silk stockings and motor-bicycles carried Magnolia Street away from what it was, and the cinema and the lipstick and the dirt-track and the dance-hall and Clausens' Pompeian Rooms? Not very far, Mr Emmanuel believed; Life was good twenty years ago; it was not much better now, but would be soon. Not very far, Mary Cooper believed. It was wretched twenty years ago, was now, and would remain so world without end.

They did not disagree, however, about Kate Ritchie, who once had a black-man for a husband. Her house in the old days was like a little palace; but it was now a blot upon the street. Her front steps were not scrubbed for months at a time. No curtains hung before her windows, or if they did, they stayed there till they dropped. From no bamboo tables did the proud aspidistras soar. She was once the trimmest woman in the street. She was now down at heels, her skirts were all up and around, she wore a boa generations old.

She was not poor. She got a lump sum of money twice a year, and she did needlework. She made up pyjamas and nightgowns quite cleverly, when she felt like it. She could do almost anything with a needle, and she had so little sense of money, that you could get her to do it for next to nothing if you talked nicely to her.

But the point was — where did that lump sum of money come from that she called for at the bank twice a year? It had been coming about ten years now.

The most picturesque explanations were current in the

Lamb and Lion, and all of them were bound up with Pete Ritchie, her negro man. Nobody had ever found out whether or not he died during the War. They were just beginning to give him up, when Kate Ritchie marched off to the bank one fine morning and drew the first installment of her mysterious endowment. It was a tidy sum of money, judging from the goings-on of the next few weeks.

It was immediately decided that Ritchie was sending his woman conscience-money for having let her down. Everybody remembered how he loved her, with a love surpassing the love of white for white. One or two flamboyant imaginations suggested that, unknown to himself, all the time that he was a sailor and Kate Ritchie's man, he was a person of high estate. As a small child he had been kidnapped by some usurper from the Court of Dahomey or Ethiopia. During the War he found out who he was, and returned to his capital to claim his birthright.

It was also suggested that he had given up the sea to join some international gang of traffickers in cocaine; and now that the turnover was showing a real profit, he could not ignore Kate Ritchie any longer, for he still loved her in his heart, whatever his relations were with the cocaine princesses of Vienna and Buenos Ayres.

Nobody had ever found out whether either of these hypotheses had anything to do with it; perhaps they both had. But it was certain that Kate Ritchie went off twice a year to the bank. She did not need to show any identification papers now. They knew her.

"Pound notes as usual?" they asked. "Yes, if you please!" she said, with her nose slightly tilted. For she was a lady that morning and would be a lady again six months from then. And as for what went on in between times, it was no concern of the bank clerks.

On leaving the bank she walked along Begley Hill Road to the corner of the next street. The leather bag with the pound notes was pressed tight under her arm. A man had been leaning heavily against a pillar box for the last few minutes.

"Got 'em?" he asked. His voice was not pleasant.

"Yes!" she said. She clasped the bag tighter under her arm.

"Right!" he grunted. He said no more. He plodded beside her to Magnolia Street on his large splay feet.

We have made the acquaintance of this gentleman already —

a tough one, he seemed, but no American. He was, in fact, the blue and silent cavalier of Kate Ritchie in the private bar of the Lamb and Lion three or four nights ago, the night they sang odes to Mick Shulman. Nobody knew who he might be. The rivers of beer that flowed down his throat that night did not loosen his tongue — that night, or any other night. Kate Ritchie, also, uttered no word regarding him.

He had again appeared in Magnolia Street, as he had done six months earlier, as he would six months later. As regular as clockwork he turned up in Magnolia Street.

For, evidently, Kate Ritchie's money fell due in three or four days....

The cavalier plodded on beside her. When they got in, he stayed downstairs in the kitchen, while she went upstairs to her tin trunk. It all seemed a familiar routine to both of them. She locked up the greater part of her money in the tin trunk, then she came down again with three pound notes.

Then they sent out for drink. They sent out for food also, but they forgot about that quite soon. They started drinking and went on drinking for a day or two. For about a day or two he remained silent. It was considered wiser not to approach him. The proceedings still remained more or less private.

But after two days the fun started. All the *fire-goyahs* from the streets of the flowering shrubs with a taste for liquor, came and paid their respects to Kate Ritchie. For the *fire-goyahs* were as persistent as the greybeards of the Lithuanian Brotherhood. Mrs Edelman and Mrs Poyser would as soon have done a *danse du ventre* on the pavement as turn out their own gas on the Sabbath evening. But of the *fire-goyahs* that paid court to Kate Ritchie only the face of one was familiar — May Agnes Hartley. She still occupied the attic in the Berman house, where Ada Hummel, Mrs Berman's younger daughter, lived, and sold home-made sweets, as her mother had done. If ever Ada Hummel went to live anywhere else, May Agnes Hartley would have stayed on. She went with the house, like the cupboards.

She came to Kate Ritchie's house, and sang, as she sang in her attic, as she sang in the middle of the roadway. After a few hours of Kate Ritchie and her friends, she went off to Blenheim Road, and took up her stand just off the pavement. And she sang. Tram-drivers, chauffeurs, cyclists, gave up the effort to get her to move out of their way. They accepted her as part of the landscape, like a road-island. There was a moon that night, against which she loomed up enormously. She sang in her frail voice things that had been and were to be. There was a curious unreality about her. She seemed as if she had never existed at all, as if she were an emanation from Mrs Poyser's sacks. Or had she existed once, and did she die long ago?

She came back to Ada Hummel's attic and slept for a few hours. Then she took the shawl off her bed, put it round herself and went forth again to the company of her sisters, in the house of Kate Ritchie. Some of the *fire-goyahs* had lain about the floor all night. Others, from the last recesses of the flowering shrubs, came this forenoon for the first time. With her skirt more lop-sided than usual and her hair in her eyes, Kate Ritchie went up to her tin trunk, found the keyhole with great difficulty and brought out two or three more pound notes. She had made the journey once or twice already.

That evening Mrs Derricks made her appearance. She did not add much to the gaiety of the proceedings, but a party of undertakers would have been welcomed with as much exuberance. Her son, Wilfred, had an engagement that night at one of those cinema theatres that included a few variety turns between films. Henry, her husband, was busy doing fretwork in his room. So she managed to slip away. An engagement at a talkie-theatre was about all Wilfred could hope for nowadays. His performance fitted very well into that background, for he had to convulse his face so desperately to produce his treble that there seemed as little true relation between his mouth and the sound issuing from it as there was between the mouth of a talkie-actor and the sound that did not issue from it.

Henry was upstairs doing fretwork. He had been pensioned off for nearly ten years, so he had lots of leisure time now to practice his hobby. He was not at all so meek a little man as he used to be, but that was chiefly because his wife, Bridget, was not at all so fierce a woman as she used to be. He was the head of the household now. He ruled it with a rod of iron.

But he still applied himself to the art of fretwork, as sternly as he used to twenty years ago. He still fretted countless cigarette boxes, photo-frames and menu-card-holders. What he did with them all after he had fretted them, was a mystery. A certain quantity were absorbed by church bazaars, at which Wilfred sang occasionally. He had the satisfaction of knowing that now at last, in the houses of some of the parishioners who attended those bazaars, some of those menu-card-holders actually held menus.

But he made much more fretwork than those church bazaars could get through. What became of those photo-frames and letter-racks? You hardly ever saw their corpses, so to speak, as you hardly ever see the corpses of birds or rabbits in the woodlands.

Mr Derricks used to get up in the morning to make the fire while Bridget and Wilfred were still asleep. Perhaps that helps to one explanation of the mystery. Perhaps he made the fire with the corpses. In some ways it is a magnificent thought. After half a century devoted to the art of fretwork, Henry Derricks was still not quite convinced he had turned out the perfect menu-card-holder.

And that evening, Henry being bent over his bench, pursuing the Platonic phantasm of a menu-card-holder, and Wilfred being away on an engagement, Bridget Derricks slipped off to Kate Ritchie's house. It seemed quite like old times to Mrs Derricks, the good old times when she queened it over the Boys and gave parties which were famous through all Longton.

But the Boys never came to see them now. For she herself was only a ghost of the woman that she was, and as for Wilfred, an unsuspected strain of piety had revealed itself in him. The Hubbard business seemed to upset him a lot. At all events that was about the time he started church-going, though his attendance was rather spasmodic for some years. Latterly, however, he attended church every Sunday morning. He sang at church bazaars whenever he was invited. At those same bazaars they sold a good deal of his father's fretwork. Altogether there was a strong Derricks note at church functions these days.

And yet, two or three years after the War stopped, there seemed some chance of the famous theatrical parties going back again to their pre-war strength, if not their pre-war virulence. They had never really stopped, even in the darkest days of the War. And after the War, quite a number of the old Boys found their way back to Magnolia Street. A new generation of Boys was springing up, too. There was one perfectly magnificent party in

450

1923, worthy of the best Derricks traditions. Of course nobody nowadays said "Smoggy van Jew!" at Rabbi Shulman or any member of his family. That was partly because Mick Shulman, the future light-weight champion, was quite dangerous at sixteen. It was also because people did not feel that way so much in the post-war years in England. They left that for the Derrickses of Austria and Bavaria. But it was a grand party just the same. You can always find somebody to jeer at when you get merry.

And then Mrs Derricks, the incomparable hostess, fell ill. For weeks and weeks she was almost unconscious. The doctors in the hospital shook their heads and muttered and twittered. They were quite excited. It was one of the earliest cases of *encephalitis lethargica*, sleepy sickness, they had in Doomington at that time.

She seemed to get better, but she never did really. The vigour and sparkle went out of her. The Boys still came for a time and there were a few more parties, but they were half-hearted. Sometimes, even when there wasn't a party, Mrs Derricks would stand on the edge of the pavement and try to say something when Rabbi Shulman or some other greybeard came into sight.

But she couldn't remember what it was she wanted to say. So she went in to Wilfred, and Wilfred and she went along to the Lamb and Lion, and they had a glass or two, and he sat there stroking her hand, as if he were a large fine man and she were a little undeveloped dwarf of fifteen. He looked after her very nicely indeed. Henry never went into the Lamb and Lion with her. He had never overcome the nausea produced by the very smell of beer. After all, he had been a clerk in a brewery for over half a century, so he had really had enough of beer by this time.

She did not drink much that evening in Kate Ritchie's. For when she started a glass, she forgot about it, if Wilfred was not on hand to remind her what she was doing. But after two or three hours she got up and went out of the house in which was a perpetual movement of *fire-goyahs* going out with empty jugs and returning with full ones. And Mrs Derricks stood upon the edge of the pavement and said something. It was not clear what she said, though the word 'Americans' came out clearer than the rest. "Them Americans!" she repeated, and shook her fist vaguely.

And then Wilfred returned from the cinema theatre and saw her issue from Kate Ritchie's house and take up her place at the edge of the pavement. He never had those rages with the old lady nowadays, when he used to tear her new hats to shreds with his even little teeth. How could anyone behave that way nowadays with the poor old thing? But his voice was quite shrill with anger when he came up to her: "You wicked old woman!" he cried. "How often have I told you not to go into that house? Come along at once! Do you hear?"

She gave him her hand timidly and shuffled off after him. Wilfred pecked and tweeted like a scandalised bird. He determined he must get up that petition among the neighbours, as he had more than once threatened to do. It was disgraceful that such goings-on should be tolerated in a respectable street — every half year the same thing. Representations had been made to the landlord, who had more than once promised to eject Kate Ritchie, but he had taken no action yet. Nobody liked to tackle the situation while Kate's companion was still about. After he left, Kate's house was as quiet as a mortuary for six months.

"But really, really," exclaimed the Longton Nightingale, "this time it's gone too far! I'll get up a round robin the first thing tomorrow morning! Really I will! You've not taken your Sanatogen, mother! How'll you ever get better if you don't take your Sanatogen?"

By now Kate Ritchie's companion was in an extremely good humour. He acted as host for her whenever she was indisposed for an hour or two. The festivities went on for some days, and every now and again Kate Ritchie went up to her trunk and extracted another couple of pound notes. The Mick Shulman excitement got tied up with it somehow. While the millionaire stocking-manufacturers and pants-manufacturers and furniture-manufacturers on Riverside Drive, their wives, their sons, and, most fervently, their daughters, were shaking cocktail-mixers in Mick Shulman's honour, Kate Ritchie and her guests drained countless jugs of beer in his honour. Kate's cavalier, who had expressed no interest in him at all on the night when they celebrated his triumph in the Lamb and Lion, became extremely maudlin over him.

"Good ole Mick!" he stuttered. "Plucky lil bastard! I always shed he'd got the right shtuff in 'im! Didn' I, Kate? What? Did I or didn' I? I *did*! There y'are!"

From the maudlin stage he proceeded to the skittish. He went

452

about on all fours playing bear. Sometimes, still on all fours, he went upstairs to Kate's room where her tin trunk was. But however drunk Kate got, she never forgot to lock the trunk and she did not leave the key about. So her friend came down a little disappointed but still full of fun. He went on making deep bear-like noises and all the guests screeched with laughter.

It continued like that till Kate had extracted her last pound note and she had nothing but silver coins left. There were quite a lot of them. She got them as change all the time the pound notes were being spent. After having spent about half of these silver coins, it occurred to her that it would be nice to have a few laid by for after the party. There would not be any more pound notes for six whole months and when the party was over she wouldn't feel much like needlework, for a long time.

So she tried to hide the silver coins in various odd places. Usually he found out where she had put them and he slipped them into his pocket. The *fire-goyahs* also came upon them here and there. Weeks later, one or two of the nicest *fire-goyahs* might come back and say: "'Ere you are, Kate, 'ere's that 'alf-crown you lent me, that time when we was all so jolly like!"

And "Thank you very much indeed!" Kate would answer weakly. And very pleased she was to have a half-crown dropping from Heaven like that, and herself with hardly a spoonful of tea in the house.

But only one or two of the *fire-goyahs* would bring back the half-crowns, she knew from experience. The fancy man certainly would not. It was pathetic what places she put her last few coins into in the hope he would not notice them. For several parties running she managed to bury quite seven shillings worth of silver in the butter and five shillings worth in the tea-pot. But at the last party he had found out, so the butter and tea-pot were of no use any more.

Then the party at length was all over. The *fire-goyahs* went back to their attics. The rough man lurched off round the corner into Blenheim Road. He would not be seen again for six months.

Chapter 4

I

She was the same Mrs Poyser who stood like Justice, upright and oracular, behind her pair of scales. The barrel of salt herrings, the jar of pickled cucumbers, the marching sacks of sugar, the bins of lentils — all these were the same, too. But the pair of scales was not. It was a clumsy lump of pig iron in the old time. It was now a shining thing of glass and brass, with a fastidiously exact dial finger that came to rest against the appointed ounce.

The pair of scales was a concession to Time and Science. But Mrs Poyser made no concession. Her pointed nose was the same, her tightly screwed-back hair, her apophthegms.

Mr Poyser who, as of old, did the weighing, the packing, the wrapping, had conceded more to Time than Mrs Poyser. His hair was quite grey and his shoulders stooped. He blinked rather absent-mindedly through his glasses. His heart was more often than not across the Pennines with his daughter, Becky, who lived in Leeds. He sighed. He wondered how soon his wife would let him take another Sunday excursion to see Becky, and dandle his grandchildren on his knee.

There was the usual group of women in the shop, in this quiet half-hour before they had to get busy with the midday dinner. But today, in Mrs Poyser's shop, the half-hour was by no means quiet. Several of the women were strangers so far as we are concerned. They lived in other streets, or came to live in Magnolia Street since we were last this way. Some were not strangers. Here was Mrs Emmanuel. A certain air of resignation lay on her. She believed, for her own part, that the millennium which the Great War was to usher in was not really going to happen next Christmas but one. Her husband, on the other hand, was still rather of the opinion that it would. Here also was Mrs Edelman, an old lady now, and not such a fierce one. Time had mellowed her. Mrs Hummel, who kept the home-made-sweets shop, ran in a moment ago for some powdered ginger, and was too excited to run back again.

Here, finally, was the Rabbi's wife, Mrs Shulman.

What had happened to the Rabbi's wife? Her lips used to be drawn down in a pout of perpetual disappointment. She used to look like an old sack. Where did she get that handsome silk dress from? And this gold cable that hung massively down her bosom? And the watch that was hooked on to the gold cable? Why did she stand there purring like a cockatoo?

No, the answer was not merely her son, Battling Kid Shulman, though he had knocked out Young Benny Marcus and made himself the world's light-weight champion. That news had come through about a fortnight ago now; and though the women realised it was something to exult over, for it meant the winning of many thousands of pounds, and reporters coming to the Kid's house in Magnolia Street, and the photographs in the papers of the Kid's father and mother and sister and brothers — though the women had exulted, they had been puzzled, too. Why should you earn thousands of pounds by hitting people on the nose? When they were girls in Russia, they used to see *moujiks* hitting Jews on the nose, and sometimes Jews hitting *moujiks* on the nose, but nothing like such sums of money used to pass from hand to hand.

What was the world coming to? It was all very mystifying.

But this morning they were beginning to get things into focus. Mrs Shulman had a lot to tell them. That was why she was purring like a cockatoo. She waved a letter about in her hand, and purred like a cockatoo.

First, she had got her gold watch that morning. She unhooked it from the gold cable. Mick had promised her a gold watch to hang on her gold chain if he beat Young Benny Marcus. He had beaten Benny Marcus. The amount of duty she had to pay on that gold watch was enough to buy the Town Hall Clock. But he had sent a fat bundle of dollars to cover the duty, and a lot more beside.

Second, Mick was coming home. He was on the high seas already. He would be landing in Liverpool in a week. He was going to spend a couple of months in Doomington; he would, perhaps, even have a box-fight in Doomington, if they made it worth his while. Then he was going back again to New York. He would take his old father and mother back with him for a few months' holiday.

Rabbi and Mrs Shulman were to be the guests of Berman P. Teitelbaum. Mr Teitelbaum was the father of the young lady to whom Benny had got engaged the night after his great box-fight in Madison Square Garden. Mr Teitelbaum was one of the

455

richest Jews in New York. He was the biggest of all the New York pants-manufacturers.

No wonder Mrs Shulman made those pleased noises. No wonder the other women did not know whether they were standing on their heads or their heels. No wonder the air pattered like hail with their good luck wishes.... *Mazel tov, mazel tov*!

"So I shall not have to take him to see Mr Billig," said a sepulchral voice. The voice seemed to come from the depths of a sack of rice, but it came actually, from the cavernous mouth of Mr Poyser.

"What do you say?" Mrs Shulman wanted to know. "He shall go to see Mr Billig? My son?" She paused a moment, to decide whether she and her son had been insulted or not. Mr Poyser relapsed into the sack of rice. Mrs Shulman decided to postpone the issue. For she hadn't finished yet. It seemed impossible that there could be anything left of marvel to recount. But there was.

"And do you know, Mrs Poyser," Mrs Shulman asked, fiddling about with her gold cable. "Do you know who was there at the engagement party? You can guess ten times! A lady!"

"Not... You don't mean... Can it be possible?"

These remarks came from various members of the group. But, of course, Mrs Shulman *did* mean it. The question provoked the only possible answer. Of all the millions of ladies in the United States of America, Mrs Shulman could only mean one lady. It would not have impressed them in the least had the lady been Mrs Hoover or Fannie Hurst or Ethel Barrymore.

"Yes," said Mrs Shulman, "should I so live! Bella Winberg was there, too. She's a great friend of the Teitelbaum family! She lives just near, in the next apartment house, in Riverside Drive. They're always in each other's houses, like sisters and brothers." She attempted to make her tone as casual as possible, but it was tremulous with triumph. "Ah!" A sigh went round the company. "Bella Winberg!" (She had always remained Winberg to them. Her married Swedish name had never caught on.)

That helped them at last to get Micky's glory into a clear focus. So that was the exalted society to which his prowess had elevated him? He was engaged into a family which ate off gold plate and Bella Winberg came in and out casually, like it was the grocery-shop.

"Well, *mazel tov*, again!" breathed Mrs Emmanuel. And then she remembered suddenly, and somewhat defiantly, that she, too, was not the least distinguished of mothers. "My boy, Max, he also goes to good houses!" she pointed out.

"Of course, of course!" said Mrs Shulman. She could afford to be charitable. Max Emmanuel had not won the world's oil-painting championship. "A credit he is, too, your Max! Perhaps my Micky will let him paint his picture, yes?"

Mrs Emmanuel pouted. "He was painting a Lord his portrait last week!" she pointed out.

"Well, Mrs Emmanuel!" Mrs Poyser remarked. "When news comes from your Max that he also is engaged to a nice Yiddish girl, like Micky, it'll be like a holiday to me!"

"There's time, there's time!" insisted Mrs Emmanuel. "Zangwill, he was thirty-seven when he got married!"

Mrs Shulman felt the conversation had absented itself from her baby long enough.

"So he'll arrive in Liverpool a week next Tuesday!" she pointed out. "And Bella Winberg —"

"Yes?"

"Well, my Micky says she was going to London by Southampton. But neighbours remain neighbours. So they're travelling to Liverpool together on the same ship just to be company for each other. Well, and what do you think of that?"

"On the same ship?" marvelled old Mrs Edelman.

"My potatoes!" cried Mrs Emmanuel suddenly. "I left them boiling on the fire! They will be burnt to a cinder! The pot will make an explosion! Give me my packet of self-raising flour, quick, Mrs Poyser!" She turned to Mrs Shulman. "You should have a great comfort, a *nachuss*, out of your son and your daughter-in-law that is to be, Mrs Shulman. It would be nice to be rich!" she added wistfully.

"I must be going, too, Mrs Poyser!" cried Ada Hummel. "Did I say a ha'penny pepper, too? Well, Mrs Shulman, it should be in a lucky hour! Travelling on the same ship as Bella Winberg!" She retreated, shaking her head in incredulous wonder.

II

But before the ship which bore Mick Shulman back home berthed in Liverpool, he sent a phantom of himself before him to

457

announce his coming. They had made a talkie of him in New York, for the *Movietone News*. As fast as liner could bring the film to Ireland and aeroplane to England, the Mick Shulman film news item travelled. On the night of its first presentation in the Palasseum Theatre in Doomington, the whole of Magnolia Street rallied forth to acclaim its paragon. The management sent a special invitation to the Shulman family. The whole family went, including the Rabbi, who had never been to a cinema in his life before, talkie or silent. The Rabbi got more and more wild-eyed as the titan noises possessed the atmosphere and the giant shapes jigged across the screen. When his son came on at length, his jaw dropped, his hands fastened like talons on the edge of the seat before him.

"It's all right, father!" his son, Solly, the doctor, yelled at him across the roars of acclamation. "It's only machinery!" The Rabbi was disposed to accept things from Solly that he would not credit from any other source.

"Yes! Yes!" said the Rabbi weakly. But he was not convinced. He mopped his brow with a large red handkerchief.

That was Micky, his son — not in the flesh, it seemed. No, certainly, his flesh was not a mere flat flicker of whitenesses and blacknesses. On both sides of him were taller Israelites. (These were his trainers and managers.) He looked like a young King of Israel with his bodyguard flanking him, from the foothills of Samaria round about Shechem.

That was not Micky in the flesh. But this was his voice, his small son's voice. "Hello, folks!" said Micky. "How are you all? I'm coming back to you right now!" (He had been in America only a year, but he already had a decided American twang). "Who says it won't be good to be back in little old England?"

There was so much enthusiasm in the Palasseum that two women had to be carried out in a dead faint. One of them lived in Oleander Street, in the house whose back door faced the back door of the house where Mick Shulman was born. Mrs Shulman looked on calmly when the attendants carried the two women out.

"I wonder what time it is?" she asked loudly for the tenth time. She lifted out of her bodice the enormous gold watch her son had sent her from America to hook on to her gold chain. "It's getting late," she said. But she did not know if it was late or early, night or day, winter or summer. She was too happy to care.

Chapter 5

I

There is less than an hour to go before the SS *Calibantic* swings out for Liverpool from the Twenty-Third Street dock in New York. There is the usual last minute welter on board ship — stewards staggering up the gangways with luggage, distraught ladies who have mislaid their bags, children shrieking, nurses trying to calm them, lovers hugging desperately the last time for the hundredth time, wheedlings of the purser for better cabins, arrivals of boys with telegrams, flowers, books, baskets of fruit, boxes of chocolates.

But all the excitement on board is as nothing to compare with the pushing and swaying of the huge mob assembled on the dockside to see the *Calibantic* off. This is obviously something more than the usual send off, there are more than the usual friends, relatives, business partners. There must be some distinguished personage who bids goodbye to America, the bountiful mother, this morning. Who can it be? A Nobel Prize winner? Oh certainly not. An illustrious politician? He can't be illustrious enough for this. A film star? That is not at all improbable.

Actually it is Battling Kid Shulman, light-weight champion of the world, who beat Young Benny Marcus for the title so gloriously about a month ago. He is now, at this very moment, approaching the gangway, with a woman on either hand. The officials are doing all they can to clear a way for him, but it is all he can do to force his way forward. The whole 'fancy' of New York is here, to wish the Kid 'Godspeed'. It is noted on all hands that, though he's a limey, he's a reg'lar feller. All England in New York that could get away from its job — if it had any job to get away from — is here, too. But the hoarsest, the most abandoned, of the Englanders are the Doomington contingent. They haven't got any throats left. It is odd to hear so much hefty Doomington among all that downtown yelping and southern chanting and mid-western rattling and universal roaring.

Doomington is here today. But the white heat of the flame is Longton, the streets of the flowering shrubs, Magnolia Street. Magnolia Street is here today to bid its most distinguished son

'Godspeed' to Magnolia Street. The whole Seipel family has got the morning off on various pretexts — except Reb Feivel. The occasion would have been a little too strenuous for the old man.

But Mr Seipel has been cheering till his tongue is swollen, though he is not quite clear in his mind what it is that young Shulman has done exactly. Mrs Seipel has spent most of her time crying, though she interrupted her tears to utter an occasional shrill cheer. She is not crying because Mick has become a world champion. She is crying because he is going back to Magnolia Street and she is not. He will be able to go in to Mrs Poyser's grocery-shop any day he likes and drop in to have a cup of tea with the Emmanuels, the Edelmans — all of whom seem to her across the mist of time and sea a little more glorious than they actually are. She mops her eyes. Her handkerchief is quite wet. Then she opens her mouth again and cheers wildly. But her voice makes no more impression on that tumult than the buzzing of a fly.

The three boys are there, Sam, Eli and Berel. They have cheered so fiercely that they are all quite blue in the face.

Jane Seipel is there. But she has hardly raised her voice. She had hoped to be able to get up to Mick Shulman and slip into his hand a letter addressed to Enid Cooper. It would have been so lovely if Enid could have received a letter from her which had been taken in person across the Atlantic. She knew there would be a crowd, of course, but she did not suspect so vast a multitude. There was not the least hope of getting within yards of him.

And when young Shulman came into sight at length he had a woman on each arm. One of them, older than himself, was none other than Bella Winberg, even in her travelling clothes a mass of platinum and diamonds. Jane had read in the eminent Walter Winchell's gossip column the romantic story of how the two old-time neighbours had met — she, one of the richest Jewesses in New York, he the world's boxing champion, whose gloves dripped gold pieces.

Born in the same small street in an English ghetto, they had met again, after many years, in the fabulous apartment of Berman P. Teitelbaum, the steam-heated cave of a Hebrew Aladdin. The pen even of the hard-boiled Mr Winchell had quivered a little with emotion. How well preserved Bella Winberg looked, how good-tempered! She moved with so complete an unselfconsciousness, that you might have concluded the ovation was for her rather than for her escort.

460

The other woman was a few years younger than Mick. It was evidently Mick's fiancée, Clara Teitelbaum. Jane recognised her from the photographs. Was the tale true, Jane wondered, that they had published in a thousand chatty paragraphs? Was it a shade too symmetrically romantic? Was it a final blare on the trumpets of publicity? The young lady had previously been engaged, it was said, to Young Benny Marcus. But when the referee counted eight and he still didn't get up, she felt she could not bear him any more. Her affections turned right about turn. She knew she could not live another day without the Kid from Doomington. He had a flattened nose, but at least he had not got a cauliflower ear, like Young Benny Marcus. It was all fixed up then and and there in Mick's dressing-room.

They don't mark time in New York. The engagement took place next night in Riverside Drive.

Or was it all the work, Jane wondered, of some super Mr Billig?

Miss Teitelbaum was dabbing her eyes industriously. The cinema operators were turning their handles industriously.

"Don't you take on so, honey!" he was saying to her — or words like them. "You know I'm just going over to pick up the old folks and bring 'em back with me to New York! Wipe away them tears, baby!"

But seeing that the space between them and the cinema operator just to the left of the gangway was quite clear, she threw her arms round her little champion impulsively and sobbed bitterly upon his chest.

The final gong shuddered throughout all the decks. The gangways were removed. The great liner thrust her nose towards the open sea.

The crowd melted. No-one was left but a few loiterers. Mr and Mrs Seipel moved away with their two younger sons between them.

"Well, Janey," her eldest brother wanted to know, "Aren't you ever coming?"

She turned round at a gentle touch upon her arm. "All right, Sam," she said, "I'm coming. I was just thinking."

Chapter 6

I

There were many attractive women and distinguished men on the passenger list of the SS *Calibantic*, but none more attractive and distinguished than Bella Winberg and Mick Shulman. The actresses who had been making talkies in Hollywood and the authors who had been lecturing and signing copies of their works behind Macy's book-counter, had their followings. But these did not compare with the crowds that surged after Mick and Bella, from lounge to bar, from bar to boat deck.

It was not at all what Mick and Bella wanted. They had both had a hectic time lately in their various ways, and they both wanted to take things quietly. That was where Alfred M. Turnbull, their stockbroker friend from Chicago, was so useful. After a day or two he managed to keep their party down to an inner ring of never more than twenty people. Mick, of course, couldn't do anything in that line himself. He couldn't elbow anyone out of the way without cracking his collar-bone. But Alfred M. Turnbull, coming from Chicago, was allowed to exercise any persuasion short of a machine-gun.

Of course it wasn't the fault of the male passengers that they clustered round Bella Winberg. (That was not her name now, but she would not be our Bella by any other.) Men had always clustered round her, from the days when she disposed herself on a red plush sofa in Magnolia Street till now, when her enormous drawing room — all brocade, silk, satin, handpainted oil paintings in hand-carved frames, crystal chandeliers, trays of candy, vases of priceless flowers, radio-cabinet, four inch thick carpet — was the salon of the most *recherché* Jewish aristocracy of Riverside Drive. She did nothing but sit down and stay there and by the mere fact of staying there brought all the men for miles dancing about her like moths round a candle.

She had a husband, of course. He was a Swedish Jew. He was blond — or had been blond, for he was bald now. He had blue eyes. He sold to rich intellectuals electric light fittings that looked as if the sewers had got into the wrong place. He sold to ordinary people fittings to light up their houses. He was rich. He was sharp and mysterious. Secret actresses were imputed to him. He combined the chief faults of the Nordic and Mediterranean races.

No wonder Bella liked to go to Europe or Florida as often as she could without fatiguing herself. No wonder her husband loaded her neck, arms and hands, with platinum collarettes, bracelets and rings, so that she should not be cold when she travelled.

But she did not need to wear platinum and diamonds to attract the men. She would have attracted them as much if she wore nothing at all.

And of course it was not the fault of the women that they clustered round Mick Shulman, light-weight champion of the world. Not a few of them had paid many dollars to see him knock out Young Marcus. What arms he had! What thighs they were! A doctor had declared that he had never met an athlete with such terrific lungs. His nose was not good. But he was a boxer, wasn't he? He wasn't a Ziegfeld Folly Girl.

It was a good thing that in addition to her maid and chauffeur and his trainer and manager, they had Alfred M. Turnbull in their retinue. He was not an employee of theirs, of course. He was a first-class passenger, who was taking a month's trip to Europe for the good of his health. He sold real estate to the Chicago racketry and bought and sold stock for them on the stock market. One of his clients, apparently, had developed a grievance against him. Another of his clients had told him to go to Europe for a month and have a holiday. When he came back the first client would not have a grievance any longer. He wouldn't have anything to keep it in.

So Alfred M. Turnbull booked a berth on the *Calibantic* and wondered what he was going to do with himself. Life wasn't life to him unless he was arranging things and managing things. "I'm the boy," he told his clients, "who put the serve in Service."

And then he saw the excitement on the dock-side when Mick Shulman said goodbye to New York. His eye fell on Bella and Mick and he became their servant at once. Quietly and enormously he appropriated them. They became his nurselings, his gangsters, his stock exchange. He wasn't out to make anything. Was it not he who had put the serve in Service? He had been a man without an aim or guiding star for four whole weeks to come. And four weeks means a lot to a man from Chicago, where they do as much in a day as an Englishman in a fortnight and a Spaniard in six months.

But now... he was their steward, their masseur, their saxophonist, their duenna. He put money for them on the two daily sweeps, the decimal sweep and the noon-to-noon mileage sweep. And Bella Winberg won one or both with cloying regularity. (For she was born under a star which was Zeus to her Danae and embraced her in a shower of gold. In the excitements that had disturbed the New York stock exchange for the last year or two, she had been a little bear or a little bull at exactly the right moments.)

He put money on sweeps for Bella and Mick, he mixed the cocktails for the holy-of-holy cocktail parties she gave in her suite. When Bella did not dance with Mick, he humbly took Mick's place, and danced more divinely than any of the gigolos to whom Bella paid vast sums at Biarritz — the gigolos with whom she danced, not because she was in need of men to dance with, but because the rich American women always competed for the most expensive gigolos. He always saw to it that the deck-tennis court was empty when Bella and Mick wanted to play, and always contrived to lose to Bella in singles, though she just smiled and never moved an inch. He was their chattel and their shah, their doormat and their halo.

It wasn't quite like that until the second day at sea. During the first two days he lived some sort of a life of his own. He even had a drink with another group after dinner on the second day. Then he came back again to Mick and Bella.

And then the thing happened, the thing that wrapped him up in a parcel and tied him round with string and wrote their names on a label. The conversation had strayed in the direction of a rather fat and elderly gentleman sitting a few tables away. He had two gold teeth and chewed his cigar and had tried to be pleasant to Bella. Bella did not like him.

Alfred M. Turnbull thought this was the moment in which to show a little of the rough stuff. It would not displease Bella to know she had two henchmen to fight her fights for her, not merely one. He protruded his lower lip.

"If that dirty little Jew —" he said. He did not say more than that. For the next moment Mick Shulman, the son of the Rabbi of the Lithuanian Brotherhood, brought forward his left fist in that same hook which did all the damage to Benny Marcus at

Madison Square Garden. Alfred M. Turnbull crashed through the screening behind him and fell among the whisky and brandy glasses of the next table. Everybody was very interested, of course; and it was felt that the moment Turnbull came round, he would shoot the light-weight champion, for he came from Chicago.

He did not. He did nothing. He said nothing. He judged it was not necessary to apologise, for Mick was certain to understand how sorry he was. Of course he had not intended to hurt Mick's feelings. He now realised Mick was a Jew and had not realised it before. There are human beings so illustrious that the mind does not enquire of them are they Christians or Jews or Moslems. Who pauses to enquire whether a Sarah Bernhardt, a Lord Reading, an Edna Ferber, is a Jew or whether a Mussolini, a Pierre Benoit, is a Christian?

So it was that Alfred M. Turnbull became a fifth limb to Bella and Mick during the next four weeks. So it was that he became organiser and master of ceremonies, at the celebrated Magnolia Street Party towards which the S.S. *Calibantic* was now speeding full steam ahead, cutting the water with her strong bows.

II

Bella and Mick never quite decided from which of them the idea actually sprang. It was Bella, almost certainly, who was responsible for the idea of a party as a party. She was always giving parties in Riverside Drive or the Negresco in Nice or the Crillon in Paris, wherever she happened to be. She was always giving them and always going to them. It was the natural rhythm of her existence.

She was not particularly interested in them. She much preferred to sit on a sofa, the only woman in a room, with lots of men fluttering all round her. But it never occurred to her not to give and not to go to parties. If it had, the thought would have alarmed her. What on earth would she do with all her money? There is, after all, a limit to the amount of space a woman has on which to display platinum and diamonds. And what on earth would she do with her time? So she gave parties and went to them. So she suggested to Mick that he and she should give a party.

She had not been to Doomington for several years. Her people had never moved from the house in Didsbury which they bought when they became, according to Doomington standards, rich. She did not like the house. It was small and cold. Her parents could come and stay with her at the Ritz, if they liked. They did so, once or twice. But this time she had arranged to put in a week or two in Doomington. It was about time she paid the old folk a visit. And she liked Mick. He was a good person to be with; he was a change after all the New York business-men and smart alecks. It was cosy and homely, being with him — it brought back the old old days.

"Let's have a party," she said, "while I'm in Doomington. What do you say, Micky?"

"Sure!" said Mick. "Wouldn't that be fine!" And then the words were on his lips before he knew that he was uttering them.

"Say, why not a Magnolia Street Party?"

She threw back her head and laughed her low gurgling eastern laugh. "A Magnolia Street Party? Ha, ha, ha! Ha, ha, ha!"

Then suddenly she stopped laughing. A sudden flicker of the wild glory of the idea crackled before her eyes.

"What do you say? A Magnolia Street Party?"

"Yes, yes!" he said. "Why not?"

He was a little crestfallen. After all was it not exactly Magnolia Street they had in common, that and no more? Was she ashamed of Magnolia Street? Was she? Well, *he* wasn't! He still had no clear idea at all of what the words proposed. But a feeling of profound loyalty towards the little street where he was born, where he had lived these more than twenty years, where he had fought his first fights and won his first victories, surged up in him.

"Yes, yes!" he cried. "Let's have a Magnolia Street Party!" Then he shoved his jaw out. His eyes grew fierce. "And if you won't I will!"

But even as he spoke she saw the party in all its virginal and serene beauty take shape between the table and the portholes that soared above and swooped below the edge of the green sea. She rose from her easy chair and threw her arms about the young boxer and kissed him.

"How wonnerful!" she cried. "How perfectly wonnerful!"

She cast her mind back over the infinite chain of parties along which she had dragged herself link by link — platinum parties, diamond parties, the men playing poker for huge sums, the women sitting together comparing platinum and diamonds.

Mick blushed. He was no longer the whirlwind light-weight who had brought vast crowds to Madison Square Garden and sent his voice through the microphone hallooing over lands and seas. He was a small boy of Magnolia Street again, blushing because a beautiful school-miss had kissed him before all the boys.

"Yes, wouldn't it be fine?" he said shyly.

Bella sank into her chair again. A silence fell between them. Alfred M. Turnbull would not for his life have intruded upon it. Then Bella said quietly: "But tell me, Micky, what exactly do we mean by Magnolia Street?"

He looked puzzled for a moment. "I don't know!" he confessed. "Oh everybody!" He made a vague comprehensive gesture with his right hand.

"Everybody? Yes!" Bella endorsed cordially. "That's just what it must be! Jews, Christians —"

"Of course!" assented Mick. The throats which had so hoarsely acclaimed him were neither Jewish nor Christian throats. From the high eminence where he stood these distinctions became infinitesimal... excepting when someone suddenly shouted in his ear. "If that dirty Jew —"

"We must have a big hall!" he suggested.

"The biggest we can get! You remember? The Convention Rooms, in Begley Hill Road!"

"Oo-oo!" said Mick. He forgot for the moment he was wealthy, and engaged to a wealthy heiress. He forgot Bella's millions. He only remembered that all his life long the Convention Rooms were associated in his mind with motor-cars, crystal chandeliers, expensive weddings, unapproachable functions where there was no place for little ghetto boys.

"You see?" Bella went on. "It must be the biggest hall in the Magnolia Street district, otherwise some of the old folk will have trouble in getting there!"

"Of course!" Mick agreed.

"I'll know practically nobody who lives there now!" announced Bella wistfully. It was the voice in which she announced she had never met Douglas Fairbanks or Lord Rothschild. "Most of them will have moved!"

"Look here!" said Mick. He suddenly remembered how rich he was. And how rich Clara Teitelbaum was. "We must have everybody! Everybody who lived there when you did. Let 'em all come!"

"And since?" asked Bella,

Alfred M. Turnbull permitted himself to say a word. "Say, folks," he said, "How many houses are there in this yer street?"

"Twelve a side!" said Mick promptly.

"When did you leave, Bella?"

Bella paused a moment. She didn't mind being Magnolia Street with the distinguished young man who had been her neighbour. It wasn't quite the same thing with a Chicago stockbroker. She licked her lips with her little pink tongue.

"Oh couple of years before the War!" she said. "Maybe more!"

Alfred M. Turnbull closed his eyes and made a quick calculation. "Couldn't be more than a coupla hundred people at most, I guess! Would that be too many?"

"No!" said Bella, smiling at him sweetly. "Not with *you* to organise things, Alfred!"

Then she suddenly had a vision of a tall gentleman, pale and tall, with broad shoulders and a head balanced insecurely on his neck. An industrious gentleman. An enthusiastic gentleman. He had been clerk to the Jewish Board of Guardians.

Then her hands tightened on the padded arms of her chair. She had a further vision of this same tall gentleman. He was standing on a platform, the sweat pouring from his forehead. Faint and clear came a drumming and thudding across the years, across the drum and thud of the liner's engines, above the swish of the long seas. Drumming and thudding of feet. Rhythmic clapping of hands. *We want Benny! We want Benny! We want Benny!*

"Ladies and gentlemen," shrieked Mr Emmanuel. "I want Benny, too! We all want Benny! He's on his way now! He'll be here at any moment...!"

But Benny Edelman had not turned up.

"Tell me!" cried Bella Winberg. "Does Mr Emmanuel still live in Magnolia Street?"

"He did a year ago! He won't have moved! Why?"

468

"Why, honey, why? I'll tell you why! There was a Magnolia Street Party once before. It was Mr Emmanuel's party. You weren't born then, Micky!"

"Oh yes, I was!" said Micky. "You mean when Benny Edelman ran off with the *goyah*? I've heard all about it often! I was born right enough! I was three!"

"Why, yes! So you *were*, Micky! My God, what a party! It mustn't be that sort of a party, Micky!"

"It won't!" said Micky, setting his jaw. It was the way he set his jaw when he promised the managers he wouldn't let the match go beyond the third round.

"It won't!" corroborated Alfred M. Turnbull. He didn't know what it was all about, but he realised that Magnolia Street had once been mixed up with a "flop," and "flops" kept back-stage when Alfred M. Turnbull took the footlights.

"No, it won't!" summed up Bella Winberg. She had had something to do with that earlier party, but she had been a slip of a girl then. She had organised parties since that time. They had not been "flops." They had been "wows." She appraised her two lieutenants, the stock-broker and the prize-fighter. She looked down at the enormous solitaire glittering on her finger.

"No, it won't!" she repeated. Then she went on: "We'll need him, just the same, this Mr Emmanuel. He'll be all right, so long as he's looked after properly. Who's going to work out the list of guests? It'll take whole days and nights to find out where they all are now. Who's going to send out the invitations? Gee, I'm so excited I can't see straight!" Then she stopped. "What was the name of that smart baby who walked off with the gold watch? At least they all swore he did. Derricks, wasn't it?" She looked down once more at her solitaire, at her platinum bracelets, this time a little apprehensively. "Oh yes, they're insured!" she said. "But I think he'd best get no invitation, just the same!"

"It wouldn't reach him," said Mick. "He's probably doing a turn in Dartmoor!"

She sighed. "That boy had talent," she said, "and such a nice clean face... What am I talking about, *that boy*! It's twenty years ago, now! And poor Benny Edelman," she continued. "He was too busy to turn up at the last party! Wouldn't it be grand if he could turn up at this one! But there's no chance of that, I suppose. His old mother's still alive, is she?"

"Of course he will," said Mick. "Haven't you heard about Benny Edelman?"

She smiled faintly, but Mick did not notice it. The air for him was too full of Magnolia Street shadows. "No," she said. "I've been out of touch for a long time. Alfred!" she turned round to her stock-broker. "Alfred, get us some drinks! Micky! Tell me about George Derricks! Tell me about his brother, the Longton Nightingale! Tell me about Benny Edelman! It wasn't a happy marriage, was it? Tell me about that sailor! He *did* marry the Berman girl? Yes, her name was Rose. How it all comes back! It might have been yesterday! Tell me all you know, Micky!"

III

So, during the next few days, Mick Shulman told Bella Winberg all he knew about Magnolia Street. It was surprising how much he knew, seeing that he had spent most of his time since he was a small boy preparing to knock noses in, and knocking them in. He surprised himself by the amount he knew. He was not a good raconteur. He had a limited vocabulary and an artless method of telling his tale. But Bella Winberg listened entranced. When Ruth Draper or Otis Skinner told their tales on New York stages or in expensive drawing rooms, she had not listened half so breathlessly.

Alfred M. Turnbull had a thin time. He had nothing much to do but mix drinks and wrap rugs round Bella's knees. Then he sat down and looked at her, listening the while to the tales Mick Shulman told of a tribe of inconceivable people who lived in a slum street in a dark English town. The people seemed stranger to him than the pygmies of the African jungle or the Sakais of Malaya, who live up in the hills and make their clothes out of the bark of trees.

It was as if the people of Magnolia Street, living or dead, came forward from their city and the shore of their land, and trod the heaving waters till they found the ship where their two kinsmen were sailing, and slid viewlessly from deck to deck until they found them; and, finding them, whispered in their ear with not quite the sound of the waters whispering. And they said: You may go far. You may dazzle all eyes with jewels. You may make great arenas resound with acclamation. But you will not leave us behind utterly, for ever and ever. You will remember us again, and come back to us.

He told her of Kate Ritchie and the black man who had not come again and the silent courtier who paid court twice a year. He told her the tragic tale of the tram-conductor, Hubbard. He told her how Mr Billig now lived in front Begley Hill Road, and of Becky Poyser, her husband and her children. He told her the tale of old Mrs Durbin. (There were many details that he was ignorant of, or that eluded him. These she learned later and added to the blunt outline he had sketched for her.)

Mrs Durbin's barber-saloon had gone to rack and ruin. She gave up being a lather-boy, because all the strength went out of the edges of her palms. She would sit all day long passing two papier-mâché disks through her fingers. They had the name 'A. Durbin' stamped in them, with his regiment and number and religion. One of the disks was oval and had two holes punched in it, as if he had worn it on a bracelet. The other was circular and had one hole. He wore that on a necklet.

The disks did not make Mrs Durbin believe one bit that her son, Arthur, was really dead. It's quite easy to snip a boy's disks off when he's lying unconscious or wandering about with a lost memory. She got more and more certain he was coming back any day now. He didn't of course. She got a nice letter from King George in which he wrote:

"I join with my grateful people in sending you this memorial of a brave life given for others in the Great War."

Accompanying the letter was a certificate in beautiful black capital letters. There was a painted shield on top with a lion on one side and a unicorn on the other. Underneath was Arthur's name and regiment written in lovely red ink.

But it threw her into an awful state. She tore the letter and certificate into fragments and threw them into the fire, and then came into the shop, shouting and shaking her fist. Now that sort of behaviour doesn't do any sort of business any good, least of all a barber-shop. And Bill Stephens, her barber, wasn't very steady at the best of times. Andy Dexter, Steve Tawnie's son-in-law, was in the chair at the moment, being shaved by Bill Stephens. He got up an awful sight, with a lump of ear hanging loose.

The thing was that she knew for positive Arthur was coming back. She'd seen it in the cards and the tea-leaves. And in the old

471

days if any woman in Magnolia Street had jeered at cards and tea-leaves, that woman had been Mrs Durbin. She used to fair hold her sides skitting and jeering. Which shows what happens if you start playing about with such things, even in fun.

So she died. The stock and goodwill were going very cheap. And a young Dutch couple, seeing Albert Durbin's advertisement in the *Hairdressers' Journal* and knowing a cheap thing when they saw it, snapped it up. That was why the place was called Clausen's Pompeian Rooms now, not Durbin's Barber-Saloon. Albert Durbin, the other brother, had a room in Aubrey Street. He had been blinded in the War and wore a large pair of blue spectacles. You often saw him up and down, with a big volume of Braille under his arm.

Then there was George Derricks, who had taken Benny Edelman's watch that time, sure as eggs were eggs, though no-one could actually swear they had seen him do it. He had not come back again to Magnolia Street since his triumphant home-coming with the DCM in 1916. Mick was nine at the time. He remembered that home-coming very vividly. George had been brought to mind by the Sunday papers from time to time, during the last few years, though he had not appeared in person. Not those arid papers which devote columns and columns to books and music and pictures, so much as those more right-minded sheets which appreciate the aroma of a good piece of adultery, embezzlement, murder or perversion when it hits their noses.

When news was published about George Derricks, they generally published his photograph, too. But that was not much help as a rule, because they always seemed to publish the same photograph, whatever the man's name was, and whatever crime he had committed. It makes the criminal look like a draper's assistant, with plastered-down hair, thin eyebrows and a stiff collar; which was, however, exactly what George Derricks had always looked like.

Whenever the papers published George Derricks's photograph they published several names be had been known by, for he had had a number of careers, all separated by a longer or shorter period of retirement. But it was not to be imagined that he was a violent person. He did not knock people on the head or kidnap schoolgirls. He was usually associated with respectable matrons in Soho night-clubs. She introduced gentlemen of position to her young ladyfriends and George obtained possession of their wallets. And their watches, of course. He had always had a great weakness for watches. But he was fastidious about them, too. If any of those watches were the reward paid for an industrious accumulation of cigarette coupons, he replaced them in the pockets or on the wrists of his clients. The ethics of such presentations shocked him. He did not believe in the principle of something for nothing.

And then Mick told her the tale of Benny Edelman and his old mother; here again, he told her only the bare outline. She learned a good deal more from Mick's sister, Rachel, when she took her off to the dressmaker in St. Anne's Square, to fit her out properly for the Party.

Old Mrs Edelman was an unforgiving woman. When her son, Benny, married a gentile, she sat on a low stool for seven days and mourned him for dead. Merely because he went to the War and had his leg blown off he did not come back again to life for her. He remained dead, unforgiven.

She hastened the marriage of Norman, her younger son, in order that a small boy might be born to take the dead one's place. A boy was duly born, but his mother went out walking on the clay-croft and drowned him.

She did not actually assert that Fanny tied a brick round his neck and threw him into the water. But that was her attitude. The boy's father came back from internment in Holland, and found out what had happened, though his wife had kept it from him. He forgave her, but his mother did not. The old woman went about the house with stern eyes and grim lips. She did her duties and spent as much time as she might in the synagogue. But even on a summer day, after she had been in the house again for five minutes, she made the air seem cold and harsh.

The strain was doing Fanny no good, so Norman took her to live in a small house in Rosemary Street. There was nothing else for it. He helped his mother with so much a week and she took in lodgers, as she had always done. She was a lonely old woman, sitting in the kitchen with the *Pentateuch* before her and the spectacles slipping down her thin nose. There was no sound except the cat mewing for milk sometimes. Her lips moved rapidly as she spelled out the holy words, but no sound left them.

Of course Benny was not dead merely because he had married a gentile woman. He often wished he were. His marriage had not been a success. He was handsome enough, but as a lover not at all subtle. His wife often remembered her first husband, the insurance agent, and realised with dismay that elderly and scraggy as he had been, he could give the Jew points in lots of things. Benny was good-looking but his soul was soft as dough. She was good looking, but her soul was hard as nails.

And then he went to the War and lost his leg. She was quite pleased and excited about it for a long time and talked about her hero and walked about Laburnum Street as if she owned the place. He came back to her with an artificial leg after a long sojourn in a hospital near London. That renewed her pleasure for a time and she showed him off with great pride to her customers till the War ended, and even for some months after.

But the creaking the leg made had already started to worry her. She got more and more irritable about it. And when he took his leg off at night to get into bed beside her it made her quite sick. After a time she said she couldn't stand it any more. So she made up a mattress for him in the stock-room and he had to sleep there. She was a vigorous woman, and a strong male was a necessity to her. She had already had recourse to one or two while Benny was at the front, and even earlier, it was said. So a man named Jim Hawkins used to come in and visit her. He was a good-looking fellow. He and Tommie used to go off to football matches on Saturday afternoon; when they came back a hot bath and a fine tea awaited them. And Benny and Tommie looked after the shop while Mrs Edelman and Jim Hawkins had a good time together.

It soon got to the point that they spent the whole night together, while poor Benny lay tossing about on his mattress alone in the stock-room. Whenever Jim Hawkins spent the night, the phantom toes of the leg Benny hadn't got itched like anything.

He was a timid person and he might have put up with the situation, if it hadn't been for Tommie. He and Tommie were fond of each other, for, after all, he had saved Tommie's life. The boy used often to take him along to the cinema out of his pocket-money and provide him with smokes. He could have stood Jessie's snubs if Tommie hadn't been there. The presence of the lad hurt him dreadfully.

474

Yet the situation was only tolerable just because Tommie *was* there. He was a free nice-minded kid. If it hadn't been for Tommie, he'd have stumped off long ago, wooden leg and all. He hadn't a clear idea where he'd go to, of course, and what he'd do when he got there. He wouldn't go and fling himself on Norman, his younger brother. His pride wouldn't let him. As for going back to his mother in Magnolia Street... Benny sighed mournfully and scratched his head. He knew that he had been dead a good many years now.

And now he was pretty well dead so far as his wife was concerned, too. Jim Hawkins treated him rather like that, too, as if he were a dead piece of junk in the cistern cupboard.

But it wasn't like that with the people who lived in Magnolia Street. They kept him carefully alive. He knew that if ever a word was breathed regarding a Jew boy or girl and a Christian sweetheart, the first thing that was pointed out to them was Benny Edelman, whom God had punished in so many ways.

Benny Edelman was very miserable No wonder he sometimes wept a little in the darkness of the stock-room, amid the cases of cigarettes, while the sharp peals of Jessie's laughter rang through the house and Jim Hawkins urged hoarsely; "Quiet, you fool! Do you want the 'ole street to 'ear?"

When Hawkins first appeared on the scene, Tommie didn't quite know what it was about. But he didn't remain long in ignorance. He refused to go to football matches on Saturday afternoons with his mother's friend. He glowered at him. Bad blood developed between them. The crisis was not long delayed. It seemed to Jim Hawkins that the only thing to do was to learn the young brat. He learned him savagely, when Tommie next gave him a chance. He had a bad time of it himself.

It was just before dawn next day, that the door of the stock-room opened very softly.

"Hello!" asked Benny. "Who's that?"

"Ssh!" said Tommie. "It's only me!"

"What's wrong? Where you going to? What you dressed for?"

"Ssh, Benny! I'm running away. I just want to say goodbye to you. I'm going to be a soldier!"

"Oh Tommie!" It was a piteous voice. "It'll be like... like bloody hell without you, Tommie lad!"

"I can't stick it no longer, Benny! So long! I'll send you a postcard!"

"Tommie, listen here! Don't go!"

"I must go! Why?"

"Wait for me! Come in while I get dressed! I've had enough!"

"Jesus!"

"Ssh! I'll be two-twos!"

"Benny, where'll you go? You can't be a soldier with that gammy leg!"

"I'm getting out of here!" Benny dressed. He had a small store of silver coins he'd been collecting in the chimney against a rainy day. He put them in his pocket. The two stole quietly downstairs.

"Lean on me!" said Tommie. "Then your leg... it won't crack so much!"

They slipped the bolts of the back door. They were free.

"Well, Benny?"

"You look here, Tommie! I know where I'm going! I've been wanting to for a long time, oh years and years. Perhaps they won't want me! In that case, I'll come back to you and we'll see what. If they do want me, I'll stay. I won't come back, so you'll understand why. That's not till this evening. Do you want to get out of it now, at once?"

"Do I hellaslike? It's all right to me, today, tomorrow, or next week I've got a quid put by. What shall we do, Benny?"

"Well, what shall we do?"

"First a bite of breakfast. Then, what d'you say? We can go over to the Zoo this morning! And this afternoon, City's playing Aston Villa! What a pity you can't wait till after tonight. Buster Frogley's trying to break the record on the dirt-track!"

"I don't know! I may be back again in time for that. Anyhow, let's have breakfast first! Wait, I can't walk so fast!"

"Gee!" said Tommie. "It's going to be a fine day, too! What the hell we waited so long for? Ain't this like the pictures?"

"Is Mrs Edelman in?" asked Benny Edelman.

It was one of the lodgers who had come to the door.

"No!" said the lodger. He was about to close the door.

"Is she far?" asked Benny.

"She is at the synagogue, at the corner there. She goes every evening!"

"Oh, then I'll wait!" said Benny. He came in and walked straight through to the kitchen and sat down on the metal stool near the fire.

The lodger was only a new lodger. He shook his head and went upstairs. Evidently the visitor knew his way about. Benny Edelman sat down. He knew that his mother had gone to the synagogue. He had been waiting about at the corner till he saw her go in. He had not sat on that stool for twenty years. A good deal had happened since then. He had saved a small gentile boy from a pond. His brother's small boy had been drowned in that pond. There had been a War. He had lost a leg. His wooden leg creaked in the twilight of the kitchen. Jehovah shows his pleasure in strange ways....

He did not know how long he sat there, his hands on his knees, his head on his hands. The fire was banked up with slack. The flames burst through at length. His long shadow swayed along the scrubbed linoleum.

He heard the sound of a key in the front door lock. He heard the steps of his mother coming along the lobby. They were firm steps despite her years.

She came down into the kitchen. She caught sight of a man sitting beside the fire, on the metal stool.

"Who is it?" she said.

Benny lifted his head from between his hands. "It is I, your son, Benny!"

She stopped. Her heart seemed to stop, too, arrested in an empty space. She had had a son Benny who died. She had had a grandson Jacky who was drowned. She was an old woman.

Neither of them moved or said another word for some time. But his head drooped towards his hands. His leg creaked in its socket.

She came nearer. A current flowed in short sharp waves into her heart and out again. Her cheeks were flushed. The rims of her eyes were hot.

"The kettle!" she said. "Why didn't you boil the kettle? Fill the kettle at once!"

"So that we can expect Benny Edelman to come to the party after all!" breathed Bella Winberg.

"Not without his Mamma!" said Mick. "Mamma won't let him out of her sight in a hurry!"

"And he's quite grown up now," Bella murmured wistfully. "We've all quite grown up!"

"You?" objected Mick. He fished about for something gallant to say, but was not equal to it. "Jeeze!" he said. "It's going to be a swell party! Have a drink, Bella? What? Say, Bella, you look all dopy! What's wrong?"

"Nothing's wrong, Micky!" murmured Bella. She rested her elbows on her knees, and her chin on her cupped palms. Her eyes took on a far focus, as if they looked beyond the small table they were sitting at, beyond the rail of the liner, beyond the sliding seas. Then she turned suddenly to Micky.

"Did you know the Seipels?" she asked.

"The Seipels?" he said vaguely. "What Seipels?"

"They used to live in Magnolia Street!"

"Did they? Oh you mean the *Seipels*. Oh yes, I know. Berel Seipel was a lance-corporal in the brigade when I was a sergeant. But they lived in Oleander Street. Berel and I used to talk to each other from the back room windows. But what on earth puts the Seipels into your head?"

"No, they lived in Magnolia Street when we lived there," she said quietly. "They went off to live in Hulme during the War and ran a candy-store. Then Mr Seipel came back from the War. I suppose he got the habit of being careless with his cigarette ends in the army. It's a bad thing in a candy-store with all those shavings and wrappings about. So he burned the whole place down."

"I seem to remember something about it," murmured Mick. "I was only about eleven then. But where on earth do you get all this dope from?"

"They came back to Longton. They wanted to come back to Magnolia Street, but there was only one house empty, the one where there'd been a murder."

"Yes," said Mick. "Hubbard's."

"That's right. Hubbard's. And they didn't fancy that. So they took a house in Oleander Street instead."

"I give it up," exclaimed Mick helplessly. "What size boots did they wear?"

She turned her face towards him again. "You want to know how I know all this?"

"You've got second sight."

"There was a big crowd at the dock when we sailed. Did you notice it?"

"I did," said Mick.

"You didn't notice the Seipel family was there, too?"

"Now, Bella, you're trying to get a free ride on me."

"Oh yes they were."

"Nothing much escapes you."

"You're quite right."

"And you mean to tell me they told you all this, on the dock, with half New York —"

"No, I mean to say, it was all kinda queer. Seeing the big eyes of that Seipel girl —" Then she broke off suddenly. "Mick, do you know anything about Uncle Adolf?"

"Uncle Adolf? What Uncle Adolf?"

"Now think. Didn't your pal from the brigade ever tell you he had a rich uncle?"

"Did he? He may have done! Say, Bella, hadn't you better lie down?"

"Well, I'm going to tell you a tale about Magnolia Street, see? One *you* don't know. One nobody else knows this side of the Statue of Liberty. Do you think you're the only one who can tell Magnolia Street tales?"

"But where — how —?"

"Jane Seipel. Now you know. She's one of the leading saleswomen in our firm. Strange, isn't it? When she came to America, she had ideas about going to a university and doing welfare work. But there wasn't any Uncle Adolf: so she went into business, instead. Two years ago she came into *our* business. Every year, on my birthday, my husband gives a little supper in our apartment to the head employees. That's how I met Jane Seipel. That's how I heard about Uncle Adolf. I'd always wanted to learn the truth about Uncle Adolf. Though he didn't actually live in Magnolia Street, he seemed to belong to it, quite as much as... Mr Billig, or the old barber-woman, or any of them.

"Do you want to hear about Uncle Adolf, Micky? Or don't you?"

"Shoot!" said Micky.

So as the liner snorted eastward on its way, and the stewards moved from table to table, deftly balancing their trays, Bella Winberg told Mick Shulman her Magnolia Street tale. She told him of the golden letters of Uncle Adolf, of the Ready Money that never quite happened to be ready, of the hope that burned hardly less brightly in the hearts of the Seipels as the difficult years went by.

Excepting in the heart of Jane Seipel. She had never been quite taken in, from the beginning. But for the others — he was

479

the keystone of their arch. They felt they would crumble all of a heap if they gave up believing in him.

However, they determined that Mr Seipel should go first, off his own bat. They managed to scrape the money for his fare, somehow. He went about 1922. Uncle Adolf was waiting for him on the docks in a fever of anxiety. He was a tall shabby haggard creature, Jane Seipel said. She herself did not see him till two years later. All this high talk about his wealth, his business — he was a tremendous Real Estate merchant — was his 'fantasy,' his 'compensation' that was how Jane Seipel called it. He lived alone in a wretched little wooden shanty in Newark, New Jersey. He drank a little. He played cards a lot. Pinochle, of course. Now and again he got a travelling agency for some shoddy vacuum cleaner or coffee-percolator — the sort of stuff they tout round Paterson, New Jersey, or White Plains, New York, on the installment plan.

But he was nothing — nothing! Like a puffball. You touched him and he wasn't there. However, that was not the real point of the story. The real point was the way the Seipels behaved, all of them, one after another.

Uncle Adolf was sweating with anxiety when Mr Seipel arrived at New York. He had not quite known whether to run away or throw himself on his brother-in-law's mercy. That was what he decided to do. He arrived at the docks a good twelve hours before the passengers got off. He walked up and down chewing his lips and tugging at his hair. He must have looked a fine sight.

Mr Seipel was not a very astute person. But he only needed to set eyes on Uncle Adolf to see through him and the whole business in a flash. It was not that it was *all* a tissue of lies. He *had* had a bit of a position twenty-five or thirty years earlier. But of course not the faintest shadow of what he had made out. The picture he painted was of the business it was going to be. He speculated. Obviously he had not the faintest idea of things. So he just collapsed into the dirt.

But he had his pride — like his sister, Mrs Seipel, like Jane Seipel, like all of them. He simply could not bear to let them know how he really stood. And he was fool enough to hope that some coup might any day, in half an hour, put him on his feet again. So those foolish letters went steaming across the Atlantic, month after month, year after year... It was not only foolish, it was wicked. Mr Seipel thought so, anyhow.

But Uncle Adolf just threw himself on his mercy. He was such a wretched creature that Mr Seipel must have felt a positive Napoleon. He could not live without his lie. He could not bear to think his sister over in England knew him for the fool and idiot he was.

So he induced Mr Seipel to back him up. Mr Seipel promised. He tried to avoid the subject in his letters as far as possible, and when they forced him to say something, he admitted that Uncle Adolf's business wasn't going so grand as he had hoped. Which was, of course, quite true. But he didn't give them an inkling of the nasty truth. By now the Seipels no longer expected Uncle Adolf to send over a steam yacht for them. But they still felt he would turn up trumps some time in the vague future. Except Jane Seipel. And *she* didn't know how tragic and comic it all was.

She was the next to go over. She, too, entered the Uncle Adolf conspiracy. She didn't let him down. Her eldest brother went over the year after. He joined the club, too. The rest of the family didn't get across till about 1928. Mrs Seipel was a Russian subject and she couldn't get into America till her husband had taken out his full citizen papers... So they all knew now. But they wrote not one single word to their relatives and friends in Doomington, not one single word. They wouldn't let the poor wretch down, though he had let them down so horribly for so long.

"He's dead now," concluded Bella. "I met Jane Seipel in the office a few months ago. I asked about him, and she told me. But we won't say a word about Uncle Adolf, will we, Mick, not to a soul?"

"What?" cried Mick. "What did you say?" He perceived from the expression on Bella's face that the expected answer was in the negative. "No! No!" he said, hurriedly.

Bella Winberg sighed. "I think it a *swell* story," she said petulantly. "Yes, yes, so do I!"

"Why didn't you listen? Why did you let me go on, if you weren't listening?" She thought it would do the celebrity no harm if she rapped him over the knuckles a little. He looked down at the floor, crestfallen, like a small boy.

"The fact is —" she started severely.

At that moment Alfred M. Turnbull thrust an excited red face round the door of the saloon. Perhaps he judged the moment called for a little judicious interruption.

"Why? What's wrong?" cried Bella.

"Say, babies!" exclaimed Alfred. "Come along and say how d'you do! Here's England! Strikes me as a damp kinda place! Come on now, be respectful!"

Bella and Mick arose and followed him to the deck railings. England was a dark blur athwart a slant of rain. They stood staring out, all three of them, towards England. What England was to Alfred M. Turnbull, it is not easy to say. It was Anne Hathaway's Cottage, perhaps, and the Nelson Monument and a large blue policeman controlling traffic. But to the plump little millionairess and the steel-built boxer alike, England was a small street in Doomington, with a public-house at one corner and a grocery-shop at the corner opposite. A handful of old men went up the stairway of the synagogue to say their prayers.

Chapter 7

I

Bister, the first footman, valeted Max Emmanuel when he went to stay with the Staidlows at Staidlow Towers. Max never opened an eyelid till half-past ten, so at half-past ten Bister tugged respectfully at a blanket. Max, with one eyelid open, but still quite asleep, projected himself out of bed as out of a catapult, through the open door that led to his bathroom and into the bath which Bister had prepared at exactly the right temperature. During the trajectory movement he had miraculously delivered himself of his pyjamas. It was a feat of genius which some of Lord Staidlow's guests appreciated much more than his paintings; sometimes quite a fair section of the house-party gathered at Max's door to see him perform it. For, after all, Houdini was both awake and stationary when he extracted himself from his padlocked coats of mail, whilst Max was both asleep and moving rapidly when he extracted himself from his pyjamas.

Arrived in the bath, both eyelids opened. He was awake. He bathed. He shaved. Fourteen minutes later, with a more decorous motion, he returned to bed. One minute after that Bister set his breakfast down on his bed. Bister knew Max hated kedgeree and adored kidneys.

"Thank you, Bister!" said Max. "Oh, letters!"

"Yes, sir!" said Bister. He went to the wardrobe and proceeded to concern himself with trousers and braces.

Max opened his letters. There were the usual invitations to dances and private views. His agent implored him to have the Lady Staidlow portrait ready for his next show a month or two ahead. Max was thirty-four but he was still a Bright Young Painter, much younger and brighter than all the Confusionalists and Chaotics who exploded like rockets every season in a shower of cheap colour and were never seen again. He was so bright and young that his agent had to employ a journalistic ghost for him in order that the world should know what Max Emmanuel thought of the new coiffure, M. Chiappe, provincial cooking in England and the latest Charing Cross Scheme. He was still a bright young painter and it was impossible for him not to show a portrait of Lady Staidlow at his next show, and the show after that, until such time as the next Society hostess took her place as the indispensable sitter.

He opened his last letter without excitement. The address was typewritten. It contained a stiff card, evidently another invitation. He slit the envelope nonchalantly.

"Bister," he asked yawning, "did Lady Staidlow send word with you this morning?"

"Yes, sir," said Bister. "You were not to hurry, sir, but her ladyship will be waiting in the studio at quarter past eleven."

"Thank you, Bister." He extracted the card of invitation from the envelope. A letter came out with it. He recognised his father's delicate handwriting immediately.

"Of course," said Max. "One of his meetings. More love. Lots more. Buckets. But what does he want to invite *me* for?"

He glanced indifferently at the card. Then his eyelids drew back as if an elastic thread had pulled them. His eyes nearly dropped out of his head. These were the terms of the invitation:

MME JONSEN (MISS BELLA WINBERG) OF NEW YORK
AND
MR MICK SHULMAN OF DOOMINGTON
LIGHT-WEIGHT CHAMPION OF THE WORLD
HAVE MUCH PLEASURE IN INVITING YOU
TO A GRAND MAGNOLIA STREET REUNION
ON NOVEMBER THE NINETEENTH 1930, AT 7.30PM
AT THE CONVENTION ROOMS, BEGLEY HILL ROAD
CANTOR WEINGARTEN WILL SING SECULAR SONGS
JIMMIE DUCLANE WILL ENTERTAIN AT THE PIANO
ED LAMPERT'S ORCHESTRA
REFRESHMENTS — DANCING
RSVP TO MR ISAAC EMMANUEL.
13 MAGNOLIA STREET, LONGTON
ADMISSION STRICTLY BY TICKET ONLY
MR EMMANUEL WILL BE GLAD TO CONSIDER
APPLICATIONS FOR
RAILWAY FARE

"Excuse me, sir," said Bister, "is there anything the matter?"

"The matter, Bister? Oh my God, where's the nearest drink?"

"In the smoking room, just under the stairs. Sir, what can I get you?"

484

"Oh, it's all right, Bister, it's perfectly all right. But I think just a dash of gin in a teaspoon of lemonade —"

"Certainly! At once, sir!"

Bister left the room swiftly with a troubled face. Max read his father's letter.

MY DEAR MAX

You will be surprised to receive this invitation. Well, so was I when Madame Jonsen — you remember, she was Bella Winberg, the daughter of the rainproofs in Magnolia Street, you know she lives in New York now and is worth millions. Last Monday evening she drives up to our house in a motor-car half as big as the street. She has brought it from America with her. Inside it is like the dressing room of an opera star. She has with her young Shulman. All the papers are full of him. You have read, haven't you? Also there is a Mr Turnbull with her, a big businessman from Chicago.

She and Shulman are giving a party to bring together Magnolia Street. Does it sound like a madness to you when you first read it? So it did to me, but no longer. I am as excited as they are. It is an idea so beautiful it nearly makes me cry.

It is all arranged, expenses no object. They said I would be the best person to send out the invitations and do all the clerical work and Mr Turnbull will see about the music and the entertainments and manage it on the night. It is to be kosher, of course, for while the Jews cannot eat the Christian food, the Christians can eat the Jewish food, so long as it does not look too kosher. We have got Silverstone the big caterers of Begley Hill Road to do the food with your mother to look after it. She will also make knishehs, varennikas, creplach and blintsies for the old-fashioned Jewish people who will not like the mushroom patés and the mayonnaise.

It works in something wonderful that Winberg's daughter and young Shulman should be working together in giving this affair. You see all the Jewish people would travel a thousand miles to see this girl from Magnolia Street who is now worth all these millions. It is said her husband bought her some pearls from a Rajah in India who went bankrupt and she doesn't even need to insure them; because nobody would believe such big pearls are real ones, so why take the trouble to steal them?

All the Jewish people will come to see her! Has it not always been so with our people? They will do anything to see a rich person but if there was a meeting organised about international friendship, would they stir a foot unless you throw in a few songs free?

Now perhaps some of the goyim *would not have come just to see her, to show they stand above money. But to come and see Mick Shulman because he can hit people on the jaw stronger than other boys can hit on the jaw — if it was Shakespeare come to life again they would not be so excited.*

But I admit my head also is simply turning round with excitement so I am afraid this letter is not clear. You do not understand how much work there is to do. Everybody who has lived in Magnolia Street since Bella Winberg was a girl, must be invited. I am doing it all in the office of the Board of Guardians and I have no time at all for my ordinary work. But the Guardians understand what a great occasion it is and they do not say anything. It is bringing the Jews and the Christians together in a great simchah. *It looks like the dawn of a brighter day, when all races and peoples will go hand in hand together along the road of universal love and the crowds on both sides of the road will throw flowers at them.*

Max paused a moment to think that out. "Let me see now. If all the races and peoples are walking hand-in-hand along the Great West Road, where are the crowds to come from who are going to throw all those flowers?" He decided to postpone the problem. He resumed his reading.

But already people who never lived in Magnolia Street are applying for tickets, or they say they were lodgers and it is not fair they should not get tickets. And it is impossible to tell you how much work it is sometimes to trace one single family, where it has got to, let alone a whole street. Thank God, there are still a number of people left in Magnolia Street who lived here when Bella was a girl. There are the Poysers and the Edelmans and the Tawnies from the public-house and the Derrickses — did you hear about the poor old lady getting sleepy sickness? — and Mr and Mrs Carter, but he is an invalid and I don't expect he can come. And Albert Durbin is only round the corner. And Mrs Ritchie, she used to be married to the shvartzer. *You remember?*

She is still there. She is not respectable now — but Bella and Mick say I am to ask everybody, everybody.

Oh Max, it is very hard work. But it is in a glorious cause. And I will be very unhappy if you cannot come. You are the only one left now, so you must. Did you hear that your brother, Moisheh, has had another baby in Palestine? Mazel tov! He is now the secretary of the new colony behind Acre! Fancy Moisheh being a secretary! He is said to be the best horse dealer in the colonies. He was always good with horses.

Your mother tells me to tell you that she will make you those special varennikas you used to like, in chicken fat. But I think it was David, peace be upon him, who liked them, not you. So you must eat some when you come or she will remember it was not you, but David, peace be upon him. I rely on you to come.

I am your affectionate father,

Isaac Emmanuel

The letter fluttered from Max's fingers on to the breakfast tray.

"Excuse me, sir," said Bister, retrieving it. He held it out.

But Max did not lift a finger to take it from him. The thing had happened to Max which sometimes befell him in places as remote from Magnolia Street as the jewelled light and shade of an African bazaar, or the tubular steel drawing room of a London hostess. He was in Magnolia Street again. His brother, David, was in the room with him again, hunched up against the door, whilst he himself stood before his easel, thrusting away fiercely.

He had that queer taste at the root of his tongue again, a dissatisfaction, a sickness, a sense of betrayal. David, who had died for him, that he should go on painting...

He made a wry face as if he were swallowing some unpleasant physic. Bister made a step towards him. He blinked. He shook his head violently.

What a fool he was! How David would have exulted in it all! He would have gone about among the chaps, telling them that his brother, the genius...

"Excuse me, sir," Bister repeated.

"Oh of course," said Max, taking the letter from him.

"Thank you, Bister."

"This drop of gin and lemon, sir, it's been waiting."

Max swallowed it. The premature alcohol slid insidiously along his veins. He stretched out his legs luxuriously. He refreshed his eyes in the primrose and silver harmonies of the walls. He took up the invitation card again and read it.

"Listen, Bister!" he cried. "Mr Emmanuel will be glad to consider applications for railway fare! Can you beat that, Bister?"

"Sir!" said Bister non-commitally. He may have thought it was a little early in the day for a gentleman to begin. But, of course, this was not a *gentleman*, in the academic sense of the word.

"I tell you, Bister," Max proclaimed, "I'd come all the way from Djerba not to miss that party! I'd sneak from my own private view not to miss that party! What a whale of an inspiration!"

"I beg your pardon, sir!"

"I beg yours! My trousers, please! I mustn't keep Lady Staidlow waiting!"

II

It was so regular a thing for Lady Staidlow's house-parties to include a fashionable young painter painting herself, or one of her charming daughters, that she had had a mid-Victorian conservatory converted into a sort of studio for their convenience. Lord Staidlow's grandmother had had it built up against a lovely Jacobean room to house vivid tropical flowers. They were nothing like so vivid as the canvas flowers that bloomed there now.

"I'm dreadfully sorry," said Max. "I say, I hope you've not been here long."

"No, my dear, only a minute or two. How are you feeling? Like work?"

"I don't know, Letty, I don't know. I want to find out. I'm so excited — won't you take your pose? — I'm going to be either marvellous or rotten! Rotten, I think! Where's that jam-jar? Yes, I know I'm not ready yet. But don't move, please, don't move! I'm looking at you all the time. No, really, your hands *weren't* like that, Letty. *Left* fingers in the *right* palm!"

She smiled. She liked painters and poets to call her Letty, if they had been born in the... in the lower classes. She couldn't bear the least familiarity from Knights of the Garter. She liked the irritable note in Max's voice. She liked it in all her painters. It meant they were more interested in painting than social glory.

"Like this?" she asked humbly.

"That's right!" said Max.

Nothing was said for some seconds while Max squeezed tubes of paint on to his palette. "Is this to be a silent morning or a talky morning?" asked Lady Staidlow respectfully.

Max viciously squeezed some paint which wasn't there out of a half-inch of tube. "Talky, I think! And nothing else, I shouldn't wonder!"

"What's it about, Max? May I know?"

"Your profile a little more to the left, and chin down. *Down*, I said! That's right! Of course, you may! I've had an invitation to a party!"

"Is that all?" She was disappointed. A young man who received invitations as a matter of course to *her* house-parties, had no right to be excited by any invitation from any hostess in the kingdom.

"I should say it *is* all!" gloated Max. "The most stunning party! Talk about your Quatz' Arts and Covent Garden and Inverterry House!"

"If I may enquire —"

"Magnolia Street!" he exploded. "It's the Magnolia Street Party!"

"I beg your pardon?"

"You *know*, Letty! You can't pretend I've not told you. The little street I was born in, in Doomington! Jews and gentiles, twelve a side! You remember?"

"Of course, Max, of course! How stupid of me! The name slipped my memory. Magnolia Street, you said?"

"Yes!"

"A party? In Magnolia Street?"

"Yes!"

That was the thing people simply adored about Max Emmanuel. It didn't embarrass him in the least that he had emerged from a little slum street in Doomington. It didn't occur to him to be embarrassed. He was an artist. Magnolia Street still remained his supreme experience. The Longton Nightingale, the red-haired Becky Poyser, the kind Mr Billig — he talked of these people with extraordinary vividness, not as a writer might, of their comedies and tragedies, but as a painter, their clothes, their movements, their eyebrows.

The Lady Staidlows listened, fascinated. It was as if he clothed with flesh the incredible creatures presented in a mediaeval bestiary and set them walking before their eyes.

He told her of the rich Jewess who had come back from New York, and had driven up to his father's house in a car half as large as the street. He told her of the lad who had become the world's light-weight champion. (She knew his name already.) He speculated as to how the idea of the party arose. He set the guests dancing to the music of Ed Lampert's orchestra, whilst the old Jews stroked their beards. He told her there would be *knishehs* to eat, and *varennikas*. But there would be fruit sundaes, too, and mushroom patés and cakes that looked more like jewellery than pastry.

"It will be marvellous!" he said.

"You are going, of course?" she said.

"I should jolly well think so!"

"What night did you say it was?"

"The night of November the nineteenth!"

"Do you remember, by any chance, you've accepted my invitation to the ball I'm giving that night?"

"Oh, Letty!" His jaw fell. "Oh, I say! Oh, of course —"

"Don't worry, Max old boy! There'll be lots more parties in Staidlow House. There mightn't be another Magnolia Street party for a long time! I wish I was coming too, Max! It'll be lots more fun than mine!"

His eyes danced. "By jove what fun it would be if you came!"

"Well, well, I suppose they'll need me in London that night. Do you know you've not done a stroke of work for half an hour?"

"Oh I say, shall we drop it? My hand feels like a broomstick!"

"You promise to get on with it tomorrow? I insist on your having it ready for the show!"

"Trust me, Letty!" She could trust him. He had too keen a sense of exhibitional politics *not* to have his portrait of Lady Staidlow ready for the show.

"Shall we go for a stroll somewhere ?" she asked.

"Through the cypress walks! That'll be fine! So sorry I've brought you here for nothing this morning! May I just put these brushes and things away?"

They went out into the crisp autumn air. The rimy leaves crackled under their feet. A great red setter came bounding up to them.

"Charles!" she cried. "Darling!"

They kissed each other. She flung twigs and gravel for him. Charles was far too lordly to go chasing twigs and gravel.

"Snob!" she said.

"Bow-wow!" he replied.

"Isn't he rude?" she asked.

"He thinks you shouldn't be seen about in the morning with painters," Max interpreted. "It's not respectable!"

"They're the only people a woman may trust herself with nowadays. As for these *bishops*..."

"Yes," agreed Max. "They're a dangerous crowd — these *bishops*!"

"Oh by the way," she said. "I think I ought to mention it. You know Lady Swetenham?"

"Do I?"

"We drove over to tea last Sunday!"

"Oh of course!"

"She's got Fedora staying with her!"

"Fedora?"

"Surely you know who Fedora is?"

"Sounds like a film-vamp. Or a toothpaste. Is she?"

"No, no! Fedora! Of Hanover Square!"

"Oh, a dressmaker, isn't she?"

"No! *The* dressmaker!"

"I congratulate her!"

"Congratulate me!"

"Why on earth?"

"She's coming here to tea today. Molly Swetenham's bringing her."

"How gorgeous!"

"Let me explain. She's not merely a dressmaker. She's an artist. She won't dress everybody by any manner of means. Molly pumped her about me and found out she approved. She's seen me about, of course. I come up to scratch. I've got a Fedora shape!"

"Which means?"

"It means she's an artist just in the way you are. You'll only accept Emmanuel shapes."

"I see."

"And she's coming this afternoon. Officially it's to tea. But she'll be studying me out of the corner of her eyes all the time. That's another of your tricks, too. She doesn't go straight at it, like a cart-horse!"

"Who is she?"

"A Russian. Most mysterious. Very fascinating. That's what I wanted to warn you about. I'm convinced she's the perfect Emmanuel shape. She might have stepped out of one of your pictures. I won't have you throw over my portrait and go rushing off to Molly Swetenham's to paint her!"

"I say! She sounds rather good stuff!"

"She is! She can take ten years off your age!"

"Do you want her to make you look like a schoolgirl?"

"Oh no! Only ten years less than a grandmother!"

"But really? Who is she?"

"It's said she's one of the late Tzar's daughters. But no Russian isn't! She's very anxious not to be thought one of the late Tzar's daughters! She has a very seductive accent!"

"That's odd! Russians don't have accents!"

"Oh I suppose there's a little Hapsburg in her to account for the accent."

"It'll be great fun! Oh I say! That blaze of chrysanthemum there! It's like a noise! It's like a band!"

"Ed Lampert's Orchestra!" she said. "Cantor Weingarten will sing secular melodies!" he added.

III

Lady Swetenham duly brought Fedora to tea that afternoon. He knew who she was at once. No mixture of Romanoff and Hapsburg blood flowed in her veins. Her blood was purer than that.

He had a flawless memory for faces and their minute particularities. He knew at once who Fedora was though he had not set eyes on her for many years. He did not need the small dark speck beside her mouth to tell him who she was.

It was Dora Winberg, of course, Bella's sister. *She* was Fedora of Hanover Square. He remembered hearing from his father that one of the Winberg girls had gone to London and become a

492

fashionable dressmaker. But she wasn't a fashion. She was a religion — Fedora who dressed a duchess or two and the best countesses.

They were introduced.

"How do you do!" he said.

"How do you do!" she said. She was charming. Her pale square forehead, her dark eyes, her waves of intense dark hair. Her voice was musical — the ghost of a bewitching foreign accent.

Of course Letty Staidlow suggested she had his sort of face, the sort of face he loved to paint. It was pure Magnolia Street. All his best portraits, whoever the sitter, were, in fact, pure Magnolia Street — the delicacy of Rose Berman's face, the mournfulness of Rachel Shulman's, the roguish sweetness of Nellie Tawnie's, who, by now, was probably not so sweet and roguish.

He listened. He was delighted by her. How well she played her part: "We Russians, you know, it is so always with us..."

He did not resent it. He knew that every artist has a part to play before his patrons will recognise him as an artist. It is a duty only second to being a good artist, to play the expected part well.

His heart brimmed with affection for her. She was good, the little woman was *good*. How well Magnolia Street held its own in the shires! He found himself getting quite giddy with local patriotism.

She permitted attention to be withdrawn from her for one moment. He seized his opportunity.

"Hello!" he said to her under his breath jovially. "I know who you are, of course! You know who I am?"

She bowed a little stiffly. She looked at him a little coldly. "You are Meester Emmanuel, the painter, is it not?"

"Yes, yes!" he said. "It's all right! Don't bother with me! I think you're perfectly stunning!"

She bowed again, just a little more stiffly. There was quite a lot of bowing and curtseying and this and that expected from mysterious Russian ladies of quality.

"I say," he said. His voice was just a little uneasy. "You'll have got an invitation from my father, haven't you?"

"I have not the pleasure of knowing your father!"

"But I say, Miss Winberg. You *are* going to Bella's party... the Magnolia Street Party? I won't tell a soul, if you'd rather it wasn't mentioned! I say, let's go up together!"

493

"I am afraid I do not know what you are talking about!" she said. She turned away. At that moment Charles, the great red setter, appeared at the French windows, shaking his imperial plume of a tail.

" Bow-wow!" he went.

"Snob!" cried Lady Staidlow, making faces at him. "Snob!"

Chapter 8

I

It was surprising to see a woman so smartly dressed turn into Magnolia Street from Blenheim Road. Her pupils at the fashionable girls' school where she was chief assistant would have been disconcerted to find that their adored Miss Cooper had business in so mean a street. The surprise would have been shared by her colleagues among the Northenden Players, who were, perhaps, the most accomplished team of amateur actors in the North of England.

But to us it would not have been so surprising. We would have remembered that Enid Cooper once actually lived in this street. We would have had a clear memory of the young lady in her straw hat, her gymnasium skirt and knickers, her long stockinged legs, coming in from school, with her nose tilted slightly upward. The memory would be accompanied by a dimmer vision of a little Jewish girl on the other side of the street, Janey Seipel by name, blushing with joy merely because the heavenly creature trod the same pavements as she, and breathed the same air.

And why should not Enid Cooper go back to Magnolia Street? Did not her sister, Mary, still live there? Did she not fear that Mary might live there till the day she died? Had she not gone back that day to see whether, by strength and cunning, that fear might not be cast out?

She turned in upon the Jewish pavement. She wished to look across the street to find out if Mary was once more sitting at the parlour window behind the half-drawn curtains, doing nothing, seeing nothing. Every time she came to Magnolia Street, Mary was at that window like some carved figure.

There used to be an old woman lower down the street who did exactly the same thing. Miss Tregunter her name was. She died of shock a number of years ago when the dreadful Hubbard tragedy took place. The house had been empty since then. The sight of Mary sitting motionless at her window made you feel that the old woman's ghost had come back to Magnolia Street to occupy another woman's body. But Mary Cooper never moved. Miss Tregunter did occasionally get up to shoo the cats away from her little box-hedge; and if the little Jewish boys started playing too near her window, she would shake her fist and cry: "Go away! Go away! I'll tell Mr Furniss, the High Master!"

It was bad enough that it was impossible to move Mary out of Magnolia Street. But it was wretched to see her becoming a Magnolia Street oddity, like Mrs Durbin, the black-eyed little barber-woman, who used to tramp about all night long with a cap stuck on to her hair with hatpins.

She would not move; for Dick, her brother, whom she had idolised, had died in that house. Enid tried to remonstrate with her, to get her to keep inside the room, at least, so that people shouldn't get talking about the queer silent lady that lived at number six.

"Listen, Mary, there's a dear!" she said. "Are you listening?"

"I am!" Her voice was dull, as if all its edges were planed off.

"I'd be so pleased if you wouldn't sit at the window here all day long, so soon as your work is finished. I mean read a book, go out, go to the pictures! Your crochet used to be so good once! Anything, Mary dear! You see... these people... they'll talk about you. Do you remember Miss Tregunter? I do wish —"

"Miss Tregunter! Yes, they do talk about me. I know. I knew a long time ago I should be Miss Tregunter. Almost the first moment I set foot in the street. Even before I saw Miss Tregunter herself, sitting behind her curtains..."

"Mary darling! How silly! How can you talk such nonsense!"

"It *was* like that!"

"Oh no, no, it wasn't!" Enid stamped her foot. Mary sat pale and silent and did not move.

"I don't want to upset you, Mary darling! I don't get round often enough to start scolding you when I do! But I do wish you'd try not to... you know...."

"I'll try!" said Mary.

But the force which brought Mary to that window was something stronger than herself. She was sitting there that day, as she had done a month ago, a year ago, that day that Enid went back to Magnolia Street with a lever to dislodge her, that Mr and Mrs John Cooper had put into her hands.

Enid was about to cross the road to her sister's house when her nostrils were assailed by a sharp smell, released by the opening of a door in the house on her right hand. It was a sharp and pleasant smell, the odour of boiling ginger spiced with cinnamon.

Enid stopped. This was the house of Ada Hummel who sold home-made sweets. Ada Hummel's sister, Rose, had married her own brother, John. They were sisters-in-law. She had a relative by marriage as well as by blood in Magnolia Street,

"But of course!" Enid said to herself. "I can't possibly not go in! She's just as much in it as I am!"

She did not as a rule visit her sister-in-law when she came to Magnolia Street. In fact, she had never entered the house before. But she and Ada had once overlapped by a day at Shipscar, John's little house in the New Forest. She was a pretty little woman. She had had a dreadful time, Enid remembered, with a brute of a husband, who had deserted her.

She mounted the three stairs, walked a few feet along the lobby and turned into the parlour which had long ago been converted into a sweets-shop, reconverted into a parlour, and converted once more into a sweets-shop by John Cooper himself.

The bell tinkled as she pushed the door open. There was a pleasant smell of *ingber*, the ginger sweet, and apples baked in treacle, and *strudel* rich with raisins and spicy with cinnamon. Ada was slicing the *ingber* into rhomboids in the dish where it had hardened. The knife dropped from her hands.

"Oh Miss Cooper! Is it you?" she exclaimed. "What a pleasure! What a pleasure!"

"You've heard the good news, Mrs Hummel?"

"Have I heard the good news?" The news was too good for both of them. The two women leaned across the counter and kissed each other. The little maidens from the fashionable school would have opened their eyes wide to see Miss Cooper engaged in such irreticent embraces with a little Jewish shopkeeper, across the trays of *ingber* and baked apples.

"Please take this chair, Miss Cooper! That's right! We say *mazel tov* at such a time! That means good luck!"

"How do you say it? *Mazel tov!*" echoed Enid.

For the news had come to them both only yesterday morning that a son had been born at last to Rose and John Cooper. They had three girls already, one named after Rose's mother, one after John's mother, and one named Ailsa, because they both thought it so lovely a name.

"I would have cried my eyes out if it had been another girl!" said Ada.

"Oh it wouldn't have been so tragic as all that!" hoped Enid.

"I cried my eyes out just the same, though it was a boy!" said Ada. "I cry for good news and bad news just the same! Oh what a pity!" she exclaimed.

"Why? What!"

"If I'd have known you were coming I'd have had a drop of wine in the house! When it's *mazel tov* with us, we take wine and cake! Won't you let me go and —"

"Oh please, please! I wouldn't dream of letting you bother like that! Won't you let me taste a little of this sweet? It looks delicious!"

"My *ingber*? You are laughing at me. I am ashamed! Yes, please take!" She broke off a piece and handed it with a pair of tongs to her sister-in-law. Enid took her gloves off and lifted the sweet delicately to her mouth.

"But it's lovely!" she said. "It's lovely!" Ada was almost beside herself with pride.

"Come, let me wrap some up for you! Please! I insist! You must take this bag! Rose will kill herself laughing to think we toasted the baby with *ingber*! I got a letter, as well, from John this morning, Miss Cooper. Did you? He said Rose said I must come for Christmas. Will you be there? It will be grand if you are there, too!"

Ada's eyes shone. Enid's eyes twinkled. She was the sort of woman whom women fall down and worship the moment they set eyes on her. There was a queer admixture in her crisp femaleness of a certain masculinity, which her tailor-made clothes and short hair did not diminish.

"Indeed! Mrs Hummel! Or now that we've got the same nephew, mayn't it be Ada? I got a letter from John, too! Of course I'll be there at Christmas! I'm off to Shipscar the moment term ends. But he insists on one thing. He says he'll show me the door if I fail him again. You know Mary, of course, my sister, opposite?"

"Of course, Miss Cooper!"

"Enid!"

"Enid!"

"That's right. John says I mustn't dream of coming without her. They've tried year after year to get her down, and she's always agreed in a vague sort of way. And then when it came to it, there was no moving her... It's as if she feels she'll be leaving Dick behind. You remember, our poor brother, Dick?"

"Oh the poor boy! With the gold hair he had! Like a girl's! And those blue eyes!" Ada mopped her own.

"Yes. He was a sweet youth. Poor Dick! And the idea is that now at last we've got a lever to make her move. There's a new Dick. Naturally, they're going to call him Dick."

"Richard, that is? Richard Cooper! A lovely name! He'll grow up to be a film star with a name like that!" vowed Ada.

"So they're hoping to get her to come, and when she comes, she stays! You know what John is! That bulldog chin of his! We all know the country's the only place for her! It'll put some new ideas into her head — the dogs, the ponies, the rock-garden.... The only time in all her life she's been happy was when she lived in the country with an aunt of ours. That was before we... before we came to live here!"

"And if you hadn't... oi! oi!" said Ada. "It would have been awful! John and Rose would never have met each other!"

"You never know. John was a dreadful gadabout! If he'd have heard there was a pretty girl in Magnolia Street "

"I remember. Oh yes. He made eyes at me a few times, too. Perhaps he thought I was Rose!"

"Oh no, he didn't! John didn't make mistakes like that! There they are now anyhow, down in the New Forest. At least there she is! And when he comes back, she opens up... like a flower. It's lovely to be there when they're both together!"

"To think that Rose should go straight from Magnolia Street and win prizes with her roses!"

"And that she can get John carting rocks about for hours for her rock-garden! And John sweating like a pig!"

"And how clever she is with those animals!"

"Did you know Whisky foaled last week?"

"Foaled?"

"Had a baby pony!"

"Oh all these babies! I will cry again soon! Yes, I will!" She fumbled for her handkerchief.

"No, Ada, you mustn't! I've got to go in a minute and I want your help!"

"My help?... Oh please!"

"You must help with Mary — to get her away. The appearance of the young Dick is going to make that comparatively easy, at least far easier than it's been till now. We're going to make use of the young gentleman for all he's worth. And this is where you come in. How long will you be able to spend at Shipscar, by the way?"

"I don't know. A week, yes?"

"That's capital. We'll tell her that you've got to come back after a few days. Let's tell Mary it's only a few days.

"She'll give you the keys and you will just go in and have a look round, won't you?"

"But yes, of course, I will!"

"You see what's at the bottom of it all? If Mary had any idea that we were going to prevent her returning to Magnolia Street, we'd never get her to move."

"Yes."

"And then, when we've got her there, Rose will beg her to stay on to give a hand while the baby's so tiny. That part should be fairly easy. And you'll go off and tell her you'll look after things a bit for her. You see, she just thinks of it as Dick's house. That's what makes it all so difficult. The new Dick will be doing *his* job all this time. We can reckon on that. But she'll get fidgety now and again as the weeks go by, and then we'll have you to fall back on. And before she knows where she is, I'll be round in Magnolia Street to pack up and send off to Shipscar anything that's worth keeping. Oh I know how unscrupulous it sounds, but you do see how desperate it is, don't you? And you *will* help, please ?"

"And if I should scrub the floors for Rose's sister-in-law, should I not do it?"

"Oh it won't come to that. You're busy enough here. How are your children? Annie and Leo, aren't they?"

"God bless them! Like roses! And you remember their names, too!"

"But of course! Aren't they my niece- and nephew-in-law?"

"My Leo won a new scholarship last month! Did you know? He's going to be a doctor like Dr Shulman! He's going to go special for confinement cases! And my Annie's walking out already! Her boy's a cotton salesman!"

"Isn't that splendid! I know you're all going to be frightfully happy! I suppose they're both out now? I liked them awfully down at Shipscar! But of course! I'll see them at the Party, won't I?"

"So you have got an invitation, too, Enid? How wonderful! You must come! You must surely come!"

500

"Of course I've got an invitation! Isn't it the Magnolia Street Party? I won't be cold-shouldered! It's going to be colossal fun! That's another thing I've got to talk to Mary about. She's jolly well coming, too! John said she must. It'll prepare the ground, he says. The great thing is to take her out of herself. I'll come down on the nineteenth and get her dressed nicely. Then we'll carry her off between us, shall we, Ada?"

"So Rose and John got an invitation, too?"

"Of course they did! Everybody! All Magnolia Street that ever was, I understand. Since 1910, at least. I had a word or two on the phone with Mr Emmanuel. John will be away unfortunately! And of course Rose couldn't travel all that way so soon!"

"What, Rose? In two weeks she is always strong as an ox!"

"Yes, quite, Ada dear. But I suppose the Jewish people here feel —"

"Yes, yes, I know what you mean! Such nonsense! Perhaps if I had married a nice *goy* sailor..." Her lip quivered a little, she brought out a handkerchief. Then she got herself in hand again. "Never mind, thank God, I am happy. I have a little house — like a palace. I have my two children — God bless them — like doves! What more should I want?"

"Yes, yes, my dear," said Enid softly, "You are much to be envied." She spoke so gently that Ada hardly heard her.

"What they would all like," Ada continued indignantly, "when a Jew and a Christian marry, it should turn out like Benny Edelman. Then they are all satisfied. But when it is a Rose and a John — a Garden of Eden — then it pricks them in their eyes!"

"You mustn't upset yourself, Ada! For John and Rose are happy, aren't they, tremendously? And so are you! With those great jolly devoted children of yours! Put that handkerchief away now!"

"And you?" cried Ada suddenly. "No, you must not be angry with me! Are we not relations? And you? When do you get married? When do *you* have children? They, too, will be my nieces and nephews! I will knit coats for them. And when they grow up, they will come and see me, and I will fill large bags for them with *ingber* and *strudel* and *lekkach*. Yes, it is foreign. But they will like it. Well, say, Enid!"

Enid smiled, a little sadly, perhaps. There were few people in the world from whom she would not have resented such questioning. It was impossible to resent it from a woman so gentle, so simple, as Ada, whom fortune had dealt with so cruelly.

"I, my dear? I shan't get married! I'm not what they call a man's woman. It's the little girls that fall for me. Shall I tell you a secret? I mean — while we're on the subject?"

"Yes," said Ada. She looked a little bewildered.

"I was engaged until about a month ago. He's an actor. He acts in the same company as I do." Enid stopped. It was ridiculous that she should be baring her heart's secrets in this way to a little Jewish woman who sold sweets in Magnolia Street. It was ridiculous. She had not breathed a word of her affair with Andrew Poyndester to anyone in the world, not even to John, or Mary. Yet it eased her, somehow. It made the loneliness not quite so hard to bear.

"I knew of course," she went on, " that Andrew wasn't quite the cave-man type. I knew he wouldn't get hold of me by the hair and whirl me round his head." She knew that what she was saying was gibberish to Ada. Ada's eyes were wide as two saucers. But she had to get the thing said, now and never again. "It was no good, my dear. It wasn't really that I wanted to be pulled into a cave by the hair. That isn't my taste, really. But it was no good. It was the same as before. He was a little girl, too, like the other little girls."

"I don't understand," quivered Ada.

"Never mind!" said Enid briskly. "It doesn't matter much. He wrote the most *dreadful* plays. It's going to be marvellous, isn't it? The Party, I mean. O good heavens! Look at the time! I must run over at once and see Mary.

"I wonder if she saw me come in. She was at the window!"

"Yes, she always is!"

"We're going to dislodge her from that window, you and I! Goodbye, Ada, you've been so kind! *Mazel* how did you say it?"

"*Mazel tov!*"

"*Mazel tov!* Till the Magnolia Street Party!"

II

Mary Cooper had not noticed her sister go into the little sweets-shop opposite her window. She had never been very much aware of what was happening in Magnolia Street, excepting if she was waiting for Dick to come home from work. But it was a long time

502

now since Dick had stopped working... nearly ten years.

Enid swung open the gate, entered the tiny bare garden and went up to the window where Mary was sitting. She tapped at the glass. Mary did not lift her head. She seemed neither to see nor hear. Enid tapped more sharply. This time the sound pierced the veil. Mary lifted her head, saw it was Enid, and smiled faintly. She went out of the room and opened the front door.

"Mary darling!"

"Enid, I'm so glad!" Her voice was low. There was not much spirit in it. "I'm afraid I was sitting at that window again!.Are you going to be cross with me?"

Enid was not going to be cross with her. There was no need, now that the air was full of conspiracy. "My darling? Cross? With you?" She flung her arms round her sister and kissed her. "A few hours after John's baby — John wired you, of course?"

"He did, my dear! It will make them so happy!"

"And you! And me!" cried Enid tempestuously. "Come, darling, aren't you going to ask me in?" She stormed into the house and carried Mary into the parlour with her on the wind of her onset. She always behaved with a vehemence quite unnatural to her when she came to see Mary. She was normally a dignified and controlled woman, excepting when she acted, when she displayed a hardly suspected warmth. In a sense she acted whenever she came to see Mary, too. She sought to bring some keen air into that silent house, to whip her sister's face into colour, to make her laugh, even. But it was a rare achievement to make her laugh; and a ghostly one when she attained it, so thin and tinkly and unreal was Mary's laughter, like the note of a spinet long forgotten in an attic.

"I *may* sit down, Mary dear? And you don't mean to say you've not got the kettle boiling for tea? You got my card? And in any case you should have known, if I couldn't get up to see you yesterday, then I'd get here today!"

"I think I got some crumpets, Enid. You like crumpets, don't you? Do you remember how Dick loved crumpets?"

"Of course! Rather! I wonder if the new Dick will have an unholy appetite for crumpets, too!"

"What? Are they going to call him Dick?" For Mary Cooper the tone was one of great animation.

"Not so fast! It all depends on you!"

"My dear! How —"

"I've heard from John this morning. He and Rose send an ultimatum. There's to be a grand family gathering at Christmas. His company has promised he'll be home this time, you see! He's been in Penang and Casablanca and God knows where the last twenty Christmases! He says I've simply *got* to bring you down when this term's over. If not —"

"You know, my dear Enid, I can't! You know I can't!"

"I only know this! That if you don't come this time, they'll call the poor little creature Ebenezer or Melchizedek or something. It'll be your fault. *They — will — not — call — him — Dick!*"

"They must! Enid, you must see to that!"

"*You* must see to that! It wouldn't be fair, darling, to the other Dick, would it now? Well, that's settled! I'll write and tell them! Where are those crumpets? Come, come, Mary, let's get them toasted! Oh yes, and we'll eat them with these little ginger sweeties! I just went in to see Rose's sister, just across the street. I had to congratulate her on the little nephew, hadn't I? A dear little woman! She gave me these!"

"Yes, Enid, I remember them! Yes, the very same! I remember a long time ago that a young fellow across the street — he lost a leg in the War — I remember when he saved a little boy from drowning...."

"I think I remember. The small boy, Wright, from next door. Oh it's ages ago now! Yes, Mary?"

"Her mother used to make these sweets, too... in that same shop. And she stuffed Dick's pockets with them. He got so ill. I can remember as if it was yesterday."

"Yes, she was a sweet old thing! Come, let's get the kettle boiling! Shall I toast the crumpets — or will you?" For, of course, Enid's main reason for coming to Magnolia Street was not to encourage Mary talking and thinking about Dick, but to stop her. "I'm parched, I've done so much talking today!"

And indeed she was doing much more talking than was her habit. She was by no means a garrulous woman. But this quick-fire chatter was what she came to Magnolia Street for. She always saw to it that she had some bright balls of gossip to juggle with. She thrilled with delight if she was successful and caught Mary in the gay skein she wove. More often than not she did not succeed.

"But I will to-day!" vowed Enid under her breath, as she lit the gas stove. "What with John and the new Dick and Rose and

504

Ada and Battling Kid Shulman... What? What's that you're saying, Mary?"

"I can't go!"

"It's settled, my dear Mary!"

"I can't leave the house! Please, Enid!"

Enid hove to. She exerted all her arts, as sister, as schoolmistress, as actress. She worked the good Ada for all she was worth. She presented a direful portrait of the new Dick saddled with some dreadful Baptist polysyllable for a name.

She declared falsely how ill Rose had been after her three previous confinements. The newcomer (Dick or not Dick, as Mary herself decided) weighed several pounds more than his predecessors. Rose would need the help of a devoted sister by so much the more urgently. What were doctors and nurses compared with a devoted sister?

"You *must* go, darling! It's really very serious this time! I shouldn't be surprised if John never speaks to you again if you don't! And Rose will be dreadfully hurt! You must go!" She raised her voice. She caught hold of Mary by the shoulders and shook her. "You *must* go! You *must* go!"

"I'll go!" said Mary, in a flat voice. "But they must understand —"

But Enid would let her go no further. "Darling!" she cried. She threw her arms round her and kissed her. "Oh won't they be pleased! How perfectly ripping it's going to be!"

But another song of exultation was ringing in her heart. "At last! At last! We've got out of it! All of us! We've finished with Magnolia Street at last! Hallelujah! Glory be to God!"

"Let me talk!" said Mary, just a shade crossly.

"Yes, dear!" said Enid meekly. But the voice within continued gloriously: "At last! At last! At last!"

"I'll go!" repeated Mary. "But they'll understand I must come back the moment Rose is fit again. They'll understand, won't they, Enid ?"

"Of course they will!" said Enid hurriedly.

"Because it would be like leaving Dick all alone —"

"Mind, Mary, you're burning those crumpets! Yes, they'll do now! Where's the jam? I like it smeared over the butter. Thank you, Mary, quite thick! I suppose this tea's as strong as ink now. Oh do let's make some more... Then there's this Party, darling, the Magnolia Street Party," she rattled on. "You've got your

505

invitation, Mr Emmanuel told me he sent it. Ada and I are coming to fetch you —we'll look after you!"

The spirit of negation was crushed in Mary Cooper. The greater consent having been forced from her, it was not difficult to force the less. "Of course, dear, if you'd like me to come! Will it be amusing?" she asked, trying to colour her tone with a little interest.

"Will it be *amusing*, Mary? I feel in my bones it's going to be the loveliest party ever! The idea was a stroke of genius! Think! Just think who's going to be there!"

For half an hour or more Enid exercised her imagination on the subject — the hosts, the guests, the refreshments, the entertainments. She was brilliant. Her eyes shone, colour came into her cheeks. She was plaintive, she was ironical, she was enthusiastic. She had never worked harder in all her life before. And throughout, like a cat sitting before a mousehole, she was watchful. She watched Mary's face with an intense and secret scrutiny. She saw a dim reflected light start up on the rim of the grey waters of her eyes. She observed a faint wash of colour spread across her cheeks.

"Yes," whispered Mary. "I think it's going to be great fun!"

"Great fun! How many years is it," thought Enid, "since she uttered those two brief words!"

"And I wonder," continued Mary, " if that painter is going to turn up. He's so famous now. I often read about him in the newspapers."

"You mean," said Enid, "Max Emmanuel?" She was conscious that her heart paused a moment as she uttered the name.

"Yes. His father seems to have a lot to do with it."

"I don't know," said Enid. "He's probably far too grand to turn up at a Magnolia Street party. He's too much in demand at the Staidlow parties. He still paints Magnolia Street, of course," she found herself saying with a faint note of bitterness. "Of course the critics don't realise it, and I don't suppose he does himself. He'll never paint anything else... but from the safe distance of Villefranche or Tunis."

"The thought of him seems to make you quite cross," said Mary.

Enid tossed her head. "Not at all! Why?" It suddenly struck her she was being rather silly. Why shouldn't Max Emmanuel keep away from Magnolia Street? It was a grim place, a shabby place, after all. Wasn't her own head nearly cracking with joy that she had at length managed, or very nearly managed, to break the last link that bound her family to Magnolia Street?

"Well? Who knows: perhaps he will be there!" she said lightly. She thought it was unlikely. She dismissed the thought of him from her mind. They talked clothes for a minute or two. Then Enid suddenly caught sight of her watch.

"My darling!" she cried. "The time! I've got heaps and heaps of homework to correct tonight! It's been lovely, Mary! Good-bye, darling!"

"Good-bye, Enid dear!"

"My bag of sweets!" cried Enid. "You haven't scoffed them all? No, thank heavens! Good-bye again!"

She went to the front door and opened it. Yes, it was exactly as if her head was cracking. She was dizzy with fatigue and joy. She was afraid that if she stayed a minute longer, the voice that sang inside her would force its way through her lips: "At last! At last! We've got out of it! We've finished with Magnolia Street! Hallelujah! Glory be to God!"

She did not doubt that the Magnolia Street Party would be amusing. It was certainly going to be expensive. She had galvanised herself into excitement over it, in the hope of injecting a little into Mary. She smiled. Madame Jonsen and Mr Shulman did not know it, but the Party was going to be not only a welcome to the wanderers coming back home to Magnolia Street. It was also going to be a farewell to the strangers who had tarried in Magnolia Street so long, and had now at last found their way out.

She descended the steps into the little bare garden. She stopped. On the other side of the pavement, walking towards his father's house, was Max Emmanuel. She had not seen him for many years, but she recognised him instantly. He had not noticed her. It was clear that he, too, was going to be a guest at the Magnolia Street Party.

The noises that made a glad clamour in her heart stopped of a sudden. It was as if, for some reason, it was not going to be so easy to get away from Magnolia Street, after all.

"I'm run down!" said Enid to herself. "I'll need that holiday at Shipscar by the time Christmas comes round!"

A few minutes later she got on the tram-car. "I wonder what I'd better wear," she was considering, "for that Magnolia Street

507

Party? The plain black frock with the crystals? Or that green frock from Jay's? The black one, I think! With a spray of orchids, perhaps!"

"As if it matters!" she laughed to herself. "As if anyone will take the least notice!... A threepenny one, please!" she told the conductor.

Chapter 9

"*Mazel tov!*" said Mick.
"*Mazel tov!*" said Bella.
"Whoopee!" said Alfred M. Turnbull.
"Boom-boom!" said Ed Lampert's Orchestra.
"Plop!" said the champagne corks.
The Magnolia Street Party.

The Rabbi has a new silk hat and a new frock-coat. The cuffs that protrude an inch or two beyond the sleeves are not a separate garment. They belong to the dazzling white shirt that shows behind his frock-coat. That finery will not be wasted. He will need it when he and Mrs Shulman go over to New York, to stay with the family of Clara Teitelbaum, who is going to get married to their son next spring. It is a beautiful silk hat, and he is proud of it. He does not change it for his skull-cap, as he usually does, when he comes indoors. He would like the people to see the beautiful silk hat that his son, Mick, bought for him.

Then he falls into a reverie. His chin droops upon his breast and the long sparse black beard is bent up upon his shirt front. The laughter, the popping of corks, the crash and blare of the orchestra, do not disturb him. Who knows where his mind is straying now? In Jabneh, in Tiberias, where the holy colleges were? His mind is not absent from them long.

But Alfred Turnbull will not have it. This is going to be a hundred per cent whoopee night, and then some!

"Say, old son, have a drink!" He reaches forward a glass of wine. It is a pleasant wine, a dry château wine.

"No, no!" cries Mr Emmanuel, hastening up. "Let it be sweet wine from Palestine! He will not like that, it is too sour!"

"Me too!" says Alfred M. Turnbull. "I like the sweet hooch best!"

"Take!" says Mr Emmanuel. He hands a glass of sweet wine from Richon-le-Zion to the Rabbi from the Dnieper and the stock-broker from Lake Michigan. He pours out a glass for himself.

"Here's mud in your eye!" says the Chicagoan.

"*Lechayim*! To Life!" says Mr Emmanuel. He turns to the Rabbi. "That it should be a wonderful wedding between your son and his bride in New York!"

The old man smiles gently. Then he mutters a few words.

"What? What does he say?" asks Alfred M. Turnbull.

"That is the prayer before wine!" Mr Emmanuel explains.

"That's a swell idea!" exclaims Mr Turnbull, "A little prayer before liquor now and again might decrease the casualty lists in Chicago! Say, Mr Emmanuel, where did we get this stuff? That's just as I like it — sweet as molasses or hot as hell! Hello! Here's the old dame!" Mrs Shulman has come sailing up to them majestically. "Well, ma, how are ye?"

"Couldn't grumble!" she replies. She has used the same formula for thirty years. But she has grumbled often enough. She does not grumble tonight. "Ah Mrs Shulman! *Mazel tov!*" proclaims Mr Emmanuel, warmly.

"*Mazel tov!*" replies Mrs Shulman. The reference is clearly to Mick's impending nuptials with Clara Teitelbaum. No party with Jews in it can fail to develop a nuptial flavour sooner or later.

What a grand old woman she looks tonight, with her heavy shot-grey satin dress and gold cables enough on her to bridge a river! She is bearing up magnificently under her disappointment, though she was quite angry when she first heard about it. She has learnt from Mick that light-weights, however illustrious, are seldom quite so irresistible a catch as heavy-weights.

"Then you must be a — how do you say it? — A heavy-weight, at once! Do you hear, Mick, at once!"

Mick has managed to convince her that the transformation is beyond his power, for the time being, at least.

"Then the moment I get to New York, I will go to Madison Square Garden! I will! It is a shame! A heavy-weight should be more of a catch than my son!"

"Don't worry, mamma!" her daughter, Rachel, soothed her. "He will get so fat and happy when he marries Clara, he will soon be a heavy-weight."

Mick looked a little alarmed. That was not the sort of heavy-weight he wanted to be. Mrs Shulman was reassured.

"You think so, Rachel?"

It could all be safely left to Rachel. Everything had been safely left to Rachel for nearly thirty years.

Rachel Shulman looked quite a young girl tonight. (She was still Shulman. But she wouldn't be Shulman much longer if she could do things like that to herself.) Bella had taken her in hand. She had made an appointment for her at the best hairdresser's in Doomington. She had got a frock for her from the smartest dressmaker. She had spent ages matching up her shoes with her frock. She had sent her a little spray of pink rosebuds, just the colour of her frock and her shoes. She was wearing the brooch, the bracelet, the earrings, that Mick had bought her. She did Mick and Bella credit.

"After all, Rachel," Bella had cooed. "You mustn't forget you're hostess for Micky. So in one way it's really your party! You must look your best!" It had amused Bella far more to dress up Rachel for the party than to dress up herself.

A long, long time ago John Cooper had a suspicion that she was probably quite a pretty girl if somebody could only get her to pull her hair back from flopping over her face. It is a pity he is not here tonight, to see how accurate his instinct was. But then his instincts about girls were always accurate.

John Cooper sails the high seas tonight. An invitation was duly sent to him and his wife, Rose. And Rose has sent a charming little note saying how sorry she is, but what with the new baby and one thing and another... It is of course, a good thing John and Rose are not here tonight. It would have been a little embarrassing to everybody. To John and Rose it would have been a little puzzling, too. Once, long ago, there had been so much beard-wagging and tongue-clacking because it was suspected of a gentile youth and a Jewish maiden that they went out walking together, and loved each other, perhaps.

And tonight, because Bella Winberg wore platinum bracelets and Mick Shulman had a fist like the kick of a horse — tonight the gentiles and the Jews loved each other like brothers and sisters. To the strains of the luscious orchestra, they went up and down and round about, locked in each other's arms.

Like brothers and sisters. That was about the truth of it. Brothers and sisters, not more.

Yes, Rose Cooper and John Cooper would have been a little puzzled by the Magnolia Street Party. But it would have pleased them both to see Rachel Shulman looking so sweet and tasty.

"So in one way, Rachel, it's really your party!" said Bella.

Rachel Shulman's party! It had always been her dearest dream to give a party. Actually it was to be a garden party. But

511

no garden party, not even the annual one at Buckingham Palace, could be half as glorious as this!

She looked round the heaped tables. There was nothing there the Jews could not eat, and nothing so exotic that the gentiles mistrusted it. It was a stand-up supper. Everybody stood up to it lustily. There were slabs of smoked salmon large enough to build a bank. There were whole roosts of roast chicken. There were enormous pyramids of fruit, their apexes shaggy with the foliage of pineapple. The bottles of mineral waters and wine and whisky and brandy retreated tier beyond tier. Elegant gentlemen in tail coats were decanting them. They said "Yes, sir! Yes, madam!" as if it were King George himself giving a party to the House of Lords.

"A garden party! Pah!" Rachel was a little scornful at the recollection. "Any Lord Mayor can give a garden party!" She remembered the exiguous refreshments she would have provided. Pink cakes! Pink ices! Pah! she went again. Her eye caught the glint of the gold foil of the champagne bottles. Her bosom heaved proudly under her pink crêpe-de-chine frock.

Yes, yes, the frock had to be pink, even if the ices weren't.

"Please, Bella!" she had insisted. "Let it be pink!" Bella cocked her head and looked at her critically.

"Yes, you're probably right! With those eyes and that hair! But as my sister, Fedora, from the Kremlin and the Hofburg, would tell you, there's pink *and* pink!"

Rachel looked down at her frock with satisfaction. She looked across to the champagne bottles with pride. She looked across to Mick and Bella starting off the dance, with love, with adoration.

She remembered the entertainers. Could it be true?

Cantor Weingarten?

Jimmie Duclane at the piano?

Ed Lampert's Orchestra?

There was no doubt about Ed Lampert's Orchestra! Could you doubt that saxophone? (Wasn't that how you call it?). Could you doubt that megaphone?

"Hi! Hi!" called the man through the megaphone. He wore a paper hat. He was so funny. "Hi! Hi! What you standing about there for? Get 'em round the waist! Seize 'em! Don't let 'em go!"

And that wasn't all...

They'd only got to know about it tonight. About Johnnie Winkworth's Young Ladies. Alfred M. Turnbull had brought it off at the last moment. Heaven knows what it's cost him in wines and what it's going to cost him in drinks and flowers and boxes of chocolate...

Johnnie Winkworth is putting on his mammoth musical show, 'Sweet Seventeen', for a couple of weeks tryout in Doomington — prior to its presentation in the West End. And Alfred M. Turnbull has persuaded him to let his Young Ladies come and do a few dances at the Magnolia Street party after the show....

"Hi! Hi!" calls the man through the megaphone. "Shake that thing!"

"Can I have this one, please?" a young man asks awkwardly. He is in khaki. His name is Corporal Tommie Wright.

"Delighted!" Rachel says. In his awkwardness he holds her away from him as if she might blow up at any moment.

"A little closer!" She smiles upon him graciously like a princess in a story book. In his awkwardness he holds her so tight she can hardly breathe. She closes her eyes. She likes it like that.

Max Emmanuel, the painter, is here. He is the only one of the three Emmanuel sons present at the Magnolia Street Party. His younger brother, David, never came back from France. His elder brother, Moisheh, is buying horses for a Jewish colony in Palestine.

His father was talking to two women. One of them he knew to be Mary Cooper. Who was the woman with her, with dancing green eyes, who carried herself with such ease? She wore a black frock with a line that conformed to her body at once simply and exquisitely. It was a line he often pursued on paper with his charcoal. It often eluded him. She wore a collar and necklace of crystals, and three white orchids below her shoulder.

She laughed. It was not a noise that belonged to these noises. It was a clear pleasant tinkle, like spring water. It was not a face that belonged to these faces, with its fine hair, thin nose, its suspicion of a cleft in the chin.

"How do you do, Miss Cooper?"

"Oh, Mr Emmanuel! I wondered if you'd be here!"

She smiled. They both smiled, as if they were each quite certain that the Magnolia Street Party would have lost much of its meaning if the other had not been here.

"How many years is it, Miss Cooper?"

"Please! I implore you!"

"Isn't it... isn't it immense?" said Max.

"Heavenly!" she declared. Her voice had too much fervour in it. She coughed. "Awfully jolly, I think!" she modified.

His eyes twinkled. "Awfully jolly!" he repeated. "Every party I'll ever go to now will be bread and cheese!"

"Rye bread!" she stipulated.

"It *is* a good band!" said Max.

"*Such* a good floor!" Enid insisted.

"The floor! The band!" They both burst into loud laughter. The people near them looked round, wondering what had amused them.

"As if it were a Free Foresters' Social in Wimbledon!" he said.

"It's like .. it's like..."

"Yes?" he enquired.

"A scene in Ben Jonson? Oh, no! Like nothing I know at all!"

"Or a painting by Brueghel? No, that's not it, either! Brueghel is too — too — homogen... What's the word?"

"Homogeneous!"

"Thank you!"

"Let's dance!" suggested Max.

"Shall we?"

"Oh, please!"

She danced beautifully. He danced well, too.

"Who's that old man there?" Enid asked. "I adore him!" (It was odd. She adored that old man. A few days ago her head had nearly cracked with joy because she was going to leave that old man for ever and ever.)

"The very old one? With a beard — that isn't like a beard at all? Like a few puffs of smoke?"

"Yes."

"That's Reb Berel! He's looked like that since the day I was born. And for a hundred and sixty years before that. He's the beadle at the synagogue. He goes about at weddings and funerals, shaking a tin box for charity. That's why he looks so lost! He's wondering where his tin box is... *That* was a quick one!"

"Much too quick! Lovely tune!"

"Will you give me the next?"

"Here's your father! I promised it him!"

"The one after?"

514

"Delighted!"

"Max!" cried his mother. "Come at once! You must try some of my *varennikas*. You know how you love them!" He took one of the patties from her hand obediently and started eating it. But he did not finish it. His eyes moved where Enid Cooper moved, under the glancing chandeliers.

Two gentlemen are sitting behind a palm. They do not look like dancing gentlemen. They are both drinking beer, which is the philosopher's drink. One is a pure philosopher, the other an applied philosopher — a sociologist, to be exact. The name of the first is Charles Stanley. He has a hare-lip, but a magnificent white brow. Although he is a philosopher, Charles Stanley has found it impossible to resist the invitation to the Magnolia Street Party. Or perhaps because he is a philosopher. It is actually so far from Magnolia Street as Wolverhampton, in its University College, that he expounds philosophy, with his slightly defective palate. But with the trenchant pen he expounds it in the abstract pages of *Brain* of London, *La Cervelle* of Paris, *Das Gehirn* of Berlin.

The name of the sociologist is Albert Durbin, who was once a barber. He is delighted to have this opportunity of comparing notes with an expert, on the writings of Adam Smith and John Stuart Mill.

"That's what the Bolsheviks don't understand," explained Albert Durbin. "You can't get behind the fundamental laws of sociology."

"Let me get some more beer for you!" requests Charles Stanley solicitously.

Dr Shulman, Mick's eldest brother, is at the Party, of course. So is his wife, a lady from Brondesbury. She has taken him in hand to good effect and shown him just how a successful doctor should dress, and just what sort of a motor-car to do his rounds in. Dr Shulman is keeping his eye on his patient, Bill Carter, an acute case of renal dropsy. Bill Carter's wife, Sally, had implored him to let her bring her husband to the Party.

"Please, Doctor," she begged. "It will buck him up no end! It'll be like old times! May I bring him, Doctor?"

Dr Shulman wondered what and when these old times may have been. He knew she had not left her wash-tub for fifteen steamy years.

515

"You mustn't let him stay more than an hour. And take this! Yes, you must! It's for a taxi back. I won't let you bring him otherwise!"

"Oh, Doctor, Doctor!" she breathed. She held his hands between her two seamed hands.

"Please!" he said uncomfortably. "This room," he muttered, his eyes travelling between the damp door and the dripping window, "with its fire and smoke going up perpetually — it's not like a slum kitchen. It's a chapel in a cathedral."

"She should be taking him away in ten minutes!" muttered Dr Shulman, looking at his watch. "Oh, I'll give them another half hour! They both look as if they're in heaven!"

He strode over to Bill Carter with a couple of cushions he had picked up in an anteroom.

"You must rest your legs on these, Carter!" he ordered.

"Yes, Doctor!" said Bill meekly.

"Please," Sally whispered in his ear. "He says he'd like a drop of whisky. Shall I let him?"

"I think you might. What about yourself? A drop of champagne will do you all the good in the world. Wait. I'll get you some."

Mick's other brothers are here — Benjamin the research chemist, Yossel the lawyer, Isaac the chartered accountant, Issy, a doctor like his eldest brother. They all have wives. They all have children. They all have spectacles. They all have dinner jackets. They exchange wives solemnly and dance, not very skillfully, to Ed Lampert's blues. It seems a little strange to them that Mick should be a world celebrity and a rich man. Mick is the only member of the family who has never studied and won scholarships. He has never read a single book in his life. They have read thousands upon thousands of books. They are not celebrated. They are not rich.

"It's a little strange!" they think, the platoon of the brothers of Battling Kid Shulman.

There are quite a lot of people here tonight whom we do not know at all, people who came to Magnolia Street after we left it in 1910 and 1916, and went again before we returned in 1916 and 1930.

516

The Higginses, what do we know of them? Only that Mrs Derricks sometimes broke their windows thinking that Elsa Stanley still lived there.

The Noviks, what do we know of them? Only that they live in the house where the Billigs once lived. That they have not such a magnificent walnut sideboard as the Billigs once had — and still have. That they will never have such a magnificent walnut sideboard so long as Mrs Novik spends all Mr Novik's wages on patent pills.

The Tuchuerderbers, what do we know of them? That they live in the house of the Seipels and there are five Tuchuerderber girls each taller than the last.

What do we know of the Poledniks? The Poledniks, who are Jews, live on the gentile pavement. They live in Miss Tregunter's house. They live in the house where Walter Hubbard murdered Dolly Hubbard, and it stood empty for a long time. It stood empty till the Poledniks came. Mr Polednik is very devoted to Mrs Polednik. They have a child a year regularly, and their children win all the local baby prizes.

All these are here tonight — the Higginses, the Noviks, the Poledniks, the Tuchuerderbers. So are the Huxtables, who live where the Briggses once lived. Alas! The Briggses are not here tonight! All Mr Emmanuel's secretarial diligence has not succeeded in running the surviving Briggses to earth. There is only one Stanley present out of the whole Stanley family.

But the Billigs are here, pink as school-children, smiling all over their pretty faces.

"Mr Billig! Mr Billig!" cries Bella joyously "I can't believe it! You are Mr Billig's son!"

"Now, now!" Mr Billig warns her, tapping the side of his nose with his finger.

She smiles at him mischievously. "You didn't really love me," she whispers. "You've not cut off that beard!"

His pink cheeks go red as a beetroot. "For that," he exclaims, "I will kiss you! Once! Twice!" He kisses her on each cheek like a champagne cork going off.

Old Mr Derricks (who does not like beer) has discovered he does not dislike champagne. He likes it.

"Come, madame, come!" He seizes Mrs Billig by the waist.

"Gershon! Gershon!" Her cry becomes fainter as the fretwork expert whirls her further and further away.

517

"My wife! My wife!" calls Mr Billig apprehensively.

"I will be your wife!" insists Bella. "Come! Let us dance!"

"I thought you'd turned me down!" grumbled Max Emmanuel.

"I *had* to dance with my host when he asked me," insisted Enid Cooper, " I felt sure you wouldn't mind."

"I suppose not."

"I'm glad you danced with Ada."

"Ada?"

"That was the dark little woman you just danced with! Isn't she a dear?"

"Yes, she's all right."

"She's a relative of mine — my sister-in-law."

"Oh, I see. Then she's Rose Berman's sister?"

"Rose Cooper."

"Of course. Rose Cooper. Lovely creature she was — such a beautiful mouth. I give all my pretty women Rose Berman's mouth. They prefer it to their own."

"I'll tell Rose."

"Don't tell her husband! How are they getting on?"

"Fine! They had a boy last week. After three girls. Wish me *Mazel tov*!"

"I say! How clever of you!"

"Magnolia Street!" she smiled.

"It's taught us both a thing or two!" He looked at her. She had exactly the right distance, the right perspective. He liked that nose, ever so slightly tip-tilted. And what a throat she had! And what lips she had! No, not for painting. Rose Berman's lips would do for painting.

"I say," he whispered. "I like you awfully!"

She obviously had not heard what he said. "We're going to call him Dick."

They danced in silence for a minute or two.

"You had a brother once," he said softly. "Wasn't Dick his name?"

"Yes, that's the idea!"

"A lovely kid — I remember! Dark blue eyes, dark lashes! And yellow hair!"

"You heard about it then?"

"I did!"

"And you had a brother, too. He died in the War, Mary told me."

"David." He stopped. It was as if a tiny claw tugged at his heart-strings. He went on again. "He was a good kid. I came home from France one day and found a lot of women gathered in the kitchen. The news had come that same day. Your sister came over to say a word to me. I've never forgotten it."

"How they'd have enjoyed it if they'd been here!"

"Yes." The word came out a little harsh and clipped. "The Party isn't quite complete," he said. He took himself in hand. There had been other lads who died. "There was such a nice youth named Durbin, at the barber-shop. There were two. He was the younger one. He also went west."

"Do you see that poor fellow there — in the corner?" she said softly. How accurately their moods chimed with each other! "Those big blue spectacles? He's blind, of course! That must be the other one. It's good to see the little boxer so nice to him. America has done him more good than it usually does. At least," she observed more briskly, "My friend, Jane Seipel, is not very keen on the place."

"Oh the Seipels!" He was quite himself again. "I remember! Such dear people!"

"They'd have given ten years off their lives, each of them, to be here tonight. I'll write and tell Jane everything — everything."

"Everything?" mused Max. "I wonder!"

"What are you saying?"

"I said shall we slide along and drink to the absent ones?"

"Splendid idea!" she said.

A lady has just entered the room. She is wearing her best boa, but it is not a very good boa. Her steps are a little unsteady, as if she is not certain of her welcome. Her name is Kate Ritchie — or it used to be. She is not sure herself what it is now.

Another lady has just entered the room by another door. There are lots of doors in the Convention Rooms so that people keep on appearing and disappearing without warning.

Who is this second lady? Do we know her? If we do, it's ages since we set eyes on her. That skirt slipping over on one side... That slide which has just slid out of her hair on to the parquet floor...

The two ladies have met half-way between the two doors.

"Mrs Ritchie!" cries one.

"Mrs Winter!" cries the other.

"Well I never!"

"Goodness gracious me!"

They have their arms round each other like two long-lost sisters. They rush away to a quiet corner. They ignore food and drink and music. They ignore the years that have run. They ignore the hair that is grown grey. They talk. And they talk. Then they talk more. They would talk still more than that, but Alfred M. Turnbull has spotted them....

"Hi!" he calls to two Shulman brothers, the lawyer and the chartered accountant. "Serve them dames some eats! Give 'em a drink! Shake 'em up a bit!"

A handful of *fire-goyas* has assembled. They don't quite know what to make of it all. Alfred M. Turnbull hands each of them a glass of champagne. They hold the glasses away from their faces a little distrustfully, as if they were kittens and might scratch. There are as many cherries on their combined bonnets as on a Herefordshire cherry tree. May Agnes Hartley stands away from the group, in the centre of the dance hall. She stands there and sings, as if it were the centre of Blenheim Road. The dancing couples swerve by her like taxis avoiding a road island. She sings, and prophesies. If everybody stopped talking and laughing, and the band stopped playing, and the feet stopped shuffling, we might learn what will befall in Magnolia Street twenty years from now. But the band goes on playing, the dancers dancing. We cannot hear her.

Sport is well represented at the Magnolia Street Party. First and foremost, there is Mick himself, very handsome with his black hair shining like glass and a well-cut suit of tails. There is Steve Tawnie. He used to keep goal for Doomington United in the brave days of Billy Meredith, the toothpick-chewer. Tonight he beams like a harvest moon. There is no shadow across the face of things for him. His old team has more than once broken the spell of bad luck which has made this season the most doleful in its history.

All this autumn he had been getting more and more wretched. "Won't touch his food!" deplored his wife, Maggie. "Not even faggots!" Certainly he had not borne as woeful a visage during the darkest days of the Great European War.

And then came the match with Birmingham under a lucky star! He breathed again. He smiled again. He returned piously to his faggots.

"Cheero, Mick!" cried Steve, lifting a glass of champagne to his young friend. He and Mick, after all, were brothers. Had they not both heard the enormous huzzas of multitudes acclaiming their handiwork?

"Cheero, Mick!" repeated Steve's son-in-law, Andy Dexter, who played for Lancashire.

"Cheero, Steve, Andy!" replied Mick. He felt like a school-boy coming back to his old school, who finds that his masters expect him to drop the 'Mister' when he addresses them.

Andy Dexter! Who made three consecutive centuries for Lancashire last year! A few years ago Mick traded an old pair of boxing gloves for his autograph...

Who is that little old man in the corner, with a long thin nose, rather hollow-cheeked? Why, it's Bella's father, Mr Winberg! He is, after all, the fountain from which a good deal of this milk and honey flow. It's a pity nobody takes much notice of him. Excepting, of course, Alfred M. Turnbull. But there's something rather professional about the way Alfred M. Turnbull takes notice. He's very much the official life-and-soul-of-the-party.

But then Mr Winberg is like that. He is enormously rich now. His rainproof factory extends for acres like a black Versailles along the Mitchen. He makes the wheels go round. But you never notice *him* — as a man, that is to say. He is a brain with not much flesh attached. You hardly notice him even in his own factory. But God help you if you slack off at your machine for half a minute.

That's Mrs Winberg, sitting by him. She is just a little disgruntled. She thinks too much fuss is being made of Mrs Shulman. After all, who is she? What is her son, that they're all so excited about him? A boxer, a common fighting man! And just as you'd expect from a woman who's got rich so sudden, Mrs Shulman is wearing far too much jewellery! Mrs Winberg can't help regretting, none the less, that she's not wearing her own treble pearl necklace tonight.

A common fighting-man, that's all Mrs Shulman's son is! Take her own daughter, Dora, for instance. She makes dresses

521

for the Royal family. If a week goes by and Princess Mary doesn't ask her to tea, Dora gets worried. Princess Mary must be ill.

Or her son Isaac — Eric, he calls himself always, and why not? He goes about in America, in a country place called Virginia, chasing after foxes, with all the other born aristocrats who went over to America — how do you call the name of that ship? — on the *Sunflower*.

Or look at Bella. Look at that collar of diamonds with platinum. If it's worth a penny it's worth fifty thousand dollars!

A common fighting-man!

At this moment Andy Dexter fortunately comes along. He has already been introduced to his hostess's mother. "Won't you dance this one with me, Mrs Winberg?"

"Go away! Go away!" she protests coyly. "Can I dance?"

He will not be gainsaid. He is gay and handsome. She follows him creditably. A sack of flour could dance to Ed Lampert's Orchestra.

Nellie Dexter is looking extremely handsome tonight. Her hair is the exactly right shade of red, as Becky Poyser's hair is the exactly wrong shade. Becky Poyser that used to be. She is Mrs Freesner tonight. She has interpreted the invitation rather liberally and brought Mr Freesner with her and her own two children and his four children... five children, that is to say, for the thirteen-year-old girl, Rita, who looks so much like Becky, is, curiously enough, *his* child by his first marriage. Husband and wife often get to look like each other after living together for a long time. It isn't often that the same thing happens between step-daughter and step-mother.

She has really brought along her husband and all the children as a sort of barricade against Bella. She used to hate Bella and is afraid that Bella will try to make her feel small. But after all, with all her millions, has Bella been able to produce *one* child — an illegitimate one, even?

She soon finds she has nothing at all to fear from Bella.

"Oh Becky, I *am* so pleased to see you! And all these little ones? They can't all be yours?"

"No, my husband has been married twice. This one is mine. And this one. Say good evening, children! It is good to see you, Mrs — er — er."

"Oh please, *Bella* from you! Like it always was!"

"Like it always wasn't!" Becky said to herself. "But how beautiful she is! No wonder all the men run after her! She is fat, yet look at her feet! How small they are! Are those real diamonds on the shoe buckles?"

Nellie Dexter was dancing with Harry, one of the Poyser twins. Both were married. Their wives and children were here. They both liked dancing with other men's wives rather than their own. Joe, the other twin, was tapping his foot impatiently till Harry got through with it. Then a voice twittered coyly in his ear:

"Won't you give me a dance, Joe? You're doing nothing!" said Miss Tuchuerderber. She was one of the five Miss Tuchuerderbers who lived in the house where the Seipels used to live. They were unattractive Miss Tuchuerderbers. They all dressed ten years below their age, and the ten years gaped like a hole in a sock. The touch of a Fedora was lacking.

"By all means, Ethel!" said Joe, biting his moustache. "That will be lovely!"

"Hee-hee-hee!" tittered Miss Tuchuerderber. "I'm not Ethel! I'm Dinah!"

Mr Polednik was dancing with Mrs Clausen of the Pompeian Rooms. After all, was he not the only Jew who lived on the gentile pavement? Should he dance with a mere Jewess?

But Mrs Polednik and the small Poledniks who had won all the baby prizes were over at the buffet, where Mrs Emmanuel had put out the *knishehs*, the *varennikas*, the *blintsies*. The odorous dainties were keeping piping hot in entrée-dishes that stood on trays heated by methylated spirit lamps. These Poledniks would win no more baby prizes if they ate many more *knishehs* and *varennikas* and *blintsies*.

"Take more! More!" urged Mrs Emmanuel beaming on them, in the intervals of her conversation with Mrs Poyser. Or her monologue, rather. Mrs Poyser was rather off her stroke tonight. It disquieted her not to be in charge of things. It dazzled her to see such food and drink on the tables — merchandise as unfamiliar to her as Urbino Majolica and Old Masters. She was like someone who leans over a swift stream, and feels the current sweep past her, whatever her paddling fingers might do... the current of this music, these refreshments, these entertainments, these dancings together of Jewish maiden and gentile youth, Jewish youth and gentile maiden.

523

And the old people, too... The way Mrs Winberg was dancing about with the son-in-law of the public-house! It was a scandal!

Or was it? She couldn't work up any real indignation tonight. She had drunk such good wine, and such a lot.

"I agree with you, Mrs Emmanuel. Don't you, Ada?" asked Mrs Poyser. But Ada wasn't there any longer. She was whirling round with Wilfred Derricks, who was wearing a little dinner-jacket tonight — not that awful Eton suit he used to wear all the time.

Wilfred had left his mother in charge of Issy Shulman. Mrs Derricks was grinning from ear to ear. Issy Shulman could tell funny tales, if he liked. He was a doctor, like Solly, his elder brother.

"I agree with you, Mrs Emmanuel," repeated Mrs Poyser.

It really was the only thing to do tonight with Mrs Emmanuel, to agree with her. She was holding forth as if it was a public meeting. It seemed that Bella Winberg and Mick Shulman were only the *official* hosts. It really was Mr Emmanuel's party... a love party... to bring together the Jews and the gentiles.

"I agree with you, Mrs Emmanuel." But no. She suddenly realised she didn't. Bring together the Jews and the gentiles? Well, and why not? No, no, certainly not! Oh what else could you do tonight but agree with Mrs Emmanuel?

So long as Isrol, her husband, showed no signs of agreeing with Mrs Emmanuel. She didn't want Isrol to hold any heretical views about Jews and gentiles coming together. He didn't. He was much too busy watching Becky, his darling. She was dancing in the arms of the hero of the evening, young Shulman. She was like a grand actress, the way she held herself.

"No, no!" Mr Emmanuel was saying to Mary Cooper. "It is not so gloomy a world!"

"Not now, not now! But the lights will go out! There will be wine stains on the cloths! The broken wine glasses will be lying under the tables!"

"There is more wine left in the bottles! There is a lot more in the grapes for next year!"

"Not *this* wine! This wine is spilt for ever!"

"Ah, but it is fun spilling it, no? Do you dance, Miss Cooper?"

"I have not danced for — I think it must be over twenty years!"

"Then it is time to begin again! Come, let us dance!"

"I do not know these dances!"

"The dances are now the same as when you danced yourself... twenty years ago. The wine is *not* left on the tablecloth! It unspills itself. It comes up from the tablecloth to the glass again!"

"I wish it *had* been possible to meet you earlier, Mr Emmanuel."

"You must come and see us often, often. Are we not neighbours? We have been neighbours so long. My wife would be so proud if you would come!"

"I will be happy. I go to stay with my brother in the New Forest next month. When I come back, Mr Emmanuel... Yes, let us dance! But tell me —" She stopped and looked at him. She looked outward through her eyes, she whose habit it had been for so long to look only inward upon so dark a spectacle. "Tell me! Are you not tired?"

He had not known how tired he was, or that he was tired at all. Suddenly he felt himself so tired that he tottered, his feet almost slipped under him. How queer it was that this woman, more strange to him than any stranger, should be more sensitive to his fatigue than he himself was!

Tired? What foolishness! Was not this night victory? Had he not for long decades worked for this night?

Tired? He was so tired that his eyelids might be of lead, so hard was it to keep them drawn back! What was this night worth that had come at length? Everything? Anything?

"I think, Mr Emmanuel —" she started.

"No!" he said with a hoarse urgency. "Let us dance! We will dance, yes?"

They danced. She moved a little stiffly, but there was beauty in her carriage; and her partner looked like a poet, with his fair hair rising and falling and his cheeks flushed. His left hand beat time to the music. There was love in his eyes for all men.

"Hey, folks! Quiet! Quiet, everybody!" roared Alfred M. Turnbull. "The famous Cantor has arrived! The Rev. Weingarten of the Eighty-Fifth Street Temple! And those of you who haven't heard him on Eighty-Fifth Street have heard him in the greatest of all talkies — 'The Heart of a Rabbi'! Quiet for the Rev. Weingarten!"

Alfred M. Turnbull was sweating profusely. He was having one hell of a good time. His heart was as clear and sweet as a small child's tonight. He was doing it all for Bella and Mick. He himself wasn't getting a cent out of it, not one cent. At his Chicago parties he had always to keep one eye open to see if he couldn't sell a lot to or for one of his guests. He had to keep the other eye open to see some dago hadn't crept in, who felt he'd got a date with Alfred M. Turnbull.

It wasn't at all like that tonight. The sweat poured. The veins stood out on his forehead.

"Quiet for the Rev. Weingarten!"

The Rev. Weingarten sang. He was a small man, with a bushy black beard, twinkling black eyes, a long black frock-coat, a small black skull-cap.

He had sung more than once at Bella Winberg's more orthodox parties at Riverside Drive. After his appearance in 'The Heart of a Rabbi', he sang at her more heterodox parties, too. He commanded enormous fees. He happened to be on a visit to London that autumn and Alfred M. Turnbull had been requested to seize him by the frock-coat. He never sang religious ditties out of the pulpit nowadays — for money, that is to say. He had done so once — but it broke his heart every time he remembered it. So nowadays he only sang Yiddish folk songs and airs from the more rococo operas.

He had the temperament of a prima donna and the eagle eye of a school-teacher. He did not begin till there was complete silence. Then he gave tongue.

It was ravishing. It was soul-searing. Jews and gentiles, old and young, wept till their handkerchiefs were soaking. Alfred M. Turnbull sweated. The Rev. Weingarten sweated too. This was the sort of audience worth singing for. He often sang the praises of the Magnolia Street audience in later years, to less enraptured congregations in New York.

He sang opera and more opera; then the cry for Yiddish folk songs arose. Mr and Mrs Polednik led the cry. They were both a little under the weather.

"*A brievele der Mamen!*" they implored. The Rev. Weingarten wiped his brow, and sang.

Then the mothers took up the cry: "*Rozhenkes und Mandeln!* Raisins and Almonds!" they implored. The mothers love that song. It is a lullaby. They themselves were lulled to sleep with it by their own dead mothers, long ago, in the Russian villages.

He sang that too, his ineffable voice spiralling thinly among the gilded roof carvings!

Rozhenkes und Mandeln
  Dos werd sein dein Beruf,
Mit dermit west du, Iddele, handlen,
  Shlufshe, iddele, shluf!

Raisins, almonds and raisins
  This will earn your keep.
You'll sell them over the seasons,
  Sleep, little Jew-child, sleep.

That was the way it went. It was too much, indeed it was too much. Old Mrs Edelman's mouth was twitching. Mrs Billig was sobbing gently. The *fire-goyahs* were crying their hearts out. Alfred M. Turnbull, too, was somewhat affected, but he did not lose grip of the situation. The moment had clearly arrived for the not less expensive but much more hilarious entertainment of Mr Duclane.

"Thank you kindly, Rev!" he proclaimed. "No wonder, folks, they call him the Skylark Rabbi! And now who d'you think's waiting kinda bashful in the conservatory? I'll give you three guesses! Prince of Wales? Wrong this time! Lindy? No, not either! Yes, mother! You're right! You got it!" He addressed himself to Becky Freesner. She blushed to the roots of her red hair. "Jimmie Duclane! As well known on the Great White Way as he is in Shaftesbury Avenoo. Now, boys and girls, give him a great big hand! Step on it now! Step on it!"

Mr Duclane, too, was ravishing. That was his voice. He, too, was soul searing. That was his face. The Tuchuerderber maidens didn't get a wink of sleep for the next three nights, thinking of his face.

As for his jokes... Well, they were... yes, they *were* a little. Fortunately Mrs Edelman didn't understand them, or she would have disapproved, and Mrs Derricks didn't catch them, or she would have shrieked with laughter and made everyone self-conscious. Fortunately, too, some of the greybeards had gone already.

The Longton Nightingale, it must be admitted, was a little embarrassed; but the young people, boys and girls, didn't mind at all, while the noise the Poyser twins made was enough to bring the gilding off the ceiling in flakes.

Then Ed Lampert and his orchestra got to work again. There was more dancing. There was more eating, more drinking. It was amazing how the Polednik children at this stage could keep their eyes open, let alone stuff away those masses of meat patties and potato cakes, as if they had just this moment been landed from a month's stay on a desert island.

Then Johnnie Winkworth's Young Ladies arrived. It was, perhaps, fortunate that Rabbi Shulman and Reb Berel had fallen asleep in their places. Mrs Derricks said "Whoops!" once or twice uncertainly, then subsided. They were lovely Young Ladies. They danced superbly.

Mrs Poyser was not at all sure that such an exhibition was quite salutary for Mr Poyser. Mr Poyser, however, was nursing his latest grandson against his bosom. "*Shlufshe, Iddele, shluf!*" he was murmuring gently into the child's ear.

"Or perhaps it isn't really happening?" whispered Max Emmanuel to Enid Cooper. Their cheeks were flushed. Their eyes shone.

They were sitting in a recess from which they commanded the main stream and several of the minor eddies of the merry-making. On the table before them were a bottle of wine with two wine glasses, a casket of cigarettes, and an enormous bowl of scarlet roses.

"I'm always coming up against it in this strange way!" he went on. "One night during the War just before I left Salonica... Oh I'll tell you about that another time... Are those Johnnie Winkworth's Young Ladies dancing up on that platform? Are they or aren't they? Are they wearing anything above their waists? Are they or aren't they?

"Is there a party going on here? Am I? Or does it? Why have they stopped? They never started! Or did they?"

"Oh, please!" implored Enid. "Let there be a party! Not for my sake! I want it to be happening for Mary's sake!"

"Please, Enid, for our sakes too! May it be Enid?"

"But —"

"Please!"

"Yes, Max!"

"For our sakes too, Enid! What? Who are they calling for?"

"We want Wil-fred! Wil-fred Derricks!" the Poyser twins were crying rhythmically. "We want Wil-fred! We want Wil-fred!"

Andy Dexter, Benny Edelman, Tommie Wright, Issy Shulman one after another took up the refrain. Feet stamped to the rhythm. "We want Wilfred! We'll *have* Wilfred!"

The eyes of Max and his father met suddenly. There was the look in them of those who see ghosts.

"My God!" said Max. "Can it be possible?" said Enid. "It isn't *now*! It's *then*! We've dreamed everything since then!"

"Yes! You're right! It's twenty years ago!"

"Look!" cried Enid. "Your father's signalling to you!"

"He remembers! He's the only one in the whole place who remembers! And us!"

Mr Emmanuel lifted his glass. He saluted Enid with it, then Max. There was a queer look in his eyes. His eyes were sad, yet there was triumph in them. Tears seemed to tremble on their lashes. He pointed to Benny Edelman.

Yes, Benny Edelman was here tonight, though twenty years ago, at the great love-party in Unity Hall, he had not turned up.

"To Benny!" his lips went.

"To Benny! To Benny!" went the lips of Max and Enid. All three drank. The innocent Benny took another puff at his rich cigar, then he added his voice again to the chorus.

"We want Wilfred! We want Wilfred! We'll *have* Wilfred!"

For, after all, the professional stuff was all very well in its way, these Weingartens and Duclanes, but we have our local talent, too, in Magnolia Street.

"Hello, what's all this?" enquired Alfred M. Turnbull, a little bewildered. "Who's this they're shouting for, Bella?"

Bella Winberg was whispering into his ear.

"The little fellow over there, with the old lady. The one with the golden hair. He lives in Magnolia Street. It's a man, not a boy! He's a singer! They want him to sing!"

"All right by me! What's his name, do you say?"

"Derricks — Wilfred Derricks!"

"Oke!" whispered Alfred M. Turnbull. Then he proclaimed: "Mr Wilfred Derricks, the famous Magnolia Street star, has kindly consented to sing! Now, Mr Derricks! This way, please!"

There was a great roar from both pavements. "Wilfred! Wilfred!" For the first time in his career, Wilfred Derricks had to be pressed to sing. The combined efforts of the Poyser twins and Alfred M. Turnbull prevailed on him at length.

"I'm quite out of voice!" he warned them, "Quite out of voice!"

"Bull!" said the three gentlemen.

"Very well then!" He shrugged his shoulders. He ascended to the stage amid deafening cheers. He stood up on tiptoe and whispered into the ear of the pianist. The pianist nodded. Wilfred took the note. He began to sing. It was a familiar song at that moment. It went:

> *There's a rainbow round my shoulder*
> *And it fits me like a glove.*
> *The world's all bright and I'm all right,*
> *For I'm in love.*

His voice sounded quite pleasant this evening and he brought it out easily. He had softened its quality with some good wine. Mr Emmanuel stood just under the platform, beaming, his head swaying somewhat loosely on his neck. He had taken his pince-nez off and was beating time with them.

It was as if he were saying: "Yes, yes, everybody! That's just how I feel, too! And you all, don't you?"

"I adore your father!" said Enid Cooper, turning to Max impulsively. "What a different world this might be with a few more Emmanuels dotted about the place!"

"Yes," murmured Max. "That's his idea. It's quite a different world he's after." His eyes looked a long way beyond the massed flowers, the heaped tables, the gilded walls. His voice was so low that she could not catch what he said.

"What do you say, Max?"

"I should have brought his letter along," he went on, as if he were talking to himself. "You would have adored that, too." His voice was still very indistinct. She waited for him to go on.

"It went like this," he said "Are you listening?"

"Please!"

"It looks like the dawn of a brighter day, when all races and peoples... how did it go on now, how *did* it go on? ... Oh yes... like the dawn of a brighter day, when all races and peoples will go hand in hand together along the road of universal love and the crowds on both sides of the road will throw flowers at them."

He turned round towards her. "Isn't that marvellous?" he exclaimed, his eyes shining. "Isn't that just marvellous?"

"Lovely!" she said.

Then he stopped and pondered for a few seconds. "But it stumped me before, when I got the letter, and it stumps me again. Enid!" he cried. "If all the races and peoples are walking hand in hand along the Great West Road, where are the crowds to come from who are going to throw all those flowers?"

Then suddenly, as if a single set of nerves controlled them both, they got up from their chairs, and thrust their hands into the great bowl of scarlet roses on the table before them.

"Here!" he cried.

"Here!" she cried.

They were flinging roses at each other as if they were both mad. All Magnolia Street stopped dead and turned round to look at them.

"Here!" they cried wildly, pelting each other with roses. "*We'll* throw the flowers. *We'll* throw the flowers!" Their cheeks flamed scarlet like the hurtling roses.

From all Magnolia Street not a sound rose, Magnolia Street was turned to stone.

"*We'll* throw the flowers!" cried Enid Cooper and Max Emmanuel.

Then they stopped. Their hands fell. They stared steadily and somewhat sombrely into each other's eyes.

Hamburg–Berlin–London
April 1930–June 1931

THE END

531